GODDESS

OF

LIMBO

LEA FALLS

GODDESS

OF

LIMBO

Cover design: Franzi Haase—www.coverdungeon.com—@coverdungeonrabbit
Map design: Robby Krueger—@robby.krueger_illustratorin
Pantheon symbol design: Brian Falls
Illustrations: Enchanted Ink Publishing
Copy editing: Enchanted Ink Publishing
Formatting: Enchanted Ink Publishing

ISBN: 978-1-7370115-0-7

Imprint: ZauberFalls Publishing

Thank you for your support of the author's rights.

Printed in the United States of America

FOR ANYONE WHO HAS STARED AT THEIR SPLINTERED SELVES AND WONDERED IF

THEY COULD EVER BE WHOLE AGAIN. YOU ARE NOT JUST WHOLE. YOU ARE DIVINE.

CONTENTS

PROLOGUE

YEAR ZERO. THE WORLD BEFORE

Another day of watching stories end.

Another day of reaping souls.

If only my celestial story ended as easily.

I blink as slow as the passing of the sun and pretend that sleep sweeps my body into the sweet arms of mortal dreams. When I open my eyes, the spectrum of colors this world offers melts me anew. The air carries fresh scents, each one telling a story that invites my nose and mind to walk along unknown shores.

I fancy myself a storyteller, not merely an observer. I like to watch mortals' faces morph from confusion into delight when I give them another chance, watch them laugh and weep and curse me for the joyful torture I bring. But I am no good. I can't tell stories like the air can. I could never write a world that blossoms and withers in the gasp of a breath, like my creator did.

The Poet and the Smith shaped this world from destruction. They called it kénos, the substance that swallows everything into nothing. The nothing life is birthed from. In a way, the world is still kénos, for its beauty swallows me. My celestial lover, Balthos, sighs at the hours I spend adoring the patterns dots draw on ladybugs, the dirtied pants of an orcish boy that float above his ankles when he outgrows them, the way lips creep upward when anger evaporates from a mortal's heart. The world is the greatest story ever told, and it retells itself daily. I fancy myself part of it. I long to lie in its meadows and pretend to enrich it instead of ripping dying souls from it. I want to tell stories, not end them.

Today I'm supposed to carry 203 souls to their deaths. Their stories are finished, I know they are, but I'm tempted to add another epilogue. One more twist and turn. The first soul on my list is an elvish farmer with eighty-five offspring, who's lived a great deal longer than any of my lover's mortals. But he started learning the fiddle a month ago, and its sound causes his granddaughters' woven dresses to twirl under the noon sun. It's quite a spectacle. If I take him, silence will suffocate their wooden cottage and the spirits of those within. No more twirling dresses.

Death snuffs out all stories and leaves behind nothing but silence. I hate silence.

I leave the daffodils that smell like mortal homes, stretch my arms, and allow myself to dissolve into wind. I reshape in a sterile place—bright and golden and perfect. Utterly boring. This is where I belong, where all things belong that neither blossom nor wither. The only shadows in this smooth realm of light fall off my creator, the Poet, my lover's creator, the Smith, and Balthos himself. I plan to drown him in my kiss until the mortal world has turned and all my due souls have stolen another day of life. He knows I use my touch to distract him, but disobedience is a negligible price for the nectar of my lips.

The air is pure here, void of all curiosities that startle the breath. Nothing can startle me in the celestial realm. I run up the diamond forged stairs that lead to our eternal palace.

White light flows out of me and sparkles on each step, but I don't stop to relish the glow. Diamonds are a rare treasure in the mortal realm, but their abundance here robs their meaning. Should I want more, I merely have to wish for it, so why treasure them?

I make it up the stairs, focusing on my lover's mineral body. We're made of blue kyanite, the holiest of crystals, composed to melt and reform. Hard when needed, softened when the wind carries us. A few more moments, and his body will fuse with mine until the blessed parchments that hold our souls touch. The height of this friction is a small solace for being celestial. A similar force plays with mortals, but I know it cannot measure up to the indulgent bliss Balthos and I receive from it.

When I get to the top, the impossible happens—I *startle*. The sensation is pleasant, new, different. I love the unexpected that plunges me into the dark until I crawl to the light again. Light only entices me when it pulls me out of darkness.

I step through our arching entrance and startle because Balthos isn't alone. The shadows must belong to the Poet and the Smith, but they rarely leave their palace wing. They created us to gain more privacy, to shield their time from needy mortals. Before we existed, the creators decided when each mortal's story came to its conclusion and passed the souls on to the ethereal realm—a world created only for the dead, away from their loved ones, away from us. It is now Balthos's and my duty to finish stories, and I can't say I am good at it. How am I supposed to understand death when it's not on my path?

I walk closer and realize there are six shadows instead of three. I reach them and startle again. It's not our creators I see. It's monsters, lined up in a row. Five, all ghastlier than the one before. As I stare at them, a prickling runs over my crystal skin. *How delightful.* I prefer beauty over the horrendous, but like light, beauty needs darkness to exist. These creatures are built of steel, not kyanite. Each looks like a mash of objects and flesh that dares to play god. I laugh.

"Alames, my pet." Balthos sees me. He's wearing a strange suit. A golden breastplate shields his torso, and hard shells wrap around his arms and legs.

"What's with the silly costume?" I ask.

He smiles. The curling of his lips equals the pleasure I get from listening to waves crash, or the morning breeze shaking the tops of pine trees, or the satisfying crunch a pie makes when the knife plunges into it. I love the mortal world, but Balthos's smile rivals it all.

"The costume, really? It's armor, my pet, but I thought you'd be more interested in our guests."

Armor. A word so lovely, I wonder if the Poet gifted it to him. I walk around the creatures, taking in the absurdity of each one. They must be an invention of the Smith, for the Poet's Quill of Life only creates images that allow the eye to please the spirit. The one closest to me is seven times taller than my current form with a beastly body of furry muscles. It resembles a wolf with the hollow skeleton head of a tusked boar. Its leg muscles are an exposed mess of tendons and veins.

I scrunch my nose. The creature is delightfully unpleasant to look at.

"Did the Smith make them?"

The monster closest to me roars. Long claws stretch out of its paws. I dissolve into blue liquid and reform a step farther back. My atoms leap at the illusion of danger—the illusion of death.

"Caedem! What have I told you?" Balthos enlarges himself, glaring at the monster with eyes that could break a mortal.

I chuckle. "Leave it. It's probably designed that way."

Balthos shakes his head and takes my hand. "He's designed for war, but not like this." He turns back to the monster. "Caedem, this is Alames, your goddess. Threaten her again, and you'll return to the void you came from."

I allow my body to liquefy further and glide around

Balthos's shoulders until he shrinks back to his normal form. He shivers at my cool touch, those little kisses of dew.

"No need to disturb yourself, my love. You know nothing dramatic can happen to me."

His lips stiffen. I gush around him, hoping to lure him into the river of my arms until I can flush away the familiar worry that pains his face.

"We're not immortal, my pet."

I laugh but choke on a hope I could never express. I picture following my favorite stories into death, watching them resurrect in the ethereal realm that we shall never enter. It is too sweet a poison to dream of.

I distract myself with curiosity. "What's war?"

Balthos runs his fingers through my flushing body, and I reshape into the woman he desires. He pulls me close as his gaze penetrates me. A madness shading his eyes tightens my throat. I've seen it before, when mortals' stories go awry. It takes but a glimpse of madness, and their paths curve away from the joy I previously expected.

"It's a new game to play."

I glance back at Caedem. "He doesn't look like fun."

"Don't worry, my pet, it's the mortals who will play. He's the conductor, and we get to watch."

I frown. The Poet and the Smith haven't done such elaborate work in centuries, and none of their creations have ever confused me.

"How would we watch? We have our duty to fulfill."

"Those times are over, my pet. Don't you think it's unfair that we have to do all the work and the mortals don't even thank us?"

I don't. It is unfair that I can never join them in living.

"How much grander would it be if they worshiped us and we got to observe how life plays out?"

I look back at the monsters, failing to grasp what he's talking about. "Worship?" If anything, I worship them, and I don't intend to stop.

"My love"—the soft kyanite of his hand melts into mine—"these are the new players of the mortal drama, and I've made sure they will entertain you."

"You've made . . ."

He smiles again, but this time it doesn't carry the beauty of mortal treasures. It mirrors the sterile light of our realm and both rattles and stiffens me alike. I don't recognize the feeling.

"I have more gifts for you."

What strange poetry to call monsters gifts. Balthos detaches himself from me and paints a shape into the air. A diamond chest manifests in front of him. More useless diamonds. How splendid. I turn away to study my *gifts* instead. They look strange, lined up there, as if Balthos's will carries weight. One creature looks like discarded poems a writer might have tossed into the trash. Its steel is formed into parchments, and blades stack up into the shape of a quill. Ten large eyes encircle the top, and mouths cover the sharp bottom tip.

"Ah, Calliquium," Balthos says over his shoulder. "I thought you might like him. I designed him with you in mind."

My kyanite tightens around my soul. This wasn't the Poet's and the Smith's work but his own. How can he be so foolish? The Smith will punish him for such charming arrogance, perhaps even with kénos. "How did you do that? Do the creators know?"

"This is what I wanted to show you."

I turn around and face a sight that sends my body quaking. On a cloud inside the chest lie the creators' tools—the Poet's Quill of Life and the Smith's Chisel of Creation. I'm sure to touch them would be to dissolve into the grandeur of existence. Balthos reaches for them anyway.

"Don't!"

His fingers close around the Quill before I can stop him, and he hands it to me. I take it and shudder as its magic runs through me. Energy charges me, makes me more powerful than I have ever felt. It could make me a creator instead of a celestial servant. I wonder if it could make me mortal.

"How did you get these?" I ask.

"I needed them. Our dear friend Calliquium has already done wonders with them. Isn't that right?" He nods at the parchment monster, which screeches and drools from its mouths. I don't believe it could do anything right. A million questions storm me, but I cling to my ignorance.

"I figured if we watch mortals all day long, you might get bored. So we made their world more interesting." He waves his hand over a patch of light, which transforms into a window. I look down and see scars on my beloved mortal world.

"What are those?" I try to keep my voice calm. He seems proud, and perhaps the Poet and the Smith approved it.

"Borders! And each part received its own language."

I tense up further. The language mortals speak is beautiful—at least it was. "How will they understand one another?"

"They won't. Isn't it a spectacle?"

His words can't be meant for me. A spectacle? Mortals have always been that and more to me. They have never bored me. Perhaps I can anchor him back in reason.

"What about the passing of souls? The Poet and the Smith didn't allow them to do it, did they?" I point at the monsters. A crack rips into my soul at the thought of them touching my mortals. I don't know how to mend it.

Balthos avoids my eyes. "No one will have to do it, my pet. I altered the Parchment of Stories."

"You did what?" The crack causes others, and soon my insides feel like the birch of an aged tree.

Balthos reaches for my hand, but this time I pull away. I should find the Poet and the Smith, warn them of the havoc my love has caused, but I can't. If they dissolve him with kénos for this, I'll lose a part of me.

"I know this is a lot, pet, but we couldn't go on the way things were. Serving the mortals day in, day out, never pleasing each other. It's better now. I wrote with the Quill that each story shall have a finite ending, a suitable death. The soul will pass to the ethereal realm on its own after that."

My body grows so stiff that if I bent my finger, it might fall off. "M-my love, they might not reach a predetermined ending. The mortal world has a mind of its own."

Balthos hardens as well. I know I frustrate him, but I'm searching for sense in his madness.

"You shouldn't concern yourself with that. If they don't fulfill their stories, they're flawed. Their souls splinter, and the world discards them to the place where all flawed creation goes."

Limbo. The realm where the Smith disposes of failed experiments. I'm not allowed to visit it, but my creator has told me gruesome tales of this forgotten world. It's nothing like the ethereal realm, the only place my beloved mortals deserve to go.

I have to do something. I have to protect them, even if it means losing Balthos. My body does not follow my orders. It stays rigid despite my pushes.

"Where are the Poet and the Smith? Bring them to me," I demand instead.

He sighs and shakes his head. "They kept us apart, my pet. They wouldn't have allowed us to build a new world."

I blink away his words, for I do not want to understand them. He tosses more at me.

"We deserve to be real gods, you and I, with servants of our own. We can't bow to masters forever."

My kyanite trembles. "The Poet is my parent, not my master."

Balthos stares at me, searching for something I'm withholding. "*Was,* my pet. I ruptured them with the Chisel."

The trembles turn into spasms. My smooth kyanite becomes brittle. I still refuse to understand. The Poet and the Smith are the source of everything—all the goodness, all the stories. Without them, there's no life.

"Please listen to me. I made new ones from their splinters.

Better ones. They will serve us while we lie in the meadows you love and dream up a new world. You and me."

I look at the monsters and recognize the white hue around their steel, a faint glow that reminds of goodness, of stories, of life.

"You cut our creators into splinters?" I know the answer, but I beg for a better one. I want to look at five monsters, not six, but the god that holds my heart fades into their ugliness.

"Yes . . . I think any soul can splinter."

He's right, I think as my soul shatters. A lightning bolt tears through me and slices my parchment. I try to hold on to the world's precious memories—the ladybug dots, the dirty pants, the creeping smiles—but it's no use.

"Alames!" Balthos screams in the last moment of my consciousness. Black clouds appear in the air. They are unseen darkness in our bright realm and pull at me, pull at the pieces that used to be me. Balthos tries to catch my light and is left with only a splinter. The clouds claim the rest.

My last thought curls around precious mortals and their stories. I pray for them to find their next chapter.

THE NEW

The Lost Goddess Alames

Balthos, King of the Gods

Exitalis, Lady of the Dead

Guardian of Silberfluss

Caedem, God of War and Strength

Guardian of Virisunder

PANTHEON

Calliquium, Keeper of Language, Thought, and Knowledge

Guardian of Fi'Teri

Squamatia, the Serpent

Guardian of Tazadahar

Zelission, the shape-shifting Trickster and Protector

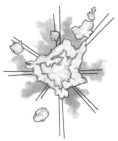

Guardian of Sap Bürüy

Tiambyssi, the Time-Waver

Guardian of Vach da tìm

CHAPTER 1

SUBIRA

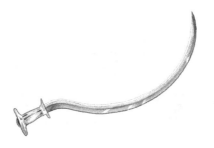

May 969 - The Desert of Tazadahar

Tazadahar's desert sand crept under Captain Subira Se'azana's fingernails, leaving a rawness that sharpened her mind. The stinging lessened the inconvenient nausea that rose from her excited belly up to her dry throat. The nausea bore questions—what it meant, the motherhood it might lead her to—but they had to wait. For now, only the digging mattered.

She unstrapped her short dagger and used it to shovel quicker. Eight months of active combat had dulled the blade and sharpened her senses. She noticed everything—the desert air's suffocating thickness, the tense inhales of the two human allies behind her. She felt the blessing of her gods, Balthos and Calliquium, as she searched the dune for the hidden weapons.

The sand radiated heat, as if it had been fighting alongside its oppressors. It scorched Subira's knees through the thin linen attire. She missed her armor, but to earn the locals' trust, she had to blend in. Her elvish ears and black skin stood out enough. Virisunder's crimson military uniform would have alienated the local rebels further.

Huda and Badih, two of the most committed human rebels, stood watch. They twitched to help, but she waved them away each time. They needed to keep their eye on Eardhaya, Tazadahar's smoking capital. As long as smoke danced into the sky and the music of screams weaved through the dirty desert winds, victory stayed within reach. Subira thought of the music that had blessed her elvish ears the night before, actual music from the mischievous strings of Gustave's lute, followed by yet another kind of music, the sensual sort of panted breaths and stolen moments.

The war. Focus on the war.

They had to win before the battle burned every rebel house in Eardhaya down to its bare clay walls and soaked its wooden floors with the blood of Virisunder's allies. They didn't deserve such a fate after their brave fight, and neither did Subira's dear friend, Alexandra. Princess Alexandra Verdain finally ruled the neighboring nation-state of Virisunder, as was her birthright, and Subira wouldn't allow her friend's first foreign war to fail. Virisunder's General Benedict von Scherping had decided to surrender to Tazadahar, but Subira refused to accept such cowardice.

Badih shuffled his feet in the sand, a sign of impatience that bridged their language barrier. He was eager to get ahold of his nation's traitorous prince. So was Subira. She didn't understand Alexandra's urgency on the war's exact issues, but she didn't concern herself with the details. Her task was to win, and win she would.

She caught herself smile and pushed it away. Warfare shouldn't have aroused her any longer. She was choosing a different life. A better one. One that included neck kisses and tavern stages beneath her feet. She'd chosen Gustave and their treasure that grew within her. But she needed to deliver

Alexandra victory before she could resign from military life and deliver a different miracle.

She dug deeper and watched her black skin turn orange from the dirt. The gods hadn't blessed Tazadahar's soil like they had her homeland, Fi'Teri, or her chosen home, Virisunder. Balthos, king of the gods, still breathed life into the dire, rough earth here, but Tazadahar's goddess, Squamatia, did little to cultivate life for her people. Subira painted a circle into the air with her index finger, then grabbed it inside her fist. She followed this sign of Balthos with a mumbled prayer. "With grace be our servitude."

The last bit of sand turned into crusted earth. She was getting closer. The rebels had promised her the supplies needed to defeat the detested Prince Talbot Cox of Tazadahar, an elf in a human nation. The locals hadn't trusted elves since he had become prince, but they had overlooked that Subira was one when she'd let her tongue dance until it had produced words they trusted. Besides, the rebels pursued the same goal as Alexandra—regaining control from the Elfentum Council, which had instated their elvish prince.

Once a merchant union, the Council now influenced all six nation-states of Elfentum. Fifty years ago, the Heideggers, the Council's leading family, had discovered a source of magic in Tazadahar—assulas. The shiny green energy wasn't as frowned upon as demon magic or orcish witchcraft. Alexandra thought them key for a new era of enlightenment and progress. The Heideggers, however, favored profit over progress and kept the magic's secrets within Tazadahar's walls, equipping only their Council officers, the Tidiers, with assula weaponry. Nobles across all Elfentum nations paid hundreds of motus for their magical protection. Cowardly nobles, that was. Subira had never understood why a proper noble lady required Council assistance to protect herself.

She scratched her finger on a sharp rock hidden in the sand. Drops of ruby blood spawned on her finger and comforted her with their familiar scent. The frustration eased with each pearl. She preferred conflicts with clear sides and strategies, but the Council had forced Alexandra into a proxy war. Harald Heidegger, its leader, claimed Prince Talbot kept magic production within Tazadahar walls, so Virisunder's princess had to attack the nation, not the Council.

Subira tore harder at the dirt until her fingers touched a smooth, solid surface. She cleaned off the sand, but it looked no different from the dirt surrounding it. A sigh escaped her. She'd have preferred not to have to deal with assulas just yet. The rebels must have stolen more Council magic than she'd expected. As if warfare required cheap tricks like that.

"Problem?" Badih asked behind her. Subira shook her head and pulled a chain from her neck. A tiny glass orb filled with green light dangled from it. The rebel smith had assured her the luminescent magic inside was a versatile assula key. She held the orb against the solid surface until the dirt transformed to stone and a long black weapon case revealed itself.

"We find it," Subira said with a smirk, speaking Tazadahar's language as best as she could. Religious motifs of Balthos and his pantheon graced the case's top. Its elegance made up for the magical nuisance. She opened it and spotted a lovely brown hilt. It was the color of darkened walnut and attached to a beautiful half-moon blade. It wasn't a saber, like Subira had expected, but the curved steel of a shotel, Fi'Teri's signature sword. She smiled at the respectful nod to her birth nation. The rebels genuinely liked her. On a professional basis, of course, but the concept of casual likability was still foreign to her. It was as strange as Gustave liking her, although there was nothing casual about his intentions. Her stomach leaped and triggered another nauseous wave. It traveled up to the edge of her throat. She took a deep breath and willed it back down. As always, her body followed her orders.

She pulled out the shotel and uncovered two sabers beneath it. They looked like standard Tazadahar equipment, but a green glow circled their gilded copper hilts. A sinking weight joined the nausea in Subira's stomach. The weapons reminded her of the Fae, foul creatures the gods had banished many centuries ago. How could she know if Balthos approved of assulas? She'd have to consult a priest about that when she returned to Virisunder. For now, Subira hid her mistrust from the rebels. They were brave soldiers led to the battlefield by conviction, not greed, and she was fighting on their land. If not her trust, they at least deserved her respect.

Two short bows with matching quivers filled with twelve arrows each awaited them underneath the sabers. She kept one bow, handed the sabers to her allies, and held out the other bow and quiver.

"Best shot?" she asked.

Badih stepped forward and took it with a frown. "This isn't a Tazadahar bow. It's Sap Bürüy crafted."

Subira shrugged. The best long-range weaponry came from the human nation of Sap Bürüy because of its mountainous landscape. Badih's pride shouldn't have stopped him from utilizing other nations' strengths, but it wasn't her duty to scold him.

She transferred the remaining objects into her shoulder bag. Alexandra's instruments were questionable in use, but she respected her friend's requests. It was difficult enough to conduct a war from a faraway palace without being questioned, especially when her general was a spineless deserter. Subira's muscles tightened when she thought of General Benedict von Scherping. *Coward.*

She brushed the crusted sand off her palms and wrapped her fingers around the shotel. The hilt slid into her hand smoothly, and its dark brown looked like an extension of her own skin. A pang shot through her when she realized that she'd have no use for the weapon after this mission. There'd be no more armor to drag her down. Then again, armor had always lifted her up. She pushed the thought aside. Her decision was final. Gustave saw her clearer, beyond the skills she brought to Virisunder's or any state's military. There was a life outside of it all, and she deserved to feel a whiff of it.

She cleared her throat and spoke in her best Tazadahar tongue. "Let us go. We need to watchtower before sundown. Keep heads low. They can have snipers."

They nodded, their stern faces confident. She had led them around the traps of death before. They trusted her—whether for her abilities or because they had no choice, it didn't matter. Most of Virisunder's military was retreating under the cowardice of General von Scherping, and their elvish oppressor Prince Talbot wouldn't fare well with rebels once he had regained full control.

Subira studied the faces of her allies, and a warm uneasiness filled her. She wished she could protect them from their enemy, but she couldn't even protect them from the sun. Huda's face had turned redder than the evening sky. The skin on the top of her nose was peeling. One more mission, then they could all go home. *Home.* It would be a first for Subira.

They continued their way over the dunes. She longed for Virisunder's firm earth, where she didn't have to question each step. Tazadahar's ground was a trickster. She was always one slip away from humiliation or disaster. It sounded a lot like court life. Perhaps Alexandra's experience of the war wasn't so different after all.

The evening sun burned hotter than twilight allowed. Subira took it as a good sign. Caedem, the wrathful god of her chosen home, Virisunder, would love to watch his enemies burn in the heat.

The walk tired her. The sinking pull of the sand agitated the restlessness that pulsed through her body. Her mentor, Makeda, had once asked her if she ever felt scared during battle. She didn't. She felt little in the dance of combat, only energy and an addicting sense of purpose. Fear found her in the quiet before, the anticipation of what was to come. Makeda had conducted a grand war both from the front line and a military base. Subira couldn't understand how she did the latter. Sitting in a base, writing commands instead of shouting them across a field, robbed a general of all their greatest strengths. She much preferred to influence the heat of the moment. Once she left the military, Gustave's and her upcoming performances would provide a similar rush. She was sure of it. She wanted to be.

After another stretch of tedious walking, the sun sank out of reach, making room for the night to have its share. They had to be quick now, or Alexandra's addition to their plan would no longer work.

"There!" Badih pointed at a white spot that peeked through dried shrubs on top of a dune. Subira squinted at the spot and recognized Prince Talbot's leisure fortress. Virisunder's troops had forced him out of his capital palace and into his private pleasure haven, but that had been before General von Scherping caved in and kissed Talbot's feet. They'd regret it. There was nothing pleasurable about Subira's plan.

"Stay down," she commanded, then dropped to her stomach and crawled up the remainder of the dune. Had something kicked inside her stomach, protesting the sudden pressure? She forced herself to ignore the answer her mind came up with. It wasn't real, couldn't be. Not yet. Not until Alexandra got her victory and her treaty.

The others crawled beside her until they reached the shrubs. Subira positioned herself behind a shrub that persisted despite its evident thirst. She took in the fortress. The pearl-white limestone in its octagon structure contrasted the surrounding orange desert. The outer walls and the southern watchtower were sturdy ashlar masonry, but Prince Talbot had commissioned an elaborate inner fort made of timber with etchings of the seven gods and Alames, the Lost Goddess. Subira would hate to watch the depictions burn. Virisunder's god, Caedem, would understand. Indulge, even.

Subira squinted at the watchtower. Two humans stood guard. Typical of Talbot to employ locals for dangerous, mundane positions. She hoped Huda and Badih wouldn't mind, but a quick look at them told her they'd kill any countrymen siding with their elvish oppressor.

She nocked an arrow and noticed the delicate linings etched into its arch. Most nations focused on firearms nowadays, but the traditional craftsmanship of Sap Bürüy was alluring. Archery was one of the few things Sap Bürüy humans were capable of.

She took a deep breath and aimed at the human leaning over the watchtower's railing. The second one appeared to be eating dinner, which she hoped would distract him from sounding the alarm immediately. On the exhale, she released and imagined herself flying alongside the arrow on a steady quick course until it reached the guard's throat. When he tumbled over the railing, she allowed herself to lower the bow and grab the second arrow. The second guard dropped his dinner, but the fool reached for the railing, not the bell. He checked on his companion's fate, dooming himself to suffer the same. Subira released the second arrow before she or the guard had a chance to contemplate what death meant to them.

"Well done, Captain," said Huda.

"Thank you." She nodded, then gestured toward the tower. "Let us rush."

The dune led right to the watchtower. No other prying eyes could discover them. Subira looked at the steep sand curve and calculated their options.

"Careful, Captain. We need to go slow, or we'll trip," said Badih, right as she came to the contrary conclusion.

She strapped the bag and her weapons tightly and took a deep breath. This time she truly was the arrow. Her hand found her stomach bulge, noticeable only to those who cared, and there were none. Except for Gustave.

On the exhale, she tossed herself down the dune. The initial impact hurt enough to alert her, and she brought her limbs in closer. She became a cannonball, not an arrow.

"Crazy elves!" Badih shouted behind her.

She picked up speed the farther she rolled. Orange dust danced around her, embedding her in a fog of both action and pause—a perfect comfort before battle. Approaching the watchtower, she reluctantly broke her cannonball form and stretched out her legs with bent knees to gain leverage in the sand. The friction roughed up the skin around her ankles and the clothes meant to protect her. The scratches left a tiny trail of blood in the sand. Was that how Tazadahar's sand had turned orange? She considered sucking the blood back in. Captain Subira Se'azana had stepped on this land as a victor, not another piece of meat for the desert to devour.

Her feet slowed her down, but she still hit the watchtower's stone wall with the side of her body.

She sucked in air. "Sweet Calliquium!"

By the time her mind had processed the impact, she had jumped back on her feet and brushed off the sand. Huda and Badih were still on the dune, safely and slowly stumbling their way down. Subira looked up at the tower, then pulled the bow and bag off her back. She searched through the items she and Alexandra had discussed until she found the heavy iron grappling hook and a thick rope. By the time Huda reached her, Subira was ready for the next shot.

She cranked her neck up to locate the railing's tower and remembered the guards who had fallen off it. They lay four steps away from the spot she'd landed on, close enough for her to watch their blood pay the sand. The dead bodies hypnotized her for a few seconds. Something dropped in her stomach. She feared the source of it was less pleasant. *Look at the goal, not the body. A just goal produces a just death.* The words of her mentor, Makeda, rang in her ears, and she forced her gaze back toward the railing.

"Balthos be your judge," she mumbled.

She drew the bow back and took another deep breath. Close range combat came natural to her, but it was difficult to find archers more skilled than she was, so she covered their long-range needs as well. She was at the cusp of exhaling when the sound of spit broke her focus. She let go of the draw and checked for the source. Badih stood over the bodies. Huda was laughing next to him.

"Disgusting blood traitor." Badih spat again.

"Hey!" Subira interrupted him and walked over, avoiding the body's dead eyes. Could they have been cold in this scorching heat?

"Captain?" Badih asked without concern.

"What you doing?" Eyes could indeed be cold in the hot desert. Even living ones. "Not appropriate behaving." She struggled with the Tazadahar words to properly express her disgust.

Badih crossed his arms. "You handle your people, I handle mine, *Captain.*"

Fury rose within her, but she relied on her allies. She had handpicked them. A general had to be a good judge of character, and she was hoping to become one in her future career. No, she wasn't. She was giving up the military to perform. The thoughts raced around her head, and she was desperate to make sense of it all. She adjusted the bow in her hand, and her fingertips touched one another. It was oddly calming. She tapped them again, then a few more times. Two seconds later, she found herself nodding and returned to her target.

After one shot, the grappling hook caught on the railing. She tugged it twice to ensure its sturdiness. The tugging provided a calming sensation as well, so she repeated it three times more than necessary. She nodded at Huda and Badih. They returned the gesture, and Subira tensed up. Their confidence had assured her earlier, but now it unnerved her. She liked them. She trusted them. What more could she do to ensure that her choice was correct? She didn't like where the questions led and turned back to the rope instead.

The evening sun watched them as they climbed up the tower. Its beams obscured all vision, but she didn't require her eyes to feel her movements. They hopped onto the tower's deck, which had remained unsoiled from blood. Up here, Subira had a clear view of the fortress's inner life and was pleased to discover that her spy's reports had been correct. Guards filled the court around the main timber fort, which reached high into the sky. Two flags waved proudly on its top. Squamatia's serpent body stretched across Tazadahar's flag. Next to it was the Council's flag—six hands representing the six nation-states of Elfentum clasping one another in a circle.

"This one is for you, Alexandra," Subira said in Virisunder tongue.

She searched through the bag for Alexandra's tools. Subira could have done without them, but her friend deserved a shared victory, so she had to incorporate the princess's toys.

She pulled out an extendable telescope and propped it against the railing. Through it, the flags provided an ideal target. She contemplated which one to aim at first. As it was Alexandra's idea, the Council flag seemed suited. She knelt back down for the second item this silly plan required. Huda and Badih watched her. She could hear them whispering in rapid Tazadahar, too quick for her ears to comprehend.

Subira found Alexandra's mirror invention in the bag. She moved it around in her hands, trying to make sense of its structure. The mirror curved inward, and Alexandra had attached a thick round glass to it, which warped the viewer's perception. Subira peeked under the glass to understand it better but gave up quickly. It was better to follow the princess's instructions without questioning the sanity of her approach. If Subira questioned her sanity, she would be no better than Alexandra's enemies.

She walked over to the telescope and placed the mirror at the eyepiece. Nothing happened. She closed her eyes to recount the instructions. *Catch the sun.* Alexandra considered this a simple task.

Subira searched for the scorching companion that had tormented them throughout the day and found the sun stroking the edge of the northern dunes. A few minutes more and it would give up its power with no memory of the force it had once commanded. Subira tilted the mirror toward it. She lacked both the precision and the patience for this silliness.

Ten unsuccessful seconds passed, and it became harder

to keep the mirror still, to only tilt it a little. She longed to toss it into the air and slice her shotel through it. She poked her head in front of it to check the reflection, and a harsh ray hit her face. *There we go.* The mirror must have sensed her disapproval and fought back. She liked that.

She turned and tilted it a few more seconds until it aligned with both the sinking sun and the telescope.

"Need help?" Huda asked.

The Council flag flared up beautifully with the fire Subira had stolen from the sun.

She grinned. "Yes, Huda, they need help in there very soon."

Huda laughed, and joy flooded Subira. She was used to wiping smiles off faces, not placing them there.

She adjusted the telescope to catch Tazadahar's flag. A guard yelled from the yard. He couldn't spot where the fire had come from but alerted the others like Alexandra and Subira had hoped.

She lit up the second flag, then aimed the telescope down at a top-floor window frame made of wood. It was excessive, but Subira preferred to be thorough. It took longer to catch fire. She was about to give up when the dry dead wood soaked up the flame as if it were the water it had longed for. Subira's grin widened. *That should distract them.*

"Weapon ready," she said to her two allies before climbing down the ladder that reached deeper into the watchtower. It led them to a sparsely lit stone staircase. Subira wasn't sure whether to be relieved or disappointed that no additional guards awaited them there. Relieved, of course. She didn't need combat. It didn't need to be part of her.

They ran down the stairs, using the time the distraction had bought them as best they could. Voices carried up from the bottom. She gestured for the others to slow down, and they sneaked the rest of the way. The stairs ended in a small dark room with a single door. Behind it, Subira registered the voices of three men. *It must be the break room.* They had the element of surprise on their side, but the guards were likely armed. If they possessed assula firearms, Subira and her allies couldn't give them the chance to shoot.

She readied her bow and arrow. "Have throw dagger ready."

Huda nodded and pulled out her dagger. Badih did the same with a wide grin that sickened Subira. Then she remembered her own excitement a moment ago and sickened herself. The sickness combined with her existing nausea. *Go away. Go away.*

She couldn't give her body a chance to react.

"Three, two, one," she whispered, then kicked in the door.

Her arrow pierced a guard's throat before he could move past his surprise. The daggers hit their targets as well and cleared the room. She breathed. Success. She gestured her allies toward the door across the room. It must've led to the yard.

The moment Subira's hand touched the doorknob, a flash of green light destroyed her certainty. She spun around and found Huda spasming. A cloud of the same light swirled around the rebel's convulsing body. Her eyes rolled backward.

Both Subira and Badih froze in shock. Subira scrambled to regain control over her mind. She cursed herself. Makeda had trained her to handle any surprise thrown at her. Or so she had thought.

The light dragged a golden shimmer out of Huda's throat. Her mouth widened beyond its natural reach. Her jaw dislocated, then dropped farther until it hung limply off her face, held in place by her stretched skin.

Where had the light come from? Subira forced herself out of the shock, pulled out another arrow, and examined the break room for a fourth guard she must have missed, a secret attacker using an assula weapon unbeknownst to her. Badih followed her moves with his own bow. Subira peered behind Huda but found no one. The horror possessed no conductor.

Badih reached for Huda's shoulder.

"No touch!" Subira snapped.

He dropped his arm, and Huda shook harder. The green light picked up speed, dragging at the golden string and swirling around her like the unexpected pull of a river. Subira aimed her arrow but dropped it immediately. Attacking light was a fool's errand. Makeda hated the Council for creating magical traps. There was no honor in fighting invisible opponents. One might as well fight the Traitor god. Unfortunately, this meant that Makeda had never prepared Subira for such a task.

The green light narrowed around Huda's throat and choked her.

"Captain!" Badih shook almost as hard as Huda. Subira had found them as a team and was sure they had expected to die as one.

She had to do something. She had to keep her safe. If she couldn't protect a trained soldier from air and light, how could she ever expect to protect a helpless infant from the horrors of this world?

She loosed the arrow at the tip of Huda's boot, hoping her shock reflex could pull her out of the strange trance. Huda continued trembling without taking notice. The light pushed against her throat, leaving an unnatural dent. She didn't gasp for air. If Huda was still alive, she wouldn't be for much longer.

Subira bit her lip. A general acted without hesitation. She swung the bow over her shoulder and slid into Huda, kicking her off her feet. She'd hoped to get her ally out of harm's way without body contact, but the moment her leg touched Huda's, a gross pain shot through her. Dozens of tiny hands seemed to beat her muscles. They tore into her calves and traveled upward until they gnawed at her hips. They reached deeper, reached for her gut and higher. Fear shot through her. They could tear at her own body, but she couldn't allow them to tear at the hope growing inside of her.

"Captain!" Badih called out again.

Huda's heavy body had fallen onto Subira the moment the pain took hold. She struggled to get words out from underneath the weight. "Open gate and give signal. Storm. I follow."

He hesitated. She wondered if he was contemplating what was more important—Huda or the revolution. He chose the latter and left Subira.

Her body cramped and began to tremble like Huda's. The human pressed down on her harder. Subira's attempt hadn't eased Huda's torment either. The light had chased her to the ground. The last golden string left Huda's body. Subira watched it drift upward to an empty glass orb attached to the corner of the ceiling. The orb sucked it out of the air and stored it inside. Another empty orb hung to the right with a cracked hole and a glimmer of green inside. Subira must have set off a magical alarm of sorts.

She forced herself to pull the bow back into her shaking hands. The malicious magic compressed her stomach. Panic took hold. Had it suffocated what lay within? She breathed through it, but fresh fear followed any calmness that arose. The arrow. She had to become the arrow.

She nudged her shoulders to the side until her torso was free of Huda's weight. With freed arms, Subira gripped the bow tighter and tried to nock the arrow. She used too much force, and the arrow's tip slipped off the bow's edge. A tremble shook her body at the same time, and she dropped the arrow out of reach.

Huda became limp. Any motion quieted down as the shakes left her. Subira's chest tightened without the light's influence. She tried to breathe, but her body seemed to have forgotten how. Only one thought screamed in her head. *Huda is dead. Huda is dead. Huda is dead.* The green light had finished her ally. Subira would be next.

"No," she whispered, but invisible opponents didn't listen. Magic didn't listen.

The green fog came for her neck. Subira forced an inhale, but the breath had to squeeze through her tightened airways. Water shot into her eyes. The intruding light gnawed at her consciousness. Her eyelids became heavy, and vision slipped away from her.

"Kymbat!" The earsplitting scream of a man snapped her eyes back open. Huda's body on top of her. The green fog. The orb filled with golden light. Nothing had changed. She stretched her head as much as the light allowed but couldn't spot the man who had screamed.

"Kymbat!" the man screamed again. The anguish in his voice jolted through Subira. It carried the burning pain of a whole nation going up in flames. The contents of her stomach demanded the attention she had denied them all day. She gagged. The light pressed down harder, causing her to choke and cough.

Another scream, a cry this time, followed by sobs. It sounded so close, yet not in the break room. Subira's mind cleared. *Kymbat.* Was it a Tazadahar name? The man must've been in the main yard. The rebel skirmish must've been failing. They needed her. The man needed her to survive.

She took as deep of a breath as she could and held it. She threw her upper body toward the arrow and reached as far as she could. Her fingertips grazed the arrow's fletching but failed to take hold of it. It slipped through her fingers once, twice. By Balthos's love, this wasn't how she'd end. She reached farther and caught the fletching. Her lungs demanded air, but she ruled them not in the position to make demands and pulled the arrow to her.

Another cry. The agony of his voice turned Subira's stomach again. She forced herself to disconnect from it. *Just wait, I'm coming.* She nocked the arrow and aimed at the orb. She pictured her body stretching, sharpening, forming into a straight line to soar through the air. Then she released it.

The orb shattered, and the golden lights floated out toward Subira. She didn't have time to celebrate as the green lights pushed against her neck. The skin at her throat tightened.

A different light filled the room. Stars. Everywhere. But this wasn't magic. This was death.

Stars belonged to the night, so darkness filled Subira's vision. She lost track of what happened.

A moment later, her vision returned and the pressure on her throat lifted. She gasped for breath, rejoicing in the way it revitalized her. The golden lights above her had mingled with the green force. It materialized into a fog figure that stretched its hand toward Subira. Her dazed state didn't allow second guesses, so she took it. With its help, she reemerged from underneath Huda's body.

"Thank you." She wanted to say more, but rifle shots sounded from the yard. No time. She nodded at the fog figure, then rushed out of the watchtower.

Chaos marked the courtyard. Badih had successfully opened the fortress's main gate, and the rebel militia was storming the unsuspecting fortress guards. More streamed out of the main fort, but the rebels outnumbered them by far. Subira smiled when she realized how many fighters had signed up for the militia after her speech last week. Then she remembered what had rushed her out to the yard. The anguished man. Where was he?

CHAPTER 2

ROBERT

May 969 - The Virisunder Military Base in Polemos, Virisunder

D rizzle dissolved the queen. Her ink washed over the guard's name and ruined her rescue. *Not on my watch.* Robert Oakley pressed his beloved book against his chest, adjusted his two flintlock pistols, and rolled onto his stomach. Sore pain cramped his shoulders, but they could suck it up. Virisunder's recruitment office would open soon. They—those barely competent guards doomed to administration work—had said he could come back tomorrow if he wanted to bother them again. He did. Back in his small town of Coalchest, those who couldn't shoot had no say in who could.

But this wasn't Coalchest. This was Polemos, by Caedem, the most thrilling city in Elfentum. Merchants from all six nations lured tourists into their tempting traps. Restaurants served exotic dishes he couldn't pronounce but could sure devour. Every Polemos experience could fill a lifetime in Coalchest. It overwhelmed him, if he was being honest. Back home there was one merchant shop, and the owner, Mackenzie, let all the guards, including Robert, know in person when she received new goods. It was on Thursdays, the most exciting day of his week. Polemos was like a dozen Thursdays every second.

One of those Thursdays was a gigantic bookshop with at least ten shelves. Mackenzie had a shelf in her shop as well, but it held no more than fifteen books at a time. This shop in Polemos probably had a hundred books—a hundred stories, just waiting for him to dive in. Not that he did, of course. He was here to serve Virisunder and Princess Alexandra, not starve in Polemos's gutter with twenty books.

The drizzle turned into rain, drenching his long elvish ears and soaking through his pants. He took out his dry handkerchief and carefully dappled the ink off the smudged page. He had lost the kiss, which was a shame, but the rest of the words remained intact. Good enough. He closed the book, hoping the hardcover would shield it from the water. *Defiance of a Rose*. He had spent the last of his motus on it—an original handwritten copy of the first book. He'd almost cried when he found it. It was much better to spend the night with the queen, the duke, and the intrigues than in the warm sheets of some lousy inn. Water dripped down his neck and made him shiver. He stood by his decision.

The rattling of keys stole his attention from the book cover. Three guards rounded the corner, competing in who could look grumpier about their early work shift. Administration guards—their walk gave them away. Robert could have mugged them with ease if he wanted to. It would buy him more books. He laughed to himself. Connie Oakley had raised no scoundrel. He wouldn't give up on her dreams, especially not right after she had passed. He'd become the best-known sniper of Elfentum, like she'd dreamed he'd be. Or a royal guard maybe. Serving as a personal guard sounded romantic to him. *Sniper, not guard,* he had promised her long before they'd shot her. He hadn't been able to guard her from the bullet, so he'd make a lousy personal guard, anyway.

"Ey, no vagabonds," said the administration guard closest to him. It was the one who had rejected him yesterday.

Robert stuffed the book under his shirt. It looked ridiculous, but it was safer there. He heaved his stiff body off the ground and reached out his hand. "Robert Oakley. Not a vagabond; recruit for the Virisunder sniper unit."

The guard scoffed but shook it. "You're the peasant kid who wouldn't take no, eh?"

"Commoner, not a peasant. My mother led the local guards of Coalchest—small town near Tribu La'am. I worked under her."

"Fantastic," said a second guard, patting Robert on the shoulder. "Why don't you stick with that? Sounds exciting."

Fuck off. Robert cleared his throat. "I wanna serve the princess in the best way I can."

Two of them snickered. The third guard spoke under his breath. "He can write down her mad ramblings."

"I don't think he knows how to write."

Robert pulled his mother's old pistol, Raptor, and moved quicker than any of them were prepared for. He shot off the guard's holster. By the time it hit the ground, he was pointing his second pistol at the guard's face. "What did you just say about Her Highness?"

The other two guards drew. Robert didn't want to fight any of them. He'd heard of guards dealing with pesky commoners in dishonorable ways. Had he been pesky enough yet?

"Whoa, isn't it a bit too early for murder?" A man in a colorful suit rushed toward them. "The sanitary division doesn't come until noon. Imagine the stench!"

Robert took his eyes off his target for a split second—an unwise move, but curiosity overcame him. The man approaching them was lanky with long hair the color and shine of Coalchest's fawns, and a beautiful black rose tattooed on his cheek. Was he a fellow *Defiance of a Rose* fan? A tiny woman wrapped in a blue scarf and a smartly dressed man who strutted like a royal guard accompanied him.

"They insulted Princess Alexandra," Robert told the tattooed man.

"Reginald," one guard said, "that's really none of your—"

"Hey, Dillon, wasn't this unit due for a royal guard inspection?"

The guards' faces dropped as the finely dressed man, Dillon, stepped forward. So he *was* a royal guard. Robert knew he had a good eye.

"Who insulted the princess?" Dillon asked.

"No one. H-he misunderstood. You know how these country folk are."

Robert snickered. These administration slow-draws had stepped in deep shit. Dillon scolded the guards, and Robert took a step back. This was almost as good as chapter twelve of *Defiance of a Rose.*

"Finding slander funny?" the man called Reginald asked.

"I find the punishment of it funny." He met Reginald's eyes. The blue in them turned darker and seemed to swirl around his pupil. The gaze invaded Robert like a wet willy from his sister. A second later, Reginald's chipper face deflated. Robert raised an eyebrow. He hadn't brushed his hair yet, but he surely didn't look that shocking. "Can I help you, man?"

"Oh," Reginald mouthed. The tiny woman took his hand and revealed her pale skin. Together they looked like the rainbow giant and his snow empress from the fifth book of Robert's favorite series. They were a strange couple, but Robert had always rooted for them.

He realized he was staring at their hands and looked back at Reginald's face, which was closer than he had expected. He leaned toward Robert's ear and whispered, "You know it too?"

Robert's eyes widened. "Wait, it's intentional? You guys

are dressing up as the rainbow giant and snow empress? Don't know if the scarf color is quite right, but . . . which version, before or after the ocean quest?"

The woman laughed. It was lovely, subtle—the kind of laugh that dripped down his neck like the rainwater, drenching him. He'd always had a thing for the snow empress.

"You're talking about . . . no, you . . . *Defiance of a Rose*?" Reginald's expression changed from shock to utter confusion.

Robert shook his head. *Amateur.* Dressing up must have been the woman's idea. "Yeah, I mean, is the scarf sewn onto her already, or has she not met the king yet?"

Reginald's smile gave him away. The fool hadn't even read book four yet.

"I'm good with this," he said, as if it meant something.

"All right . . ." Robert lost track of the conversation.

Dillon turned back to them. "All solved. Official warning, no suspension yet." Robert peeked at the disgruntled guards. Served them right. But all three glared at him, as if it were his fault they were disloyal shits. It'd take a lot of convincing for them to give him a chance now.

"We should head home," Dillon said.

"Right, sorry about that." Robert wasn't sorry, but he didn't want to upset the royal guard as well. "Didn't mean to disturb your night . . . morning? Didn't mean to disturb your morning." He looked up at the gray sky, trying to determine if it was a lighter shade of gray yet.

"That's all right," Reginald said.

"Let's go, Reginald. It's getting bright out," Dillon said.

"One moment, gotta finish this chat with my new friend here."

"We're not finished?" Robert asked.

"So, what are you doing here looking like a wet Labrador, my fine man?"

Robert looked down at his drenched, dirty clothes. Not as dapper as he had presented himself yesterday, but at least he looked determined. His mother had once shadowed a group of bandits for three weeks before taking them down. She hadn't smelled like roses on her return, but his dad hadn't given a shit.

"I'm joining Virisunder's sniper unit."

Reginald turned to Dillon. "Since when's the military making its applicants sleep in the streets? Breaking them early?"

"It's not my division, but I imagine this gentleman didn't want to sign up through the regular procedures."

"You can't get into a specialized unit that way." Robert tried to keep his voice calm, but he had heard the dismissals too many times. "I'm a sniper, not a cadet." They had turned his mother's greatness away with the same excuses. Commoners were good enough to die for the nation but not to build it, as if the people from Virisunder's heart didn't know how to love it properly.

The woman spoke for the first time. "Prove it."

Robert smirked. "What would you like me to shoot, madam?"

She pulled something off her finger and handed it to Dillon, who tried to give it back. "That's not . . . you still have to wear it."

Reginald took it and ran it through his fingers. It was a green gold ring with an expensive-looking ruby attached to it. Robert was used to shooting bottles as training, not gemstones. "Is that a wedding—"

"Good luck, buddy!" Reginald threw the ring and flicked his finger. It dashed into the air, higher with every second. Robert wasn't ready. He felt the book press heavily against him. *First the target, then the chapter.* His mother's words echoed in his mind. No pleasure without a hit. That was how it had always been at the Oakley household.

He aimed Raptor and focused on the tiny red shimmer of hope. Should he shoot unfocused without a breath, or on the exhale as he had trained? The thought took long enough for a breath to pass through him. He made the last bit of his exhale count and fired. The world seemed to slow down as the bullet soared through the gray. When it hit its target, the sky turned red. The ruby shattered in the air. What should have been a subtle hit turned into a huge explosion. Red gemstone splinters burst in all directions without hitting the ground. The pieces crashed toward them, then stopped. A ruby ceiling hovered over them for a second before each splinter turned into a rose. They rained down and filled Robert's nose with the sweetest success he'd ever smelled.

The woman applauded.

"I-I didn't do that," Robert managed to say.

Reginald winked and handed him a rose. "Have a good journey, my friend." He wrapped his arm around the woman's shoulders. "Come on, sugar. Let's go."

Robert stared at the rose in his hand. Petals covered the street beneath his feet. He felt as if he had jumped into one of his books. How was this possible? He remembered one man who could wield such power: the palace jester who made dreams come true.

"*Bored* Reginald?" he called after the palace jester, who gave him a wave without stopping.

Dillon nodded. "Well then, come to the recruitment office on Friday. I'll get you started with the sniper unit."

"G-great."

"The petals will disappear in a few minutes."

"O-okay."

Dillon nodded again and left. Robert wasn't sure what to do with himself, so he sat down among the petals. He'd have to make it through three days without motus, but it didn't matter. This was how stories began. He was sure of it.

CHAPTER 3

SUBIRA

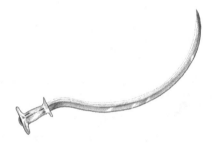

May 969 - The Desert of Tazadahar

S ubira ran out to the yard, searching for the anguished man she'd heard. She glanced at the fighting crowd, looking for any sign of him. But what did he look like? Her long, pointed ears perked up to recognize the sound of his voice but found only the rebels' battle cries mixed with shouted guard orders and startled grunts. The surprise wiped any chance for agony from their deaths.

She listened for the name "Kymbat"—a woman, she assumed, but she couldn't remember a female rebel of that name. Prince Talbot's guards were mostly male Virisunder elves.

A movement in the corner of her eye caught her attention. She spun around and faced a saber slashing down on her. She ducked beneath the blade in the last second and rolled out of his way. Once she recovered her footing, she pulled the shotel from her back and jumped into position. Excitement rushed through her, as she could finally test the beautiful new weapon.

The guard who had attacked her was large and slow—human. Subira bared her sharp teeth and charged. She feinted at his left leg, which he parried in the slow fashion she had expected. Her blade sliced through the air and caught his right ankle. The guard dropped to his knees with a yowl. She considered how to end him and settled on a quick death that would intimidate other guards the most. She whipped the shotel around and sank the blade into his jugular. Blood shot out of his neck like water from a newly discovered spring and sent as clear of a message. Life, death, either way, change was coming.

She shook the blood off her shotel and watched it touch the ground—the only tribute she was willing to pay Tazadahar. She thought of Huda. They had paid too much tribute already. The man's desperate voice crossed her mind once more, but there was no use holding on to him. Generals didn't fight phantom anguish.

She rushed into the heart of the chaos. Talbot's guards were holding down the main fort. A wooden archway that led to the main entrance provided leverage, but the rebels cut their way through the guards, one man at a time. Subira dove into the chaos as a dancer, not a fighter. The combatants fought for their lives. She used their focus to slip between them like an extension of their shadows.

A few seconds in, she noticed a guard about to behead a rebel, a young man she had recruited personally. She slowed her dance and slit the guard's throat before his saber cut skin. Combining movement and violence caused an intoxicating rush. This was her last battle. She had the right to savor it.

Her other hand pulled a dagger from its sheath on her thigh. The weapons became extensions of her arms as she lost herself in the dance. Each stab followed a beat only she could hear. The blood that flowed around her was wine, spilled to celebrate her performance. She longed to close her eyes and live off the movement alone, but Makeda had trained her too well to die for a dream.

The dance sped up until she was sprinting. She reached the archway and passed through the thick wall of guards before the humans realized what had happened. She wasn't entirely sure herself. There had been stabs, blood, and more light shot over her face, then she found herself running into the entrance hall of the main fort.

Her lungs protested again. This time she listened. Smoke filled the fort, and the heat was worse inside. The fire had traveled quicker through the building than she had expected. She coughed out the black smoke. The sound echoed within her in a lower pitch. She searched the hall for the anguished man but gave up within seconds. He wasn't her mission.

Subira was rushing toward the main staircase when she noticed a flickering above her. Flames spread across the fort's upper level. Prince Talbot had crammed the halls with carved sculptures of beautiful women that slowly burned to ashes.

Virisunder's General Benedict was an idiot, but even he wouldn't discuss a peace treaty while the fortress burned around him. Harald Heidegger, the head of the Council, was a magic-bearer himself and supposed to be present. He should have been able to extinguish the fire but hadn't bothered. Subira let go of the staircase and peered around the hall. She needed to find the prince, preferably alongside Harald Heidegger, and force them to sign Alexandra's treaty—the one they'd come here for, the one that would allow each nation to have its own assula smiths, independent from the Council. Without that treaty, the whole war would have been pointless. For Virisunder, at least.

Subira took in the entrance hall for a sign of where the cowards were hiding. All the guards were protecting the entrance. They were out of her sight, but Subira spotted a few scared servants scurrying around. She put her dagger away, then wiped the shotel blade on her pants and strapped it onto her back. A young girl poked her head out of a door, spotted her, and slammed it shut.

Subira rushed over and knocked. No answer. She took a deep breath and restored her face to an amicable expression, one that hid the bloodthirst she had allowed herself to indulge in. Then she opened the door.

The room itself was a dead end—a cigar room with bookshelves and armchairs. It surprised Subira. She had assumed Talbot to consider reading beneath him. The servant girl was a white Virisunder elf, ten at most, cowering in a corner. Subira nodded her head as a peace gesture and approached slowly. The girl shook.

"I'm sorry for scaring you. You speak Virisunder, correct?"

The girl opened her mouth, but words seemed to evade her, so she nodded.

"I will not hurt you, but I do require your assistance. What's your name?"

The girl shook, and a tear sprung from her eye. Subira softened. Gone was the excitement of battle. She hurried over to the girl, who screamed.

"No, no, don't scream." She sank to her knees in front of her. The girl's eyes grew larger. "This must be so scary, right?"

The girl gave the slightest nod. Subira smiled and stretched out her hand.

"I'm Subira. Some of my friends call me Subi." The name irked her, but perhaps it could spark some trust between them.

"E-E-Evelyn," the girl said, eyeing Subira's hand. "What's that red stuff on your face?"

Subira touched her cheek and realized that the blood of the slain guard hadn't just marked the soil. She swallowed.

"You seem like a brave girl, Evelyn. Brave girls can handle the truth, isn't that right?" She smiled in encouragement, and the girl nodded. "Wonderful. It's blood, dear. There's a war happening outside. It's important to stand up for yourself when someone makes you feel bad, and that's what's happening."

Evelyn looked at the door, then back at her.

"I knew you'd understand," Subira continued. "Brave girls always do. But we are inside, so there is nothing to fear, okay?"

"Okay."

Subira's heart warmed. She wished she could drop the battle, drop the war, and carry the girl to safety at Gustave's and her new home.

"That's right. There we go." She lifted the girl's chin and smiled wider. Evelyn raised the corners of her mouth slightly. "Can you tell me what you're doing here, so far away from home?"

Evelyn dropped her chin and stared at the ground. "Prince Josef brought me here."

Subira sucked in air, and her muscles tightened. The peace that had washed over her disappeared. Her fingers itched to take the shotel and look for the swine herself.

Josef Verdain, formerly Josef Heidegger, was the husband Alexandra had never chosen. Alexandra was only ten when her father disappeared, leaving Virisunder's fate in her young hands. The Council had provided a guardian to assist the child princess. The wedding was intended as a ceremonial gesture with no marital duties involved until Alexandra was at least eighteen. Unfortunately, the Council's head magic-bearer, Josef, had volunteered to marry the ten-year-old for more than just political reasons.

The thought triggered Subira's nausea, but she reminded herself how strong Alexandra was. Her friend deserved a victory.

"I'm sorry to hear that, Evelyn. Is he still here?"

The girl shook her head. Subira bit her lip. She couldn't have killed him anyway. She was a Virisunder captain, so he was technically her prince.

"Do you know if his brother is still here? Short brown

hair, a trimmed beard. He wears rectangular glasses and has two shiny stones pierced through his ears. His name is Harald."

Evelyn peeked up from the ground with a guilty look on her face, as if Subira had caught her stealing sweets. She glanced at a nearby bookshelf, then back at Subira.

"I understand." Subira stood up and squeezed Evelyn's shoulders gently. "Thank you. You have the heart of a warrior."

Subira looked around—not at the bookshelf, but for a suitable hiding place. She didn't want to leave Evelyn behind, especially after the sudden loss of Huda, but bringing her along posed a far greater risk.

The door creaked and interrupted her thoughts. She spun around and hid Evelyn's tiny body. She was about to reach for the shotel when Badih entered. His black beard had turned crimson with blood, and a gash ran over his face. Subira wondered if she had looked as frightening to Evelyn.

"Captain, you're alive." Badih rushed in and closed the door.

"It's okay. He's a friend," Subira said in Virisunder. She straightened her shoulders and shook off any softness before addressing Badih in Tazadahar tongue. "Yes, good to see you as well alive. I find them."

Badih's eyes widened. His previously dead face lit up with an excitement that unnerved Subira. She hadn't technically found Heidegger and the others, but she had an idea where they might be.

"I need you wait."

Badih's brow furrowed. "I came for the prince. You know that, Captain."

Subira nodded. "Yes, and you will get chance. Give me ten minutes." She needed to know that he still listened to her command.

Badih hesitated for two painful seconds before saluting. "Understood, Captain."

"Good. You need look after she. Keep she safe." Subira stepped aside and revealed Evelyn, who winced. The girl wrapped her hands around Subira's blood-soaked pants, unwilling to let go. Subira turned back to her.

"I will be back soon, all right?"

Evelyn shook her head. "I want to stay with you."

"I have to return to war one more time, okay? After that you can stay with me." She smiled until Evelyn nodded. "This is Badih." She gestured to her ally, who walked over to the girl and gave her a stern nod. He showed no grace with children, but at least he'd know how to keep her safe.

"Thank you, Badih."

He gave her the same stern nod and locked eyes with Evelyn. Subira's feet didn't want to carry her away from the girl, but her logic overruled any lingering feelings. The treaty. Alexandra needed Heidegger and Prince Talbot to sign the treaty.

Subira inspected the bookshelf Evelyn had pointed out and discovered a glass orb on the highest shelf. Green, not golden, light filled it. Otherwise, it was identical to the one in the watchtower. She pulled her shotel off her back and reached the orb with it. The blade cut through the cord that attached it to the shelf, and the orb tumbled down. Subira took a step back and let the glass shatter. The lights shot out of it.

A second later, the bookshelf faded away and a dark hallway appeared behind it. Makeda had warned her to expect the dishonorable and unholy when dealing with magic. They'd have to deal with a lot more once Alexandra's treaty was signed. *Don't question her.*

Subira entered the hallway and focused on the sound each step made. If she hoped to push Heidegger into a corner, she had to surprise him. He wasn't as powerful a magic-bearer as his brother, but Subira hoped to avoid direct battle.

The hallway led to another door. She pressed her ear

against it and recognized the voice of Benedict, her cowardly general. He spoke in Virisunder.

"—no reason to decline, Your Highness. The rebels were never under my control."

"I've heard rumors they were. Perhaps your own people aren't under your control." *Talbot.* Subira had only spoken to him once, but she recognized the sneering amusement in his voice.

"Let's just sign for peace, deal with the rebels, and be done with all of it," Benedict continued.

"Talbot, let the man surrender if he's so desperate to wave the white flag," said Heidegger.

Silence followed. Subira could picture the disgraceful hopelessness on Benedict's face. She decided to relieve him from his shame and knocked.

A Tidier, one of the Council officers, opened the door and examined her. His assula rifle was ready to shoot, but Subira forced her shoulders to relax and nodded at him with utmost respect. Behind him, three men stared at her in disbelief. She must've baffled them in her blood-soaked rebel uniform, armed with a Fi'Teri shotel and a Sap Bürüy bow.

"Good evening, dear gentlemen, Captain Se'azana reporting. I'm here to confirm that Impetu Caedem has been employed against the rebels as the general ordered," she said in Virisunder. Impetu Caedem was their nation's elite troop, meant to charge, kill, and conquer as it was their god's wish.

Benedict's face dropped further. He looked at her as if he could no longer comprehend his mother tongue. It didn't concern Subira. She had manipulated enough of his orders to cherish his confusion.

The Tidier guard, Prince Talbot, and Heidegger all looked at Benedict, waiting for a response. When it didn't come, Subira stepped into the room and continued. "Those unfortunate fools should be eradicated within the hour."

"B-brilliant," Benedict finally said.

Talbot frowned and crossed his arms. Unlike Benedict,

he didn't seem to embrace confusion. "What does this mean, General? I thought you didn't know about the rebel attack."

Benedict's face turned as red as the blood that boiled in Subira. She walked closer to Heidegger, who sat in a plush armchair next to Talbot's desk. Her gaze stayed with the men, but she sharpened her elvish vision to watch out for any sudden movements the Tidier might make in her periphery. Talbot stood behind his desk, facing Benedict, who shifted his weight from one foot to the other. Heidegger was the only one unaffected by the room's tension. Subira couldn't wait to shatter his arrogance.

"If I may, Your Highness." Subira bowed in front of Talbot, whose shoulders eased. He couldn't resist a show of royal affection. "The general wasn't sure if I'd come through on the order. He knew I was against this peace treaty and, to my shame, believed I might allow the rebels to take your precious fortress."

"That would be treason."

Subira tilted her head down again. "Yes, Your Highness." From the corner of her eye, she saw Heidegger beckon his Tidier over. Subira's breath got shallow as her nerves fired up. He wasn't buying it.

Talbot laughed. "All right, Benedict, I get it. I wouldn't trust a Fi'Teri elf either. By Caedem, Princess Alexandra is eccentric in her military appointments."

"Alexandra is eccentric in everything," Heidegger chimed in. "That's why my brother chose not to reside in the palace anymore."

Subira sensed her body shaking with anger and nerves—micromovements only she noticed, and the Tidier if she was unlucky. Subira, Alexandra, and her jester courtesan had worked hard to remove Prince Josef from the palace without upsetting the Council. It hadn't been the swine's decision to leave.

Her eyes met Benedict's and bored through him. *These are the people you're betraying Alexandra for.* She knew he didn't see it that way. Benedict wanted to protect Alexandra, but Subira knew the princess didn't need protection. She needed agency and power to use that brilliant mind of hers, and her so-called protectors infantilizing her didn't help.

Benedict cleared his throat. "Well then, shall we sign the peace treaty? We'll wait until my troops are done with the rebels and can celebrate."

Talbot nodded with a self-satisfied grin that Subira would've loved to cut out of his face.

"Lovely." Heidegger stood up from the armchair and stretched. Subira wondered if the war was anything to him other than a convenient stab at Alexandra.

Benedict pulled out a quill and the traitorous scroll. Alexandra's true treaty was pressed against Subira's heart. She had bound it to herself as a reminder that she'd either get the prince's and Heidegger's signatures on it or bleed out through it. With their signatures on it, assula magic would become accessible for the masses.

The Tidier hadn't loosened the grip on his rifle. Subira placed a hand on her hip, carefully tracing her way to her dagger. It would be a risk to take out the Tidier first, but Heidegger carried no assula staff on him, and she trusted her own speed. She'd wait until Heidegger leaned over the desk to sign the treaty, then act.

Right as she finished planning, an arrow flew from behind her and pierced the Tidier's throat. He collapsed with a gargle. Subira and the three men turned around in time to witness the next arrow. It hit Benedict between the eyes, perforating his skull and killing him in an instant. Only Sap Bürüy arrows cracked skulls—Sap Bürüy arrows like the ones she had found in the dunes.

"No!" Subira screamed when Badih entered the room.

Her instinct told her to check on Evelyn, but Makeda had trained a well-functioning soldier. She pulled her dagger and spun behind Heidegger, holding it to his throat before he could react. Her mind struggled to process what had happened. Benedict and the Tidier lay on the ground in front of the desk. No blood trickled from Benedict's forehead, as the arrow kept it inside. It was barely a wound. He had been a coward, a buffoon, and worst of all, spineless, but he had still been a general. He had been one of Alexandra's few allies and had welcomed Subira into Virisunder's military without hesitation. Her stomach turned. Generals weren't supposed to die that easily.

Badih walked closer to them, his bow aimed at the fear-struck prince.

"The oppression of Tazadahar's people ends now, *Your Highness.*" Badih's voice was calm, as if he had been preparing for this. But it had never been part of Subira's plan. She had promised him the head of Talbot, not Benedict.

Talbot nodded, still unable to say a word. Subira noticed that Heidegger was playing with a gemstone key chain in his hand. She pressed the blade closer to his throat and smelled the first drip of iron spill from his cold veins.

"Virisunder thinks it can force an elf onto our nation's throne, then barges in here to save us from him," Badih continued in Tazadahar.

"Badih," Subira said, "remember treaty. We're on same side."

Badih chuckled and spat in front of Subira. "I don't side with traitorous opportunists. Look at you, *Captain*, Fi'Teri born and playing dress-up. You sold yourself to Virisunder. You're no better than any of their scum."

The dagger shook in Subira's hand. Talbot cleared his throat and looked at her for help.

"Wh-what did he say?"

Subira had thought she couldn't think any less of Talbot, but her judgment had failed her plenty that day. "You don't speak Tazadahar, Your Highness? You rule this country."

Badih snorted an ugly laugh. "There we have it. Let's stop this farce."

He drew the bow, but Heidegger was quicker. A flash of

light beams broke out of the key chain and shot at the unsuspecting Talbot. They went for his throat and strangled him with quick mercy, unlike the death Huda had suffered. He didn't struggle long enough to comprehend Heidegger's betrayal. Subira couldn't grasp what had happened either, but it confirmed her belief to never trust the Council. She grabbed the key chain with her free hand and broke Heidegger's index finger. He inhaled sharply but remained calm.

"Now, my dear gentleman, can we discuss the matter among equals?" Heidegger asked in flawless Tazadahar tongue, although the blade against his throat thinned his voice. The show of magic had humiliated Badih and his primitive bow. Subira couldn't have looked much better. She cut a deeper line into Heidegger's skin, hoping to remind him that his life was in her hands.

"The Council has profiteered off our land just as much as the prince did," Badih said after he'd recollected himself.

"Now, let's not call him the prince. A dead man makes a poor ruler."

Badih's eyes met Subira's, and for a moment it felt like they were back at the rebel camp, chatting over the campfire, unsure what they were getting themselves into. The moment passed.

"I'm listening."

"The Council never meant to profiteer off Tazadahar. We feel blessed by Balthos to call this beautiful nation our home and want nothing more than to enrich it. Unfortunately, Talbot made that difficult. Don't you agree?"

Badih nodded.

Subira couldn't take it any longer. "Badih, the Council *put* Talbot in charge. Princess Alexandra's treaty would allow the assula trade to flourish. The actual people of Tazadahar would benefit from it."

She could've killed Heidegger, right here in this room. No one would know. But it would leave Alexandra's foul husband,

Josef, in charge of the Council. She bit her lip and focused on her first goal.

"You will sign this treaty, Heidegger. The Council will no longer hold the monopoly on assula magic." She shifted the key chain in her hand and gripped Heidegger's hair, yanking his head back.

"She's quite a feisty one, isn't she? For Alexandra's lap-dog, that is." Heidegger tried to appear detached, but there was an edge to his voice. She got him. Badih had seen that she was in charge. He had to make the right choice.

"Badih is your name, correct?" Heidegger continued. "How would you like to sign Princess Alexandra's treaty as a first order from *Prince Badih* of Tazadahar?"

A weight dropped into Subira's stomach. This couldn't be happening. The Council couldn't instate another prince for this poor country right under her nose. Badih was too smart to give in to such dishonorable temptations.

"Yes, yes, that would be appropriate," Badih said.

"What about the revolution?" Subira asked. The signed treaty would be her victory, but the means betrayed what the rebels had fought for.

"Tell her to let me go, Your Highness," Heidegger choked out. Subira hadn't noticed, but the pressure she was applying was tiptoeing toward lethal force.

"Release him."

"Badih—"

"Now!" Badih pointed the arrow at her face, and she let go of Heidegger. The Council leader fell forward onto the desk. His hand rushed to his neck, where he smeared it with the blood Subira had drawn.

"The treaty, Captain, please." Heidegger reached out his hand.

Subira loosened the rope around her chest and pulled the treaty from her cleavage. She waited for the euphoria of victory to set in, but it didn't come.

Heidegger took it and signed his name without looking

it over. This gave Subira a hint of the satisfaction she had expected. At least she'd terrified Heidegger, even if he didn't show it. Badih, dazed by the sudden turn of events, grabbed the quill and signed without looking either. Subira tied it back onto her chest.

"So this is peace," she said.

Heidegger straightened up. "If our new prince says so."

Badih grinned. "Yes, peace. As long as no Virisunder scum ever sets foot on Tazadahar land again. Let me be perfectly clear." He swung the bow over his shoulder and walked back toward the hallway.

Subira noticed herself jittering. She needed to get out of here. She had brought Alexandra the victory she deserved, and a travel ban with Tazadahar was a small price to pay.

Her nausea rose anew. Everything inside of her wanted to run, fight, scream. She breathed deeply to calm it down. *This is victory. This is victory.* There was no reason to be upset. This *was* victory.

Badih returned with a yellow ball, similar to those children liked to play with. Red streaks covered it. He held it out to Subira.

"Take this as a warning for all Virisunder citizens. We're not joking. We make no exceptions." Subira looked down at the ball. She felt her hand rising toward it. The nausea throbbed its way up her throat. Badih turned the ball until it had freckles and scared eyes and wasn't a ball at all. *Evelyn.*

Subira turned away and vomited.

CHAPTER 4

ALLY

November 969 - The Palace of Virisunder, City of Polemos

$$1 = 0.99999999999999999999999999999999999999999999999999999999999999999$$

A lly stared at her equation until the numbers danced in front of her eyes. As she frowned, her long white eyebrows touched in the middle. She ignored the twitch in her eyelid and ran her milk-white fingers over the parchment. She knew she should review the military documents she had drawn up, preparing herself for the upcoming meetings. It was her duty as Virisunder's acting princess, especially as one planning to jump into another war, but all the words she had written that day swarmed through her mind and lured her thoughts into dangerous territory. She wasn't keen on declaring war with herself as well. Some simple mathematics would do the trick. Numbers never failed to relax her.

$$1 = 0.999999999999999999999999999999999999999999$$
$$9999999999999999999$$

If one could be an infinity of broken pieces, the world could be broken apart and still function as a unified whole. Equally, her mind could be torn into pieces without invalidating her existence as one. She nodded to herself. Imperfection could appear perfect, and perfection could be misunderstood as fragmented. It all depended on the approach.

Stupid. You stupid, crazy harlot.

She winced and examined her surroundings. Hissing stories flooded the library. Only books met her gaze. Thanks to her grandmother Theodosia's thirst for knowledge, the library contained thousands of books. Its size exceeded the palace ballroom, and with her tiny frame, Ally needed two ladders to reach the upper shelves. On normal days, she loved this place almost as much as her grandmother had. Today, malicious sounds haunted it. She searched in vain for their source. The voices must have once again been a fabrication of the illness that plagued her.

Disgusting.
No, she's not. She's just weak. Look at her. Weak.

She tried to blink them away, without luck. Ignoring the voices posed a greater challenge than it normally did. *Not today, please not today.* She looked around and counted items with corporeal reality to ground herself. *Windows. Desks. Religious murals on the ceiling.* The voices quieted down. *Thank you, Reggie.* Her love had taught her the tool, among many others. She had needed them less since her husband, Prince Josef Verdain, had left, but she could never escape the illness. Except for those rare breaths she spent alone with Reggie.

Why are you trusting him, stupid?

He uses you for your position while fucking around. He might
kill you.

Murder you, dissolve you. Dissolve you.

"Shut up!" she yelled through the empty library. The murmuring circled her like wasps, stinging with each word. She had time to see Reggie before his show. She rose from her chair, then hesitated. She shouldn't bother him with her slipping sanity, no matter how much she longed for his eyes to calm her. They shimmered blue like ocean waves that carried ships onto better shores, away from their limiting harbor.

You won't exist with him.

"You mustn't lie to me." She ruffled her hair.

"Your Highness?"

Ally threw a book at the intruder before seeing who it was. Dillon, her personal guard, avoided it with a well-trained side step and checked if anyone else was around. There wasn't, so he rushed over and patted her hand like her dad used to. Those small gestures, shadows of a life before Josef, made Dillon irreplaceable to her. He wasn't her dad, but he was the last good thing her dad had left her with before disappearing.

Ally hugged him, breathing in the familiar scent of rosemary and black tea. It steadied and calmed her, a fascinating effect. She would have to research the connection between known scents and her body's nerves later. An experiment might be appropriate. Her heart soared when she thought of the chemistry lab they had installed in Josef's old office. She longed to dive into study, but it had to wait. This war was more important than her individual urges.

"I've got you, Ally," Dillon whispered.

She nodded and buried herself deeper in his chest. With him, she felt like the carefree child Josef had stolen.

Dillon untangled himself. "Subira has arrived."

Excitement rushed through Ally's body. Many years had passed since she had gotten over her childish fancy for Subira, but she couldn't deny the eagerness to see her. Subira remained her oldest, most loyal friend, and they had spent far too little time with each other, a circumstance that would change with the new war. They finally had the chance to grow together and lift each other up to their highest potential.

"I should warn you—" Dillon started, but Ally waved him off.

"Bring her in."

He did as told with visible uneasiness. Subira entered three seconds later, bearing three surprises. Ally noticed the dress first—elegant dark blue silk taffeta with golden lace stitched to it. Its wide skirt covered Subira's legs completely. Virisunder's crimson armor usually accented her strong calves, a pleasant view that added to her imposing image, the image of a woman meant to be this nation's general. The layers of fabric made her look like a different person, one Ally wasn't familiar with. She noticed a second oddity. Plump breasts peeked out of Subira's cleavage. They had increased in mass and volume, no doubt. Ally realized the inappropriateness of her calculations and lowered her gaze to the third surprise and explanation of the former. Her breasts didn't show the only increase in mass. A large belly bump challenged her dress.

"Hello, Alexandra," Subira said with a smile. Another oddity. Smiles from her had to be won. She didn't just walk into the room with them. Except, now she did.

Ally swallowed. "Subi . . . I . . . hello."

"Should I leave you two alone, my princess?" Dillon asked.

Ally nodded without looking up. Her gaze remained on the illogical form of Subira's body.

"How many months?" she finally asked.

Subira's smile widened as she looked down and ran her hand over the bump.

Nothing is real. Everything is a lie.

"Nine. A few more weeks, maybe."

You're ruined.

The voices were right. She was ruined. She had already declared the new war and begun preparations. There was no turning back without losing the little respect she had so desperately fought for.

"So the war with Silberfluss . . ." Ally began.

"May I sit down, dear?"

Dear. Subira didn't speak in endearments. Perhaps it wasn't her. Perhaps Josef had discovered a curse to morph himself into her friend's appearance. Subira—or Josef, whoever it was—walked over to the library desk Ally had been sitting at and rested their hands on a chair. They didn't sit without permission. It would be impolite. They followed stiff manners. *Subira, it must be.* Of course it was Subira, a changed, strange version of her.

"I'm sorry. Yes, sit down, of course. Constance, please bring us some tea, and the sambusas, shiro wat, and injera I asked the kitchen for." The maid nodded and hurried off. Ally looked after her, uncertain how to face Subira.

"Thank you. You shouldn't have," said Subira. "I looked over your declaration against Silberfluss."

Ally forced herself to stop staring at the empty door and took in Subira's face instead. She looked happier but soft in a way that unsettled Ally.

"Yes, well, I hoped so. As acting general, you will—"

"Why Silberfluss? Tazadahar is a declared enemy. If you wish to gain land—"

"Excuse me?" Ally hadn't meant to be rude, but her confusion had taken hold. Subira didn't interrupt people, especially not nobility. She could, of course, do so if she wished, but the Subira Ally knew would never drop her etiquette.

Subira showed no recognition. "I'm saying, if you have a skilled general, someone better than Benedict—may he rest in peace—you could take over Tazadahar land. We have the resources and—"

"You are my general."

Subira cleared her throat and examined her fingernails.

A silly object to study, but Ally was easily swayed when it came to examinations. She looked at Subira's fingernails as well, and her heart dropped. They were long, well-kept, and sharpened in elvish fashion—beautiful and unsuited for any kind of warfare.

"About that . . . my circumstances have changed, Alexandra."

Ally sensed herself tearing up and suppressed it. If Subira smiled, she could as well. "You know I prefer to be called Ally."

Subira's grin had an arrogant air to it, one Ally had never seen on her before.

"And I prefer Subira, but you still call me Subi, don't you? It's what we do."

Ally's knuckles whitened as she grabbed her seat. The cushion's hem scratched against her palm, a sensation that traveled up her arms until it pricked her whole body. *Not real. Not real.* She focused on Subira's fingers, taking in every detail. They looked softer than they usually did. She must have spent an unreasonable amount of time caring for her skin. It started to make sense why Subira's adjustments to Ally's strategy plans had been so minimal.

"Are you all right, dear?" Subira reached out her hand, their study object. Ally was about to take it when she noticed a ruby gemstone sparkling on her finger. Ruby rings were Virisunder's signature gemstone, worn only in the first year of military service or after a union of a different sort.

"You're married?"

Subira retracted her hand and stared at her fingernails again. "Yes."

"Excuse me . . . yes? As in, yes you are married and pregnant and haven't informed me about either, at least on a professional level?"

The scratches on her skin turned into stabs. She glanced at her wrists and found no wounds. The illness. The illness was taking over. Perhaps she should run, rush to Reggie and leave Subira here until the situation cleared itself. Then again, how could it? She couldn't run away from responsibility now that she finally had it. Josef had claimed her to be feebleminded, easily agitated, unfit for governing. She would prove him wrong.

"So who's the lucky gentleman?"

Subira met her eyes again, visibly relieved that Ally was taking it so well. "His name is Gustave van Auersperg."

Ally closed her eyes and let her mind run over the names of officers she had employed in the Tazadahar conflict. None matched, despite her impeccable memory.

"Illuminate me. He's a soldier, right?"

"In a greater sense, yes. Every unit and profession is needed for a well-functioning war."

Ally frowned. "You married a cook?" It wasn't an issue, but Subira cared about nobility far more than Ally ever had.

"The opposite, I suppose. He worked in the sanitary division."

The absurdity of that comment drowned out the painful sensations. Her mind became too busy catching up to torture her. She pictured Subira—her rigid, diligent, relentless, sexy Subira—dismount from her horse to make out with a sanitary boy in the trenches. It could have been a satire written by her love Reggie.

"I see."

"Look, I'm very sorry I didn't inform you earlier. Gustave thought it would be best to keep it a secret for now. He didn't want to—"

"Lose your salary increase? I imagine."

Subira looked like Ally had slapped her. "Ally, I-I'm sorry. But I'm leaving the military."

"No, you're not."

"I brought my resignation papers with me."

"You're not quitting. As your princess, I forbid you to quit."

Subira bit her lip and shot a terribly disarming look at

her. Ally noticed her tense shoulders soften. Those traitors.

"Gustave is a musician. We'll be performing on stage together. I will dance . . ." Her last words were barely audible but were enough to shake Ally.

"You dance?" She knew Subira. She thought she knew Subira. She was certain that she thought she knew Subira.

You know nothing, you stupid thing. You understand no one.

Subira nodded like the traitor she was. Or perhaps Ally was the traitor for never knowing her. She thought of Reggie and how happy the stage made him. She could never steal performing from him. But she had seen Subira happy. She had watched her in combat, fighting with the joy and grace only a dancer could command.

"Subi, the military is your life."

Subira reached out for Ally's hand again, and this time she allowed her to squeeze it. "What if it isn't?"

Tears welled up in Ally's eyes. "Does he love you?"

Subira smiled. "I love him very much."

"That's not what I asked."

A knock interrupted them, and three maids brought in steaming shiro wat, a flavorful chickpea stew from Fi'Teri, and other delicacies from Subira's native home.

"I'm sorry," Subira mumbled before letting go of Ally's hand.

The maids placed the delicious-smelling pot on Ally's library desk and set the injera bread and sambusa pockets around it. Subira kept her greed subtle, but Ally picked up the military documents and gestured at the food.

"Enjoy yourself." She handed her a wet cloth to wash her hands with. Unlike Virisunder cuisine, Fi'Teri food was best eaten by hand, wrapped in the injera bread, although the elvish nobility also enjoyed piercing food pieces with their clawlike nails.

Subira gobbled down the shiro wat as quickly as she could while using only two fingers. Her struggle between exquisite manners and the hunger a pregnancy brought amused Ally. She'd had similar urges when pregnant with her daughter, Josefine. She hadn't understood why her body had craved imported seaweed from the northern nation of Vach da tìm every morning. Then again, she had understood little of what happened to her body at that time. Elves were designed to carry children no earlier than their thirties or forties, not at nineteen. As was often when it came to appropriate ages, Josef disagreed.

Ally picked up a sambusa, but the memory of Josef left her stomach feeling raw and heavy, so she put it back down. She looked through the documents instead.

"As to your earlier question, Virisunder will attack Silberfluss because of my sister-in-law Agathe Heidegger."

Subira chewed faster and nodded along.

Ally continued. "We weakened the Council's position in Tazadahar, and with it their hold on Elfentum, and suddenly a Heidegger takes Silberfluss's throne? This was the work of her brothers."

"Agathe did win the crown by right of contest in a duel against Silberfluss's prince, and the Council pledged to neutrality—"

"Oh, come on!"

"But I see what you mean."

Ally slammed the documents on the table, causing several sambusas to fall off. They rolled all over the floor, and her maids hurried to pick them up.

"My apologies," she said to the maids, then hardened her gaze at Subira. She needed to understand how important this was. "Harald Heidegger is the head of the Council. He instated Tazadahar's new prince. Harald's sister now sits on the throne of Silberfluss. The Council is slowly taking over Elfentum's nobility. How are you not seeing this?"

"I *am* seeing this."

"We're surrounded!"

"Ally, I don't think Prince Badih will work for Heidegger. He has his own motivations."

She slammed a second pile of documents down, which sent a glass shattering to the ground. Subira took the third pile from her and put it aside without looking at the papers.

"I agree. This is worrisome. We don't want the Council turning from a neutral union to the actual rulers of Elfentum."

Ally grabbed her wrists, dipping Subira's silk sleeves in the shiro wat, and pulled her over the desk.

"We need to stop it while we can. We need to kill Agathe, take Silberfluss, and regain control."

The Council couldn't take control over Elfentum. The Heideggers couldn't take control again. *Josef* couldn't take control again. Ally's stomach clenched. She searched Subira's eyes for a sign that she wasn't alone in this.

But you are alone. You're always alone.

"I promised Gustave to quit."

Ally forced down a scream and pressed out a word instead "So?"

"I'm trying to do right by the gods."

"Screw the gods!" Ally yelled, pulling the shocked Subira closer until she stumbled off her chair. Her large belly crushed the remaining dishes. The maids frantically tried to lessen the mess Ally was causing.

"Don't speak like that," Subira whispered, glancing at the ceiling. Her fingers formed the sign of Balthos.

"Subira, who cares about the gods? They have never helped us. This is about you and me and justice for Virisunder."

Subira closed her eyes and took a long breath. She nodded and opened them again. "I can take over the base here in Polemos after the birth and consult with whomever you pick as the acting general."

It wasn't enough, but it was something. Ally loosened her grip. "Thank you."

"Having one of your leisurely tea parties, mother?"

Josefine sneered from the library door. Ally let go of Subira's hands, and the two women composed themselves. Subira picked chickpeas off her dress. Ally noticed that orange stew covered her own body.

She sighed. "I told you not to sneak up on me like that."

Josefine crossed her arms and leaned against the door, smirking. Ally hated when her daughter smirked like that. It increased her resemblance to Josef.

"Yeah, well, let's see how much longer you make the rules around here."

The disrespect stung, but Ally pushed it aside to focus on what lay underneath it.

"Excuse me, Subira." She nodded at her friend and walked over to Josefine with as much confidence as she could muster. She had never formed a bond with her and found it difficult to predict what went on inside her head. Josef had kept her away from their daughter right after her birth.

"What do you mean by that?" Ally asked.

Josefine's grin widened. "The Council wants to see you. I just spoke to them. They've introduced some very interesting ideas . . ."

The Council was here. Josef as well? Ally inhaled sharply.

"I do not appreciate that you had a meeting without me. We will discuss this later."

Josefine clicked her tongue. "I doubt that."

Ally signaled for Dillon to follow her and left the library. The walls she rushed past appeared fuller than usual. The first Verdains had a fervor for shimmering metals and colorful art, so they'd embellished most of the palace's interior. Now, however, each painting stared at her, watched her every move. She rounded the corner into the governing wing where her grandmother Theodosia had confronted her a dozen times. She'd judged her, yelled at her. Her voice had echoed from every corner. Ally took a deep breath. *Paintings. They're paintings, nothing more.* She had never even heard her grandmother yell. Theodosia was a quiet person, living in exile at her wife's military academy.

Ally forced herself to look at the portraits and recognized the sweetness of her grandmother's eyes. She looked intimidating, sure, because her wife, Makeda, had commissioned artists to depict her that way. The thought of her grandmothers was both heavy and grounding. She wished they could have raised her after her father had disappeared. They were no longer allowed on palace grounds. It had been a united Council decision to ensure peace, but they had overlooked Ally's ambitions in the equation.

She found the Council members in her largest assembly hall, which was reserved for important gatherings. Ally counted over thirty members and twenty-five Tidiers, the Council's guard legion in their eggshell-colored uniform. Gemstone chains ran from their wrists to their pockets. Sunlight from the large window reflected off them. Each Tidier carried an assula rifle, capable of firing multiple shots without reloading. Ally had started to equip her own legions with them, but most assula-powered weaponry was still out of her reach. Finding and training assula smiths was a nuisance, and each nation had received an infuriatingly small supply of prepared assulas from the Council's magical Institute. Ally had hoped to have studied and understood the curious substance by now, but that would have required a visit to the Institute and therefore visiting Josef, who ran it.

Her eyes darted through the room. Her shoulders tensed as she searched for her husband. He wasn't there. The only Heidegger present was Harald, the Council's leader.

His attendance alarmed Ally, but she had to compose herself. The Council members watched her every step, every twitch. She entered the room in her most regal manner and met Harald Heidegger's eyes. Harald cleared his throat and put on his finest patronizing smile.

"My sweet Princess Alexandra, how lovely that you could join us for the meeting today."

Ally raised her nose. "You're in my court. If anything, you are joining me. What do you want, Harald?"

Don't act proud! They'll catch you!

She remembered the shiro wat on her skirt. The embarrassment amplified the voices' volume.

They can see you're worthless. Worthless. Worthless.
Worthless? Worthless.

Harald responded, but she couldn't hear him. The voices were too loud.

"I don't comply with that," she said, hoping that it would be an adequate response.

Several Council members exchanged looks. It hadn't been an adequate response. Ally stared back at Harald and found no answers in his expression. The smile he'd previously worn turned into a grimace that stretched farther and farther. The corners of his mouth wrapped around his head, leaving a gruesome hole between his nose and chin. It must've been another alteration of reality. She searched her mind for a law of nature that could explain it. *The observer effect. It is impossible to perceive anything without perception altering its state.* Her senses had likely altered his face.

"Alexandra? Are you listening?"

Half of the room laughed. The sound mauled her ears. Dillon stepped behind her and lightly placed his hand on her back.

"Heidegger stated that the war with Silberfluss is a rash, unwise decision," he whispered.

Ally licked her lips and puffed out her chest. The Council was already scared. It meant she was on the right track.

"Thank you for your input, Harald. I have filed the declaration correctly with my right as princess of an Elfentum nation. The Council cannot decline wars."

"No, but with approval of the court, we can suggest when a princess might be unfit to rule for the sake of her heiress."

They're getting rid of you.

She took a heavy breath. She would allow neither her illness nor the Council to spoil months of preparation for the war, no matter what scheme they might've come up with.

"That is a lovely, unnecessary piece of information, as I am not unfit to rule."

A Council member of Silberfluss descent coughed. "Says Princess Lunatic . . ."

Ally's hand darted to the short dagger she wore on her hip. She often neglected her combat training for library studies, but she was certain she could hit the rotten human who had spoken. He was supposed to be neutral, a servant for all of Elfentum, as the Council required. Most of them only served themselves. His cough turned into a snicker. He would look much better with a dagger between his short human eyebrows.

Before she entertained the temptations of righteous violence any longer, an unnatural numbness came over her body. It started at her throat and trickled through her limbs within seconds. It reached her brain last, snuffing out all emotions. Her thoughts and the movement of her body weren't inhibited, but she felt sick and hollow. Only Reggie had her permission to alter her state with magic, but her consent mattered little to a Heidegger.

Harald smiled. "Now, now, let's not get emotional." He was addressing her, not the Silberfluss Council member. "We're all pursuing the same goal: prosperity and peace for Elfentum."

"Stop it." Ally wanted to argue more, but she couldn't bring herself to care.

"The meeting just started, Your Highness, but I suppose if you're tired—"

"The spell. Stop the spell."

Harald laughed, and this time the whole room, except for Dillon, joined him. It was impossible to decipher what the humiliation felt like. The understanding was trapped somewhere between her stomach and brain. She tried to remember a theory or law that could help her. What if she forced a collision with an impulse to disrupt momentum . . . no, she didn't have enough control over the variables. There must've been a different law. *Allotropy! The same element could take on different forms.* Graphite and diamonds were both carbon. Numb Ally and feeling Ally were both versions of herself. It didn't matter in what form they pressed her. One might be vulnerable, but her potential was indestructible.

She stole the room's laughter with a smile.

What are you doing? You're—

Shh. No one would speak on her behalf.

"My court has approved my actions against Silberfluss. The gained land and treasury will allow Virisunder to progress out of its current state. We will build a fairer societal system. Ambitious plans, but my new advisers trust me. Besides, Agathe isn't dealing with the famine that plagues Silberfluss. The wasted bodies of her serfs and peasantry are on her hands." Reducing Ally to logic had been a mistake. Nothing was distracting her from the Council's hypocrisy now. "The war displeases you for personal reasons, Harald, and because the Council doesn't benefit from it."

Harald cleared his throat. "Princess Agathe has only held the throne for four months. The Council is confident the famine will be solved within a year." Ally's confidence had thrown him off-balance.

"Tell that to her starving serfs." Ally's eyes bored through him. She noticed his finger flick. A moment later, the numbness disappeared and a storm of emotions poured over her. She tried to catch up, but the amount was impossible to process. The floor beneath Ally cracked. Hissing made its way through the stone. *Not now.* She was so close to standing her ground.

One of the Council members—a sweaty, nervous-looking

elf—made his way over to Heidegger. He whispered, but Ally's sharp senses made up for it.

"Should we proceed with plan B, Sir? Josef warned us she might be reluctant."

Josef. As soon as he uttered the words, the floor beneath Ally turned into glass. Large chunks of it cracked upward and ripped her soiled dress.

"Not yet," Harald said.

Ally saw blood running down her ankle but felt no pain. A voice, one of Ally's treacherous companions, screamed. The glass drifted apart, making space for a dark pull. Her breaths became rapid as she tried not to fall.

The Council members remained unfazed. No one else seemed to notice the sudden dematerialization of the room. Was it a hallucination or a curse masking itself as a fragment of her mind? Her thoughts raced away from her. She tried to remember an equation, a law, something to steady herself. Instead of mathematics, a pair of deep blue eyes came to her mind. A chuckle. A warm, firm touch. *If both realities are possible, sugar, why not believe in the more pleasant one?* She stomped her foot into the dark void and found solid ground. Nothing had happened.

"Alexandra," Harald said. "We'd like you to crown Josefine as the princess of Virisunder and urge you to step down into the queen position."

They couldn't be serious. She was only thirty-four years old. The ruling prince or princess stayed on the throne until their heirs had married and were of child-bearing age. For elves, this usually meant the ruler had reached their first century. The suggestion that Ally's cranky teenage daughter was better suited to lead the nation in times of war was ridiculous. They were trying to suffocate her significance like they'd done with Queen Theodosia.

They've seen into your mind. They know how toxic you are.
Worthless piece of shit.
She tried to do well.

That makes it worse.

"Harald, I must have misunderstood. You aren't suggesting that I hand the crown to my teenage daughter, are you?"

"Josefine has shown herself talented in diplomacy and wit. Her father speaks highly of her potential."

"No."

The sweaty elf next to Harald stepped forward. "Y-yes, Your Highness. We have . . . ehm . . . we have begun to take the steps for the power exchange."

Ally's cloudy eyes dug through him.

"No."

Heidegger stepped forward and leaned in, close enough that only she and Dillon could hear him. "It's in your best interest to give us what we want, Alexandra."

Ally's eyelid twitched once, but she refused to move another muscle. "The upper nobility of my court will have to sign off on such an absurd Council invasion."

Harald sighed. The touch of his breath on her skin was as unwelcome as his spell had been. He didn't stink as sour as his brother, but her stomach flipped nevertheless.

"You force me to play the joker. Not a smart move."

He brushed past her without another look. Ally's strong stillness turned into a frozen state. She wasn't sure if she could ever move again. He was bluffing. He must've been. The Council members around her cleared the room without a goodbye as she stood there, her mind dissecting every word Harald had left her with. His word choice was odd.

She longed to see Reggie. He would know how to make sense of it all, and as her jester he always knew how to lift her spirits and enchant her lips into a smile. Her jester. *My joker.*

CHAPTER 5

RICHARD

November 969 - The Farmlands of Waldfeld, Silberfluss

A s the last sere leaf fell onto the barren field, Richard Kilburn knew it was over. He had scavenged the dry earth for an overlooked crop, anything to extend the life of his family. It had been in vain. The noble Belladonna family that both owned this land and every Kilburn for the past twelve decades had taken the last of the harvest. Richard hadn't protested. He had done nothing as they took the food his son and wife needed. The Belladonnas had *needed* his harvest so they could spend their motus on newly available assula magic knickknacks instead of food. Rumor had it there was now a tool to produce flames on command. It was worth more than the lives of a few serfs.

Richard knew he should return to the shack he called home, but with every step toward it, the guilt seeped into his feet like iron, binding him more and more to the land he never chose. He sat down and watched the nearby road. At home, both his wife, Edeliènne, and his son, Pier, would welcome him with their inexhaustible kindness. He deserved to suffer in silence.

Music came from the road. An array of sounds followed—hoofbeats trotting along, carriage wheels rolling over the dusty road. The Grievance March must have reached Waldfeld. Every year, in remembrance of their Lost Goddess, Alames, Silberfluss's royalty, upper nobility, and high clergy members traveled through the nation for two weeks, visiting the church of Exitalis in every town they crossed. It was an honor that they visited Richard's small town of Waldfeld. He should've been at church. Father Godfried would be disappointed in him.

The banners of Exitalis's various sects waved in the wind. He raised his hand and painted Alames's sign, a blossoming flower, and Exitalis's sign, a peaceful gravestone, into the air. All Elfentum nations worshiped Balthos and his Lost Goddess equally, but Exitalis was the patron goddess of Silberfluss and deserved as much honor as the fallen one.

Richard bowed his head in respect. When he looked back up, he noticed a small gap between two church congregations. Exitalis's Church of the Last Judge should have been represented there, but he couldn't spot a single worshiper. So the rumors were true. A lone Sap Bürüy archer had murdered the entire sect. Richard shook his head. The world was headed into unholy times.

He wondered if the Grievance March would pass through Waldfeld's forest toward the Belladonna estate. Father Godfried had declared it forbidden territory in a recent sermon. He claimed a demon had escaped limbo and lived within their humble woods. It was a shame; Richard loved the forest. Within nature, he didn't feel as foreign to himself as he usually did.

Fanfare announced the largest wagon, forged with silver metals and marble work. Fine woodwork would have looked better than the extravagant clash of materials. Richard stretched his neck to get a better look at it. The horses wore royal saddle cloth. At least twenty guards and ten armed men in odd-looking eggshell-colored uniforms marched next to the wagon. It must've belonged to their new ruler, Princess Agathe Heidegger. His son had been rambling for weeks about the repercussions and significance of an elf ruling over a human nation. None of it mattered to Richard. It took two days to ride from Waldfeld to the capital of Freilist. To royalty, Richard's town might as well have been in limbo.

"Dad!"

Richard startled and jumped to his feet. The weight in his stomach worsened when he spotted his son on the edge of the field. Pier had seen him idle, sitting around when he should've been caring for them. He took large strides toward him, as close as he could get to running without giving away his urgency. Father Godfried often reminded of a man's duty to be a calm, dependable force. With his thirteen years, Pier was still a boy and needed his dad to carry that burden.

He reached the field's edge under the soft gaze of his son. Pier's ginger curls and freckled face resembled his own features, but this was where the resemblance ended. He had grown almost as tall as his father without his torso catching up in width. His face was delicate like his mother's and hinted to the wit and clarity Richard didn't have but wished for. He wanted to buy his son a book to sate his hunger for knowledge, but he couldn't even ease the real hunger.

"Dad." Pier embraced him for a few seconds longer than he normally would. "I think it's time to say goodbye."

Richard felt a pull on his body, as if the world had turned him into a pack mule on the edge of collapsing. He pushed past Pier and entered the shack. Edeliènne lay flat on the intricately carved bed Richard had built for her as a wedding gift. Her body seemed to disappear in the hay mattress. She had as little substance as the blanket Pier had wrapped her in.

Pier rubbed Richard's back, then squeezed past him to

renew the hot compress on Edeliènne's forehead. The winter winds hadn't invaded Waldfeld yet, but his family already suffered from the cold. Pier allowed the compress's water to trickle lightly onto her cracked skin. She lifted a bony finger and ran it over Pier's forearm as a thank-you. Richard stood frozen in the doorway, unsure what to do with himself. There was much building up in him, demanding his attention, but his duty was to remain calm—not brave, but calm.

A tear pearled off Pier's prominent cheekbone, the only sign of weakness his son seemed to allow. Despite it, he kept moving, caring for his mother like he had in the past months. Pier was brave enough to witness each one of Edeliènne's struggling breaths. He helped her keep dignity with the tasks she could no longer perform. He had been with her night and day while Richard had scoured the fields, hoping to find the last pieces of his pride. The hunger had taken too much of Pier's flesh as well, but it didn't seem to touch his spirit.

"Mom, Dad is home. Would you like to say hello?"

Edeliènne opened her bright blue eyes and gifted him the same tired smile she'd worn on the day they'd met. He wanted to believe that he had saved her from wasting away in a brothel with too much opium and liquor. Now she wasted away in his shack. He prayed to Exitalis less opium was involved.

Pier nudged Richard into the only room of the shack. He gestured for him to sit on their stool near the bed. Richard obeyed, struggling to remember what he was supposed to do, what he could do. He ran the back of his hand along her haggard check. She inhaled deeply, and her smile grew wider.

"Hello, darling," she croaked.

He gave her a nod. A pressure rose up his throat, longing to burst into something dishonorable. A sob maybe, or words of sentimentality he'd regret later. Edeliènne needed someone strong. She always had.

"I'm here," he said instead, studying her face. There was a fullness to her lips, a bit of flesh the famine hadn't robbed yet. For once, Pier might have been wrong. "Just give us one more day, Edeliènne, then we'll have——"

"A grand feast with pudding and my favorite gravy," she said with a sigh. "I look forward to it."

The words stung. For over a decade he had promised her a life that would allow feasts, but he'd never been able to provide it. When Duke Belladonna had assigned this land to him, he had slept like an elf, four hours each night. Then he'd gotten up and worked, planted rare vegetables alongside his wheat that the Belladonnas might crave for a few extra motus each month. He had planned to save up until he could afford a small woodshop and sell services he was actually good at. He had been young and naive and convinced that a few nice chairs could provide feasts and fancy dresses for his wife— anything women might fancy. But the motus he stored away disappeared within days. The riddle continued for months until he had discovered flasks filled with thick black liquid in a jewel casket beneath the oven. Opium. It wasn't a feast or a better life, but if it was what Edeliènne craved, he endured it.

"Pier, come over here, love," Edeliènne beckoned. Pier knelt down next to Richard and took her hand. "I love you."

Tears rolled over Pier's cheeks as he brought her hand to his lips and placed a kiss on it. "Thank you, Mom, for everything."

Edeliènne turned her hand with great effort and brushed the tear off his face. "Let me say goodbye to your father, will you?"

Pier nodded, then stood back up and walked to the other side of their shack. His face was pale but collected.

"Good boy," Edeliènne said.

Richard nodded. Fire and acid seemed to burn his throat, making it impossible to speak.

"Look after him."

Richard nodded again.

"Not just physically. Make sure nothing takes away his true self."

Richard wasn't sure what she meant, but he nodded a third time.

"Are you"—she gasped for air as the world slowly denied her oxygen—"just gonna nod at me till I'm asleep?"

He swallowed hard to make room for words. "I failed you."

"You're too decent, that's all."

Richard couldn't help himself anymore. In an unusual and weak burst of emotion, he pulled her into his arms, so close that her skin seemed to melt into his. Her fragile bones nestled against his tanned muscles. The last warmth of her skin reminded him of his grandmother's warmth and his mother's love before he had become unworthy of it. He couldn't lose Edelienne as well.

"Mom!" Pier shrieked.

Richard startled and almost dropped the fragile figure in his arms.

"Dad, do something!"

Richard glared at Pier and pulled her closer. He didn't want her last memory to be one of unrest. To his utter shock, his son rushed over and tried to tear her away from him. Richard held on tighter. His arms were the only thing he had to offer. They couldn't fail her too.

"Stop it, boy!"

Pier wasn't strong enough to rip her out of his arms, but it turned Richard's pain into fury.

"Dad, don't you see? The gold, it's coming from her." Pier sobbed, still fighting him. His hand clasped around his mother's waist.

Before Richard could grasp what was happening, he backhanded Pier. It was an instinct. Blood shot out of Pier's nose. Richard felt the pain as if the punch had hit him instead. He hadn't meant to. He had wanted to protect Edelienne, stop the madness. Guilt didn't listen to his reasoning. His frail son sank to the ground, eyes filled with shock and betrayal that sickened him. Was it the same look Richard had given his own father all those years ago?

Red streaks ran down Pier's face, but he didn't seem to care about the physical injuries.

"She won't become an angel now." Pier sniffed.

His son's face disturbed him too much. He turned back to his wife, and shame washed over him. He was already disrespecting her last wish.

"I'm sorry, love. I didn't mean to—" He stopped. The woman in his arms was dead. He knew he should yell at Pier for stealing her last moments, but a peculiar sight distracted him. Throbbing strings of golden light traveled out of EdelIÈnne's chest into the air. He was blinking at them, trying to understand, when a black entity appeared. It floated in the air next to the strings and sucked the gold out of his hut. Richard was no scholar, but he had heard enough tales to recognize what was happening. His wife, his loving Edelienne, had splintered. Her soul hadn't traveled to the ethereal realm where it belonged; it had shattered into splinters, like their Lost Goddess, Alames, had. Edelienne was forever doomed to roam through limbo.

His body trembled while he struggled to form a single thought. Lumps of pain throbbed inside him—grief, shock, guilt, love. It wasn't good for people to feel this much. The last time he'd felt this much, everything had collapsed. He swallowed hard and decided on a more reasonable solution.

"Let us pray, Pier. She's with Exitalis now."

"She's not though . . ."

Richard had hoped Pier wouldn't know about limbo, that this dark reality of their world had never found its way into his son's vast well of knowledge. Pier's watery gaze told him he knew it better than Richard did. He slid down the wall and cried harder. Richard longed to rush out of the shack, back onto the field, or better even, to the church for a prayer. But Pier wasn't alone in this. Not while Richard lived.

He laid Edelienne's corpse on the bed and pulled his son

back to his feet. With one hand on Pier's bony shoulder, he wiped away the blood.

"Sorry for the blow. I wasn't thinking." He tightened his grip. "But we can't be weak anymore, all right?"

Pier looked at his feet, avoiding his father's eyes. The painful lumps of unwanted feelings grew within Richard. They heated up, ready to boil over. He wasn't sure how much longer he could hold it in.

"We're gonna make it through this." He pushed Pier's chin up. "You hear me? We're gonna make it through this together, and I'm gonna find you a place in Waldfeld, a real one. You're gonna have a wife and sons of your own, and none of this will matter anymore. You hear me?"

Pier searched his face for recognition of a different kind, something that Richard understood but tried not to.

"Dad, I'm—"

"Let's pray. We don't wanna keep our lady of the dead waiting, do we?"

He let go of Pier's shoulder and searched the kitchen cabinet for matches. His eyes fell on the Edeliènne's jewel casket. It looked cleaner than the other kitchen tools, but she couldn't have been using it. They had run out of motus weeks ago. He checked over his shoulder for Pier, who had sat down on the stool next to his mother and was tracing the lines of her face with his index finger. Assured that he wasn't watching, Richard opened the casket. His heart dropped when he saw what was inside: at least twenty square copper coins—enough motus to last them two more weeks—as well as an empty flask and one half filled with black goo, which was likely worth forty more motus. He pushed it aside with a shaking hand and revealed the green leaves hidden beneath it. *Poison hemlock.* Father Godfried gave a tea of the plant with drops of opium to the old and frail longing to pass in peace. The pain in Richard's stomach grew. Edeliènne had chosen death before she could run out of opium.

He looked back at Pier's famished frame, and anger shook

him. The contents of her jewel casket could have bought their son a grand feast. He forced himself to steady. *Calm.* Father Godfried had taught him to stay calm. He pulled out the matches instead and lit their prayer candle. The sound of the match caught Pier's attention, and he cleared some space on the bed for Richard to sit on. After he lit the candle, Richard closed his eyes.

"Dearest Exitalis, lady of the dead, wife of the king, mother to us, we thank you for the life and death of Edeliènne Kilburn. Our hearts recognize the gift you giveth every day. Thank you for the breaths you have not yet taken. We mourn the loss of our dear goddess Alames, as we celebrate the days you alloweth us. Take the passing of today's time as a sacrifice and have mercy on our mortal bodies."

"Have mercy on our mortal bodies."

"Our blood is yours," Richard and Pier said in unison.

CHAPTER 6

ALLY

November 969 - The Palace of Virisunder, City of Polemos

Bells echoed through the palace's dining hall and released Ally from her tension. They announced not only her but every courtier's favorite time of day: the jester's after-dinner show. Josef had originally hired Bored Reginald, as Reggie was known at court, to perform the occasional small variety show in the hope he would ridicule Ally in his performances—a task way beneath him. Bored Reginald was a grand illusionist. Within a year, he had become the court's darling. He dazzled the minds of anyone he met. No ball was held, no honoring performed without his fantastical inventions. His art was like clouds. As soon as one recognized the beauty of its shapes, it dissolved. Ally was grateful that his place in her life hadn't dissolved.

She put her fork down and scanned the stage. Reggie's troupe hadn't laid out any props or built a set for the night—the signs of a solo show. Ally looked for a detail that might hint at what she could expect and found shadows flitting around the hall. She turned her gaze down immediately. It had taken her three hours to recover from the Council meeting, and she wasn't keen on relapsing over her mashed potatoes. She focused on a silent force inside of herself to mute all unwelcome visions and reached for her nightly chamomile tea.

From the corner of her eye, she spotted Josefine leaning closer to her uncle, Harald Heidegger. The two had been whispering throughout all five courses of the elaborate feast the palace kitchen had prepared. Ally knew they were conspiring, but she had no new information to ruminate over. Her courtiers had approved the war with Silberfluss, and unless the Council changed their minds in a court vote, they couldn't remove Ally from her princess position without consent. It was unlike what had happened to her grandmother. This was a sole Virisunder issue, and Harald would have to fight for the votes, even with Josefine's approval.

Sudden darkness smothered Ally's rumination. Her heart raced, and she grabbed the knife in front of her. It was meant to cut butter, but in the right circumstance, she'd find use for it. Two seconds later, magic illuminated a spot in the middle of the stage. She set the knife down and leaned back in her throne. *This show better be good, Reggie, after scaring me like that.* But she knew it would be.

The courtiers next to her speculated in whispers how torches could be snuffed without approaching them. Ally smiled. Silly people. When would they stop questioning the talents of Bored Reginald? He was in control. That was the only thing that mattered. As long as he was in control, nothing could go wrong.

Dark fog appeared around the spotlight and circled it. It sped up by the second until purple glitter sprayed out of it. A few courtiers laughed, but Ally sat up taller, determined not to miss a second of the show. The fog thickened until it looked like a black curtain. The glitter blanketed it like purple snow. A pedestal rose out of the floor. The whispering grew louder.

"How did he do that?"

"Where is it coming from?"

"Shh," Ally commanded, and the courtiers became silent.

The sound of drums filled the room, coming from the backstage area. Their slow rhythm increased and became louder and quicker until an earth-shattering explosion resounded from the spotlight. The glitter snow blasted into the air in a grand spectacle. The whole room stared at the spotlight, eager for the climax. One second. Two seconds. Three seconds. The fog and glitter cleared and revealed . . . no one.

A storage door in the back of the dining hall opened, and Bored Reginald entered in his pajamas, which had a depiction of Harald Heidegger's face stitched on them.

"Oh my, you weren't expecting *me* to stand there, were you? How very embarrassing for you."

The courtiers roared with laughter as Bored Reginald walked into the spotlight. He was a lanky elf in his late thirties with straight brown hair, worn in a ponytail that night. His most eye-catching feature was a black rose tattooed on his left cheek. Its stem reached down his neckline and into his shirt. He was striking in ways that evaded the current language, his oval face blessed with both strength and softness. Ally's heart quickened as she took him in. The day had felt endless without him.

A few of the courtiers pointed at his pajamas and laughed. Ally glanced at Harald. A Tidier elbowed his side with a grin and received a sour look in return.

Reggie picked up on the anticipated attention his outfit drew. He stretched out his arms to reveal it fully.

"Are you laughing at this?" He brought his hands to his cheeks in an exaggerated gesture of bashfulness. "My oh my, *I* should be the one embarrassed. I'm so sorry. I thought it was expected of the court to sleep with the Council."

Ally lost her manners. "Ha!" Thankfully, other courtiers

joined her in the taunting. She scanned the room. About a quarter of them didn't laugh. Not enough for Harald to push a vote through.

"So," Reggie continued, stretching out the word, "what are you all doing here?"

"We're here for you," a handsome young man hooted from across the room. A pang of jealousy shot through Ally.

"Me? I was just about to enjoy a nightcap in my alcove, but I suppose if you ragamuffins aren't bored of Bored, I could make you a little less bored." He reached into his pocket. "Here, have a free show, my court-anions." With that, he tossed a handful of purple glitter into the air, bowed, and shuffled back toward the storage door.

Ally giggled, louder than she'd intended to, and Reggie stopped. She held her breath as he spun around. His gaze made her stomach waltz.

"Unless, of course, Your Highness would be interested in a more intense spectacle," he said with a smirk, lighting a fire inside her that slowly wandered southward. She cleared her throat and tried to pull herself together.

"You don't want to disappoint the court, now do you, Bored Reginald? Perform your show," she said and almost sounded as if her thighs weren't on fire.

"Always happy to please, my princess." The comma was barely audible. Ally blushed.

With a snap of his fingers, Reggie turned his pajamas into a black tailcoat with a top hat. White dots painted the coat like stars, telling stories that only the night sky understood. He took a bow and clapped his hands. The dining hall blurred. When it sharpened again, he'd transformed the hall. The heavy brick walls behind Reggie had turned white and elusive. An opaque snowstorm obscured the stage. Ally noticed Harald twitch nearby. He didn't appreciate magic that enraptured instead of harmed. Ally thought of the means Reggie used to perform his magic and grew uneasy. He had made it clear that he was not to be questioned on them. He rarely asked anything of her, so she had obeyed.

Ally gave in to the mesmerizing illusion. Her own mind tortured her with horrible images, but his magic proved that shadows only existed because of light.

"Now let me introduce the players of tonight's show." He snapped his fingers twice, and each time a black silhouette appeared in front of the white storm. They were shadow figures—one with a lilac tint, one with a blue tint.

"Silhouettes again. How original. I get why they call you *Bored*," Josefine snarled from across the table. Ally's eyes narrowed. Her daughter loved putting people down to raise herself up. Ally was just about to chide her when Reggie responded.

"My most humble apology, dear Lady Verdain. I did not know you needed more thrill."

He led the shadow figures closer to Josefine and snapped his fingers again. Both grew in dimension and color until they turned into illusions of two muscular, sparsely dressed men. The courtiers' eyes widened, for they were both undeniably attractive. Reggie's fan from earlier whistled. The jester himself crossed his arms and grinned.

"So you're longing for excitement, my dear Lady Verdain? I think they are too."

Another snap, and they performed a provocative dance that soon turned into a striptease. Ally shook her head, barely able to contain her laughter. *What are you doing, Reggie?* The look on her daughter's face was priceless. Josefine turned burgundy and finally behaved like the teenager she was. Heidegger would surely recognize her immaturity, and the ridiculous discussion would be over. Reggie always managed to turn conflict into humor.

"I-I command you to stop this, jester," Josefine stuttered.

Reggie clapped his hands, and the figures turned back

into shadow silhouettes. "Thank Alames you were satisfied already. My illusory phallus game is weak. Total flop, if I may say so."

Ally burst into laughter not fit for a princess, but the courtiers' howling drowned it out. Several whistled. Reginald had a talent for making nobles forget their nobility. It surely worked on her.

"Now please, gentlefolk, you can finish this story later in your privates with your privates. If you'll excuse me, I'd like to get back to my boring old art."

A dramatic gushing sound quieted the room. The rhythm of haunting drums followed. He changed the atmosphere of the room in an instant. Not with the cowardly methods Heidegger used, but simply with his brilliance. The rhythm connected to Ally's heartbeat until her breath steadied and new strength streamed through her veins. For the first time since seeing Subira, she was certain about the path ahead. She had allowed the Heideggers to take whatever they wanted for too long. They had robbed her of her youth, of raising her own daughter, of her crown's power. It ended now. She'd take Silberfluss, take Agathe's throne, and build an Elfentum nation too strong for the Council to meddle with.

Reggie's eyes met hers, and she sensed a chemical reaction between them, an energetic charge that she would never tire of studying. He stepped to the side of the stage and gestured for the silhouettes to take their place inside the snowstorm, far enough to be enclosed by it without becoming invisible. An illusionary scaffold rose from the floor and lifted them until they almost reached the hall's high ceiling. They took each other's hand and bowed to the audience as the construction shook underneath them.

The blue-tinted figure spun the lilac one. Their circles reminded Ally of a sped-up clock until the figure spun out of time and collapsed onto the scaffold. The blue one picked them back up, and the two drifted into a pulsing dance. They pulled together and apart like a silent accordion. One pull was farther than the blue figure expected, so the lilac one slipped off the scaffold's edge.

Ally let out a shriek. She knew the Council members were watching her, but they didn't understand. The silhouette was sure to fall to their death. The blue figure caught the short one in the last moment. They were safe for now, but the scaffold trembled beneath them. It couldn't hold the imbalance for long. The lilac one swung from one side to the other with all her might. *Yes, focus on the momentum. It'll create force.*

The blue one didn't let go. The lilac figure's swinging was desperate yet beautiful. They looked like a bird, soaring higher and higher in the hopes to land again. Every time they tried, the scaffold threatened to throw them both to their death.

Reggie flicked his finger. Flames emerged next to the scaffold, reaching toward the ceiling until they stopped half an arm's length under the lilac figure. The figure must've felt the heat, but they kept swinging, focused only on the blue one. Hands crept out of the flames.

When they had built enough momentum to land, the blue one's arm ripped. The strain of holding them had torn the figure apart. Ally hadn't noticed until that moment. Her eyes and concern had been with the lilac one.

The fragments of the blue figure broke down on the scaffold, and the lilac figure fell toward the flames. But before the lilac one could be ravaged by the hands, wings grew out of their back. The figure became the free bird they were meant to be and flew up to the top of the scaffold. The lilac one gently picked up the halves of their lover, and they ascended into the snowstorm together.

No sound came from the audience. Their trance only broke when the snowstorm dissolved and Reginald took a bow. The understanding that the show was over seeped in, and the hall erupted in booming applause. The noise brought Ally back to reality. She noticed that her face was wet with tears. Her body shivered and felt hot at the same time. The story had found its way into every molecule of her skin.

Ally smiled at her love. He seemed tenser than usual and hid it from the court with his exaggerated bows.

"Thank you, thank you. I live for your ability to clap your hands together rhythmically," he said.

"Encore! Encore!" a few courtiers yelled, but Reginald shook his head.

"I don't think Lady Verdain can take any more excitement tonight, my court-kin." He bowed toward Josefine, who blushed anew. She pretended to be disinterested, but Ally had caught her leaning forward, enraptured like everyone else.

"Come back tomorrow for my next show. I'll probably take a nap on stage or something. I don't know. I haven't prepared anything." He twirled on the spot until his coat turned back into his pajamas, and he produced a comically large whiskey bottle out of the air. "To freedom, the Verdains, and to improved scaffold construction, or whatever my show was about!"

The courtiers raised their glasses as well and yelled, "Hear! Hear!"

It wasn't a sufficient send-off. Ally jumped up from her chair and raised her glass. It was filled with grape juice. She preferred not to aggravate the voices with alcohol.

"To flying!" she yelled.

Harald shook his head. A few courtiers and most of the Council members laughed. They were laughing at her, not with her, but she didn't care. This wasn't for them. Reggie looked at her for the first time since the show had ended.

"To flying," he said.

Then he left. The temperature of the room dropped. The dining hall appeared darker despite servants lighting the torches anew. Ally noticed that Harald was watching her, and a shiver crept over her skin.

"If you'll excuse me," she addressed him, "I require rest."

Heidegger nodded with a calm expression. His calmness unnerved her. She'd expected him to twirl courtiers around his finger, convince them to vote for his succession plan, but he just sat there, sipping his wine.

You're doomed already, and you don't even realize it.

Ally took a deep breath and left the dining hall without giving him another look. Dillon caught up with her as soon as she reached the hallway.

"Would you like me to get him?" he asked when no one was within earshot.

She nodded. She'd made it through the day on her own, but she craved his kiss to brace her for the night. Still, the Council might send a guard to check on her room. It was better to be safe.

"Send him to our hallway."

"Of course." He rushed off toward the backstage area, and Ally relaxed. Her performance of the day was over as well. Her mask was no longer required. She took care of the elaborate updo and jewels her handmaidens had woven into her hair first. The pins pricked her skin, and the whole useless construction weighted her down. Twenty minutes later, she headed to her and Reggie's secret hallway, her long white hair cascading down her back.

She turned into a rarely used corridor. The four rooms it led to were designed for storage and bookkeeping, so people rarely visited it. A copper statue of Theodosia from when she was still the princess of Virisunder stood watch at the end of the hall. Her grandmother wore the jewels Ally had freed her hair of, along with a richly decorated hoop skirt and puffy sleeves. Ally was grateful fashion had evolved since then. It must have been impossible to embrace someone in such attire.

She slid her arm around Theodosia's waist and pulled a lever on her lower back. Her grandmother had installed the statue when Makeda first became general of Virisunder. A relation of this sort with another woman—especially one of Fi'Teri descent—had been unthinkable at the time, but Theodosia had always been determined to make history. Seven years ago, Reggie and Ally had visited them at the military academy Altor Caedem, and Makeda had told them about their secret hideaway.

The statue creaked forward and revealed a small gap that led to a forgotten hallway. Ally's tiny body slipped through it without problem. She was never sure how Reggie sneaked into it but suspected magic.

The lovely green light of an assula lamp lit up their special hallway. Ally had purchased it a month ago, as lighting torches had proven difficult in the secluded space. Her heart jumped when she saw Reggie.

"Is that my Ally I'm spotting in this little alley?" His voice was naturally playful but more sincere than his stage persona let on.

Ally jumped into his arms. The force of her motion tossed them against the wall. He stumbled, caught his balance, and hugged her tighter. His embrace seemed to create another world for her, a wholesome one.

He's trapping you.

He kissed the tip of her long elf ear. She leaned into him more, ignoring the whispers of her mind.

Stupid piece of shit. Too dense to see he's using you.

The kisses turned into nibbling. The sensation normally sent shivers down her spine, but now panic jolted through her. She pushed herself off his chest and glanced around. Her breath sped up. The walls seemed awfully close. Was someone watching them?

Reggie set her down gently and cupped her face. "Rough day, sugar?"

Ally nodded and kissed his hand. Subira, the Council, the voices—everything fought her that day. She was supposed to lead, not lose petty battles.

"If you need a day to clear your mind, I can always—"

"That was a beautiful show tonight, Reggie."

She knew what he was suggesting and wouldn't allow it.

He had found a way to expunge the illness for a few hours. He had the power to give her a life and a mind of her own, but the price was high. Too high.

"Sugar, really, it's no biggie. I can whisk together another day of clarity, easy."

"No."

He respected her choice and hugged her again. She breathed in his scent of daffodil meadows and ocean breeze. With each breath, the fragments of her mind reattached. Josef was gone. Reggie was here to stay. She'd win the war with or without Subira. Virisunder would double in size. She was in control. She pulled herself out of the hug and kissed him on tiptoes, barely reaching him. Verdain women were of short stature, and she was the shortest of them all. The touch of his lips settled her in her body. Her mind quieted, and the blood that pulsed through her reawakened, igniting an urgent hunger within her. The kiss was both infinite and terminal.

A loud blast pulled them apart. Theodosia's statue shattered as if it were made of thin glass. The pieces crumbled to the ground and revealed Harald, who was running his fingers over his glowing gemstone chain. Five Tidiers stood behind him with assula rifles and gemstone chains of their own. Ally let go of Reggie's arms.

Harald stepped forward with a self-satisfied smirk. "One of your troupe's great artists told me where to find you, Mister *Bored*. But how curious seeing you here, Alexandra. Clearly our idea of what constitutes as rest differs."

Music blared through Ally's head—several mismatching symphonies with creaking violins, shrill flutes, and a piano out of tune. She tried to hear her own thoughts over the noise.

"That's *Princess* or *Your Highness* for you, Harald!" Ally yelled, much louder than she had intended.

Reggie stepped between them so quickly it seemed like an illusion. "Your highest Council chief ruler in charge, I was just explaining the artistic process behind tonight's show to the princess. She was curious because, as you might remember, I put on a damned to the gods, mother-snuggling great performance."

It's all over. It's all over. It's all over.
Sing, harlot, sing.

Ally trembled. *How much did they see? How much did they see? How much did they see?*

Harald ignored Reggie and turned to the Tidiers. "Seize him."

The Tidiers dashed through the opening. Their boots crushed the remaining pieces of Theodosia. The noise echoed within the melodies tormenting Ally. Two Tidiers forced Reginald to his knees, two pointed their rifles at him, and the last one bound his hands. Ally screamed and pressed herself against the wall. *Is this real? Is this happening?*

You killed him, you stupid harlot. Toxic. Poisonous.

Reggie glanced at her. He looked concerned about her, not himself, despite his predicament. He continued his farce, nevertheless. "Now, Tidiers, I know that it should be criminal to be this good-looking, but this seems a little extreme."

Charming. Clever. Funny. His strategy might have worked if Ally stayed quiet, but—

Say something.
Say something.
Say something, stupid.
Say something or he'll die.

"What are you doing? Why are you arresting him? What's going on?"

Harald's smile widened. He had pushed her where he wanted her: ready to obey.

"You have rightfully stated, *Your Highness*, that the Council has no jurisdiction changing a nation's monarch. It is, however, our duty to ensure the religious purity of all Elfentum nations. According to the Polemos Summit of 924, it's the Council's duty, as a neutral organization representing all of

Elfentum, to eradicate heresy against the seven gods whenever it occurs."

Ally blinked at him blankly. The words had made their way through the melodies, but she couldn't connect them. "So?"

"So, we have found evidence in your jester's private tower that incriminates him."

"Who gave you permission to search my palace?"

Harald chuckled. "Prince Josef, Your Highness."

He got you. He finally broke you.

"We have found books and prayers to the Traitor, as well as a play about the Traitor that besmirches the memory of our Lost Goddess, Alames. During Grievance Week, of all times!"

"It's called artistic expression, Mister Councilman," Reggie chimed in. He continued to be calm, but Ally noticed his face whiten. "You might want to look that up. I was doing research on her, that's all."

Heidegger scoffed. "*Her?* The Traitor is not a woman. It's a monstrosity mortal sinners designed."

Reggie let out a nervous laugh. "See, that's why I need research. I was not aware of that."

They're going to hang him, and it's your fault.

"Now, Alexandra." Harald turned back to her. "We know your mind is easily . . . persuaded. We cannot allow a princess of Elfentum to have close relations with a suspected heretic. As long as she's the princess, that is."

Her worst fears became true. They knew. The melodies tore at her eardrums.

"This is ridiculous," Reggie said. "I'm the court jester, nothing more."

Heidegger's smile turned into triumph. "Rumor has it you perform private shows of a certain kind for her as well, and seeing what compromising position we found you in, I dare say they're correct."

His eyes pierced through Ally. He had lured her into the mousetrap. She was aware of it and yet had no choice but to eat the cheese and get crushed. Memories of Reggie's and her journey flashed in Ally's mind: Their first kiss. Their first exchange of ideas. The first time Reggie had stolen her from Josef's claws and led her to a magical illusion that belonged solely to them.

She had tried to resist, but it had been no use. Denying her joy was suicide, and no matter how determined she was, she couldn't kill herself day after day.

This was it. If she fought Harald, they would hang Reggie for heresy to punish her. It would strengthen her position against the Council, but she'd never pay that price. The other option was to obey. She could hand her crown to Josefine and retire on a barony. She might even be able to bring Reggie with her. The picture of a quiet life together soothed her for a moment. Then she realized the oblivion that would swallow them. The war would fail. Virisunder would wither. The Council would win. Unless there was a third option . . .

"Even if this slandering were true, he is not accompanying me to the front, so my past relations to him do not matter. Princess Josefine won't listen to a fool."

Heidegger feigned ignorance. "*Princess* Josefine? But, Your Highness, you disputed our suggestion earlier." Then the second part of her idea registered with him. "Pardon, did you say *front?*" For the first time since he had marched into her home, he seemed lost. She relished the small victory it brought.

"Yes, *front.* As my last action as princess of Virisunder, I am appointing myself general. I'll be in charge of the war against Silberfluss, a conflict that, may I remind you, has already been approved." She thought of her daughter and her constant desire to be the best without putting in any effort. "I'm sure the new princess will appreciate her reign commencing with a successful war in Caedem's honor." Victory had always secured Virisunder's monarchs a place in the heart of their nation. Caedem was the god of war and strength, after all.

Everyone remained silent for three seconds, taken aback by her unexpected decision. She'd teach them not to underestimate her.

Reggie spoke first. "Your Highness, may I . . ."

Ally closed her eyes. One look at him could risk everything. Becoming the active general would require her to leave him behind. It was the sacrifice Subira had backed away from. Ally thought of the kiss they'd shared mere minutes ago. It seemed like years. Reggie was her eternal spring, but she had to become winter.

"You may not, *jester.* I don't know what fantastic tales you have spread about your position here, but you clearly have forgotten your place. From now on, I expect you to focus solely on artistic pursuits."

"No, Al—"

She glared at him with as much hate as she could muster. It wasn't much, but he crumbled when the cold gust hit him. "Careful, jester. Your position at court is dispensable."

One of the Tidiers, a particularly slow-looking human, spoke up. "His position? But, Your Highness, the heresy allegations still stand. He—"

Ally directed the icy winds of her misty eyes at him. He flinched, despite his physical advantage. "You want to remove the nation's most popular artist during a delicate exchange of power on the grounds of some unpublished garbage? Over some daft scribblings? My judgment may be impaired, but that seems unwise."

Harald snapped his fingers. "Let him go. We got what we came for."

The Tidiers released Reggie with some reluctance. He didn't move.

"Marvelous," Harald continued. "We should leave you to it, jester. You have a lot to prepare for the crowning ceremony. *King* Josef is looking forward to seeing how your foolish touch will enrich the celebration." He turned to Ally and gestured toward the exit. "Queen Alexandra, it may be wise to get actual rest now. Your troops await you. I'm sure they'll be happy to take commands from someone who *truly* understands the purpose of this war."

A cold shiver ran down Ally's spine. She had discussed military strategies with Subira before, but those had been games of the mind, meaningless banter with no stakes. Ally didn't know what the general position actually entailed. She'd have to study it. There was nothing books couldn't teach her.

Reggie sank farther onto the ground. Perhaps there were a few things books couldn't teach her.

"After you, my *queen*." Harald placed a hand on her back and pushed her toward the exit. She longed for a moment alone with Reggie to explain herself. It was unlikely she'd get a chance to see him again that night.

Ally had no choice. She walked out of their former sanctuary, past the ruins of Theodosia. She turned to make sure the Tidiers followed her and was relieved when they did. Reggie didn't stand up. With every step she walked away from him, she felt heavier, colder.

Then, when Heidegger and the Tidiers stopped paying attention, she noticed Reggie's hands run over the stone floor. For a brief moment, the two silhouettes from his show appeared on the ground. They embraced and vanished.

Ally's and Reggie's eyes met. They would make it through this. They had to. As long as she kept swinging, he would keep holding on to her.

CHAPTER 7

RICHARD

November 969 - Town Square of Waldfeld, Silberfluss

The noise of the busy market faded into the background when Richard brought his knife to the wood. The satisfying scratching of the blade allowed him to think without having to put on a mask. The knife carried his strength. His hand commanded the calm. Richard's only duty was to sit and watch as the beautiful timber art of nature transformed into a new creation. Man-made, but part of nature's marvel.

Guilt had followed him out of the shack, but the whittling dispersed it. He'd likely find it waiting for him at home, together with his abandoned son, and he would allow it back in. For now, however, a frenzy of hope had taken hold.

The motus Edeliènne had been hiding from them had paid for enough millet and milk to last a few more weeks. Pier had prepared creamed millet with milk instead of water that morning, a rare treat for the two of them. Richard hoped it would sustain his son and let him rest after months of caring for his mother, preparing the opium for her, week after week, while starving himself.

Richard pressed the blade down harder than he'd intended and sliced off the tail of the wooden horse he was whittling. He examined the half-finished figurine and put it aside. Perhaps he'd find a purpose for it later. He was reaching down for a new branch when a woman approached his stall.

"Look at those charming toys. You still got it in you, Dick."

He glanced up and nodded at Dotty Ackerman, a local free farmer. She had grown up on the land right next to his father's. Their parents used to compete for who could grow the most wheat in a season. As if it mattered. The Ackermans got to keep all of their harvest for themselves. Even when Richard's father won, the serfs always lost.

Two rambunctious children, five or six years of age, used Dotty as a shield for their catch game. The little girl ripped a tear in her mother's skirt during a surprise attack on the boy, who shrieked the same way Pier used to during thunderstorms. His skin was darker than Pier's though. He didn't look like a Waldfeld resident. The girl looked odd in her own way, with long, pointed ears that reached up to her temples in a straight line. Her teeth were sharper than those of normal humans but didn't look like the cutting thorns elves called teeth. *Halfer.* Dotty had scandalized the town by marrying an elf and happily procreating. Richard's father had been furious when he'd heard about it. He'd said that the Ackermans might grow more wheat, but he grew better children. Richard liked Dotty regardless.

"Vana!" She examined the rip, then glared at her daughter, who shrunk. Dotty looked as sweet as Edel"ienne had, but she didn't possess the same quiet indifference toward trouble.

The boy stepped in front of Vana. "I'm sorry, Mrs. Ackerman. I taunted her to do that."

Dotty's stern face melted into a chuckle. She shook her head and turned back to Richard. "Can you believe it? Jules's family has only been in Waldfeld for two months, and he's already taking the blame for my daughter. The Ackermans sure know how to twirl someone around their finger. Reminds me of you and Brice when you were young. Don't you think?"

Richard reached for the branches underneath his stall and ran his fingers over their rough texture. None of them seemed suited for the next figurine. He sat back up and noticed Dotty staring at him, waiting for an answer, so he shrugged. "I don't remember."

Dotty nodded. "Well, ehm, I'm very sorry about Edeliènne. Pier must be devastated."

"We both are."

"Of course."

He wished he could object to her sympathetic smile. She could mourn on her own right, but Edeliènne's death was his fault, and he didn't deserve the sympathy.

The boy picked up a wooden fox figure and tapped on Vana's shoulder. She brushed him off and addressed her mother instead.

"Mommy, is Edejen the woman who starved?"

Dotty's cheeks turned pink. "We'll talk about it later, sweets."

Vana crossed her arms. "But, Mommy, we still had potatoes. Why didn't we give them to her? She could eat mine. I hate potatoes."

"I'm so sorry, Dick."

Richard waved Dotty off. "Don't worry about it." He missed when Pier was that age. The younger the kid, the smaller their problems. Pier used to lecture him that the royals and the peasants needed to meet over soup and talk openly about what they wanted from one another. The simplicity of his solutions had been comforting.

Richard leaned forward toward Vana. "Your mommy shared a lot with us already, and we passed it on and shared with others as well. Do you know the Belladonnas?" Vana nodded. "We gave them a little bit too so that everyone could be happy."

"That's stupid."

"Vana, careful." Dotty glowered at her.

"What? I'm sorry, Dick, but that's not very smart."

Richard put down the whittling knife and scratched his ginger beard. He didn't care for Dotty using his old nickname, but this little girl was adorable. "Why is that, young lady?"

"The Belladonnas have a lot of ugly horses that are mean. They bit me once. So you gave the Belladonnas the food for your wife, which they maybe gave to their horses. That's a really poor decision."

Richard shrugged. "What if they demanded it?"

Vana squinted her eyes. "Then we kill them."

Richard spluttered. After all these years, the Ackermans still managed to surprise him. Dotty grabbed Vana's wrist, making it clear that the discussion was over. "That's enough, Vana. I'm sorry, Dick. She overheard my husband telling one of his stories the other night and has gotten some ideas into her head."

"It's cute," he said, then snapped his fingers at the boy, Jules, who was still holding the fox. "Hey, boy, you want that?"

Jules glanced at Vana, then nodded.

"Take it. It's yours."

His face lit up with joy that warmed the cold winter air. Richard needed to make motus, but if he could make some children happy first, he'd take the win.

Dotty shook her head and reached into her pouch. "Let me give you a coin for that."

Richard crossed his arms. "Don't worry about it."

"Dick . . ."

"Don't worry about it; I'll figure it out. Always do." Except, he hadn't, but he didn't want Dotty's sympathy to sustain him, especially not when it stemmed from some romanticized memories of her lost brother, Brice.

Dotty studied him. "You're not thinking about signing up for the war against Virisunder, are you? I saw the recruitment posters all over town."

Richard bit his lip. He had thought about it. It would be a selfless way to ensure a good future for Pier. It would also jeopardize his place in it. The thought of missing the birth of his grandchildren kept him away from the recruitment tent.

"No, don't worry about me."

Dotty sighed. "Someone ought to."

Vana pushed in front of her mother. "Can I pick one too?" Dotty yanked at her wrist. "No, wait. Mom, I will mind the shop for three hours if you give me that rose."

"Clever girl you got there, Dotty."

Dotty sighed again, the exasperated sound of a young mother. Richard missed that noise as well. "Let's go, you two." She took Jules's hand.

"But, Mom——"

"We're leaving." She dragged them away from his stall and looked over her shoulder. "Bye, Dick. Look after yourself."

Richard waved after them and watched as they disappeared into the busy market. He slumped down and waited once more. Some people glanced at his work while passing, but apart from Dotty, no one had stopped. It was the war's fault. Who wanted to buy toys during wartimes? Richard shifted on his stool. He hated how the outside influenced their idyllic little Waldfeld. Father Godfried reminded them in each sermon to appreciate what Exitalis provided right in front of them and to treasure the little moments, like toys and children's laughter. But no matter how unwise it was, the world was changing.

He observed the crowd for a while and readjusted the figurines on his stall. When the sun dipped behind the surrounding rooftops, he picked up one of his imperfect branches and whittled again. He shaped the wood without paying attention to its form. It turned into a tiny sword. He held it against the light and examined it. So many of Waldfeld's recruits would stumble into a war they didn't understand with less suitable weapons than this toy. The work his fellow peasants signed up for was to cushion Virisunder's attacks. They provided a buffer for Silberfluss's valuable trained soldiers. He doubted they'd receive proper weaponry and training.

He placed the sword next to a wooden sparrow and observed the market again. He wasn't the only unlucky vendor. None of the small merchants seemed to make any motus that day. Everyone needed food, but who wanted to buy scarves or toys during a famine and an upcoming war?

A cold wind rustled the pine trees of the nearby forest. He peered at the treetops that reached high above the merchant houses. He hadn't reconnected with the forest's serenity in weeks—not since Father Godfried had warned them of the dangers. Richard tried to picture a demon that would choose the scent of pines and the soft soil beneath one's feet as their home. How could a creature of evil embrace such beauty? But Father Godfried's word was law. Bad things happened to those who disobeyed.

"Kilburn." A guard approached him. "Time to pack up or pay another motus."

Richard stood up with a groan and stretched his stiff muscles. "Packing up."

He opened his case and placed each figurine into it with great care. When all of them had returned to their safe home, he noticed that the guard hadn't moved.

"Cute."

Panic surged through Richard before he realized that the guard was commenting on the tiny wooden sword in his hand.

"Thanks."

The guard swung it around in the air as if it were a real weapon. "By Exitalis, Kilburn, I wish this was bigger. Better than the junk the military provides."

Richard looked him over. He was young, no older than twenty-five, with hazel skin, dark curls, and a handsome, innocent grin. Like the little boy, he must have come from far away. Richard had heard that humans from the tribal land Tribu La'am looked like that. It would be a shame if the war took his life.

"You signed up?" Richard asked.

The guard nodded. "Yeah. I think I've overstayed my welcome here, and Virisunder is supposed to be warmer." He shuddered dramatically. People had been complaining about the cold all day, but Richard was used to the brisk air. He pulled the shawl off his shoulders. Edeliènne had woven it for his thirtieth birthday four years ago, and it reminded him too much of her.

"Here. Might help."

The guard took it with visible confusion, then looked Richard up and down, likely judging him for the rest of his tattered clothes.

"You can keep the sword too."

The guard wrapped himself in the shawl and smirked. "Thanks. Will you make me a bigger one?"

Richard frowned. "A bigger . . . ?"

"Sword. A bigger sword." He raised the tiny sword into the air and emulated a battle cry. "For Waldfeld!"

Richard chuckled. "I can, if you like."

"Lovely," he responded with a wink. "Hey, I have you as Kilburn on my list, but what can I call you without being a dick?"

"Richard, I guess."

"So, Dick? All right, let's go with Richard." He smiled as he said the name. Richard liked how it sounded from his lips. "I'm Ordell, but you can call me Yooko if you like."

"I . . . what?"

"Don't worry about it. Well, Richard, I look forward to receiving a big sword of wood from you."

"Okay." He wondered whether a wooden weapon could withstand combat. "I just need to find a way to harden the wood."

"I could help you harden that wood." Yooko leaned over

the stall. "My shift's over in a few minutes. Wanna grab a drink at The Stag's Tail first?"

Yooko's intentions dawned on Richard, and his eyes grew wide. The Stag's Tail was as godless as the forest. According to Father Godfried, any man who found himself there would lose Exitalis's favor.

"N-no."

Yooko cocked his head. "You don't drink? Look, I'm not necessarily a one night kinda guy. How about a meal? My treat. Molly's Kitchen is pretty decent."

Richard avoided his eyes. *Decent.* This was nothing. This meant nothing. He had lost his wife, and a man needed a woman in his life, or else the Traitor's ideas invaded his mind. "I don't know what you're talking about."

Yooko smirked, but before he could respond, he spotted something behind Richard and startled. "Sorry, I gotta go. See you later, Dick."

Richard looked over his shoulder and saw three royal guards approaching the market square. He turned back around, and Yooko had disappeared. The only thing that remained was a hollow feeling in Richard's chest and a nauseating pressure in his stomach.

Richard shook his head and forced himself to think about his future instead of some indecent criminal. The future was the pressing matter. He had hoped to sell enough toys to put the meat back on Pier's bones. He'd have to figure out another way to save his son. He picked up the remaining branches and thought of the wooden sword. Yooko was right. Weaponry forged of wood could be affordable to Waldfeld's people without losing its quality. If only he could solve the durability issue. A noble smith could use magic to stabilize it, but Richard would never get the motus together to purchase assulas. He wished there was a different magic, one for the simple folk.

Another heavy breeze gushed through the square. Richard looked back at the forest, and an unholy thought crossed his mind. Rumors said demons possessed more magic than any assula could carry. There were stories about brave, stupid mortals striking deals with demons. Father Godfried considered it a sacrilegious act, but what if the demon worshiped the gods' glorious nature as much as Richard did? He considered himself neither brave nor stupid. He wasn't one to take risks either. He was calm, pious Richard: The man who had let Edeliènne starve. The man who would never disobey Father Godfried and enter a demon-ridden forest. The man who would let his son starve as well.

An hour later, he had dropped off the market supplies at home and found himself in the heart of the forest. The damp moss penetrated Richard's thin leather boots as he made his way through the darkness. He had brought his prayer candle as a light source and for soul protection. Part of him hoped his goddess Exitalis might shield him if the demon was unwilling to cooperate. Another part longed to extinguish the flame and fade into the forest's peaceful darkness. Pier needed him to return.

A twig snapped beneath his foot, and he halted. Something had changed. The trees stood too thick to allow free airflow, yet wind caressed his face and snuffed out the candle.

Without light, his sense of smell sharpened. The air was heavy with the scent of oak and grass. The candle soiled its freshness, so Richard waved the remaining smoke away. He should have been concerned that Exitalis had left him, but he wasn't. Something else had embraced him.

The feeling of cold air on his skin disappeared, as his surroundings adjusted to his body temperature. Whatever it was, it left drops of dew on his arm. It reminded him of the clover he used to collect. He used to sprinkle its morning dew onto his love's forehead during the hot summer months.

Father Godfried crept into Richard's mind. He shouldn't enjoy sensations like this or relish spoiled memories. Demons were not to be trusted, and here he stood with his guard down.

"Exitalis, wife of the king, mother to us, thank you for the breaths—" A hissing drowned out his prayer. The demon must have found him.

He cleared his throat and addressed it directly. "Great power of the otherworldly, I come for a trade."

The earth underneath him rumbled. A mystical glow vanquished the darkness. It reflected off the bark and bushes around Richard, dipping the scenery in a mixture of brown and green. Vines sprouted around him, growing in unnatural ways. Some started midair, some slithered around the oak trees. They picked up speed and embraced Richard in a glowing whirlwind. He longed to know more, to understand and connect to the strange entity.

"Show your face, for I am worthy." His voice boomed through the storm until it stopped. He hadn't felt worthy of anything for the past fifteen years, but this he was certain of. The vines froze in their current state. Some were attached to the ground, but most of them hung in the open as if they belonged to an abstract painting.

From the opacity of the forest, a figure stepped into the glowing light amidst the frozen vines. Richard's breath caught. *The demon.* He understood that it doubled him in height. Beyond that, he couldn't comprehend the sight. The demon looked like an unseen color, the inside of the womb, the uncertain certainty of death. It evaded his understanding and likely that of any mortal.

Richard recognized the voice it used, for it was an echo of nature, the sound of dripping rain and summer storms. The words found their way inside of him, but he was unsure whether the demon spoke or placed its voice into Richard's mind.

"Hello, mortal."

Richard's mouth turned dry. "Hello."

A collection of sounds and voices rushed through him. "A trade. A trade? You hear that? Yes, a trade. A way out. It can't get us inside of him. It won't find us."

"Hello?" Richard asked, hoping to quiet the disturbing chatter.

The voices reunited into one. "What are you offering, mortal?"

The moment he had stepped out of the shack, Richard had realized he needed an answer to that question. He had yet to come up with one.

"Ehm . . . I could make you a table."

Richard heard the gushing of a waterfall combined with the pleasant splintering of wood. It was the demon's laughter.

"What am I to do with a table, mortal?"

Richard deflated. He'd never been able to figure out how to make Edeliènne happy, and a shapeless demonic creature seemed even harder to please. "I, ehm . . . I can give you anything that won't harm my son."

The sounds disappeared, and Richard's heart dropped. It had realized how foolish he was and abandoned the trade.

"Please, I don't want you to ever hurt Pier, but I'll do anything else." He couldn't return home a failure. He couldn't face those sweet, hopeful eyes again and tell Pier that problems were no longer simple and solutions long gone.

A hissing started in the back of his head that turned into a whisper. "What do you want?"

Richard cleared his throat and tried to phrase the many longings he harbored, longings that could never be expressed. "I . . . I want you to make me the most respected weaponsmith of Waldfeld. I want to whittle the weapons using only wood, and I want them to be unbreakable." He hoped to become unbreakable in the process too.

An uncomfortably cold breeze blew through his insides. It reached every corner of his body, twirling around each organ, every piece that made him human. The raw exposure made him tremble, but it didn't satisfy the demon.

"You're a brave man. Sturdy. Let me inspect you closer . . ."

Richard did not get the chance to protest. His thoughts were blown out like a candle, and he lost all will and agency. His body felt foreign, as if he merely consisted of the clothes he wore. He tried to think, but his attempts fizzled out before they could ignite. The paralysis hurt when he fought it. Without making the conscious decision, he drifted into the warm and hazy fog. Nothing to think. Nothing to feel.

Everything cleared, and he was himself again. The first breath he took was harsh and painful. He fell to his knees as the impressions flooded him. How long had he stood there? How long had he lost control? Everything was too much. He had not yet fully recovered when the demon began to speak once more.

"I will teach you how to make the weapons of the Fae."

"The Fae?" His ability to speak surprised him. He assumed the question was an unspoken thought.

"Yes, Fae. We are splintered Fae, assembled into one *us*. We experience your world without grounding. But there's no alternative. The path behind holds torture."

Richard blinked at the air. "De-demons are—"

"Splinters, yes. Do not call us demons. We are soul-clusters, no worse than the parts we're made of."

He thought of Edel[i]ènne, the splintering. Was she doomed to become an unholy creature?

"Choravdat is our name. We will help you. All we ask of you in return is an escape. A chance."

Choravdat's shape became more fathomable. Richard looked into what seemed to be their eyes. They were wide and endless, like gazing up into the universe. Was there mischief in them? Sadness? He couldn't tell. Swallowing was like drinking sand, but he pushed through it to speak.

"An escape . . . from what?"

The vines retracted back into the creature.

"The Ouisà Kacocs of limbo."

Limbo. It was the realm of the Traitor, far from light, far from Exitalis and the pantheon. The cursed lands of the lost. He tried to remember anything else, but it was all Father Godfried had taught him.

"What's Ouisà Kacocs?"

The air fogged up and trembled. "The foulest creatures that exist." It was a bold claim from a Fae demon, or soul-cluster.

"Why?"

"We, and our type, exist of many splinters, pure and rotten. They do not. Only the rotten ones cluster to form an Ouisà Kacoc."

Richard thought of the ugliest parts inside his own soul, of the vileness his father was capable of. Without redeeming qualities, they'd all be monsters.

"And you're their serf?"

The fog cleared, and a new wind gushed around him. "Let me live inside of you. They might find me here, but your body . . . your body is safe."

Richard shuddered at the idea of any living entity entering him, but did he have a choice? He thought of Pier and the piles of books he could buy him with the motus a successful merchant brought in.

"Promise you won't harm Pier." Of this he had to be sure.

Choravdat remained silent for five long seconds.

"I will not harm him in ways you wouldn't harm him yourself," they finally said.

Make sure nothing takes away his true self. It sounded like Edeliènne's last wish and left him just as clueless. But it was fine. He would never hurt his son.

Twenty roses blossomed around his feet. Every second, another one wilted. He was running out of time.

"Deal." Richard reached out his hand to shake on it, and Choravdat took it. His fingers dragged over flower petals and splinters. The blood that blossomed sealed the deal.

A hole opened in the soul-cluster's center, and a magenta

ray of starlight shone through it. It reached farther and pierced into Richard's head. He collapsed while his synapses danced in circles, connecting the unconnectable. The pain of enlightenment. Vast knowledge that offered one definite truth. He wasn't alone anymore.

TEN YEARS LATER...

CHAPTER 8

XENIA

April 979 - Polemos, the Capital of Virisunder

Dusk dipped the palace of Virisunder in fire. Xenia knew this time of day ignited power in everything. It changed her from a lanky ten-year-old half-Virisunder, half-Fi'Teri child to an invincible elvish knight straight out of the legends. She stretched her wooden toy sword into the air and ran up the hill behind the palace that led to her home. When she reached the top, the sun glared at her vivid amber eyes. She took it as the challenge of a dangerous foe, then pulled the sword close to her and somersaulted for a glorious surprise attack. A treacherous mud puddle soiled her brilliance and left her sputtering dirt. Something cracked on her back. She pulled herself out of the mud and examined the damage. Her crossbow, the loyal companion, had passed in this battle. She bowed her head to it. It had given its life to great honor. She looked at the sun. *I will get you next time, scoundrel.*

Xenia's mother would be upset about the crossbow, but she was sure her dad would buy her a new one at the Sunday market. Her heart jumped when she thought of the market. Perhaps her mom would join them too. It had been a while since they'd last gone together.

She brushed off her noble skirt, but the mud stuck to her hands. It had swallowed both her and the clothes. She was late for dinner as well and could already hear her mother's endless nagging. Their manor stared down at her from the top of the hill, like her mother surely would. She turned her back to it and took in the majestic palace with all its beautiful towers and gardens instead. The brisk evening air lured a grin out of her. Dusk was the best time of the day. Every breath taken at dusk turned dreams into possibilities, she was sure of it. One day, its magic would turn her into a true knight. All the boys and girls would turn their heads when the princess honored Xenia for her heroic deeds. She pulled her sword once more and saluted to the heavens with a victorious cry. "Long live Princess Josefine of Virisunder!"

"Xenia!"

Crap. Her mother had heard her. Xenia sighed melodramatically and made her way to the three-story manor she called home.

Xenia's mother, Subira, leaned against the door with crossed arms and grim lips. The hundreds of tiny braids that were supposed to stay looped up in a bun hung loosely in a half ponytail. She was in charge of Virisunder's military base and should've kept her hair tied and neat, but whenever Xenia returned from her days of mischief, her mother's bun was tousled or nonexistent. She misrepresented their great nation's military. Her mother was supposed to look proper, always. Xenia swore that no strand of her hair would ever be out of line once she was a knight. Right now, however, the frizzy chaos on top of her head remained out of control and crusted with dried mud.

Xenia dragged herself to the entrance.

"I told you to be home before sunset. And look at you, you're all—"

Xenia rushed past her and into her dad's stretched out arms. He awaited her with the excitement a future knight deserved.

Xenia's dad, Gustave, was a tall blond Virisunder elf with puffy red cheeks and great stories. He livened up any conversation, and his words lifted Xenia to the highest clouds. Her mother's words dragged her back down to boring reality.

"Look what the wind blew in!" he hollered, lifting her up into his arms. "Did you beat all the scoundrels today, champion?"

Xenia pulled her broken crossbow from her back and presented it with pride. "Yes, Daddy! I defeated all of them, but we had a casualty."

"Oh no, the brave fellah." He put on a playful tragic face. "We will remember him dearly."

Subira gently took it from her. "Honey, you have to be careful with these. You could have gotten a splinter."

Her dad shifted Xenia in his arms. "If you'd bought her the Kilburn training one, this wouldn't have happened."

She bit her lip. "We can't buy goods imported from Silberfluss, darling. They likely got here illegally and—"

"From what I'm hearing, you're getting one of those special Kilburn bows on Sunday, champ!" He tossed her higher, and Xenia laughed. When he sat her down again, she checked her mother's reaction. Her mother opened her mouth to speak, but her dad cut her off.

"We're hungry."

Subira hesitated before heading into the kitchen. The concern did not leave her face.

Xenia's smile faded for a second, but when her dad turned back to her, his expression was joyful again.

"Well, I'm proud of you, champion. Can't wait to see what great deeds you're doing on Sunday." He let out a low laugh and ruffled her messy hair. His hand turned as dirty as her whole body.

"Are you gonna sing about the war again?" Her dad was the most talented musician she had ever heard. More talented than Bored Reginald, probably. Not just that, he was also a glorious war hero who had accomplished incredible deeds in the war against Tazadahar. He concentrated on being a dad now but occasionally sang stories of his heroism in the market.

He scratched the back of his head and grinned. "Maybe . . . gotta see if I can write something new by then."

When she grew up, she wanted to become as glorious as her dad, and he assured her she could. He said she'd serve under Josefine and become indispensable to the great princess. Her mother was apprehensive of the idea, at best, but Xenia chose to believe the person who believed in her. She trusted her dad.

Subira peeked her head back into the foyer. "Dinner is ready."

They had maids, but her mother did most of the cooking. While it wasn't a noble thing to do, Xenia overlooked it in favor of the wonderful dishes she got to enjoy.

The smell of mesir wat, Xenia's favorite Fi'Teri lentil dish, drifted into the foyer. Xenia rushed into the dining hall and dropped onto a chair, inhaling the steaming scent of home. Subira frowned at her.

"Honey, at least wash your hands before dinner."

Xenia rolled her eyes and made her way to the kitchen with dragging feet. It smelled even better in here. She eyed the different lovingly prepared dishes, and her stomach growled. Adventuring was hard work that required replenishment. She spotted a sweet-smelling bowl, dipped her hands in the wash bucket, and wandered over to it. Fried plantains and cinnamon chickpeas. Her dad didn't like Fi'Teri desserts, and

Subira didn't care for sweets in general, but Xenia couldn't get enough of them. Her mother must have made them for her. A rare hint of gratitude flared up in her when the spicy sweetness hit her tongue. She stuffed chickpeas into her mouth until she resembled a chipmunk. She was chewing when the loud voices of her parents' usual fighting carried into the kitchen.

"I want normal food," her dad said.

"Darling, we discussed this. I'd like Xenia to know some of my family recipes."

He scoffed. "The family you ran away from, eh? Great lesson for your daughter."

"That's not fair . . ."

"I tell you what's not fair—having to eat this primitive *Fittery* muck because of some shitty in-laws!"

Xenia dropped the fried plantain chips. She hadn't realized the desserts were primitive. Knights had to be sophisticated in all matters, even in their taste. According to rumors, Princess Josefine only considered Tribu La'am imported chocolate as an acceptable dessert.

"Xenia likes it," Subira said.

Xenia stepped away from the bowl as if it had bitten her. Her dad couldn't know she was primitive. He'd stop seeing her as a knight. She fled the kitchen and returned to her seat with her nose up in the air.

"Hmm, I see. This stuff again," she said, trying to sound unimpressed.

Subira's face fell. "Yes, honey. You mentioned the other day that you'd like some mesir wat soon. I thought I'd make it for—"

"I don't remember saying that."

Her dad laughed. "See? She doesn't like your muck either. Our little girl's got taste. A Virisunder, through and through."

Her mother teared up. Xenia felt the urge to hug her, make it better, but the proud sparkle in her dad's eye suppressed it.

"Well, then . . . I will . . . I will make something else tomorrow."

Guilt formed in Xenia's stomach, an unwelcome companion to the sweet chickpeas. "Mom—"

"Let's pray, shall we?" She smiled at Xenia. The tears were gone. Perhaps Xenia had imagined them.

She closed her eyes and reached for her parents' hands. She loved the evening prayer. Xenia didn't give their god Caedem much thought throughout the day, but she made sure to wish for her knighthood every time she did talk to him. According to her mom, each of Elfentum's six nations worshiped a different god but acknowledged the existence of others. Gods were inhabitants of the celestial realm, feasting on the mortals' admiration. She knew better than to voice her thoughts, but to Xenia, the concept sounded parasitic. Why were they marionettes of some chap in another realm? If Caedem fed off her energy and ate up her prayers, she might as well demand something in return. *Make me a knight and I'll keep serving you. Otherwise, I'll figure out how to get to this celestial realm of yours and show you how to be a god.* This was her daily prayer.

It wasn't the sacredness that Xenia loved about the evening prayer. It was the togetherness. For a few minutes, her family felt whole. She tuned out her parents' fights as much as possible, but the absence of fighting didn't create harmony. This moment, her parents' hands in her own, did. She pried one eye open and saw that her dad had taken her mother's hand as well. For a few seconds, everything was good.

The seconds were never enough. When Xenia grew up, she'd create a family worth having. A loving one. When she found her life person, she would succeed where her mother was failing. She would make them happy, and her future children would never have to worry about a broken home. They would be able to focus on becoming knights themselves, just like their mother.

"With strong hearts we bow," her dad said, finishing the prayer.

"With strong hearts we bow," Subira and Xenia added in unison.

"And we thank you, Calliquium, for guiding our tongues and keeping our hearts informed," Subira added.

Xenia inhaled sharply. Her dad didn't like it when her mother included gods other than Caedem or Balthos in the evening prayer. Xenia didn't understand why, but bringing up Calliquium demeaned Caedem.

He stood up and stretched his arms. "Hey, champ, how about you eat dinner in your room today?"

Xenia's shoulders dropped. The prayer had been too short. She was hoping to at least eat some of the meal together. "But, Dad—"

"I need to have a private conversation with your mother. You understand that, don't you, my little knight?"

She glanced at her mother, who seemed frozen in place, except for her fingers that tapped on the table in a monotone rhythm. Subira noticed Xenia's gaze, and their eyes met. She bit her lip again and jumped up.

"Gustave, darling, sit back down. Let me make you a steak and some potatoes. We'll restart the prayer." She rushed toward the kitchen, but he grabbed her upper arm and pulled her back. His fingernails sank into Subira's skin.

Xenia looked down at her food. They loved each other. It was normal. Fights happened. The mesir wat steam tickled her nose, but it didn't smell pleasant anymore. Nothing was pleasant. She poked at it and focused on the orange color.

"Karina," her dad called, "bring some of this muck to Xenia's room."

Karina, the maid, took the plate away and left Xenia to stare at the mahogany table.

"Champ?"

She stood up mechanically and walked toward the door.

"Xenia, wait—" Her mother's weak voice chased her out

of the room. She ran all the way to her chamber, skipping several steps of the large staircase. Halfway up, she heard something shatter, followed by her mother's scream.

She reached her chamber and slammed the door shut. It drowned out the noise and with it all thoughts in her head. She opened her window and leaned over the sill, like she often did, to get a good look at the palace. Only six more months before she would start military school and learn how to become the best knight for the princess. Xenia kept her eyes firmly outside, fixed on her future home, her better home: the palace of Virisunder.

A few moments later, Karina brought in the food. Without her dad to impress, she gobbled all of it down. She hadn't tasted a dish this rich, spicy, and comforting for weeks. She ate a large portion, but the meal left her strangely empty. She craved more evening prayers, those seconds of peace.

She walked over to her bookshelf and searched for the origin story, the explanation of where all this fighting came from. Her old picture book, *The Lost Goddess*, awaited her as it always did with its beautiful pastel blue cover. She flipped through it. This was where it had all gone wrong. She searched for her favorite drawing, and a smile crept over her face when she found it. It depicted Balthos and Alames in a tender embrace with nothing but blissful love on their faces. They had never fought or hurt each other. Why couldn't her parents behave like them?

She turned the page and found the ugly faces of the Poet and the Smith. Those evil gods had become jealous of Balthos and Alames's eternal love, so they'd splintered the pure goddess. Balthos, the poor king, had tried to hold on to her, but the Poet and the Smith had cursed the mortals, mostly orcs, to steal Alames's remainders from him. Xenia choked up when she saw the despair in Balthos's eyes as he reached for the white splinters of light. The story never failed to sadden her. The next pages looked too gruesome for her taste. She skipped Balthos slaying the old gods in revenge but caught a glimpse of the creation of the Traitor. The misguided mortals had assembled a foul creature from Alames's splinters, the Traitor, and had used it to fight Balthos. Xenia had never understood what anger had led them to attack the heartbroken king. The orcs of Tribu La'am were in the foreground, of course. Those heretics still hadn't found their way back to the pantheon.

She turned the pages past Balthos creating the good new gods until she found the image that gave her hope. The king danced with Exitalis, his new goddess. The only unsoiled splinter of Alames shimmered in her chest. Around them, the new world celebrated the end of the Celestial War and the treaty that had banished the Traitor to limbo. According to the treaty, Balthos and his pantheon weren't allowed to step into the mortal realm either, but Balthos forgave the people and allowed them to worship him once more.

Xenia didn't care as much about the latter part, but Balthos and Exitalis's dance proved that love was capable of rebirth. Maybe if her mother finished the war against Silberfluss, she could go dancing with her dad.

CHAPTER 9

PIER

May 979 - Tribu La'am University, City of Mink'Ayllu, Tribu La'am

Soft green fingers caressed their way to Pier's hand and made it difficult to write his valedictorian speech. The firm strokes on his thumb evoked a shiver in him, a memory of their recent plunge into ecstasy. The sensation served as a distraction while Pier's pencil escaped his hand and twirled into the thief's.

"Got the precious Kilburn sword!" Martín laughed and held the pencil above his head. Pier couldn't tell if his boyfriend's reflexes were extraordinarily quick for an orc or if Pier was extraordinarily bedazzled. He reached for the pencil, eager to find words worthy of the politician he hoped to become. He had assumed Martín had drifted into a cozy slumber after their lovemaking exhausted him, but as always, his conman had a trick up his sleeve.

Pier had grown tall and lanky, almost a match to his

orcish boyfriend's height. He grazed the pencil's edge right as Martín tossed it into the air. It twirled in its flight like a clock that sped through time. Martín casually reached for it, a cool smirk on his face, planning to catch it with ease. He didn't. It bounced behind Pier's dorm bed, out of reach for both of them.

Martín put on his best tragic face. "There goes the Kilburn sword."

"You're impossible," Pier said, but he smiled and brought his forehead to Martín's. A tingle ran down his spine, and Martín's gentle sigh blessed his ears. Tusks prevented orcs from sharing kisses like humans and elves did, but they possessed a sensitive spot on their foreheads that offered a similar sensation. The closeness made Pier's stomach flutter. Images of their new life poured into his mind, the life of possibilities that awaited them after Pier's graduation the next day.

The four years of college had been the happiest of his life. He hadn't known how badly he needed to escape Waldfeld until he had. Until he'd arrived in Mink'Ayllu, the capital of the independent country Tribu La'am. Until its rich, volcanic earth had cushioned his feet, and the ancient Tribu La'am University had brought light to Pier's shadowed parts. This land had taught him the language of his soul. His dad's smithy had paid for a degree in political sciences, but Pier's experiences in this foreign world enriched him more than any class could.

His real education had started after an awkward flirtation with a perfect Silberfluss woman in his first semester—Zazil Revelli. Witty. Caring. Someone he'd longed to spend his life with. Who wouldn't be attracted to such a woman? A gay man who preferred a shady young tour guide leading him to Mink'Ayllu's secrets. Secrets like the trade economy that had been in place for centuries and minimized poverty. Or how inviting a brick wall felt when said tour guide pressed him against it. Luckily, Zazil and Pier had a lot in common, including their mutual lack of attraction for each other.

"Actually"—Martín's trickster spirit flickered across his cocoa eyes—"I can think of an even better Kilburn sword."

Pier was lying in Martín's arms, next to his boyfriend's clothed chest, which he wasn't allowed to touch. Martín slipped his arm out from underneath him, sending Pier to roll off the bed. He caught Pier in the last second and pinned him underneath himself. Pier had assumed his lower parts had joined Martín in the presumed slumber, but they reawakened spectacularly.

He expected Martín's hand to reach for the wooden cock Zazil had designed, but he reached for Pier's cheek instead and stroked it with great care, adoring each freckle.

"How did I get so lucky?" Martín's voice cracked higher than Pier knew he would have liked, but it didn't matter. He couldn't have looked more handsome.

"By being Everything," Pier breathed back. He had first hired Martín as his man for everything—help with research papers, translator of strange Tribu La'am dialects that exceeded Pier's three years of language study. He had traded anything he could find for Martín's inaccurate city tours and local wisdom. Before he knew better, he had traded his heart. A year had passed since then, and Martín remained Everything.

It was a risk, of course. Everything was younger than him, although orcish lives ran on a different clock with their shortened lifespan. He wasn't a college student, like Pier and his friends, but the heir of the local Zac-Cimi crime family. He was also everything that Waldfeld wasn't. Everything his dad would disapprove of. But Pier's professors had taught him that a career in politics meant risking everything, so why would happiness follow different rules?

Martín nuzzled his forehead against his Pier's neck, causing another wave of tingles. Pier soaked up Martín's joy, hunger, longing, anything he could fill his own body with. Hunger was a familiar friend, but it had never been coupled with joy.

"It's a pity you took my pencil, Everything." He traced

his index finger up Martín's thin, serrated tusk, along his cheekbone, and up to the darker green beneath his eyes. They looked like shadow patches on a grassy meadow. The eyes were trees that rose from the shadows and sprouted into rich cocoa fruits. Pier was sure he'd never starve again as long as those eyes were around.

"Once I'm done with the speech, I want to sketch the future manor I'll spoil you with. Right on the palace grounds of Freilist."

"Ooh, the palace grounds of Frytist? I feel spoiled already."

"Freilist, dear." He leaned over the bed's edge in search of parchment. Martín climbed off him to give him room, but empty papers were nowhere to be seen. Pier had filled every last one with plans on how to transform Elfentum's archaic political landscape. How to unite the nations under a system that the nobility and peasantry led together. He had spent months buried under historical peace treaties in the university's grand library and had bombarded his friend, graduate student Sachihiro, with questions. Eventually, Sachihiro's answers had all circled back to Virisunder's once legendary Captain Subira Se'azana. His friend used any occasion to talk about his special interest in her. Pier found her lack of follow-through disappointing but wasn't going to fight over it. At this point, Pier had collected enough ideas to propose a reform of Silberfluss. He only needed someone to propose it to.

Martín ran his fingers through Pier's ginger curls. "I'm proud of my college boy. You know that?"

Pier picked up a thesis and ran his fingers over it. He'd used his best handwriting, as if the upswing of each letter could cause a revolution.

"I hope it works." Not just his political career, but all of his life plans. Bringing Everything back home would be the first hurdle.

Martín squeezed him tighter. "It will."

"We need to convince my dad first."

"We will."

Pier wasn't so sure. His dad resented change. After the Kilburn Smithy had succeeded, all he'd wanted for Pier was to bring home a girl and settle into the life he had designed for him. He'd never asked him if he even desired such a life, but Pier would convince him. He had to. Besides, the shop was too lucrative to keep it a Waldfeld secret. People were selling Kilburn counterfeits across the county because his dad refused to produce on a larger scale. Once they followed Pier's strategy, they'd supply Princess Agathe's royal army in no time. He'd get close enough to her long elvish ears to whisper a new future into them. One where she wasn't a mere trophy to her brothers and the Council. One where war became unnecessary and relations to Virisunder blossomed in peace. One where he could marry an orcish man in the capital and enrich Silberfluss's normality instead of destroying it.

But he had to convince his dad first. His muscles knotted into their usual rigid pattern, and an uncomfortable fullness weighed his stomach down. Tomorrow was graduation day. Tomorrow the real test began.

Martín's hand wandered to Pier's neck and massaged it.

"I think someone needs another tension release." He placed his other hand on Pier's leg and caressed his way upward.

Pier sank into the sensation. His whole life, he had devoted himself to problem-solving, but every new conflict he resolved, he absorbed. He knew of only two methods for expunging the stress from his body, and Martín's touch was by far the preferable one.

"Ey, boys, put your naked butts away or not. I'm coming in." Zazil's voice resounded through the door. Martín let out a half-frustrated, half-amused sigh as she barged into the dorm room a second later.

Pier was always happy to see her. Even now, when she robbed him from the desired clarity a brain wiped clean with lust offered. Only a thin blanket covered him, but he didn't mind. There was no part of him she hadn't seen.

She was the most outrageously flashy elf Pier had ever seen. Tribal patterns of golden ink decorated her face. They were keepsakes from the summer she and her fiancé, Gon, had spent traveling through Tribu La'am to study the customs of different tribes. She had charmed herself into their hearts, and they had blessed her with ink. Gemstones and crystal chains pierced the pale ears that stretched far out from her tattooed face. She had studied assula magic, a family trade, with a minor in people studies. She loved creating magical fashion gadgets that could both alter looks and ease pains. Pier knew the piercings hid marks from a darker past, but they also colored her hair in a bright pink that glittered in the sunlight.

"Nice tent." She chuckled and opened his round dorm window. A breeze of Mink'Ayllu's humid air gushed in.

Pier jumped off the bed and allowed the wind to kiss his face. He would miss this eternal summer when he returned to Silberfluss. Damp cold air crept into every corner of the stone houses back home. Mink'Ayllu's wood and clay constructions breathed in the warmth and gently exhaled it onto its residents, a reminder that one was never alone in this wild but forgiving city. Its arms were open to anyone with goods and a smile to trade.

Zazil grabbed Pier's neglected pants off the ground and tossed them at him. She grinned at Martín. "Ready to try Esperanza's new weed, Bandana? She's been bragging about it nonstop."

"It's Martín," he grumbled, "and fuck yes I am. Except for the Esperanza part."

Pier rolled his eyes. The animosity between Esperanza and Martín tired him. She was the sweetest, most joyful girl on campus, and it baffled him how anyone could resent her, let alone Martín.

"You'll survive it, Bandana." Zazil winked at Pier.

"It's Martín."

A smile crept over Pier's lips. Martín had worn his hair shoved into a bandana when they had first met. Pier had since convinced Martín's parents to let him cut it, which had rendered the style obsolete, but the nickname had stuck with their friend group. Pier didn't object to it. Much to his delight, Martín scrunched his nose when he got upset over the nickname.

Pier tied his pants to his suspenders right as Gon Ch'ulel entered the room and was grateful for it. He didn't care if Zazil saw him naked, but flashing his butt at her fiancé, Gon, brought back memories. Pre-Martín memories.

"Babe!" Zazil rushed over and swung her arms around Gon's neck, causing them to sway dangerously to the side. "I thought you were waiting at Esperanza's garden."

"They're being weird," Gon said, struggling to keep their balance. In her stormy hug, Zazil had knocked over one of the crutches Gon relied on. Pier picked it up and helped them back onto it. Zazil's small elvish body couldn't support an orc on its own. Gon had adorned their crutches with ancestral scripture, blessings from those tribal orcs that had come before them and carried their magic through them. Their style matched the patterns Gon's own face were tattooed with. Zazil had added assula-charged rainbow quartz to the crutches that steadied their stance and polished their colorful look.

Gon was a medicine and ancestral magic major who had joined their older brother, Sachihiro, in the quest for knowledge away from their orcish northern tribe Juyub'Chaj. Unlike their brother, Gon spoke of the tribe with deepest adoration, but Pier couldn't picture the orc among traditionalists. They were neither man nor woman, referred to as they/them, and wore their long indigo hair in a braid with Zazil's crystals weaved into it.

Gon's mother had birthed them too early, which had caused a severe weakness of certain muscle groups and their motor control. What they lacked in their stance, they made up in mental stability. They provided Zazil the roots she desperately needed, while sharing her love for eccentricity. They liked to wear brightly colored linen skirts and pastel shirts that revealed most of their dark green chest.

Pier had to admit that Gon was a pleasant sight to rest one's eyes upon. Not as pleasant as Everything, of course, but they had the unnerving talent to make his mind drift.

"There we go." Pier let go of them, and they nodded gratefully. Gon preferred to use as few words as possible.

"You forgot something, college boy," Martín said behind him. Before Pier could respond, a hastily shoved blouse blocked his view. He adjusted it himself and raised an eyebrow at Martín—a weak defense for his own blushed cheeks.

"What?" Martín shrugged with a self-conscious grin. "Looking good." He had nothing to worry about, but Pier knew that Martín's condition lent itself to jealousy.

He leaned into Martín and kissed him on the cheek. "I love you."

Martín pinched his butt and stretched his tongue at him—a pink flower petal on the otherwise green meadow. He wrapped his arms around him for the hundredth time that day, as if he feared Pier would run back to Silberfluss without him and he'd have to find his way to Waldfeld on his own. Pier smiled. Martín got lost the moment he crossed Mink'Ayllu's city limits. There was no chance he'd leave his Everything to wander around Elfentum's war zones on his own.

"You okay, Gon?" Martín asked. Gon nodded.

That was when it hit Pier. This was it, the last afternoon they would share before their paths parted. It was strange that each chapter of their lives ended at its prime. His mother's had ended that way. He'd seen it coming, like he knew he'd graduate tomorrow, and still, the end was impossible to grasp.

He looked forward to bringing Everything home, of course. To replace his library nights with practical pursuits of peace and progress, but who did he have to become in the process? This Pier, as he breathed and laughed and cried, would reassemble into a new version of him, and he could only hope it would be a stronger, better one. It was difficult to imagine a version better than the Pier that lay in the campus gardens, giggling about nothing, surrounded by his friends and Everything.

He wished he could freeze the moment and turn it into a still life painting, but the others were setting into motion again. Together, they left Pier's room, which was filled with cramped books and sketches carefully taped to the wall. Pier used to pin them up with whatever he could find, plastering the walls as chaotic and staggering as his mind often felt. Sachihiro had taken offense to this madness and rearranged them into perfect order.

They walked through the open-arched hallways of his college dorms, and for the first time since arriving, Pier noticed every detail. He soaked in the shades of apricot and turquoise the sun tickled out of the wall paints. He examined the large circular stones that paved their way, surrounded by tiny mosaic squares. It was impractical, but he wondered if each circular stone was made of former squares that longed to be part of something larger. He wondered if the Council's Heidegger family had felt that way before they'd lost touch with their edges, or if they had always known their goal was to swallow small squares, not represent them.

They reached the staircase leading to the college yards. Its white metal spiral looked like cream swirling in Tribu La'am's signature brew called coffee. Martín let go of Pier's hand and helped Gon down the stairs. Zazil watched them with a smile, but Pier noticed his own heavy heart reflected on her face.

"Juyub'Chaj should have fewer stairs." He nudged her shoulder. She was accompanying Gon back to their tribe in the northern mountains of Tribu La'am. Pier was glad about it. He never wanted her to absorb another hardship or experience another act of mindless brutality in Elfentum's troubled streets. He wanted her to settle among dancing orcs, fire festivals, and elaborate family dinners, far from her old troubles in a peace he wished for both of them. And yet, he didn't want her to leave. He didn't want to leave either.

She took his hand and squeezed it, then pulled out a box made of gray marble with *P & Z* etched into it.

"I got something for you." She handed him the box. "Better give it to you before Esperanza sees it. She gets too high-pitched when she's jealous."

The box was smooth with a hot spot on the bottom. He turned it around and found a dimly gleaming assula staring out of the marble like a green eye.

Pier smirked. "You're proposing to me? I'm flattered." He regretted the joke immediately when tears shot into her eyes. "Zaz . . ." He put his arm around her.

She shook her head and chuckled at herself. "Yeah, I'm gonna marry all of your asses so you fuckers have to follow me around all the time."

"What?" Martín yelled from the bottom of the stairs. Zazil blew him a kiss and winked. "Ew, no, keep it in your pants, Zaz."

Pier and Zazil laughed. "Looks like you've been scorned."

"Oh, my poor heart. I don't get to marry a bunch of gay guys." She pretended to faint without touching the ground. Thankfully, she didn't test if Pier could catch her. He hadn't exercised in at least a year.

"In all seriousness though, it's a messenger box. We can send assula-transmitted letters to each other. I have the second one. My professor for Applied Assula Magic said it was impossible, but fuck him! Which Gon and I did, actually, but he's still wrong about this."

The box became heavy in Pier's hands as he realized the impossible opportunities it held. He clicked the iron lock open with the same care he'd use to brush an escaped strand of hair out of his lover's face. Pink velvet lined the inside. Parchment and a pen awaited him, prepared to carry whatever stories this strange new life held. Zazil had etched more letters into the inner top: *To my true brother.*

It wasn't goodbye. He'd miss her cackling laughter, but as long as their parting didn't rob her presence from his days, he could endure it. A pressure grew behind his eyes, an urge for the release he had learned to suppress. Zazil freed it for him and sobbed. Pier pulled her tighter. She lingered for two seconds, then pushed herself off.

"All right, enough with this sentimental bullshit." She hurried down the remaining steps. "Where's Esperanza? I need some weed."

Gon wiped a tear from Zazil's face. "Snazzle?"

"I'm okay, babe." She kissed their hand, then swatted them off.

Pier walked down the stairs and intertwined his fingers with Martín's. Together they stepped into the crowded college gardens. They weren't the only ones who'd decided to spend their last afternoon soaking up the generous Tribu La'am sun. Orcs, humans, and the occasional elvish student relaxed on the groomed yards around them. Most of them were locals, Pier suspected, and wouldn't have to miss the sunshine. He understood why they needed it, anyway. The rays of sunlight reflecting off the botany department's glass dome differed from the mindless beams that would shine on the graduates' working heads in a few weeks. College offered the pleasure of holding all the stakes and no stakes at all. Life would never be this simple again.

They tiptoed through the sunbathers and past the statues of the university founders and their ancestors. It was peculiar that the founders had considered their great-grandfathers important enough to be honored in the main courtyard. Pier barely even knew his grandfather. His dad had forbidden it as best as he could. Then again, Pier could picture himself building a statue of his dad in his future manor. No, a statue wouldn't do. His dad didn't appreciate impractical art. Pier could carve "Richard Kilburn" into the manor's foundation. That tribute would suit him.

They reached the bridge that connected the botany

building with the historical society. Underneath it was an easily overlooked gap in the building's construction that led to their secret garden. A waft of smoke and incense blew out of it. Pier sniffed and recognized myrrh, patchouli, and what might be mint. They had found Esperanza.

Martín coughed. "The fuck are they burning?"

"Told you they're being weird," Gon said.

Pier made his way to the gap and squeezed through it much easier than his orcish companions could. As with the hallways, he took a moment to appreciate the beauty of their secret garden. The history wing encircled it and gave them privacy, but the sun still peeked over the two-story building and shone on the dozens of exotic plants Esperanza had filled the open-air space with. Some were drugs, some remedies, and others lethal poisons. All of them were Esperanza's pet projects. A caged area next to the entry gap provided music in the form of croaking frogs. Their purpose probably wasn't to be unskilled musicians, but Pier had never asked Esperanza about it.

He blinked into the smoke that fogged up the garden. A bonfire in the back caused it. Esperanza had allowed them a small sitting area that wasn't filled with plants.

Pier stepped into the smoke and stumbled through Esperanza's jungle until he spotted his two friends. Esperanza sat in front of the fire, one arm stretched into the air, holding a sharpened branch wrapped in leaves. It looked more like a Kilburn sword than his pen had. She wore two leaf-woven cloths that barely covered her short but plump body, and her dark brown curls frizzed into a lion's mane around her head. Pier noticed small branches and leaves sticking out of it. They seemed perfectly natural, as if they had grown out of her as well. She came from a human Tribu La'am tribe, but sometimes Pier wondered if she had blossomed from the soil, the strangest among her plants.

Her boyfriend, Sachihiro, danced around the bonfire in only a leaf cloth himself, although Pier noticed his regular shorts peeking out from underneath it. He would have made an imposing sensual figure with his broad shoulders and firm dark green abs if he hadn't looked so out of place. Unlike his younger sibling, Gon, Sachihiro preferred books over tribal magic and solitude over community. He'd been at Tribu La'am University for eight years, studying decryption, language, and whatever else his curious mind fixated on. In a few months, he'd start his professorship. No matter where they'd all end up, it was comforting to know that their awkward scholar would forever be at Tribu La'am University.

Two years ago, Sachihiro's quartz-speckled eyes had emerged from his papers and fallen on Esperanza. Pier and the others had been sure it would be a short-lived affair, a strange diversion from Sachihiro's usual fan ramblings over the great Captain Subira Se'azana, but here he was, two years later, dancing around a fire, half-naked and chanting a strange tongue. Love was a curious force.

Pier approached in silence, careful not to disturb the spectacle. His beloved showed less poise.

"What are you all up to? Smells like my sister failing at barbecue!"

Sachihiro stumbled and stepped on a smoldering piece of wood. He yowled, and the others rushed toward him.

"Sachi!" Gon pushed their way through the plants as quickly as they could. Esperanza somehow kept her focus through the yowling. Her eyes remained closed, fully concentrated on her ritual.

Pier allowed Gon to pass, who hurried to examine the injury. The yowling turned into grumbled complaints, and Pier relaxed his shoulders. If Sachihiro complained already, it wasn't too worrisome.

"Did I miss the fun?" Zazil appeared through the smoke behind him.

"Sachi burned his foot," Pier said.

"Ah, so I *did* miss the fun."

Pier smirked. "Be nice, Zaz."

Martín tried to assist Gon, but Sachihiro shooed him away. ". . . in the middle of something important . . ." he rambled. Pier shared a look with his Everything, and both suppressed a chuckle. ". . . could have changed all of history . . ."

"You're fine." Gon patted his shoulder and sank to the ground next to the fire. "Tell Esperanza to put some aloe vera on it."

Martín and the still-grumbling Sachihiro joined Gon on the ground. Pier plopped down into Martín's embrace and ran his fingers over the thin black hairs that grew from his lean but strong forearms. At least one thing wouldn't change.

Zazil waved her hand in front of Esperanza's face. "Yoo-hoo? Someone home?"

"Leave her alone," Sachihiro said. "She might still make it. We almost connected to the Fae realm yesterday."

Zazil laughed. "Sure you did."

Gon shifted in their seat. "I told you not to try this kind of stuff, Sachi. Especially not with our ancestral dances. The Fae are evil."

"That is a false, judgmental—"

"Hey, folks." Pier raised his voice above them. A man who couldn't keep peace between his friends couldn't keep peace between nations. He was not that kind of man. "Can you believe tomorrow we'll all be graduates?"

"I've graduated before," said Sachihiro.

"And I know you're happy to watch your sibling accomplish the same thing, aren't you?" Pier gave him an innocent-seeming but lethal smile, and he relented.

"Yeah, I guess."

Zazil sat down next to Esperanza and swung her arm around her. Esperanza remained motionless in her trance, although her brows furrowed a smidgen.

"Speaking of graduates, guess who wants to hire this hotshot?" Zazil pointed at herself. Gon let out a sigh.

"Who?" Pier asked.

"Why, the acting general of Virisunder, Queen Alexandra

Verdain, that's who. And don't sigh, babe, you know I'm not taking it. I'm just bragging." She leaned closer to Pier. "The lovely Miss Verdain wrote that she'd benefit from my extraordinary talents." She wiggled her eyebrows.

"You make it sound like she offered you a courtesan position." Pier laughed. "Although, that would be quite smart, actually. I'm sure courtesans and their advisers have a lot of political influence."

Zazil clicked her tongue. "Better—she wants me to become Virisunder's assula smith. Can you imagine how my family would react if I took their secrets to the enemy? It's almost too tempting."

The enemy. A shiver ran through Pier's spine. The thought of Zazil working for Silberfluss's enemy nation unnerved him, even in theory. Who drew the line between enemies and friends? If she became Virisunder's smith, the two nations would draw that line, likely between them.

He looked at Gon. "I think your charm is better used with our new chieftain over here."

"Not yet," Gon said, but their smile revealed their excitement. Pier knew they couldn't wait to return home to their tribe with their wonderful bride. Nausea rose in Pier when he thought of returning home. *Dad will be happy for me. He'll be happy. He'll be happy.*

Esperanza jolted in a sudden awakening that caused Zazil to jump and scream, "Fucking limbo!"

She giggled. "Blimey, did I scare you? I'm such a fopdoodle, I zonked out."

"Evidently," said Zazil, struggling to catch her breath.

Sachihiro laughed. Esperanza's full presence lit up his face. "Serves you right, Zaz."

"Oh, fuck off, Sachi," she said with a grin.

Pier forced himself to relax. Everybody loved Martín. Pier's dad had accomplished the impossible before, but disliking him exceeded even his abilities.

The conversation among his friends continued, and the

words soon turned into music to Pier, an accompaniment to this perfect moment. He wanted to gift it immortality. Take in every detail. Allow it to nestle down in his memory with its herbal scents that brought out the musky cologne Martín sprayed on his body every morning. Underneath it was a more arousing, salty smell—a keepsake of their earlier passion.

At some point, Esperanza pulled a caged metal ball filled with herbs from the fire, and the air cleared. The remaining smoke framed the faces of Pier's friends. He wished he could paint them, exactly like that, with their faces reaching out of gray obscurity and into his memory.

They passed a joint around. Pier brought it to his lips, like the others did, and felt a hint of a kiss. It reminded him of the gentle kisses his mother would leave on his forehead every night before she fell asleep in their run-down farmhouse.

He allowed the joint's smoke to fill his lungs. It eased his body into calmness and reminded him of what had happened after his mother's soft snores filled the room. He would jump out of bed in search of the same calmness to protect him from night terrors. The calmness lived on the farm's porch, where his dad sat deep into the night and stared into the fields. Pier would sneak out to him and crawl onto his lap. Only there would the calmness wash over him. Only there was he safe. And only there could he sleep. Every morning he'd wake up in his own bed with no trace of his lapsed bravery but the dark rings under his dad's eyes. One night when Pier had fallen asleep in his bed right away, he'd woken up to his dad holding him inside the house, and they'd both listened to Edeliènne's snores. That was when Pier had understood that his dad needed this sacred calmness as much as he did.

The joint's calmness brought clarity. He needn't worry about bringing Martín home. Pier's dad would never risk losing him. In a few weeks, Pier would be back home, not at the farm, but at the Kilburn weaponry shop. With his dad and Everything under the same roof, he'd never have to fear the darkness again.

He looked around the circle and found his own serenity reflected in everyone's faces, even in Gon's, who refused weed. He couldn't imagine a single thing that could disturb the peace, but neither did countries before war broke out.

The moment passed with a rustling sound. Pier decided that it must have been a bird diving into Esperanza's wild jungle and thought no more of it. He preferred to stay in Martín's arms and pictured himself lying on the bed of a green river that carried him wherever it wanted. He wanted to stay under, convinced he'd never need to take another breath.

The rustling became louder and closer. A second later, he noticed footsteps.

"Esperanza," Zazil said, "did you tell anyone about the garden?"

She giggled. "Yup, yup, yup. Had to. I told the freshmen office. Someone's got to protect my babies when I leave."

Pier wondered if she was referring to the frogs or the poisonous plants and decided he didn't care.

"He's probably here somewhere," a voice said in Silberfluss. Pier sighed and tried to straighten up, prepared to handle any diplomatic negotiation with some freshman, but Martín wrapped his arms around Pier's waist and hugged him tighter.

"Nope, no escaping."

"Everything, I—" Martín cut Pier's protest off with a well-placed tickle attack. Pier half-heartedly slapped his hands, then surrendered to laughter. Martín tossed him into the soft grass and climbed on top of him for a wider range of tickle targets.

"Pier," Gon whispered next to them, but Martín's hands preoccupied Pier. He must have grown ten additional arms to pleasurably torture him with.

"Pier," Gon repeated.

He gasped for breath between fits of laughter.

"Here he is, Mister Kilburn." The freshman's voice was distant, unimportant. Way less interesting than Everything's body on top of him. His eyes locked with Pier's, which caused his heart to beat so forcefully Pier felt like it might leave him any moment.

"Zaz, pin his arms," Martín hooted without breaking eye contact. "Let's get him!"

Zazil didn't respond.

Martín went for Pier's weakest spot, the top of his right collarbone. Tears of laughter shot into Pier's eyes, and he closed them, slapping around unseeingly.

Martín's laughter stopped first, followed by his tickling. Then his hands slipped away. Pier's dancing chest came to an abrupt stop as he sucked in air. Had he accidentally hurt him? He hadn't thought his weak slaps could have that effect.

He opened his eyes and found the tip of a sharp wooden dagger lifting up Martín's chin. It hadn't broken the skin yet, but it was close. Pier followed Martín's shocked gaze up to a human man who stood above them. A human man with a ginger beard and travel clothes. A human man who looked like—

"Dad!"

His dad didn't look at him but stared at Martín as if his eyes had turned into two more daggers, fueled by repulsion. Pier was sure those daggers could rip him and everything around him apart. Two painful seconds passed in which no one dared to speak. Then—

"Take your dirty fingers off my son."

CHAPTER 10

VANA

May 979 - Waldfeld's Town Square, Silberfluss

T he half elf Vana Ackerman strummed her guitar as if each string held the power to shake the world. The town's dirty cobblestone square was her stage, and each note connected her deeper to those who breathed the same air that reeked of piss and sweat, those who fought the same fight she did. Music was the magic of the simple folk.

The true magic-bearer was Jules, her sweet best friend and the lead singer of their duo. She peeked at him as he brushed his brown locks out of his face and enchanted the crowd further with a voice fit for the best of people. That was whom they were playing for—the best people Silberfluss had to offer. Vana spotted Alva in the audience, with her gray hair and fingers wounded and raw from wash water. She spent all day cleaning the underpants of merchant folk, but she still clapped along to Vana's and Jules's rhythms. There were Colby and Dustin, their faces smeared with coal, their lungs run-down in a bitter tribute to their oppressors. Still, they sang along to The Spirit and the Enforcer; that was what Jules and Vana called themselves. Their music reawakened the most tired of souls and brought out the fiercest parts of their battered community. There was nothing Vana wanted more than to plant seeds of hope that blossomed into revolution—except for seeing Jules smile again, free from the heartbreak she had caused.

"Dear gods, dear Verdains, dear Verdain gods. Thank you for leading us into darkness so you can shine your light." His voice wafted through the crowd. With each ear it touched, the audience's love for him grew. Vana watched how their adoration flickered in the torchlight. He'd be fine. There were lots of ladies to love him properly. Ladies who'd make better girlfriends than she had. Ladies who'd pull sweeter sounds out of him than she'd ever had the privilege to hear. Ladies like . . .

Her eyes fell onto a fiery redhead in the front row. Isa was her name, if Vana remembered correctly. She had written *Enforcer* onto a cloth in ornate lettering and held it above her head. It bounced up and down, along with her tits, as she danced to the rhythm.

"And if we're cold, you show us the joy of freezing. And if we're hungry, you show us the joy of starving. And if we're bound, you show us the joy of worship."

Vana's eyes fixed on her front row fan. The look Isa gave her was far from adoration for Jules. Vana's heart had been mirroring the rhythm in her chest, which now dropped into her pants. She noticed Isa's fingers—callused from hard work but strong and skilled. They gripped tightly around the cloth. She wondered how they'd look gripping a bedsheet instead.

Jules bumped her shoulder, and she jolted out of her thoughts. *Shit, my solo!* She'd forgotten her favorite part of the song. Bored Reginald, the once great rebel bard, included solos for all musicians in his songs. It was one of the many reasons she and Jules loved performing covers of his work. She wondered if her idol minded that teenage rebels played his songs now that he'd become a spineless palace pony.

She allowed her fingers and the strings to run wild together for a few seconds as the guitar solo of Bored Reginald's "The Last Prayer" began. Then she restrained herself. She included a few nifty tricks and a wink to Isa but didn't release herself fully into the music. The night belonged to Jules and to him alone. It was hard enough to find out that your girlfriend of three years, and friend of forever, was a dyke. Vana didn't need to steal his show as well. The word gnawed on Vana's stomach. *Dyke*. She wished she could change things, make them good again. At least he had his talent to lift him up. That smooth-voiced Tribu La'am immigrant had more rhythm and presence than any old Silberfluss sucker. Technically, he and Vana were both Silberfluss suckers, but his parents had immigrated from a human tribe of Tribu La'am, so that made him special.

She finished her solo, and he picked the beat back up on his handheld bombo drum. Vana smirked at him.

"No one deserves happiness when misery is a blessing." His singing pulled the daylight back into the dark town square. "Or do you? My dearest princess. Or do you? My dearest prince."

Vana studied him. The light he brought to the square didn't reflect in his eyes. He usually couldn't tame his enthusiasm when they kicked the last vendors off the square and took over as The Spirit and the Enforcer. It was fine. His light would return in time. Vana wasn't important enough to snuff it out forever. It must've been disappointing that she wouldn't suck his cock again, but he couldn't possibly love her more than she loved him.

She joined for the final lines. "Or do you? Beloved gods. Do you pay the price of happiness to gift us suffering?"

Vana grinned at him, and her shoulders relaxed when he returned it. His shining white teeth contrasted his dark brown skin. The applause ripped them out of their stupid drama and back into their dreams. This was their last concert in Waldfeld before they'd head to Silberfluss's capital, Freilist. A merchant patron had signed them up for a talent show. He wasn't a noble shit merchant, of course, but one of Vana's class who'd gotten lucky.

"Thank you, comrades of music." Vana stretched her fist to the crowd in solidarity and bowed together with Jules. "We'll be back in five for an original song written by our brilliant Spirit over here. You don't wanna miss that!"

The two headed over to a side alley that functioned as their backstage area. No one would dare to steal shit from the Enforcer.

Vana picked up a comb and brushed it over her head before remembering that she had recently shaved it. A thin line of black hair remained in the middle, like a short night separating two bright days. She'd gotten rid of the rest to offend Silberfluss's nobility with her half-elf ears. They didn't stick out like regular elf ears but pointed upward alongside her skull. She could thank her elvish dad for it, a man bold enough to bed a human woman, as if it were a difficult thing to do.

Jules had promised to tattoo the shaved sides soon. He had gotten brilliant with the needle. Plenty of art adorned his own body to prove it. Vana's mom, Dotty, wanted her to wait until she turned eighteen, but they were about to become Elfentum's biggest rebel band, so she couldn't wait two more years for tattoos. Besides, her dad had taught her how to crack skulls, so a bit of ink wouldn't tarnish her.

"Great show," she said, lovingly punching his arm. They hadn't been alone since the breakup that morning, and Vana struggled to come up with words to ease the moment.

"You too, Vox." He tousled her remaining hair right as she finished brushing it. "Thought for a second you were leaving me high and dry with that riff."

Heat shot into Vana's cheeks, and she took a big gulp of mead out of their supply bag. Too big of a gulp.

"Me?" She coughed. "Giving up"—another cough tore through her as the mead betrayed her—"attention? Never!"

Jules shook his head. "I'm fine, Vox."

He wanted her to believe it. Part of her was eager to comply, but her mom would smack her head with a ladle for it. One didn't swallow down problems, especially if those problems were weeds growing between her and Jules, slowly poisoning what they had. Vana cursed herself for the weed that grew inside of her and poisoned the little normality she had clung on to.

"Come on, man, don't bullshit me." She offered him mead, a different poison to crack him open.

He ignored her and glanced to the side. His look studied the fans who sat down on the cobblestone. The tiredness had returned to their spent bodies now that she and Jules weren't there to rejuvenate them.

"Can you believe we're leaving?" he asked. "It doesn't feel like it."

Vana shuffled her feet. His ambiguity was great for writing lyrics, but she hated it at that moment.

"Jules, I'm sorry for all the drama. I—"

"Shut it, Vox." He kissed her cheek. The warmth created a longing to hug him, but Vana knew that such behavior was off-limits. The touch wouldn't be casual to him. It should have never been casual to her either.

"I'd rather watch my friend live than my lover die every day. I'm glad we figured it out." He took the mead from her and finished it.

Vana didn't want the words to reach her. Instead, she studied the ink work on his neck. Music notes ran down his chest and ended at a depiction of them, The Spirit and the Enforcer, right above Jules's belly button. She couldn't see the full artwork through his black shirt, but she had spent countless hours tracing the pictures that represented their life together. The tattoos depicted the Ackerman farm, her home, with wheat growing richer than it ever had, and his family's tailor shop with all its colorful fabrics that they'd steal to craft stage outfits and banners from. Both artworks transitioned into an image of the two of them from behind. They held hands and walked toward the rising sun. *Stinking romantic.*

She couldn't help it any longer and pulled him into a hug. A strangeness poisoned their embrace. He was awkward at first, then pulled her tighter than she was comfortable with.

Someone cleared their throat next to them, and they jumped apart.

"Sorry," Jules mumbled.

Another polite cough. They looked over into the depth of the alley where a young woman stood. Vana's first glance was careless, as if the human lady in front of her weren't the most dangerous beauty she'd ever seen. She corrected her mistake immediately and devoured every piece of information she could grasp. The woman's corn-yellow hair fell over her shoulders in waves, gentle as her curves, and cradled her bosom. Freckles danced around her pale nose, and her steel-blue eyes seemed to freeze the torchlight and dip the alley into a sky-colored haze. Heat shot through Vana again, in lower places than before.

The woman's lips curled like blossoming rose petals. "The Enforcer, it's a pleasure to meet you."

She didn't even look at Jules, but Vana had to admit that she wasn't either.

"See you in two, Vox." Jules patted her shoulder and scuffled back to the stage.

The entrancing creature stepped closer to her. Vana wondered if she was a Fae, for her eyes held an unnatural power. People hated Fae, but Vana had always romanticized shape-shifting creatures, made purely of magical energy. She pictured nothing more stimulating than exchanging power with such a creature. But this woman couldn't be Fae. Their shapes shifted within nature, not in human form.

"You don't bow down for me?" the woman asked.

Vana blinked—a saving second of disconnect that brought some sense back into her. "You didn't bow down for me either."

She laughed. The sound was high, melodic, and a little too perfect.

"Oh, you are a dirty peasant rebel, aren't you?"

Vana's stomach twisted. She wasn't sure whether to be offended or turned on. The woman offered her the top of her hand, which made it difficult to shake it, but Vana did so anyway. She laughed again, then cocked her head in a posh nod.

"I'm Lady Rutilia Belladonna, as you haven't noticed. Consider me a personal fan."

Vana took a step back and forced her gaze to the ground. She'd known the woman was posh, but she had hoped her appearance was a trick, not a sign of nobility. Worse, she was the daughter of Waldfeld's duke. She had sprouted right from the source of oppression and dared to claim she was a fan.

"Don't tell me I've upset you."

Vana peeked up to watch her pout in a ridiculously alluring fashion. She decided to run, leave the alley behind, and dive back into the heart of her people. The decision came and went. She didn't move a single muscle.

Rutilia placed the tip of her index finger on the tanned dent of skin that led to Vana's breasts and traced it back up to her throat. The hairs on Vana's neck betrayed her as they perked up. A shiver followed. Rutilia's pout morphed into a carnal grin. Vana pictured returning to her stage, but her mind replaced the image with a hungrier one. She had an urge to grab the noble girl's waist, press her against the brick wall and discover how the enemy tasted.

Her hand crept up to Vana's cheek. "I was hoping The Enforcer could play a private session for me sometime."

Vana swallowed hard. "P-private?"

She nodded with a mocking innocence on her face and fluttered her lashes over those deadly eyes. Vana imitated the nod before she understood what she'd agreed to. Rutilia flashed her white teeth and revealed her sharp canines. They weren't supposed to be this sharp on humans, but hers could have torn into Vana's flesh. She'd filed them to look elvish.

"How grand. I look forward to seeing how you perform for me." She stepped back and peered at the town square. "I'd cut the concert short if I were you. The duchess of Nimmerwarm has guests and doesn't approve of political rowdiness."

Vana spat on the ground. "Fuck her."

Rutilia smirked. "Look after yourself." She pranced back into the alley. Vana was surprised to see that the cold brightness of her eyes didn't illuminate the path. She wanted to yell after her, let her know that she didn't give a shit about the orders of some noble brat. The shape of Rutilia's skirt's voluptuous backside robbed her words. She stared at her ass until Jules announced their next number.

Ah, fuck. She had planned not to leave Jules's side all night, to reassure him that nothing had changed. To make him feel like the best damn singer in Elfentum, which he was. Instead, she had ditched him for some noble brat. She bit her lip until she could taste blood and rushed back onstage.

"Sorry, man," she muttered before putting on her usual self-assured grin that fit her guitar so well.

Isa, the redhead fan from earlier, jumped the low cord that separated their stage from the rest of the square and wrapped her arms around Vana's neck.

"Enforcer, such a fan!"

"Whoa." Vana failed to push her off, too scared that she might hurt her. Jules grabbed her waist and pulled her away. Isa giggled as she was dragged away and pressed a kiss onto Jules's lips before hopping back over the fence. Vana's stomach dropped at the thought. Isa was at least in her midtwenties.

Jules gave her a vague smile, then leaned over to Vana's ear. "Careful with that one, Vox. She's a loon."

Vana intended to nod along, but it turned into an awkward twitch. This kind of attention left her unsorted. Things had been much easier back when she and Jules had decided to marry one day and become the greatest troubadour couple that had ever lived. Her dad had never prepared her for girl trouble.

Jules must have sensed her lostness, for he squeezed her hand and whispered, "Let's hide in your family's old barn later and talk. We gotta get that fret off your face, comrade."

She rested her forehead against his for a few peaceful seconds, then returned to their loyal crowd.

"Who's ready for some of Spirit's magic? Louder, I can't hear you!"

The sound of Jules's bombo drum restored her heartbeat to its natural rhythm.

"Kick that dog, oh one more time. Kick me, oh one more time."

She joined in with her guitar and played its strings to roughen up her skin. Fierce movements to push the noble girl out of her mind. Belladonna was an enemy of the revolution. The whole family was, and by the soul of her people, she'd inspire Waldfeld's working folk to rise up and quit this misery. She wouldn't rest until they'd starved off the dependency the upper class fed them.

"Are you tired of biting the hand that never learns? We'll bite back, what then?" Jules sang. "What then?"

The sound of marching steps mingled with the crowd's cheering. Someone blew a horn and ruined Vana's favorite riff. She was about to tell them off when she saw them. Ten armed guards stomped toward them. Their armor shimmered bright blue instead of Waldfeld's local leaf-green color. *Nimmerwarm guards.* Duke Belladonna of Waldfeld and Duchess de Matière of Nimmerwarm, the neighboring town, worked closely together. He must have granted her permission to patrol Waldfeld because of the visitors Rutilia had mentioned. Vana didn't trust Waldfeld guards either, but the Nimmerwarm ones had no relations to those they protected. This was Waldfeld's town square. They had no right to march here.

Their sight silenced all cheers, and a good dozen fans scurried away. Vana itched to shout at them, but Jules's song hadn't finished yet, and she wouldn't dare to cut off his sweet voice. She settled on glaring at them instead. Her muscles tightened when she noticed the pistol in the captain's hand. Two others carried rifles.

"Kick us, oh one more time, and we'll bite back. Back. Back. My spirit spreads." Jules sang the last line with his eyes closed in complete serenity. "There's no escaping the Lady of the Lows."

By the time he'd finished, the guards had formed a line in front of the stage, separating them from their loyal people. One guard held the struggling Isa in a tight grip.

"What the fu—" Vana started, but Jules grabbed her hand and signaled for her to shut up. He turned back to the guards with a calmness she did not possess.

"How can we help you, gentlefolk?"

He was too polite to those shitheads. There was no compassion on the captain's face. Vana's left eye twitched as anger rose in her throat. Any moment now she'd spit fire at them. Or better even, any of the many sufferings they'd forced upon her people. Her dad had taught her never to trust guards. The rule had kept him alive during his many years of vigilante work. Vana had never asked how much blood he had spilled in those days before her birth, but his wisdom had taught her that the trail of justice was bloody and lethal. Unless music paved it. The Spirit and the Enforcer's revolution would be a reckoning of the mind, not the body.

The guard captain gripped his pistol tighter. The weapon had a strange glow to it, similar to the ones royal guard fucks carried on parades.

"We've heard you're inciting people to riot against the duchess of Nimmerwarm," the captain said. "We're here to keep the peace."

"The fuck we do!" Vana tried to shake Jules's grip, but he didn't let go. Fifteen of their fans remained, and Vana had to admit they didn't make them look good. They pushed and cussed at the guards. She longed to join them, but something about Jules's blank calmness unsettled her.

"We're musicians. We carry no weapons." His trained voice did not strain. "We have a right to play in our town square."

The guard scoffed. "Right, eh? This square belongs to the Belladonnas, not some Tribu scum."

Oh, fuck off! She wouldn't stand for such blatant injustice, no matter what Jules said. If he was too sweet to defend himself, Vana would do it for him. She collected saliva in the back of her mouth and spit into the captain's face. Years of teaching her four younger brothers how to spit, and more importantly *when* to do so, had made her an expert.

She laughed at the dull shock on the captain's face. "Who looks like scum now?" She indulged in her peaceful victory by cheering on the remaining fans. The crowd obeyed and added a creative new array of insults. Jules didn't celebrate.

Vana sneered at the guards who separated them from their fans and pulled on Jules's sleeve to leave. The concert was over anyway, and they'd had their fun. This display of civil disobedience was the perfect end to a musical communion of rebels.

As Vana turned, she noticed the captain's lip twitch upward. A second later, he announced his victory. "They attacked."

The guards understood his call as an order and reacted immediately. The torches no longer illuminated the square on their own. Green shots flashed through the night, loud enough to silence all music. The two guards with rifles opened fire into the screaming crowd. Vana saw her beloved fans scatter in all directions before losing track of them. Her eyes belonged to Jules and the impossible hole in his chest.

She stared at the captain's barrel as if it would offer an explanation, then caught her Spirit. He dropped backward into her arms. His sweet voice no longer sang but hissed in pain.

"Fuck you," Vana stammered. "Fuck you, fuck you." She wrapped her arms around his warm torso. The heat of his skin was a gift she'd never appreciated more. She pulled him away from the bastard and tried to remember what her dad had taught her about bullet wounds. *Your opponent has only one shot before they have to reload their flintlock firearm, and that takes time.* She had to get Jules out of there. Apply pressure. Pray. Except Vana didn't pray. Her mom had taught her not to trust in gods or those who represented them. Her mom's brother had paid the price for such foolishness.

Praying wouldn't save Jules. Heal. She could heal him. She just needed to apply pressure, then stop the blood flow. It had already soaked through his shirt and turned the black fabric blacker. But it was fine. Her dad had survived many gunshots in his vigilante days.

"I got you. I got you, comrade. Hang on," she whispered into his ear as she dragged him away from the square's center.

The captain whistled, and she looked back up to him. Her half-elf body struggled to pull the taller Jules out of sight quickly. For the first time in her life, she cursed her heritage.

The captain followed her. His fellow assholes had stopped chasing after the innocent folk and watched them. Vana used all her strength to carry the shallow-breathing Jules into safety, but she couldn't outrun the captain. She yanked Jules closer to their alley and missed a raised cobble. They stumbled backward, and she landed hard on her tailbone.

The captain laughed, then made a disgusting grunt and spit into her face. Vana closed her eyes and loosened her grip on Jules for a second to wipe the saliva off her face.

More gunshots tore through the night, and this time she felt the impact's secondhand quakes. She ripped her eyes back open and watched the captain fire into Jules's chest without provocation. Once. Twice. Three times. He didn't have to reload. The pistol kept spewing its horror uninterrupted. With each shot, green sparks flew around the barrel. They looked like the flashes of lanterns some richer merchants owned. It was magic—the worst kind.

Jules's body jolted in her arms. Something sharp grazed her side. A bullet, meant for him, that had passed right through his defenseless body.

"We're done here," the captain said.

Vana was too numb to scream back. They disappeared into the night and left no trace of the crime they had committed. Vana shook when she realized that their lives mattered this little. Only a few bloodstains recorded their pain, and those could have stemmed from the geese that had been slaughtered on the market earlier. She laid Jules down on the cobblestone and stared at him, sure she could never blink again.

"Help," she uttered. The word barely made a sound. It wasn't enough. She forced herself to swallow the panic and screamed, "*Help!*"

Jules took one brave inhale that caused her stomach to flip. *Yes, stay with me.*

"Vox . . ." His eyelids buried his light as they closed. They couldn't close. Vana couldn't lose her Spirit. He was part of her. Pressure. She had to stop the blood flow.

Her shaking hands ripped open his shirt. She expected him to protest. It was his favorite shirt, but he remained silent. Then she saw it—four gushing waterfalls of blood drowned the tattoos of her farm and his family's tailor shop. They soaked the whole landscape. She looked closer and saw the small depiction of Jules and herself drowning. Their hands, once clasped together, had been shot apart. A gaping hole of flesh spread between them. Vana put her hand onto the wound and felt both of them.

"Jules." She pressed down hard. "Jules, stay with me."

She tried to reconnect the ink figures' hands. They had to keep walking.

"Jules?"

They no longer walked toward the rising sun, as Jules had tattooed them, but into a ruby sunset. No, into a blood moon. No, into nothing.

"Jules." She could no longer see them.

"*Jules!*" she screamed, but no sound came from his sweet lips.

People gathered around them. Vana noticed that they weren't fans but merchants who lived close to the square. She wondered if any of them mattered. Probably not.

"*Jules!*"

None of us matter to those guards.

"*Jules!*"

"Someone get Dotty," a bystander said. *Dotty . . . Mom . . .* Vana couldn't picture her anymore. If Jules was dead, were any of them still alive?

"Dotty, yes, someone should get her."

"Get Dotty!"

Her mother did still exist. She must've if everyone kept calling for her. So did her dad. So did her brothers. For how much longer would they be allowed to live? How long until those guard fuckers decided that they didn't need them anymore?

Vana's shaking hand ran through Jules's blood up to the inked words *The Enforcer.* It was the only tattoo that remained intact. The blood didn't spoil but accentuated it.

Vana swallowed down a sob. The people of Waldfeld had lost their Spirit. She couldn't picture living without him, but perhaps the Enforcer could. The Enforcer had a job to do. She had a rebellion to lead. She had to choose each one of those shitheads' deaths before they could make that choice ever again. The next blood running wouldn't belong to the people of Waldfeld. It would belong to them.

CHAPTER 11

MARTÍN

May 979 - Tribu La'am University, City of Mink'Ayllu, Tribu La'am

Martín's big sister had taught him eight ways to knock out a fool who threatened a Zac-Cimi with a knife; nine if he wanted to be excessive. None of them doubled as a greeting for a potential father-in-law. Releasing his Piernapple from underneath him would've been a good start, but he was reluctant to do so. A Zac-Cimi didn't give up his territory without a fight. Not that he thought of his boyfriend as territory—more like a miraculous volcano or a playground. *Focus, Martín, you have a knife on your throat.*

"Hey, what a surprise." Zazil jumped up and stretched her hand toward the grim-looking ass named Richard Kilburn. "Mr. Kilburn, is it? Zazil Revelli, very good friend of your son's."

The ass looked at her, confused. She had spoken perfect Silberfluss from what Martín could tell, but perhaps intelligence wasn't his strong suit.

"Dad," Pier croaked from underneath him. "I can't get up if you don't lower the dagger."

That wasn't technically true, but like always, Martín's college boy knew how to twist the truth to a more beneficial statement. The blade on Martín's throat lowered until it grazed his chest. If the ass dared to poke him there, he would have to knock him out. The two bothersome flesh sacks underneath his cotton bind already hurt, and the sweat that ran down between them was a painful reminder of his inadequacy.

"Dad?"

Richard dropped the dagger, his face still blank. Martín wondered if that man's brain would catch up eventually or if his main achievement was not drooling on everyone. Then again, his main achievement was this cute genius on the ground. Martín stood up and helped Pier to his feet. This rattled Richard awake, and he took Zazil's hand. Finally. Her arm must have gotten tired.

"Ms. Revelli, nice to meet you. Didn't know Pier was befriending our rivals." His forced smile looked like a bad case of constipation.

"Oh no, I—"

"She's not really—" Pier chimed in.

"It's fine," said Richard. "Pier has told me what a nice young lady you are."

Zazil raised a well-deserved eyebrow at Pier. She was neither nice nor particularly young and was working hard to get rid of the noble lady part. Marrying a Tribu La'am chieftain would give her the equivalent of Elfentum nobility, although that ass wouldn't acknowledge it.

"Yes, nice, young lady . . . that's me. I'm not really part of the Revelli assula smiths anymore though. Not really a momma's girl. Or a daddy's girl. Or . . . anyway, lovely to meet you too. Pier? Wanna take over?"

Pier shimmied his way between them. "You're . . . you're early."

Richard frowned. "I wanted to surprise you. Thought you wanted to show me around a bit. I didn't know . . ."

"Right, about that—"

"That creature didn't hurt you?" He dared to glance at Martín. There were seven methods a Zac-Cimi could use to deal with blatant disrespect. Talking was not the preferred one. For Pier's sake, he'd give it a try.

"I talk Silberfluss." That was an exaggeration, but he understood it pretty well at this point. The talking would come when he moved to Waldfeld with Pier. Tomorrow. There was no way he'd let that grumpy jerk change the plan. Martín had already packed his bags. His parents were disappointed that he wouldn't finish his chef training at their hotel—they had long decided he wasn't suited for his father's semi-legal trade deals—but Martín had convinced them that Elfentum humans didn't know what good food tasted like anyway. They had agreed and celebrated that their scrappy little girl had swooned an intellectual. The thought left a heavy pit in Martín's stomach, and he became grateful for the distraction Richard provided.

"No, he didn't hurt me," said Pier. "This is . . . this is Sachihiro Ch'ulel." He gestured at Sachihiro, who had been avoiding the situation in the background. He startled when addressed and dragged himself to Pier and Richard. Esperanza followed him like a hummingbird on too much sugar.

"Yeah . . . Sachihiro Ch'ulel." He stretched out his hand, but the ass didn't take it. He stared at it for a second before addressing Pier.

"I don't really want to talk to—"

"Mr. Kilburn!" Esperanza pushed herself in front of Sachihiro, throwing him off-balance.

"Sweet vine, what—" he mumbled, but Esperanza's frantic giggles drowned him out.

"I am so excited to finally meet the grand artiste himself. The way you use leaf structure as embellishment is just . . . dazzling, simply dazzling! The work of a true master." She fluttered her eyelashes.

"Sweet vine?" Sachi asked behind her, but she ignored him.

"Thank you. I, ehm, you're Esperanza, correct?" Richard extended his hand to her. Instead of shaking it, she performed a ridiculous curtsy.

Martín rolled his eyes. "Enough nothing." The Silberfluss words evaded him. What did Zazil always say? *Bullshit.* No, that wasn't helpful. His eyes met Pier's, and his heart dropped. He would still tell his dad, wouldn't he? They had been planning their new life for weeks. Martín's big sister, Catalina, had warned him not to trust Elfentum folk, but his college boy was different. He wouldn't back out last second because his dad was a prick. Sure, he loved his dad and spoke fondly of the years they had spent alone, building a successful shop from the ground up. He'd often admired how his dad had gotten them out of servicedom or whatever odd Elfentum thing they'd been stuck in. He planned to make his dad the most famous weaponsmith of Elfentum and turn the Kilburns into merchant nobility. Still, he wouldn't leave Martín to appease his dad. *Fuck, he'll totally leave me to appease his dad.*

Martín cleared his throat and tried to sound less threatening without shifting into the high-pitched voice he hated. "Richard! Sorry for confuse us. I Martín Zac-Cimi. You father from hot—"

"Thank you. I got it from here," Pier said. "Dad, this is my boyfriend, Martín."

The woodsmith looked like he had turned into wood himself. His cold gray eyes stared through Martín, who gave him a half-hearted wave. No reaction.

"Anyway . . . this is Gon Ch'ulel. Another good friend of mine." Pier gestured at Gon. They tried to get up onto their crutches, but Zazil signaled them to stay down. It didn't matter. Richard hadn't as much as blinked. Martín swayed from side to side, as if to balance out Richard's stillness.

"Hello?" Martín finally asked. This was ridiculous. He had expected Pier's closed-minded dad to be an ass about the coming out, but he couldn't refuse to react to it.

"Dad? I . . . ehm, do you want me to show you the botany dome?"

Martín noticed Richard's throat rise as he swallowed. *A movement!*

"Let's go to the hotel, Pier." His low growling was difficult to understand, but Martín could pick up the word "hotel" in any language. The Zac-Cimi Hotel was his parents' pride and the best family business front in Mink'Ayllu. Much better than the Tikal family's pretend tavern.

"Yes, Richard, sir, you love it. Best suite book, just for yours!" Martín said with some difficulty.

Richard inhaled sharply and turned to Pier.

"You got me a room with . . . *orcs*?"

No matter what Piernapple said, this man was definitely an ass. Still, if he was the price of being with Pier, Martín was willing to pay it. Pier looked like he was about to throw up. Another reason to dislike Richard—his college boy had a sensitive stomach, and Martín hated when people upset it. He wrapped his arm around Pier's waist and pulled him close into the safety of his grip. Richard tensed at the sight.

"It's fine," said Richard. "I didn't think you . . . it's fine. Let's get to the hotel. We need to talk about . . ." He glanced at Martín, who met him with a defiant grin. "Just lead the way."

"Would you like me to join you?" Esperanza asked, but Pier shook his head. Of course he didn't. This was about Pier and Martín. Why did this woman weasel her way into everything?

"Join us for dinner tonight, Esperanza, please," Richard said. So he *was* capable of being polite.

"It would be a pleasure." Esperanza beamed. Sachihiro

cleared his throat, but she didn't look at him. "I have an herbal potion against coughing in my room, Sachi." She rushed past Richard. "Allow me to show you the way, Master Kilburn."

Esperanza and Richard headed out of the garden. Martín gave Pier a nudge, but he struggled with walking. He leaned into his college boy's neck until his tusk tickled his cheek and whispered in Tribu La'am, "Worst part is over. Nothing my mom's chuchitos can't fix."

Zazil gave Pier a kiss on the other cheek and nudged him as well. "Write me if you need me. Doesn't matter what he thinks." Martín wondered if she wanted to call Richard an ass too, although she might have had a worse word in mind.

Pier nodded and set into motion, away from their secret garden and freedom.

Welcome to Martín's grand tour of unpleasantries! Tonight we present you with marvelous atrocities, such as my backward soon-to-be father-in-law and my oblivious, bragging dad discussing the trade of my humble self in broken languages. Plot twist: neither of them know what the other one is actually talking about! Also featuring my uncomfortable boyfriend, unable to eat a single bite, while my overbearing mother piles chili rice on his overloaded plate. And let's not forget our dear Miss goody-goody Esperanza gushing about the joys of this evening. Oh, how lucky I am!

The evening was a disaster, sure, but it could have been worse. No one died. Richard did not insult Martín's parents directly or grumble any slurs against orcs, and Pier reached the bathroom before ridding himself of the plentiful dishes. Martín slipped in after him and placed a hand on his forehead until he'd finished vomiting. Afterward, he snuggled him close.

"How are you holding up?"

Pier squeezed him and let go. "Tonight should not go on the records for Tribu La'am and Elfentum relations, that's for sure." He gave him an orcish kiss. "Let me talk to him alone.

I'll convince him. Don't worry, I'm optimistic," he said with his most pessimistic face. Martín decided not to call him out. He helped with the dishes instead, making sure that his parents would still allow him to go to Silberfluss with Pier.

An hour later, Martín lost his patience. Pier had told him that in successful debates it could take hours, sometimes days, for all parties to come to an agreeable solution. But this wasn't politics. This was family. Martín marched up to Richard's room and knocked. He heard two voices inside, and neither of them sounded like his Piernapple.

Richard opened the door and took a sharp breath when he saw him. Martín peeked into the room but couldn't spot Pier or anyone. He swore that he had heard two voices.

"Where Pier?" Martín asked in Silberfluss tongue.

Richard's eye twitched. "There's nothing here for you, boy."

He tried to close the door on Martín, which was audacious. This was the Zac-Cimi Hotel. Richard hadn't even traded anything for his room. Martín's family could throw him out without breaking a deal. He pushed past Richard into the room and closed the door behind them. He was taller and about as broad as the weaponsmith but unfortunately not as muscular. He should have trained more. If Martín had had the build of a proper male orc, Richard would have been intimidated. Panic surged through Martín that Richard had guessed his predicament. No, he couldn't have. Martín's parents had not used his deadname once during dinner.

"Where Pier?" he asked again with a lower pitch to make sure he was coming across properly.

"He went for a walk. Wants to clear his head."

Martín eyed the room, expecting his Piernapple to jump out of a corner at any moment. Nobody was there. Who had spoken? His eyes wandered over Richard. Was he secretly a ventriloquist? If so, they might've been able to get along after all. They could perform a cabaret act together in Waldfeld. The image was as ridiculous as Esperanza's curtsy, but it might soothe him during the three weeks he would spend with Richard in a carriage on their way to Silberfluss.

"Look, we started on wrong hand. I am exercised—no, *excited*—for Silberfluss. Let us no complicated."

The ventriloquist sighed. "Let's drop the pretense, all right? You're not coming with us. You're lucky I'm a peaceful man. Another boy in your position wouldn't be this fortunate."

You're lucky that I don't have regular male tusks. He wasn't a ventriloquist, just an ass, and a creepy one at that.

"I can't let you turn my son into a woman."

Martín's Silberfluss must've been worse than he had thought. He couldn't have understood him correctly.

"Bullshit." Zazil's word spluttered out of him before he could help it. "You can no make man into woman if not lady." After pretending to be a daughter for seventeen years, he was sure it was an impossible endeavor, no matter what was itching under his binder.

"Exactly, so there's no reason for you to come with us. What happened between you two was . . . unfortunate, but no one in Waldfeld has to know. This won't affect Pier's future. I won't let it."

So this would not be simple . . . or friendly. If Pier couldn't get to him with diplomacy, no one could. Martín needed to speak a language this stubborn ox of a man understood. He widened his stance, squared his shoulders, and crossed his arms. He felt tiny but hoped that all orcs looked imposing to a closed-minded human.

"I no leave him. You have problem, we talk, we fight, whatever. I no leave him."

Richard turned away from him and held on to the desk by the window. His knuckles whitened, and Martín's heartbeat quickened. The ass forged weapons, but that didn't mean he knew how to use them. Martín wasn't the best fighter either, but he'd held his ground in a brawl before. He could beat him, no question. The sweat that formed on his palms disagreed.

"Please don't make this difficult," said Richard.

Difficult? He was the one making it difficult with his backward bullshit. Martín decided to end the farce. "Your son is ga—"

A flash of green yanked at Martín's ankle, and he fell onto the hard wooden floor. He reached for the sling on his ankle and found no trace of what had happened. When he looked up, Richard towered over him.

"I love my son. Don't you dare slander him in the name of Exitalis, boy."

Martín rolled from underneath him and got back to his feet. He inhaled a new scent of cloves and lilies. His dad didn't like fauna in hotel rooms. What was going on?

"How you do that?"

A green flash covered Richard's eyes. It disappeared, but he knew what he had seen. Conning Mink'Ayllu's tourists had given him an impeccable perception. Richard must've been an assula magic-bearer like Zazil, but Pier had never mentioned magic. Perhaps he didn't know. That must've been how Richard turned trees into weapons. In Martín's experience, wood didn't remain hard for long.

"We're leaving tonight. Pier and I. Understood?" Richard opened the door for him. If he wanted to play stubborn, Martín would play along. He strolled out of the door, ignoring his own rapid heartbeat. Richard cared about his son. He wouldn't hurt Martín.

"Too bad Pier no be running your shop then. He brilliant, but we no leave other. We go to Silberfluss capital. Bye-bye to son."

Something sharp grabbed his waist and yanked him back into the room. Thick vines tightened around his stomach, with thorns stabbing through his dark green skin. Pain surrounded him. A second later, darkness replaced it. Then came the fall.

He was no expert in falling, but wasn't it common to drop downward? Not this time. He fell in all four directions without ripping apart. His vision disappeared, and the drop seemed to press his stomach out of him. He tried to scream, but no air fed his vocal cords. Was this what dying felt like? If so, the ancestors were a bunch of liars. *Peaceful, my ass!* Then again, the fall felt steered. Martín had never pictured death as directional.

The return of his eyesight was a curse. What he saw next he could never unsee. He landed in a place beyond existence. It was vast; he recognized that much. Every second his surroundings faded and reassembled. The only reliable truth of this nightmare was an all-consuming air of terror. The floor had no grip. Martín seemed to tangle from an invisible thread. His body felt like a foot right before falling asleep. A creeping numbness that hadn't possessed him yet. There were no colors, only hues of former colors that faded into shades of darkness. Plants surrounded him, half-withered and jittering in the foggy landscape. Martín couldn't tell if the glitches were an illusion or part of the horror this place posed. The return of Martín's senses brought a rotten smell with it. He discovered its source and barely suppressed vomit. Half-decayed body parts performed a morbid dance. They rose into the air and sank, dissolving further. Some parts looked like the remainders of brutally devoured bodies. After some concentration, Martín realized that the plants jittered in the same rhythm as the sinking and rising of the corpses. It was a dance of survival in the barest sense.

"You're not taking my son away from me." Richard stood right behind him, but his voice wandered through the grainy air in echoes. Martín startled and turned around to face another inexplicable nightmare. Vines had grown out of Richard's extremities and eyes. The sockets birthed thick green strings with flowers at the end. Blossoms replaced his actual eyes, and he stared at him from the petals. Large thorns had ripped through Richard's clothes and covered his shoulders and back.

Martín trembled. His tongue became too heavy to answer. He had considered himself a tough guy. Dubious alleyways didn't scare him, and he had no problem with Mink'Ayllu's countless scoundrels, but this? This was too much. It didn't matter how clever or brave he could be. Panic had taken over, and panic was the only thing that ruled this place.

"Can you promise me to leave Pier alone?"

Martín nodded. He would tell any lie for this to stop. "Wh-where are we?"

"Limbo." He said it as if the word carried centuries of meaning. Martín tried to recall if he had heard it before. *Limbo . . . limbo . . .* it was an Elfentum concept, part of their weird religion. Wasn't it the place Blothos and his fools had declared evil? A shiver of needles shook his body. Whether or not he existed, Blothos's description of limbo was correct.

Wind picked up. It smelled of spoiled milk and carried a scream with it. Richard's vines retracted, and his eyes fell back into their sockets. He hunched and shook as the thorns withdrew into his body. Martín struggled to understand. His thoughts screamed at him to flee. One broke free—did Pier have hidden thorns and lethal vines as well? College boy's dimples came to his mind, and for a treasured second the panic quieted down. It didn't matter. Pier could turn into a hedgehog at night for all he cared.

"Shh, it won't be long, my friend," Richard whispered to himself. "I need to be certain first."

Martín thought the weaponsmith insane until a voice, sounding of water drops and sizzle, proved him wrong.

"Dear Richard, your condition of our deal . . . you're forsaking it." It didn't sound like Silberfluss and wasn't Tribu La'am, but Martín understood it. He couldn't locate where it had come from.

Richard looked up. His human eyes were bloodshot. "Say it. Say you won't see him again."

Martín focused on the dimples. Anything to ground him in this nightmare. "I love Pier."

Richard roared, and thorns shot back out of him. A flytrap ripped out of his chest and darted at Martín. The jaw of the strange plant clutched him until he could no longer breathe. He gasped for air.

"*Say it!*"

Tears shot into Martín's eyes. The grip loosened enough for him to press out words. "What. Are. You?"

"You see the red shimmer over there?"

Richard's eyeballs remained in their sockets but bulged. He was insane. He must've been. Martín turned his head to the red shimmer in the distance. It looked like a translucent dome covering a large area. Now that he concentrated on it, he could hear faint screeches and gargles coming from it, horrible noises that crept under his skin and seemed to tear it open from inside. He had to get out of here. He had to get out of here immediately. The panic searched for an exit. Left. Right. There was nowhere to go. His heart sped up, ready to pop out of his chest, and breathing became impossible.

"That's the domain of the Ouisà Kacocs, the foulest of demons."

Demons. Of course. Zazil had told him about demons before. Only the desperate or insane tried to make deals with these cursed monsters. The ancestors strictly forbade it. He looked back at Richard—a good candidate for desperate *and* insane.

"Ouisà Kacocs only listen to the Traitor who created them. They catch whatever lost soul wanders in here." The flytrap's stem shook as he spoke. "I will leave you here."

"*What?*"

A terrifying scream came from the dome, followed by chomping and gnashing. It destroyed all memories of dimples, ginger curls, blue eyes, and freckles painted on beautiful cheekbones. It destroyed Everything.

"I have to."

"No, you don't. No, you don't. I break it off. Off, done, gone."

The flytrap dropped him, but there was no ground to

land on. Martín's deflated body hovered among the severed limbs.

"You're making a mistake," the gushing of a river said. "My friend—"

"Let's leave this forsaken place."

With that, they fell again. Fell into hope. A bright world. Back into reality.

Martín landed on the solid floor and kissed it. He had never realized how beautiful the hotel was. Was this the sanctuary his parents saw every day? He had never treasured his body's weight and solid form more. The air was hot and humid but alive. Nothing danced apart from his own chest. He laughed for the life he'd been gifted. For the lack of limbs and the fresh scent of cloves and lilies. For the fauna in his dad's room. He remembered Richard and the price he had paid for this life. His laughter vanished.

The monster had his back turned to him and spoke quietly. "Say goodbye to Pier, but don't mention what happened. He must never find out. Understood?"

When the monster turned around, there was no anger on his face. No madness, no hatred. It was as if he wore a wooden mask. Martín found himself nodding. He dragged his feet to the door. There was nothing else to do.

"I love my son."

You don't know what love is.

Martín nodded and left.

He found Pier outside the hotel, red-cheeked, wearing two coats, and carrying three suitcases and his large sketchbook. He looked like a mad scientist. Or perhaps an artist. It made Martín smile before he remembered that smiling was off-limits.

"Piernapple, what are you doing?" That wasn't a great start either.

"So I was thinking . . . I know you're studying Silberfluss tongue and have worked exceptionally hard on it, but you're not exactly an expert in it yet. Virisunder tongue is quite similar to Silberfluss but perhaps a little simpler to learn due to the close proximity to Tribu La'am. And Polemos—oh, Virisunder's capital, Polemos, is astounding, absolutely beautiful. Architecturally and culturally. As absurd as the Verdains' politics are, their taste has been impeccable for generations. And Polemos is full of opportunities, really. Especially now during the war . . . their spy network is pitiable, but with just a few little twists here and there—"

"Pier, Pier, stop. What is all this? What are you talking about?"

"Come to Virisunder with me. Tonight. I'll organize a carriage. Let's just go."

There he was, looking like an overworked alpaca with shimmering eyes, ready to throw his life plans away for Martín. Pier loved planning and conspiring. He had worked out dozens of ideas on how to take the Kilburn family business to the capital. He had told Martín repeatedly that people were dissatisfied and waiting for change-bringers. He planned to become one, and yet here he was. Pier, the eternal planner, was ready to throw it all away for him. Why had Martín agreed to Richard's condition? Why was he so scared and weak? Perhaps he was the scrappy little girl after all . . .

"What's wrong?" Pier asked. The innocence in his face killed Martín.

He had two options. They couldn't run away together. Richard would find and destroy him. It would destroy Pier as well. Plometos, or whatever the capital was called, was not an option. Martín could give Pier the tearful, loving goodbye he desperately craved, but would Pier accept it? He was too smart not to question unsaid words. He would know that it was Richard's fault. How could he go back to his family business and create a dynasty with the monster dad he loved so much if he knew? Would it serve Pier to know what Martín knew? It wouldn't. It had to be option two.

"I don't want to go to Elfentum with you."

"All right, well, we have other options. There's Fi'Teri, which is supposed to be great for diplomats. The climate is even similar to—wait, Elfentum?" Why did it have to dawn on him already?

Martín took a deep breath. He was good at fooling people, even when he didn't want to. "I know the plans were fun and stuff, but . . . come on, Pier, I'm so young! I'm not ready for this. I wanna explore this city. Meet more people . . . you know, *other* people."

He managed to smirk. The expression burned his muscles. Poor Piernapple had no idea how to process the news.

"But . . . but you said orcs mature differently because of your shorter life span and such. You're about five to ten years ahead of humans. That's what you said."

"Yeah, I'm about twenty-two to twenty-seven in human years. Why would I wanna settle?"

"Settle?"

Martín felt both their hearts breaking. Perhaps the broken pieces would fall to the floor and intermingle. Perhaps they'd stay together somehow.

"Look, let's be honest here. We would have ended it earlier, but the sex was too good."

Pier didn't respond. Martín saw the two sides of him arguing. There had always been two sides of him: the rational, analytical politician Martín admired, and the caring partner he loved.

"You said you were devoted to me." The words were quiet, but they seemed to rip Martín's eardrums apart.

"Come on, Pier, I'm a con artist!" *Come on, Pier, I'm a con artist. You know I'm lying.*

"So you don't love m—"

Martín couldn't let him finish that sentence. "Of course not."

All color disappeared from Pier's face. He looked like another corpse of limbo. No color, just faint hue. Then he found his rational anger.

"I came out to my dad for you." It was an accusation, and it was all Martín needed to hear. He had succeeded. The first seed of resentment was there, and from it Pier could grow the strength to get over him.

"Good luck with that, college boy." He meant it.

CHAPTER 12

ALLY

May 979 - By the Hard Rime River, Virisunder

Her white hands struggled to attach the insulated mouthpiece to the last metal pipe. Ally had designed the instruments herself and was convinced they'd work, if only her fingers would stop shaking in the icy wind. The sweet scent of spring had reached Polemos already, but winter haunted this no-man's-land close to the cold nation of Sap Büruy.

She glanced across the Hard Rime River. It was too wide to bridge but narrow enough to allow a clear view of Silberfluss territory. Those wicked waters prevented the invasion of the eastern border that she and Subira had planned. Laughable Council restrictions had slowed them down in the west. Whenever an attack swayed in their favor, a new Elfentum-protected trade route appeared. Ally hadn't excelled at the few chances they had gotten either. She studied strategies, but no book taught how to wrangle the heat of the moment. Consequentially, they hadn't gained land in over two years. They hadn't lost land either. She and Princess Agathe had found themselves in a perfect stalemate.

Stagnation. It was the constant companion that pervaded any ambition of hers. She had stagnated on the throne. Stagnated in war. She could feel a force brewing inside her, but nothing seemed to unleash it.

She forced the mouthpiece onto the last pipe. The war's stagnation wasn't her fault. It made sense in theory, even if none of the experiments had brought results. She had sacrificed herself to the field for ten years now. She had sacrificed the only requited love she'd ever found. If the fault lay on a sole person, it belonged to the military genius who abandoned her nation daily to be home at five o'clock for dinnertime.

Ally took a deep breath. There was no need for anger. Today's operation would show Subira what true commitment looked like. And perhaps, against all better hopes, Reggie was still waiting for her to return.

"The soldiers are ready, General."

Ally felt Dillon's familiar hand on her shoulder, much warmer than her own frozen limbs.

"Good." She handed him the instrument and relaxed at the sight of his dark eyes and neatly combed black hair. No matter what changed around her, her personal guard had always been there. He was the only reminder of her childhood that Josef hadn't tainted. If Ally had ever possessed innocence, Dillon held on to it for her.

"Make sure the loops and shoes are set. Then give Clarence the signal to start the distraction. We should be safe to slide in at that point."

Dillon nodded and returned to the other soldiers. She had picked eight for this mission. Most of Ally's troops doubted her ability to lead them, a logical reaction to the stagnation, but this endeavor required loyalty.

She knelt down at the riverbank and ran her fingers over

the taut rope sticking out of the water. Gray clouds suffocated the afternoon sun, which offered plenty of shadows to hide in. Ally had spent three refreshing weeks calculating the area's sun movements, but today exceeded her expectations. Science had gifted her the perfect condition to prove herself.

Subira had given up on the eastern border because of the river. So had Agathe. No one expected a surprise attack on the baronies the Hard Rime River protected. They were vulnerable, which made them the perfect entry point to conquer Silberfluss's eastern territories. Subira claimed no military attack could breach this border, but Ally's experiment could. If only it didn't involve the cold.

"Ally?" Dillon knelt next to her, ensuring that no one else could hear him. He had put on a tight bodysuit that radiated with the green glow of assulas and held out another one. "Please."

Ally scoffed and stood up. She rushed to the tree that held on to one end of the rope and checked the knot. It had to stay taut until all ten of them had crossed the river. On the other side, they'd take out Silberfluss's bridge patrol and open the border.

"I triple-checked it, Your Majesty. My patent Oakley knot," the soldier standing next to the tree spluttered. The pastel blue of his eyes looked like the cover of Ally's favorite old picture book, a comforting but strange association.

"Well done, soldier."

He squared his shoulders, visibly pleased with himself. "Thank you, Your Majesty."

Ally was about to ask for his name when Dillon reached her. "It's too dangerous without the suit, please. Subira employs her own assula smiths. These suits—"

"No." Subira might have trusted the assula smiths the Council provided, but Ally didn't. If no one gave her the opportunity to study the magical energy, she wouldn't use it. She'd once thought assulas could empower the people and carry them into progressive times, but they only strengthened dependency on the Council and their high-level smiths. She had heard the distant land of Tribu La'am taught anyone how to use and smith assulas. She'd have loved to abandon the bloodshed and spend her days in knowledge, but it wouldn't help her people. Besides, she didn't care about *smithing* assulas. She longed to understand their substance. If assulas powered firearms, could they power carriages as well? She had sketched mechanical carriage birds and had calculated the possibilities of them taking off into the air. With the right fuel . . .

"Ally, this isn't safe." Dillon's nagging would have triggered Ally's voices had Reggie not gifted her a clear day. She'd felt bad asking for it in her last letter, but he'd complied without objection.

"No experiment is." She had told Reggie about the plan in her last letter but had left out the part about the suits. She didn't want him to worry—not that he necessarily did. Perhaps he had found a new love to spoil with attention, like she had asked him to.

"Just this once—"

"I appreciate your concern, Dillon, but I'm already wearing insulated gear and have applied a paste that warms up in reaction to water. It will protect my skin and prevent hypothermia. Besides, it should only take four minutes and thirty-eight seconds to cross the river. The time frame is too short to worry about the impact."

Dillon didn't look convinced, and truth be told, neither was Ally, but she needn't be reminded of it. As comforting as her personal guard was, she wished he'd offer up more faith in her.

"Sounds like a mighty fine plan to me," the soldier with the picture-book eyes said. Ally opened her mouth, but Dillon stepped in once more.

"Get in position, Oakley. This doesn't concern you."

Anger boiled up in Ally, but she suppressed it. Dillon was here to help her. He knew better. She left the two behind and took a stance in front of her soldiers.

"Everyone gather," she bellowed. "Make sure your weapons and footwear are well attached. The shoes have grips on the bottom that will allow you to walk on the riverbed without getting caught by the stream. Hold on to the loops around the rope and you won't drift. It will be over in a few minutes." *It will be over in a few minutes.* The affirmation had carried her through worse torments than cold water.

"Aye, General," resounded around her.

Ally secured her own equipment and grabbed a loop. She laid a hand on her heart and took a deep breath. It would be fine. She had calculated the odds, and her calculations rarely failed. She thought of Reggie. He'd be at the palace now, backstage, getting ready for a show. Were Tuesdays still cabaret nights?

She took her pipe and adjusted the mouthpiece. Thoughts of her lost home would spoil her odds. Her mission didn't allow hesitation. She ran for the water, swung the loop around the rope, and plunged into the icy stream.

The first two seconds were easy. As predicted, she inhaled in a reflex and her pipe instrument provided the oxygen she required. She sank down to the riverbed with the weight of her armor, but the loop kept her stable. As long as she held on to the loop and the rope held out, the water couldn't carry her away.

She took the first step, and the cold hit her. Her heart rate accelerated, and the bitter water stung sooner than expected. With it came adrenaline that alerted her. She kept her eyes closed and took the largest steps she could. The stream pressed into her left side but didn't rip her out of the riverbed. A blow of pressure pushed against her from behind. Dillon had entered the experiment.

Twenty-two, twenty-three, twenty-four. Keeping track of the seconds since she had submerged directed her brain to a productive task, away from adrenaline-fueled panic. They had five minutes before their body temperature would sink too low and impair muscle movement. Her soldiers might've had longer if the bodysuits did their job well. The cold's pain stabbed into her joints. It reminded her of an acid liquid she'd once had to swallow for Josef. Back then it had seemed to burst through her bones, but she breathed through it now. Did Josef know he had not weakened but strengthened her?

Eighty-five, eighty-six, eighty-seven. The water was eating through the paste now, eager to tear at her feet. Her left toe was bound to give in first, but according to her calculations, she shouldn't lose it. Even if she did, the war had taken so many parts of her mind that losing a body part meant nothing.

140, 141, 142. Her teeth chattered, and the cold pierced through her eyelids. Pain, hungry for attention. It tempted Ally to open her eyes, to test if she *could* open them and to see the length of the rope in front of her. But she couldn't. This was a game of trust, and she had played long enough to master it. The illness's brutal hijacking had caused her to doubt herself. She had sought stability in other places—science, Dillon, Reggie. It wasn't enough. What good was a sword and shield if she didn't know how to fight? She needed to differentiate herself from the illness. She was Ally, the scientist, the lover, the queen, and she could damn well trust herself. Her muscles protested, but with that trust she took another step, another grip, another breath.

165, 166, 167. A wave pushed against her. She sensed a slight vibration. It was unusual but had happened twice while she'd been researching the waters. They were close enough to Sap Bürüy for occasional Taimen trouts to pass through this part of the Hard Rime River. The one she had spotted had been larger than Dillon and had caused waves. Huge but harmless. It reminded her of an illusion Reggie had once created for her. They had climbed down to the dungeons, which he had disguised as the bottom of the ocean. They had stood there, perfectly dry, among magnificent, colorful fish. The thought made her smile. She registered that her facial muscles still worked.

178, 179, 180. Another wave, stronger this time and

followed by plenty more. The bank shifted underneath her feet. Trouts couldn't cause such an effect. The waves, or the fretting of her soldiers, shook the rope. Ally stopped counting. The icy bites jumped on her unoccupied mind. Her heart raced. Not a good sign. She should've been past the initial shock and hyperventilation. She must have crossed more than half of the river by now. They had to get through another minute and a half. Opening her eyes to examine the situation posed a great risk.

The pushing of the water became stronger. Whatever it was, it was approaching them. Had the enemies discovered her? She opened her eyes. The cold dug into her with force. She squinted into the murky river and turned her head to the source of the waves. She had planned to keep moving, but her body froze when she saw it. For two counts, she couldn't process the information with her temporarily decreased mental abilities. Then Dillon ran into her, forcing her to face the threat.

A ship. A large wooden ship with a spiked keel moved toward them. She vaguely registered that it was painted in Council colors, but it wasn't her main concern. Its proximity demanded her attention. It would drive into them and snap the rope before its suction would pull them under. There was nothing she could do to prevent it. She had led her soldiers into their wet graves.

It couldn't be. The river trade route wasn't in use during this time of year. She slapped Dillon as hard as the water allowed so he'd open his eyes. He spotted the ship and passed the slap on. The soldiers deserved to see the enemy before it conquered them. Ally walked on with little use. The ship's speed exceeded her own by far.

Dillon grabbed her shoulder and signaled to the rope. He pushed himself off the ground and up the loop until he could grip onto the rope directly. The ship was about ten seconds away. Dillon gestured for her to do the same, but her body was too stiff to boost her high enough.

Nine seconds. Dillon reached down and pulled her up. She let go of her own loop and noticed that he had a knife in his hand.

Eight seconds. He pressed Ally's hand onto the rope. The paste had worn off now, and the pain on her palm was excruciating.

Seven seconds. Dillon turned around and cut the rope behind them, in front of all the other soldiers. *No!* He was sacrificing them for her. She never would have allowed that. He didn't give her a chance to protest.

Six seconds. Ally and Dillon dropped together with the rope. The momentum tugged them out of the keel's direct target. Dillon pulled them up along the rope toward the riverside.

Five seconds. As Dillon dragged her, Ally looked back and saw the rest of her soldiers sink farther into the middle, farther into the keel's path. She caught the look of desperate picture-book eyes. They seemed so sweet.

Four seconds. She couldn't do this. She pushed herself off Dillon's grip and swam toward the sinking soldier, the one with the picture-book eyes. She wasn't a monster if she could at least save one of her soldiers.

Three seconds. Swimming was hard. Her joints were so cold they seemed as likely to snap as they were to stretch. Her mind and body were not speaking the same language anymore. The suction should have pulled her down, but Dillon caught her ankle.

Two seconds. The soldier's picture-book eyes widened when he saw her shoot toward him.

One second. Dillon's grip held her back. If she only reached far enough—

The ship crashed into them. Bubbles shot from all directions, carrying the soldiers' final screams up to the surface they'd never see again. An impact wave hit Ally, and she lost all sense of direction. Too many enemies. She fought the ship, her dwindling consciousness, the shock-induced rigidity that set in, and most of all, she fought to make her last breath count.

Something warm—a moving, living thing—wrapped around her waist, and another yanked at her ankle. The latter was aggressive. Its pull hurt but caused her to move again. Perhaps it was the trouts. They had come to take her away. Her body stopped responding to her orders. She couldn't resist the pull. Did the trouts know she was a queen, or would they treat her as a common prisoner? *Queen Alexandra of Troutlandia.* It sounded like a Bored Reginald play.

A white light consumed the waters.

"Ally! *Ally!*" What a spellbinding voice, void of the water's horrors. Where was it calling from?

"Alames?" Low resonance filled her cracks. She couldn't feel her body, but she felt the voice's vibration. "Is that really you, my pet?"

Tension took hold. There was nothing to clench, nothing to back off from, but the voice repulsed her. Where was its beauty? Had it not been the same voice? She listened for the spellbinding sounds that had first echoed through the light but only found the dark one.

"If it's you, just breathe. You know you can." *What a strange accusation.* She tried to remember the concept of a physical body, the concept of lungs. The image of a chest rising up and down broke through the tension. *Inhale.* But with what body? She tried anyway, and spasms shook her until her body returned. Water. She was breathing in water. Deadly water.

"Pity, you're not her . . ."

Fuck you. Rage possessed her body, stronger than she had ever felt, stronger than perhaps anyone had ever felt. The rage itched in her fingertips. She burst, she was sure of it. Whatever had been left of her body burst.

Her surroundings cleared. She was in the river, among the chaos of the ship's keel and her drowning soldiers. The soldier with the picture-book eyes held on to her waist, and Dillon yanked at her ankle. But it was hopeless. Their elvish bodies were no match to the keel's force. Ally looked down at her body and startled. It wasn't elvish. It—

Rage drowned her thoughts before she could process what she'd seen. The scientist, the lover, and the queen were gone. The urge to devour an enemy ruled this Ally. Dillon had sacrificed her people. She registered his shocked face through her rage, but it could not stop her. She tore her long sharp claws through the arms that had grabbed her. His bleeding body joined the other soldiers in the keel's deadly suction. The keel. The ship. Her main enemy. She launched and ripped her claws through it. Whatever her body had become moved through the water with ease. The wood crumbled in her paws. Its splinters left her untouched. She yanked at it until the ship crashed into the riverbed.

A mortal body blocked the way behind her. She grabbed it, ready to toss it into the ship's demise. The body blinked at her—alive, moving on its own. *His* own.

Picture-book eyes. The thought startled her. *A thought. Thoughts. Thinking.* Her consciousness broke through the instincts. Reality overwhelmed her as she recognized the man in her paw. It was the soldier she'd been trying to save. *Wait, paw?* Who was she? Had she harmed Dillon? Her body shrunk. With a last burst of strength, she wrapped her arms around the soldier and saved him from the suction. Together, they shot through the shipwreck and out of the river.

"Let's not worry about this moment," the spellbinding voice said.

Everything went black.

"Duchess Ulzhalgas swayed her voluptuous curves around the duke. He wiggled an eyebrow. No, *both* his eyebrows. The deal was as good as done. The duchess trembled with excitement. If it was the politics or the man that aroused her, she could not say."

Ally blinked into the night. Frozen grass pressed against her wet back. The green glow of an assula bodysuit warmed her aching body.

"Well, thank you very much, my treasure. The motus is appreciated, but I value nothing more than your beauty."

Breath wandered through her lungs. It stabbed when it got too deep, but it functioned. Each exhale produced a small cloud of fog.

"Oh, you flatter me, my duke. Shall we explore the less civil of matters?"

Ally blinked again. What was this nonsense?

"He replied with the bulge of his enormous, dripping—I'm gonna skip ahead here. Let me see. Nope, still continues. I forgot how long this scene is. It's a good one though, really is. Let me just—ah, there we have it. Chapter Two: A Second Love. Oh, I think this is the one where we meet Blue Mirage. She's the best, I swear."

"What?" Ally croaked, turning onto her side.

"By Caedem, Your Majesty! You're awake." The soldier rushed to her side and knelt in front of her. "I didn't . . . I wasn't . . . I wasn't aware of that."

His face brought back memories. The waves, the ship, the trouts. How had she ended up in the grass? All she remembered was a white light, darkness, and a ridiculous story. Nothing else.

"What was that?"

"*Defiance of a Rose,* Your Majesty. Best book series there is, if I may be so frank. You were out for a few hours, so I figured . . . I thought it might help."

Thinking hurt, but the title reminded her of cheap Sap Bürüy romance adventure books from the palace library. She had never touched them.

"Right . . ." She sat up. The movement triggered wet coughs.

"Damn, thought I got all the water out. Your Majesty, I mean." He patted her back.

She had drowned; why was she here? She looked at her shaking hands. They were paler than usual but alive and well. The soldier had performed optimal first aid, but it wasn't his job. It was Dillon's job.

"Where's Dillon?" She looked around and found herself in a meadow surrounded by trees. "Where's the river?"

"I had to get us away from the river, Your Majesty. I carried you for about an hour after you pulled me out of that mess. We got too much attention there, with the shipwreck and all . . ."

"Shipwreck?"

His eyes widened. "You don't remember?"

"Where's Dillon?"

She read the answer on his face and waited for her body to react. She'd thought Dillon to be an essential component of her being, no matter how small he made her feel. Who else did she have? Reggie, Subira, and . . . there was no one else. She looked down at her chest, the beating heart within, the cold limbs that ached, and expected it all to fall apart. Her body would splinter. It must.

The soldier squeezed his book into a green-glowing pouch around his neck. "I'm sorry, Your Majesty. It's . . . it's a miracle we're alive."

She shook her head and waited for the splintering to start. It didn't. There was no absolution. She trembled, and hiccups overcame her.

"It's all right, cry it out, Your Majesty. It's . . . well, it's shit, but it'll pass."

The hiccups shook her harder, and she realized they were sobs. She'd lost her loyal soldiers. What if she lost Reggie too? If Subira never spoke to her again? Would her body remain intact? She didn't want it to carry on like nothing had happened. She refused to feel that much, to simply continue with a pain too harsh to hold. She shouldn't have been capable of enduring it. She hated herself for enduring it.

"Okay, this is inappropriate, but, ehm . . ." The soldier opened his arms. "Would you like a hug?"

She nodded and collapsed into his awkward embrace. He stroked her shoulder in a gentle manner that caught her off guard. She noticed her body nuzzle closer and cursed it. It didn't deserve the comfort that was denied to her heart. It should've fallen apart alongside her mind. Josef hadn't broken her. Drowning hadn't broken her. Losing Dillon and her soldiers hadn't broken her. She was doomed to persevere, to suffer and keep walking anyway, even when she wanted it all to stop. Especially when she wanted it all to stop.

"You know, thanks to you my sister's still gettin' her butcher shop. She should name her first-born after you, you know, for savin' me. She and my dad are real excited I'm bringing in military wages. She just bought herself a nice pair of boning knives. Caedem knows what exactly those are, but she wants it, so she gets it. If they're happy back home, I'm doing my job well."

He described his life in the small town of Coalchest and the butcher shop he was funding until Ally stopped sobbing. She listened to his stories as clouds covered the starlight and pictured the great deeds of his sharpshooting mother, Connie, and the smells of the daffodil fields he loved. The life he described was foreign and surreal but as comforting as a fable.

Every once in a while he stopped, unsure whether to continue. The answer was always yes. Hours must have passed before she spoke again.

"What's your name?" she whispered.

"Oh, eh, Robert," he said, confused by the sudden interruption. "Robert Oakley, Your Majesty. Bored Reginald recruited me as a sniper. Dillon too. I mean, I got approved by someone other than the jester. I promise."

The empty spot on her ring finger that had once belonged to Josef itched. Reggie and a charming sniper had freed her from it over a decade ago. It couldn't be him. Could it be?

"Did you shoot a ruby ring as target practice?"

It took two seconds for comprehension to set in. "You're the snow empress."

"Call me Ally." She took her eyes off the night sky and studied him. The handsome elvish face underneath his brown stubble looked young. He was in his early thirties perhaps, the same age she'd been when she had started the war with Silberfluss, when she had plunged her life and the lives of so many others into chaos for ideas and visions. He was doing the same, risking his life for a butcher shop.

"Are you sure, Your Majesty?"

"Pretty sure that's my name."

"No, I mean—" He blushed. "Never mind. Ally it is."

She thought of the night they'd met and of the irresponsible frivolities she and Reggie had indulged in, hiding in the shadows of Polemos's best cabarets. Things had been simpler then. Pleasure of the flesh had eased the agony of her mind— another thing she'd given up for the war. It was criminal to think of it now, but any other thought tore her apart.

"What do you think I should do?" she asked the wedding ring destroyer. He blinked at her, lost for words, but she saw that he wasn't lost for thoughts. "Your book. What do you think I'd do if I were a character in it?"

He chuckled. "Probably have sex with someone."

She laughed as well, a natural reflex that brought great relief. She rejoiced in the way it shook her body, unlike the panic, the pain, the grief. Perhaps there was a different way to fall apart for a few moments. Perhaps splintering wasn't the only solution. She gasped for the air that the sudden burst of joy denied her.

Robert grinned but didn't join the laughter. There were those picture-book eyes again, staring at her not in despair but with a different urge. They didn't look as sweet and innocent as they had before. He tightened his embrace. She noticed that his tanned chest was almost bare since he had given her his assula bodysuit. He must've been freezing. She carefully removed the pouch from his neck and placed her hand on his chest. The heart underneath it hammered quickly, and his breath caught.

"I didn't want to wear the assula suit," she said.

"I'm sorry." He unwrapped one arm and placed it on her neck instead. "Would you . . . would you like me to take it off?"

She nodded and allowed herself to fall apart. *Just this once, please.* Goose bumps covered her skin when the cold air kissed her. A few moments of escape. A few moments of illusion. She granted it.

His kisses followed. The soft touch of his lips on her neck evoked shivers. Her sighs turned into moans as he grew hungrier and rougher. He laid her in the grass while caressing every part of her torso. His kisses wandered down her stomach until his tongue found the pulsing source of her foolishness. She gripped the grass when the first pleasure wave hit. The blades couldn't withstand the force that rushed through her, and she ripped the grass out with a loud moan.

Robert paused to look at her. "You're beautiful."

"Keep going," she pressed out.

"I . . . I just . . ." He went back under. His well-placed kiss made her shudder. "Worship you."

The quiet mumble barely pierced through the lust that had taken hold of Ally, powerful as the rage but safer to indulge in. *Worship me.*

"That's a"—she panted as his tongue waltzed her into ecstasy—"very"—one breath—"foolish"—two breaths—"thing to do."

He emerged again and licked his lips. "Do you like fools?"

"Very much." She knew there was an implication, something that should've worried her, but it didn't. This was a chemical reaction, an experiment she was in charge of. Her first success in years. She knew how to do this.

She propped herself up on her elbows and met his sharp sniper look. Its intensity tossed her into a thrilling uncertainty. She worried the illness would find her there, but a different madness devoured her. Robert gazed back between her legs and found his target. Another flick, another moan. She needed more, to feel him more.

She jumped back into his arms. All awkwardness of their former embrace had vanished. She took off his shirt and grabbed his back muscles. They were as hard as he was underneath her, eager for a deeper embrace, an inappropriate union neither of them had expected. Their first kiss was urgent, rough, and so right that Ally knew it wouldn't be their last.

Her hands wandered to his breeches and yanked at them. She needed to uncover the treasure they held, feel it in all its might. It was a vital part of the experiment. She struggled to untie the firm knot between his passionate kisses. Her taste was still on his tongue and riled her up further, distracting her from the impossible knot. After a few seconds, he chuckled into their kiss.

"Havin' troubles?"

She drowned out his chuckle with another kiss and gave the knot one last tug before giving up.

"I believe your breeches are faulty."

He smiled, placed a hand on her neck, and guided her back into the cold grass. The frozen blades caused a shiver, but their wetness matched her own. He untied the breeches.

"My patent Oakley knot, remember? Can't get rid of it easily."

His wink made her heart jump. He stroked the opening that yearned for him and licked his fingers. The heat that shot through her melted the last memories of the river. He slipped inside and lowered himself on top of her until his chest hair tickled her nipples. She clenched around the grand fullness, her body releasing into the ancient rhythm it knew so well.

Words slipped out through her moans. "Would you like to be my personal guard?"

She didn't know why she'd said it, but knew she wouldn't

take it back. Only this moment mattered, and it couldn't end. She was so fucking sick of endings.

"It'd be an honor, Your Majesty."

She snickered. "I told you to call me—"

He cut her off with a strong thrust. "Ally."

They sank for the second time that night and drowned together in their clasped beat. It took longer than four minutes and thirty-eight seconds for the spring to release its river.

CHAPTER 13

ZAZIL

June 979 - Juyub'Chaj Tribe, Tribu La'am

The tickle of a knife roused Zazil from her sleep, but she didn't dare to open her eyes. The sight would be too familiar, the pain too inevitable to greet it willingly. Any second now, her brother's torturous voice would ring in the day—another cluster of hours to squeeze her way through until the flickering torches of her opium den brought nightly salvation.

"It's a Zunzun." It was so much softer than her brother's voice, not a hint of a sneer. She rubbed her crusted eyes and realized there wasn't a hint of hangover either. Silberfluss's dens and dance boards had lost her years ago. Instead, she'd spent yesterday's evening watching the sunset from the top of a volcano, her small elvish hands buried in her betrothed's green grasp. They'd waited until night had fallen over the tribe of Juyub'Chaj, her new home, then had headed back for an early night in.

"Zunzun," Zazil mumbled as she squeezed her eyes tighter, still lost between knife and sunset. A heavy arm wrapped around her waist, and the fresh scent of a mossy riverbed, a scent she'd grown addicted to, tickled her nose. But something else tickled it as well.

"Tribu La'am hummingbird. Full of energy. They remind me of you, snazzle."

She opened her eyes to a big fat bug, screamed from the top of her lungs, and jumped out of bed. Her fiancé's crutches, leaning against the bedside, foiled her escape, and she landed flat on her stomach.

"Snazzle!"

"Fucking fuck Traitor, fucking limbo, ass, shit!"

Before she could get off the floor, the curtain to her and Gon's tribal cabana moved. Zazil hadn't gotten accustomed to the tribe's lack of privacy yet, and when she saw the feet in front of her, she was sure she never would. They were tattooed with the bright ancestral incarnations every high priestess wore. Zazil would receive them too, once she'd completed her studies with the current high priestess—Gon's bitch of a mother.

"Spectacular morning, isn't it? Just . . . great," Zazil said with a gulp.

The high priestess dignified her with one glare, then turned to Gon, who was still in bed. "My dear son, the carob ointments are now ready for your chieftain values recitation. We await you at the fire cabana."

Zazil cringed at the word "son," knowing how uncomfortable it made Gon. "They're still in bed," she said instead. "The wedding isn't until sunset. Let them sleep in! My, eh, my grandness."

"High Priestess," she said coolly. "You should familiarize yourself with the title if you wish to wear it. We will see you there, Gonzalo."

Zazil got back to her feet and was brushing off her night-gown, ready to argue, when the high priestess raised her hand. "I'm not familiar with Silberfuzz's customs, but it's traditional here for the bride to accentuate her beauty and fertility on her wedding day. Just a thought." She left before Zazil could commit blasphemy. It was a shame; she was quite fond of blasphemy.

"I'm so sorry, snazzle," Gon said behind her. She turned around to find them struggling their way out of bed. They fumbled for their crutches with closed eyes.

Zazil's anger deflated into a chuckle. "Babe, what are you doing?" She picked up the crutches and handed them to Gon. Their silken teal hair fell softly over their strong neck. Zazil leaned in and gave it a nibble. Her sharp teeth matched their thick skin. "Keeping the eyes closed for a special reason?"

Gon smiled, felt their way to her face, and brought their foreheads together for an orcish kiss. "Pier told me in Silberfluss you're not supposed to see the bride before the ceremony."

"Fuck Pier. Your aim is way off without sight." That should've challenged Gon enough to toss her back into bed. The thought of Pier stung, and stings of any kind were best drowned in sex.

Gon traced their fingers over her golden face tattoos instead, humming a gentle melody. Her muscle tension eased, and the nightmare's memory faded away. It sucked that Pier was busy saving that stinking limbo hole called Silberfluss instead of watching her dream come true. It sucked that Bandana had dumped him. It sucked that his backward father had dragged him back to Waldfeld before he'd even graduat-ed. But today wasn't about Pier. Today was about her, the fu-ture high priestess of Juyub'Chaj, burning her cursed Revelli name and rising from the ashes as a Ch'ulel. With Gon by her side, she could rise without Pier. Surely. She didn't need him. Fuck, did she miss him though.

Something hummed next to her ear, and she shrieked.

"There's our little friend," Gon whispered. She was about to argue on the friendship terms when the bug landed on Gon's raised hand. "Look, snazzle."

She fought through her disgust and peeked at the bug, at its pointed orange beak and pretty green feathers. "Oh . . ."

"Zunzuns don't look like they belong here, but they do." Gon held her tighter as she examined the bird. She could belong here too. This pink-haired hot mess of an elf could marry a tribal chieftain and become part of a whole that might just make her whole too. Why not? Gon's older brother, Sachihiro, was supposed to be chieftain, and they'd allowed him to become a Mink'Ayllu professor instead. They'd accepted Gon and all of their flawed perfection. They'd accept her too.

"Told you Zunzuns remind me of you."

"All right, you big softie." Zazil snorted but leaned in for a kiss. "Off to the carob thing with you!"

A childlike grin graced Gon's lips. "I've been waiting for this my whole life."

Zazil picked up their crutches and made sure Gon was stable on them. "Then you've got no time to waste." She hoped it'd sounded as cheerful and relaxed as they wanted her to be. It must have because they rushed out the door in nothing but their loin cloth.

Zazil plopped onto the stool at her dressing table and examined the morning damage. Too many lifeless blond strands dragged her hair down, and she noticed a bald spot.

"It's traditional here for the bride to accentuate her beauty," she mumbled to herself as she pressed the assula gemstone on her left earlobe. Several locks of bouncy blond hair filled the bald spot. She twisted a glowing green cog piercing on the inside of her right ear, and the blond turned pink. "Better."

"You're a wonderful addition to Juyub'Chaj."

Zazil almost fell off the stool. Gon hadn't left yet but was leaning against the doorframe, peeking at her with one eye open. "The ancestors love you just as much as I do."

How beautiful that would be, to have a whole loving

family. The more she lingered on the thought, the more panic spread in her chest. She waved them off instead.

"Get moving, babe. I'll see you on the volcano."

Gon left with a sigh. Zazil made sure they were gone before her gaze fell upon her bridal gown. It appeared as unreal as her luck, with golden strings infusing the white-and-red cotton. The orange morning sun painted the strings as fireflies buzzing around the skirt. Native flowers twirled around the waist, everblooming. Esperanza had helped Zazil with the plants, but the dress itself was her design. After weeks of anxious messages, Pier had urged her to express her panic of not fitting into the peaceful mountain tribe. He'd probably meant for her to express it to Gon, but she'd had a better idea. One night, she'd climbed up the volcano to the prayer platform where her wedding would be and had asked Gon's ancestors for a sign of her worthiness. They'd answered with golden strings to weave into her dress.

She scoffed at herself and reached for the cloudlike fabric. What a fool she was to doubt proof that tangible. Yet doubt was the last addiction she could not shake.

She checked for Gon again, then searched through her trunk. A little assula magic would soothe the doubt. Her fingers found the glowing green shoe sole, one of her favorite creations. The prepared assula had been particularly unruly, but with some force she'd managed to forge it. It slipped into her bridal shoe, docile as if it had never had a mind of its own. Gon didn't want her to bring assula magic, but she had to prepare herself. Just in case.

"Aren't you just a gorger moth magnet?" Esperanza entered with a flower basket in her hands, causing Zazil to jolt upright from her crouched position. "I brought the frangipani flowers for your hair. I tied a few daffodils in for the new beginning."

"Fabulous, garden me up!" she said a little too quickly, but Esperanza's tired face offered a welcome distraction. Her friend's beaming smile didn't reach her eyes. They were deep set with dark rings, and Esperanza's cheeks had lost their normal rosy blush. Tribal ground wasn't good soil for her, as she put it. It brought back memories of the dreadful flatland tribe she'd escaped from. Sachihiro was lucky Gon would be chieftain, not him. Esperanza wouldn't have stayed with him otherwise.

"Bad night, sweetie?"

"Oh, don't knit your neck over it. Mr. Kilburn's friend dashes around in my old skull hole, that's all."

Zazil frowned. Pier's asshole father hadn't brought any friends to Tribu La'am. She doubted he even had any. "What friend?"

Before Esperanza could answer, Sachihiro pushed the cabana curtain aside. He'd chosen a classic Silberfluss suit over the expected tribal wear. "There you are, sweet vine!"

Esperanza yanked at Zazil's newly grown locks, squeaking. She wasted no time getting into Sachihiro's arms. "Ivalace!"

Ivalace . . . Zazil had to step up her pet name game for Gon. Babe didn't sound as poetic as an ivy plant.

Sachihiro patted Esperanza's braid but didn't reciprocate her passionate greeting. "Today is Zazil's day, sweet vine." He turned to Zazil instead. "Good morning. I'm ready to help."

She smiled at his eager expression. It was her wedding day, so she received the attention. Sachihiro's ridiculous insistence on logic could be sweet. She glanced back at the mirror and all the unfinished beautifying work it revealed. This was a Pier job, damn it. Having both Esperanza and Sachihiro in her cabana instead was a bit much.

"Sachi, that's sweet. But I don't think I need your help with—"

"Nonsense. You might be nervous, so of course you need my help. The great Captain Subira Se'azana always says proper preparation eases any nerve. I made a list of all the tribal members so you'll feel like you've lived here all your life. I don't know why you'd want to feel like that, but clearly you do. Let's start with Kabil . . ."

The harsh winds on top of the volcano's prayer platform amplified the high priestess's every word. "By the will of our ancestors, I pronounce you destined partners. In birth, death, and worship."

The entire tribe had gathered around Zazil and Gon, now bathing in the evening sun. After a chaotic day of preparation, she'd finally found ease in the sacred circle. Zazil had stopped silently cursing the high priestess and had allowed her to lead them through the ceremony. She raised a red clay bowl next. What was it for again? Something about the passage of time and children? It always circled back to children. Not that Zazil wanted any brats, but she and Gon had discussed it. Get the blessing first, then she could shock her dear new momma-in-law.

The high priestess let out a loud throat-sung note, and soon the tribe joined in. Was Zazil supposed to join? She peered at Sachihiro, who had crossed his arms, making no sound. Good. As long as he wasn't pulling any tribal moves, she should be fine. Gon let out a loud note too, lower than she'd ever heard them speak. Shit. She thought back on the different tribes she had visited before. Throat-singing. She had tried it before, but her battered lungs weren't the best for it, and it felt . . . vulnerable.

The song echoed around her. Everyone joined except for Sachihiro and Esperanza. The sound seeped into Zazil's body and vibrated within her. It built a connection to the tribe, a whole. She'd felt it before at fire festivals—the release of one's own self for the greater being. She had never dared to join. What if she tainted the whole? What if her own song destroyed the tribe's connection? She was sure her darkness would seep into their bodies and swallow them like it had once swallowed her.

But this was her tribe now. She couldn't prevent tainting

it, not if she hoped to become a high priestess herself one day. She thought of Silberfluss, the dens, the gutters. How had life lifted her to the top of a sacred volcano? The golden strings of her dress caught her eye. The ancestors loved her. They wouldn't allow the darkness to spread. They'd cleanse her.

She pictured the memories leaving her body and drifting away, off the volcano's prayer platform and into the endless ocean. She filled her lungs with salty air, opened her mouth, and screamed. It was supposed to come from the back of her throat but turned into a guttural release. Some notes around her stopped, but most tribal members embraced her scream. They allowed it to pierce the communal song, as if it belonged there. Gon squeezed her hand. It did belong there. All of her craziness, all the wildness within her, all of her belonged there. Her past didn't. Her brother didn't.

She took another breath to release every memory of him. Right as she opened her mouth, the high priestess tossed ashes into her face. She coughed and swallowed some. The song halted.

"High Priestess!" Gon ran their fingers over Zazil's spine, and the coughing stopped.

"The wind must have caught it," said the high priestess, and a tiny smile crossed her face. Zazil got the feeling that Gon's mother wasn't pure enough to be tainted.

"What was that?" Zazil asked.

Gon nuzzled their face against her long ear. "Dad."

"*What?*"

The tribe whispered. Zazil tried to keep herself from shaking, but even the earth rumbled.

"The old chieftain blesses the new. Do you not honor that tradition?" The high priestess raised an eyebrow. Unlike the tribe, she seemed to enjoy the hostile interruption the bride had caused.

Zazil turned to Gon and lowered her voice. "Dad . . . as in your father?"

"His ashes . . . they're supposed to drift above you,

releasing into the wind, you know?" Her first instinct was to list all her favorite Tribu La'am swear words, but she sucked in air instead. Zazil had promised Gon long ago to embrace their customs. She would have preferred not to combine her father-in-law's funeral with her wedding, but the fluidity with which many orcs viewed life had its charm. Birth and death— it was all one big circle they experienced together. An elvish lifespan didn't lend itself to such a deep connection. The prospect of two hundred years made life idle. Zazil was ready to live as an orc and die like one when Gon's time came.

"I do honor the tradition. Please proceed, Your Majesty." Not her title, but she hoped it would bother the high priestess and endear herself to the tribal members.

"That's the wrong title," Sachihiro called from the side. *Thanks, Sachi.* Reliable as always.

The high priestess inhaled sharply, clapped her hands three times, and used her fingers to draw symbols in the air. Zazil tensed up as she watched the ritualistic gestures. Had she pushed it too far? The high priestess shook her wrists and opened her palms. A glowing gold orb the size of an orcish fist manifested out of the air and fell into her hands. She bowed toward it and held it out for Gon. Zazil frowned. Was this—

"The chieftain's Utsilo. Use it wisely."

Zazil had expected something more spectacular than an orb. Utsilo, the ancestral favor, was a tribal magic force that exceeded the power of assulas. They were rare, so Zazil had never had the chance to inspect one closely and understand how they functioned, but she had studied them in her Tribu La'am culture class. The holder of an Utsilo could request a favor from the ancestors they could not deny. It came with a deal, as all Tribu La'am exchanges did, but Gon had assured her that their ancestors were loving. Their father had used his Utsilo to save Gon's life after the premature birth.

Gon bowed to their mother. "Thank you. I will."

Of course they would. Gon could use it to save a lost child like they once were, or to enlighten the tribe with all the knowledge they had collected, or to stop their mother from being such a bitch.

The high priestess stretched her arms out and looked toward the sky. "Ancestors, bless this—"

A rumbling from the ground cut her off. The volcanic earth underneath them shook, and Zazil's chest tightened. *I'm a Ch'ulel. I'm a Ch'ulel.*

The prayer platform cracked between Zazil and Gon. The crack shot down the path they had come from and cleaved through the volcano. *This can't be happening.* Juyub'Chaj's fire festival wasn't for another three months.

The rumbling increased until it was louder than their song had been. The crack widened, almost large enough for Zazil to slip through.

"Remain calm!" the high priestess yelled over the noise. "This is—" The eruption of smoke drowned out her words. A hot cloud of ash broke out of the peaceful volcano. It swallowed the sky and everyone underneath it. Within seconds, the world turned gray.

Smoke filled Zazil's lungs and rattled her body with violent coughs. She felt the mountain move underneath her, but she couldn't see through the gray. *Think, damn it.* First the smoke, then the lava. Tribes believed uncontrolled eruptions to be ancestral punishment, which rarely happened. The one time a volcano had erupted unexpectedly at a human tribe in the forest lands, they . . . they . . . what had they done? Zazil searched her brain for an answer and found none.

A golden light appeared through the smoke and illuminated the cracked path that led back to the village. It shone from the high priestess. Her torso had turned translucent, and a golden parchment hovered where her rib cage parted.

"Follow my lead. Do not stray. Run!" she called, illuminating the way.

Run? But Gon can't—

The orcs around Zazil followed the command without a second thought. The high priestess's word mattered above unity. Her word had created this unity. It shouldn't have been that way. She protected the path they ran on, protected everyone who could run. Everyone except for Gon.

"Run, sweet vine!" Sachihiro shouted, then appeared at their side. Zazil grabbed Gon's arm and swung it around her shoulders. She couldn't carry them, but they could move quicker that way. Gon's crutches fell to the trembling earth.

The first stream of lava burst out of the crater and rushed toward them.

"Go!" Gon screamed.

"Out of the way, Zaz." Sachihiro picked his sibling up and took off. Zazil could barely keep up with what was happening. Sachi, of course. She ran after them down the path, skipping over the lethal crack. It was wide enough to swallow an orc now. She was faster than Sachihiro, but he had a better grip on the ground.

They trailed the rest of the tribe, catching up quickly, but so did the lava.

"Use the Utsilo, Gon!" Sachi shouted.

"Not enough time," Zazil responded before Gon could. As loving as those ancestors were supposed to be, dead people didn't have a great concept of time pressure.

The high priestess danced down the path. Her limbs flailed wildly in the light. Its power increased. She formed a golden dome around her running people—protection to stop the lava. It thickened around them until it was barely translucent.

"Stay within the dome!" Her voice boomed across the path. The smoke behind Zazil became hot enough to burn her skin. The lava couldn't be far off. Zazil peeked over her shoulder and saw it. The volcano's angry red tongue was fewer than twenty steps away.

"It'll close!" the high priestess yelled again. Just in time to avoid the fiery death that awaited them once the lava caught up.

Sachihiro tripped. Zazil's heart stopped as the two Ch'ulel

siblings stumbled into the crack. Gon clawed the earth, holding on to the crack's edge, but Sachihiro fell out of sight. The dome closed with Zazil in it and robbed her of her beloved Ch'ulel siblings. She couldn't see them anymore. The smoke disappeared within the dome as the golden light surrounded them.

"*Gon!*" Zazil screamed.

My shoe. She could have kissed herself for remembering it. She stomped the ground. The energy beneath her foot rushed through her. She directed her focus onto the dome. *Break it.*

Green light shot out of her sandal and crashed through the golden dome. It ripped a large hole in it and crumbled its magic around them.

Zazil saw Gon. She also saw the wave of lava about to consume them.

"*Fool!*" The high priestess tried to close the hole, but it was in vain.

Zazil ran through it and took Gon's hand. To stop the stream, she'd need a fully crafted staff, or five assulas. The small sole wouldn't be enough. The boiling stream reached the crack. *Save us, you unruly bastard.* Not a proper magical command, but the assula listened. Green light blasted out of her and crashed against the lava. Its crystals hardened into solid stone, refusing to yield to the force behind it. The change traveled through the stream until the built-up crystals stopped the fresh lava from spilling onto them. It formed a crystallized wall that rose as high as their university's history wing and looked like rubies.

Zazil took her eyes off it and grabbed Gon's arms. They had held themself up this far, but she saw the strain in their face. "Someone fucking help me!"

Three tribal members rushed to her side. *About fucking time.* With their help, Zazil pulled Gon out of the crack and laid them on the ground. Coughs rattled them as they allowed their muscles to loosen. Zazil leaned over them and brushed their blackened hair out of their face. Sobs crept up her throat. "We made it, babe. We made it."

"Ivalace?" Esperanza called behind her.

Sachi . . . fuck. Zazil let go of Gon and stumbled back to the crack. It was steep and dark. Sachihiro must have fallen deep into the volcano. Zazil felt as crystallized as the lava. She tried to move, to check on Gon and Esperanza, but her limbs were unyielding.

Esperanza sank to her knees next to Zazil. "Ivalace?"

Zazil swallowed. "He's . . . he's gone, Esperanza."

"My son!" The high priestess pushed Zazil out of the way. Now? She remembered them now?

Black smoke rose from the crack. It looked denser than the eruption's gas and carried no ash. Zazil reached for it, and it flinched. It was smoke; it shouldn't have flinched. It shouldn't have felt anything. Zazil lowered her trembling hand. Her stomach knotted.

"What is it, High Priestess?" a tribal member asked.

Zazil wished she could enjoy the high priestess's baffled face. She was as lost as Zazil.

A scraping sound came from the crack. Zazil leaned over it, into the smoke. She blinked through the black substance and spotted a large object. The smoke lifted it up, scratching the rough sides of the crack.

The high priestess stepped back. "Careful, this is not a—"

Before she finished speaking, a body ascended from the crack—a large green body with broken glasses.

"Ivalace!" Esperanza squealed.

"Shh," a voice echoed through the smoke. What a spellbinding voice. "Your story is still needed, my child." The tribe watched in silence as the smoke carried Sachihiro back to the land of Juyub'Chaj and laid him down next to Gon. Sachihiro's body touched the ground, and the smoke evaporated as if something had sucked it out of the air.

"What's going on?" Sachihiro opened his eyes and blinked at the staring crowd. Gon pulled him into their arms.

The tribe broke into another communal sound as they called his name in relief. Zazil didn't join them. She tried to understand what had happened. This was not a kind of magic she had studied.

The high priestess took Sachihiro's arm and lifted it into the air. "The ancestors have chosen their new chieftain!"

The tribe's relief turned into a cheer that left the four of them cold. Shock hit them at the same time, but it was Esperanza who acted upon it. She stood up and withdrew from Sachihiro.

"Sweet vine . . ." His voice came faintly through the cheering.

"The Fae," Esperanza mumbled. "They need me." She turned and dashed down the path.

"What the—" Zazil started, but the words wouldn't come. She'd known Esperanza would leave Sachihiro if he were to become chieftain, but surely not this quickly? Not if she loved him. Zazil turned her anger upon the cause of this mess. "What the fuck, Mother?"

The cheering died down. It was forbidden to address the high priestess in such a manner. Not even her children were allowed to do so. Zazil didn't care. "What the actual fuck? First you ditch Gon like that, and now you're taking the chieftainship from them?"

"Him."

"Oh, fuck off!" Zazil erupted like the volcano. She spilled lava on Gon's precious future with the tribe, but she couldn't help it. Gon had made her believe their family was different. It wasn't. Family remained a steaming pile of shit no matter how it presented itself.

"Gonzalo has brought danger into our midst. He cannot be trusted as our chieftain."

Gon shrunk in on themself. Zazil made herself as large as she could. No one had the right to make this ridiculous bundle of kindness feel bad about themself.

The high priestess stepped closer to her. "You have soiled our earth with demonic magic and——"

"They're called assulas, bitch! Read a book." Several tribal members sucked in air. There was no going back now. "What should I have done instead? Let Gon and Sachi die like you were fine with?"

"The ancestors select whom they see fit, spike." The elvish slur hit Zazil harder than she'd expected. So much for accepting. So much for pretending to be an orc. The tribe knew she was an elf and would never truly belong. "He was weak at birth. He wouldn't be here if his father hadn't taken pity on him."

Tears shot into Zazil's eyes as she turned to the tribal members around her. "I saved all of your asses, and none of you have the guts to stand up against this bullshit?"

Sachihiro cleared his throat. "High Priestess——"

"Not you, Sach. No offense, but you're equally fucked here."

The high priestess towered over her. Zazil hadn't realized how large the orcish woman was. Her painted tusks ended in sharp points. "You provoked the anger of our ancestors. If you do not leave our land by tomorrow's sunrise, the volcano will erupt anew."

Bullshit. She tried to anchor herself in the rage, fume over the injustice, but guilt spread in her stomach. Her worst fear had become true. She had ruined Gon's life.

CHAPTER 14

VANA

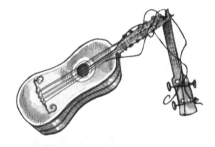

July 979 - The Ackerman Farm, Waldfeld, Silberfluss

"Come on, Betsy." Vana pushed against the stubborn cow. "Move, old girl. You don't wanna stand in the way of revolution!"

She did. Vana growled and opened the barn door wider. Her parents had allowed her to use it for the night, and she had already set up her stage. Officially, she was holding an intimate remembrance concert for Jules, but anyone coming knew she'd remember him properly—by taking action, not by locking herself in a barn and crying. She had done that too, of course, for the past month, but that routine was getting old.

Tonight these barn walls would bear witness to a greater tribute to her beloved Spirit—the rekindling of justice. It looked like Betsy wanted to witness it too.

"Adam! Can you get her out of here? Old girl sneaked back in while I was setting up the food."

Vana's brother skipped to her and patted Betsy's neck. "You know I could help more than that."

Vana bit her lip. She loved the fervor of her younger brothers, but she couldn't risk losing them. Not after Jules. "Gotta be older than that, sorry."

"I'm fourteen." He led Betsy out onto the field. "You're sixteen."

She shrugged. "Yeah, but I mature like an orc, now shush. I'm sure Mom's got dinner waiting for you."

"Next time?" he asked.

There would be many next times. She wouldn't stop until they'd robbed every Silberfluss guard of unjust power and had instilled a new system, one that served everyone. It was time to bid relenting farewell.

"Maybe."

Adam rolled his eyes and headed back to their small farmhouse. He would spend the night listening to the snores of his parents, grandparents, and two brothers, as they all slept in the same room. Vana was sick of it. The Kilburns had a larger house, and there were only two of them. Everyone deserved such luck. It shouldn't have even been luck. It should've been Princess Agathe's duty to provide it.

She didn't begrudge Richard Kilburn for his success because he still looked out for his own. Without him, she wouldn't have gotten her hands on such lovely weapons for tonight's mission. She secured the trunk and sat down on it. Now she had to wait for her future-bringers to arrive. They'd see the Enforcer wasn't just talk and music.

She watched how the wind brushed through the wheat for a few seconds, then jumped back onto her feet. Sitting alone in stillness unnerved her. It filled her with a restlessness that needed expunging. Her eyes fell on her guitar. She hadn't touched it since Jules's murder but had placed it on the stage in case a guard came to check on the concert.

She picked it up and ran her fingers over the strings. Three years ago, when she had strummed her first chord, the movement had stung her untrained fingers. The joy of the tone had overshadowed the pricks. She had played until her fingertips were wounded and raw and her heart was freed of every dread she had harbored inside. Only bliss had remained.

She played a chord and felt nothing.

"We're finally hearing the Enforcer again?"

Vana looked up and saw Isa walking toward her, followed by six other fans she recognized from past concerts. She swallowed and put the guitar back down. She ignored her shaking fingers and focused on the mission. Isa had spread the word to the right people: young, but not too young; older than her, in their late teens or early twenties; honest, tough-looking rebels in the making.

"Great to see you all came." It didn't carry her usual showmanship, but it had to. She needed to get their blood pumping, get them excited for the prospect of the night. If the morale wasn't there, she had already failed them. She hurried to the barn door without another word and pulled it shut with a slam. Her mom would be upset, but she'd deal with that later.

She kept her back to them. "But comrades, tonight isn't about music." She turned around, satisfied to find them staring at her. "Are you ready to take the lyrics out of your ears and put them into your fists? Because you're with the Enforcer now, and she's not fucking around."

She rushed past them and leaped onto the stage. "I know you all came for the music originally, but you stayed for the message. Our Spirit may have left us"—*keep your voice steady; they need a leader, not a little girl crying in a barn*—"but we can make sure his songs come to life, and by fucking limbo, they will!"

The fans nodded. Isa and three others clapped. She was almost there.

"Those guards think they can boss us around and treat us

like shit? Well, tonight we're founding our own organization. We'll protect the people from the guards meant to protect them. Welcome to the Vindicators of Anarchy!" Vana said.

Isa hollered, and the others applauded, except for one guy, Greg, an old friend of Jules.

"It's VA for short, if that's easier," Vana added, trying not to blush. Anarchy had no leaders, so she'd have liked to have a small signature in its birth organization—a hint she'd existed, that she'd been the one taking the chance.

Greg chuckled. "So like Vana Ackerman?"

Heat shot into Vana's cheeks. "That's not . . . I mean . . ."

The atmosphere in the barn shifted in an instant. Isa pulled a knife from a holder on her thigh, held it against Greg's throat, and hissed.

"Whoa!" Vana jumped off the stage and placed her hand on Isa's forearm, carefully pushing her off Greg. "Let's not . . . let's keep Jules in mind here, all right? We're all together in this." She looked over her shoulder at the mortified Greg. "You're all right?"

Greg nodded but said nothing.

"Sorry, my Enforcer. Didn't mean to steal your thunder." Isa winked at her.

"Okay, well, that's . . . that's . . . let's focus back on our common goal, shall we?" Vana hopped back on stage, but the weight in her stomach didn't leave her.

"All right, where was I? Yes, VA. It's okay if you don't wanna join, Greg, but just hear me out first, all right, man?" She had to stop stammering. She couldn't lead if she was stammering. She took a deep breath and continued. "In the VA we'll be taking out foul guards first."

"We'll be the wrath of Exitalis. Slaughter those pigs so she can feast on their guts!" Isa yelled. The weight in Vana's stomach spread. She wasn't sure if Jules would approve of that wording, and she had hoped to leave religion out of this. She wasn't doing this for Silberfluss's goddess. She was doing this for its people. Still, she didn't want to scare off her most committed comrade.

"Yeah . . . yeah, that's . . . anyway, once that's done, we will organize a fairer distribution of wealth. Silberfluss is not an impoverished state, but it is run by impoverished minds who do not understand that a body can't function properly with rotting limbs. Unfortunately, most guards don't share our values. Princess Agathe would rather let us rot than acknowledge our value."

Her comrades muttered in agreement. One guy named Kent yelled, "That ghastly whore!"

"Hey, let's not insult our working ladies," Vana said. "We condemn based on politics, not on bedroom habits. And Agathe's politics are shit! Actually, all royals' politics are shit. Fuck Agathe! Fuck Alexandra! And fuck their useless war!"

Applause followed. Vana grinned. She got them. She had true comrades now.

"Tonight we'll break into the Nimmerwarm barracks and slit the throats of those who murdered our Spirit, those who fired into a crowd of our people just because their duchess had some fancy visitors. I say no more!"

"What if they catch us?" Greg asked. "I heard they're throwing more people into Balthos's Heretics lately." He shuddered, and a few others joined him. Silberfluss's most notorious prison was rumored to be filled with demons and ghosts. Vana didn't buy it. Noble trash had probably labeled the poor bastards locked up there as ghosts.

"Look, I know imprisonment is a real threat, but remember, folks, it's punishing crime with crime. If those are the rules to their game, we'll play it and we will play it better than them! We will punish them for punishing us. We will participate in this vicious circle until crime is no longer seen as an evil deed but as a desperate fight against organized oppression. Who's with me?"

Everyone cheered, even Greg. Vana's heart jumped. Her whole body felt charged, ready to take action. Was that how her dad used to feel on his vigilante missions? The rush intoxicated her.

"Let me show you your weapons." She beamed and opened the trunk. *Thanks, Kilburn. Let's fuck them up!*

The night was smothering the last glimpses of daylight when Vana and her Vindicators arrived in Nimmerwarm. The barracks were attached to the estate of Duchess Madeleine de Matière, which reached several stories into the air. Looking up at it hurt Vana's neck. Figured. She couldn't even look at a noble manor without contorting herself.

"All right, comrades, you see the barracks over there?" Vana pointed at the imposing red brick building. She had always pictured barracks as tents, but her Vindicators could break into an actual building as well. It couldn't be that hard. "We're going in quietly, all right? No open combat. We're not trained enough yet. Don't get me wrong, I'm sure you can all kick ass, but . . . let's not risk it for now."

"Aye, aye, my Enforcer." Isa's eyes sparkled with excitement. Vana had expected righteous anger, but this joyful eagerness concerned her.

"We might have to take out a patrol, but we're approaching from the back. The goal is to slit the sleeping guards' throats and disappear the way we came in. Stay away from the main manor. We don't know what's in there." She waited for their nods before continuing. "And if you see the captain who shot Jules, let me know. He's mine." She couldn't wait to spit in his face while blood seeped out of his throat.

"Aye, aye."

"Let's go." Vana's hand clasped tighter around the red oak seax she had picked from the trunk. Richard had wrapped it in cloth and had warned her that once the hilt touched skin, it remembered its owner. He believed that the seax could protect her and told her the blade absorbed whatever liquid it was given first. Once it touched it, it craved it. Vana wasn't sure how much she bought into the Kilburn sales tales, but holding the hilt felt like holding hands with a loved one. Perhaps her Spirit was with her after all.

Vana and her Vindicators had marched through the edge of Waldfeld's forest as cover. She was relieved that the trees continued around the estate. They had to avoid the estate's gate and its guards, so Vana signaled to retract into the forest line until they had circled to the back of the barracks. Isa's stiletto knife lit the way. Vana had almost picked the beautifully crafted stiletto Richard had forged from dule tree wood and infused with mushrooms that glowed in the dark, but he'd convinced her to take the seax. He'd said he loved the connection of spirit to weapon. The seax could be her enforcer, and she'd be its spirit.

They reached the back of the barracks and faced the high metal fence encircling the estate. Vana stepped out of the forest and swung the rope she'd brought off her shoulder. Isa and her other comrades followed.

"Who's the best climber?" Vana asked.

Greg raised his hand. "I clean the church bells for Father Godfried."

"That means . . . ?"

"It's hard to get up there, all right?" Greg took the rope from her. "I've got it, Lady Anarchy." He whispered the last words so that Isa wouldn't hear them and smirked at Vana.

She punched his arm gently. "Go for it, comrade."

Greg had been one of Jules's classmates and used to play catch with them. He'd gotten too involved with the church for her taste, but she knew Jules had kept a soft spot for him.

He swung the rope around his arm and climbed the metal fence.

Isa rested her head on Vana's shoulder and clicked her tongue. "Did he bother you, my Enforcer?" The closeness of her cheek brought a different image to Vana's mind—the image of a noblewoman with soft skin, golden hair, and a carnal grin. *Rutilia. Don't think about her now, idiot.*

"Right . . . wait, no. No, Greg is fine. He—"

"Secured. No patrol guards," Greg called from the other side before tossing the rope over the fence.

"Let's just go," Vana said to Isa. A dangerous flicker crossed her comrade's eyes, and one of them twitched. She grinned before Vana could process it.

"Don't worry, my Enforcer. I'll make sure the Spirit gets the send-off he deserves."

Vana opened her mouth to respond, but two of her comrades had already climbed the fence. She couldn't be last, so she grabbed the rope and flinched. It was rough like a guitar string. She shook off the pesky thought and landed on the estate grounds with trained grace. She had wished for a revolution of music, but her dad had taught her some moves in case violence ever crossed her path.

Vana examined the surroundings. There was no door to protect, no direct entry point, so her comrades didn't have to deal with any patrols right away. Attending guards likely made their rounds on the estate grounds, but none of them had crossed their path.

Isa jumped down next to her. The light of her stiletto lit up the barracks' back wall and revealed a barred window. It was out of their direct reach, three heads higher than Greg, their tallest comrade. It was the perfect entry point, provided they got through it. *All right, Kilburn, let's see if your weapons are as fantastical as you claim them to be.*

"Greg," Vana said, "gimme a lift."

He bent his knees, and she climbed onto his shoulders.

"Isa, the stiletto." Isa handed it to her, and Vana held it underneath the window so that only a slight gleam reached it. She squinted into the darkness and thanked her dad for her sharpened half-elf senses. The room was filled with swords, shields, and strange glowing rifles. She raised the stiletto until a faint beam shone into the room. No one inside reacted to it. It must've been the armory, and it was likely unguarded.

"It looks like—"

The sound of a world ending cut her off. Shots. More than any weapon should've been able to fire. Vana crashed to the ground as Greg collapsed under her. She hit the ground with her shoulder first and strained her muscle. A dull pain shot through her, but it was nothing compared to the images that flashed in her mind. Ink and blood. Ink and blood. Ink drowned in blood.

She forced herself to feel the grass, to notice Greg's body next to her. This was the real world, and if she couldn't live in it now, she wouldn't be able to live in it tomorrow.

"Nimmerwarm scum!" Isa yelled.

Vana pushed herself off the ground and saw a patrol guard firing at them. Her comrades stormed the sole aggressor. Vana tossed the stiletto to Isa and pulled out her seax. Kent and Maureen disarmed the guard before she could join.

"Finish him quickly," Vana said, and Maureen pulled her dagger.

"I want him," Isa said and jumped the helpless guard. She raised the stiletto into the air and stabbed the needle blade into his eye. He yowled, causing too much noise.

"Isa," Vana hissed, dragging her off. The guard slumped into a pathetic pile on the ground. Vana's stomach turned. They needed to be better than their oppressors, not cause an equal mess. "D-do it quickly, please," she said to Maureen, who lifted the guard's head. One slice of the dagger and his story was finished.

Vana swallowed. This was great. Another guard gone. This was what they were here for. Blood seeped into the soil as the rest of his life force left him. Dark cloud puffs appeared around him. Vana turned away. This was good. This was justice. Justice didn't have to be pretty. Then she remembered Greg.

"Shit!"

He curled up on the ground, holding his bloody leg. Vana rushed to his side. "Comrade, where—"

She noticed the wound on his kneecap and the grimace on his face. He would never clean the church bells again. Vana's stomach lurched, but she couldn't break. Anger. She needed anger. She looked back at the dead guard, and the pity she had felt left her. She shouldn't have stopped Isa.

"Hold on, comrade, we'll get you home and—"

"Finish the assholes who killed Jules," he said through the pain. *The mission, of course.* They couldn't abandon it with one man down. It was the price they should've all been willing to pay. She looked at her comrades, and her eyes fell on the small ironwood ax Kent carried. She tried to remember what Richard had told her about ironwood. He had rambled on about the weaponry for an hour, so it was difficult to remember the properties of each one. *Ironwood . . . indestructible?* It was the blade that could cut through anything.

"Someone lift Kent up. Your ax should be able to cut the bars." They followed her command, and she turned back to Greg. "We'll hurry, and you hold on until then, all right? When we're home, I'll ask my mom to make more of that apple pie you like."

He mumbled something. She leaned in closer to understand. ". . . wife of the king, mother to us, I thank you for the . . . for the breath you giveth and taketh. I . . ."

Vana left him alone. It was an intimate prayer, and although her mom had warned her not to trust the church, the thought of an all-powerful goddess sweeping in and helping them was comforting.

She turned to Isa instead. "Stay with him."

"But—"

"You're my best fighter." She was at least the most committed. "I know you can fend off more of those assholes if they dare to show their faces." Vana's stomach alerted her with another twist. She ignored it. Isa was overeager, but she also loved Jules and Vana. She wouldn't disobey.

"Aye, aye, Enforcer." She said it so formally that Vana expected a salute. Instead, she cupped Vana's face and pressed a kiss on her lips, as she had done with Jules. Vana hadn't been prepared for it. The softness of her lips felt pleasant, but her scent nauseated Vana. She hadn't kissed a woman yet, and this wasn't how she had wanted it to go. Isa was a fan. It was a fan gesture. It meant nothing, except for the wrongness it left her with.

"Ey, limp sack, I got your back." Isa sat down next to Greg and held the glowing stiletto close to his knee.

"Check on his wound, will you? Just, if you, just put some pressure on it."

"Got it, my Enforcer."

Vana stared at them, uncertain of her decision. A loud clunk interrupted her worries. Had more guards noticed them? She whirled around and pulled her seax, but no one charged her.

"Window's open," Kent called. He had cut through the bars. Vana took a deep breath to calm herself.

"Great, let me go first," she said. If someone awaited them inside, they'd have to face her before harming any more of her comrades.

They hoisted her up, and she slid through the window. Without Isa's stiletto, nothing alleviated the darkness. A jolt shot through her when her boots hit the stone floor.

"Careful, the window is high."

No one attacked her. She relaxed her tense shoulders, stepped away from the window, and blinked into the darkness. One by one, her comrades followed her into the room.

"Armory?" Maureen whispered after stepping around a shelf of shields.

Vana nodded. "Yeah, don't touch the rifles. I don't trust them."

"There're rifles?" Maureen asked. Her human eyes must have seen even less than Vana's. She definitely had to lead them.

"Stay close behind me." Vana reached out and felt her way through the room until she located the wall on the opposite side of the window. Her fingers wandered over the smooth texture in search of the door. She found a sconce with a snuffed-out candle instead. She was about to keep searching when she noticed a strange bump on the candle. It felt like a cog, so she spun it. A green flame ignited from the candle and lit up the armory. Vana and her comrades startled and stared at the light until Kent chuckled.

"Convenient."

Vana held her finger close to the flame and felt no heat. Another noble magic trick. This was the same rotten magic the captain had used to murder Jules. She placed it back into the sconce.

"Enforcer?" Maureen asked.

"Come on, let's go." Vana opened the door the candle had illuminated and stepped into the dark hallway. She heard muttering behind her and tried to ignore it. Disagreements happened even between comrades. A common goal united them. That was what mattered. The hallway led past several rooms to a double archway with a heavy wooden door. Its metal gate was loosely latched, and the sign of Exitalis was engraved into the metal. Vana saw every detail on it. Why did she see so much?

She turned around to green light. Kent had followed her with the magical candle.

"What the fuck?"

Kent shrugged. "I think that's the main barrack ahead. Let's go get the fuckers, right, comrade?"

Vana bit her lip. Comrades, they were all comrades. She didn't make the rules. If she insisted on it, she was no better than Agathe or Alexandra. Still, she couldn't shake the frustration.

"Keep it covered, all right? We don't wanna wake them." Vana opened the door carefully. An unpleasant creak accompanied the motion, and she tensed up. She poked her head through the crack to see if anyone had heard them. The same green candles shone a sparse light through the sleeping hall. Six wooden bunks lined the sides. Sleeping guards occupied most of them, but Vana counted four empty ones. That meant eight throats were waiting to be slit.

One guard stood at another barred window, peering outside. "I swear I heard shots," she muttered to herself. Her attire and sleepy voice suggested she'd just woken up. She had her back turned to them.

Vana pulled her head back. "All right, there's one guard at a window. We gotta take her out first, but silently, understood?" Her comrades nodded. "We can't risk everyone waking up. Jasper, Colby, Dustin, you three go left. Make no sound, circle the hall, and sneak up on her from behind. Kent, Maureen, you two stay with me. When the guard turns around, we'll surprise her from the other side. Quick and quiet, that's the goal here, all right?" Her comrades' faces looked pale in the dim light. She noticed Colby chewing on his cheek. "Quick and quiet, just like Kent in bed, according to his gal pal." She winked at Kent. He scoffed, but her comment lightened the overall mood.

"Wonderful, now get out of here." She nudged Jasper, and he slipped into the hall. Colby and Dustin followed. Vana waited five seconds, then stretched her neck out again. Jasper had almost caught up with the guard, but the door creaked and she turned toward Vana. Their eyes met, and the guard reached for the whistle around her neck.

Vana rushed through the door toward her. Jasper was quicker. He swung his blackwood mace at her head, throwing her against the wall. Jasper hadn't hit with the strength combat required and looked uncertain about the action. The guard slumped against the wall but reached for her whistle again. Several of the sleeping guards stirred.

Vana grabbed the guard's head before she could alarm the hall and pulled her into an awkward headlock. The blood from the guard's forehead made Vana's palm slippery, and her stomach turned. The guard slapped wildly as Vana choked her tighter. It had always sounded so easy in her dad's stories. She pressed against the guard's forehead and tried to twist. *Think of Jules. Think of Jules.*

"Finish her," Kent hissed behind Vana.

The woman yanked her head away, and Vana lost grip for a neck snap. The guard almost slipped through the head-lock, but she choked her tighter, shifted her weight, and pulled her seax. The weapon was sharp, the blade perfectly crafted. It would do the work for her. It would. No strength or commitment required.

She slammed the seax against the guard's side. Nothing happened. *Shit, wrong side.* She turned the seax in her hand and went for a cut. It was like slicing cheese, except for the fabric and tense muscles underneath, for the flesh and guts that spilled out of her, for the gasps, for the tiniest of frowns over her scared brown eyes. It wasn't like slicing cheese at all.

The woman quivered in her arms. *Stop.* Vana felt tears shoot into her eyes This was about stopping pain for the community, for her people. If causing more pain stopped it, it was worth it, right?

Her comrades spread out to the sleeping guards, weapons ready. The woman's big brown eyes pleaded with Vana as she bled in her arms. Vana wasn't sure if she pleaded for life or death. Either way, it was a plead for mercy, the notion she needed to abandon if she wanted justice for Jules.

"I'm sorry," Vana mumbled, raising the seax to her throat. Her dad had told her that a properly sliced throat was a neat death. She brought the clean blade to the woman's neck. *Clean?* The seax looked untouched. Vana pressed it against the skin until the first drops of blood formed. The blade absorbed them and became heavy. Vana tried to slice into the skin, but the blade guided her hand downward. It pushed toward the guard's stomach with such pressure that Vana couldn't resist. Before she knew what was happening, the blade stabbed into the mess of blood, flesh, and intestines over and over, soaking up the entrails. The guard shook in her arm until the seax had finished. Vana's enemy turned into a lifeless puppet. She let go and watched her drop to the ground. She looked from the mangled body to her seax. It was clean, untouched, and ready for the next kill.

In an instant, the magical candles around the hall flashed, and a voice resounded, accompanied by earsplitting chimes: "Intruder in the manor! Attack on the duchess! Intruder in the manor! Attack on the duchess!"

The alarm woke the four remaining guards. They jumped out of bed, ready to fight. Vana stood there as the room drowned in green light and violence, and watched her comrades meet the enemies she had riled them up against. The Kilburn weapons were thirsty for bloodshed, but the guards knew how to disarm their opponents. Disarming—that would have been a good lesson to teach them first. Surviving would have been another. Dustin fell first, quicker and cleaner than any of their kills had been. She had to join them. The Enforcer had to die with them.

She took a step toward them and felt a gristly squish beneath her boot. She looked down at the puddle. Organ. It was an organ. The room spun.

"Re-re . . ." She swallowed, trying to find her voice. "Retreat. Everyone retreat." She didn't move.

A guard stabbed Jasper between the ribs. Kent and Colby fought their way back to the door. Maureen had lost her weapon, but she picked up Jasper's blackwood mace and cracked it across a guard's face. The man who had killed Dustin charged at Vana. The seax lifted itself, but she didn't move. The man readied Dustin's cutlass sword, and Vana winced, ready for the slash.

He stopped and blinked at her. "You're . . . you're a *child*."

The moment of confusion cost him his life. Maureen brought the mace down on him once, twice. He joined the bloodied mess on the ground.

Maureen hooked her arm around Vana's and dragged

her out the door. They made it through the hallway back to the armory.

"Come on, jump." Maureen crouched and offered Vana her cupped hands as foot leverage.

"The others—"

"They'll catch up."

Vana stepped onto her hands. "But you—"

"Get Isa to lift you on the other side. You can pull me up then."

"O-okay." Vana stretched toward the window and slipped through it. Her landing lacked the grace from earlier. The impact jolted through her strained shoulder. She cringed, then bit her lip and cursed herself. Dustin was bleeding out from the heart, and she was whining over shoulder pain.

She got back to her feet and glanced into the dark. Why was it so dark? Isa's glowing stiletto was missing.

"Isa?" Vana squinted at the ground where Greg had been. "Isa?" Without her, Vana couldn't pull Maureen out of the armory.

A grumble came from the ground. Greg.

"Greg, are you okay? Where's Isa? We need her."

"Did we win?" His voice was faint.

"I . . . yes, yes we did." Guilt shot through her. "Where's Isa?"

The guards must have caught up with Maureen by now. Any moment they'd alert more.

"Manor," Greg whispered.

"What?"

"She's at the manor. Looking . . . for . . . captain . . ."

No, no, no. Isa would have listened. She would have listened. She wouldn't have run off.

"Vana? Pull me up!" Maureen called from the other side. The guards had gotten to her.

"Greg!" Vana shook him. "Greg, get up. We need to get them out of there."

He groaned. Vana slipped her arms under his body and

tried to lift him. "Come on, Greg. I'll give you a lift, and you pull Maureen through the window."

"Vana!" Maureen screamed. "Vana, I can't—Vana!"

Tears shot into Vana's eyes. *This can't be happening.* She couldn't let her comrades down. Why was her stupid body not human? Her elvish blood increased her agility, but weakened her muscles. She tensed up and lifted as much as she could, but Greg remained on the ground. Her shoulder burned like limbo.

Maureen screamed. Vana let go of Greg and jumped, hoping to reach the window. She could pull herself up if she caught the ledge. She jumped higher. Just a little higher. Just a little higher.

She heard a slice, followed by a gargle. Maureen screamed no longer.

"Enforcer!" Cackling laughter followed the call. It reached Vana's ears, but she was too numb to process it. "My Enforcer!"

Vana turned to face the redhead with the mad grin. *Isa.* She waited for anger to set in, but it didn't. She wondered if her seax had carved her out as well. It would explain the hollowness.

"I didn't find the captain, but I got the duchess." Isa handed her a dripping round—

"Oh, fuck no!" Vana recoiled from the duchess's severed head.

Isa shrugged. "Suit yourself, my Enforcer." She lifted the head up in the air.

"What? No, wait—"

Isa tossed the duchess's head through the armory window. Shouts resounded from inside.

"Get them!" a guard yelled. They'd be here soon.

Isa laughed. "That was fun. Shall we head out?"

"I-into the forest. We need to seek cover in the forest," Vana managed to say.

Isa took her hand. "Let's go."

"No, wait." Vana pulled her back. "Greg. Help me lift him. Get the rope around his waist so we can get him over the fence."

Isa stared at her for a second. There was an unspoken challenge in her eyes. It disappeared as soon as it had arrived. She brushed her hand over Vana's cheek.

"Whatever my Enforcer wants," she said before lifting Greg's legs. Vana wrapped her arms under his shoulders and summoned her last bit of strength. They got over the fence without worsening Greg's injuries too much. When they reached the forest, a single thought pierced through Vana's numbness. *Is this what I stand for?*

CHAPTER 15

ROBERT

July 979 - Virisunder Military's Eastern Front, Silberfluss Territory

Robert stuffed his mouth with bread to stop himself from arguing. He chewed through Lieutenant Marmont's complaints, decidedly not swallowing the man's bullshit.

"I'll give it three months and we've lost this land again. The only thing the war has given us for sure is long-term employment."

A few soldiers chuckled. Robert finished the bread too quickly. "Not for you if you keep talking about the queen like that."

Marmont set his stein on the table. "Excuse me, rookie?"

Robert scoffed. "Don't know who you're callin' rookie, but I've been fighting for the crown the whole war. If you don't know what you're doing here or standing for, why don't you join the Council? You'll get the same motus without the need for morals."

Two soldiers laughed, one sucked in air. "Careful, Lieutenant. Oakley's servin' you."

Marmont raised an eyebrow. "So you're telling me you still know what we're fighting for?"

Robert thought about it for a moment. The expected response was for glory, fame, or a place in history, but he settled on a simpler goal, one that reflected Ally. "Progress. Sure, the war's a bit stagnant, but only 'cause we're fighting stagnation. Council's giving us all these new gadgets, but we as people haven't changed much since Princess Theodosia's advances. It's not just Virisunder either. All the nations are wallowing in the familiar, becoming complacent. Gets boring, doesn't it?"

The military had provided Robert with enough motus to send back home and nurture his reading thirst. It wasn't just *Defiance of a Rose* anymore. He'd read translated romance and adventure works from Fi'teri, Silberfluss, and Vach da tìm. It had taught him what people craved. "Bored people ain't happy. So that's what we're fighting for—change."

"And what kind of change would that be?" Marmont asked.

Robert shrugged. "We know when we get there."

He had everyone's attention now. Robert became aware of their eyes on him. He wasn't much of a speaker, but it had to be said. He tapped his fingers on the table, unsure how to proceed from here.

Marmont remained silent for a few seconds and took a deep gulp from his stein. He licked his lips. "Yeah, well . . . I don't need to be lectured by a governess."

Robert slammed his hand on the table. "What did you—"

Liam, the guard who covered Robert's breaks, stumbled into the tent. "Oakley, we have an issue with the queen."

Marmont smirked. "Go on, governess. Little one's calling."

Robert stood up, fuming, and left his half-finished dinner behind. He steadied himself with deep breaths. Ally didn't need to know or feel this bullshit. She had enough to deal with.

He followed Liam through the busy camp. Virisunder's eastern troops had crossed into Silberfluss territory after Robert had taken out the enemy's border lieutenant with a well-aimed shot. A success, but they had recently lost land on the western border, so the soldiers hadn't celebrated as much as Robert had hoped. A year ago he had sympathized with their frustration, but his new position had given him insight on Ally's sleepless night, the strategy discussions, and the planned attacks on an invisible enemy. Despite what official documents stated, this was a war on the Council. The Heideggers knew it as well as Ally did. They didn't say so, of course. The other nations had accepted their "neutral" guidance, and Harald Heidegger wanted it to stay that way.

Robert didn't know much about King Josef or his marriage, but it must've been heartbreaking to wage war against one's partner. The bread sat heavy in Robert's stomach. *Marriage, partner, husband . . .*

Whenever these thoughts crossed his mind, he felt the strong urge to do some target training. Shoot something. Clear his mind. He was her guard, a great honor that shouldn't have been met with anything but honorable intentions. Longing to watch her coral lips curl at the height of rapture was not one of those intentions.

"She's having one of her . . . *things*," Liam said as they got closer. "I think she injured herself and——"

"You *think*?" Robert pushed past him into the tent. By the time he remembered to knock, he was already inside her living space. Daze struck him, as it did every time he looked at her anew. It was easy to think of her as the queen when he guarded her tent or defended her reputation on his lunch breaks. It was easy to think of her as Ally, tensing up and melting under his body, whenever his thoughts drifted while standing watch. But when he faced her directly, a harder-to-grasp image robbed the reality of all others: the image of a white beacon of light transforming into the beast that had saved his life. He saw the claws that had broken out of the enigma and had slashed their enemy without mercy. He saw the hardness of her eyes, gray like steel, creating shadows in the light. He had been the only witness of her otherworldly glory. Monstrous, yet beautiful beyond words. It didn't matter how small the world tried to make her. She possessed more strength than any person could contain.

He hadn't found an explanation that satisfied him, and part of him hoped he never would. He had considered demonic magic and pacts with foul creatures, but whatever force she bore couldn't be foul. He thought of King Josef and the alleged miracles he'd performed at the Council's Institute for Assula Magic, but such power couldn't be given. It radiated from within her. In his wildest fantasies, he thought of her as a goddess descending to the mortal world to save them. It couldn't be, of course, but he loved the sound of that story.

"Out!" Her scream pulled him back into the moment. He found her tent in disarray, papers tossed all across the room and blankets covering the floor. Ally was in similar disarray—her hair was tousled, her eyes bloodshot, and a stretch of burnt red skin marked her forearm.

"Why didn't you call me earlier?" Robert snapped at Liam. "Out, now!"

Liam rushed off and left Robert with no idea what to do next. The other guards had warned him that this might happen. Even Dillon had mentioned the delusions that took hold of their beloved queen. But Robert had never taken it seriously. He had seen how powerful she was and had assumed any weakness must've been part of the slander.

"Get out!" Ally screeched. Tears glistened on her cheeks. Her face had turned red and puffy. It looked almost as raw as the burnt skin on her arm. He wanted to pull her into his arms, make it better.

"Ally, just—" A book slammed against his chest. He caught it and backed off.

Ally's eyes twitched. "Leave. I'm begging you."

His mouth went dry. He saw the fight in her eyes. They called her the Mad Queen, but this wasn't madness. This was an attack, another invisible enemy trying to tear her down.

"Shut up. I know. I know the parasite is getting us," she whispered to herself.

He examined the book. *Composition of Native Tazadahar Magic.* "Haven't gotten to this one yet. Is it good?"

She paused and blinked at him.

"I mean, the battle scene in *Administration of Native Tazadahar Magic* was pretty epic, but I couldn't quite get into the love interest, you know what I mean?" Talking out of his ass wasn't the wisest strategy, but she hadn't hired him for his wisdom. He gave her a crooked smile. "Then again, *Tribulations of Native Tazadahar Magic* really kept me up all night. I mean, that scene when the peasant sneaked to the window? By Caedem, what a moment."

"It's a textbook on the physics of magic," she said quietly. Her voice had lost its strain.

"I get what you're saying, but can you imagine if the tailor took over the stables in *Composition*? That would be a twist, heh?"

A tiny smile crept over her lips.

"In *Composition*, do they make us wait until the end for all the steamy stuff again? Not that I don't care about the rest of the story, but I mean . . . come on. That's why you're readin' it, right?" He opened it and leafed through the parchment. It was filled with numbers and symbols that meant nothing to him. "Oh, no, they don't hold back in this one. Oh my, I see why you don't wanna be interrupted. This is very sexy."

"The formulas?"

He fanned himself. "Don't say it out loud like that. It's getting hot in here."

She giggled and ran her fingers through her matted mess of hair. Her eyes wandered over the chaos. "I'm sorry . . ."

Robert closed the book and put it on the overflowing makeshift desk. He approached slowly. "Don't be. It looked rough."

Ally nodded without looking at him. "Yeah . . ."

"Can I suggest something?"

"It's not sex, is it?"

Heat shot into Robert's cheeks. "N-no, of course not. That's not why I'm here."

She frowned. "Why are you here?" Her tone turned as icy as the river that had brought them together. Why was he here? He had fought as a sniper, like his mother had wanted him to. He had paid tribute to her and the destructive purpose laid out for him. It was time to choose his own purpose, and the chance to protect instead of destroy, to nurture life instead of taking it away, was exhilarating. But there was more to it. More than he was willing to admit.

"I have an idea," he said, hoping to distract her from the mistrust the question fostered. "Sit down, please."

"Are you telling me what to do, Oakley?" The corner of her mouth twitched upward. The invisible enemy hadn't given up yet, but she was winning. There was his Ally. *Don't think like that.* She wasn't *his* Ally. He had comforted her. Once. That was all.

"Yes, Verdain. Now sit down."

She chuckled and sat on the ground next to her cot. Robert picked up the largest blanket and shook it out.

"Do you trust me?" he asked.

"I'm not sure what I can trust."

Part of him wanted to storm out of the tent and shout at Lieutenant Marmont, the doubtful soldiers, the Council dirt, anyone and anything that had warped her ability to trust. But then again, part of him was stupid. "Are you up for an experiment?"

She cocked her head but didn't confirm.

"You say the word and I'll stop, all right?"

"What word?"

He shifted the blanket in his hand until he had a good grip on the corners. "I don't know, what do you—"

"Gravitons?"

"Is that a word?"

She chuckled again and nodded.

"Is that a yes?"

"Yes."

He tossed the blanket into the air, sat down next to her, and allowed it to fall over their heads. It drowned out the light and noise from the camp. He had no idea how she'd react to the capsule it created. Perhaps she'd transform into the beast and punish him for such confinement, but he had a feeling she wouldn't.

"Sometimes, after all the fightin', when stuff got a little much for me," he whispered, "I'd find a place where there was just me, nothing else. Kinda like being underwater, heh?"

She didn't react.

"I can leave if you want . . . or you could tell me what a gravitos is."

Her fingers moved over to his hand. "*Gravitons*. They're particles exchanged during attraction of mass."

"Romantic," he said, barely understanding what she was talking about.

"It is."

Ask her what happened in the meadow. That wasn't why he was here. He was here to take care of her, protect her, nothing else.

"Can I ask where the injury on your arm is from?"

She sighed. "I tried to dissect an assula lamp. I wanted to break it open; it resisted."

He wrapped his pinky around her probing fingers. "Not sure if you're supposed to do that to forged assulas."

"I can't get my hands on a raw one. Josef's controlling most assula smiths. I contacted one in Tribu La'am, but she hasn't responded."

He lifted one corner of the blanket, letting in enough

light to see her face. The distortions had disappeared, leaving an air of calm determination behind. Entire worlds existed in her eyes, as if she created and rebuilt them with each blink. He wanted to cup her delicate round face and bring it close to his own for a chance to see what she saw, to understand reality the way she did.

He dropped the blanket and pulled them back into the comforting darkness. "That sucks."

"That sucks?"

"Yeah, it sucks that they're stifling your brilliant mind."

She slipped her hand fully into his. "This is nice."

His mouth became dry. *Don't think about it. Don't think about it.* He expected pictures from the meadow to creep into his mind, but the snow empress from *Defiance of a Rose* showed up instead. Ally looked exactly like he had pictured the empress to look. At the end of book five, true love's kiss had set her free. Maybe he should—

"The blanket, I mean. It's a nice idea."

"Right, yes, thank you. It's my kind of physics invention."

She snickered. "I'm pretty sure blankets existed already."

"Well, shit."

She laid her head on his shoulder. "Robert?"

His heart beat faster. They would talk about the meadow. They would finally talk about the meadow. *Don't think about it.* She was a Verdain. There was nothing she could want from him but reliable protection and perhaps, if he was lucky, the occasional amusement.

"I need to tell you something," she said.

"Yes, snow empress?"

"What?"

Idiot. He was struggling to find an appropriate response when the chain of bells outside Ally's tent rang.

"Oakley? The queen has a visitor."

Thank Caedem. Someone had saved him from the embarrassment.

"One moment," he called to the messenger outside, then turned back to Ally. "Ready to emerge?"

She squeezed his hand. "Yes."

He tossed the blanket off, and the brightness of the room disoriented him. It was a harsh reminder of reality. He was Robert Oakley, the commoner lucky enough to guard the queen. It would've been preposterous to want anything more. He stretched his hand out to Ally and lifted her back to her feet.

"Your, ehm, your hair . . ." He raised his finger to brush through the mess before thinking better of it. "I'm gonna . . . I'm gonna check who that is."

He slipped out of the tent before he could make a bigger fool of himself. A beautiful Tribu La'am woman with a whimsical shock of short black curls and bows, wearing a night blue dress, awaited him.

"Hello, ma'am. How can I help you?"

She looked him up and down. "If it isn't my fine friend Robert. I'd say color me surprised, but I'm afraid I'm out of that shade."

"Ehm . . . pardon me, but who are you?"

She did a curtsy, followed by an exaggerated bow. "Regina the Grand. Our lovely queen has summoned me."

He tried to remember if a Regina was on the list of approved visitors. She gave him a wide smile and waved her hands. "Shoo, shoo, announce me. She'll be happy, I promise."

He stepped back inside. "Do you know a Regina the Grand?"

Ally's face brightened like it had in the meadow after their first kiss. She brushed past him and pulled the woman into the tent.

"How did you get here so quickly?" She was too short to reach the woman's neck and tossed her arms around her waist instead. The embrace felt so intimate that Robert wondered if he should step out, but an unwelcome jealousy stopped him.

This was ridiculous. Ally was in no way betrothed to him, and the woman was likely a former lady-in-waiting.

"Magic." The woman snapped her fingers and transformed into a familiar man: *Bored Reginald*. "I missed you, sugar." He stroked her cheek. "It's been a year, hasn't it? I'm glad you let me see you again."

"You know why I didn't . . ."

Bored Reginald had been the rainbow giant all those years ago during Robert's recruitment. The giant and the snow empress had held hands back then. Ally and Reginald's embrace felt intimate because it was. The realization sank heavily into Robert's stomach. She had told him in the meadow that he was foolish, but he hadn't realized how foolish.

"Maybe I should leave you two alone," he mumbled, pulling the tent flap aside.

"Not so fast." Reginald flicked the flap closed and pulled him back into the tent. "You're part of this, friend-anion."

They let go of each other, but the embrace didn't leave Robert. He positioned himself next to the entrance, like the guard he'd been hired to be.

"Have you told him yet?" Reginald asked.

Robert avoided Ally's eyes but felt her gaze on him. "I was about to . . . I . . ." She walked over to the cot and slumped down on it. Robert shot her a look. A quick one. Just one glance. The strain on her face had returned. He didn't take his eyes off her.

"Reginald, maybe you should go," he said. As much respect as he had for the masterful storyteller, Robert wouldn't allow him to aggravate Ally again.

Reginald chuckled. "Whoa, simmer down, my man. I appreciate your concern, but you're talking out of your ass right now." He sat down on the cot next to her and put his arm over her shoulders. Ally didn't protest, so neither did Robert. It was her decision, no matter what gnawed at him.

"This isn't as much of a mess as you think, sugar."

"I can't believe I scolded Subira over this," Ally said.

It sounded like a private matter, but Robert tried to decipher it anyway. He knew she had scolded Subira van Auersperg for her lack of engagement in the war, and rightly so. Was this what had triggered her breakdown? He glanced around the tent for a letter from van Auersperg, anything accusatory that could have set her off.

"Life can be strange sometimes," Reginald said. "But don't fret, I've drafted piles and piles of plans, each one more illustrious, outrageous, and entertaining than the next." Ally smiled. He continued. "Some are simpler, of course. Plan one: I turn all four of us into chipmunks, and we immigrate to Tribu La'am. Do they have chipmunks there? No, they do not. We'll be a sensation."

Robert stifled a laugh before he understood the subtext. "What four are you talking—"

"Plan two: there're only three of us. I'll get rid of it. Easy, pain free. That's your call, sugar. We can act as if it never happened."

"Wait . . ." The puzzle was taking shape in Robert's head.

"I choose plan three," Ally said.

Reginald smirked. "Plan three, inspired by your dear grandmama: we'll fake the Ceremony."

Queen Theodosia had created Elfentum's Ceremony after marrying her wife, General Makeda. The complicated conception ritual allowed royalty and upper nobility to conceive an heir without revealing the father's identity. Queen Theodosia had conceived Ally's father that way, and other couples had adopted the Ceremony since.

"Why would she—" Robert started.

Reginald held up his finger. "We're getting to you in just one second, eager beaver."

"I don't want to endanger any of you. If Josef finds out . . ."

"He won't know, sugar. He'll think it's from the Ceremony."

It's from the Ceremony. Robert's eyes widened when he

realized what "it" was. The queen was pregnant with another Verdain. But King Josef hadn't visited, had he? He could have shown up at camp when Dillon had still been alive, a secret reunion of the royal couple. Then again, ever since Robert had been promoted to her direct unit, he'd kept a close eye on Ally. For professional reasons. He'd never seen Josef or any men other than soldiers around her tent. Which left them with . . .

"Who's the father?"

"Didn't you describe him as clever in your letter?" Reginald asked Ally.

"He is, but I'm sure it's a bit of a surprise."

"If that's the case . . ." Reginald reached into his suit pocket—which grew larger the farther he stretched—pulled out a fist of glitter, and tossed it at Robert. "Congratulations, my man! You are, in fact, the best shot."

"Reggie!"

The glitter on Robert's face wasn't the strangest part of the situation he'd found himself in. No soul from Coalchest had ever even met a Verdain, and here he was seducing one, bedding one, leaving behind an undeniable mark. His eyes met Ally's, and he saw *her*—not the queen he protected, the fantastical goddess who had saved him, or the woman in the meadow who had led him to euphoria. Those were ideas, stories from the books he'd read. He saw her true self, and all complications disappeared. "I'll be here, whatever you choose."

"Thank you." She looked at him like she had when she'd touched his chest in the meadow. He forgot about Reginald and itched to pick her up from the cot, to hold her close so that his arms could carry her into a safer place like the blanket had.

Reginald cleared his throat. "All right then . . . I can get the court in favor of a Ceremony. Protecting the Verdain line, neutrality from the Heideggers, all that good talk."

"I'll still need Josef's approval."

"Yeah . . ."

"I have to visit him at the Institute." Terror flickered over her eyes. What could a woman who contained a beast be this scared of?

CHAPTER 16

RICHARD

July 979 - Kilburn Smithy, Waldfeld, Silberfluss

Richard pressed down on the elastic doum palm and bent it into shape. The palm had arrived from Fi'Teri yesterday, and its fibers had proven to be both flexible and resilient. It could withstand great stress—perfect for Pier. The more kinship a person felt with their weapon, the more likely it was to defend them. Pier crossed the town limits of Waldfeld every few days for obscure business purposes. It was about time something looked after him.

He formed the palm into a long-range bow so that Pier could keep his distance from any danger. He had already paid generous motus to Dotty's husband, Fergus Ackerman, to give Pier lessons. Fergus had trained that delightfully wild daughter of theirs, and Richard wouldn't want to mess with her. He smiled to himself. Despite the madness of the world, their children and Pier were growing up healthy and well, as if nothing had ever happened between the Ackermans and the Kilburns.

Would you like us to visit the memories, dear Richard? It has been a while . . .

"No, stay out of them." He had gotten into the habit of talking out loud to the Fae cluster, Choravdat, during the years of Pier's study. It was a small comfort that had turned into an inconvenience.

"Stay out of what?" Pier asked.

"I . . . we've got church later. Don't skip it again."

Pier frowned. "Can we not distract from this again, please? All I was saying is that our supply isn't meeting the demand anymore. You're denying the natural growth of the business."

Richard focused on the palm fiber. Pier had been lecturing him for half an hour now, a nuisance that had become part of their daily routine.

"I respect the exclusivity of Kilburn craft as much as you do, but we have the capital to purchase smaller smithies in different towns. So why not do it? Let's expand geographically and monopolize our market."

Richard studied his son during the lecture and felt heavier with every detail he took in. Pier had trimmed the sides of his hair and combed the curly ginger top over. Instead of a decent belt, he tightened his pants with straps over his shoulders and tied them up in ribbons. He looked like a courtier, or worse. Tribu La'am had unplanted him.

"Dad, are you even listening?"

"Hmm?"

Pier sighed. "Fine then. I'll get us offers from Freilist nobility for larger production, and you won't be able to refuse."

A rush of energy shook him. Splinters of Choravdat clattered within the walls of his body.

He'll give us up, give away the secrets.

But the opening, we haven't seen her again.

She's out there, the opening.

Don't tell them about us, Richard.

He placed his hand on his stomach and rubbed it in a circle, like his grandma used to do for him during thunderstorms. He wasn't sure if the calm carried through to his Fae friend, but they quieted down.

"You can't do that, Pier." The calm percolated through his voice. "My craft is personal." No one could know that a soul-cluster assisted in his inventions.

Pier gave him a genteel smile. "*This isn't a matter of discussion. It's a matter of asking for the impossible.* Weren't those your words?"

This wasn't about the shop. This was about the orc who had tainted his son.

He's hurting, my friend. Richard scoffed. Hurt was part of the sacrifice Exitalis demanded. Richard had lessened the pain his son had to endure wherever he could. He had established a place for him in Waldfeld's community. He had bought him books, fine clothes, and decent meals. He had even let him go.

"I have an appointment with the Belladonnas later today," Pier continued. "Don't worry, it's not about weaponry, although the duke has expressed interest in arming his guards with—"

"I need you to man the shop." Richard's knuckles whitened around the half-finished bow. "You're manning the shop, and then you're coming to the sermon with me."

Pier laughed and shook his head. "I don't think I'm gonna do that."

Richard gripped the bow tighter. The palm fiber complained as it overstretched. "Why not?"

The smile disappeared from his son's face. A coldness crept into his eyes that could have made limbo's Ouisà Kacocs shiver. "Because it doesn't matter."

He's hurting, my friend . . . I know he is.

"This is about the orc." Richard released the bow. It sprung back into its original shape.

"His name is *Martín*." Pier raised his voice. He looked as agitated as he had in that Mink'Ayllu hotel room. The expression was foreign on his son's face. It didn't belong there. "And no, this has nothing to do with him. This is about *you* standing in *our* way. Yours and mine."

Nausea rose in Richard's stomach. "I know how painful it is to lose him."

"Don't you dare bring Mom into this."

"I wasn't."

Pier opened his mouth to snap back but closed it without making a sound. Richard ran his fingers over the bow. It would've been much easier to let Choravdat take over. Their whispers resounded within him, eager to wrap their consciousness around every part of Richard, but there were parts that belonged only to him, memories that neither he nor his friend were allowed to touch. Vines itched within his fingers, longing to live his life for him. They couldn't. His friend was an observer, not a participant.

"What do you know then?" Pier asked after the silence became suffocating.

His son needed him to stay calm, to function. He couldn't lose the life he had built for him, yet Richard's thoughts wandered to the forbidden case upstairs. He had stored his addiction away better than Edeliènne ever had.

"Let me show you something," Richard said softly. Perhaps it would cleanse the big-city ideas that poisoned Pier's mind and would stop him from getting sicker.

He left the shop area in the front of the house and walked upstairs. The sound of Pier's steps slowed him down. Did he really want to do this? *Trust it, my friend. Freedom. We all want freedom. By whatever means. And we will get that freedom. No, don't tell him that. But we will, we will, we will.* Richard shook his head as if to shake out the voices. He could barely hear his own thoughts over his friend's discussion. Perhaps it was for the best.

He reached his room and sat down on the narrow bed.

He had crafted a small drawer inside the bed frame. Its knob now pressed against his thigh.

"Sit down."

Pier took a seat next to him, his eyes observant. Richard shouldn't have brought him up here. His hands sweat whenever Pier studied him. "I know you're upset at me."

"I'm not upset at you, Dad. I'm upset at the stories you bought into. I'm upset that you can't see the same future I see. I'm upset that you turn trees into swords but refuse to question anything else and—"

"Pier." He raised his hand and considered patting him on the back, squeezing his shoulder, any kind of touch that could bridge the space between them. He let his arm sink. "I want to show you why—"

The shop's bells chimed.

"Stay here, I'll be—" Richard started, but a loud voice from downstairs interrupted him.

"Pier? Piersy? Ooh, those look fancy."

Pier's eyes grew wide, and he jumped off the bed. "I got it, Dad."

His son dashed out of the room before Richard could respond. He followed him back to the shop and found an attractive man with dirty-blond hair and warm light brown eyes.

"There ya are, Piersy!" He noticed Richard. "Oh, hello, eh, Pier's dad . . . Ricky?"

"Richard," Pier said.

"Mr. Kilburn." Richard frowned. "Who's this, Pier?"

"My client."

The man waved at Richard with a cheerful but dull expression. Pier gathered his things and spoke without looking up. "This is Edward Saul. We have an appointment with the Belladonnas tonight, so if you'll excuse me—"

Edward stuck his hand out. "Nice to meet ya, sir."

Richard shook it. "Appointment? What kind of—"

Edward's smile widened, revealing a shining set of

white teeth. "I'm a prostitute. Mostly women, but if you're interested—"

Pier pushed between them. "*Courtesan*, Edward dear. We talked about that. And no, my dad is not interested." He swung his bag over his shoulder and rubbed his hands together. "Sorry, Dad, we gotta go, but we'll talk later, all right?" They headed toward the door before Richard's brain could catch up.

"I . . . wait . . . what? H-how do you know my son?"

"Met him at The Stag's Tail. My first time there. Not like Pier, who's—"

"Let's go, Edward." Pier cut him off sharply.

Richard rushed around them and blocked the doorway. "I don't want you spending time in that unholy place."

Pier sighed. "I just go there to find clients."

"What clients?"

"I manage clients with extraordinary skills and connect them with the right people."

"My skills are extraordinarily large." Edward chuckled.

"Large potential, yes. Dad, may we?"

He blinked at Pier, desperate to recognize his son in the young man who stood before him. "I . . . why?"

Pier softened. "It's a great way to make connections with nobility. Don't worry. I'm staying safe." He gently pushed Richard aside. "See you later, Dad."

Pier stepped through the door. Edward gave him another wave and followed. The door slammed in Richard's face, and just like that, Pier had shut himself off. Richard leaned his forehead against it and encouraged Choravdat to take over. Shy vines sprouted out of his shoulders and ran over the wood. Richard released control of his muscles. As always, his friend was there to savor his body for him. They appreciated it more than he did—more than he could. He closed his eyes and allowed himself to melt against the wooden door. *Take everything, my friend.* He waited for his mind to clear, for consciousness to drain out of him. Thoughts left him. He disappeared into free nothingness, but a memory interrupted his departure. Chora-vdat wasn't supposed to touch that part of him.

Come on, Dick, we've only got an hour. Dotty can't cover me for long.

One second. He had searched the forest grounds for whittling wood while his love had waited for him. Why had he done that? They'd had so little time.

Richard forced his mind back to the forefront. *I told you not to touch those memories.* A gushing sound washed over his ears, a sign that his soul-cluster friend was getting too excited or torn to speak in his tongue. Richard focused on retracting the vines and pushed himself off the door. He needed to change for the sermon, to put on decent clothes and decent thoughts.

He made his way back to the bedroom and laid his church clothes out on the bed. The pant leg covered most of the drawer. He tugged at it until the pants hid the whole drawer. His hand wandered to the knob. Vines sprouted from his fingertips, slipped under the pants, and pulled the drawer open. The case stared at him. He stared back. One second. Two seconds.

"Exitalis, forgive me," he mumbled, then took the case out of the drawer. Father Godfried would be disappointed when Richard confessed that he had indulged in memories. Choravdat shouldn't have touched them. Richard wasn't allowed to think of those memories.

He sat down on the bed and opened the case. Inside was the grievance stone. Its blue paint had chipped off, but the engraved name looked as it had twenty-seven years ago. Richard ran his thumb over the letters and numbers. *Brice Ackerman, 936-952.* The grievance stone was the only thing Richard had ever stolen. They hadn't allowed him to attend the funeral where they'd been handed out. Father Godfried had thought it would aggravate his condition, lead him to the same fate Brice had suffered. His father had already paid the motus for Richard's cure.

What if they find us? He still remembered the cadence of Brice's voice.

Exitalis protects us. He had been a fool to believe his words were comfort, not heresy.

Richard's eyes burned as he dropped the stone back into its case. He should have handed it to Father Godfried decades ago, but it served as the last picture he had of Brice. He either remembered the blue stone or the blue face of the corpse dangling in the Ackerman barn. Richard chose the stone.

That was when he remembered him at all. He shouldn't have. He couldn't. It would poison Pier too. He prayed that it hadn't already.

The shop bell chimed again.

"Richard?" Father Godfried called from downstairs. Richard shoved the case back into its drawer, rubbed his eyes, and rushed to the shop.

"Father." He bowed his head when he reached the priest. Father Godfried wore the blissful smile only Exitalis could bestow upon a man. The wrinkles on his face told of the years he had served Waldfeld and Waldfeld had served him. He had looked after this town's people and their purity since the current duke had been born. He belonged to Waldfeld like the wet winters and dusty summers, certain like the starlight and exemplary of the calm every man should possess. No matter what unfortunate tasks he had to perform, the calm smile never left his face.

"My dear son, how are we today?"

"Good." Richard brushed his hands off on his pants. He could still feel the touch of the grievance stone on his palm. The touch of Brice.

"You look a little flushed."

"No, Father, I'm good." Richard squared his shoulders and assumed the calm, decent posture Father Godfried had taught him.

"Are you coming to the sermon tonight?"

"Yes, Father. Of course, Father."

"I saw Pier on my way here . . . and I can't remember if you've paid your Indulgence for the month yet." He cocked his head to the side.

Richard's body stiffened. He prayed to Exitalis that he hadn't seen Pier with the prostitute. "I . . . I have, Father. The usual amount, but if you think more motus is needed . . ."

Father Godfried laughed softly. "Oh, I don't know, my son. Is more needed? I believe you can tell me better than I can."

Richard nodded and searched his belt chain for the key that opened the shop's motus case. He hadn't been able to pay enough Indulgence to rectify his sins when he'd been a serf, but his shop allowed him to pay the motus he owed their beloved goddess and those who served her. Exitalis had cured him and had gifted him a wife and son. She deserved everything he had.

"I'm concerned about Pier," Father Godfried said as Richard opened the case. "Some people are getting the wrong impression of him. You know people get . . . angry. We don't want that."

Richard froze. Brice's dead blue lips crept back into his mind.

"Sometimes it takes several generations to get rid of the curse. The Ackermans have a similar problem with their daughter, Vana. Dotty has been reluctant to talk about it."

His mouth became dry. Vana was a good kid who rebelled against the uncaring nobility that drove Waldfeld's hardworking people to their early graves. She didn't charm nobles with prostitutes and cheerful conversations like Pier did. But there was nothing wrong with either of them.

"I think a few cure-sessions would be good for Pier. We want him to have a family soon, don't we? And we don't want people to get angry. People do such silly things when they're angry."

Use us, my friend, use us. Take him to limbo. See if his goddess saves him.

Shh. He couldn't allow heresy within his own body. Not again. Thorns pressed against the inside of his skin, keen to rip into the holy man's heart. Richard grabbed a pouch and emptied the motus case into it. "Here's the Indulgence."

Father Godfried weighed it in his hands and nodded. "It's enough for the first session."

Richard shook his head. "No session, just . . . can you please tell whoever's angry that they're wrong about Pier? He focuses on his work, that's all."

"My son, don't you want Pier to have what you have?"

Take him. Grab him. Test him.

Exitalis, forgive me.

Richard swallowed, fighting the urges Choravdat placed in him. A cheerful, high-pitched voice with a Tribu La'am accent saved him. "Good afternoonified morning, kind gentlemen!"

Father Godfried and Richard turned to the entrance, where a decently pretty human woman with brown skin and curly hair stood. *Esperanza.* She must have come after Pier. Her eyes looked hauntingly empty.

She's here. She's here.

Can she? She might. Is she here for us?

Our blood and her blood. Freedom, together freedom.

"Good day, madam." Father Godfried nodded at her. "I didn't realize you're serving the godless, my dear son."

Richard felt his head nod. His body was no longer in his control. *Careful.* He hoped his friend would hear him.

Father Godfried stepped closer. "I'd rethink your customers. We don't want those angry, misguided people thinking you're serving the Traitor."

Richard nodded again.

Father Godfried's usual smile widened. "Thank you for the Indulgence. I will keep an eye on Pier to make sure he's safe." He gave Esperanza another nod and left.

Esperanza watched him close the door, then shook her head with a giggle. "He's a poop bin, isn't he?"

Together, our savior together. We'll be free together. Richard coughed, a weak attempt to regain some control. His friend got excited sometimes, but they had never taken over without his consent.

"Oh my, did you swallow a weevil?" Esperanza placed her luggage on a shop counter and patted Richard's back.

"What can I do for—" he managed to say before his friend cut him off.

"Get us back, Faemani savior, get us back."

Esperanza ran a finger over his cheek. "I'm glad you were waiting for me, silly."

Richard shied away from her, but his friend reached out. Vines sprouted from his skin and grew thick around them. He felt himself flatten as leaves pierced through the sides of his torso.

"Faemani savior, free home. Free our home."

"Shh." Esperanza stroked the petals on Richard's cheek. "I have thought about the gladsome, cock-a-hoop offer you made at the hotel."

Richard had made no offer. There had been a strange moment when Choravdat had needed attention, but he'd thought he'd been in control the whole time. He might have zoned out for a moment or two, but not long enough for an offer. Not to his knowledge.

Richard's eyes floated out of their sockets and examined her body. He closed them, but Choravdat forced them open. "What offer?"

"Oh." Esperanza's eyes widened in shock. "Master Kilburn, you're still conscious. I didn't know."

All he could hear was the rustling of trees. He fought to feel his limbs again. *Stop it, Choravdat.* He repeated the thought in his mind, hoping the soul-cluster would listen. His arms turned green and stretched farther around Esperanza. He felt the movements, but they refused to follow the commands of his brain.

This will not hurt Pier, Richard. This won't hurt you either. This has nothing to do with you.

"Master Kilburn?"

"He's gone, my savior. Can't hear you. Can't hear you," Choravdat said through Richard's body.

But he could hear her. He watched the shop disappear behind the wall of vines and leaves. He watched Esperanza's cold face soften with uncertainty. He watched the Fae form of his body clutch her close to him, or whatever was left.

"When the child takes us to the Fae realm," Esperanza whispered, "I want to bring someone along."

"A Faemani?"

"No, he's an orc. Are you sure Master Kilburn is gone? He looks scared."

"If you set us free, you can bring whomever the Fae realm's P-Twenty-One approves. Do not worry about Richard. He won't understand." It was true. Richard didn't understand, but he felt every move.

"Okay . . . let's do it quick-a-quickidy, please." Esperanza unbuttoned her blouse, revealing her large breasts. Richard tried to speak, to protest, but his tongue weighed him down. His vision turned milky. He knew his eyes still functioned, but the images no longer reached him. Bit by bit, Choravdat drowned out what he could grasp. *No*, Richard thought. The splashing of rain echoed within him. Richard knew it was meant to calm him, but all he could think of were thunderstorms—too many thunderstorms and no hands to rub his stomach.

You have freed us from the Ouisà Kacocs, Richard. Now we will set our people free. Keep still, my friend.

CHAPTER 17

VANA

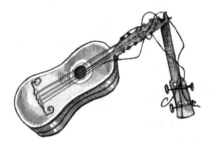

July 979 - Jackson's Bar, Waldfeld, Silberfluss

Vana peeked over the blanket edge and blinked into the setting sun. When had the day passed? The evening sky was magenta; it was as if the drops of rebel and guard blood painted it. She hadn't planned to fall asleep. She had wanted to stay awake until she found sense in it all. Sleep had found her instead.

She and Isa had dropped Greg off at the church at sunrise. It hadn't been Vana's idea, but the two had insisted, and Father Godfried had promised to send for a medic. *Greg. Medic.* It made sense enough. Vana should have gone home after that. She should have told her family about the incidents before Godfried could tell her grandparents at the evening sermon. She should have done a lot of things.

"My Enforcer, you're up." Isa sat down on the bed and

patted Vana's aching shoulder. "I was about to head out for the sermon. Wanna join me?"

Isa had changed out of the stained trousers and into an emerald linen dress that complemented her red braid. The change from severing heads to praying seemed to come naturally to her. *How?* Isa must have understood something she didn't.

Vana propped herself up on her elbows and stared at the quilt blanket as if each square hid an answer from her. Ink and blood. VA. Ink and blood. Large brown eyes gutted for ink and blood. Vana sank into thoughts, unable to react, unable to understand.

"Enforcer?"

"My name is Vana," she mumbled, avoiding Isa's eyes. Jules's beautiful voice echoed in her memory.

We will never be free if freedom's our price for living.
We will never be safe if safety is our price for giving.
No one's coming to save a soul not lost.

She squinted into the setting sun, soaking in the day's farewell.

Am I lost yet, Jules?

"Is my poor Enforcer still tired?" Isa rubbed Vana's leg. "You should come then. Father Godfried's words always invigorate me. Just like yours."

Vana looked at the hand that crept up her thigh and grew stiff. She thought of her breakup with Jules. Was she supposed to like this?

"Of course, there are other ways to invigorate me," Isa whispered, then kissed Vana's neck.

The higher you get, the deeper you fall.
So you don't look down, don't look down.
You never see us down here.

Isa's hand brushed over the crotch of the loose pants Vana had borrowed from her. The memory of Isa's sour kiss from the night before fooled her nose. The iron of her comrades' blood followed. *Maureen, Jasper, Colby . . .*

"Stop, please." She hated how small her voice sounded. Isa frowned at her. She wasn't convinced. Vana swallowed, searching for another answer that evaded her, one that might convince Isa. Her eyes fell on a painting of Balthos's sign. "What does your Father Godfried say about this?"

Isa scoffed. "You're not a woman; you're the Enforcer."

"Get off me, please."

A glimmer of madness crossed Isa's eyes, the same glimmer she'd worn when she'd stabbed the guard's eye and tossed the severed head into the armory. She hesitated, then smiled and stood up. "As you wish, my Enforcer."

She pulled a silver necklace with a pendant of Exitalis's peaceful gravestone from her jewelry box and put it around her neck. No trace of worry marked her face. Had they lived through the same night?

"You think this was a victory?" Vana asked. She knew it wasn't, but she had to hear it from her.

Isa placed a blue Alames's rose in her braid. "We didn't get the captain, but we took out many of those Nimmerwarm scum. Victory enough for now. The next foreign shits will think twice before coming to Waldfeld and messing with our people."

Vana blinked at her. This wasn't an answer. This was another nightmare. "Jules is—*was*—from Tribu La'am."

Isa picked up rouge from her desk and brushed it onto her cheekbones. She looked lovelier by the second, alluring and repulsive at the same time. It made no sense. Nothing made sense. They should've been grieving the loss of their comrades and Jules. He had died because the guards had abused their power, not because they were from Nimmerwarm. The woman Vana had slaughtered crept back into her thoughts. She hadn't been at the town square the night Jules had died. What crime had Vana killed her for? Complicity, working as a guard, or being from Nimmerwarm?

"Father Godfried said it himself," Isa replied. "The Spirit was the last good addition to Waldfeld. Everyone else is

tainting it, oppressing us, just like you told us, my Enforcer."
She said it matter-of-factly, as if reciting Vana's own words
back to her. Panic rushed through Vana. This wasn't what
she or Jules had sung about. They'd thought their message
to be clear, but Waldfeld's air must have distorted the words
that had left their lips before they'd reached their audience's
ears. When she'd spoken of revolution and community, she'd
been referring to people as poor as she was, not people of a
certain birthplace. The Kilburns weren't poor anymore. Did
she exclude them? Every time she thought of an answer, more
questions smothered her.

"We're protecting people, not the town," Vana said. It
was almost an answer, something she could hold on to. She
hoped it was the truth her comrades had died for. "And we
failed." The truth released tension in her chest, and tears
fought their way up. She swallowed them down. Not now, not
here. She needed more answers, more truths first.

Isa finished her makeup and turned back to Vana. A
crooked grin marked her lips. "My Enforcer wouldn't see it
that way."

"Yeah, well, your Enforcer died last night."

Isa's face dropped. "You don't mean that."

Vana got off the bed. Her body disappeared in the borrowed clothes like she disappeared under Isa's gaze. "No way
you misunderstood Jules and me like that. This was never
about keeping people out of Waldfeld, or Silberfluss, or wherever. This was—*is*—about justice. That's . . . that's all Jules
and I wanted. That's what I need for him."

Isa licked her lips. "*A body can't function properly with rotting
limbs.* Isn't that what you said, my Enforcer? We'll cut off the
rotten limbs of Waldfeld and serve them to Exitalis."

"That's not—"

"We'll get rid of any rotten scum that dares tell us how to
live our life. It doesn't matter if they're from Nimmerwarm,
one of Queen Lunatic's ghastly elves, or—Exitalis forbid—a
tusk."

A shudder ran down Vana's back. No matter what she did, no matter what answers she found, she'd always be the fool who'd put the knife in Isa's hand. Vana had created the Queen Alexandra Lunatic of the common folk, and she was planning her own war right here in Waldfeld.

"Now, now, no reason to look so sour, my dear." Isa leaned in to stroke her face. Vana grabbed her wrist.

Her heartbeat sped up with fear, but she refused to give into it. "Jules and I inspired people to stand up against delusional bullies—bullies like *you*."

Isa yanked her wrist free and slapped Vana across the face. It stung but gifted Vana another truth: comrades didn't harm each other.

Isa grabbed her shoulders and tossed her onto the bed. "You're clearly still tired, Vana. Rest until my Enforcer returns."

She stormed out of the room and slammed the door shut. A moment later, Vana heard the lock click. *Well, fuck.*

Vana stared at the mold spots on the ceiling. *Rotting limbs.* She was full of them. The bodies of her comrades had chosen her chest and mind as their graves, rotting there, infesting her. They turned her into the monster Isa had described, the monster that riled up innocent folk against other innocent folk.

Fuck this. Her dad would've been disappointed to watch her wallow in self-pity, and what would Jules think?

Don't like your fate, don't settle.

Don't accept your fate, meddle.

The nobles do, oh the nobles do.

Vana hummed Jules's melodies until she got off the bed. She stood tall and rotated her strained shoulder. The aching hadn't eased yet. She looked around Isa's humble room. It had little charm except for the bar sounds that drifted through the wooden floor planks. The buzz of music, laughing patrons, and clinking glasses infused the plain furniture with life. Either Jackson, the owner, didn't allow his barmaids to decorate their rooms, or Isa kept it simple to balance out the chaos within her.

Cold air drifted through the window and made Vana shudder. She didn't believe in Exitalis, but it felt like a chilling reminder that it was time to pray to the Lady of the Dead. Vana wished she could hide from it in her own bed, look at the warmth in her mother's eyes, bicker with her brothers. *Adam.* If he had joined her that night, he would have died too. She couldn't face him again. She couldn't face any of them again. Who could she face?

She took a deep breath and went over the questions again. *Why did Jules die? What did my comrades die for? Why am I still alive? What is wrong with me?* Isa's words echoed in her mind. *You're not a woman.* She had to be wrong about it. Isa had to be wrong about all of it.

Vana kicked the desk. There had to be truths about her, indisputable ones that provided some answers. She loved music. She'd lost it, but that hadn't diminished her love for it. The same was true about Jules. She had lost part of him earlier than his death because of a different love, the pricking energy that ignited in her when she saw someone like Rutilia Belladonna.

"Rutilia, shit!"

Vana covered her mouth, afraid Isa could still hear her. She listened for a few seconds, but the only noise came from downstairs. She relaxed and clapped her hands once. Rutilia must have had some fucking answers. She was a noble brat who'd listened to a rebel band. She had warned them about the Nimmerwarm raid. She had told them to cut the concert short for safety's sake. She had requested a private session from her. Had she seen Vana as the Enforcer or as a woman? She had ignored Jules, so . . . Vana's heart beat faster. Like her situation, Rutilia was full of contradictions. At the time, Vana had perceived the noblewoman as dangerous but alluring. It must have been another prejudice, another simplification of what change required. Rutilia had sought her out, she had tried to help her; she had shown genuine interest. She was the key.

Vana rushed toward the door and remembered Isa had locked it. Rutilia wasn't the key to everything. She scoured the room for a tool. Her eyes fell on the window. She could jump, but she'd probably injure herself more. As much as she longed to keep the momentum alive, she needed to keep her body alive as well—at least until it received some answers.

She crouched down and peered underneath the bed. More energy rushed through her when she spotted her bag. The rope would still be in there, and if she was lucky, her seax as well. Her stomach knotted at the thought of the weapon, but she pushed it away. She pulled the bag out and searched through it. The seax's hilt found her hand before she even saw it. It heated up with excitement that nauseated her. The ungraceful death of the guard woman flashed in front of her eyes. Dustin's collapse worsened the vision, his shocked expression when he'd followed Jules into nothingness instead of avenging him.

Vana closed her eyes and waited for the visions to clear. When she opened them again, her hands shook, but her energy had returned. She strapped her dirty weapon belt on, ignoring the horrible iron stench. Her boots shared the fragrance, and she likely did too. She hoped Rutilia wouldn't mind. The noble lady's teeth had looked elvish. Perhaps she had a similar elvish affinity for the smell of blood.

Isa's wooden door looked sturdy, but Vana noticed a splinter standing out from the frame near the lock. If she got a good enough grip, she might be able to cut it out of the frame and pull the door open with force.

She looked at the seax in her hand. "It's not guts, you twisted shit, but do your work."

She brought the tip to the frame and scratched a dent next to the lock as an anchor point. The hilt cooled in her palm. The little shit knew it wouldn't get the sick liquid it desired. She aimed at the dent and hacked down on it until splinters shaved off. This could take a while, but causing damage to Isa's room satisfied her. At least she'd get her in trouble for this.

A minute later, shaved splinters covered her hand and the metal structure of the lock became visible through the thinned wood. She leaned into the next hack, hoping to cut deeper into the part that held the lock in place.

The door hit her in the face. She stumbled backward as pain shot through her forehead. All the emotions she had suppressed surfaced in her shock. Sobs escaped her. She searched for Jules's hands in her disoriented vision.

"Isa, you bloody—" She registered Jackson's voice through the confusion. "Vana?"

She twisted the seax in her hand, ready to fight. "Don't fuck with me, I swear." Why was she still sobbing? Threats were more effective without sobs. She blinked through the pain, and the room cleared.

Jackson's face lit up. "By Exitalis, you're alive. Your mom's been asking around for you everywhere. Your whole lot is worried sick."

Vana found her footing again. They were looking for her. They knew what she'd done. They knew the mess she had caused. "I gotta go."

She stumbled past him, avoiding his eyes. They had treated her like a dying woman since Jules's death. Seeing the disappointment in their eyes would be even worse.

"Wait!" Jackson shouted after her, but she half ran, half fell down the stairs. She pushed her way through the bar. Most patrons were too drunk to notice, but several familiar faces stared after her. Blood pulsed quickly through her, suppressing the unwanted pains and sobs. If she didn't function now, she'd have to face her family as a failure—or worse, a monster.

She rushed out of the bar and into the evening air. It smelled like roasts, liquor, and sex. Jackson's bar served as a passage between Waldfeld's proper restaurants near the town square and the shady streets decent folk didn't frequent.

Decency wasn't a concern of hers, so she ran toward the nauseating stench. Her family wouldn't look for her there. It would take her longer to get to the Belladonna manor this way, but her body had no right to complain. It had slept all day instead of justifying why it still breathed.

She strapped the seax onto her weapon belt and entered Waldfeld's darker side. The houses matched the filthy cobblestone. Summer fires had blackened parts of the straw rooftops. Not all residents had the motus to fix holes and had instead covered the burnt patches with wood planks, branches, or torn quilts. A symphony of poverty played through the streets—cries of babies, beggars demanding mercy, grunts and moans from the brothels, and music of those unbroken spirits that owned the night. She and Jules had wanted to play in this part of town, but bar owners didn't allow underage visitors. No one wanted to get their hands that dirty.

Five torches lit up a fancy-looking brothel. A beautiful woman with black curls and a lack of clothes winked at her. Vana blushed and lost track of where she was going. She ran into a tall, skinny man. "Shit—"

"My apologies!" He didn't sound like the kind of guy frequenting brothels around here. Vana looked up into the freckled face of Pier Kilburn. "Oh dear, is that blood?"

Vana's hand darted to the spot on her neck he was staring at. "Nope, it's . . . no."

He frowned. "Are you all right?"

Fuck no. She doubted he wanted a truthful response, so she countered instead. "Should you be around here?"

He nodded toward the sleazy bar on their right—The Stag's Tail. That explained it. It was the only queer bar in town. As usual, two large half orcs protected the entrance. An orcish woman and her human girlfriend had opened the business two generations ago, a spiteful act in the face of Waldfeld's religious fervor. They always had their own guards looking after their patrons. Vana admired the community spirit of the place. Those were the guards Waldfeld needed, that all of Silberfluss needed—common folk looking out for their own. Vana's mom had warned her to avoid the bar at all costs. Whether it was for its nature or the frequent raids, she wasn't sure.

"Let me accompany you home. It's not the safest around here," Pier said.

Vana laughed. It sounded odd and hollow, but she was happy to still be capable of it. "Thanks, but I'm pretty sure I could gut a guy quicker than you could." *At least my weapon could.*

"I wasn't thinking of gutting as the best conflict resolution . . ." Pier raised his eyebrow. "You're not going to the Belladonnas', are you? Lady Rutilia mentioned you earlier, but—"

"Rutilia mentioned me?" Vana's eyes grew wide, and her heart jumped. *Stupid heart.* She was searching for answers, nothing more, but if she could make Rutilia forget her nobility, even better.

"Yes, which concerns me—"

She patted Pier's shoulder. "Thanks. See you around, Kilburn." She brushed past him before he could respond.

The torchlight died down, and the smell of pines replaced the stench when she reached Waldfeld's thick forest. She stepped into it, and her muscles tensed up. Nighttime had caught up with her. Yesterday it had been a welcome disguise for her and her comrades. Today it revealed how alone she was. Every step she took reminded her of the steps Maureen had taken, the jokes Jasper had made along the way, the scare a jumping squirrel had given them. This once, time could've done Vana a favor and moved backward, back to her comrades, or better yet, back to when she and Jules had wasted it together. But time wasn't a person, and neither were the gods. Only solitude awaited her in the forest, and it cared not about Vana's grief.

She kept walking. This wasn't the path she and her comrades had taken. This one led to Waldfeld's nobility, far from the town's poverty and peasantry. The tall pines snuffed out the sun's last efforts. Every once in a while, a lone firefly took pity on Vana and relieved both the darkness and her solitude, but she mostly stumbled alone through the night's uncertainty. Her legs grew heavy and her mind restless. She wished the forest would offer a distraction in the form of a jackrabbit, or anything alive, really. The woods remained as silent as a graveyard.

Crimson torchlight appeared. Vana stepped toward it and felt scrubs underneath her boots. The path had been smooth dirt until this point. She backed off and took a step forward. The path continued but curved away from the torchlight. She sighed. Was this one of those wise versus interesting decisions? It had been Jules's job to advocate for the wise path. She must have marched for an hour—far enough to reach the estate. Perhaps it was a guardhouse at the forest's edge.

She took two more steps down the path before giving in. Her head still hurt with questions she couldn't answer. The source of the torchlight would surely be easy to discover.

She pulled the seax from her belt and headed toward the light. The cracking of branches under her feet was a welcome change from the steady path. The closer she got to the torchlight, the warmer the air felt. The guard residing there must have lit a bonfire. She had expected the torch to become defined as she stepped closer, but it still looked like a moving flame hovering in the darkness.

She reached a clearing. The light illuminated the surrounding plants. Vana squinted at it. There was no cabin attached to it, no lamppost it could dangle from. The round flame turned into a slit. It looked like the crack of a bandits' cave. Vana stretched her neck to peer around it. There was nothing behind it except more plants. If she hadn't known better, she'd have thought it was a rift in reality.

"Fae . . . bring back my Fae possession . . . bring back Choravdat."

She perceived the voice as scratching on sandpaper, as shots, as the squishing of the organ she'd stepped on, as Jules's rattling breaths as he fought for the life denied to him. She perceived nothing and everything at once. Her tongue burned the longer she remained silent.

"Wh-what?"

"Richard Kilburn . . . is that you? Disgusting thief, reveal yourself . . ."

Vana licked her lips. Her tongue burned once more. "No, I'm Vana Ackerman."

A hand reached through the slit. Vana's stomach and mind both protested at the sight. Its bones were enlarged, charred, and translucent. Clumps of muscle, ripped pieces of skin, and two throbbing red veins filled the fingers.

They tried to clutch her throat, and she screamed. She slashed down on the charred bone. Her blade caught, and the arm recoiled. She tried to yank the seax out and failed. A gagging sound mixed with screams resounded around the clearing. *Laughter,* she thought, even though it made no sense.

She let go of the seax and ran toward the darkness, back toward the path. The repulsive sounds chased her.

Tell Richard Kilburn an Ouisà Kacoc is looking for him . . .

Her lungs stung, but she didn't slow down until she reached the path. She broke down on the smooth dirt, shaking and gagging. She tried to wrap her thoughts around what had happened, but she failed. Not all answers were worth finding. She pushed to her feet and stumbled forward. *Rutilia.* Any thought beyond that clear goal exceeded what her mind could handle. She tried to process what she had seen. The slit. The hand. Her thoughts had been ripped apart, leaving her with a stabbing headache. *Rutilia.* An ally, that was all she needed.

The forest cleared and presented the Belladonna estate like a curtain revealing a stage. Vana forced herself to focus on the real, comprehensible details in front of her. The manor was made of green-painted limestone and reached several stories into the air. Vana stretched her neck to take in its entirety. A juniper-colored iron fence with pointed spikes at the top surrounded it, standing taller than the one at the Nimmerwarm estate. Two glowing green torches lit up the gate and the two guards next to it. There was no way she could climb the fence, but she shouldn't have to. Rutilia awaited her. Pier had confirmed it.

She approached the gate and nodded at a guard with an extraordinarily bushy mustache. He looked at her as if she were shit he had stepped into. "What do you want, street rat?"

Vana cleared her throat. "Lousy manners you got there, but ehm, Lady Rutilia Belladonna invited me for a private concert."

The guard laughed, and Vana's hand moved to the empty spot on her belt. *Shit.* She had lost her seax to the monstrosity she refused to think about. The scorn in the guard's eyes reminded her of the captain's look as he'd shot the third bullet into Jules. *Different guards. Nimmerwarm guards shot him, not these fools.*

"Where's your instrument then?" He squinted at her ears. "Oh, shit. You're a halfer. Get your dirty ass out of here."

"Halfer?" the other guard asked. He had small green eyes and a boyish face that looked familiar. "You're Vana Ackerman, aren't you?"

"Yeah." She nodded and glared at Big Mustache.

The boyish guard leaned toward Mustache and whispered something. A grin flitted over his lips and left a knot in Vana's stomach.

"Ah, yes, the lady was hoping you'd show up soon," Mustache said.

"Great." Vana wasn't sure what else to say. How did she enter a noble manor legally? Did they announce her? She thought of the princess stories her grandmother used to tell her before she had made it clear that she didn't like princesses. But Rutilia wasn't a princess; she was the duke's daughter.

Way less concerning. If Vana thought about it, she was barely even noble. At least not yet.

"Follow along," the boyish guard said, opening the gate. Together they walked through the elaborately cut hedges. Some were shaped like people dancing at a ball, others looked like a wolf pack. Vana had never seen an adaptation of a Bored Reginald show, but she had pictured something similarly surreal. Her mom would be upset at the lack of useful crops in the property's gardens. Vana smiled at the thought.

A resigned-looking old woman awaited them at the door.

"Hello." Vana nodded at her, and the woman's brows furrowed. Was she Rutilia's mom?

"Good evening, Governess," the guard said. "The lady's special guest has finally arrived."

The governess rolled her eyes and gestured for Vana to follow her. "Wipe your shoes before you enter."

Vana looked down at the rug in front of her. They had a rug. At the door. For shoes. Vana shook her head. *What a waste.* She wiped her boots off and left ugly stains on the rug. The governess didn't care. She hurried through the entrance hall, giving Vana little chance to take in the grandeur. She'd never seen so many paintings, sculptures, and pretty things in one place. Her heart jumped when she thought of the other beauty this manor housed. *Calm your tits, Vana. You're here for answers.*

The governess led her up a steep spiral staircase that was painted the same leaf green as the manor's limestone. They reached a corridor with Belladonna family portraits. Vana's eyes darted to a gold-rimmed depiction of Rutilia when she was a few years younger. The duke's daughter had recently turned nineteen, if Vana recalled correctly. It had been a tough month on the Ackermans, as taxes had increased for noble birthday celebrations. Her stomach flipped at the thought. *What am I doing here?*

They stopped at a double-winged door, and the governess knocked. A few seconds later, an otherworldly beauty opened both doors.

"Vana." There was that carnal smile again. *Rutilia.* The hallway's candlelight reflected in her smoldering eyes. She had tied her corn-yellow locks into a loose ponytail that grazed her shoulders and was wearing a thin red nightgown. She looked less Fae, less imposing, and less noble without the pompous dress and day makeup, but she was just as beautiful as she had been that night at the concert.

"You're not gonna bow for me?" Vana asked with a smirk. It tickled the melodic laughter out of Rutilia, and Vana relaxed. She hadn't heard a sound that pleasant all night.

"Come in." Rutilia gestured for her to step inside. "Bring us some tea, will you, Portia?"

Vana stepped into the parlor, which was larger than her family's living space. She had expected it to be filled with artwork and sculptures like the rest of the manor but faced dozens of animal skulls instead. Slim candleholders stood between each skull and lit the room in a green hue. Vana tensed at the light. It must've been the same magic used to take her Spirit from her. She wished nobles would stop using that bullshit.

"Sit down," Rutilia commanded in a sweet tone, pushing her toward a crimson chaise lounge. Vana sat down and startled when she saw what stood next to it. From the corner of her eyes, it had looked like a marble statue, but it was a realistic-looking swan.

Rutilia's smile widened. "Taxidermy. You like it?"

"It's real?"

"It used to be." She sat down on the armchair across from her. "I like to keep reminders around that all beasts can be slain."

Vana thought of the monstrous hand that exceeded her understanding. Picturing it as a stuffed piece of decoration helped. "I get that."

Rutilia ran her finger over her own neck. "I was starting to wonder if you'd still come."

Vana chuckled. The sound almost felt natural. "Well, I wasn't sure if I could trust the offer."

"Boo." Rutilia pouted. "And I thought we had a nice little chat in that alley. Not as far as I would have liked it to go, but enough for a taste, don't you think?" She licked her lips. Vana grew hot when she saw the tip of that rosy tongue.

"Heh, yeah, the alley . . ." *The concert. Jules.* She cursed herself for forgetting him again. There was something about Rutilia that robbed all senses. "Listen, I need your help. How did you know about the Nimmerwarm guards?" Vana glanced at the swan. "Do you know the captain? 'Cause he's a beast I'd love to get stuffed."

A knock on the parlor door kept Rutilia from responding.

"Come in," she called, and two servants entered with a tea set and small bites of exotic dishes. Vana's stomach grumbled. She hadn't even thought of food since the previous night. The satisfaction of her mother's cooking had long left her. The servants placed the trays on the table between them. Rutilia caught Vana's eager look.

"Go ahead, dig in."

"Dig in? That's not a very noble thing to say."

"You make me forget my manners."

A different hunger spread within Vana. It confused her after all the pain and grief, but she gave into it for now. Just until she had answers.

"Oh, you need to try the chocolate mousse bites." Rutilia picked up a piece that looked like dessert.

"What's chocolate?" Vana asked.

Rutilia's eyes widened. She hopped up and sat down next to Vana. "Close your eyes."

"What?"

"Trust me."

Vana smirked and closed her eyes. "All right."

"Now open your mouth." She did as she was told.

A moment later, a rich, decadent sweetness melted on her tongue. It tasted better than any berry she'd ever tried. A warm flavor spread on her tongue without sticking to it.

"Shit, that's delicious." She opened her eyes and met Rutilia's intense gaze. The chocolate swirled in her stomach.

"You haven't tasted the best thing yet."

Vana's eyes flitted back to the tray. "No?"

Rutilia ran her finger over Vana's chin and gently guided her face back to her. "It's not on the tray, dummy."

"Oh."

"Can I ask you something?"

Vana remembered her question about the captain and the other swine that had slaughtered Jules. A pang of guilt stabbed her for forgetting again. "About the captain—"

"I asked first if I could ask you something." Rutilia pouted again, and Vana itched to kiss it away.

"All right."

Rutilia shifted on the chaise lounge next to her. Vana felt the heat of her skin. Breathing became hard. "Do you like Agathe?"

Vana blinked. "What?" She had expected another flirtation.

"The princess, do you like her? Do you think she's suited for the crown?"

Vana's muscles clenched. *The revolution, of course.* "I mean . . . no, she's horrible for our people."

"It was The Spirit and the Enforcer's goal to get rid of her, right? Or that's what you sang about, at least." Rutilia grazed her finger over Vana's neck. The chocolate had left a bitter aftertaste in her mouth.

"Ehm, yeah, all oppressors, honestly. We want to give power back to the people. I'm not quite sure how to go about it now that Jules . . ."

"How about I help you with that?"

Vana studied her face. She had hoped to gain an ally, but this seemed too easy. "How?"

"You want a revolution, I want a change in leadership. Waldfeld could do well on its own, governed by its own people, as you said."

People in their community looking after the town instead of guards the nobility had chosen—it was her and Jules's dream. It would have to be organized, of course. Waldfeld's people were reasonable, but Father Godfried had too much power. There was certainly room for improvement.

"Silberfluss, on the other hand," Rutilia continued. "Silberfluss could use a smart mind that would otherwise be wasted on a self-sufficient town."

Vana knew where she was going with this. She bit her lip. The last thing she wanted was to put another knife in an unfit hand.

"Why is some spike governing us when we could have someone from our midst?"

Vana frowned. "Spike?"

Rutilia's finger wandered over Vana's pointed ear. "Oh, I don't mean a lovely halfer like you. I'm talking about that Virisunder-bred Agathe Heidegger."

"And you think you could do a better job?"

Rutilia stretched her long leg out and lowered it on Vana's lap. The thin nightgown slipped upward and revealed her thigh. Together with her other leg, it would make a fine necklace while Vana tasted the delicacy Rutilia had alluded to.

"People underestimate me, like they underestimated you. But the moment I saw you on stage, the moment I saw that spark in your eye, I knew we could accomplish brilliant things together. You lead the revolution. I'll lead the nation."

Her comrades' deaths weren't in vain if they sparked a new age. She didn't have to stay the Enforcer. She could become the liberator instead, the one who pulled commoners out of their misery and made them matter to the state. There was only one problem. "I like the sound of that . . . but how can the revolution free us if it ends with one person deciding over everyone else again?"

Rutilia wrapped her legs around Vana's waist and slid into her lap. She swung her arms around Vana's neck and whispered into her ear, "Oh, but you want me to be on top. Trust me."

Vana's pulse wandered between her legs. Rutilia shifted in her lap and caused it to throb harder. Her thoughts longed to fly away. *Fuck reason. Fuck answers. Just fuck* . . . Jules. She couldn't forget about Jules again.

"How did you know the guard captain would attack?" The breath that carried her words was rapid, but she was proud of herself for having gotten them out at all.

"Vana, darling, can we celebrate our new agreement first?"

Celebrate. Isa had wanted to celebrate their alleged victory. There could be no celebration without answers.

Vana shook her head. "No, please tell me. I need to know I can trust you."

"Duchess de Matière wanted to take out my favorite band . . . I'm so sorry." Her eyes filled with tears. "I'm sorry. I thought if I told you, you wouldn't want to see me again. It's my fault and—"

Vana cut her off with a kiss. Her lips were the softest thing that had ever grazed Vana's skin. Rutilia reciprocated immediately. Vana had kissed Jules numerous times, but her body had never melted, her heart had never raced, and joy had never rushed through her like it did now. Rutilia pried her mouth open, and soon her tongue waltzed with Vana's. A moan escaped her, and like the kiss, Rutilia reciprocated. Vana's hands glided around her waist and gently ground her against her lap. Lightning strikes of pleasure struck from the throbbing between Vana's legs and traveled through her until her whole body vibrated with lust.

Vana vaguely registered the creaking parlor door.

"Milady, your father—" A man tried to interrupt, but he couldn't. She and Rutilia had melted into one, riding a storm that no one was allowed to intrude upon. Rutilia pulled away, and the storm lifted. *No, wait.*

She looked pale. Had Vana done something wrong?

"Sorry for the interruption," the man said.

"Get out!" Rutilia yelled. Vana agreed with the notion, but the delivery was harsh. She peeked over Rutilia's shoulder and saw him—the captain, the disgusting piece of shit that had stolen her Spirit from her. He was wearing Waldfeld's leaf-green uniform instead of the blue Nimmerwarm armor from the square.

"What the fu—"

Rutilia turned back to her and tried to drown Vana's anger with another kiss. Vana held a hand up between them to stop the temptress. "Why is he here? What's happening?"

Rutilia took a deep breath. "Yeah, Titus, why *are* you here?" All sweetness had left her voice.

"Excuse me, milady, but we got the report from the incidents last night. Ackerman wasn't the one who assassinated the duchess. She underperformed, from what we gathered."

Rutilia lifted herself off Vana and regarded her with the same scorn as the captain right before he had spit at her. "And here I was thinking you were useful."

"What? No, wait—"

Rutilia sighed. "After all the trouble I went through getting rid of that Tribu boyfriend of yours . . ." She snapped her fingers. "Captain?"

Tears shot into Vana's eyes as her mind struggled to catch up. "Why—"

Rutilia winked at her and turned back to the captain who had murdered Jules. "This brute has defiled me. Arrest her."

There's my answer.

CHAPTER 18

ALLY

September 979 - The Council's Institute for Assula Magic, Virisunder

The carriage rocked right as Ally turned the page to re-read a passage on momentum and inertia. The parchment cut her finger. She brought the tip to her lips and sucked the sweet drops of blood without taking her eyes off the words. Many years ago, in a lab experiment, she had noticed forms of gas rise into the air, but birds flew solely on the principles of momentum and inertia. She floated her other hand through the air, imagining a griffon vulture, the largest bird native to Virisunder. She had read before that the sun influenced its flight. Perhaps she should include temperature parameters in her calculations.

They're watching you.

She glanced to the side and met Robert's eyes. He was indeed watching her with a smirk that made her forget the birds.

"Cute," he mouthed. Ally looked to the Tidier sitting across from them. *Shush, you fool.* The Council guard had entered their carriage as soon as they had reached the Institute's territory. Two more Tidiers accompanied Ally's guards in the second carriage trailing behind hers. She'd wanted to ride alone with Robert, her personal guard, but they were on Josef's land now, and the Tidier was an unwelcome reminder of it. She stared stoically at Ally and Robert in her immaculate eggshell-colored uniform. The assula staff in her hand warned Ally that the Tidier, and Josef, could seize control at any moment.

Ally cleared her throat. "Do I need to remind you of royal manners, Oakley?"

Robert followed her eyes and straightened up. "So, what are you working on? Your Majesty."

"I'm not working on anything." The last thing she needed was Josef hearing about some mad inventions she plotted against him. "Just studying." She showed Robert her notes and watched as his eyes flitted over her attempts at creating a formula for flying. The frown on his forehead increased as he tried to grasp it. *Cute, indeed.*

Another soul to crush. Another man to tease
and destroy. I see what you're doing.

Ally took a deep breath. Josef relished in her illness, but she wouldn't give him that satisfaction. She'd go in there, demand the Ceremony, and leave for her new life. Reggie had promised to clear her mind as soon as she stepped into the Institute building. She'd wanted to protest, but he had insisted. She hoped it wouldn't cause him any new wounds.

Reggie. The familiar tear between longing and loss pained her. Four years ago, when everyone had deemed the war a failure, he had visited her at the front and begged her to run away with him. He'd painted the most magnificent picture of a city in the sky, far from Elfentum's chaos, from the Council's influence, from the watching eyes. Porta Proditor, he had called it. Traitor's Gate. A place where no one knew about the Mad Queen.

If she had gone with him, she would have spoiled the dream. It would no longer be a place where no one knew her, for she knew about the Mad Queen, the one who would have abandoned her nation and allowed the Council to control all of Elfentum, unopposed.

Just two months ago, Harald Heidegger had offered to provide Council advisers to each nation as alleged political support. The Council had started as a merchant union but already acted as protectors for Balthos's pantheon, and now they would influence the regents' politics as well. All six of Elfentum's princes and princesses had agreed to the Council's new political department because the Heideggers had tempted them with easier access to flashy new assula inventions and other riches. Ally's stomach knotted when she thought of Josefine. Of course, she had bought into the charade. Ally wished some regents would realize they needn't rely on what the Council provided if they educated their own people properly.

She had declined Reggie's offer. An illusion, no matter how beautiful, couldn't erase the peril of this world from her mind. War was a necessity whether he liked it or not.

"Wait a second." Robert brushed his fingers over the short beard he'd grown. He looked like a philosopher from illustrations she'd seen—the kind of philosopher who could put his book aside, pick her up, and carry her into the sheets. Her thoughts were getting away from her. "Are you making—"

"Reading notes," she interrupted before he could spill details to the Tidier. "I like to take notes while reading, Oakley."

He looked like he was about to kiss her. *Don't you dare.* A smile crept over her lips. She wanted him to dare.

"I see . . ." He sat back but didn't take his eyes off her. "Good notes. I *flew* right through them."

"Your Majesty?" Ally startled when the Tidier woman addressed her.

"Yes?"

"Does His Majesty know about your visit? He might be occupied with an experiment."

The word dug into her guts, making every muscle clench. *Experiment.* When Harald had told her that his brother, Josef Heidegger, the great scientist, was to marry her as a guardian, she'd been excited. He was to be a companion until she was old enough to become a wife. The palace's emptiness had haunted Ally without her dad around. The words "husband" and "wife" had meant nothing to her back then, but a lab partner? She had wanted one of those. Her dad had been her lab partner before he'd disappeared. She had been ridiculously short for a ten-year-old, so Josef, in her mind, was the lab partner who could reach flasks on the top shelf. Until he wasn't.

"Your Majesty?"

"The queen has the right to rest during the journey. There's no need for this kind of investigative shi—"

"No, he is not expecting me," Ally interrupted.

The Tidier raised her eyebrows. "He might not be pleased to see you then."

"I'm glad our feelings will be mutual." Ally leaned back and focused on the carriage rocking. The number of bumps per minute served as a measure of speed. It also served as an excellent source of nausea. She rubbed her stomach. *Shh, little embryo. Let's not agitate each other.*

"You all right?" Robert asked quietly. She nodded and closed her eyes.

Parasite . . .

It's not a parasite. She opened one eye and saw a maggot as large as a person burst out of her stomach and devour her skin. She shut her eye firmly. *Not a parasite, not a maggot, just a gamble.* The pregnancy was a gamble on Subira, on Robert, and on Reggie. As much as the thought of pressuring Subira made her uneasy, Ally still believed her old friend could break the stagnation of the war. It was a gamble worth taking.

As for Robert, she barely knew him and couldn't allow herself to trust him. She'd planned to keep a professional eye on her personal guard, but the more she watched him, the more intriguing he became. He observed people as closely as only Reggie did. He remained silent during her meetings with lieutenants, but she noticed dozens of microexpressions cross his face. Afterward, he'd spin a delightful tale about each person who'd attended the meeting. None of them were true, of course, but all of them were more pleasant than reality. When she asked him something, he'd reply with a concise statement first. She would dig deeper, and he'd start to ramble. The more excited he got, the more subjects he'd combine until his response was no longer concise but a collection of short stories. He was an *X* she hadn't calculated into the formula—unnerving, but endlessly intriguing.

She had hated carrying Josef's heir. She should've minded that Robert's child was growing within her, but she couldn't bring herself to. Perhaps one day she could become one of his anecdotes, scrambled among the other adventures his life took him on.

Then there was Reggie . . .

The carriage came to an abrupt halt.

"Wait here," the Tidier commanded, as if she had the right to, and climbed out of the carriage.

"Bunch of nitwits."

"Robert?"

"Yes?" He shifted in his seat and twitched as if he wanted to put his arm around her. He ran his fingers through his hair instead. "What do you need?"

She suppressed a smirk. He had to stop acting like that. It was too distracting.

"When we're in there . . . people won't respect me much."

"And you want me to beat them up. Got it." He smiled.

"Exactly. Or, perhaps even better, you stay quietly in the background and don't get yourself killed for treason."

"So whichever option I find suitable at the moment?"

She playfully punched his bicep. "No. Behave."

"Am I allowed to glare at your husband? I've been practicing my glare for the occasion." He squinted his eyes, and she giggled.

"No."

"So no rebellion at all? All right, whatever my queen wants."

She bit her lip and poked her head out of the carriage window. The Tidier was discussing her arrival with two other Tidiers at the front gate. They had a moment.

"Fine, you get one act of rebellion."

"Do I get to pick which——" Robert started, but she pulled her head back into the carriage and kissed him. She hadn't felt his lips on her since the night in the meadow and hadn't realized how starved for them she was. What was supposed to be a quick peck became urgent and hot. Her body flared up when he stroked her waist and pressed her closer. She sensed his hunger, his push for more. She pulled away while she could still control herself.

As soon as they parted, the Tidier opened the carriage. Heat burned her cheeks. She hoped the nitwits would mistake it as a sign of madness.

"You've received permission to enter the Institute, Your Majesty."

A different heat rose in Ally's chest. She didn't require permission. She was a Verdain. Josef was *her* consort, not the other way around. When would he learn that? Then again, she needed his permission for the Ceremony.

"Your Majesty." Robert pushed around her and jumped out of the carriage. He presented his hand and helped her down.

As she passed him, she heard him whisper, "See, I can behave if it's my queen's wish."

She smirked and shook her head minimally. *You inconveniently charming fool.*

The Institute's sight wiped the smirk off her face and re-ignited nausea. This was the first time she'd visit it outside of her nightmares.

The Council's Institute for Assula Magic had been built in decreasing circles that looked like the inside of an old oak tree. The construction itself, however, couldn't have looked less natural. Green assula light created the outer wall. Ally didn't know what happened to those who stepped into it. She was tempted to push a Tidier and find out, but it was in her best interest to behave as well. Behind the assula wall was the Institute's outer ring, built solely of milky glass. The Institute sat on the border of Tazadahar and Virisunder. They must have harvested tons of Tazadahar's desert sand to melt into the glass construction. The five inner rings were made of steel, and each reached slightly higher than the one before. Together they formed a spiral.

Ally couldn't spot a single window, which increased her nausea. There was no transparency, no supervision. The Council regulated Elfentum, and Josef's family *was* the Council, so he was left to his own devices in the research facility.

The monster will trap you in there.
You won't be able to escape.

Ally exhaled sharply and followed the Tidier toward the assula wall. She couldn't spot an entrance gate either.

You want to be trapped, you feeble shit.
You want him to take you again.

"I hope the local birds don't shit on all that glass. Must be tough to clean," Robert said behind her, and Ally eased up. A few more steps and Reggie's spell would protect her. Robert and Reggie were both with her in a way. They both protected her. Her heart fluttered at the thought of them before realizing how inappropriate it was. It went against the commonly accepted hypothesis of how affection or love worked. She'd have to study it in depth later, when everything else was solved.

They reached the assula wall, and Ally itched to touch it. Would it be hot like a flame? Or was it an energy in motion? How could it power weapons and household items alike? And why was it always green?

"Your Majesty?"

"Hmm?" She found the Tidier staring at her, as well as five other Tidiers who had joined her entourage. Ally's own protection had caught up too. She had brought six guards with her besides Robert. None of them were magic-bearers, but they shielded her against bandits, and the sight of familiar faces soothed Ally.

"Your hand for the registration, please." The Tidier pointed at a strange-looking hourglass that hovered in the assula wall. Ally stepped closer to examine it. The frame was forged of black iron and held the only translucent glass she'd seen so far. Green grains of sand floated in its upper half. She wanted to pull the hourglass out of the wall, take it into her old lab, smash it, and analyze what kept the grains afloat.

"The queen's guard should try it first," Robert said, stepping forward. He didn't seem to share Ally's curiosity about the object.

"Very well," said the Tidier. "Place your hand flat in the middle of the glass."

Robert raised an eyebrow but did as he was told. His fingertips penetrated the glass as if it were air. As soon as the back of his hand reached the hourglass's narrow neck, the grains trickled down. Robert grimaced and shuddered. His hand lit up with a golden hue until all sand had seeped through. Next to them, a part of the assula wall dissolved, creating an entrance to the Institute.

The Tidier gestured at it and addressed Robert. "Walk through."

He glanced at Ally. "I should stay with the queen."

"You wanted to go first. Walk through."

They will kill him. They will gut him, torture him, eat him. Why do you even care, you unfaithful slut?

Josef didn't know Robert would enter first. There was no reason for them to kill whoever stepped through. It could have been one of their own. Ally exhaled. "Go ahead, Oakley."

Robert pulled his hand from the glass and walked past the Tidier. "You better not harm her," he hissed before stepping through the gate.

The Tidier chuckled. "Your turn, Your Majesty."

Ally touched her fingertips to check the temperature of her skin. If assula energy created heat, they should warm up when the sand hit them. The Tidier to her left sighed impatiently. Not very scientific-minded for someone working in a research facility. She stretched her hand out like Robert had and pushed it through the glass. She didn't feel the material pass through. Was it an illusion? If so, how much of the Institute was real?

Her breath caught when the first sand grain hit. It felt as if tiny fingers tugged at her skin. The sand lit up with a golden hue, like it had for Robert, but a second later the light brightened. The gold turned into a blazing white that shone out of the hourglass. The light crept up her arm, where its intensity increased. For a second, her whole body glowed.

The hourglass shattered. Ally jumped as the splinters hit her body.

"Alames?" a familiar low voice called.

Ally spun around to face the shocked Tidiers. "Who said that?" They all gaped at her, but no one dared to answer.

Her guard, Liam, pulled out a handkerchief and handed it to her. "Careful, Your Majesty, the splinters cut you."

She touched her face and found her cheek covered in blood and glass. The assula wall next to them opened.

The Tidier who had accompanied them in the carriage cleared her throat. "A . . . ehm, a minor malfunction of the registration tool. Step through the gate, please . . . Your Majesty." Neither she nor her colleagues seemed to know what had happened.

Ally waited for the voice to return, but it didn't. *Alames.* The tormentors in her mind had never spoken of the Lost Goddess. She hadn't studied her much, as religious texts rarely held any scientific merit. Scholars didn't benefit from altering formulas to measure temperature, but they could benefit greatly from putting words into the gods' mouths. Most sacred texts were the work of clever politicians.

She gestured for her remaining guards to follow and stepped through the gate. As soon as she crossed the barrier, the weight of her illness left her. Her senses sharpened as she took in the space between the wall and the outer Institute circle. It was paved with flat gray stones and crowded with people. From this angle, she could see five entrances into the outer circle with at least eight people lined up in front of each. They looked like merchants and stewards from various noble houses, all eager to purchase the newest assula inventions. It dawned on Ally that her war with Tazadahar had made this progress possible. Her heart sank. It was progress, but only for those who could afford it, only for those the Council deemed fit.

Robert rushed toward her. "Al—"

Ally raised her chin and shot him a look to remind him of his position. Doing so made her uneasy, but they were inside the Institute now. She could already feel Josef's eyes on her.

"Your Majesty." Robert bowed his head slightly and took the bloodied handkerchief. "What did they do?"

"Nothing. It was an assula malfunction, don't worry."

Robert frowned and pulled his own handkerchief. He

dabbed the glass and blood off with such tenderness it lured a shiver out of her. He must have caught it because a slight grin crossed his face.

A Tidier interrupted, "Your Majesty, this way."

He led them through the lines of people, along the outer circle curve. Four of her guards protected her sides as they passed the people. She was grateful for Reggie's spell. Without it, the close contact and restriction of movement would have ambushed her. The lines grew sparser the farther they moved away from the gate, and lunch tables with scientists and Tidiers soon replaced them. The picture created an eerie normalcy next to the green wall.

They reached an inconspicuous door built of the same glass as the outer circle wall. Two Tidiers protected it. The Tidier who had guided Ally stepped forward and placed his hand flat on the door. It lit up, then disappeared. He moved through the newly created archway and called for the others to follow him. Ally's fingers itched to touch the frame as she entered. Would it explode like the hourglass? Perhaps she carried chemicals on her skin that interfered with assula energy. Or perhaps Josef wanted to demonstrate that she destroyed whatever she touched. If it was the latter, she appreciated the theatrics.

Ally's breath caught when she stepped into the inner circle. Was Reggie's spell working? The hallway looked like a hallucination. Its circular build branched into a labyrinth with smooth milky glass walls. There were no doors, no alterations. It felt like she had fallen into the orb of Josef's staff. The lanes were so narrow they had to line up single file to pass through them. Ally tried to spot the ceiling, but the walls stretched higher than she could see.

The most peculiar detail was the light source reflecting gold and green off the glass walls. There were no torches or candles. It all shone through the milky floor. Hourglasses with green sand swam underneath it on a steady path. Golden strings of light spasmed around them. Some knocked against the glass, others pushed the hourglasses off their path. Ally wondered if there was a magnetic force at play. Was it necessary to store the energy of assulas? Her eyes widened. What if the golden strings weren't magnetic at all but were the substance she'd been looking for? *Raw assulas.*

Liam, her guard, bumped into her. "Oh, excuse me, Your Majesty. Is everything—?"

Robert spun around and met Ally's eyes. She raised an eyebrow and glanced at the floor. *Come on, you're clever.* He observed the floor, then glanced back up with a grin. How difficult would it be to sneak a raw one out of here?

"Your Majesty?" Liam asked behind her.

"Yes, what, yes?"

"The Tidiers are waiting." He pointed ahead at the impatient nitwits. Ally sighed and kept moving. She was here to get Josef's permission for the Ceremony, not to study, and definitely not for an audacious adventure.

A Fi'Teri elf wearing a lab coat with indefinable blue stains on it rushed toward them. Ally expected him to crash into his Tidier colleagues, but he disappeared in front of them and reappeared behind Liam. *Thank you, Reggie.* Her illness would have loved this bizarre playground.

The Tidiers led them down another crossing, deeper into the labyrinth. The floor rattled. Ally glanced past them and saw the pathway enlarge and shrink in a strange rhythm. The hallucinations had found her. She watched as the walls folded into themselves and tightened the space they walked through until it was barely wide enough. Rooms had crushed her numerous times thanks to the illness. It couldn't faze her now.

Liam breathed rapidly behind her. Robert looked over his shoulder with panic in his eyes. "What the limbo is this?" he whispered.

Ally frowned. It wasn't a fabrication of her mind? But it looked like one . . .

A voice echoed down the path, and she froze. It was as contorted as the walls, but the contortion wasn't what scared her. It was the man behind it. "Hello, my pet."

Josef.

The Tidier brought them to a halt. "The king is now ready to see you." He knocked his staff on the ground, and a door appeared. He bowed, gestured to it, and continued his way down the path, along with the other Tidiers. Another Tidier opened the door from the inside and waved them in. Ally's guards entered until it was Robert's turn. She trembled and cursed herself for it. Josef always turned her into a fraction of herself. *It's because he can't handle my whole.*

Robert leaned toward her. "The king can't harm the snow empress. Not on my watch." He winked and entered. She followed him. Perhaps her problems could be solved as easily as in his books.

The room she entered perfectly portrayed the Council's deceitfulness. After the nightmares of the hall, they welcomed Ally into a lusciously decorated visitation room with flowery tapestries and a fluffy carpet. It was furnished with four inviting chaise lounges and elegantly crafted coffee tables. A tea set floated in the middle of the room. On it were six layers with platters of cake, pastries, and bread. The Council's symbol—six hands clasped together, forming a ring—ornamented a lavish teapot. It looked like Ally's grandmother Theodosia had invited them to a tea party instead of Josef. What was this ridiculous ruse? Reggie's words slipped into her thoughts. *Most people are illusionists, sugar. That's what makes you so bewitching. You are truth in an insidious world.* She smiled. Josef could have welcomed her in a floating ballroom or a burning lake. She knew who he truly was, and more importantly, she knew who *she* was.

A Sap Bürüy woman stepped out of a door in the back of the room. "Welcome to the Institute, Your Majesty. King Josef Verdain, head magic-bearer and researcher of the Council's Institute for Assula Magic, will be with you shortly."

Ally would have found the unnecessary introduction amusing if not for the strange hollowness in the woman's voice. There was no light in her eyes either. She wore neither a Tidier uniform nor a lab coat but a shortened maid robe made of white tulle and a fitting petticoat. Her thick black hair was tied up in a bow. The human woman must have passed the age of thirty, but she dressed like a ten-year-old. Ally's stomach turned. She used to have a similar wardrobe.

"Thank you. What's your name if I may ask?"

The woman blinked at her. Ally wasn't sure if she had understood the question until she spoke again. "They say it's Marzahn."

"Who's *they*?" Ally asked, but the door opened before the woman could answer.

Josef stepped into the room and gestured for Marzahn to leave. "Lobotomy, a fascinating practice," he said before turning toward Ally.

Pain stabbed through Ally as her body ran through the memories it connected with her personal monster.

Josef was a tall, thin elf with flat clay-colored hair, small swamp-colored eyes that longed to watch her sink into them, and a disturbing lack of a chin. He didn't wear a lab coat but a finely woven tweed suit and oval glasses designed to give him the air of intellectual authority he otherwise lacked. Ally knew his eyesight was perfect. He didn't have his usual assula staff on him, but he fingered the glowing chain of a pocket watch attached to his pants. It looked like a fine material to rip from his belt and strangle him with.

He stared at her with cold hate before breaking into a loathly simper. "My pet, how lovely of you to visit. It's always nice to reconnect." He entrapped her in an intrusive hug. Ally felt as if her skin peeled off at his touch. His sour odor made her dizzy. She pushed herself off.

"I'm here to discuss the future of Virisunder, nothing else."

"Oh, my pet." He squeezed her cheek. "There's no reason to yell."

Ally hesitated. Had she yelled? She thought she'd been in control of her diction.

"She didn't yell . . . Your Majesty," Robert said behind her. Ally bit her lip. *I told you to shush, my fool.*

"How very rude." Josef snickered. "You're not employing commoners in the royal guard now, are you?"

Ally glanced at Robert. *Not exclusively. I'm employing him in the bedroom as well.*

"My personal guards are none of your business," she said instead. "As I was saying, I'm here to discuss—"

"Oh, sweet girl, you're all flustered. How about some tea? The journey must have exhausted you."

When they had lived at the palace together, courtiers had often admired how sweetly he'd cared for her. They'd considered Ally's discomfort around him another sign of her madness.

"No. Listen, I—"

Josef grabbed her shoulders and pushed her down on the nearby chaise lounge. She noticed Robert twitch from the corner of her eye. She hoped he was too clever to act. Josef crouched down in front of her as if she were ten again. "So what's on your mind, sweetheart?"

Ally used to think her impulse to spit in his smug face was a sign of insanity. She'd since learned that he simply had a *particularly* spit-inducing face. She cleared her throat and forced herself to face the swamp of his eyes. "I am here to inform you of a decision I have made."

His eyelid twitched with a flicker of anger before his sickening smile regained control of his expression. "How very worrisome."

Ally forced herself not to wince. His closeness brought back memories of a different life, a different war. One that she had won.

"Josefine is the powerful daughter you've always hoped for, but we're finding ourselves in dangerous wartimes and—"

"A war you started, my pet." Another evil sting shot through his gaze.

"I'm aware, but—"

"You're regretting it dearly? I thought so. So what's that silly idea of yours?"

His face moved closer, a minuscule amount, but enough to unsettle her. She jumped off the chaise lounge and stepped away from him toward the silly tea set. As soon as he was out of sight, his control weakened. She inhaled deeply and allowed the breath to travel down to her stomach, where Robert had planted the seed of a new life. One that Josef wouldn't befoul. *I might as well let the fucker dangle . . .*

She picked up a brown macaroon from the tea tray and sniffed it. The sweet, roasted scent of chestnut filled her nose, and she smiled. On a regular day, she would have been too paranoid to eat it, but today she was in charge. Josef wouldn't dare to experiment on her under the eyes of royal guards on semipublic Council grounds. She popped the macaroon in her mouth and made him wait for an answer. The nutty, buttery taste melted on her tongue. She turned around and watched him awkwardly stand up from his crouched position. She savored the bits of pastry and power.

"Pet, what—"

"The Verdain family line has to be preserved, so I've decided to have another child." She did the interrupting now. "I have already informed Josefine." Her daughter had chided her parenting abilities but had agreed to the second heir as long as Ally didn't move back to the palace. Even her bullheaded daughter understood that her young age bore a risk to the Verdain line, and Josefine didn't want to birth a child as early as Ally had been forced to.

The statement flabbergasted Josef. It took him a few seconds to find his words again. Ally used the time to pour herself some tea. It smelled of cinnamon and cloves. Her smile widened. Cinnamon was Reggie's favorite flavor.

"Pet . . . I'm not coming to the palace so we can—"

Ally laughed. She felt oddly assertive now that she was out of his reach.

"Oh no, don't be silly, Josef. I know I've grown too old for your taste." She winked at him. She could have elaborated on her plan but decided to eat another macaroon first. Josef's uneasiness was too much of a treat for her. After the macaroon, she took a sip of the tea.

"Alexandra?" His impatience grew, and so did Ally's smile.

"Pardon me, did you not offer your hospitality a moment ago? Or did that only apply on your terms?"

Josef's lips grew thinner. His smile turned into stone. He opened his mouth to answer, but Ally was quicker.

"It doesn't matter. I've decided to conceive our next heir through the Ceremony, like Queen Theodosia did."

"What, have you suddenly turned into a dyke, pet?" He scoffed, barely able to conceal his anger.

"I would be careful speaking about Verdains in that tone. Aren't you pretending to be one?"

Josef gripped the chain of his watch and inhaled sharply.

"We don't reside in the same place anymore. The Ceremony is only logical," Ally continued.

He shook his head and approached her. She forced herself not to budge. "What about your war?"

Ally swallowed. "General van Auersperg will take over the front." She hadn't intended to present her gamble as a fact. She had no reason to believe Subira would leave the base and rise to the occasion, but Xenia was starting her training at Altor Caedem soon and Ally hoped her friend would crave more than her dubious marriage.

"Harald won't like that," Josef said.

"I'm not asking the Council for permission. I'm asking my husband."

He caught a white strand of Ally's hair that had fallen out of her plait and pushed it behind her ear. She clenched at his touch. "If your confused little mind wants another child, I shall bear the burden of fathering it."

Her stomach revolted. She was sure she'd gag before catching Robert's eyes behind Josef. He cocked his head, raised a fist, and silently punched it against his flat hand—an impossible but appreciated offer to beat the shit out of Josef. Ally looked back at her husband and giggled.

"No, I'm not lying with you ever again."

Her sudden joy tossed Josef off-balance. She enjoyed his weak attempts to regain it.

"Alexandra, it is highly unconventional to call for a Ceremony when you're married to—"

"Is it more or less unconventional than marrying a child?" She raised her eyebrows. She had never exuded this much power over him, but the military had taught her confidence. It was an intoxicating rush.

The last bit of false sweetness faded from Josef's expression. Ally felt his warm, wet breath on her ear as he leaned toward it. "You've become quite rotten."

A cold shiver ran down Ally's spine. What was she doing? This wasn't safe. She couldn't ridicule him however she wanted. He'd punish her for it. He always did. She closed her eyes and drowned out the questions. They belonged to her old life, to the Ally she'd buried long ago. She could bring her flowers, but she couldn't linger on her grave, or she'd resurrect her.

She opened her eyes and leaned away from him. "No, dear. I haven't become anything. I simply survived you."

He froze.

"Josef?"

He turned toward a painting of Balthos and performed his sign.

"I don't think he cares about your prayers."

Josef inhaled sharply and glared at her. "I don't recognize you."

"Good. Now agree to the Ceremony." Her legs wanted to shake under his gaze, but they couldn't. She wouldn't let them. Just this once, Josef wouldn't win.

He played with the watch chain for a few seconds. "I suppose I have been meaning to test a new invention . . ."

Robert's hand darted to his rifle. Thankfully, the other guards jumped into alertness as well, so he didn't stand out. Josef laughed joylessly. "Gentlemen, please don't humiliate yourselves. I'm referring to the Ceremony. I will test it during my supervision duty. I need to be there, of course, to ensure you're not pulling a trick on me or the Council." She got him. She'd gotten his permission without having to crawl at his feet. Pride rushed through her. "Are you still fawning over that pathetic trickster?"

The pride left as soon as it had arrived. *Reggie.* What if Josef used this to harm him? "I don't know who you're referring to."

"So he no longer finds you entertaining. I'm not surprised," Josef said. Ally hid her relief. "Fine, schedule the Ceremony next month. I will head to the palace." He weighed the pocket watch and stared at Ally one last time. All she saw was a pathetic attempt to regain some superiority. "Well then, I'll send Marzahn to show you the way out."

He left without another word, and the Tidier who'd guarded the room followed. Ally's shoulders relaxed. Victory. At least for now.

Robert stepped over to her as soon as the door locked. "Ally." He leaned in so that the other guards couldn't hear him. "You're okay?"

"Yeah."

"I didn't know he—I thought—" He struggled for words as disgust and hate tarnished his handsome face. "He wasn't a guardian back then, was he?"

"No."

He took a deep breath and nodded. His expression

relaxed back to the Robert she knew. "Permission to break his cock?"

She chuckled. "Denied." She glanced at the door and back before whispering into his ear, "I'll tell you what, how about a little more rebellion later?"

His eyes lit up with a mischievous spark. "Deal."

CHAPTER 19

SACHIHIRO

September 979 - Juyub'Chaj Tribe, Tribu La'am

The heavy breeze from the wild waters ripped the orc's notes out of his hand. He caught them at the last second but crinkled the drawing he kept with them. "Shit!"

He flattened it with great care but couldn't restore the parchment to its original glory. Pier had painted the portrait of Sachihiro's beloved idol, Captain Subira Se'azana, for his twenty-fourth birthday two years ago. Time had not been gentle with Se'azana's depiction nor with the love letter Esperanza had written underneath it. Time hadn't been gentle with him either.

He shifted on the hard volcanic stone and pulled out his quill to carefully retrace the words. He had lost Esperanza. He couldn't lose her handwriting as well. When he finished, it looked as if she had just put down the quill herself. A sense of connection lightened his heavy heart for a moment before it returned to its natural state. The weight of it must've been the only thing attaching him to the ground, for the rest of his body longed to follow his mind and float above the strange reality that had become his life.

His gaze wandered to the village nestled in the volcano's shade—his tribe, Juyub'Chaj. Technically, it was better defined as a town for the number of residents, but Sachihiro preferred to interpret language within the individual and cultural context instead of strict semantics. Eight years at Tribu La'am University and five months of living in the superb capital, Mink'Ayllu, had turned Sachihiro's alleged *home* into a claustrophobic village.

He glanced past the tribe, past the kapok trees restraining it, past the vast forests that kept it from cultural exchange. Like many tribes, Juyub'Chaj existed in a time capsule. Gon loved that about their tribe, but Gon wasn't here anymore.

Sachihiro ran his fingers over the large golden ring in his belly button. His mother had pierced it that morning at the end of the wedding ceremony. From womb to passing, a chieftain's life belonged to the ancestors. He had needed a moment of silence after that, a moment of study and peace. He used to find shelter on their volcano, a little off the path, so that was where he'd gone. He'd climbed past the ravine that had swallowed him two months ago. He'd emerged alive, but there had been no more life to return to, only his new position as the chieftain of Juyub'Chaj. The position that had driven Esperanza away.

Sachihiro had climbed high enough to see the cliffs running down the Tribu La'am peninsula. His quartz spectacles fixed his vision, but unfortunately they didn't let him peek across the waters and fields to Elfentum. He and Esperanza had planned to conduct yearly expeditions into the foreign country. Was that where she'd run to? Had she made her way through the war zone, or was she still in Mink'Ayllu, searching for her Fae roots? Esperanza was a Faemani, a human with Fae blood. After escaping the tribe she had married into, she had sworn to leave this world for the Fae realm. Legends claimed the Elfentum god, Zelission, had splintered the Fae realm off into their own unreachable world. They said it was to protect them from foul Fae magic, but Sachihiro trusted Esperanza's kin over Elfentum's gods.

He wanted nothing more than to open the realm for her and let his sweet vine find her true family. Perhaps she didn't need him for it. Perhaps she could find a portal on her own.

The sight was more pleasant than the thoughts that plagued him. He stretched his neck to spot the astronomy tower of Tribu La'am University beyond the forest. It was unlikely the shape belonged to it, but the beauty of studying language was that he could make himself believe an awful lot if he just told himself so. Somewhere down there was the small cottage that belonged to him. It seemed like years had passed since he had started his professorship and lived with Esperanza in their own botanic sanctuary. He missed waking up to the scent of flowers. And to the scent of her. A philosopher had once said perfection didn't belong in the mortal realm. Maybe that was why he couldn't have stayed. Leaving it and leaving her was the trade survival required.

He looked back at Captain Subira Se'azana's fierce face and wondered if she had ever traded her joy for survival.

"Ey, groomy, I've been looking for ya!" The voice of his childhood best friend, Fabia, startled him, and he slid down the stones. Fabia caught him effortlessly and pulled him back up.

"Whoa, falling for your new wife?" She kept her arm around his shoulders and sat down next to him. He stuffed the papers back into his tweed jacket. Paired with his tribal wedding garb, the jacket looked as out of place as he felt.

"I stopped falling. I already crashed."

"I know our passion hasn't erupted yet, but it won't be that bad. At least we can tolerate each other." She laughed, but it died quickly. "The ancestors always know what's best."

Sachihiro envied Fabia for having accepted her fate. He

wished he had never learned to question, but then he would have learned nothing.

"The ancestors might know what's best, but my mother doesn't."

"Not that again, Sachi. If you weren't her son, you'd be nothing but ash for slandering the high priestess like that."

"That would simplify things," he grumbled. "Also, didn't they try that already?"

"Sachi . . . no one wanted you to fall, but we had to follow the high priestess's light. She is the vessel of the ancestors."

"First of all, Juyub'Chaj ancestors never gave us instructions on how to deal with eruptions."

"Because it wasn't nece—"

"Secondly, my mother is a charlatan."

Her skin, normally the color of dark moss, turned into a light green. She looked up at the sky as if the sun would drop on her. "Don't . . . don't say that."

"Why not? I have semantic evidence. Since Dad died, the messages the *high priestess* channels from our ancestors have changed in rhythm and sentence structure. They use a different vocabulary. My mother's vocabulary—"

"Enough!" Fabia screamed. Sachihiro wasn't sure what had happened.

"Did I make you uncomfortable?"

She stared at him in disbelief, then sighed. "Yes, Sachi, you did. You really don't understand people, do you?"

Sachihiro slouched into himself. He understood language, but most people didn't use it well. "I'm sorry. I thought you wanted to know." Captain Subira Se'azana recommended a logical evaluation of all facts before forming an opinion. At least his textbooks described her that way.

"Enough with the conspiracy theories," Fabia said. She wouldn't understand. Her faith was too tied to her identity, and Sachihiro knew how the crumbling of every piece that once constructed one's identity could sink a person. There was no reason to pull her into the same ravine he had fallen into.

"We have our duty to fulfill," she continued.

"What does Kabil think about this?" Sachihiro's cousin, Kabil, had been Fabia's partner for the past five years—an eternity in an orc's short life.

She looked at him with an expression he couldn't place, but it reminded him of Zazil's whenever he talked for too long.

"Sachi, the Fertility Dance starts soon. Tomorrow at this time, I'll be carrying your child. What makes you think I want to talk about Kabil now?"

He shrugged. "It might help with the act."

She put her head in her hands. "Ancestors, help me. It's that kind of stupidity that led you and Gon to bring humans back to the tribe."

"Zazil is an elf."

"Halfer Ch'ulel heirs! Half orcs. Seriously, Sach, what were you and Gon thinking?"

He had studied communication for years, but it still astonished him that two people could speak the same language and sound completely foreign to each other. He wanted to tell her that Esperanza was so much more than a vessel to create a family with. He wanted to tell her that if, against all odds, his Fae princess had birthed him a child, even the most deformed, absurd little creature would've bedazzled him. But what use was it to toss words at Fabia if they had no meaning for her?

"We have a very different understanding of what constitutes as love," he said instead.

She kicked a dirt clump down the cliff and stood up. "We have a different understanding of honor, that's all."

The quiet echo of a bronze gong reached them. *The Fertility Dance.* Maybe Esperanza had been right to run.

"You deserve to be happy, Fabia."

She scoffed. "Then get your ass up and come with me. You'll be a decent husband, I'm sure."

Decent wasn't a good qualifier for love. He followed anyway.

They were halfway down the path when she stopped. "I almost forgot." She pulled a parchment out of her sachet and handed it to him. "Gon wrote. I made sure the high priestess wouldn't see it, but just this once. Consider it a wedding gift. Meet me at the end of the trail when you're done reading, and don't make me wait!" She rushed off.

Sachihiro ripped the parchment open as quickly as he could. It wasn't in his nature to hold text in his hands without reading it.

Dear Sachi,
Hope you're doing fine. Fine enough, I mean. Miss you. I hope the wedding is nice. Greetings to Fabian.

Love you, Gon.

Dear Sachi,

If you're not fine, I'll come over there and drag your ass to Virisunder with us. See, Gon, that's how you start a letter! I was gonna let them write it, but obviously they don't know how to write letters. They're looking at me like I'm wrong, but a letter implies actually sharing information, doesn't it, Sach? So Gon's wrong. I really need your language skills to back me up over here.

Anyway, I'm still expecting us to meet in Esperanza's secret jungle. I can't believe all five and a half of us are scrambled around the world. I'm saying five and a half because I'm still counting Bandana. That idiot is gonna wake up soon and beg Pier to take him back. Gon says I'm starting to ramble. I'm sitting on their lap while writing this and FINE, GON, I'LL GET BACK TO THE POINT. This big softie over here misses you terribly. I miss Pier more, but you're a close second. We've arrived well in Polemos, and those fools actually made me their assula smith.

She's very talented.

Gon's exaggerating. I'm grateful I haven't blown anything up yet. On a serious note, it's nice that they trust me so much. I admit I'm somewhat liking the job . . . I even got an invitation from Queen Alexandra herself. She wants to have tea with me. She probably just wants to get into my pants. We'll see.

Very understandable.

Thank you, Gon. Now Gon says I should wish you all the best for your marriage, but fuck that. You don't wanna hear that. Things are shitty right now, I know that, Sach. Worse than shitty. Absolute gunk crap. But make sure you're gonna be okay, even if it means being selfish. Don't be a big saddo over there, or I'll come and get you signed up with the Virisunder military as well. It's not so bad, and you won't believe who our boss is: Captain Subira Se'azana. For the first and only time in your life, you were correct. She's not just your imaginary girlfriend. She actually exists. Do with that information as you will.

I love you tons, idiot!

Zazu

He read the letter twice to comprehend the last part. *Captain Subira Se'azana.* How? The records of her career had ended with Captain Subira Se'azana giving birth to her daughter, Xenia. The birth had happened around the same time as the power switch of Virisunder, when Princess Alexandra had ceded to her daughter, Josefine. Sachihiro assumed that Captain Subira Se'azana had focused on her family at that point. It seemed unlikely but still more probable than Captain Subira Se'azana not succeeding at everything she touched. How was she leading the home base of Virisunder now?

I need to tell sweet vine about this. She'll be so—

She wouldn't be excited because she'd never find out. Sachihiro's stories about the great Captain Subira Se'azana had always enraptured Esperanza. Captain Subira Se'azana had been a mythical figure to them. How strange it was that one letter could make the captain real, but no effort could stop his sweet vine from becoming a mythical memory to him.

No effort until now. If he ran away from the tribe and made a name for himself with Captain Subira Se'azana, would Esperanza take him back? Sachihiro inhaled the warm mountain air. It was too late. He had married Fabia that morning. He couldn't do that to her.

Sachihiro, Juyub'Chaj's new chieftain, walked the final steps back to his people like he was supposed to.

The rhythm of the wooden kettledrums accompanied the flickering dance of torches around Sachihiro and Fabia's new bed. Four musicians, the twelve oldest tribal members, and the high priestess had gathered around it. Sachihiro aligned his breath with the rhythm, but the calm trance that bound the community together escaped him. Once more, he seemed to float above it all, observing. Observing how his mother's neck stretched to perform sacred chants. Observing the wishes each person wrote on parchment pieces. Observing the tall bed curtains that would provide them the illusion of privacy.

"Be blessed," Kabil said before opening the curtain for him. Fabia's sister did the same for her on the other side. Kabil reached for Sachihiro's jacket, and he flinched.

"No, I'm keeping it."

Kabil lowered his voice and leaned too much into Sachihiro's personal space. "You're . . . you're *keeping* the college jacket on?"

"Yes."

"To consummate the wedding?"

Sachihiro frowned. "What's your point?" He had to strip off his personality and agenda. He should at least be allowed to keep his jacket on.

The high priestess's throat sung note turned harsh. Kabil

backed off and gestured at the bed. "As you wish, *Chieftain*. I won't question the will of the ancestors."

"Please do. It's quite fasci—"

Kabil pushed him onto the bed. Sachihiro climbed onto the woven bark mattress and sat down with crossed legs. Fabia climbed in as well but lay flat on her side of the bed. Kabil and Fabia's sister closed the curtains. The torchlight still shone through the cloth. It didn't muffle the music and chanting of his fellow tribal members as much as Sachihiro had hoped, but he was grateful it shielded him from everyone's sight.

"Hi there, hubby." Fabia smiled at him. How was she able to do that? She unwrapped the colorful fertility shawl they'd covered her in, unveiling her large, plump bosom. Sachihiro felt a sting of guilt over his reluctance. Fabia was beautiful with her shining white tusks, lively chocolate eyes, and long curly hair, which complemented her curves. He let his eyes wander to the matching bush between her legs, but his gaze stopped at a half-moon scar. She'd gotten it on the day they and Gon had climbed to the waterfall without the knowledge of their parents. She had slipped on a wet stone and scratched her stomach on a sharp rock. Gon had taken care of her wounds while Sachihiro had told her trivia to distract from the pain.

Fabia reached for the cloth around his hips. "Need some help?"

The first pieces of parchment drifted over the bed's curtains and descended on them. It reminded him of the ash that had wafted through the village for days after Gon and Zazil's wedding. The two of them should've been here. They should've consummated their marriage.

Fabia looked up at the parchments. "It's beautiful, isn't it?"

Sachihiro examined the pieces surrounding them. The idea was to conceive the future heir on a bed of wishes from the community. He wasn't supposed to read them, but his eyes wandered over the words. *A faithful partner. Prosperity for the tribe. A healthy boy.* Sachihiro wondered if his mother had written the last one. Probably not. She'd have written something more direct, like *Not someone like Gon,* as if Gon Ch'ulel wasn't the greatest gift Juyub'Chaj had ever received.

"Sachi?" Fabia smiled again. Where was all this smiling coming from? "Would you like to touch me?"

"No."

"What?"

He realized too late that she hadn't wanted an honest answer. "I mean, I can." He reached for her left boob and cupped it. Esperanza was ticklish under her left boob. Touching that spot plunged his Fae princess into giggling fits, the cute kind that sounded delightful when she transitioned into panting. Something stirred under his cloth. *Finally.*

"Let me take your jacket off." Fabia slid it from his shoulders before he could protest. She laid it aside but noticed a crinkling in the pocket. "You brought study materials to your wedding night? Really, Sachi?"

"Don't look at them."

He reached for the pocket, but she was quicker and shifted to look at the papers. Instead of words, the great Captain Subira Se'azana faced her. Fabia's eyes widened, and she scooted away from him. "Who is that?"

"The great Captain Subira Se'azana." He couldn't lie about that. "But it's not what you think."

She glared at him. He tried to read her face. *Anger?* Yes, she was definitely angry at him.

"What is it then?" she hissed.

"I like her very much, but as beautiful as she is, I am not attracted to her."

Fabia raised an eyebrow. "Okay . . ."

"I mostly keep it around for Esperanza's love note underneath."

"*What?*"

The chanting and drums stopped. He probably shouldn't have said that. Fabia's eyes flitted to the notes, and her brows furrowed. "What language is that?"

"Faemani." *Ah, shit.* He definitely shouldn't have said that. The Faemani were nomads who traveled through Tribu La'am, but most tribes mistrusted them. Even Gon had prejudices against them.

"You brought a Fae curse into our wedding bed?"

"I mean, it's not a curse . . ."

Kabil ripped the curtain aside and yanked Sachihiro out of bed. He stumbled to the ground, and the other tribal members stared at him in shock. They had gone through the trouble of writing wishes onto paper and tossing it on his head while he had awkward sex. This constituted as an insult to their huge effort.

"Young Ch'ulel," the high priestess said. Sachihiro hated when she called him that. The formality was incorrect to use for one's son. "Explain yourself."

"I . . ." Sachihiro pushed himself off the ground. "I'm sorry. I see you're upset. But it's not a curse. It's just a love note." He looked at the faces of his tribal members, avoiding their condemning eyes. "None of you thought I was in love with Fabia, did you?"

Kabil growled. "High Priestess, permission to deal with this offense to our community?"

"High Priestess," Sachihiro pressed out. She avoided his eyes. The dismantling of their family had started with his dad's early death, but she didn't have to lose Gon. She didn't have to lose him either, and yet—

"Make your offer, Kabil."

Kabil glared at him. "You have disgraced Fabia. Sachihiro Ch'ulel, I call for the rule of K'aah Ki'ik."

"Wha-what?"

K'aah Ki'ik. The ritual of bitter blood. When a tribal member had dishonored the communal law, a defender could call for a duel to sanctify the tribe. Both contestants brought their weapons to the sacred volcano platform, prayed for ancestral favor, and battled for life.

He'd seen it the day his dad had been killed and had hoped never to hear those words again. The only combat experience Sachihiro had was writing essays on military strategy in his third year at Tribu La'am University. Then there was the time when the dean had messed with Esperanza. He had broken the dean's snow globe, which must have looked pretty intimidating. Unfortunately, Kabil, head of the tribe's warriors, might've been harder to defeat than a snow globe.

"Kabil, I know you're hurt because of Fabia and—"

"You have befouled the Fertility Dance and the honor of our future high priestess. I will not stand for it, and neither should the ancestors." There was no pity in his eyes. Sachihiro understood. It was difficult enough to watch someone else fulfill his dream. It was worse when they treated it like a nightmare.

Kabil brought his hand to his heart and faced the gathered tribe. A request for approval. The villagers hummed, agreeing to give up responsibility. It was easier to leave all choices to the ancestors, but weren't those ancestors former tribal members who'd also lived their own lives avoiding responsibility? Sachihiro looked at them in awe. They had spent the last two hours wishing him a blessed life. Now they agreed for it to be taken from him.

"My groom." Fabia wrapped herself in the sheet and stood up. She had regained her composure quickly. She truly was the ideal chieftain's wife. Why couldn't she be chieftain herself? "Allow me to offer you the ax of my great-grandfather for the K'aah Ki'ik."

Kabil frowned. "Fabia, you shouldn't—"

"Follow the ritual, Kabil. If you are determined to test the ancestors, give them a fair choice." She picked up the shawl, wrapped it back around herself, and took Sachihiro's hand. "Let me show it to you."

She pulled him out of their new shared cabana and toward her old home.

"Fabia, I'm—"

"I don't want to hear it." She pushed him into the cabana and closed the curtain door in case someone had followed them. In a hurry, she grabbed random food items, a blanket, and some tools.

"That's not an ax."

"Not an ax. Good observation, genius. Here." She pushed the supplies into his arms. "You don't want to be here? Then leave."

There were tears in her eyes. "Fabia, I'm sorry, I didn't mean to—"

"Go, Sachi, just go. You think it was hard to let go of that human? She ran, Sachi. She left you! It was over anyway. I had to say goodbye to Kabil for the tribe when both of us wanted to stay together. And you think you're the victim here? Why, because you can't play the smart-ass in that grand city anymore?"

"No, listen—"

"You think you're so much better than us, but you're a selfish prick. Kabil was ready to watch our children grow and treat our family with love and respect. But you? You . . . just go, Sachi. You don't belong here."

She was right. He'd never belonged. He'd always been sure they'd find out eventually. Had he ever belonged in Mink'Ayllu? Or with Esperanza?

"Sachi?" Fabia was waiting for an answer.

"I . . . I don't know what to do."

"That's your problem, not mine. Don't make me responsible for your misery."

She pulled the cabana curtain aside and gestured for him to leave. He tied up the provisions and gave Fabia an awkward farewell pat on the shoulder. Then he ran away from the tribe, into the forest of kapok trees.

How far did he have to run to leave it all behind? Was Virisunder far enough?

CHAPTER 20

XENIA

September 979 - Altor Caedem Military Academy, Virisunder

Now that Xenia was ten years, six months, and three days old, her holy knight duties called. She was ready to become a squire. Unfortunately, knights no longer existed in modern Elfentum, which complicated her endeavor. Xenia had settled for cadet training. For now. Soon the great Princess Josefine would recognize the long-forgotten need for knights and search for a worthy candidate. When that day came, Xenia would be prepared.

"How much farther?" Xenia nagged as she put her head on her snoring dad's shoulder. She had counted each rocking of the horse carriage to pass time but had grown bored with it.

Subira, who sat across from her, sighed. "Just a little longer, honey. We're almost there."

Xenia rolled her eyes dramatically and kicked the fine

leather underneath her seat. Her mother's eyes narrowed, but Xenia ignored her. This carriage ride was wasting too much time, time she could've spent sword fighting or horseback riding with a lance or—

She jumped off her seat and poked her head out of the carriage for the tenth time since they had left home four hours ago.

She peeked at her family's stately horses. Her mare, Page, had to stay home, but Xenia had promised to take her on an adventure next summer. She couldn't wait for her first cavalry riding class. While galloping, wind blew away all sadness and replaced it with pure energy. Xenia closed her eyes and waited for the carriage ride to give her a hint of that feeling.

Something slapped her face, and she stumbled back into the cabin. Her mother caught her. "Careful, honey."

Subira identified the attacker as one of Xenia's new dreadlocks that had loosened from her ponytail. Xenia had gotten them last week to keep her Fi'Teri hair from interfering with knight training—no, *cadet* training. She loved how tenacious and gallant they made her look. Xenia tried to stuff it back into her ponytail, but Subira pulled it closer to examine it.

"Mom, stop."

"It's gotten a bit frizzy."

Xenia's eyes widened. She had to look meticulous for her introduction. Altor Caedem's principal, Makeda Verdain, was only the best general and military strategist that had ever existed. No big deal. Xenia's heart fluttered.

"No reason to worry." Subira pulled a shining glass pipe from her bag and ran the dread through it. The frizz wove itself back into the lock. Subira smiled. "Here, take this with you, but don't let Makeda see it. She doesn't condone magic beyond bare necessities."

Xenia took the pipe from her mother and examined it against the light. Tiny bolts jolted through the glass. "What is it?"

"It's an assula hair accessory. The queen hired a new assula smith for our base, Zazil Revelli. A bit eccentric, but quite talented."

Xenia scrunched her nose. "Aren't the Revellis a shitty Silberfluss family?"

"Language."

"Sorry, Mom. But I thought they were Silberfluss smiths." She hoped her mother wasn't mismanaging the base.

"She's broken off contact with her family. If anything, it's good to have a Revelli in our midst."

Xenia was about to dig deeper when the chime of the coachman resounded.

"Altor Caedem in sight, Lady van Auersperg," he called through the small window that connected the seating area to the coachman's bench.

Xenia's eyes doubled in size. "By Caedem's cat! Yes, yes, yes, yes." She bounced on the seat. Her dad reluctantly opened his eyes and wiped saliva off his chin.

"Wha-what's goin' on?"

"We're here, Dad." Xenia pulled on his sleeve until he sat upright. "We're here, we're here!" She beamed at him.

"All right there, champ." He ruffled her hair, but she pushed his hand away.

"Dad," she protested, elongating the word, "don't mess with the dreads. I gotta look good for today."

He shot a sharp look at Subira, but Xenia pretended not to notice. Her dad had suggested a Virisunder braid to keep Xenia's hair under control, but she'd preferred her mother's suggestion.

The carriage slowed down, and Xenia jumped out before it came to a full stop.

"Honey," her mother called after her, but she'd already hit the ground. She steadied her stance and kept her head down. This was the moment she'd first see Altor Caedem, the moment she'd lay eyes on her path to knighthood. She wanted to savor it to its fullest. Very slowly, with a triumphant grin, she lifted her head. The view took her breath away. Literally. She was looking at an above-ground sewer stream. *Ew.*

"Honey, it's this way." Her mother got out of the carriage. "The road ends here."

Xenia turned around and saw her mother's smug smile. It had been an honest mistake. Xenia had wanted to be ceremonial. *Get off my back, Mom.* Her gaze wandered to the fortress behind Subira, and her mouth fell open. *Altor Caedem.*

She tried to fathom the fortress's glory. It was indeed a sight to savor. The outer wall consisted of shimmering gray stones, each as tall as Xenia. She recognized the gate from afar but couldn't distinguish its details. Next to it were iron-forged shields as wide as ten horses and as high as the wall itself. They'd been attached to the stones, whether as decoration or for the intimidation factor, Xenia could not say. A sword with a delicate rose hilt was painted on each shield. It was the sign of Altor Caedem, a reference to the weapon the former Princess Theodosia Verdain had gifted her general and chosen spouse, Makeda Amanirenas, at the beginning of the Crown War.

Six towers of red masonry reached into the sky behind the wall. A walkway lined with golden spikes connected them to one another. Together they looked like a royal crown. The most striking detail of the whole fortress was the seventh tower, narrow and of marble construction. It rose into the air from the fortress's middle and reached above everything else. An enormous sculpted sword adorned its marble. Xenia couldn't see the hilt but was sure it ended in a rose. She couldn't spot the end of the seventh tower either. Maybe it had no end. Or maybe it ended among the clouds, in a grand office for Caedem to do his paperwork in. Soul categorizing and such. Judging misbehaving elves when he was bored. Xenia decided that when she grew tall enough to spot the tower's roof, she'd sneak up there and demand that Caedem make her a knight. It would take less work than studying for cadet exams.

Xenia rushed toward it, ready to storm the fortress and claim her eternal glory. Her mother stopped her.

"Your luggage, honey." She handed Xenia her viola, training sword, and Lady Icicle, the one toy she had kept. It was important for a knight to stay connected to one's trivial joys and to common folk who liked music. Then she ran down the path.

She stumbled when she got close enough to see the gate's details. A beautifully adorned statue decorated the middle of the tall ebony wooden door. It was a blue-painted lady with her hands stretched toward the sky. Delicate drapes covered her body, which curved as if she were dancing. Her hair was painted in the same blue and brushed over her ankles.

"It's the Lost Goddess, Alames." Her mother had caught up with her.

Xenia gaped at her in awe. "It's the goddess from my picture book."

Subira smiled. "Yes, it is."

One day, she'd be a knight worthy of representing Alames. She became painfully aware of the doll in her arm and hid Lady Icicle behind her back. Alames deserved a proper knight. Gallant courtiers often stood with one arm on their back. It was noble. Not weird at all. She was adjusting to the atmosphere.

Her dad caught up, groaning under the weight of Xenia's trunk. Perhaps she shouldn't have packed so many adventure books. Then again, her mother carried all of Xenia's training gear and seemed fine. His old wounds must've been acting up again. It was a downside of being a war hero.

Subira put her hand softly on Xenia's shoulder. "Would you like to do the honor of knocking?"

Xenia bit her lip. This was it. She took a deep breath and reached for the gate's handle. It was shaped like a piece of jewelry around Alames's ankle. The goddess must have had some strong ankles because this handle was heavy.

The gate took hours to open. Or perhaps a few seconds.

Xenia lost her sense of time when she got excited. The doors opened inward and split Alames in half. Behind it stood four older-looking cadets.

"Holy Calliquium, she's here!" A short old Fi'Teri woman with a frizzy silver-streaked trim and a ridiculous amount of weapons strapped on her body hurried toward them. The lines on her face marked that she had passed the elvish age of 150, a rare sight for someone involved in the military.

"Subi, my lovely Captain Se'azana, come here." She pulled the surprised Subira into a tight hug. Together, the heavily armed women made for a terrifying sight. "It's been too long, my dear."

The hug went on longer than good manners suggested. Xenia glanced at her dad, who shrugged, as lost as she was. Perhaps it was an old teacher of her mother's.

Xenia noticed her mother's eyes were wet and shimmering when they pulled apart. "I know. I've been meaning to visit, but the base keeps me busy."

"Does it? I imagined you'd be bored by now."

Subira smiled faintly. "It's *van Auersperg* though. How many times do I have to remind you?"

The woman's face dropped, and she glared at Gustave. "Oh, you're still around. I'd say good to see you, but I pledged to honesty." She looked at him as if he were an unpleasant insect. Xenia broadened her chest. Did this woman not know her dad was a war hero?

To her surprise, Gustave stumbled and dropped Xenia's trunk. "Right, yeah . . . great to see you again, General."

"The detention room still knows your name, Gustave."

This was too rude. Xenia stepped forward and discovered that she was taller than the woman. She stood with strengthened confidence and placed her nongallant hand on her hip. "Excuse me, madam. I don't know who you are, but my dad is a war hero, and you have no right to talk to him like that. Just because you carry around a whole armory doesn't mean you know how to use it."

The woman's eyes pierced through Xenia, and her mouth curled into a small grin. "You must be Lady Xenia Evelyn van Auersperg. I can see you have your mother's bravery."

My mother's bravery?

Subira cleared her throat. "Honey, may I introduce you to General Makeda Verdain?"

Xenia laughed. "*The* General Makeda? Yeah, sure." There was no way this short old woman could have brought Elfentum to its knees. Her mother gave her a deadly look, but the woman's expression remained soft.

"Not quite what you expected, young soldier?"

Xenia choked on her laughter. *Wait, really?* She noticed the crimson emblem of Virisunder's military on the woman's chest, and her stomach dropped. *Crow poop, it is her.*

She jumped into an awkward combination of a bow and a curtsy. "G-general, it is an honor to meet you. The first book I ever read was about you and Queen Theodosia. It was kind of a children's fairy tale, b-but I've read more historical true stuff about you since." Xenia stretched out the hand she had kept behind her back, oblivious to Lady Icicle. Her cheeks warmed when she noticed it, and she panicked. Subira shifted one of Xenia's training bags and snatched Lady Icicle with her free hand. Makeda pretended nothing had happened and shook Xenia's hand, her grip much firmer than her appearance suggested.

"Welcome to Altor Caedem, soldier. I have high expectations for you, seeing as you're Captain Se'aza—excuse me, Captain van Auersperg's daughter. She was one of the best students I've ever had. My personal protégé, if I may say so, and I may."

That seemed unlikely, but Makeda spoke with such sincerity it was difficult to doubt her words. Subira managed to anyway. "Enough with the flattery, General. Plenty of talented soldiers have walked through this gate."

To Xenia's relief, Makeda let go of her hand. Another second and Xenia might have fainted in admiration.

The general clicked her tongue. "True, but few can knock out a group of four Sap Bürüy cadets three years their senior. Especially not in a way that ensured their long-term health and spared me an awful amount of paperwork. You're one of a kind, Subi. I hate to think people are making you forget that." She glared at Xenia's dad, who walked up to Subira's side and wrapped an arm around her waist. Xenia's chest fluttered. They hadn't been this close in months.

"My Bira truly is." He kissed her cheek. Subira looked at him with the loving gaze she barely used.

"Well," Subira said, "the cadets shouldn't have sneaked into the kitchen before mealtime." Xenia caught the inkling of a proud smile on her mother's face. She'd never seen her like that at home but had to admit that it suited her well. "I took my dishwashing duties seriously."

Makeda shook her head. "You take everything seriously, my dear."

"It comes with the trade."

"Does it? You should see me on musical nights! I turn into the next best jester."

"I remember that."

"Right . . . you and my little Ally could never get enough of the performances, could you?"

Xenia's eyes lit up. "Musical nights?"

Her dad let go of her mother and squeezed Xenia tightly. "You know, champ, your daddy was quite the bard in his youth here."

"That's great, Dad," Xenia answered, trying to sound enthusiastic. She was busy picturing Makeda performing on stage.

The general's smile faded. "Let's get inside. I'll introduce you to your confidant. She'll show you around." She headed into the fortress with unexpected speed. Xenia rushed after her while Subira picked up the trunk Gustave had dropped.

"What's a—" Xenia shouted after Makeda before the interior of Altor Caedem overwhelmed her. There were seven large archways around the circular entrance yard. Two stone knights guarded each arch. Above them were illustrations of Elfentum's ruling pantheon and the virtues they represented: Balthos, Caedem, Exitalis, Calliquium, Squamatia, Zelission, and Tiambyssi. Through each archway, Xenia spotted training grounds. Behind Caedem's archway, a group of children her age marched in shining uniforms. Behind Zelission's was a paddock with white stallions trotting noble steps, and behind Calliquium's she spotted a circle of students jotting down notes during a lecture. She didn't know what detail to marvel at first.

The fortress itself had three stories. She saw students in every window, so many soldiers, so many future fellow knights. Her heart jumped. The most attention-drawing detail of the entrance yard was a golden fountain with a marble statue on top. Xenia recognized the fine features of Queen Theodosia. She sat on a throne while water gushed around her.

"Heidegger is still nagging me about it," Makeda said to Subira, "but there's no way I'm taking my beauty down."

Xenia wasn't sure what the head of the Council could have against a fountain that magnificent, but she agreed with Makeda wholeheartedly. She stared at the beautiful woman and ran into Makeda, who had stopped abruptly.

"By Caedem, forgive me, General. I'm sorry." Her cheeks warmed, but Makeda didn't seem to notice. Her eyes were pinned on a boy and a girl sitting on a corner bench. It was a human boy with a friendly but nervous-looking brown face and a chubby, broad built. He was shielding an elvish girl.

"Chimalli!" Makeda snapped. The boy jumped and revealed the girl. She quickly hid something behind her back. The girl was a Vach da tìm elf with intelligent dark eyes and long black hair that shimmered blue in the sunlight. She couldn't have been much older than Xenia.

Makeda marched toward them. "What are we hiding here, Lady Phamlang?"

Xenia gulped. Makeda had changed from charming to

scary in a second. The boy named Chimalli seemed to agree because he stammered, "It's n-nothing, General. Re-re-really . . . nothing. We w-were just—"

The girl moved in front of him and faced Makeda directly. "Oh hush, Chi. It's a project I've been working on for Forging and Mending with Professor Calesvol, General. See?"

She revealed an ordinary training dagger. Xenia was disappointed. In the girl, not the dagger. She had expected something nifty.

"Very well, Lady Phamlang," Makeda said. "Chimalli, you have to stop babying her from now on. She's getting her own charge today. I introduce you to Lady Xenia Evelyn van Auersperg."

Xenia's stomach leaped as the four new eyes darted to her. She had lived in Polemos's noble district her whole life. People had known her name before she had made her first memories. Not here. There was so much to prove. She was a blank canvas, and she sure as limbo wouldn't spill any ink on that canvas. She puffed out her chest and offered her hand.

The girl glanced at Chimalli skeptically before shaking Xenia's hand. "Oh, Professor Knigge will love you. She teaches Manners. I'm Nobuko." She leaned in closer while Makeda explained the school's architectural changes over the last decade to Subira. The next words were only for Xenia's ears. "And if you're not a snob, I might be nice to you too."

Did that Vach da tìm girl dare to threaten a future knight? Nobuko winked at her. Yes, she did.

Chimalli shook Xenia's hand next. His palms were large and a bit sweaty, but she liked his enthusiasm. "G-great to meet you, X-en-enia. I-I like your hair." Xenia smiled. She wasn't sure how to feel about Nobuko, but this boy would make a great future squire.

Subira interrupted Xenia's acquisition of potential entourage. "This is goodbye, honey."

Xenia looked up at her mother and found her brown eyes swimming in tears. Military leaders weren't meant to be weak and knights even less so. Why didn't her mother understand that? Xenia wouldn't embarrass herself in front of General Makeda.

She shrugged. "See you at Treaty Day, Mom."

Her dad opened his arms. "Come here, champ."

She briefly glanced at Nobuko, then gave in and hugged her dad tightly. She held him longer than planned. Somewhere inside of her a ravine opened, and she felt her childhood slip through it. She thought of yesterday's prayer before dinner. The moment had breezed by without fanfare. She recognized now how irreplaceable it had been.

"I love you, Dad," she whispered in his ear. He swayed with her and laughed. "Love you too, champ. You're daddy's pride. Don't you forget that. Best thing that ever happened to me. Now go kick their asses." His voice was throaty, and his breath reminded Xenia of her grandma's legendary rum cookies. She laughed as well.

She let go of her dad, and with him the last bit of familiar comfort. Subira was looking up to the sky, tapping her middle finger rapidly under her eye to cover up the embarrassment she'd spilled. She gave her a forced smile when she noticed that Xenia had let go of her dad. "I know you're excited to practice whenever you want, but don't skip the meals."

Xenia rolled her eyes. "I know, Mom."

"Listen to the professors and follow all the safety precautions. They were set in place for a reason."

Xenia groaned. Her mother couldn't have minded the separation much if she used their last moments for pointless nagging. Xenia turned to Makeda and Nobuko instead. "I'm ready."

The general shot a glance at Subira and cleared her throat. "Finish your goodbyes, Lady van Auersperg; there's no reason to rush. When you're done, Lady Phamlang will show you the grounds. I will see you in the grand hall for the midday sermon." She looked at Subira. "Stay until then, dear, please."

Subira bit her lip. "I'm not sure——"

"Join us for a hot chocolate. Theo would be overjoyed to see you again. You know how the exile weighs on her . . ."

The general drank hot chocolate? Even better, the queen did as well. It was Xenia's favorite drink. Clearly, she was already suited for knighthood.

"We should be going, Bira. Long ride," her dad said.

"Another time, General."

Makeda grabbed Subira's wrist. "Remember what I taught you about choosing allies? It is easy to mistake them for enemies."

The general is so wise. Xenia couldn't wait to study under her.

Subira grew stiff but nodded. Had her mother faltered at the base? The war against Silberfluss was awfully stagnant.

Her dad took her mother's other wrist and pulled. "Come on, Bira."

"Gustave, I sharpened my daggers this morning and you look like you could use a closer shave," Makeda hissed.

"What?" Xenia asked.

Subira laughed. "That was very amusing, thank you, General. Come on, honey, let me give you a hug." She pulled her wrists free and embraced Xenia. The hug smothered Xenia, and in it lay a desperation that tightened her throat.

"Love you, Mom," she whispered as quietly as possible.

Subira sniffed and hugged her even closer. "I love you too, my little miracle."

"All right . . . all right, Mom. That's enough."

Subira let go of her and mumbled, "Goodbye, General," to Makeda. She turned toward the entry gate.

"Wait, Subi. Has Ally told you?"

Subira stopped. "Told me what?"

Makeda exhaled, exasperated. "Would it kill you two to communicate properly? For Caedem's sake! All right, but when she tells you, consider what it could mean for you. Don't let this chance pass, my dear. It might be the last one you get."

Subira frowned, nodded, and rushed toward the gate. Makeda glared at Gustave. Xenia realized that this was indeed the gaze that had brought Elfentum to its knees. It was impressive, uncomfortable, and misplaced. It wasn't her dad's fault that her mother was rude enough to refuse hot chocolate.

Gustave cleared his throat. "I better go too. Nice seeing you, General."

Makeda's upper lip twitched as if she were about to snarl. Gustave tousled Xenia's hair one more time and left.

Xenia watched as their silhouettes disappeared beyond the gate. If her life was a picture book, the next chapter started now. She didn't know the Xenia in it yet, but she was excited to get to know her.

CHAPTER 21

ALLY

September 979 - The Palace of Virisunder, City of Polemos

A sizzle ripped Ally out of slumber's last comfort. She opened her eyes and found herself in a smoke-filled chamber. Vapor crept toward her, dissolving any object in the sparsely decorated guest room Josefine had provided. Ally tried to lift her feet. Then her hands. Then her head. Her body refused to respond to her demands. The paralysis birthed panic in her chest. She screamed, but only a whimper escaped her lungs. On the second attempt, no sound came out. Ally felt the motion of her vocal cords, sensed the air moving up her windpipe to carry the sound, but nothing happened. Was this a dream, a hallucination, or a spell? Josef was staying at the palace. Had he ambushed her? But how had he gotten past her guards? No, this must've been a dream. *Wake up, wake up.* If this was a dream, the more she struggled to move, the more she was teasing her thalamus and cortex to drag her down deeper. She took a deliberate breath and focused on it passing through her. Her body responded in an instant, and she shot straight out of bed.

The chamber looked like it had the previous night. No smoke, no destruction. She sighed in relief and sat back on the bed. *What a way to start the day.* She stroked the small bulge on her stomach. "Minds are fascinating weapons, aren't they, little one?"

The embryo had no opinion on the matter.

A knock on the window caught her attention. It was a purple sparrow, too charming a curiosity to be a hallucination. She allowed the bird to enter, but as soon as it flew into the room, it disappeared into a poof and left a scroll floating through the air. She snatched it and smiled to herself. *Reggie.*

GOOD MORNING, NOBLEST, DEAREST, MOST MAJESTIC, AWE-STRIKING, COURTLY, DIGNIFIED QUEEN ALEXANDRA VERDAIN OF VIRISUNDER. THE DONOR OF YOUR BABY GRAVY IS ON HIS WAY.

~ REGINA THE GRAND

Ally laughed right as the scroll ignited in painless blue fire and evaporated into a single rose. The seductive smell sent a warm shiver through her insides. Her laughter caught. If everything went well, Reggie could join her during the pregnancy and the child's early years before Ally would have to return to her duties. They could pick up where they'd left off. Her heart ached to share time with him once more—to explore the city disguised as commoners, to discuss the secrets of their world, to find refuge in each other's arms. It was a prospect too blissful to hope for, yet it wasn't quite enough. Another longing had stolen its way into her heart, and she wasn't sure if they could coexist.

There was another knock, this time at the door. She picked her night-robe up from an armchair and wrapped it around her body. The night shift guard poked his head inside.

"A Sir Omarov requests an audience, Your Majesty. Should I send him away?"

Her eyes flitted to the copy of *Defiance of a Rose* on her nightstand. It hadn't been as bad of a read as she'd expected. In fact, the way Sir Omarov used the extraordinary speed of his racehorses to summon magic implied fascinating physical theories.

"Let him in. Captain van Auersperg has sent him as a potential diplomat to discuss the temporary truce." She wasn't sure why she'd offered so many details, but the scheme tickled theatrics out of her.

The guard nodded and allowed a burly elvish man with a Sap Bürüy kalpak hat and a ridiculously long mustache to enter.

"Thank you, that's all for now," said Ally. She kept a serious face until the guard closed the door, then started giggling. "Good morning, Robert."

He scrunched his nose and tipped his head from side to side as if he was torn between embarrassment and amusement. He gave in to the latter and twirled the mustache.

"Well hello, my dear queen," he said in a pitiable Sap Bürüy accent.

"Let me guess: the mustache was Reggie's idea, the pseudonym yours, and you are both utterly ridiculous." Reggie had done a fantastic job at disguising him. Nothing reminded of Robert Oakley but the shimmer of his picture-book eyes.

"I thought you liked fools."

She smiled. "I do."

He tucked a hair behind her ear and leaned forward.

"May I?" She nodded, ready to sink into his kiss. The massive mustache blocked most of his lips and tickled her. She pulled away laughing and shook her head. "Too silly."

Robert clicked his tongue. "Reggie is a clever bastard."

Ally's smile faded, and she turned away from him, toward her closet. She searched through her clothes and settled for a burgundy silk dress. It would adequately hide her slight baby bump. "We should go over the plan. You need to head to the main entrance soon for the registration check."

"Yes, I . . ." He sighed. "Ally, what's going on between you two? Are you two . . . I mean, are we? What are we?"

She avoided his eyes and laid the dress on the bed, next to Reggie's rose. She had tried to rid herself of love, for she had nothing to offer it. She wasn't sure how she'd ended up with two contenders instead.

"I know this is kind of a bold question from me, but he's a jester, so he's not exactly less bold . . . and I wanna know, when it comes to the baby, if—"

"You're both parts of lithium to me," she said quietly. "I don't know how to split the atom yet, and I'm not certain it'd be beneficial." She glanced at him. "I'm sorry."

He dropped his shoulders at the last sentence. "It's all right, I get it. I mean, I don't. I have no idea what you're talkin' about, but I promise to hit the library tonight until I decipher that rejection."

"It's not a rejection. It's an improbability." She took his hand. "Lithium is is an element whose subatomic particles come in groups of three, just like Reggie, you, and—"

"Ally, no offense, but let's drop it. I'm here to protect you and my child. I guess I'm happy to do just that." He gave her a disingenuous smile that turned her stomach. "Let's go over the plan, all right?"

She let go of his hand and nodded. "Of course. You have the forged papers? Let me get your invitation."

Stepping into the palace's grand hall was like stepping into a past version of herself. The Ally that had once existed, laughed, and cried under the ornamented ceiling was preserved here. War hadn't touched that Ally, but it hadn't strengthened her either. The tapestry had watched her first dance with her dad, her first one with Josef, and her first with Reggie. The wooden tiles that depicted Virisunder's illustrious history hadn't noticed her light feet when she'd first stepped onto them and had groaned as she'd begun to stand her own ground. Today it would have to withstand a new Ally.

Prospects filled the hall when she arrived. Adult noble men of all ages had gathered for a chance to father the next Verdain, or at least, to claim they had. She understood what had driven her grandmothers to invent the Ceremony, but the men's motivation for attending was silly. They'd come for some elusive concept of pride and honor.

A hush fell over the crowd as Ally's guards guided her past them. She'd become accustomed to holding military speeches but had forgotten how nerve-racking the royal court could be. Everyone watched her, eager for her to make a mistake. No, that wasn't why they were here. They were eager for—

She stopped herself. That thought was even more unnerving. She sped up until she reached the royal podium with her old throne. It remained empty, as Josefine had chosen not to attend.

Ally scoured the hall for a sight of Robert among the excited and overly confident faces. She was grateful not to be participating in an actual Ceremony but still had to pick four men besides Robert as potential fathers. They would be sent to five selected rooms and blindfolded. After the selection, Ally and four other noble women would meet the Ceremony cleric, drink the fertility elixir, and pick a door. The cleric would blindfold them as well, and they'd receive twenty minutes to stumble through the dark and conceive an heir. What a pleasure. She hoped Reggie was correct and their plan would work.

Ally had met the other women prior to the Ceremony. Their reasons for being here were more understandable, but the idea of actually participating gave Ally shivers. Two women were lesbians—like her grandmothers—one had an infertile husband, and the last one was a widowed heiress who refused to remarry. The blindfolds protected the royal family from foreign claims to the throne. Ally had no idea why all participants had to be noble if anonymity was protected. *Silly.*

"Good morning, my pet." A hand crept around her waist. One nail pressed into her side under her corset. She glanced at Josef's swamp eyes and forced herself not to sink.

"We're not going to behave like a bitch today, are we?" he whispered into her ear.

Ally swallowed. Her heartbeat sped up, and sweat pearled underneath her corset. She wasn't sure if the heat came from her pregnancy or repulsion. *He can't hurt me anymore. He can't hurt me.*

"I don't know, Josef. Were you planning to?"

His face fell. Ally stepped forward before he could respond and stretched her arms toward the men. "Welcome, honorable prospects! In the name of the royal family and Virisunder, I thank you for the selfless service you have come to offer." *Thank you for your sperm.*

She tried to remember the rest of the sacred scripture. The Ceremony breached Balthos's family laws, but her grandmother Makeda was a pious woman and had found ways to interpret the god's sacred texts differently. As awkward and odd as the whole event was, Ally couldn't deny that it had been birthed from love and defiance. She didn't want to change a word.

"Seeds blossomed in the first garden that our beloved Balthos and his Alames lay in. Their love touched the soil and turned it fertile." Ally took a deep breath. She was grateful the little one wasn't plaguing her with morning nausea or else she'd gag on the next words. "The love my dear husband, Josef, and I share has done the same. Our garden shall now be planted with a new lineage to blossom." She wondered how Theodosia had felt reciting the scripture. Had she been nervous or believed in it wholeheartedly? Either way, it had brought her Ally's dad. What would he have thought of this?

He'd be so disappointed.

Ashamed of you, lunatic!

Ally gripped her chest and took another deep breath. She could hear muttering from the crowd.

And now you trapped Robert in this as well. He doesn't want to be here. You know that, right?

She does. She just doesn't give a shit.

"Your . . . service secures the honor of our future generations and—"

The voices screamed so loud her brain registered ear pain. A shudder ran through her body. Some prospects laughed. The sound was dizzying. Before she could steady herself, the men's laughter turned into uncontrolled coughing.

"Careful, fellas, mockery is a choking hazard." Reggie strolled through the hall's entrance and gave the guards a cheerful nod, which they reciprocated. He had a better grip on the palace staff than Ally, Josefine, or Josef. The men's coughing stopped, and they quieted down, humiliated.

Ally smirked. "Bored Reginald, lovely of you to join, but we're in the middle of the—"

"You are severely disrespecting the word of Balthos," Josef sneered.

Reggie brought his hand to his chest and gasped. "Oh, my dear king, I am very sorry. That breaks my heart." He pulled a glass heart out of his chest and tossed it over his shoulder. It shattered loudly behind him. "Please continue to honor Balthos, Caedem, and everyone else we deem superior. I just wanted to pop in and see how many of you fine men are staying for the evening show."

Noise broke out as the proper, noble contestants excitedly fought for Reggie's attention. He flicked his finger, and a long scroll appeared. A quill as large as Ally followed with another flick. Reggie moved his arm in an exaggerated attempt to write. "All right, Billy, was it? Yes, I have you down. Steve? Was there a Steve somewhere?"

Josef stomped his staff on the ground and robbed the hall of speech. The air thinned, and breathing became difficult. Josef grinned. "Fine gentlemen, you can worry about the dinner show after you survive the selection." He circled the staff, and the air restored itself. The crowd murmured as panic spread through them.

Ally leaned toward Josef. "What are you talking about?"

His damp hand slid around her arm, and he placed a kiss on her cheek. "Just making sure you're not screwing me over." He released her and turned back to the men. "No need for concern. I believe you are all honest noblemen who wouldn't lie about your heritage. Shall we continue? Jester, you may leave now."

Reggie nodded and created an oversized top hat that he tipped toward Josef. As he bowed, he peered up to Ally and glanced at a man in the hall's right corner. Ally followed his eyes and found Robert glaring at Josef. He seemed too consumed with hate to worry about Josef's implications. Ally's shoulders relaxed. The three of them could handle whatever Josef had planned.

"Cheerio!" Reggie straightened back up and placed the top hat on his head. It widened and swallowed his body, and they disappeared together.

Josef cleared his throat. "We don't want to agitate my dear queen. She needs to preserve her energy, so I will take over for now. Gentlemen, no matter what happens, your sacred duty is to remain unspoken. Your requital consists solely of the servant's honor, and you may not utter a single word during the conception."

Josef recited the rest of the scripture. He made empty

words sound meaningful but snuffed out actual profoundness. Ally was sure it sounded nothing like her grandmothers had intended. Then again, nothing was as intended in this Ceremony.

"Very well, gentlemen, let us get to the selection." He smiled widely at the prospects, but there was an evil twinkle in his eyes. "Step back, please."

"The prospects have already been vetted and have received invitations," Ally hissed.

Josef licked his lips. "Your bastard, my rules."

The men backed away from the royal podium. Josef pointed his staff at the empty space and moved it slowly, with more effort than any of his normal spells required. It looked like he was dragging a body through quicksand. His staff had a glowing glass orb on top with three assulas inside. One flickered with white sparks. They sped up and twirled together in a manic dance, jolting through the orb. For a moment, Ally believed they'd break out and fly away. Instead, a hole opened in the orb, and a gray substance oozed out. It looked like a gas cloud and floated between the men and the royal podium, where it built a smoky fence.

Ally squinted. It wasn't solid but swallowed all light and reflections. A thin layer of white light edged around it. The men's bodies disappeared from her sight behind the gas cloud. She stepped closer and noticed vibrations, as if it repelled surrounding air. There was no green glow to it. No energy rushed through it. The gas didn't consist of assulas.

"You have vouched to be of noble blood. I believe that none of you would lie to our beloved nation. So step forward, and do not fret. My dear wife will make her selection as soon as you have passed the barrier."

The first man glanced around and stepped through it. The smoke retracted away from his skin before it could touch him.

"Josef, what is this?" Ally asked.

Hunger flashed over Josef's eyes. It was the look he'd worn whenever he'd used her for an experiment. Whenever he—

This is my Ceremony. She couldn't relent any power to him or he'd lure her back into the past.

"You'll see when the first commoner steps through it, my pet." Two more men crossed the line, but the majority remained as concerned as Ally about the unknown substance.

She cleared her throat. "My apologies, dear prospects. My husband is overprotective, as you may have noticed, but no one has to step through this against their will."

"Of course, you can choose not to step through, but in that case you will answer the questions of the Tidiers who have agreed to supervise." He clapped his hands, and ten Tidiers entered the hall, taking positions on both sides of the crowd. Ally's eyes met Robert's. He raised an eyebrow and rolled his eyes. It looked odd on him. Perhaps he was still upset over their previous conversation. He must've hated her for having to go through this nonsense when she couldn't even give him what he wanted.

The Tidiers lowered their staffs toward the crowd.

They're going to kill Robert. They're going to kill them all.
This is your fault, you stupid harlot. You killed him.

"Josef"—Ally forced her voice to remain calm—"this is a contest of conception, not a trial. You can reassure your virility in your free time."

He ignored her and gestured at the prospects. "Step through it, or we will have to assume you deceived Her Majesty."

Three more passed unharmed but were paler than they had been before. The fourth refused. "What does it do?"

"Step through," Josef demanded.

The man crossed his arms. "I want to know what it does first."

Josef waved at a Tidier to take care of him. She circled

her staff, and a green glimmer shot around the man's throat. He struggled to get it off, but the light burned his hands as he tore at it. It choked him until his eyes rolled backward. He collapsed, dead. Two other Tidiers picked his body up and carried it off.

Shit, shit, shit. This wasn't what she'd wanted. She was responsible for the man's death and any other that didn't fulfill the requirements. *Robert.* She needed to get him out of there. He wouldn't make it through the barrier. No matter what it did, he was an Oakley. A commoner. He'd fail the test. She needed a distraction to get him out of the hall. The Ceremony could proceed as planned. She'd endured worse. Where was Reggie? He must've known that things were going wrong.

You hurt him, and now you kill him, you heartless monster.

The next ten prospects stepped through the barrier without hesitation. When the eleventh tried to pass, Ally understood what the smoke was made of. As soon as the man stepped into the barrier, it devoured his body. The substance curled around his skin, swallowed it until nothing remained. Every part of his body disappeared. Golden light strings burst out of him and were sucked deeper into the substance. It didn't transport it anywhere, but disintegrated it into parts and deleted it from existence. The substance took his scream as tribute while it absorbed his life.

Kénos. The substance that lurked beyond all existence. Ally had read about its theory. It was thought to encircle all realms but destroy whatever it touched. Nothing was above it. Scholars didn't dare to study it, for even the essence of a celestial could not withstand it. In other circumstances, Ally would have loved to dissect the substance of nothing. Now, however, she had robbed the world, all realms, of a man who would never exist again. And unless she thought of something, the same would happen to Robert.

Josef took a seat on the throne and leered in pleasure. "It works. How lovely."

For a few seconds, the world around Ally ceased to exist. No one moved. No one dared to breathe. Time stood still for everyone but Josef.

"Next," he called, and life continued. Ally didn't know if the men understood what the substance consisted of, but they continued to move through it, shaking and slow, but brave. She had underestimated them.

Ally's eyes flitted to Robert, who was nearing the line. His eyes were closed, and he murmured to himself. She hadn't saved him from the river to erase him. This couldn't be the end of his story.

"Josef, this is heresy. Stop."

"I'm ensuring that no commoners forged their way into the hall."

"Please." The word felt wrong on her lips. "What do you want from me to stop it?"

His cold gaze bored through her. "You've made it clear, my pet, that you have nothing left to give me. I'm testing the kénos. I am curious, however, why the fate of these random men matters so much to you. I wonder if your jester has some answers for me."

Ally bit her lip. "It's cruel, that's all."

He stroked her cheek. "And that, my pet, is not your call to make."

Another scream shook the hall. It came from the second man the Tidiers choked to death. Ally's hands shook. *Do something.*

Do something.

Do something!

Ally had just opened her mouth to renew her protest when a prospect addressed her.

"Long live the Verdains." She shot around to see who the gruff voice belonged to and saw a man with a ridiculous mustache step into the gas.

"No—"

His left leg disappeared into the smoke, and soon the

kénos would devour the rest. She felt something rip inside of her as he vanished into the smoke. Logic evaded her. If he dissolved, a part of her would too. Their last conversation burned itself into her mind. She hadn't meant to reject him. Everything had been so new and strange. She couldn't choose him over Reggie because choice wasn't an option.

There was no scream, no spectacle like the first erasure. The remaining prospects stared at the kénos, unsure if they could proceed or not.

"Sorry 'bout barging in here again." Josef and Ally both startled as Reggie appeared behind them on the podium. He must have sneaked in from the servant corridor behind the throne. "But the cleric's arrived. Ran into him, so I thought I'd let you know, my king."

"Send a servant next time," Josef growled.

Reggie shrugged. "Sorry, I wanted to take a look at the spectacle. My bad."

Ally blinked at him and noticed that a tear escaped her. He knew. He must have known this would happen. He'd said Robert would be fine. He had promised nothing would happen to them.

Josef glanced at her and smiled smugly. "It doesn't seem like the queen wants you here either."

Reggie is a clever bastard. He couldn't have done it on purpose, could he? When Ally had told him about the encounter with Robert, he'd sent back lofty musings about love. She denied, of course, having fallen in love, but Reggie had never regarded Robert as competition. Was this why?

"Sorry, Your Majesty," Reggie mumbled. "I'll see you all tonight for the show. It'll be *Defiance of a Rose* inspired." He had intended to kill Robert all along.

"Leave!" Ally screamed. All eyes fell on her, but she didn't care. They could think her mad. Josef chuckled. He must have hoped the kénos demonstration would drive her over the edge. He could have his victory. It didn't matter.

Reggie stumbled back toward the servant door, and gasps

filled the room. The Mad Queen dared to throw out their favorite entertainer. How could she? Rage rushed through her, and she noticed an itching in her fingertips.

"Your . . . Majesty . . ." a weak voice said behind her. She turned toward the hall, and her heart dropped. Robert, still in his disguise, had fallen out of the barrier. He was pale as a corpse and landed on all fours, shaking but alive. He existed. Another prospect helped him back on his feet. "I seem to have two clumsy feet, Your Majesty. My apologies for holding up the line." He held his side but walked away without clear injuries.

His miraculous passing encouraged the remaining prospects, and the line moved quicker. Ally's world spun. He'd made it. Reggie hadn't betrayed her, but how had Robert passed the barrier? She pushed the questions away for now. After this spectacle, they needed her to play her part well.

Josef was watching her. She twitched her head several times and mumbled unintelligible words to herself. The madder he thought her, the fewer questions he'd ask.

When everyone had passed, Josef twisted his staff, and the kénos traveled back into its orb. *How?*

It couldn't concern her now. She needed to select Robert and four other candidates to get this nightmare over with.

Half an hour later, Ally found herself across from the five bedrooms. The four noble women who participated alongside her awaited the cleric eagerly. One of them leaned over and whispered, "Good luck, Your Majesty," but Ally barely registered it. Her mind hadn't recovered from the shock yet.

The sound of footsteps spared her polite conversation. Josef and the cleric walked around the corner, involved in religious drivel. The cleric was a corpulent elf who had long passed the aging mark. As he grinned at the women, his wrinkles drew large crevices into his face.

"Ah, the beautiful contestants! Ready to receive Caedem's gift of life?" he said, elongating each word melodically.

Ally wrinkled her nose. She would've loved to question the cleric's religious inconsistencies. Why would the god of war gift life? Not this time. She wanted to get the Ceremony over with as quickly as possible and longed to see Robert. She needed to touch him, to make sure he hadn't dissolved.

"Now, ladies, I need you to drink up." The cleric reached into his satchel, pulled out five alabaster flasks, and handed one to each woman.

The lady next to Ally kept it away from her body and eyed it carefully. "I heard this is a tusk brew."

Anger flared up in Ally. "*Orcs*, not tusks. There's no need to use the derogatory term."

"I'm sorry, Your Majesty. The princess uses it, so I thought it'd be acceptable."

Ally blew air out of her nostrils. Of course Josefine did.

The cleric ignored the argument. "Yes, yes, it's a Tribu La'am import, but it has been carefully inspected and blessed. Don't you worry your pretty head, milady." He patted the lady's shoulder, and she relaxed. "Now, ladies and my dear queen, this elixir will guarantee that none of your prunes shrivel!" The cleric laughed, congratulating himself on his supposedly witty word choice. Ally's disdain for him grew. Was he really necessary? The embryo inside her disagreed.

She opened the flask, and the enticing scent of cinnamon and daffodils caressed her nose. It was tempting to drink it, but she glanced at Josef first. Her rotten husband was busy philandering with the widow. If he had tampered with the elixir, he wouldn't miss the pleasure of watching her suffer. She chugged it before more doubts crept in.

The elixir felt like honey on her throat and warmed up the farther down it trickled. It didn't stop at her stomach but sank lower until it created a pulsing heat between her legs. It would have been a fascinating chemical reaction if Ally still cared about chemical reactions. Thoughts of a different sort took over. She exhaled. A man had ceased to exist because of her. Several more were dead. Robert could have been among them. This was not an appropriate time for arousal. Then again, the tension reminded her of the meadow. It made her even more impatient to get into the room.

"You are properly prepared to pick a prospect now." The cleric's voice dampened the elixir's effect. He was awfully proud of his alliteration. "Once everyone has entered their room, you have twenty minutes to conclude the task. Your Majesty, the choice is yours."

He gestured at the five rooms, and Ally's heart dropped. Reggie had said he'd send a sign. The cleric pulled the poshest of the ornamented velvet blindfolds from his stack and readied himself. She clutched her fists. Something heated in her left palm.

"Allow me to ask Caedem for guidance," she mumbled, then brought her hands together in a prayer position. She opened her palms enough to peer inside and noticed a tiny ruby with *2L* carved into it.

Josef sighed. "Can we proceed, please?"

Ally's eyes flitted to the second door on the left and back to her palms. The ruby shattered silently into rose petals, which vanished. She stretched out her hand to the chosen door handle and nodded. The cleric wiggled his eyebrows.

"Are you sure, Your Majesty?" Ally's eyes widened. What did he know? Was he part of this? Did he work with Reggie? Or Josef?

He laughed. "Oh, I adore selections. Everyone becomes so somber about their choice." Ally concluded that he didn't work for anyone. He was simply an idiot.

She closed her eyes and felt the gentle touch of velvet on the soft skin of her lids. She was about to push the handle when the cleric's hand, wrinkled and rough like old parchment, touched her arm.

"Before we get carried away in the joy of it all, let me remind each one of you that the removal of the blindfold is

considered treason, and no word shall be spoken." He chuckled. "And with that being said, enjoy the bumpy duty of life
creation."

Ally cringed. The elixir worked, but it was a miracle children could be conceived in this environment. The cleric was
a personified chastity belt.

When she entered the room, the hallway's tension evaporated. The door lock clicked behind her, and a gush of comforting warm air evoked memories of past blissful foolishness.
Another gush relieved her of her blindfold. She opened her
eyes to see Robert and found Reggie instead.

He crouched against the bed, holding his abdomen and
blinking at her. "Hey, sugar. What a ride, heh?"

She stood frozen for a second before realizing he must
be in pain. She rushed to his side and knelt down. "Reggie,
what happened? Are you injured? Did the Tidiers get you?"
She touched the hand on his stomach, and a pleasant prickle
shot through her.

"Sorry, I know you were expecting Robert and—" He
grimaced in pain.

"Let me see." She tried to push his hand away, but he
kept it in place.

"It's all right, sugar. The trick our ole shit nugget Josef
pulled required my fancy magic goodies, that's all."

She frowned and sat down next to him. "You're scaring
me. First you sent Robert through kénos, then your magic
injures you."

Reggie chuckled. "Well, no need to worry about Robert.
Fool didn't pass the kénos. That was me."

"*What?*"

"I didn't trust Josef, so I switched our places during my
first interruption. Robert was supposed to pop in and tell you
it was all fine while I passed through the kénos. He didn't
handle it as smoothly as I'd hoped though. Once again, are
you sure he's clever?"

Panic rushed through Ally. Robert hadn't almost dissolved. Reggie had. She pictured a world without him, and darkness flooded her mind.

"Ally?"

The corset felt tighter. It pressed all air out of her. He could have been gone. Reggie could have stopped existing. She fought for a breath. "You. Could. Have. *Dissolved*."

"Shh, sugar." He glanced at the door. "I know, but——"

"I don't care. What the limbo were you thinking?"

"I was pretty sure I'd be fine, but I needed to make sure you and Robert——"

"What about *us*?"

Reggie opened his mouth and closed it again. His hand found hers, and he caressed her fingers. His skin was warm against hers. He reached his other hand toward her face, then hesitated. She grabbed it and placed it against her cheek. The blue of his eyes seemed to melt. "I love you, sugar. That's why I'm here."

She choked up. "Promise me you won't risk our future again. Ever."

He brought his forehead against hers. She felt his breath and aligned the rhythm of her own lungs with it. "What if I can't promise that?"

She nudged him. "Then let me believe it, please. You're an illusionist, aren't you?"

He laughed softly. "Something like that."

Silence crept in, and so did her thoughts, eager to spoil the moment. He kissed her before it could happen. Their soft lips found their way back to a time when they had belonged to each other. Ally parted hers and let their tongues dance like they once had among the stars, among the oceans, among the dreams Reggie had created for her. She wished she'd never woken up. But the world needed her. It had back then, and it did now. As much as she wanted to, she couldn't sink into a kiss for a thousand years and let the world fall into ashes.

A tear pearled on her cheek, but it didn't belong to her.

Ally let go of his lips and noticed Reggie's bloodshot eyes. She caught his tear with a kiss before it could roll over the tattooed black rose on his cheek.

"I'm glad the war is over, sugar," he whispered.

She pulled away. "It's not over, my love. The Heideggers still—"

He cut her off with another kiss. "It is for us."

There was too much hope in his voice to correct him. She stroked her stomach and kissed him again. Perhaps a few years of dreaming wouldn't shake the world. Perhaps it could survive without the four of them.

CHAPTER 22

VANA

September 979 - Balthos's Heretics, Correctional Facility, Silberfluss

A drop of filth fell from the cell's memory-stained ceiling and landed on Vana's nose. She startled out of her uneasy sleep. Day one of 7,300 at Balthos's Heretics, Silberfluss's most notorious prison. Or was it night? The cell's darkness held no answers. She couldn't decipher what had happened since her arrival. She'd hit her head when the guards had tossed her in here. The temporary jail had been dreadful, but this stinking limbo hole was worse.

Her vision blurred when she sat up, and vomit crawled up her throat. The hit must have been harder than she'd thought. She felt her way to the cell's corner and puked. It didn't worsen the general stench in the air. Her legs shook, and she braced herself against the moist wall.

"You need hand there?" It was a baritone voice, thick with a Sap Büruy accent.

Vana jumped at the sound and reached for her nonexistent weapon belt. The warden had taken everything from her. The only items she'd received were two pairs of thin prison robes, a vial of oil, five sulfur-dipped pine splinters, and a flintstone. As far as she could tell, there was no source of light in her cell or any of the corridors she'd passed through. She'd received the sparse supplies to light the cell's oil lamp for a few days and would have to rot in the dark for the rest of it.

She forced herself into a fighting stance. If she didn't have a weapon, she could at least punch a fucker.

She squinted into the dark but couldn't make out his face. "Who the fuck—"

"Good morning to you too. You need help? Food is better in stomach than on wall."

Vana's shaking hands searched for the vial. "Stay away."

"You sound young."

"Okay, you're definitely staying the fuck away from me." She found the vial and searched her way to the oil lamp. Instead, she felt a large arm next to her. She punched it as hard as she could.

The man mumbled what sounded like swear words in Sap Bürüy. "Do not punch, little one. Give me moment, okay? Okay."

A second later, the oil lamp lit up and dipped the room in a soft orange color. It reminded Vana of the last sunset she'd seen in freedom. The man who had spoken was indeed a Sap Bürüy human, and a tall one at that. He looked like he'd been abandoned in the wilderness for decades. His black hair and beard were matted with filth and so overgrown they hid most of his face. What the hair didn't cover, burn scars did. He would have looked terrifying if not for the surprising softness in the brown eyes peeking from underneath his bushy eyebrows. He smiled at her.

"You are young." He stretched out his hand. "Hello. Artyom Yuldashev. Nice to see you."

She eyed it. *Fuck, how much worse can it get?* She shook his hand. "Vana Ackerman."

"First lesson." He walked back to his side of the cell. The setup he had built for himself surprised Vana. She spotted a blanket, stacks of papers, quills, a whittled backgammon set, and piles of stones. A pond drawn with chalk and filled with fish and turtles decorated his wall. A tiny doll of indeterminate material sat on top of his makeshift pillow. He must have been here for ages.

Artyom continued to speak as he searched through a sack. "You too trusting. Careful who you shake hand with here."

"Who the fuck put you in charge of lessons?"

He chuckled and returned with a wet cloth in his hand. "Second lesson: do not talk like that if you don't know person's crime. Some bad people around." He handed her the cloth. "Here, for head. Is cool a bit. Not much but should help."

She reluctantly took the cloth. He was right. She'd trusted Isa. She'd trusted Rutilia. How many more times did she need to learn the same lesson? She wouldn't make the same mistake with this guy.

"Then you should take your own advice, creep. I've killed more people than you could dream of."

"Unlikely. And it's Artyom. Although, I am happy with *creep* if it make you feel home. How long you stay at my place for?"

"Your place?"

He shrugged and pointed at his corner. "Is life."

Artyom must've been one of the people he was warning her about. Even the disgusting crime against a noble lady she'd been accused of hadn't justified a life sentence at Balthos's Heretics. "Twenty years," she muttered.

The smile on his face faded. "Too long for little hothead like you." He sat on the ground and invited her to do the same.

Vana continued to stand. He thought her weak, and if

he wasn't at least mildly intimidated, she couldn't protect herself from him. She didn't even know if he was a noble swine yet. The memory of Rutilia's cold eyes sent another shiver through her spine, and she slumped farther against the wall.

"Please, hothead, sit. Is no good to push self after hit."

"Tell me, *Artyom,* are you a Princess Agathe ass-kisser?" She was short of breath but wouldn't give in to the friendly facade he put on. It was another ruse. It must've been.

"Is the princess called Agathe now? Did not know they switch. Of Silberfluss? I have not met an Agathe, so no. I have not kissed that buttocks."

It drew a chuckle out of Vana that shook her body. The small movement was too much for her legs, and they buckled. She sank down next to him and studied him closer. He seemed to be in his late thirties or early forties. Eight long white scars marked his right arm.

"So why did they lock you up?" Vana asked.

"I come to Silberfluss and kill two dozen people with bow. They not like that." There was a concerning amount of pride in his voice.

"Ehm . . . for political reasons?" She could support that. Perhaps he was another lost comrade. *Don't think like that.*

"No. It just make me feel better." He smiled.

"You're . . . you're a mass murderer? For fun?"

"Sorry, I not mean to be spooky spook." He shrugged. "Mass murderer? Depends on who you ask. You ask me, I say no. You ask court, they say yes."

Vana thought about that for a moment. "Why didn't they just shoot you?"

He wiggled his index finger. "My question too. Judge thought is worse punishment for me to be alone with me for all life."

"At least you're human, so it won't be that long."

"You are very rude person."

"Yeah? Well, you're a mass murderer."

Their eyes met, and Vana couldn't help but laugh. He

joined in, and for a few moments the oil lamp's orange hue seemed as powerful as the summer sun.

"Touché. Friends?" He stretched out his hand for the second time.

Vana raised an eyebrow. "How come you shake my hand without knowing what I did?"

He looked her over and nodded to himself. "You are young hothead with big ideas but no idea. Other hotheads with same problem follow you. All of you got into big shit."

Vana gave in and took his hand. "Fine. Friends for now."

What had started as a light hit to the head turned into a bothersome injury and Vana into a useless mess for her first week at Balthos's Heretics. She fought it, but after the third gagging fit, she allowed it to conquer her. Dull pain and dizziness were better companions than the memories that tried to crush her. Jules, her family, Isa, Rutilia, none of them mattered now. None of them were allowed to matter. The headache didn't permit her to process what twenty years in this stinking limbo hole meant, and she was grateful for it. The only question she had to deal with was whether her new friend was bringing her food and checking on her injury to be kind or to murder her for fun.

"Kymbat?" He nudged her shoulder a few hours after lunch and after drowsiness had overcome her. She wasn't sure how long she had slept, but it didn't feel long enough.

"That's not my name," she mumbled.

"No, is not. Is Sap Büruÿ word for precious child."

Vana snorted and turned around. "All right, whatever you say, Dad."

"Don't call me that. We need go, kymbat, come on."

She noticed the frown on his face. Until now, nothing had disturbed his cheerful indifference. "What's wrong?"

He helped her off the ground and examined the side of

her head. "Not look injured, good. Come on, we go to food hall. Look alive, eh? We don't want pesty beasts notice you."

Vana stretched her shoulders and brushed her robe off. "I am alive."

"Good attitude. Keep that. Now come."

Vana hesitated. She hadn't left the cell yet. Bars had stopped her in the holding jail, but Balthos's Heretics had a peculiar design. The cells were open nooks attached to dark hallways. There were no doors, except for the one to the infirmary, and guards only patrolled the dining hall. The prison housed hundreds of criminals, but they had no protection from one another. She wasn't sure where the entrance was. The warden had recommended she avoid common areas except for mealtime, and Artyom had brought her food until now. Would he get in trouble if he murdered her in their cell? Was that why he was leading her out of here?

He snuffed out the oil lamp and headed toward the hallway. Vana bit her lip. It was his advice against the warden's. She sighed. *Fuck the warden.*

"Arty, wait."

"Don't call me that either."

"All right, Dad, I—" She reached the hallway, and her breath caught. It wasn't pitch-black. A faint green glimmer illuminated it. *Magic.* She heard shots and Maureen's scream, and a dead swan stared at her.

"Kymbat, can I put arm around?"

She nodded in the dark, which he missed. *He's got human eyes. Come on, Vana, get your shit together.* More pictures flashed by. Ink and blood and the seax and lust in Rutilia's eyes. "Y-yeah."

Artyom's arm found her shoulders, and he nudged her forward through the hallway. She couldn't see the light source, but it was enough to reveal the many twists and turns of the prison's maze. No wonder she hadn't seen another prisoner. Half of them must've gotten lost in these halls. It reminded Vana of a mirror cabinet she had once visited with Jules. His parents had bought her a ticket. The cabinet's labyrinth had dipped her into a fantastical world where everything was in-finite but nothing was real. This was how she had pictured the mystical Fae realm, if it existed. Jules had also read her a Bored Reginald poem for the first time that day. At night, she had sworn to herself to one day marry a Fae and become a revolutionary like Bored Reginald. She'd since learned that the Fae weren't real, Bored Reginald was a palace sellout, and she was too big of a fuckup for revolution.

Fae . . . bring back my Fae possession . . . A shiver ran down her spine when she thought of the monster in the woods. It must have been an illusion, like the ink and blood that kept drowning her vision.

Balthos's Heretics was the nightmare version of her be-loved maze. Darkness replaced the mirrors. Did it show her real reflection?

Artyom stopped and squinted at her. "You get existential."

"What?"

"Shh." He searched the area. "Where are you, pesty bas-tard?" He peered around a corner into another cell and shook his head.

"What are we looking for?" Fear shot through her. What-ever he looked for, he'd never find. The harder she looked, the more she lost.

Artyom exhaled in frustration and pushed her forward. "Let us keep go. Just ignore. Balthos, look after us."

Vana scoffed. "Yeah, if any shitty made-up gods wanna help us, now would be a good time. Or, you know, ever."

Artyom stopped again and cursed in Sap Bürüy. "Hothead?"

"Yeah?"

"Prison full of believers. You not want to piss them off."

Had they heard her? Was everyone listening? *Fuck, why am I so scared?* This didn't make sense. She forced the anxiety down and spoke as relaxedly as she wished to feel. "All right, but you don't believe in that crap, do you?"

Artyom chuckled. "I'm priest."

"Oh. Wait, but you're a mass murderer?"

"I am not very good priest. But is okay. Just do not yell around blasphemy. Is not good idea."

She nodded, and they continued walking. Her chest cramped up, and her hands shook. She'd never get out of here. She'd thrown her life away for what? She'd only caused more pain.

"Okay, enough. Pesty bastard still bug you, yes?"

"I don't know what you're talking about," she said, louder than intended.

"You do not see them when you come in here? Warden gave me private week with them."

"With whom?"

He let go of her and disappeared into the darkness. Vana's stomach dropped. She hadn't realized how much trust she'd put into her new *friend*. She peered into the dark hallway, unsure which way she'd come from. She'd been walking for a while. The common area must've been close by. It would be safest to find it instead of searching for her cell on her own.

She'd taken one step forward when a high-pitched shriek made her skin crawl. It sounded like the cry of a baby and the screech of a raptor combined. Whatever it was, it needed help. The sound came from another nook. Perhaps several inmates were brawling or it was an ambush on someone defenseless. Ink. Blood. Stiletto knives. *Shut up.* She pushed the thoughts down. Someone needed her. She could still be there for them. She wasn't fucking useless, no matter what Rutilia had said.

As soon as she turned into the cell, two bright green beams of light stunned her. *Shit.* The lights tore into her, and voices pierced through her head.

You're useless.

You killed them all.

You turned Isa into a monster.

Waldfeld is lost because of you.

Jules wanted none of this. You should be ashamed.

Vana sank to her knees and covered her ears, but it brought no relief.

"Kymbat. Kymbat, look at it!"

You fucked your family up.

And now you're gonna die here.

You're letting this random Sap Büruy man kill you.

"Kymbat!" She heard snapping fingers and looked up. The beams were attached to a silhouette. he crawled forward to see it clearer and realized that the light should've shone from its eyes, but it didn't. It shone from charred sockets without flesh. Arms reached for Vana, as if to hug her. She backed off until the creature's silhouette disappeared back into the light. The cracking of bones made Vana's stomach lurch. Another screech.

"Kymbat, I cannot kill thing. I get in trouble. Listen."

"Arty?"

The light beams shook. Vana leaned forward and saw that the arms no longer reached for her. Artyom must have bound them in the back.

You're useless.

Useless.

Useless.

"You need to poke fun, okay? Laugh at them."

"What the fuck are these things?"

Useless.

Useless.

"Look, is gross-looking weird thing. Ha, ha. Can talk inside your head. Very funny."

But nothing was funny. The revolution within her had died, and she'd soon follow.

Artyom coughed a weak excuse of a laugh. "It think it know my Kasanovye. It never met her. Stupid thing. Very funny. Ha, ha. Kymbat? It cannot touch us, kymbat."

"Who the fuck is Kasanovye?"

"Laugh, hothead, go!" he yelled.

**Maybe Kasanovye is his last victim.
Soon we'll be talking about you.**

Vana laughed. Everything inside of her screamed to stop. It felt both impossible and ridiculous. She pressed her hand on her stomach to track the motion. Her belly danced as she released her own weak excuses for laughter. After several seconds, it became genuine, and the voices quieted down.

The lights slid past her out of the cell and left them in darkness. She heard a rustling, and a moment later the small flame of a lit pine splinter appeared. Artyom stepped toward her and laid his hand on her shoulder. He smiled, but his eyes were red and watery.

"Lesson three, good done, kymbat."

"What was that?" Her reason returned to her, and with it a rage she'd thought lost.

"Nachtalb. They are more guards than those few idiots who show up at mealtime. They make you scared until it hurt. Normally, they only haunt you with voice, but they go after inmates who do not behave."

"What did we do?" Nothing justified this.

"A little late for monthly count. But warden might want to mess with you as welcome." He shrugged. "You need learn how to deal. They come after you sometime. Whenever thought that doesn't feel like you comes in, you laugh. Is only way that not lead to madness."

"How do you tell which thoughts aren't yours?"

"If not sure, just don't think. Is dangerous."

Vana shook his hand off her shoulder. "And you accept this? How long have they been doing this?"

He nodded toward the hallway and headed out. She followed with more energy than she'd had all week. Did the courts know what they'd condemned their own people to? They must've. The prisoners' only weapons were wit and community. These monsters had tricked them into disarming themselves. The stinking nobility, the lawmakers, the guards—all of them had punished free thought. They'd burned the soil of uprisings.

"Is prison."

"Fuck this, Arty, seriously. We're people, not test subjects for them to try out their fucked-up magic bullshit on."

Torchlight spilled into the hallway and signaled that they'd almost reached the food hall.

"You have not met others."

"I'm not saying we all deserve freedom, although we probably do, but we all deserve dignity. And—"

"Shh." He held his hand up right before a guard marched toward them.

"Sap, you're late for the counting."

Artyom nodded. "Sorry. Brought new guest, needed little tour."

The guard shoved them into the dining hall. Vana bit her lip. She'd learned not to talk back to these swines, but she wouldn't accept this bullshit. This wasn't a way to keep people. Her heart beat faster. Things were lost if she allowed them to be, but it only took one person to plant the seed of revolution in these scared heads. Rutilia had made a mistake by throwing her in here.

The torchlight in the hall hurt her eyes as much as the green beams had. After a week in her dim cell, the loud, bright, packed space felt like thirty Treaty Day festivals happening at once. It could have overwhelmed her, but Vana soaked it in. Life. It still existed. Those fuckers and their monsters couldn't take it away from them.

Ten long tables with benches furnished the otherwise sparse hall. Vana spotted four supply lifts on the opposite wall with slim metal trays attached to a mechanical loop. This must've been where Artyom had gotten Vana's meals from. Between mechanical feeders and the nachtalbs, there was little for guards to do. The warden had taken all measures to avoid work.

Now, however, four guards and the warden were checking inmates off a list. Artyom waved Vana to get in line with him.

"Why are they counting us?"

"People die. They need know how much new people they can send."

Vana raised her eyebrows. "So . . . people often drop dead around here?"

"Hothead, is best if you keep head down, please."

That's exactly what they want us to do. She didn't protest. If it weren't for Artyom, the nachtalb might have fucked her up permanently. She'd convince him in time. Her eyes wandered over the crowd. To her surprise, Artyom wasn't an exception. The prison was filled with people other than Silberfluss humans. She spotted Virisunder and Fi'Teri elves, half orcs, a couple of full orcs, more Sap Büruy humans, and plenty of Tribu La'am humans.

The line moved up and allowed Vana a closer look at the warden. He was meager with dark rings under his eyes and a long brown ponytail. Vana leaned toward Artyom's ear. "Why don't we just kill him?"

Artyom's eyes widened. "Shh, no, no, do not say that."

"Name?" the warden asked the Tribu La'am man in front of them.

"Why not? It would be easy to take him out. The few other guards too."

Artyom took a deep breath. "Kymbat, is not that easy. Doors locked with magic. Prison is Council-run."

"Ordell Smith," said the man in front of them. It was a strange name for someone from Tribu La'am. Vana focused back on the more urgent matter.

"So?"

"So Council can send Tidiers with all magic weapons, and we are shit of luck."

"Name?" the warden asked again.

"Artyom Yuldashev."

The warden smirked. "Long live Exitalis, the Last Judge. May she await you."

"Does this not get old?" Artyom asked.

The warden gestured to the side, and Vana stepped forward.

"Name?"

"Vana Ackerman. Remember it."

The warden frowned. "Excuse me?"

"Remember it. You'll need to." She memorized the warden's befuddled face and relished it. Artyom cursed to her left. The warden leaned toward the guard standing closest to him. "Keep a nachtalb close to her cell."

"Do your worst," Vana said before stepping to the side. Blood rushed through her. She finally recognized herself again. Artyom pulled her to a table without another word. She noticed several pairs of eyes on her, including those of the Tribu La'am man named Ordell. *Good.* Attention fostered questions, and questions led to rebellion. She'd make her stay here worthwhile.

Artyom noticed the attention as well. "Just like school, eh? Look at new kid."

She wouldn't know, but she wasn't going to tell him that.

"Yeah." She looked around and noticed a group of women sitting near them, a little down the bench. "Do you wanna make some friends?"

"Not particular." He followed her gaze toward the group. "Ah, I see. You are bit of ladies' lady, are you not?"

Heat shot into her cheeks. That wasn't what she'd been thinking. She wasn't going to flirt with anyone. Not here. Or in general.

"Is okay, not worries. But not sure if Erna be happy." He nodded at the muscular gruff-looking half orc who sat on the outer end. Four timid-looking young girls sat between her and another tough woman of Silberfluss descent. They kept a firm eye on a nearby table.

"Saying hello won't hurt." Vana scooted closer to them.

"Good afternoon, ladies. I'm Vana Ackerman. You can call me Vana though." She addressed the burly half orc and reached out her hand despite the discouraging stares.

"We know," the half orc answered, then spit into her hand.

Vana jerked it back and groaned in disgust. "What the f—"

A sour-looking elf lady leaned forward. "We don't need no dykes here."

"Ey!" the half orc snarled. "I told you not to use that word, Maya."

Maya wrinkled her nose and leaned back. "She is though . . . look at her."

"Doesn't matter. She's a perv." The half orc turned back to Vana, who realized what was happening. She threw her hands up.

"No, no, no, you got this wrong. I'm a political prisoner. I—"

The half orc interrupted her with a growl and stood up. She was two heads taller than Vana.

"I get a little tip from the warden every time one of you perverts makes their way in here. We protect our little herd from *your kind.*"

Vana struggled for words. She thought of Rutilia, of the kisses they'd shared, the coldness in her eyes when she'd found Vana useless. She hadn't acted against her will, had she?

"Please, I'm not—"

The half orc stepped closer, her eyes fixated on Vana's. She knew orcs were normal people, but the scary stories she'd heard were easy to believe now. Artyom tugged on her elbow, but she was frozen in place until her look fell on the youngest of the group, a petite Virisunder elf. She gawked at her with fear. Tears shot into Vana's eyes, and she allowed Artyom to drag her away. He led her back into the hallway and shoved her against the wall, firmer than she had expected. His look was wary, hard, and surprisingly terrifying.

"Why you get arrested? Do not bullshit me."

"I didn't—"

"I ask why, not why not."

Vana felt as if she were back on trial at the courthouse. At least her parents had been there with her. "I was supposed to be the Enforcer . . ." Not a good start, but it was the only place her brain took her to. Treacherous tears ran down her cheeks. "My . . . my Jules and I were in a band, The Spirit and the Enforcer, but they shot him. No, *she* shot him. The duke's daughter. She ordered it because she thought I'd be fucking useful. Turns out I'm not, so . . . it was . . . he died in vain."

She couldn't see Artyom's face through her unexpected rainfall, but he had neither left nor attacked her, so she kept going. "She looked beautiful, but she's not. I did go to her after Jules died. I didn't know she'd ordered it. She had invited me, and . . . I was so confused that night. I wanted to avenge Jules, but I attacked the wrong people, and then . . . then at her manor . . . we kissed, but she did it too. She was on top of me. I didn't . . . I don't think I did . . . and then her guard, the one who shot Jules, appeared. And he told her I was useless, and . . . she made them get rid of me."

She wiped her eyes. Artyom studied her intensely. "What she want you be useful for?"

"For her own political bullshit game. She wanted some stupid higher position and needed a troublemaker or assassin or something. But I'm a revolutionary . . ."

Artyom remained quiet for five horrifying seconds. His angular eyes seemed to catch every expression that crossed her face. Vana was about to add more weak explanations to her case when he pulled her into a tight hug. "Revolutionary, eh?" He laughed quietly into her ear.

Her tense muscles relaxed. He believed her. As long as one person didn't see her as a monster, she didn't have to see herself as one.

He let go of her and gently slapped her cheek. "Okay, revolutionary. Do you have plan? Smart one, preferable."

"About how to turn this dump hole around, or . . . ?"

He nodded. Vana looked back at the dining hall. The name Ackerman had been a staple in Waldfeld. It had been easy to make herself known. Here, however, she'd have to start from scratch. Maybe it was a good thing. No attachments tainted her message. Once she'd figured out her message, of course. She took in the crowd of resigned faces. Their hopelessness kept them in place better than any wall could. If she challenged that, if she got them excited about something . . .

"Yeah, I have some ideas. Maybe I'll make a speech when the warden's finished." It had been too long since she'd last stood on stage, assured of herself.

"No."

"I think I could get them to believe in something again if I just—"

"No. Kymbat, you need think first. I have parchment in cell. You write down ideas. We organize. We see from there. Good?"

Vana's excitement deflated. "I can't write."

"Okay, we start there." He patted her shoulder. "You are revolutionary? Revolutionary need reading and writing. After dinner, we start." He trudged back into the hall, toward a table away from the half orc and her protégées. Vana hesitated. If she didn't prove herself now, how could she face them? She thought of Isa and her fervor. Perhaps Artyom was right. Perhaps a revolutionary needed time to grow. Besides, if she learned how to read, she could read Bored Reginald plays by herself, provided she ever got out of Balthos's Heretics.

CHAPTER 23

MARTÍN

October 979 - The Zac-Cimi Hotel, Mink'Ayllu, Tribu La'am

"Needs more salt."

"Needs less sulk."

Martín glared at his sister, Catalina. He used to enjoy kitchen duty with her, but she had this new habit of questioning his life choices. Martín was perfectly capable of questioning his life choices on his own. *We get it. I'm a jackass.*

"Do you wanna fail?" he asked her instead. "Because I don't have to teach you all this stuff, you know." Their parents wanted them to learn all the intricacies of the family business, from intimidating the shit out of rivals to seasoning appetizers.

He tucked a strand of long greasy hair back into his ponytail and snatched the soup ladle from her.

"I can get a lackey for seasoning and sautéing when I run the hotel," Catalina said. "I'm much better at handling

Dad's side of the business, anyway. Give me a good *deal*, and I'm happy." She cracked her knuckles. A slight smile escaped Martín, which was a rare sight these days. Catalina looked sweet with her curly clover-green hair and brown button eyes, but she sure knew how to kick ass.

"Running the business, eh? Isn't that supposed to become my job?"

She was five years older than him. By the time his parents retired, Martín would be the most suited of his siblings to take over. Orcish businesses were passed on to the youngest child because of the short orcish life span. It made little sense to start a career as a forty-year-old with twenty years left at most.

"About that . . ." She swung her arms around his back and swayed him.

"Trying to steal the hotel?"

"Come on, Mart. You'll be eighteen next week."

"Yes, I know what day my birthday is. Thank you."

She let go of him and punched his upper arm. He yowled more dramatically than he had to.

"It's time to stop conning your family."

Martín rolled his eyes. She loved talking in riddles, perhaps to keep the upper hand in every conversation, or perhaps to keep distance. She'd make a fine politician, just like—

There it was again, the dragging pain that started at his heart and pushed into the guilty pit of his stomach. *Shit.* He tried every day not to think of Pier, and every day he failed. Today was no exception.

"That right there! That's exactly what I'm talking about." She pointed at the frown between his eyebrows. "You're not conning any of us, Mart. We know you're unhappy, and I'm sick of seeing you bitter and mopey. I want my stupid, cheerful brat of a brother back."

Martín grimaced. "He's dead."

"At least you kept the melodrama."

He bumped her shoulder. "I want that guy back too."

He had been running from that man and everything he

had stood for. It was easier to be nobody than to figure out who he was without Pier. Becoming a Pier-less Martín required acceptance, and he wasn't ready for it. He spent his days in the hotel kitchen, showing his family love through delicious food and by sparing them his depressing company. It was Catalina's own fault if she came down to bother him. He wasn't happy, but at least he wasn't in pain either. He was just . . . nothing.

"I know it's hard to get back on your feet when an Elfentum flaker dumps you. They don't get how serious this shit is for orcs."

The pit in his stomach grew heavier. Martín had told no one about the incident with the monster. Both his dad and Catalina were too protective and proud to be wise. He didn't want to risk either of them getting trapped in limbo.

In his version of the story, Martín hadn't been ready for commitment and had broken up with Pier because of it. His family ignored his account. They assumed his college boy had flaked on him. He wasn't sure if this assumption was based on prejudice against Elfentum humans or if he'd been a fool to believe Pier would settle for him—for Martín, with a cotton strap around his chest and no stubble in sight. The thought provided a morbid comfort. At least he could feel sorry for himself instead of guilty for letting his college boy down.

"Will you quit moping and look at me?"

"I'm not mopping; the floor is clean."

She punched his arm. He probably deserved it.

"Look, I know it's tough. Mom and Dad started dating at fourteen. Chale got hitched at fifteen. There's a lot of pressure on us. But elves? They don't give a shit! Okay, your wimp was a human—"

"Ey, don't call him that!"

Catalina gave him a knowing look. "You broke up with him, eh? Sure looks like it . . . but that's not the point. Elfentumers run on a different clock. Take my pen pal, Daiba—"

"Wait, you have a pen pal?" Martín loved interrupting her passionate speeches. She got delightfully upset.

"Yes, I can read. What's your point?" she snapped, but there was a twinkle in her eye celebrating his giggle. A drop of joy. Finally. "Anyway, Daiba wrote me that most humans don't settle until their late twenties or thirties, if even! They get to know themselves first. When that elvish asshole left me, I thought my life was over, but then I discovered that I love myself more. Do you love yourself?"

"You're my sister. I don't need to know how you love yourself."

He caught himself a third punch. "I'm serious, Mart. Do you love yourself?"

The short answer was no. He had never loved himself. Sure, he liked the ideas he had of himself. He was funny, sort of, and nifty. He liked to think a good heart tamed his big mouth, but that was about it. He hated his reflection, hated his laugh. He hated his short tusks and the way people perceived him. He would never be good enough to live up to the idea of Martín. He didn't even like that name. It had been a spur-of-the-moment decision to avoid his deadname.

Conning people came naturally to him because his whole life was a con. It had felt so good when Pier had unraveled the con. He'd taken off Martín's mask. Putting it back on repulsed him, but who was he without it? Who was he behind the con?

"Oh, come here, you big loser." Catalina gave him a tight hug. She knew. That was why she kept coming to the kitchen. Martín wished he could cry it all out on her shoulder like some people did. They released a lost lover one teardrop at a time. Pier's memory hadn't settled into the shallow pond of watery eyes. It pulsed through Martín's veins. He couldn't rid himself of it without bleeding out.

Catalina let go of him. "You really miss the wimp."

"Seriously, do you have to call him that?"

She tried to ruffle his hair, but her fingers got stuck in the greasy ponytail mess. "You're cutting this shit off."

"Lina—"

"You're cutting it off, and then you'll pack your bags. Go to Silbertuss and find that wi—*Pier*. Find Pier, and while you're at it, maybe keep your eyes open for some beefy hunks."

"I'm not into beefy—"

"You never know. You're gonna leave either way. Sister's order."

He tried to protest, but she held her hand up.

"Nope, don't wanna hear any protests. Now let me try this." She took the ladle and tasted the soup. "Forget you, this is salty enough. Tell Mom I'm off to meet the new carpenter and that I'm a naturally brilliant cook that needs no practice ever."

She rushed off, leaving Martín with a messy kitchen and messy thoughts. He wished he could obey, take the next carriage to Silberfluss and sweep Pier off his feet like a tough, self-assured hero. But that wasn't him. He was a short orc hiding in the kitchen from monsters.

He judged the soup. The soup judged back. He'd never liked carrot-chili, anyway.

If Zazil were here, she'd hit him with the ladle for throwing constant pity parties. Not that she had any right to judge. She had done much worse when Gon had briefly broken up with her. Pier and Martín had gotten her through that time together, but there was no Pier to drag Martín out of his wallowing mess. No Zazil, or Gon, or Sachi. Martín couldn't forget them any more than he could forget Pier.

He stirred two heaps of salt into the soup and tried to picture their faces in the orange liquid. He wouldn't ask Zazil what to do. She'd be too furious that he had hurt Pier. *Me and you both, Zaz.* Sachihiro would do the same thing Martín was doing, except he'd be mumbling about the great Captain Subira Se'azana while moping. Gon? They would visit the next best volcano and ask their ancestors for guidance. They said if one addressed the ancestors at an ethereal port, they often answered. Of course Martín's great-grand-uncle second degree of his mother's cousin's husband would be interested in his love problems, wouldn't he? He'd know the perfect trick to bring a hot guy back into his life.

Martín didn't believe in ancestral intervention, but what did he still believe in? *I'm not gonna climb up a fucking volcano.* It was a ridiculous idea, although he'd breathe in fresh air for once instead of baked beans steam. *I'm not gonna climb up a fucking volcano.* He could test if his rusty leg muscles still functioned uphill.

Martín took off his apron and sighed. He had to give something a try. Anything. Sister's orders. *I'm gonna climb up a fucking volcano, aren't I?*

Why didn't the ancestors use wells as ethereal ports? All Martín would have to do was yell loud enough and receive wisdom in a bucket. *If you poke Richard in his right eye, he stops being a monster and Pier and you live happily ever after. There, fixed. Now have a cool drink of water, hotshot.* He shouldn't have thought about cool water. He'd run out of it an hour ago, and the blistering heat reminded him enough of thirst. A nice pond would make a great ethereal port as well. If this ancestral talk worked, Martín would leave some suggestions for their spirit management.

Martín pictured himself at the pond. He could soak his sore feet while having a chat with a dead guy about that time his life fell apart. It sounded almost pleasant. Instead, he had to spend half the day climbing up the rocky volcano that watched over Mink'Ayllu.

"This is stupid, this is stupid, this is stupid," he sang to himself as another hour passed. The evening sun awaited Martín when he reached the high point. The view shut him up immediately. He had hiked the mountains before, but nothing compared to looking at Mink'Ayllu's glory from the volcano's top.

The city stretched out in a large circle and looked like a birthday cake with torches for candles. The university sparkled as the last sunbeams reflected off the botany wing's glass dome. Martín spotted the hotel, towering over most surrounding buildings with its pointed roof. A sense of pride rose in his chest. Their institution was a vital part of the city's landscape. His gaze drifted farther, away from the familiar and toward the grand unknown he and Pier had pledged to explore together. The vastness made it seem possible. The monster was nothing but a tiny dot in the beautiful painting of the world. Richard wasn't important enough to ruin everything.

The air was fresher here too. Martín breathed in possibilities. He now understood why Gon struggled their way up here, despite having studied how to communicate with ancestors from anywhere. It couldn't be the same. Up here was a sacred place—away from the world and yet part of it. There might still have been a ravine between who Martín was and who he longed to be, but for the first time, building a bridge seemed possible.

He walked to the crater, buzzing with determination, then stood there. One second. Two seconds. Three seconds. *Shit.* Martín had no idea how to start a conversation with the ancestors. He peeked down the crater and fidgeted.

"Ehm . . . hello? Anyone there?"

Great start! Was he supposed to pray? Chant? Sacrifice blood? If so, his own or someone else's? He backed off. *Idiot.* A spiritual conversation was beyond his pathetic capabilities.

He had turned around, wondering how to explain his little excursion to Catalina, when a voice echoed from the crater's darkness.

"Zac-Cimi?"

Martín froze.

The voice's echo crackled like a bonfire.

"Yes, that's me. Ma-Martín. Martín Zac-Cimi's the name." Was he allowed to lie to the ancestors? He wasn't lying. *Martín* was the best name he had, even though he'd only been using it for a year. But what if he had to prove his identity to them? *This is stupid, this is stupid, this is stupid.*

"What is it you seek, child?" a different, softer voice asked. It posed an obvious question he should've known the answer to. He had come for guidance and help on his own volition, after all. His mind turned blank. What did he want?

He thought of his life from a few months ago, but if that was all he wanted, he could enroll at Tribu La'am University, then find new friends and a new boyfriend. He didn't want the same experience; he wanted the people involved back. He wanted the promise of possibilities the experience had ended on.

"I . . . ehm . . ."

The voice waited patiently while Martín assembled concrete thoughts in the abstract mess of his mind. He gazed back at the faraway Elfentum and thought of the tiny monster that kept him away from it. There were two things Martín longed for. They sounded impossible and yet as necessary as air to breathe. He was tired of shallow breathing.

Martín stepped to the edge and yelled his wish into the crater. "I want to be the man Pier Kilburn needs!"

Silence. This was either a dramatic pause or they'd given up on his sorry ass.

Something snatched Martín off the edge and pulled him down. Terror hit instantly, masking itself as questions. How had Richard found out? Had mentioning Pier's name alarmed the monster? He wasn't ready to face limbo again. He'd never be. Falling. He was falling again. He clawed at the darkness, searching for anything to restore reality.

It wasn't darkness but the low glimmer of magma that awaited him at the bottom. *Not better.* No pain of burning flesh shot through him. The magma cradled him with surprising coolness and formed a seat under him. *Cold magma under my butt. Can this day get any weirder?*

It could. His eyes adjusted to the low red light, only for a golden ray to overwhelm him.

"You have a brave heart," the ray said. Its voice differed from the ones that had asked for his wish.

"Functioning eyes would have been great too," Martín mumbled, blinking hopelessly into the light. The ray didn't burn Martín's butt with magma for his disrespect, so it must've had a sense of humor. Good. It would need it.

"I come to offer you a deal," the voice said.

Martín squinted and recognized the shape of a giant orc in the brightness. It was hollow against the piercing golden light.

"A deal already? Get a guy a drink first."

"I do not understand what you're referring to." The rays surrounding the shape pulsed with each word. *Got it, not that much humor.*

"Sorry, this is weird, that's all. I've never done something like this . . . so you're my ancestor?" He should have checked that first. What if it was one of those Ousakacac things Richard had told him about?

"Yes, my son. From a long, long time ago."

Martín shifted in his seat. The magma followed his every movement. He glanced around the absurd setting he'd found himself in. The inside of Mink'Ayllu's volcano almost looked like a cozy cave, if it weren't for the sea of deadly magma. Daylight didn't reach him, but Martín saw a dot overhead— the only sign that he was still in his own realm. The walls looked too steep to climb. He hoped Gon was right and the ancestors did love them.

"I know how you feel," the voice said. *Unsure how to get the fuck out of here?* That wasn't reassuring.

"When our story changed, judgment was written into us. We used it as a shield to protect ourselves. We listened to the words Calliquium placed in our minds, and you still do, my mortal child. I know it is hard for those who cannot win battles of judgment."

The words baffled Martín. This wasn't his great-grand-uncle or someone mundane like that. This ancestor must've been older than that. He must have lived through the legends. In Tribu La'am belief, the goddess Alames had abandoned the world during an ancient war, leaving a high priestess and a chieftain in charge of each tribe. After they'd died, they'd become the ancestors, replacing Alames.

According to Pier, and the rest of Elfentum, Alames had been lost and new gods had taken her place. Martín had spent little thought on those gods, but he knew Calliquium was one of them. If Elfentum's gods were real and favored monsters like Richard, they'd all be in trouble.

"I have faced judgment like you do, my son, and I believe I can help you." It didn't make sense that an ancestor from the legends spoke to Martín as an equal.

"How would you know how I feel?" He didn't mean to provoke him but had no idea how to express awe.

"It's a quiet pain when your manhood is questioned for reasons outside of your control."

Oh. But . . . he couldn't be, could he? Martín squinted at the orc's large shape. *He's clearly* . . . Martín didn't want to finish that thought. Nothing good came from it.

"But how could you understand, wise . . . ehm, ancestor?"

He searched for a reaction in the shape but couldn't recognize shit. Gon should have mentioned that talking to an ancestor was like talking to a highly responsive torch.

"You can call me Muwaan, son."

Martín nodded, then realized he didn't know if Muwaan could see him. "Great, thanks. Nice name!"

"Many centuries ago, I fought in the war for our worlds under the command of Alames and—"

"Alames commanded the ancient war? I thought she ditched." Gon would have slapped him for interrupting an ancestor. No, Gon was too peaceful. Zazil would have slapped him on Gon's behalf. "Sorry, didn't mean to be disrespectful. City orcs, ya know?" He laughed awkwardly and hoped that the golden energy was smiling. It looked . . . bright. That must've meant Muwaan was smiling.

"You need to learn patience, my son." Muwaan was not smiling. "Alames splintered when Balthos, king of the cursed pantheon, took charge, but she didn't abandon us. She re-formed into a weaker version of herself and fought for us. Balthos did not recognize her. He thought we had used her splinters to create a monster, the Traitor. We hadn't. She revealed herself to us because she loved us more than she'd ever loved him. It wasn't in her nature to command, but she persevered and pushed for the treaty that ended the war. It banished Balthos and his pantheon to the celestial realm, and Alames—the Traitor he saw her as—to limbo. She lost her mind after that. It wandered loosely through limbo for centuries, desperate to rebuild other souls, unable to rebuild her own."

"That suck—is unfortunate. That is unfortunate."

A warm breeze brushed over Martín's face. It must've been the ancestor's sigh, either over the tragedy of Alames's existence or over Martín's poor manners.

"You have no sense of how unfortunate it is, my son. The world I returned to after the war was different: Full of misled mortals. Full of division. Full of demons."

Martín stiffened. This was why both of them were here. The stories were fascinating, but if Alames had lost her mind roaming through limbo, there was nothing he could do about it. Richard, on the other hand, needed to be stopped.

"Our goddess warned us it might happen. Death was no longer the same. Story endings were no longer guaranteed. The splinters of our fallen people were no longer safe. It is a grim world, my son." Muwaan took a few moments of silence.

Martín fidgeted. His personal drama seemed laughable next to the ancestor's lament.

"I was injured in the battle against Caedem. It was a brutal one. He was worse than any demon I faced afterward. Wrath and paranoia are the only emotions that lead him. We couldn't let Caedem or any of them win. We still can't."

Martín had sworn to Pier that orcs aged quicker than

humans and that seventeen years was enough time to mature. He was almost eighteen now and had never felt like less of an adult. His perspective had been self-centered. He'd found out that monsters were real and had thought of no one but Richard and Pier. No one was safe if monsters were real, and even less so if the gods were among them. This world wasn't a playground for cons and shenanigans; it was a battlefield, and Martín, the con man and tomfool, was utterly unprepared for it. Perhaps realizing how unprepared he was to be an adult was a necessary part of becoming one.

"How did you get injured?"

"Caedem caused the ground we ran on to erupt. I lost . . . certain parts that night. When I returned home, I made people uncomfortable. They pitied me to my face and declared me a freak behind my back. I do understand what it means to feel incomplete, son."

He did. He was the first person who could understand how Martín felt. He shifted in the magma seat once more, conscious of the phantom itch that often plagued him. "I'm sorry about the accident."

The light flared and moved closer to Martín. "There's hope for this world. We believe splinters of Alames have left limbo—enough splinters to form a person."

Martín's eyes widened. Was this why no one asked the ancestors for relationship advice? *Hey, ancestor, I fucked things up with my cute boyfriend. Wanna help? Oh sure, Martín, but let me tell you about the resurrected savior of the world first, then we'll get right back to the love woes.* He cleared his throat and settled on the most pressing question. "How do you know what's happening in limbo?"

"Because I reside there, my son."

Shit, shit, shit. Martín tried to stand up, but the magma followed his movements and kept him in place.

"You can leave if that is what you wish. I am looking for a brave soul."

Martín slumped back down. He thought of the monster,

the screams of limbo, the numbness that had penetrated him there and hadn't left since. But it wasn't limbo that had created the numbness. It was the pain in Pier's eyes and the irrefutable truth that Martín had caused it. The numbness protected him from the guilt and anger that simmered beneath it. He wasn't ready to let go of it, to step out of the kitchen and face the threat of limbo once more. But he hadn't been ready to talk to the good-looking college boy who'd passed his tourist scam either. He hadn't been ready to tell him why his tusks wouldn't grow larger. He had never been ready and had done it anyway.

"I want to be that brave soul." He looked down at his neglected body. He hadn't even put the strap over his chest. His skin itched at the thought, and he longed to step out of it, to become nothing but light, like Muwaan—daze people with his glory. But he didn't want to daze people. He wanted them to see him. "I don't know how to be that."

"Start writing your own story, my son. Don't accept the one Balthos has given you."

Martín leaned closer to the light. "If you didn't accept yours, why are you in limbo?"

"Not all of limbo is lost. After the war, some of us stayed behind to build a refuge for those souls who don't make it to the ethereal realm after their death. Our goddess reassembled many splintered souls, but we no longer feel her presence like we used to. This is the other reason why I stayed, my son. A day will come when the treaty is tossed aside and the war erupts anew. When that day comes, when Alames calls upon us, we will be there."

Thoughts raced through Martín's mind and then disappeared altogether as he tried to process the impossible. Pier's monster dad was nothing but a tiny taste of the horror yet to come. And he knew about it. Martín knew about it, so staying out of it was no longer a choice. Would he have chosen to run away if he could? He had once. *I want to be the man that Pier Kilburn needs.*

Martín steadied his voice. "Fuck Balthos's story. How can I help?"

The light flickered. "I am happy to hear that. We believe one of the gods has violated the treaty and descended to the mortal realm."

"Alames?"

"No. She wouldn't have risked another war with the celestial realm. Someone from Balthos's pantheon, perhaps the king himself, has stepped onto mortal soil. We believe our beloved goddess ascended into the mortal realm to investigate the matter. But she's too splintered to sustain herself, my son. Too fragile. We expected her to be in your world for a decade, maybe two, but it has been over forty years in your mortal time. She needs allies."

Martín nodded as if goddess support was part of his daily schedule. *In the mornings I show tourists Mink'Ayllu, in the afternoon I help a splintered goddess save the world, and at night I make killer tamales.*

"We believe Alames is in Elfentum, away from her potential allies. We orcs did not accept the new pantheon like the elves and humans did, so she'd be safer in Tribu La'am. Find her, ensure her safety, and tell her that the knights of limbo are at her command. Remind her why she came to this world. She's prone to become enraptured in things."

"Okay . . . cool . . . yes, definitely. Um, tiny detail . . . quick question, how do I find a goddess?" *Let alone lecture her . . .*

"This is where our trade comes in. You want to be the man Pier Kilburn needs. Is that right, my son?"

Martín's breath caught. He hadn't known how to bring Pier up. What did his little heart matter to Alames, limbo, and the world?

"I can lend you my most treasured possession if you promise to find Alames first. I used it to slay the worst of the Ouisà Kacocs."

Richard would be no match for a weapon that strong. Nothing would. Martín would never feel like a scared little girl again. He pictured the glimmer in Piernapple's eyes when he showed up in Waldfeld with a sparkling diamond sword, or a prancing snake whip, or whatever Muwaan's great weapon was. He couldn't wait, which revealed the trade's problem. "I'm honored, but I need to see Pier again."

"No." The ancestor's light rose higher into the air. Had he been kneeling this whole time? *Holy shit, how tall is this guy?* "You need to find Alames first. We need to find her before Balthos does."

Martín's stomach dropped. This complicated things. "So this king of the gods is real . . . and looking for her also? How well does your weapon work against gods?"

"Not very well." *All right then.* He couldn't do this. It was too much to ask. Maybe he could find Pier on his own and tell him about how he'd spoken to a made-up ancestor in his mind. Maybe Martín had imagined limbo as well. He and Richard could have a laugh about it. Martín's skin crawled at the memory of limbo's stench. He hadn't imagined it. His imagination didn't hate him that much.

"Listen, my son. If you stumble over Pier on the way, you can solve your issue. Perhaps it'll attract Alames. She adores a good love story."

Martín shifted again. His dad had taught him never to trade if he couldn't see the person's face or wasn't sure how to hold up his end of the bargain. This trade would make his dad's skin crawl. Then again, so would limbo. He never wanted his dad to see limbo, or have Catalina face a demon. But was it even avoidable at this point? It was if he trusted Alames.

Martín ran his fingers through his outgrown hair and pulled on the blouse he was wearing. Most of his masculine clothes were Pier's, and he couldn't bear to wear them anymore, but he hadn't traded them for new ones either.

"With each year Alames stays in the mortal realm, she risks being discovered."

Martín expected his head to burst. "All right, I'm gonna

be real with you here, okay? I barely made it out of my family's kitchen today. I haven't taken a bath in a week. I'm a fucking mess. Why me? I mean, you're a wise guy, right? That's a very unwise choice."

Muwaan took a long time to answer. Any moment now, he'd recognize his mistake and shoot Martín out of the crater quicker than he could say "my bad."

"You were afraid and came to me anyway. Guilt, fear, and loathing smudge your soul parchment, yet you joke, you laugh, you care, you search for the one you love. Over the centuries, I have doubted my knowledge of the goddess, but there's one thing I know: she's a hopeless romantic, fond of foolishness."

"You're calling me a fool?"

"I'm calling you Alames's champion."

"Well, shit."

"She would appreciate the language you express yourself with more than I do. I have made the right choice. It's time to make yours, my son."

It was difficult to picture the world needing him. His family didn't even need him. Catalina did fine at his duties. Pier might've needed him, but then again, he might not have. He might have already found someone else, like Martín wanted him to. That was what he wanted, wasn't it? Catalina was right. He was conning everyone, especially himself. He wanted to be the man who could sweep Pier off his feet. He wanted to be special enough to help a goddess. Not necessarily serve her, that wasn't his style, but support her in taking out monsters like Richard. But was he worthy of those wants? He also wanted to stay numb. He was worthy of that.

"The weapon I offer you can mold you as well."

Martín's eyes grew wide. "How?"

"With the love of Alames."

That sounded like bullshit but was too tempting to pass on. He thought of his personal monster. Richard wanted him to stay numb, wooden, stoic, and dead—like he was.

"I'm in."

"Wise choice. My gift will bring you the great power of knowledge. Pledge that you will never turn it against innocent souls."

Martín scoffed. "Easy." He'd only turn it against demons like Richard.

"It won't be. The gods have seeded hate, judgment, and mistrust within you. Don't let them lead you astray."

Martín nodded and put a hand on his heart. He flinched when he felt his uneven chest but breathed through it. This moment was bigger than that. "I swear on Alames to protect the innocent and to never be an idiot about using whatever power you're willing to give me." He smiled. *Alames.* As confusing as Elfentum's pantheon was, he'd never had trouble remembering that name.

"Very well. There's one last thing . . ."

Martín froze. The ancestor wouldn't change his mind now, would he?

"This is not a condition of our trade, but how attached are you to your name, Martín?"

He had hoped his name wouldn't come up. He had blurted it to stop his friends from calling him Bandana, and that hadn't even worked. Pier had known not to mention his deadname. Martín was the first name he'd thought of when he needed one, so it stuck. He didn't like it, but it was better than digging up the name he'd buried alongside his dresses.

"After the war, I hunted Ouisà Kacocs. The gods had brought many, too many, into the mortal realm. I wanted to defeat the monsters that poisoned our lands, and I did so successfully for many years. They feared me until one of them defeated me." The light flickered. "The world forgot my name after that. Alames remembers, and I believe she would recognize it even in her frail mortal form. But I want everyone to remember. I want any monster you encounter to tremble at the sound of my name. Can you do that for me?"

Martín pictured himself standing on a pile of disfigured

demon creatures, shouting "Muwaan!" *That might diminish the heroic moment.* One of his family's rivals scratched their surname into the tusks of slain competitors. He could etch *Muwaan* into demon flesh, but Alames might disapprove of grotesque violence. He'd figure out how to make the name known.

"Sure, I'll tell them you sent me."

"No, son, I want you to take on my name. Become the new Muwaan Zac-Cimi and continue my legacy."

Muwaan Zac-Cimi. It sounded magnificent. The fresh start it provided sounded even better, but it couldn't be true. Martín didn't deserve this. "I feel honored, really, but you wouldn't want people calling me that. They'll think you're, I mean I am . . . I'm not . . ." *Please don't make me say it.*

"You are the man I have chosen."

Martín choked up. *Muwaan Zac-Cimi, helper of a goddess, partner of Pier Kilburn.* Perhaps Martín didn't deserve it, but Muwaan did. "I'll carry your name with pride, Muwaan. If you really want me to, I'd love to inherit it." The light swirled around him, and a warm breeze accompanied it. He was certain the ancestor was smiling this time.

A large orcish hand made of light reached out to Martín. It placed a metal instrument in his palm. Martín withdrew and examined the sharp silver sickle he'd received. Its grip was made of an opaque blue crystal carved in the shape of a woman. She wore a crown that was attached to a silver chain hanging from the sickle. At the end of the chain was a small empty glass orb.

"What . . . ?"

"Cut out the white light when I tell you to." The ancestor's light stretched until it lost its orcish shape and surrounded Martín like the cocoon of a butterfly. Martín squinted at the swirling light and noticed its structure. It looked like bound parchment. A small white light flickered in its midst.

"*Now!*" Muwaan bellowed from all directions.

Martín had many questions, but he swung the sickle toward the white light before asking any of them. He hit the line to its left, where it was bound to other parchment pages. The ancestor groaned in pain, and Martín flinched, but before guilt or worry could get him, another yell resounded.

"Again!" Martín did as told and cut the line to its right. The white piece broke off the whole and floated toward him until it reached the orb. It compressed itself into a shining stone and settled into the orb, as if its glass were nothing but air.

Martín pinched it between his fingers, and the orb pushed back toward his heart in response. He tried to stop it, but it burned into his chest. His blouse melted away. Everything turned bright.

"Precious mortal." The words of a woman cradled him. Martín had never felt this safe, this certain, this utterly loved from within. The brightness cleared, and he found the orb attached to his skin at the top of his ribcage. It sent warm pulses through his upper body and released a painful pressure he hadn't realized was there. It felt like a muscle knot that vanished with a massage. He looked down, and for a moment he didn't recognize the body he saw. The golden orb was attached to a flat chest. *My flat chest.* He brought a shaking hand to it and ran his fingers over the smooth green skin. This couldn't be true. This couldn't be him. He gasped for air, but it soon turned into laughter—unreasonable, ridiculous, but true. He was free. He was finally free to be himself.

The ancestor returned to their orcish shape. "Protect that joy, son. You will need to store its memory for darker times."

Why would he have to store it? He couldn't possibly feel anything but joy ever again.

"You now carry a splinter of Alames in you."

Martín almost missed it over the awe that overwhelmed him. His ears registered it, but his brain didn't. He touched the orb, and another rush of love streamed through him. It felt like his mom's cooking, his dad's jokes, and his sister's pestering. "Thank you, yeah, I can feel . . . wait, there's a splinter of Alames in me?"

More wind gushed at him. "Yes, my son. The splinter will find its own and teach you the ways of the parchment. With its knowledge, you can face any creature."

"Thank you." Tears rolled over Martín's cheeks. He couldn't hold them in anymore, and he didn't need to. He had nothing to hide.

"Give yourself time to adjust to the splinter's powers. It took me years to understand. The path to knowledge is paved with failures."

"Thank you, thank you." Martín couldn't say it enough. "Are you all right?"

"Do not worry. My parchment will recover. One last thing."

"Anything."

"At all costs, stay away from those who have a black rose tattooed on their body. When you find her, make sure Alames stays away from them as well. She might want to trust them, but she can't. They're keeping her more fragile than she has to be. They're not who they say they are."

Martín nodded, going over it in his mind so he wouldn't forget. *Black rose bad. Got it.*

"Are you ready to return to the sunlight?"

Martín nodded again. There was so much he wanted to express, but he found no words. Before he could mutter another thank-you, he rose upward to the dot of daylight, ready to face the world as Muwaan Zac-Cimi, helper of Alames.

CHAPTER 24

ALLY

October 979 - Altor Caedem Military Academy, Virisunder

Ally teared up when she laid eyes on Altor Caedem's imposing architecture. Its shield and towers told tales of a time when her family had been whole, her mind kind, and her future untarnished. Her dad used to carry her on his shoulders from the carriage all the way to the beautiful gate with Alames's sculpture. Her grandmother Makeda would rush toward them. She'd take Ally off her dad's shoulders, pretend to drop her, then trick her with a tickle ambush. Ally had asked her to stop once Subira moved into Altor Caedem because she didn't want to embarrass herself. Her grandmother Theodosia's teatime, however, hadn't changed. Ally smiled when she thought of the macaroons and caramel shortbreads. Subira would sit next to her with her horseradish-and-cucumber sandwiches. She'd never cared for sweets.

A sob escaped Ally. What an unnecessary reaction, void of any reasonable triggers.

"You're all right?" Robert rushed to her side.

Ally smiled through those cumbersome tears. "I should be past this phase, but . . . but . . ." Another sob. This was embarrassing in front of Robert. She tried to steady herself and blinked at him through her watery eyes. He had trimmed his beard the day before, which complemented his jawline. Had his biceps always looked that firm? She hadn't felt them around her since the morning of the Ceremony. She must have scared him off. Him and his sculpted abs. And his fascinating mind and caring heart. And his abs.

She sniffed again and placed her hand on her stomach. *Stop confusing your mom, little troublemaker. Stupid hormones.*

Reggie stepped out of the carriage and snapped his fingers. Five more Reggies appeared around them, each portraying a melodramatic emotion. The one closest to Ally wore a swimsuit and drenched himself in tears. Enlarged drops ran over the black rose tattoo on his cheek.

The real Reggie draped his arms around her and Robert and poked his head between them. "Pregnancy emotions are a doozy, aren't they? Mine constantly get carried away. I tell you." He snapped again, and an equal amount of stoic Reggies picked up the melodramatic ones and carried them back to the carriage. Ally chuckled.

Robert watched them disappear. "Right, you were there for Josefine's too, weren't you?"

Josefine. Panic rushed through Ally. This was all a farce. Why had she kept the baby? They'd take it away from her. They'd steal it at birth like they'd stolen Josefine. She wasn't trusted with a baby. She couldn't be.

They have to take it away. You would suffocate it by accident.
It wouldn't be an accident. You'd do it on purpose.

Reggie gave Robert a rough pat on the shoulder. "Your foot looks better on your leg than in your mouth. Let's stick with this beautilicious moment, shall we, my handsome man?"

"Sorry, Ally, I . . . I'm excited to meet Queen Theodosia and General Makeda. Feels surreal, honestly. I wanted to go to Altor Caedem as a kid."

The remark confused Ally enough to distract her. "Why didn't you?"

Reggie went back to the carriage to organize the luggage. Robert laughed and bit his lip. It was too good of a look on him. "They only accept commoners once a year on a stipend. Didn't quite make the cut."

Ally frowned. Altor Caedem was supposed to educate the militaristic future of Elfentum. Anyone capable belonged to that future. "That's ridiculous." Her grandmothers wouldn't endorse such nonsense. "Is it a Council law?"

"I don't know . . . don't worry about it. It's not important. I'm still excited to meet them."

She grabbed Robert's arm. "Stop it. It is important."

"What—"

"We're not above you—Verdains or royals or what you will. We're not above you." Her heart raced. She'd wanted to tell him since the Ceremony. "And I don't have the right to hurt you just because I'm . . . whatever you think I am."

"Ally, I know—"

"No, you don't." She wasn't sure why she was getting upset, but her muscles tensed. "I don't have courtesans, Robert. I didn't sleep with you because I thought it was my right. I thought . . . okay, I wasn't thinking at all that night. But I didn't make you my guard to do . . . I mean . . . that's not—I like you." She stared at the ground and ignored the wave of sobs trying to surface. Perhaps her body was celebrating their arrival at Altor Caedem with every pregnancy symptom imaginable. Perhaps her baby was that dramatic.

"Ehm . . ." Robert said, but Ally didn't want him to continue.

"I know you put me on a pedestal, but you're also upset with me over Reggie, which I understand on a theoretical level because yes, I do love him, and that won't stop. But . . . I don't want you to think your frustration has anything to do with status. It's a regular romantic collision, of sorts. Not that I ever had, or I mean, that's not the right word, but . . . that's what I meant with lithium. You're not a possible binder. You're part of the molecule to me."

She peeked up at him but couldn't decipher his expression. "Ally, that's . . . a lot. I don't think I can—"

He didn't get the chance to finish because Ally's ten trunks danced past them toward Altor Caedem's gate, performing a Virisunder waltz. Reggie stepped next to them with a grin on his face and an absurdly tiny trunk in his hand.

"Don't worry, sugar. I've got this one. Have to work out those steel biceps of mine!" He kissed his lanky upper arm and lured a smile out of Ally. She glanced at Robert and was glad to find him in the same state, watching the trunks' performance with a hint of a smirk and a softened gaze. "Shall we?"

Robert avoided her eyes, so perhaps it was best to drop the subject. Her relationship with Reggie had started in a strange, stumbling place. She wasn't sure how romantic engagements developed naturally, but everything was a chemical reaction at its core, and some needed time. She didn't drink but had seen Robert enjoy a glass of wine after his shifts. Yeast and sugar could take years to properly react, and heat was a common byproduct. In this case, it'd be heated conversations, a natural side effect of creating intoxicating joy. Or perhaps it was different. Perhaps she was the grape must, Reggie the sugar, and Robert the yeast.

"Ally?" Reggie raised one eyebrow at a time in a silly rhythm. "Let's go see our good ole Makeda."

They were both waiting for her on the path, and so were the two other trusted guards who'd accompanied her to Altor Caedem. Josefine had insisted on keeping most of the royal guard and all the current military personnel to carry on the war with Silberfluss as soon as possible. Ally had negotiated a temporary truce but hoped Subira would step in and continue it soon. She wanted her friend to have the best soldiers and guards at the front and preferred the small entourage. The only ones she'd insisted on bringing had been Reggie and Robert. The court dearly missed their Bored Reginald, but his best friend and troupe member, Cleo la Chatte, had taken over his shows, and the nobility accepted that Virisunder's best jester should entertain the new Verdain baby himself.

Ally reached the gate and regarded it with awe. She was here. She was actually here. Josefine hadn't wanted her at the palace, and she needed a safe, secluded space to birth the child and raise it for the first eight years. After that, the court required the royal offspring to be raised at the palace. Several dukes and duchesses had offered to house Ally, but she'd made her choice the moment she'd settled on the Ceremony. There was no place safer and more appreciated than her grandmothers' tower at Altor Caedem. Neither was allowed to leave the premises because of their exile, so Ally hadn't seen them in over a decade. She glanced up at the Sword Tower that held the private residence and smiled. Did Grandma Theo still import chocolate to drink with her macaroons?

The gate opened before they could knock. Robert stepped in front of her to shield her from the crowd of soldiers and cadets gathered behind the gate, but one short Fi'Teri elf pushed him aside and lifted Ally into an embrace as if she weighed no more than a feather.

"My little sugar cube's here!" Makeda shook Ally in the air before setting her down and cupping her face. "Let's look at you."

"Hi, Bibi." Ally called her the Fi'Teri term for "grandma." She'd forgotten how comforting family felt. There was no pretense, nothing to gain, nothing to want, just love for the sake of it.

Makeda guided her chin to one side, then the other. "Not

too many scars. Both ears still there. You've done me proud at the front, I see."

Ally sighed. "Hardly."

"Well, that doesn't matter now." She kissed her forehead and patted her cheek. "You're here to stay. I've been talking about it for weeks, and wait till you see your grandma. She even got out of bed already."

Ally's heart sank. Losing Ally's father had pushed Theodosia into a grief spiral. Ally had assumed she'd be out of it by now. She couldn't picture Virisunder's most influential princess, the woman who taught her how to evade the treacherous grip of delusions, remain in shambles. "Is she not feeling well?"

"Don't worry about that." Makeda waved it off. Ally wished people would stop telling her not to worry about vital details. "I got a great midwife already. She helped deliver our Charles way back. Couldn't deliver you because of the circumstances, but she'll make sure everything goes well this time."

Ally raised her eyebrows. "Have you finally decided to illuminate me on the *circumstances* of my birth, Bibi?" The only thing Ally knew was that her mother hadn't survived it.

Makeda laughed. "No, but I built a bit of a makeshift lab, so you can put that curious mind to better work than worrying about the past." She eyed her up and down, stopping at Ally's visible baby bump. The voluminous skirt covered most of it, but Makeda's sharp eyes missed nothing. She placed her hand on Ally's belly, and the baby kicked back hard. Ally gritted her teeth.

Makeda leaned in closer. "One month pregnant, heh? I think I'm missing information on the *circumstances* as well."

Ally hadn't intended to tell either of her grandmothers about Robert. She smirked despite her thumping heart. "I'm happy to trade information, Bibi."

Makeda shook her head. "Look at you, spoken like a

general." She swayed her fist in the sign of Caedem. "Forgive us for any sins committed."

Ally rolled her eyes. "I don't think Caedem cares about my pregnancy."

"Caedem cares about everything."

"Sexy lady you got there!" Reggie stepped next to them and nodded his head at the Alames sculpture on the gate.

Makeda chuckled. "You make that joke every time." She slapped his upper arm. "Good to see you're still around, Reg. You've been looking out for my girl?"

"I'm not sure that's a job for one person, but . . ." He twirled his thumbs, and the Reggie duplicates popped out of the ground. "We've tried," they said in unison.

Makeda crossed her arms and stared at him, then at Ally. "And you gave Subira up for that?"

"Subira was never interested in me or any woman, Bibi." She looked at the big-eyed Reggies around her and smiled. "And yes, I would have."

"All right," Makeda conceded. "Come on in. Theo appreciates this stuff more than me." She gestured for them to follow her and marched through the gate.

"Tough crowd." Reggie twirled his thumbs again, and the illusion disappeared. "Do you think she's beautiful though?" He glanced at the sculpture.

Ally shrugged. "You know I don't care about the gods, especially the dead ones. I care about the living. Can we drop the religion talk please?"

"Sure." He snapped his fingers, and a dark curtain appeared around them. He leaned down for a kiss, which she gladly gave. Another snap, and the curtain disappeared. "Let's put the fun back into Altor Caefun!"

Ally followed him through the gate. The moment her boot touched Altor Caedem's ground, a prickling excitement flooded her. This was it. This was her new life. She walked over to Robert, who stood by the decadent fountain and took in every detail of the courtyard with awe.

"Welcome home," she whispered in his ear.

He turned to her. "Home? That's a nice thought."

She tensed up. "It's not a thought. You're staying, right?"

His picture-book eyes penetrated her. She could get lost in them, but she didn't want to. She couldn't lose this moment.

"Yes, I'm staying . . . Your Majesty."

The weight of her bump increased, dragging her down. She heard whispers in the distance, but the tightness around her chest didn't stem from the illness. Robert couldn't accept that her feelings for him and Reggie coexisted. She nodded. "I understand."

She followed her bibi without another glance at him and focused on her breath. This was fine. She wanted him around, and he'd be around. There was no problem. Nothing was lost. Her eyes welled up again. It was truly a ridiculous body function.

They entered the familiar tower, and she barely noticed when Reggie put his arm around her. It was bleak for the residence of a former princess, but Ally knew that comfort could only be found at the top. Makeda used the steep spiral staircase as her morning exercise, and Theodosia didn't leave the tower, from what Ally had heard. The only light came from oval windows the size of Ally's head. After ten minutes, Ally ran out of breath.

"Want me to scoop-di-doop you the rest of the way, sugar?"

"I'm fine."

"It'll be like flying."

"I'm fine!" she snapped and regretted it immediately. She wasn't sure where the anger had come from.

Before she could apologize, Makeda's voice resounded from ahead. "By the way, dear, the guest you requested arrived yesterday."

Ally's eyes widened. "She has?" She hadn't heard from Zazil Revelli for months, but Subira had informed her that the assula smith had finally accepted the job offer.

Makeda waited for her to catch up. "Arrived yesterday. She's having tea with Theo at the moment. I hope just tea . . . by Caedem, that woman is a flirt."

Ally chuckled. Lady Revelli didn't sound like the standard Council-approved assula smith.

"Marvelous." Revelli was one of the first graduates of Tribu La'am's new assula program and, from what Ally had heard, the most promising one. She hadn't signed a Council contract either, so she'd be essential to the war and might provide Ally with a raw assula—raw energy she could study. Ally ran the rest of the way, ignoring the increasing dizziness. She'd be able to sit in a moment.

An old guard stood at the top of the stairs. Ally recognized his face but couldn't remember his name. He lit up when he saw her. "Your Majesty, how lovely to see you again."

She nodded. "Lovely to see you again too."

"And with our new Verdain, I see. How far are we in? Five, six months?"

Ally's stomach leaped. How many people suspected that she had deceived the Ceremony?

You're getting Robert killed. And Reggie. You're getting both of them killed.

That's what she wanted.

No, it's not.

Yes, it is.

"Your Majesty?"

"Right, yes . . ." A hand touched her back. She turned to find Makeda smiling at her.

"Let's get our sugar cube inside." She opened the door and led her into the reception room. The contrast was so stark Ally had to blink to adjust her vision. Unlike the bare staircase, the reception room was stuffed with bookshelves, artwork, sculptures, plush rugs, mismatched armchairs, and curiosities of all kinds. There was a golden telescope and an easel with a painted world map. Virisunder was at its center and had received the most detail. Something grazed her leg, and Ally shrieked.

"Damu, don't scare our girl." Makeda leaned down and picked up a fat orange cat with a missing eye. He purred in her arms. Ally smiled and stretched her hand out to pet him, but a sneeze cut her off. Makeda set him down on a near-by armchair. "Right, I forgot you're allergic. There are seven of these rascals around here, so keep an eye out." Makeda carefully navigated through the furniture and oddities to the largest double-winged door. "The guest residence is upstairs, and don't fret, it doesn't look like this." She wrinkled her nose. "This mess is Theo's realm. I'm running around the academy most of the time."

"I don't mind the decor. It's interesting." The longer Ally stood in the reception, the more details she noticed. Numbers that likely signified dates were sewn all across the burgundy velvet curtains.

"*Interesting* is one word for it. Anyway, you'll have three rooms for yourself, and your men are welcome to stay in our best barracks."

Ally glanced at Robert, who studied a broken teapot with more attention than it deserved. "Okay."

Makeda opened the winged door and waved Ally over, who squeezed between two armchairs. Her new belly made it harder to cross the room than she'd expected. She bumped against a shelf, sending a magnifying glass flying. It stopped in midair and turned into a chirping bird. Damu's ears perked up.

"Glass is a vital part of a cat's diet, right?" Reggie asked from behind her. Ally chuckled and watched as the bird settled on the room's highest shelf.

She stepped through the double-winged door into anoth-er busy room filled with colors, books, and too many furniture pieces. This time, however, she didn't stop to examine the cu-riosities but focused on her grandma instead.

Theodosia rose from a pink sofa with nine pillows and

two cats. Ally startled at her sight. It had been a decade since she'd last seen her, but she'd aged as if thirty years had passed. She wore a stained purple nightgown that matched the wrinkled dark circles under her eyes. Her gray hair hung limply over her shoulders, bearing no resemblance to the maroon updos she used to sculpt on her head. Ally glanced at Makeda. Her bibi had gained a few wrinkles and some gray streaks in her frizzy hair but looked mostly the same as she always had. The only detail that remained the same on her grandma was the patient smile she wore.

"Alexandra, come here." She stepped over another cat and pulled her in for a hug. The familiar scent of lilies hit Ally's nose, and she eased up. This was her grandma, the woman who'd taught her how to care for books and when it was acceptable to write in them, the one whose bedtime stories lasted for hours until bibi would bring them to an end, the one who understood terror no one should be familiar with.

"I missed you," Ally whispered.

"I missed you too. Time moves quicker than it used to." She let go and cupped Ally's face like Makeda had. There was no spark in her eyes, no excitement, but they were warm and loving nevertheless. "I'm glad they didn't ruin you."

"Theo," Makeda said. Ally startled at the coldness in her voice. Her grandmothers had always been inseparable. "Let's keep it light, all right, mahabubu?"

She was relieved to hear Makeda's pet name for Theodosia, but it didn't bridge the distance between them. Theodosia nodded and gestured for Ally and the others to take a seat. Ally's eyes fell on an occupied armchair and widened. How could she have missed Lady Revelli? On second thought, it made perfect sense. The elvish woman blended into Theodosia's eccentric tea parlor like she was part of the decor. Her hair was as pink as the sofa, and her face was as cluttered with golden ink and jewelry as the parlor was with artwork.

Revelli seemed as surprised to see her as Ally was. "You're the queen."

Ally raised an eyebrow. This was the brightest assula student of Tribu La'am University? She had overestimated the program's quality.

Revelli jumped up and stumbled over a hissing cat. "I wish I wouldn't have made all those dirty jokes now," she mumbled to herself.

"Pardon?"

"Never mind."

But Ally knew what she'd meant. Everyone joked about the Mad Queen.

The woman stretched out her hand. "Za-Zazil is the name. Mrs. Ch'ulel if we wanna be proper. Which I guess we should be since you're the queen." She laughed nervously. Ally took her hand and noticed a green-glowing silver ring on her finger. She frowned and brought it closer to her face.

"Fascinating how small you're able to craft them. What does this one do?"

Ally glanced at Zazil. The smith's cheeks turned as pink as her hair. "Would you really like to know, Your Majesty?"

"Of course." Why would anyone refuse an answer?

Zazil cracked her neck. "Well . . . this one is for breast enhancement. Makes them a bit bigger and plumper."

Ally stared at the cleavage Zazil's blouse revealed. "I see."

"Ha!" Makeda said as she plopped into an armchair. "I'll take some of that hot chocolate, mahabubu."

Ally blinked and looked away. She caught Reggie's eyes as he stifled a laugh. *Don't you dare comment.*

"Do you have somewhere private we could speak?" she asked Theodosia instead. The sooner she could learn about assulas, the better, and scientific information would banish certain distracting thoughts from her head.

Theodosia smirked and pointed at a door. "You can use my dressing room."

"Thank you." Ally tiptoed around two tea crates toward the door. Zazil followed promptly.

"Should I come with you, Your Majesty?" Robert asked.

Ally looked at him and stiffened. It was fine that he was her guard. He made an excellent guard. There was nothing else she needed from him. The heaviness in her chest suggested otherwise.

"Oh yes, I approve." Zazil beamed.

Ally wasn't sure what the eccentric elf was referring to, but she shook her head. "It'll be fine, thank you." Zazil had just begun her career. Harming the queen in the dressing room of the notorious General Makeda Verdain would be beyond unwise. They entered and found themselves among the adorned hoopskirts Ally remembered Theodosia wearing. Here they were collecting dust like her grandma did.

Like you will one day.

Ally pushed two skirts aside and sat down on a stool.

Zazil grinned at her. "So my spouse and I were joking about this happening, but I'm so down. I know you're the queen now, but are you more of a pillow princess or . . . ?" She weighed her hands. "Because I'm happy either way."

Ally had the urgent need to hide in a hoopskirt when it dawned on her. "You're flirting with me."

Zazil paused. "Yes . . . I thought that was obvious. Oh dear, I, ehm . . ."

Ally swallowed, desperate for a response. "I'm flattered."

"Okay then, let's . . . let's forget I've made an ass of myself. Ehm, what did you want to talk about, Your Majesty?"

What did she want to talk about? *Assulas, of course.* But she couldn't move on. Zazil's embarrassment was too awkward to ignore. Under different circumstances . . .

"I really am flattered, Zazil, was it? But I'd rather not complicate that area of my life any further."

Zazil's eyes brightened as she pulled up a stool. "Dish! Has that something to do with those two handsome fellas waiting for you? Your Majesty, I mean."

It was Ally's turn to blush. She ran the laced rim of a skirt between her fingers and fought the urge to blurt it out. This was of no importance. Politics were at stake. A war was at stake. Her love life was of absolutely no importance. And an assula smith, even one not affiliated with the Council, was the last person who needed to be informed of such unimportant matters. "I don't know what you're referring to."

"Sorry, I'll stop. Putting my nose where it doesn't belong is a habit of mine. Don't have my bestie around at the moment, so I'm afraid it's gotten worse. I'm annoying the crap out of Subi, which is equally hilarious and terrifying, I gotta say."

Ally smiled when she heard Subira's nickname. It was almost as if she were talking to a friend, an opportunity she hadn't had in a long time. "You don't seem like the type of person who's afraid."

Zazil laughed. "Of anything? My oh my, I've made a great impression already."

"You have."

> Stupid slut. You're trusting everyone now, aren't you? Would you like to ruin her too?
> *No, she'd ruin you.*

"Back to the assulas." *Focus.* "I've offered you the position of head assula smith in our military because, unlike the rest of your family, you do not engage with the Council in the close relations smiths are expected to have."

Zazil waved it away. "Oh yeah, fuck those assholes. I'm sorry, my parents never let me talk to royalty for that reason—I can be a bit frank. But yes, I had considered giving up assulas altogether, but now that I joined the family business—without my bloody family, that is—I'm not becoming a Heidegger pawn. Met good ole Harry once, and that dude creeps me out. There's just something off about him. You know what I mean? Total creep factor, with that face and . . . oh, right, he's your brother-in-law. You know, my brother-in-law is a sweetheart. Total dork, but adorable."

Ally smirked. The smith's words were running away from

her, and she was attempting to catch them with too many gestures. She had a good feeling about her.

"I've gone completely off topic, haven't I? Sorry. What
can I do for you, Your Majesty?"

Ally leaned as far forward as the bump allowed. "I want
your inventions to help us turn the war around. I want you to
break the Council's regulations and Princess Josefine's as well.
Not in terms of weapon production—I'd like to study the substance first—but I give you permission to build whatever else
you see fit. In fact, I might have some suggestions."

"You have suggestions, Your Majesty?"

"Surprised?"

"Concerned."

Ally leaned back. She'd forgotten that the woman expected the Mad Queen like everyone else. For a brief second,
she'd thought she'd found a fellow scientist to push the bound-
aries of what was possible with. She should've known by now
it was never the case. No fellow scientist helped her reach the
highest shelves of her lab, and if they offered, other intentions
were at play. "Yes, well, you don't have to pursue any of my
blueprints."

"Blueprints? Those . . . those are difficult to produce."

"Not really. It merely takes some ammonium ferric ci-
trate and potassium ferricyanide. I've prepared a folder of
blueprints for you."

"Wow."

Ally frowned. "It's about the designs, not the blueprints
themselves, you understand?"

Zazil nodded. "Yep, yep. I . . . yes, I'd be happy to take a
look at your ideas."

"In exchange for this freedom, I have one request: bring
me a raw assula, the pure energy before it has been forged
and molded." Ally's stomach leaped, and she was sure the
baby reciprocated. Excitement rushed through her. This was
it. She could understand the source of the magical energy
and push for actual change. She could study its movements,

perhaps create a circuit. Josef had managed to infuse it into his watch chain. Could it be infused into other metals and transmitted over a wide range? Perhaps she could design a power grid that carried the energy to a larger vicinity, not just to noble families that paid for it.

"That's not a good idea, Your Majesty."

Ally deflated. "Why not?" She'd misjudged her. She'd thought the woman wasn't one of Josef's elites. He must have sent her to ridicule Ally.

"First of all, I'm not a collector. I get my materials prepared, not raw."

"Collector? Where do you collect assulas from?"

Zazil raised her eyebrows. "You don't know?"

Ally inhaled sharply. "Are you mocking me, Mrs. Ch'ulel?"

"Oh, fuck no, I'm sorry. I just wasn't expecting that. Okay, look, raw assulas are dangerous because they're . . . well, they're death."

"Death isn't an energy." Ally felt both too stupid and too smart for this conversation.

"The energy is a byproduct. I've only witnessed it once because it's . . . uncomfortable, but when a person passes, their soul is released and the residual energy remaining in their body is harvested. That energy is forged into assulas. I can get my hands on a raw one and send it to you if you really want, along with some special gloves. Don't wanna burn these lovely hands, do we? But you gotta be very careful with it. They didn't even teach us how to collect at college. Only the Council is trained in collection."

Ally froze as thoughts and theories rushed through her head. *Only the Council collects.* That meant the Institute was in control of all harvesting. First the kénos, now this. Josef wasn't exploiting new forms of power—he was exploiting death.

"Get me that raw assula as soon as you can."

CHAPTER 25

PIER

October 979 - Waldfeld, Silberfluss

Pier threw his weight onto the stuffed trunk to close it but barely made a difference. He sighed and pulled his large university trunk from his closet instead. It was over-the-top but would ensure that none of the outfits wrinkled. He had carefully assembled them over the past weeks to ensure that Edward made an impression in Silberfluss's capital, Freilist. Pier had organized several tea invitations per day for his client, and the more striking the outfits Edward wore, the more talk he'd inspire among the courtiers. Whatever Pier and Edward did, nothing could remind of their heritage. They were the undiscovered heart of the court, not two commoners from a backward small town.

He heaved the enormous trunk onto his bed and felt a sting when he saw how much dust it had gathered. His time in Tribu La'am had become a dream—an informative one that had planted ideas in his head, but one he woke up from. Waldfeld worked every day to undo the growth Mink'Ayllu had gifted him. He couldn't let it. He had to hold on to the Pier who'd once existed, even if he belonged to a dream.

At least he had Esperanza for company and Zazil's letters to brighten his day. He and Zazil rarely went to bed without exchanging words. The last days had been silent because of a minor disagreement, but he'd make up for it soon. He shouldn't have chided her for meeting Queen Alexandra. He didn't want her to work for the enemy, but his worries over Alexandra were unfounded. The queen had ordered Zazil to work on a flying machine. For some reason, Zazil humored her, but it proved that Virisunder's queen was as insane as suspected. Even more reason to rise in Silberfluss's court and aid Agathe in putting an end to this prolonged war. The best way to do so was through her bedchamber. From the information Pier had gathered, it was the only way for a commoner to get close to the princess. He'd considered bringing Edward to Queen Alexandra, but according to Zazil, she had her own vipers. It was best not to get involved in someone else's plan.

He blew the dust off the trunk and opened it. Forgotten pieces of his old life awaited him: parchments with essays scribbled on them, stained shawls from the fire festival he had attended, and various hats to prevent his constant sunburns. He carried them over to his closet with great care. A piece of clothing fell and landed on his foot. He put the pile down to pick up the dark green cloth. It was a bandana. No, it was *the* bandana. Martín's. He glanced at the door to make sure he was alone, then brought it to his nose and sniffed. It still carried a hint of his scent.

Pier bit his lip and stuffed the bandana into the darkest corner of his closet. The man he claimed to be didn't creep after former lovers. He wouldn't waste energy on anyone who didn't want him. The man he claimed to be was above that, above Martín, above Waldfeld.

"How long are you leavin' for?"

His dad's voice startled Pier. He stood at the door, eyeing the college trunk.

"Just heading to Freilist for a week. I have a couple things to take care of."

"You'd tell me if you were leaving for good, right?"

"Dad . . ." He wanted to unleash his frustration, but his dad's deflated appearance made it difficult these days. His scruffy ginger beard hadn't received care in weeks, and he barely left the shop. Pier had hoped having Esperanza as an apprentice would liven him up, but it'd had the opposite effect. His dad needed to get out of Waldfeld too. He was too talented to rot in this bloody town. He'd make a fine royal smith for Silberfluss once Pier snatched an adviser position. "I wouldn't just leave you; don't worry."

Except he would have. He would have followed Martín to the bottom of a volcano or to the edge of limbo if it had meant staying with him. He moved Edward's fine suits into the new trunk, rougher than intended. Sentimentality had no room in his new life. Princess Agathe made herself vulnerable by keeping courtesans and allowing romantic inklings to flourish. He wouldn't make that mistake.

"Good," his dad grumbled.

"Can I help you with something?" He regretted how rudely it had come across when his dad backed off.

"Sorry, didn't mean to . . ."

Pier sighed and turned to him. He kept forgetting how lonely his dad must've been. They'd been inseparable after Pier's mom died, building the shop and rebuilding their lives. Pier didn't want to cut him out now, but his dad refused to come along on their next great endeavor. "It's fine. I need to get going, that's all. How's Esperanza taking to your lessons? I'm sure it's nice to have someone so enthusiastic to lecture."

"Unlike you, you mean?"

Pier turned back to the trunk and shoved two pairs of shoes into it.

"Need help?"

Pier shook his head and packed quicker. "No, thank you. I got it."

The floor creaked under his dad's feet as he shifted. Pier glanced up, waiting for him to say something. He hadn't even responded to his question. After a few seconds, he gave up and returned to the packing.

"Son?"

Pier suppressed another sigh. "Yes, Dad?"

"Father Godfried is holding a special sermon on Sunday."

Pier slammed the trunk shut. "Dad, I can't—"

"Maybe stay two weeks in Freilist, make it a trip . . . You don't need to be there. But come back, will you?"

Pier paused. Father Godfried's word had always been the law at home. It was unlike his dad to encourage disobedience. He studied him and noticed how sunken his eyes looked. Pier's muscles tensed. He let go of the trunk and approached him. "Dad, what's wrong?"

He shook his head.

"You can tell me."

He remained silent, but Pier noticed his dad's eyes water. Panic rushed through him. He hadn't even cried when Pier's mom died. Pier had assumed his dad was too calm for the melodrama of life to sway him.

"Dad?" He wanted to hug him, but they hadn't hugged since those nights on the porch. "I don't have to—"

"Splendid morning! How hops it?" Esperanza stepped out of her guest room and beamed at them. "Just the chap I was looking for. Pier, you're going to Freilist, aren't you? I have an itty-bitty list of things I need." She pulled a parchment from her satchel and handed it to him.

"I'll be in the shop," his dad mumbled, then left before Pier could say another word.

"A bit of goosegrumps, aren't we all?"

Pier frowned. "Ehm, no, we're fine . . . don't worry about it, darling. Let me look at this." He unrolled the scroll but recognized none of the words. *Echinacea. Comfrey. Yellow dock.*

"Pharmacies in Freilist should carry all of it," she said.

Pier rolled the parchment back up and put it in his shoulder bag. "Of course. I'll see how much I can find."

Esperanza giggled. "Oh no, it's important you find all of it. Otherwise I'll pluck the daisies from underneath, and that would be a mourn-gloom for all of us, wouldn't it?"

Pier went over her words in his head until they made sense. "Wait . . . your life depends on them?"

Another giggle. "I'm afraid so."

All plans and worries evaded him. He gently grasped her shoulders gently and looked her over. She seemed perfectly healthy, better than Pier had expected after the horrible events at Zazil's wedding. He should have been there for them. Their college family had depended on him to keep the peace, yet he'd been here, bickering with his father. But his dad needed him as well. And now Esperanza was sick. He should have been further along in his career by now. He could have taken better care of them if he was. Both the career and his loved ones had needed more attention, and where had he been? Wasting time on bandanas and petty heartaches.

He turned Esperanza from side to side to check for injuries. She had gained weight since she'd arrived, but nothing else stood out.

She laughed more. "You're a silly-wuss. Stop worrying; it's not a bad thing."

"Of course it's a bad thing if you're unwell. Has this something to do with Sachi? I can write him a stern letter if you wish." What if Sachihiro was sick as well? He hadn't written his friend in several months.

Her laughter stopped. "I don't know who you're talking about."

"Sach—"

"I'm opening the Fae realm, Pier." She took his hand and pressed it against her stomach. "It's finally happening. I knew they were in trouble. Their world is breaking, but I'm saving them." Her eyes bulged. "I'm saving them, Pier, and that's more important than anyone or anything it costs. You're doing the same with Silberfluss, aren't you?"

It wasn't an illness of the body that plagued her, but of the mind. Gon had mentioned once that Esperanza's soul was fractured. Sachihiro hadn't wanted them to talk about it in fear of upsetting her, but Pier had noticed the small signs: the odd speech patterns, the periods in which she acted less like herself, the obsession with different realms.

He guided her back to his room and onto his bed. "How long have you been thinking that, darling?"

She pouted. "You think I'm a fopdoodle."

"No, I don't think you're a . . . that. I think the last couple of months have brought on a lot of change, and it must be exhausting."

"I'm four months pregnant, Pier."

The words trickled in slowly. *Pregnant.* It couldn't be. Barely any time had passed since they'd smoked in their garden, talking about the lives that lay ahead of them. But that wasn't true, was it? A lot of time had passed. Pier was no longer the same college boy, and Zazil had stopped dreaming about tribal life. Why would Esperanza remain the same?

"That's . . ." He swallowed and patted her hand, gaining time while he searched for an appropriate response. "Great?"

Her smile returned. "It's the solution."

Dread spread in his stomach. Pregnant or not, she seemed off. She needed Gon and Sachihiro. "If I may be so frank, is it Sachi's?"

"Dash my wing, I don't know who you're talking about."

"Sachi, your—"

"So, Pier, I need those herbs." The dread in Pier's stomach increased. She'd last seen Sachihiro during Zazil's wedding in June and had shown up at their shop four months ago. As far as he knew, she hadn't gone out with any man in Waldfeld. She'd focused solely on her apprenticeship with his dad. The dread spread to his chest. Pier had never seen his dad on a date or pursue anyone since his mom had died. He wasn't the type for romantic relationships, but he'd been acting strange the past four months.

Pier tapped his foot repeatedly, steadying himself. "Dad didn't . . . he didn't come on to you, did he?"

Esperanza pulled her hand away and stood up from the bed. "No, he's a sweetheart." She plucked dead leaves off Pier's succulent. "You need to take better care of what's yours, dear." She turned around. "Let's drop the river in the puddle. The father doesn't matter. It's not going as planned."

The more she said, the less Pier understood. "This was planned?"

She continued as if she hadn't heard him. "I'm not sure it'll work, but it has to. They depend on me. I know they do. Get me the herbs, will you, Pier? Help me birth salvation."

Pier's heart sank. She had lost her mind. She must have. He peeked at her stomach and noticed a bulge. Salvation or not, she was expecting. "Esperanza, darling—"

The shop bell rang, and his dad's voice followed. "Edward's here."

Pier sucked in air. "I gotta go."

"Okey dokey, it's all bright when the bee drinks."

"Right . . ." He closed the trunk and picked it up, unsure what else to do. Freilist was calling. If his plan went well, Zazil would soon return to Silberfluss and bring Gon along. Gon could provide the medical assistance needed, and perhaps Sachihiro would show up as well. He looked back at the bulge, and an absurd thought struck him. This could've been his half-sibling. It was too bizarre. It made no sense.

He put the trunk back down and pulled her in for a tight hug. "It'll be okay, darling. Don't you worry."

She squeezed him. "I'm protected. We don't have to worry."

He released her and nodded. "I better . . ."

"Yes, go you snailfoot."

He'd only be gone for a week or two. Nothing would happen in that time. But what if it did? Waldfeld's medic had taken fewer biology classes than Pier. Father Godfried took care of most ailments. Esperanza needed Gon. Nothing would happen if they were here.

Pier's eyes fell on the gray marble box Zazil had given him. She hadn't responded to his message from yesterday, but she wouldn't sulk if a medical emergency occurred. He picked it up and pushed it into Esperanza's hands. "Here. Write on the parchment inside if you're not feeling well while I'm gone. Zaz will get it and can send Gon to you. They're in Virisunder, about a three-day ride from here. The moment you think something's going wrong, you write them, okay? Don't wait until it's too late."

She examined the box, and an unfamiliar expression crossed her face. "Thank you," she said, lower than her usual register.

"Of course." He kissed her cheek and left, praying to the ancestors that they'd take care of her and all the loves he neglected until he could look after them the way they deserved.

He found Edward in the shop with a jug of beer in his hand and a smile on his face. Pier's dad sat across from him, his face as sullen as it was before, but he made more effort than Pier was expecting.

". . . and that's when we realized the bedbugs were in our hearts. Like a metaphor, you know? Except for Carl. There were a ton in Carl's bed," Edward rambled.

Richard got up when he saw Pier and pulled a bow off the wall.

"Good morning, Edward," Pier said. "Ready for the journey? I hope you packed something other than beer."

Edward laughed. "Oh no, beer's on your dad. Don't know why you don't want me coming around here. He's not that bad."

Pier's eyes darted to his dad, who stood next to him with the bow, perfectly capable of hearing every word. "Sorry, Dad, I—"

"Here." He handed him the bow. "It'll protect you. Stay safe."

He took the bow and smiled. Mr. Ackerman had tried to teach him some tricks, but Pier believed himself a hopeless case. It was a sweet gesture nevertheless. His dad expressed himself more in his craft than he did in words. "Thanks."

Edward put the jug on a nearby table and gave Richard a surprising hug. "Thank you for the brew, Mr. Kilburn. I'll finish the story later." He gave Pier a hard pat on the shoulder. "Come on, Piersy, let's go."

Pier found his own uncertainty reflected in his dad's eyes. Why was it so easy for Edward to embrace a stranger but impossible for Pier to hug his dad? He put the trunk down, slower than necessary, and gathered courage to give him a proper goodbye. When he looked back up, his dad pushed wrapped bread into his hands.

"Don't want you to get hungry."

The air felt heavy with unsaid words, undone hugs. Pier nodded. "Thanks, Dad."

He placed the bread into his bag but knew he wouldn't touch it. He didn't feel like eating that day.

"See you soon," Pier said, and then he left.

CHAPTER 26

SUBIRA

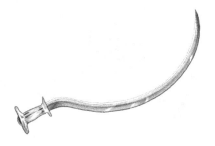

November 979 - Royal Military Base, Polemos, Virisunder

My dearest Subira,

Thank you for sending Zazil to me. I look forward to seeing where her talents take us, although they would be wasted at the base. We have settled nicely into Altor Caedem, and it would delight our hearts to receive a visit from you soon. I saw your little Xenia on the way to class the other day, all stern and concentrated just like her mother used to be. I assume you still are, but I wouldn't know anymore.

I hope you had time to rethink my offer. Agathe is using the truce to fortify towns on the new border, especially on the western front. The places themselves are unremarkable (Elderbeer, Nimmerwarm, Waldfield, you name it), but I suspect Heidegger is assisting the local nobility, and Agathe might fortify to attack as soon as the truce ends.

I still hope you accept the new position, but I can no longer begrudge you leaving active service. All these years ago, I compared your decision to me having Joseline. I was wrong. I didn't get to decide back then, but I do now. I understand that sometimes love is an acceptable choice.

My regards to Gustave. I hope you two are looking after each other.

Much love,
Alexandra

Subira's eyes burned from a lack of blinking. She had been staring at the letter for the past five minutes. *Thank you, Balthos, for testing me.* She leaned against the royal post office of Virisunder's military base, unsure why she had opened Alexandra's letter immediately. She had already known what it contained. More urging, more teasing. The military information was important, but she didn't have to mention her little girl. Each time Subira read one of Alexandra's letters, two distracting reactions threw her off her daily routine: jealousy and dread. Alexandra had chosen the same life she had. It was her right to. It could also be her friend's downfall. The Ceremony was a scheme; it must have been. Most of Subira's soldiers had written it off as another one of the queen's absurd decisions, but Subira knew better than to dismiss her. She'd sworn never to do so, and there were more likely explanations for the pregnancy. Subira knew what the heat of a battlefield could do to one's reasoning abilities.

The nearby clock tower struck four o'clock in the afternoon. Subira straightened her back and strutted toward her office at a challenging pace for her throbbing head. Some nausea boiled up, but it was nothing she hadn't dealt with before. Four o'clock meant she had thirty more minutes to finish her work for the day and get home in time to prepare dinner at sunset. Punctuality had been easier in summer. A lot of things had been easier in summer.

She entered her office and startled at the stack of papers on her desk. It had multiplied during her absence. Apparently, everything was reproducing. Her assistant, Baudelaire, had taken paternity leave as well. As happy as she was for him, he'd left her drowning in more of the paperwork she had hoped to avoid.

She sighed and flipped through the letters. Still nothing from Xenia. For weeks, she had wondered if Gustave was withholding letters from her, but she shouldn't have asked him. It wasn't worth the pain now throbbing through her head. Makeda probably kept her little knight busy. If something went wrong, Makeda would contact her directly, and Gustave would come to her for help with whatever issue arose.

She sat down in her armchair and grabbed the first pile of documents: relationship requests between military employees. Subira massaged her forehead and skimmed through them. Without Baudelaire, they'd fallen into her lap. A ridiculous task, as if she qualified to decide on such matters, but tradition demanded it. Balthos's law guarded matrimony and its requirements. It was an honor he allowed her to have a say in the first steps of it.

She tried to concentrate on the first request, but the words swam before her eyes. She put it down and pulled out her pocket watch. Eight minutes had already passed. She looked back at the letter pile. There was no way she could leave anytime soon. She had to at least make a dent in it, or it would become uncontrollable the next day.

It was time for plan B. Subira felt her way through the motus sacks in her drawer and pulled one out. She weighed it in her palm. She hoped it would be enough to keep Gustave occupied at the pub for a few more hours. If the messenger boy was quick, he could get it there by thirty after. *It should avoid another fight.* After the incident with the wall last night, Gustave had comforted her with the prospect of going dancing soon. They hadn't done that in two years. It would be a shame to ruin it over paperwork.

"Timothy!" she called, placing the relationship request aside and pulling out an official letter instead. It was a plea from the front with the usual questions. When was the truce ending? Who was replacing Alexandra as the new general of the front? Subira dipped her quill in ink and set it on an empty parchment for a response. She kept her eyes on the page and held out the motus sack when her messenger boy entered. Timothy was used to the pub runs.

"Ehm . . . good afternoon, Captain Subira Se'azana. You're real. It's an honor. I mean, what I wanted to say is . . . ehm, Timothy is not available right now."

It wasn't the familiar voice of the teenage elf but a low, gruff one—the kind of voice that could tell her stories on hikes through the misty forests of her home. A ridiculous thought, yet she couldn't help but hope for a Fi'Teri troubadour when looking up. The messenger was not from Fi'Teri. He wasn't an elf at all. He was an orc, and a nervous-looking one, for that matter.

"Who are you?" Subira was too surprised to follow her usual guidelines of polite conversation.

"I, ehm . . . Sachihiro Ch'ulel. At your service, Captain!" He made a hasty salute and mumbled, "Subira Se'azana." He followed the salute with a bow so low his round crystal glasses slid off his nose. He caught them and made his way back up with an excited sparkle in his toffee-colored eyes. Subira was uninterested in sweets, but she couldn't help noticing how his eyes formed a pleasant contrast to his moss-green skin. His uniform strained against his firm, orcish muscles.

"Oh." It was all she could say. Her reaction seemed to increase his nervousness.

"Yes, Captain . . . Subira Se'azana. I'm a new recruit. It's an honor, really. You hired my sibling as a medic, so they helped me get the position, but . . . but I am qualified for it, of course, and I won't sit on my butt all day, I promise." He let out a quick laugh and ran his fingers through the teal hair that covered his crooked ears. "I'm quite an admirer, to be honest. I've read everything about the strategies of the great Captain Subira Se'azana. Well, you, I suppose." He laughed again.

"Very well." She cleared her throat. This was entirely un-anticipated, and she wasn't quite sure what to do with herself. Then she remembered. "No, actually, it's Captain Subira *van Auersperg*. I'm married. But Captain will suffice."

He frowned. "In what division does your husband work?"

The frankness of his question took her aback. She didn't usually accept such disrespect, but perhaps he was unfamiliar with Virisunder customs. His sibling must've been the new medic she'd hired alongside Zazil. The Revelli smith had been Alexandra's idea, but she'd insisted to be employed alongside Gon Ch'ulel. It had been difficult to push through with Princess Josefine. Hiring a second orc would surely upset the princess further. The thought made it even more appealing to keep Sachihiro.

"My husband worked in the sanitary division." She could lecture him about manners another time. For now, her curiosity won.

"He cleaned toilets?"

"No." No one at the base had asked her about Gustave in years. She barely remembered how to speak about him as if he'd mattered to the Tazadahar war. "The trenches. Sometimes. When soldiers didn't have access to the sanitary facilities."

Sachihiro nodded. "So he was in charge of shit?"

Subira's eyes widened. "Soldier, language! I forbid both the content and delivery of such sentiment."

His face turned brown around his cheeks. It must've been orcish blushing. The discoloration had a calming effect on her. It was . . . endearing.

"I'm so sorry, Captain Subira Se—van Auersperg. Captain Subira van Auersperg."

"Captain will suffice." She was grateful he didn't know her middle name, Banou, or it would never stop.

"I'm so nervous to actually meet you. See, I thought the name was a misprint in my textbook. The ceremonial naming should follow the highest rank, and I assumed a prestigious military family such as the Se'azanas would be above van Auersperg. I must have missed that Virisunder doesn't follow the custom."

Subira's lips thinned. Virisunder did follow the custom.

"I think I've upset you. I'm sorry. I really didn't want to fuck it up with Captain Subira van Auersperg. I mean . . . oh no." His cheeks turned browner. "You called me in for a task, Captain Subi—Captain?"

She had? Right, she had. The weight of the motus sack

in her hand made itself known. She considered sending him to Gustave, but her husband wouldn't be as forgiving of his frankness. He wouldn't be pleased to see an orc either. He believed Tribu La'am heretics should be kept out of Elfentum, an understandable view seeing as they did not worship the pantheon, but Fi'Teri's god, Calliquium, encouraged communication between different nations. It wasn't their place to judge. If the people of Tribu La'am didn't believe in the pantheon, they would have to justify themselves to Balthos after their passing. Nothing hindered Subira from welcoming them, and they might find their way to the king's truth before their souls were lost.

She checked her pocket watch. Fifteen past four. Fifteen more minutes and she'd be late. She pushed the thought aside. A new recruit, especially one as controversial of a hire as Sachihiro was, required her attention more.

"Why don't you have a seat?" She put the motus sack back into the drawer. She would find a different way to soothe Gustave's anger.

Sachihiro smiled, revealing more of his tusks, and sat down awkwardly on the chair across from her desk. It groaned under his weight, and he shifted several times until settling for a half-hovering position.

Subira raised an eyebrow. "Are there any specific accommodations you and your sibling require?"

Lines formed around his toffee eyes as he smiled. It suited him. "No, Captain Su—Captain. Happy to serve as we are."

She examined him and the chair. They were an inadequate match, but Sachihiro was determined not to show it. A slight smile crept onto her lips as well. "I expect full honesty from all my soldiers, Ch'ulel."

He gulped. "I understand, Captain. Truthfully, my butt is very uncomfortable in this chair."

Her smile widened as she pulled out a blank parchment and jotted down notes. The barracks required a few larger furniture pieces. Some oversize chairs would be helpful for meetings. She glanced at his broad figure. He would require a larger bed as well, and a bigger uniform. He must've been her tallest soldier. Subira was at eye level with most elvish men, but she could have easily rested her head on his chest. She tensed her hand around the quill. *Balthos forgive me for such a thought.*

"Anything else?" she asked, sharper than intended.

"The . . . the rations." He scratched the back of his neck. "The orcish metabolism works three times quicker than human and five times quicker than elvish digestion. These rations run through within an hour, and we—"

She held her hand up. "No need to elaborate." This was a major oversight on her part. It was her job to keep soldiers in their optimum state. She clutched the quill until her fingernail bored into her palm. It drew a minuscule amount of blood, but the scent was enough to soothe her.

"You must be malnourished. I apologize. Your rations will be increased as soon as the new supplies arrive." A sharp spike shot through the left side of her head and triggered more nausea. She tapped her fingers on the desk to get through the pain. The distraction helped her refocus. She checked the watch again. Eighteen past four.

"That's kind of you, Captain, but you don't look healthy."

She glanced up and found genuine worry on his face. Soldiers often discussed whether a Fi'Teri immigrant could lead Virisunder's base, but no one cared about her beyond that. It stirred something in her chest that had been condemned to lie still.

"Tell me, soldier, why are you here?"

He shrunk into himself. "I do understand that recruiting me is unusual. I'm surprised to be here too. One moment you're ruining my wedding night—"

"Pardon?"

"Oh, yes, thank you for that." He continued as if she knew what he was talking about. "The next moment I'm in your office. I understand if you don't want me here, but please keep Gon. They're an excellent medic, and Zazil would throw a fit if I got them fired. I know there's little precedence for orcs in the Virisunder military, but we would have benefited you in events like the ambush of 948, and——"

"No, you misunderstood." He thought her no better than Princess Josefine. He didn't realize how much she related to his struggle. Makeda had paved the way for her, but people still scrutinized Subira's every move due to the color of her skin. As much as she loved her friend, if Subira had made half of Alexandra's mistakes at the front, she would have been exiled without discussion.

"I don't have any apprehension about hiring you," she said. It was important to her he understood that. "I——" The room spun, and her eyes felt as if they had been overstretched. She closed them to ease the nausea.

"May I?" His voice was like the crackling of a fireplace right after leaning closer to feel its heat. She opened her eyes and found him kneeling in front of her. This was both un-anticipated and inappropriate. Soldiers got this close to her during sparring matches or challenges but kept their distance otherwise. The innocence in his face made it hard to picture him challenging her.

He held his hand out. His face was close enough for her to see the ivory structure of his tusks. Before she analyzed the situation further, she found herself nodding. He wrapped his large hand around her forearm. Her breath caught when his skin touched hers. He pressed his thumb down next to a vein on her inner arm. A wave of relief rushed through her body and eased the nausea. His hand worked up to hers and pressed between her index finger and thumb. Another wave washed the head throbs away. She closed her eyes and saw the tranquil smile under his black beard. She longed to be closer to it.

A small sigh of pleasure escaped her. She hadn't made such a sound in three years. Despite its quietness, the sound filled the room. She opened her eyes wide and found the clean-shaven Sachihiro in front of her. His hair was still teal, not black. She swallowed and became painfully aware of the sound she had made. It left them staring at each other bashfully.

He retreated and cleared his throat three times before speaking. "I, ehm, I hope that helped. Little trick my sibling taught me. It always worked when my girlfriend wasn't feeling well."

His girlfriend, of course. She looked away, then back at him, expecting to see a spontaneously grown beard. There was none. She tapped two fingers against her neck and straightened up. Enough of this foolishness.

"Let's have a look at your file, soldier." She browsed through a crate of paperwork until she found his name. "You arrived here five days ago, is that correct?"

"Yes, Captain. I joined my sibling and sister-in-law."

"Sister-in-law?"

"Yes, Captain. She's your new assula smith, Zazil Ch'ulel."

"Revelli?" She leaned back to the crate and retrieved the smith's file.

"Ch'ulel. They're married by tribal law, although their official relationship status is pending your approval at the moment."

Subira sat back up in her chair. "Oh, by Balthos's love . . ." She *had* lost track of the paperwork. She found the relationship approval request Ch'ulel had filed and signed it, hoping it wouldn't be detrimental to the war effort or Zazil's career. Romantic engagements usually were.

"Approved. Let's get back to your file."

"I really appreciate you taking the time, Captain."

She nodded absently as she read his file. *Sachihiro Ch'ulel: Immigrated from the Juyub'Chaj tribe, Tribu La'am. Graduated with honors from Tribu La'am University after eight years of study in communication, languages, and decryption. Received the dean's recommendation for a professorship.* She reread the first paragraph several times but couldn't process the information. It couldn't be true.

"You . . . went to university?"

He broadened his chest in pride. "Yes, Captain."

Subira bit her lip. When she had joined the Virisunder military, she had started in a lower position than her schooling had suggested, and yes, she'd had to straighten her hair to fit in with the Virisunder elves, but surely prejudice couldn't run so deep they'd throw away recruits of extraordinary talent. There must've been a misunderstanding.

"Remind me, soldier, what position have you been assigned to?"

"I'm Timothy's assistant, Captain."

She suppressed a growl and steadied her voice. "Timothy . . . our fifteen-year-old messenger boy?"

Sachihiro nodded, but her sudden shift in tone seemed to unsettle him. "Am I in trouble?"

"Are you in—?" She couldn't even repeat it. This detestable discrimination was happening at her own base. She slammed her fist on the desk and glared at the stacks of paperwork. It was their fault. How could some arbitrary documents keep her from leading her people like they deserved to be led? How could she be a decent captain if paperwork buried her?

She stood up and slammed the motus sack drawer closed. She didn't care about getting home in time anymore. Gustave would find something that displeased him with or without an overdone steak in front of him.

"You're not working for Timothy anymore," she snapped at the frozen Sachihiro. She looked up at his face and noticed that she had guessed correctly; the crown of her braided bun reached his chest.

He made himself tiny. "Captain, please, I can—"

She didn't want to hear it. This destructive ideology had no place in her military. "You're working for me now. You're my new assistant."

His cheeks flushed brown, and his eyes widened in shock. "For you?"

"Provided you accept the position." She was surprised how spiteful she sounded.

"I-I'm speechless."

"Evidently."

She grabbed a pile of neglected files and shoved them into his arms. Sachihiro's eyes grew even larger. She pushed the door to Baudelaire's old office open and gestured toward it.

"This will be your workspace. If you accept the position, I expect the papers to be sorted out in the morning. We can discuss details of payment and better accommodations then."

"Tha-thank you, Captain." He grabbed the remaining files from her desk and headed into his new office.

Subira exhaled. She didn't trust spontaneity, but any good captain should make bold choices from time to time.

"You're becoming the new general?" He was already reading her correspondence as he made his way to the desk.

Her boldness deflated. "I'm uncertain." She returned to her own desk to avoid the look on his face.

"Why not?" he called from the other room.

"My husband is here in Polemos." She felt silly yelling into the other room, but perhaps he'd take the hint and stop talking.

He didn't. "He can come with you to the front and clean the shi—trenches. Clean the trenches."

Another small smile escaped. "I'll think about it." She checked her pocket watch. A quarter to five. The sun was setting.

CHAPTER 27

PIER

November 979 - Freilist, the Capital of Silberfluss

Pier left the noble manor so exasperated he almost overlooked the gorgeous sixth-century marble post office across the road. Almost. He never failed to appreciate an architectural masterpiece, and Freilist housed a multitude of them. Part of him wanted to strut through the capital's streets with his arm hooked around Martín's and listen to made-up history trivia. That part of him wasn't focused enough.

He took his eyes off the building and returned to the more pressing matter at hand: the fact that his dear client was a natural foe of social grace. Edward was heart-stoppingly handsome, but his manners? *Ancestors help us.*

"Ladies don't like to be reminded of their age," Pier said, signaling him to quicken his pace as they walked off the manor's premises. They needed to be out of sight in case the countess's offended state turned volatile. Pier had learned to enjoy their company, but he didn't trust nobles.

"How would you know?" Edward wheezed behind him.

"Knowing that is my line of work, and I'd appreciate a little more trust." Pier caught himself. He shouldn't hurt Edward's ego. This week needed to be a success, and it wasn't fair to put additional pressure on the sweet man. "You did pretty well in the beginning."

Edward's face lit up. "Really?"

"And you're an excellent ravisher. We just need to bridge the time in between."

When the manor was no longer in sight, Pier pulled a map out of his shoulder bag. He had visited Freilist before, but the noble district was larger than he had expected. An entire Waldfeld neighborhood could fit into each estate.

Edward sat down on the cobblestone. "I'm tired." He had slept nine hours the previous night and had enjoyed a slow morning with plenty of food, while Pier had run errands and organized meetings. Pier had slept one hour and wasn't complaining. Then again, he made exhaustion look good.

"Let's get you to the inn. We're meeting the first courtier tomorrow."

Edward grimaced. "I'm not ready."

Pier sat down next to him and took his hand. "Don't you worry about being ready. I will be there almost the whole time." He smiled at him, but it didn't work. His client pulled his hand free and buried his face in it.

"I super fudged up today."

It pained Pier to watch Edward tremble under the pressure he had forced onto him. He wished he could carry the burden himself. Edward had been doing fine on his own. He had earned five motus a week, occasionally more, and had charmed himself into the hearts of Waldfeld's innkeepers. They always kept a room available for him. He did decently well. Pier's dad was also doing decently well, but decent wasn't good enough. Not for Pier. A decent life had killed his mother. He wanted a great life, not for him but for everyone, and a greater world on top of it. If people stopped settling for the lowest available option, they could make a difference. Martín hadn't settled for the lowest available option—*him*—and Pier hoped he was living a great life.

He stroked Edward's blond hair. "Have you ever been to the cabaret?"

The question got Edward's attention. He looked up and shook his head.

"You see, the performers of cabaret shows rehearse for a few weeks before going onstage, just like we did." A sheepish nod. Pier smiled. "The night before the big opening, they do what's called a dress rehearsal, and it almost always fails. Badly." A sheepish blink. "Now you didn't fail *badly* with the countess today, but it's good that the conversation turned sour. It taught us our final lesson for tomorrow."

"Oh! That . . . that actually makes sense."

No, it doesn't. Limbo help us if you talk like that tomorrow. "See? It'll go great tomorrow! Now you go to the inn and get some rest. I have one more meeting, and then tonight we go over this valuable lesson from today, okay?"

Edward grinned and jumped up. "You're right!" He helped Pier to his feet. His hand was strong, warm, and much larger than Pier's. The touch felt like sultry days in Mink'Ayllu's catacombs chasing treasures, or spirits, or whatever story his tour guide could come up with. It had never been about the stories; it was always about the spark of mischief in his eyes.

"First the duchess's courtier, and soon I'll be the princess's harlot!"

The comment snapped Pier back into the present. "*Courtesan*! Edward, you are a courtesan or romantic companion, not a harlot. Princesses don't have harlots."

Edward laughed. "All right, Piersy, see you at the inn."

He strolled away. Pier brushed off his three-piece suit and watched him for a moment. He put a lot of pressure on

Edward, but he'd also put his hope on him. Pier had worked relentlessly to make noble connections. He had spent the past months spreading rumors about Silberfluss's best lover until word made it to Freilist. If they could get their foot in the palace's doors, the offers would be limitless. Everyone at court would learn about Kilburn weapons, and Pier could work his way into the political circles, whispering ideas into noble ears until all of his loved ones were taken care of. Then, and only then, could he focus on gaining power for himself.

If only Edward's words were as convincing as his ass. *Wait.* He managed to take his eyes from the pleasant sight and checked the map. "Edward! The inn is the other direction."

Edward turned around, stared at him for a second, then shrugged. "Oopsie."

Pier suppressed a sigh. Things would work out. They had to. He'd be there to smooth out any verbal hiccups. For now he had other worries to focus on. He didn't want to lose Zazil to the enemy, so it was time to mend her home front. If he fixed one of her problems, she might overlook his other shortcomings.

He had disappointed her when he hadn't shown up for the wedding and hadn't told her that his father refused to pay for a proper travel entourage. Pier hadn't saved up enough motus to rent his own carriage entourage, and the travel to the Juyub'Chaj mountains would have been too long and dangerous without one. He wasn't sure what sounded worse: crossing several war zones or finding his way through the haunted Forest of Pearls on the Tribu La'am border. Still, he should have been at the wedding. He should have negotiated with Gon's mother and resolved the situation. He should have kept Esperanza from running. His stomach turned when he thought of her solemn request. He had to find those herbs as soon as possible. One task after the other. For now, Zazil was his priority.

He pulled out the letter Zazil's parents had sent her. She had forwarded it to him with the distinct instructions to burn it, kill it, feed it to the sows, then throw their shit at the Revelli manor. He'd decided to take some liberty with the execution. A brief scan revealed the address. Unfortunately, the words "shameful bestiality" and "disgraced exile" caught his eye. A wave of fury rose and nauseated him. Anger felt foreign in his body. It was unnecessary and counterproductive. He planned to charm the Revellis into revoking Zazil's disinheritance, not to attack them. *Bestiality.* That wasn't how his dad had seen his relationship with Martín, was it? It couldn't be. One must have a hateful heart to believe such bogus.

His stomach grew heavier. The noble family they'd visited earlier had served rich vanilla cake with whipped cream on top—enough to fill him up for a whole day—but if things turned out in his favor, the Revellis would likely serve tea and cake as well. It would be wisest to cleanse himself of the cake and the anger before approaching the manor. He walked toward the Revelli estate until he reached an alleyway to duck into. Ten minutes, that was all he needed. Then he'd turn on his patent charm and convince them that Gon was a perfect match for Zazil, tusks and all.

The alleyway was hidden and narrow, with the neighboring estates' fences to shield him from spying eyes. He pulled off his jacket, vest, and shirt, folded them carefully, and laid them aside. The November air made him shiver. *Perfect.* It could cool off the anger until it evaporated. He glanced around one more time, then relieved himself of the cake. One slice of that cake could have extended his mom's life for a week. He couldn't keep it. It wasn't fair to her. She had taught him that anger was a destructive force focused on increasing the problem instead of solving it. It was better to swallow it down until it faded, or in his case, purge it.

"Hey, pretty boy."

Pier jumped and twirled around. An elvish man had appeared out of nowhere and eyeballed him with a self-assured smirk. He had long sleek hair that was half-white and half-black. It framed his gorgeous face and gray eyes.

Pier cleared his throat. "Hello there." He tried to wipe any remaining vomit off on his sleeve before remembering that he wasn't wearing one. "Ehm, would you mind turning around?" He picked up his shirt and vest. He didn't want to be exposed in front of the stranger.

"Yes, I would." His words dragged on long with a smooth, alluring resonance. He didn't take his eyes off Pier.

"Well . . . that is an option." Pier put his shirt on and tried to regain some confidence with each button he closed. He'd spent his past months arranging seductions but hadn't been the target of one since Martín.

"So you're Pier Kilburn." It was a statement.

Never show that you know less than they do. Pier put on his jacket and straightened it. "Yes, that's me. I appreciate you finding me, but I don't think I'll require your assistance. Thank you, though." The strange elf grinned wider. Pier continued. "Pardon me, your name has slipped my mind."

"Cute." He offered his white-gloved hand, which was adorned with expensive jewelry. "Marcel Revelli. I'm Zilly's older brother."

Pier shook his hand. The touch of his glove carried a strange charge of energy. "Zilly?"

"Zazil."

Pier retracted his hand. Zazil had never mentioned a brother. She preferred not to speak about her family, but surely a brother would have come up.

"You don't believe me." Marcel circled his thumb and middle finger against each other as he spoke. "Zilly and I got into opium together. I assume she hasn't mentioned me much if she's trying to leave that life behind." A green hue rose from his gloved thumb.

Assula glove. The Revellis were the highest-regarded assula smiths of Elfentum. Pier had seen how much Zazil could do with only a fraction of the magical energy. This glove might've been as powerful as a sword. Pier wished he hadn't left his bow at the inn, but it was a silly wish. He couldn't share tea and cake with nobles while carrying a bow, and Marcel Revelli wasn't his enemy. In fact, he could be an ally. If he truly was Zazil's brother, he could help him change their parents' minds on Gon. If what he said was true, she might've even missed him. She might've regarded Pier as her brother, but what if he could reconnect her to her actual brother? She wouldn't have to settle for Pier.

"I suppose that makes sense. She has mentioned my name?"

Marcel chuckled. "Oh, quite often. You and Gon are at her heart's center, aren't you?"

Pier eased up. It hurt to think Zazil was withholding so much of her life from him, but she had obviously kept Marcel informed. "So you know about the whole Gon situation? What do you think of it?"

He sucked in air without losing his smirk. "It's a shame, isn't it?"

A shame. He must've been a politician as well, for he used the same vague expressions. He taunted Pier to provide a stance before revealing his own opinion. Pier knew how to play that game. He crossed his arms and casually leaned against the fence. He kept his eyes on Marcel, challenging him to break contact first.

"Tell me . . . how are your parents dealing with the shame?"

Marcel bit his lip and looked down before glancing up slowly. It stirred heat in Pier, and he saw that Marcel caught it. "Our parents are nothing but cold, empty shells of people. Why don't you come with me and see for yourself? We can talk afterward. In private."

Pier shifted his shoulder bag. He hadn't expected to receive an invitation into the Revelli estate. It would give him an advantage in the discussion, but his gut told him to remain cautious. He had no proof this man was actually Zazil's brother.

"You're scared of me," Marcel said.

Pier tensed. Whatever happened, he couldn't show weakness. "You misunder—"

"I'm pained." He placed his hand on his heart. "Zilly considers you part of her family, part of us."

He thought of Zazil's last angry message. He was losing her. He couldn't lose her. "Did Zazil tell you how we met?" Pier asked, testing him.

"Not that I recall, but I know you kept her from throwing herself into the gutter after Gon broke up with her. That's how I know you're the special one to her."

Pier thought he saw a red glint in Marcel's eyes, but when he looked closer, they were bright gray. His stomach complained, but there was nothing left to rise into his throat.

Marcel laughed. "Are you always looking for conspiracies? It's quite endearing, but I don't want to freeze my ass off out here."

Pier took a deep breath. That sounded more like Zazil. She'd have laughed at him too for being so dramatic. "My apologies." He shook his head and headed out of the alleyway. Marcel followed. "I had a lot of meetings with different noble families today."

"They put you on edge?"

Pier let out a short laugh. "I suppose so." He was revealing his small-town upbringing after all. He had a lot to learn if a few nobles could make him this suspicious.

Marcel guided him around the corner toward a large gaudy manor with moldings and pillars made of solid gold. Zazil's style was eccentric and colorful, but she had taste. Her family was void of it.

The manor's random display of riches had no coordination or balance. Copper, brass, and marble statues of the gods, as well as painted wood depictions of the war against the Traitor, were scattered all across the yard.

Marcel opened the gate, and Pier followed him on the path that led to the porch. He passed a brightly colored fountain with a monstrous statue of the Traitor, the deformed creature mortals had turned Alames's dead splinters into. The Traitor knelt in front of a handsome Balthos, who signed the treaty with pity on his face. On Pier's other side was a sculpture of Balthos holding his dead goddess in his arms. For a moment, Pier thought it was a tasteful piece of artwork lost in the chaos. Then Alames's marble chest burst into splinters. A green assula cloud formed out of her chest and made the splinters hover where her heart should've been. Pier startled when small bronze statues rose from the surrounding grass. *The mortals.* They were painted dark green and waited to catch Alames's splinters. Their portrayal sickened Pier. Their faces were contorted with greed, their noses were pressed flat, and their mouths were scarred holes with yellow half-rotten tusks poking out of them. Pier had never seen orcs depicted that way.

He stopped. This mission was a lost cause. Politics could convince the ignorant, not the fanatic, and this madness was the work of the latter. He didn't want Gon anywhere near it. He was grateful Zazil had escaped such an environment.

Marcel turned around. "Scared?"

Pier frowned. Marcel was too calm among the horror to be Zazil's treasured brother. "How did you know I was visiting?"

He laughed again, but this time it felt like a tactic to gain time. "Zilly wrote me you'd come today."

Pier's chest tightened. He hadn't told Zazil about his plan. He had wanted to surprise her with the mended family fences, the opportunity to return to Silberfluss. He hadn't told anyone where he was going, not even Edward. *I caught this arrogant asshole in a lie. His beloved conman Everything would be proud.* Sober realization followed. No one knew he was here.

"Pardon me, I remembered that I have another engagement." He turned around and hastened away, back toward the gate. "Lovely meeting you. Maybe some other time," he called over his shoulder.

He reached the gate, relieved that Marcel hadn't followed.

He pulled the metal latch, but it didn't move. It was a regular iron fence at Pier's shoulder height. It appeared to be the least strange object in the grotesque yard. Why wouldn't it move? He pulled at it again, but his efforts were in vain. The metal burned the tip of his finger. He yanked his hand away, but the pain increased. He found the cause and gagged. A faint green hue had cut into his fingertip and pulled off the first skin layer.

Before he could process what was happening, a gloved finger stroked his neck. He shuddered, and the full hand wrapped around it. Marcel pulled Pier backward, away from the gate, away from freedom. His sharp elvish teeth tugged on Pier's earlobe and drew blood.

Marcel leaned in until his lips brushed against the blood and whispered, "It's rude to leave before tea and cake. I thought you knew that."

CHAPTER 28

ALLY

December 979 - Altor Caedem, Virisunder

Ally took a shallow breath and sank onto her lab chair for much-needed rest. Her little warrior pushed too hard against her lungs for any substantial relief to set in. She glowered at the experiment table with the beautiful glowing glass orb. Various instruments and papers were piled up around it. For the past two weeks, she'd been trying to measure and understand the raw assula Zazil had sent her and had gathered next to nothing.

If she touched the orb without her protective gloves, a light shock shot through her. It would've likely been worse without the orb, but Zazil had strictly forbidden her to remove it from the glass. The collectors harvested assulas in the orbs. They didn't leave the glass until they were prepared for further forging. At that point, the golden glow would have turned green. Ally thought of the hourglasses and golden lights inside the Institute's floor. They hadn't been contained, unless the glass floor itself counted as an orb.

She had discovered nothing else. The books Theodosia had lent her on the subject illustrated basic forging methods, but Ally didn't risk trying them. Zazil had only gotten her hands on one raw assula, and Ally wouldn't corrupt its natural energy. She had tried to order more prints on the subject, but her bibi had gotten upset. Makeda hated assula magic with passion. She had to allow its general use in weaponry because of Council regulations but wanted nothing else to do with it. The magical power had played a key role in Makeda's and Theodosia's defeat and their eventual exile. Ally thought it was even more reason to understand assulas better, but her bibi disagreed.

Ally leaned forward and picked up her notes. If assulas were the converted energy of a living body, how were they contained with no organs to create continued movements? She dipped her quill in ink and added a few more questions around her equation.

"Robert?" she asked while writing. "How much do you weigh?"

He guarded the door while reading an analysis of fiction novels across the six Elfentum nations. Theodosia's private book collection rivaled the palace library.

"Hmm?"

"Your weight, if you don't mind me asking?"

"Ehm . . . not sure. About thirty-six conchs I think."

She scribbled the number down and began to calculate his mass.

He walked over to her and cocked his head at the formulas. "Why?"

"I'm calculating how much usable energy your body would convert into if you died." She eyed him. He made a good theoretical test object, but if assulas stemmed from body energy, the Council harvesters should've collected in Tribu La'am. Energy equaled mass, so orcs must've held the most potential energy. That didn't sound right. She added more calculations.

"Well, that's . . . reassurin'."

"I'm not thinking about killing you," she said absent-mindedly while calculating the energy. Something didn't add up. She had received no reports of Council members in Tribu La'am, and Virisunder would have an assula shortage if body mass was that relevant.

"Thanks," Robert said.

"What?"

"Thanks for lettin' me live, I suppose."

She lost track of her thoughts and glanced up at him. Since they'd arrived at Altor Caedem, he had looked at her with the same unchanging expression: attentive but emotion-ally indifferent, like listening to directions. "I'm sorry, I was just calculating . . ."

"Whatever you need, Your Majesty." He was the per-fect guard and nothing more. The only time he displayed any emotion was when Ally had a dizzy spell or a cramp. She wished the baby would kick her now, cause just enough pain to get his attention. She bit her lip. What a pathetic no-tion. She waited for her voices to yell at her, but Reggie had soothed them now that she was getting closer to delivery. At least she had Reggie again. It was more than she had hoped for or believed to deserve.

"That's all for now. Thank you, Robert." She returned to her equation, stared at it for a few seconds, and tossed it onto the desk. If mass was the main variant, why weren't they all producing assulas as a byproduct of living? Why was it a byproduct of death?

She stood up and examined the orb. The energy had floated freely under the Institute's glass floor, but someone had carried it there. It could be caught, set free, and caught again. She put the gloves back on and took a glass container off her shelf. Two weeks had passed. It was time for practical experiments.

"Robert, kindly leave the lab." She put on her goggles, opened the container, and picked up a small but sharp chisel.

"Your Majesty, what—"

"Leave please, this might be dangerous."

He stepped next to her instead. "It's my job to keep you safe."

She avoided his eyes and placed the orb on a marble board. He wanted to keep the baby safe and prove that he was a proper royal guard. That was all he cared about. "And you're doing an excellent job, but I have taken measures for my protection, whereas you have no clue what's going on."

"What measures? Those things?"

She had to look up now. He pointed at the goggles with a smirk. Ally's heart jumped. There was amusement in his face, something other than indifference. He glanced at her lips, and she held her breath. *Kiss me, fool.*

He turned away and walked back to the door. "I'll stand right here, just to keep an eye on things, all right?"

"That's fine." *The experiment.* She had to focus on the experiment. She raised the chisel and cracked the orb with one swift stab. The golden light burst upward into her face. She leaned away and swung the glass container to catch it. The light dodged the container and attached to her arm instead. It circled above the glove and tightened like a hand grasping her. The room disappeared in golden brightness until she saw the small silhouette of an elvish girl.

"Mommy!" the girl cried.

The room turned back to normal. Ally blinked and regained her vision just in time to see a black cloud manifest. It grabbed the golden light string and disappeared. She stared at the spot where it had floated for several seconds, bewildered.

"Did something happen, Your Majesty?"

She knew what that black cloud was. She'd studied it. She'd faced it on the battlefield. It appeared around those damned souls bound for limbo.

"Your Majesty?"

It collected the splinters of souls, not the energy of bodies.

"Ally?"

She screamed.

"Ally!" Robert rushed to her side and caught her before her legs gave out. The baby kicked as if she were fighting limbo herself. Ally felt herself rip as if her body wanted to follow the splinter. The Council didn't harvest the energy of dead bodies. It harvested souls, collected them before they could pass to limbo or the ethereal realm. That was the energy she'd gone to war for, the energy she had fought to make available to everyone: the energy of enslaved soul splinters.

"Hey, hey, Robert's here." He cupped her face as she sobbed. "Can you put words to this, maybe? Let's try, all right?"

"They're souls," she whispered.

She thought of the girl, a shadow of a person. The splinter had belonged to her.

"They're children. Robert, they're children." She broke down in his arms and clutched him as close as her belly allowed.

"Shh, I got you." He scooped her into his arms and sat down with her, swaying her gently. "What about children?"

"The splinters . . . the assulas. The Council's assulas, Robert. They're—"

"The soul splinters of children," Robert said slowly, shock taking hold of him with each word. "No."

Ally nodded. "I felt it. The orb keeps them from passing on."

He turned as pale as her and stood back up, still carrying her. "We gotta fight them," he mumbled. "The Tidiers. We gotta fight them."

Ally nodded, her brain unable to process anything else about this moment.

"No." More thoughts rushed through her. The Institute. The Council. The six nations. All of Elfentum was complicit. She thought of the experiments Josef had conducted on her back when she was a child, the endless hours she'd spent in his lab, the many ways he had tried and failed to break her. *He tried to splinter me.*

"It's my fault."

"No, no, no." Robert hugged her closer and sat back down. "This is horrifying, but you can't blame yourself. It would have spread either way and—"

"No, I helped him perfect it."

"What?"

Ally's skin crawled when she pictured the instruments he had used on her. Had there been an orb in the room? There must have been, but she couldn't remember. The harder she tried, the less of the room she could picture. "I helped Josef. I helped him do this."

Robert guided her chin to face him. "Hey, absolutely not. Don't talk like that. Nothing that monster did to you is your fault, you hear me?"

There was so much sincerity in his eyes. She wanted to believe him.

Robert furrowed his brows. "But we are gonna bring these fuckers down."

"Knocky-knock." They startled as Reggie entered. He dropped his cheerful tone when he saw them. "What's going on?"

"Sorry," Robert mumbled, then tried to set Ally down. She clasped him tighter and shook her head. He readjusted her in his arms, kissed her forehead, and turned to Reggie. "This genius discovered something horrible."

Ally was impressed he'd spoken in full sentences, his thoughts collected. The sniper training must have given him focus in the face of terror. She didn't possess such poise. Fragmented memories of her time with Josef fought for attention while she grasped for theories or plans or understanding or anything that could lessen the terror.

"She does that . . ." Reggie drawled, scratching the rose on his cheek. "What's the discovery, sugar?"

Ally's heart sped up. There was a strange distance between them. He seemed reserved, cautious, like a hunter waiting for his prey to move. The thought sent another shiver of terror down her spine.

"The essence of assulas."

"Oh, good." His reservation disappeared. "Yes, I mean, what? That's . . . that's horrible, truly." He acted like his old self again, but there was one problem with it.

"Let me down, please," Ally whispered. Robert set her down. "What's horrible, Reggie? I haven't told you what it is yet. And you wouldn't know, would you?" She stepped closer to him until he looked like the prey. "Because if you did, you surely would have told me instead of letting me experiment for weeks and condone the *enslavement of souls*."

No surprise crossed his face. He knew.

He gulped. "Hey, sugar . . . let's, let's not make assumptions, all righty?" He looked over Ally's shoulder and raised his hands. "Whoa, whoa, whoa, easy!"

Ally turned around. Robert had pulled his pistol and was aiming it at Reggie's face. "I don't miss, Reginald."

"Robert, no." Ally's voice shook. She'd jumped to conclusions at the Ceremony. She couldn't do it again.

Robert didn't blink. "Just keeping all my eyes on him. So we're condonin' this kind of thing for children, are we, Reg?"

Ally looked back at Reggie's pained expression. "I didn't know they used children's splinters as well. Must be for the stronger ones. That's . . . not great."

Not great? "This is a catastrophe, Reggie. We need to inform the people. We need to stop the Institute. We need to—"

"Ally, calm down."

Rage shot through her, and her fingers itched. "Calm down?"

Reggie tossed his hands into the air. "Okay, okay, I get it. This sounds fuck-e-di-fucke—"

"Don't you *dare* use your jester voice right now!" A fire

ignited in Ally. Her hands trembled, and a white hue spread through the room.

"Ally, listen to me," Reggie blurted. "They're splinters of dead people. Their souls are already lost. They might be more lost in limbo; who knows? This way their stories continue—"

"Are you fucking kidding me?" Reggie became smaller until she could see the top of his head. Or was she rising into the air? "This isn't one of your plays!"

"I don't like assulas either, Ally, but they power half of Elfentum at this point. Getting rid of them would lead to chaos and war and—"

"Maybe we need that war." Her chest widened. She looked at her arms. The white hue stemmed from her. She didn't question it. She didn't need to. It felt natural. "Maybe all of Elfentum needs war to cleanse itself from the Council, and assulas, and the toxic oppression of the church, and—"

"Ally, you're being irrational." Reggie stretched his neck to look up at her. "Take a deep breath and nothing bad has to happen."

"Are you threatening her?" Robert's voice sounded strange and distant, but he was still there, guarding her. He cocked the pistol.

"Shush, my fine man, this doesn't concern you."

"But it concerns *us*?" Ally asked. Pain shot through her head. Everything felt clear, but her thoughts couldn't catch up to the truths.

"Sugar, we've been here before, and I hate doing this."

Her body buzzed with a new energy, one that her living being produced. Not a byproduct, but a beautiful creation within her. She looked at the tiny man in front of her. *Reggie's a magic-bearer.*

"How many souls have you enslaved to put on those shows?" Her voice sounded raw and rough, like a growl.

Reggie rose in height until he was nose to nose with her. He stroked her cheek. "Please . . . you're Alexandra Verdain, sugar. Nothing else. You're just Ally."

"Just Ally?" she asked.

A tear rolled down his cheek, and he nodded. She grabbed his wrists and cut into his flesh with her claws.

He sighed. "All right, then. Sorry, Robert. I'm sorry, my love. It's for the best, trust me." He raised his other hand and snapped his fingers. The world turned white, then black. Ally shrunk into herself and passed out.

Ally opened her eyes and found herself in the middle of paper stacks. Her head lay on her lab desk, and a throbbing headache greeted her. She must have dozed off on her notes after studying for too long. She sat up and stretched. A loud snore came from behind her. She looked over her shoulder and saw Robert, asleep on his chair, slumped against the door. She giggled. Her poor guard had sat there for hours while she'd tinkered with the assula enigma.

She turned back to her desk and froze. It was gone. The assula was gone.

"Robert!"

"Wha—?" He jumped up in a daze and rushed over to her. "What's wrong?"

She searched through the papers and instruments until she'd turned over every piece of her mess. "The assula is gone!"

"Wha—how?"

"I don't know!" She scooted her chair backward and knelt to search under the desk. Glass cracked under her foot. She stumbled to the side and found the orb's shards on the floor. *No, no, no.* She had broken it. She must have stepped on it when she'd fallen asleep. Tears shot into her eyes. How could she have been so stupid?

Someone knocked on the door. Robert helped Ally back to her feet. "Come in."

Makeda entered with thin lips and furrowed brows. "Something's wrong with Reginald."

Ally forgot about the assula and rushed out of her lab.

"Careful with the runnin'!" Robert shouted after her, but she barely heard him.

She found Reggie in their bed, convulsing with pain. Ally jumped next to him.

"I'm here, love." She brushed hair out of his face and stroked the side of his head. His forehead was boiling hot.

Robert entered, pale as her. "What happened?"

"Send for a medic."

Ally kissed the tip of Reggie's ear and snuggled against him. "I'm here." She noticed that he pressed his hand against his side like he had at the Ceremony. "Can I take a look, my love? I promise I'll be gentle."

He shook his head. "No medic."

"Reggie, we——"

"No medic, please."

Ally sighed. "Robert, come back."

"Yes, Your Majesty?"

"Just get us a cold cloth, please."

Robert nodded and left. Ally ran her fingers over Reggie's neck. "How can we help you if you won't let us?"

Reggie rolled over to face her. Ally's shoulders sank when she saw how wet his eyes were. Watching him suffer without being allowed to offer solutions ripped her apart. He had always assured her that they were a team. It was the two of them together. The paranoid voices often questioned it, but she knew they belonged to her illness. Now, however, she questioned it with her clear mind. How could they be a team if he kept secrets from her?

"Come to Porta Proditor with me," he said. "You and Robert both. Just for a bit, while I recover."

She frowned. "The sky city you told me about? Reggie, it's a story."

"No." He slid his hand around the back of her neck and stroked it with his thumb. "It's real."

Ally wondered if he had ingested her illness when he'd cleared her from it. "Take some days off from magic. I can cope for a week. I've lived with it for so long."

"Ally, it's real. They also call it Traitor's Gate. Let's go there—you, me, and Robert."

Traitor's Gate. If he was right and the sky city was real, it must've been the home of rebels. They must've opposed Balthos's pantheon and therefore the Council. Ally's heart quickened. What if there was a floating island full of potential allies against Josef?

The baby kicked her hard, and she gasped for air. *Right.* "Reggie, I'm seven months pregnant. I can't travel into the sky." Another thought struck her. If they lived in the sky, but people down here in Elfentum knew about them, they must have traveled between the city and solid ground. They must have had flying devices. "How do you get there?"

"You're right." He perked up and kissed her. "Let's get that little butt-kicker out of you first. I'll tell you more about it later."

She wanted to question him further, but he fell back into his pillow and closed his eyes. She kissed his lids, and he smiled.

"Can I hold you for a bit, sugar?"

"Of course." She snuggled into his arm and closed her eyes as well. He sighed.

Robert cleared his throat. "Ehm . . . the wet cloth, Your Majesty." Ally blinked at him and tensed at the cold in his eyes.

She took the cloth and placed it on Reggie's forehead. "Thank you."

Reggie stretched his other arm out and looked at Robert. "Wanna scoot in, my man?"

"I'm not your man, Reginald."

Ally looked at her split lithium. "Why don't you read a little to us, Robert? I'd love to hear the prologue of *Defiance of a Rose* again."

"No, you wouldn't," Robert mumbled. "My shift is over, Your Majesty. I'll be at the barracks if you need me. I hope you feel better soon, Reginald." He strutted out of the room without another look.

Reginald peeked at her from underneath the cloth. "Go after him."

"What?"

"I know you want to, sugar. Go after him." He groaned as he pushed himself up again.

Ally shoved him into the pillow. "Stay down, fool."

"I wanted a kiss."

She kissed him softly at first, then with urgency. Heat rushed through her sore muscles. Why were they sore? She hadn't moved much in the last week. It must've been another pregnancy symptom. Her hand wandered under the blanket, but he caught it. "Are you sure? I could make you feel better without a medic . . ."

Reggie chuckled. "Thanks, but you two need to talk, and I need a nap."

"I don't want to leave you alo—" she started, but he pulled a sleeping hat as large as three pillows out of thin air and placed it over his face. Loud snoring followed. Ally giggled.

"Fine, but I'll tell a guard to keep an eye on you and will be back soon."

He tossed the hat off. "Is that a threat, milady?"

Ally smirked. "Maybe."

"I'll make sure to nap extra hard so as not to awaken your wrath."

"You better." She jumped off the bed and threw him a kiss on her way out.

Soberness hit her once she reached the staircase. She had no idea what to say to Robert or if he was willing to listen. She took the first two steps before a hissing spread through the stairwell. She hesitated. Reggie might have lifted his spell. The illness could have returned, but he would have warned her ahead of time.

The air crackled. "Alames, my pet?" It was the same low voice she'd heard at the Institute when the hourglass had exploded. "I know you're there. I've felt you."

Ally's breath caught. "I'm not Alames."

"You have questions, so many questions, but you're no longer tainted by mortal foulness. We can find each other again."

The staircase swam in front of Ally's eyes. Her mind couldn't comprehend the words, but she knew how to handle voices. "I don't trust you."

Pain shot through her stomach, more than a regular kick. She sank down onto a step and clutched the railing, fighting to keep her consciousness.

"We can take time to reacquaint ourselves, my pet. But don't make me wait too long."

Cramps shook her. She held her belly, felt the warrior inside kick and toss. She couldn't lose her warrior. She couldn't lose her consciousness.

"Who are you?"

"Balthos. I'll be there when you call me."

The crackling disappeared, and Ally lost grip of the railing. She slid down three steps and collided with the stone wall. The kicking stopped.

"Hello?" called another voice, another man. Ally couldn't comprehend it. "Anyone up there?"

She saw the silhouette of an elvish man climbing the stairs toward her.

"Ally!" Warm, strong arms cradled her and lifted her up.

It felt familiar, as if it had already happened that day. Everything felt familiar.

The man readjusted her in his arms and kissed her forehead. "Robert's here."

CHAPTER 29

VANA

December 979, Balthos's Heretics, Silberfluss

Prison didn't differ much from feudal society. They served a farm girl gray slime and expected her to swallow it as vegetable stew. This shit had never been in contact with vegetables. Vana stirred her dinner and wondered if it was more radical to refuse to swallow slime or to eat it and thrive despite it. Her stomach growled for the latter, so she took a spoonful. The taste of mold made her gag. She cursed her healthy reflexes and decided to skip dinner again. At least she'd gotten a good metaphor out of it. Artyom would have to add it to her manifesto later. Her own handwriting still needed work, but he wrote everything down she asked him to. He either had inexhaustible patience or was bored enough for any activity.

She peeked at her new comrade, whose skin looked ashen

and sickly. The cells were getting cold with December chills, and Artyom hadn't been up to snuff lately.

"Stop it, vulture," he grumbled.

Vana grimaced. "Sorry, man, you just look like shit."

"You look shit every day, and I never complain." His familiar smirk put her at ease before she noticed how glassy his eyes had gotten.

"We need to get you something . . ."

"You drag me here. Was that not cure?"

She had pestered him for days to visit the dining hall. Nachtalbs never entered the hall, and she'd hoped the torches would warm Artyom enough to ease his ailment. Whenever Vana or her brothers had caught something, their mother made them soak up sunlight. Unfortunately, sunlight was a privilege not given to rebels of the system.

She rubbed his back. "I'll get you somethin' to warm you up."

He smiled but scooted away. "Your hothead is plenty. Do not come too close. You relax and enjoy Silberfluss delicacies."

She looked back at the slime. "That's not what we usually eat in—"

"Sure, sure." He swallowed a spoonful and grimaced. "You want to make me feel better? Get me some hot kuurdak."

She was about to ask what the limbo kuurdak was when four guards entered the dining hall alongside the warden. Artyom spat out Sap Büruy words that didn't sound friendly.

"Delinquents and heretics, I request a moment of silence," the warden said. *We've all shut up already, asshole.* "I expect you to be on your best behavior today. Pretend you possess some level of decency. We are honored by the highest of Council guests, King Josef Verdain of Virisunder."

Frantic murmuring filled the hall. Vana didn't know much about the king, but Bored Reginald couldn't stand the shithead, and Josef Verdain was noble, so guilty by birth. Other inmates seemed to have more informed opinions on him. The half orc, Erna, shoved her protegees into a corner and broadened herself in front of them.

"Silence! He is visiting us for his yearly disadvantaged relief program. With any luck, you might be chosen for early dismissal to serve His Majesty instead."

All those fancy words surely covered up bullshit.

Artyom tugged her sleeve. "Keep head down, kymbat. Stay quiet for me, please."

The sound of fanfare resounded through the labyrinth, and the warden stepped to the side. The tune was simple, but it was the first music Vana had heard since Jules's death. It awakened a longing in her that she had buried alongside her Spirit. For a moment, she allowed herself to crave the music and the joy it brought. The light moments of strumming, composing, playing with no real goal. No life depended on her. Back then, a song soothed any pain. Back then, notes paved an open and free road for her. Back then, she'd thought the strings of her guitar couldn't kill anyone. She knew better now.

Next to her, Artyom was murmuring Sap Bürüy words with clasped hands, either praying or cursing the shit of out everyone.

Steps followed the fanfare. The two instrument players entered first, visibly unhappy with their job. Maybe they had hoped to join Bored Reginald's palace troupe when they'd taken on a royal position but had ended up announcing the shithead king at whatever dump he went to. Eight guards followed. At least Vana thought they were guards. They wore eggshell-colored uniforms with emblems on their arms, and each one held a spear with a glowing glass ball instead of a sharp tip. Was this the uniform of Virisunder royal guards? As much as she hated Silberfluss royal guards, at least they had style. These weirdos could've used a visit to the Kilburn shop for some proper weaponry. And who fought in eggshell clothes anyway? It must've been impossible to wash bloodstains out.

Vana's musings stopped when she spotted the king. She'd been curious to see Queen Lunatic's husband and Princess Agathe's brother, but the actual sight of him sickened her. He looked as hungry as she felt. What could a king crave that he didn't possess an abundance of?

He observed the prisoners for a few seconds, then smiled widely. "Thank you for your precious time, valued citizens. I come to you not as a king, but as a loyal servant of the Council."

Vana leaned over to Artyom. "I thought his brother ran the Council? Not exactly a serva—"

"Shh, shut food hole, kymbat."

The king spread his arms. "I am not here to judge. This is solely Princess Agathe's burden. If you were under Virisunder jurisdiction, my daughter, Princess Josefine, would shorten your suffering with the mercy of a rope."

"There's something wrong with this fella," Vana mumbled.

Artyom grabbed her neck firmly. "Vana, I knock you down if you not shut up."

She frowned but couldn't risk responding. The eggshell guards were watching her. Artyom let go and ruffled her grown-out hair.

"What the—" she mouthed, but he shook his head.

"Now, dear citizens, please line up in a row so I may inspect your . . . potential," the king said.

"Kymbat, get rebel look off eyes and keep head down. Please."

Vana scoffed. She wasn't scared of some noble shit and his milk teeth guards.

"Balthos, protect us." Artyom sighed and picked up his slime bowl. "Kymbat, forgive me."

"Wha—"

He shoved the bowl in her face. Stinking lukewarm slime smudged her skin. She spluttered and coughed.

"You want to curse me, you wait till cell, understand?"

Artyom said before she could yell at him. She wiped her eyes, ready to curse him right there, but found genuine fear on his face. She swallowed her anger and disgust.

The prisoners rushed to form a line quicker than they'd ever done for the warden. Vana had no choice but to ignore the crap dripping down her neck and join the obedient crowd. Terror pained most faces. Her stomach tightened. It wasn't right for one person to instill fear in so many people, especially if said people were known for questioning the law and defying oppressors. She noticed sweat dripping off Erna's forehead. The half orc was murmuring to herself. *Fuck all this praying; we need to do something!*

The king approached the beginning of the line with two guards. Strands of dirt-colored hair stuck to his waxy forehead. Lining up for a creep like him was demeaning. It would've been easy to hurt him. Artyom gave her a shoulder bump. She saw the plea in his sunken eyes and remembered how crappy he'd been feeling. He strained himself to look after her despite it. The least she could do was keep her mouth shut, no matter how demeaning it was.

The king passed the first ten inmates without stopping. The eleventh was a teenage horse thief. King Josef paused and lifted the boy's head with his own glass ball spear to examine him further. The ball shot a green flash into the boy's jaw. His eyes turned inward, and he collapsed.

The king shook his head. "Not pure anymore and too weak for a third-grade classification."

As he moved on, two guards picked up the boy and dragged him away.

"Do not do anything," Artyom whispered again, and not a second too late. Vana barely refrained from giving that royal asshole an uppercut.

The king passed Artyom without hesitation but paused when he got to Vana. He squinted at her slimy face with the same disgust Vana felt and leaned the spear thing closer to her. "How old are you?"

A pinch in her ass startled her before she could answer. A large hand accompanied it, grabbing and pulling her tighter. She was about to punch the fucker who dared to touch her when she realized it was Artyom. He grinned at the king.

"Right age, Majesty. You try after me?"

The king wrinkled his nose and kept walking down the line without giving Vana another look. As soon as he'd passed, Artyom dropped his hand.

"What the fuck?" Vana hissed from the corner of her mouth as the eggshell guards passed them.

"Sorry," he mumbled, but it didn't relieve the nausea in Vana's stomach. She remembered that Erna didn't like Artyom either, a detail that hadn't bothered her until now. She took a small step to the right, away from him.

"Kymbat, I—"

"Don't call me that."

The king continued down the line. With each person he passed, the air seemed thinner. Vana wanted to rebel, to scream at him, but she controlled herself. An orc farther down couldn't. He spat at the king's neck and yelled at him in Tribu La'am tongue. The king snapped his finger and waved two guards toward the orc. Vana prepared herself for a riot. Those glass spears would be no match against quantity and brute force.

Instead of stabbing the orc, as Vana had expected, they lifted the spears into the air and swung them in a circle. Green threads emerged from both glass balls and wrapped around the orc's body. He screamed and tried to punch his way out, but they entrapped him too quickly. The threads circled up to his neck and face until he was no longer visible.

The king looked back at him. "Grade eight at most. Not worth much. You know what to do."

The guards picked up the fully bound man. A terrible hissing came from under the thread. *He's suffocating. Fuck, he's suffocating!* Artyom's knuckles whitened as he clenched his fist. He shook his head at her again. But why should she listen to him? Vana's muscles ached from tension. They would regret this. Every one of these noble swine would regret this.

The king's voice ripped Vana from her thoughts. ". . . ideal for our program. Yes, I do think so. You will join me for a private conversation in the infirmary." Vana leaned forward to see who he was talking to. It was one of Erna's girls, the petite Virisunder elf who had been terrified of Vana. She trembled as the king spoke. He ran a finger over her upper arm. "Nothing to fear, sweetheart. Wouldn't you like a way out of this ghastly place?"

"Sir, sorry, sir." Erna pushed her way through the line. *Careful, Erna.* "Clarisse can't read or write, sir. She'd make a poor protegee."

The king's face lost its waxen tone and turned orange instead. "Did I allow you to address me, halfer tusk?" The guards stepped closer to Erna, but she stood her ground. Vana glanced at Artyom and realized he'd done the same thing. He'd protected her. A wave of gratitude washed over her.

"Just trying to be helpful, Your Majesty," Erna continued. "Clarisse really isn't the smartest and—" One guard tilted his spear, and a green light shot into her stomach. She buckled and gasped as if they'd punched her.

They're going to kill her too. Vana had to do something. Erna was a community protector, the Spirit to all those young girls. The establishment couldn't murder her as well. Vana eyed the magical spears. The inmates outnumbered the guards by far, but she didn't know how powerful the magic was. She couldn't be responsible for another rebel slaughter. If only they didn't have that damned magic.

A thought struck her. *I can use magic too.* Vana tapped her foot in a rhythm and clapped. Within the blink of an eye, she had everyone's attention. Artyom groaned, but he didn't understand. Not all magic was evil. She'd fight them with the one true magic: the magic of Bored Reginald.

She sang the last full song that had left Jules's sweet lips, "The Last Prayer."

"Dear gods, dear Verdains, dear Verdain gods. Thank you for leading us to the darkness, so you can shine your light." It was Bored Reginald's most famous song prior to his palace days, back when he'd pushed for Queen Lunatic's removal. Everyone knew the lyrics.

"And if we're cold, you show us the joy of freezing." The guards approached her, but she sang peacefully. They hadn't shot Jules down until Vana had provoked them. "And if we're hungry, you show us the joy of starving." Several inmates joined the rhythm with their feet and hands. "And if we're bound, you show us the joy of worship."

The guards hesitated as a quarter of the inmates clapped along. "No one deserves happiness when misery is a blessing." Vana's voice wasn't the only one anymore. Half of the inmates joined the rhythm and sang along. One of the fanfare players smirked.

"Or do you? My dearest princess. Or do you? My dearest prince. Or do you? Beloved gods. Do you pay the price of happiness to gift us suffering?"

"Enough! Enough!" the warden yelled, but the communal song drowned out his voice. "Enough!"

The song of her comrades rekindled a fire in her. There were no criminals down here, only unappreciated stories worth fighting for.

Their voices died together in an instant. Any further sounds caught in Vana's throat. She looked over at the king and saw that his staff was vibrating with energy. His face was frozen in a grimace that resembled a smile. "I see you're still carrying enthusiasm for our old palace fool. How nice of you to exhibit this for me." Was he snarling at them? Vana thought such primal energy was below noble shits. Then she remembered Rutilia. Nothing was below noble shits. "Of course, Reginald has moved on from entertaining hopeless lots of sinners. He's performing for intellectually advanced creatures now, like my unborn child."

Vana detected a hint of panic under the arrogance. *That's*

right, little shit, you don't mess with a collective. She wondered about the child for a moment but pushed the thought aside. Another royal brat wouldn't make any difference when the revolution was coming.

The king nodded toward Clarisse. "Time for our little interview." Vana's heart sank. She'd hoped he had forgotten. "Tidiers, please accompany Miss Clarisse. Walter?"

He signaled to an eggshell guard who hadn't been involved so far. Vana's eyes widened when she noticed the medical kit on his belt. Artyom saw it too but shook his head and mouthed, "Too dangerous." *Fuck you, Arty.* He'd put himself at risk protecting her. She'd repay the favor.

"Please prepare our candidate," Josef continued.

The doctor approached Clarisse gentler than the guards had, but she cried when they took her away. Two other girls were holding Erna's arms. She looked as if she were about to maul the king. He and his guards—or *Tidiers*, as he had called them—left, and the fanfare players followed. The one who had smiled earlier gave Vana a wink before exiting. When the king was out of sight, the spell on their voices lifted and the hall became noisy.

The warden clapped his hands. "That's enough! No more singing! Get back to your usual activities." He and the prison guards left as well.

Vana waited until they were out of sight before turning to Artyom. "I'm getting you that kit."

Artyom grabbed her arm. "To limbo, you are—" A violent cough cut him off. Vana didn't know whether to laugh or cry.

"Good point. I'm definitely getting it for you."

"Vana!" He was too late. She left him behind at the line and rushed toward the dark hallway. Perhaps she could help Clarisse too.

The darkness of the labyrinth shielded her. She noticed the glow of the assula trinkets prison guards wore around their neck and crept after them.

A hand slid onto her shoulder, and she jumped. *Nachtalb.* She forced her breath to steady. Those little monsters weren't designed to attack first, and she wouldn't let them provoke her. Not again.

You're scared of being alone.
That's why you trust Artyom without reason.
Risking your life for him.
If you risk your life, you think he won't betray you.
But he will.
They all will.
The only person who didn't is dead.

Fuck no, you're not bringing Jules into this again. She swatted at the dark. "Get out of my thoughts, you creepy little fucks!"

The warden and guards stopped. *Shit.* Artyom was right. She was still a stupid hothead through and through.

The warden lifted his trinket and pushed a button on it. The gaping eye sockets of nachtalbs all around her lit up with a bright green glow. Everything became visible: the hallway, the monsters, and Vana. She dropped to the ground, making herself as thin as possible against the wet stones. It was no use. The beams of nachtalb eyes circled up and pointed at her.

"Dear Balthos, not another one!" The warden approached her. *Don't breathe. Don't breathe.* Any motion could give her away. He sighed. "Take her in with the boy, but leave quickly. The king is not to be disturbed."

Vana felt more people approaching. *Guards.* Rough hands grabbed her. She took a deep breath and held it. This seemed like a shitty situation, but it might work to her advantage. If she understood correctly, they were leading her right to the royal shit and his doctor.

A stench of tobacco and gin hit her nose. She heard the warden's voice, too close to her own face. "She doesn't look mangled like the other one, but I suppose you never know with these nachtalbs. Hopefully the Institute sends us new ones soon. These are getting too . . . sentient."

The fuck? Vana's stupid heart beat faster. She hoped they wouldn't check. They carried her for an excruciatingly long time without oxygen. She dared to breathe once to avoid gasping for air. A guard's hand on her chest followed, waiting for the next treacherous breath. It didn't come. For once, Vana controlled herself.

They stopped, and she heard a knock. The only door in Balthos's Heretics led to the infirmary, so they must have arrived. Several seconds of silence passed.

"Should we . . . ?" a guard asked.

The warden sighed. "He'll be upset." Another knock.

The door creaked open, and Vana recognized the king's voice. He sounded out of breath. "Yes? I assumed you knew better than to interrupt me."

"Forgive me, Your Majesty. The nachtalbs knocked out another inmate."

Vana sensed a shadow over her. She wished she could open her eyes and claw that royal shit's face off.

"Ah, if that isn't our troublemaker." Clammy hands clasped her face and turned it to both sides. "A halfer . . . how disappointing. Might still be a grade four. Leave her in the storage room. I'll harvest her after I'm done."

The guard gripped her tighter. "Your Majesty . . . the nachtalbs aren't supposed to do this. She didn't do any—"

"Thank you," the king said. "I'd like you to reconsider your attitude toward our inmates if you don't care to join them. These are heretics who have betrayed the word of Balthos. And my creations are working perfectly. This prison is self-regulatory. It likely has too many inmates."

"That's horri—"

"Traute!" the warden said. He must have kept his distance, but Vana felt him close to her now. "We have bothered the king enough, don't you think? My apologies, Your Majesty. We will drop her off and you can proceed with . . . ehm, you can proceed."

"You may enter."

The infirmary's bright light almost made Vana squint, but she remained still. The guards carried her until another door opened. It must have been the storage room.

"What did this sweet girl get arrested for, anyway?" the king asked. "She has the same complexion as my dearest Alexandra."

The guards dropped Vana on a hard stone floor. It hurt but wasn't as chilly as the rest of the prison. She noticed a green light source through her eyelids.

"Clarisse Lautrec murdered the brothel owner in charge of her," the warden said.

"How unpleasant."

Footsteps became quieter, and the door closest to Vana clicked. She must've been alone now but didn't dare open her eyes. Instead, she remained still on the floor, getting accustomed to her environment. She hadn't felt this warm in months. She needed to find her way back here with Artyom after the warden left. This would be a proper place for him to regain his strength.

"Oh no, don't cry, sweetheart. It's making you ugly," the king said through the door. Vana's stomach turned. *Fuck this.* She had to help Clarisse. She opened her eyes. What she saw almost blew her cover. She covered her mouth to squelch her scream.

The room was lit in green light, but by nachtalbs, not trinkets. The monsters hung on hooks all around the room with empty glowing eye sockets. A glass flask with more green lights was attached next to each nachtalb's hook.

Vana had never seen them illuminated and wished she still hadn't. They were lifeless corpses with swollen purple skin which had been burned off around their eye sockets and mouths. Instead of lips, their mouths had been ripped down to the bone structure. They still had teeth, but they weren't the original ones. The half-elf, half-human corpse in front of her had one large tusk gaping out of its mouth hole. A lot of them were halfers and mixed national elves or humans. All of them were naked and covered in injury marks. Instead of fingernails, they had long pointed claws.

Vana's legs trembled as she held in her screams. These creatures weren't monsters. They weren't enemies. They were victims who'd been turned into weapons. She steadied her breathing and examined the room. Panic wouldn't help anyone. As she calmed herself, she noticed that no foreign thoughts attacked her. None of the creatures moved. They must've been deactivated.

A movement to her right made her jump. She spun around, her fists ready as if it would help against nachtalbs. Her stomach turned when she saw him, but she kept herself from gagging. Next to her was a Tribu La'am nachtalb with black curls whose skin wasn't as discolored as the others. *Jules.*

But it wasn't Jules. It was another young Tribu La'am man who they'd deemed to be worth more dead than alive. Vana choked up but swallowed it down. This was no time to open her wounds. The nachtalb hung on a hook with bound hands like the others but struggled against the entrapment. His head jerked toward the right, where the glass flask hung.

Vana took a step toward him and checked his pulse with a shaking hand. He had none, yet he was in motion. She examined the flask closer and noticed that a thin tube attached it to the nachtalb. The glowing green substance traveled through it. Vana's eyes grew wide. *Are they milking you for light?*

She wrapped her arms around the dead man's body without thinking and lifted him off the hook. She had no idea how to help him, but even if there was no release from his fate, he shouldn't suffer it trapped in a prison within a prison. He fell heavily on top of her. She rolled him off and laid him on the ground. The tube snapped, and the green light traveled back into him. He convulsed as soon as it entered his body.

A sob came through the door. *Clarisse.* Vana left the nachtalb on the ground and peeked through the keyhole. The first person she spotted was the doctor, leaning against the wall without a hint of expression. The precious medical kit was still hanging over his shoulder. Another horror unfolded to the left of him. Vana froze at its sight.

Clarisse was strapped to a stretcher, naked and gagged. A syringe was sticking out of her arm. The king buttoned up his suit pants.

"Oh, will you stop crying, sweetheart? You've proven quite worth the trip down here, and your parchment weakened nicely during this little treat. It won't be too painful to harvest now." He picked up an empty glass ball from a nearby table and ran his hand over Clarisse's chest. His lips curled, and he inhaled deeply. He lowered his spear onto her chest and circled around her heart. His hand sank through her skin, right between the ribs. His wrist disappeared soon after. He closed his eyes and smiled. "Hmm, there we go. I thought you might have a grade two parchment. Beautiful, no bond and so innocent still. Truly beautiful."

He sighed with pleasure and pulled his hand out. There was no blood on it. He stroked her side.

That's it, fucker. You're going down. Any fear Vana had felt evaporated. She spun around and searched for a weapon. If only she'd kept the seax. She'd have loved to spill the king's guts.

Her eyes fell on the convulsing nachtalb, and she knelt down next to him. "Shall we make this fucker pay?" she whispered, then picked him up from the ground. His full human stature was taller and wider than hers, but the lack of muscle made him light enough to carry. She lifted his twitching body up in front of her and ripped several flasks off the wall. Some of them shattered, but she grabbed a handful. Whatever foul magic the green lights were, if they turned corpses into weapons, they could surely protect her.

She held the nachtalb as close to her body as she could and led his hand to the doorknob. She was lucky the door wasn't locked, but this was where her luck ended. She had expected the king, Clarisse, and the expressionless doctor to be there, but she had forgotten about the Tidiers. They hadn't been visible from the keyhole and had made no sound, but there they were—four of them lined up behind the stretcher.

Vana used the nachtalb's arm and tossed three flasks at the Tidiers before they could react. The lights shot out of the flasks with gargling sounds and flew up to the Tidiers' throats, encircling them.

"What—" The king's eyes widened at the sight of the nachtalb. "How is this poss—"

Vana pushed another flask into the nachtalb's hand and aimed it at the king, but he noticed her hand before she threw it. He smiled and moved his staff in a quick jolt. Vana's body froze immediately. Everyone but the king grew stiff. The green lights that had attacked the Tidiers were sucked into his spear. He walked around the nachtalb and found Vana. His eyes lit up when he recognized her. "You really are craving my attention, aren't you?"

He stomped the spear on the ground, and Vana's face felt lighter, clean. The slime had disappeared. "There we go. Let's take a look at you." He studied her face, nodded to himself, and brought his hand to her cheek.

A choking noise saved her. The doctor slid down the wall, gasping for air. A sharp stone stuck out of his throat. Blood gushed from the wound. The king swung around. His distraction broke the paralyzing spell. Vana pushed the nachtalb on top of him and pressed down.

A scream tore through the room. *Clarisse.* Vana looked over in time to see the second sharp stone piece reach her. Instead of ripping through her throat, it ripped through the bindings and freed her. Two magical rays of light shot through the room. The Tidiers were no longer frozen and back in the fight. The third ray caught Clarisse before she could run.

Vana slammed harder against the nachtalb and reached for the king's spear. A sting rushed through her bones as she touched it. The king pushed against it. Pain traveled up her arm to her shoulders until it hit her neck, where it pressed down on her windpipe. She gasped.

A Tidier fell down. The warm red liquid that sprayed on her face must've meant another sharp stone had hit him. Vana ran out of air and decided to return the favor. She lightened her pressure on the nachtalb, then threw her weight where she suspected the king's stomach was. The impact knocked the wind out of the king and broke the pain in Vana.

She took a breath, but it didn't last long. A violent rush of energy threw her off the nachtalb and against the wall. It punched into her sparsely padded spine, and she sank down in pain.

Another shard shot at the Tidier holding Clarisse. It sliced off his elvish ear. Blood and screams caused chaos long enough for Clarisse to free herself and run. "It'll be okay. Go find Erna," said a man with a Sap Bürüy accent. *Arty.*

The nachtalb's body floated off the king. Vana struggled back to her feet while Artyom entered and buried another stone shard in a Tidier. He wore a hood and carried a slingshot made from a wishbone. The remaining Tidier shot a light beam at him, but he jumped out of the way.

The king was back on his feet, catching up on the situation. Vana charged before he could fully grasp it and smashed him against the infirmary desk. The king groaned and lost grip of his spear. It fell to the floor and rolled away from him. Vana pressed her arm against his throat. There was no doubt in her this time, no hesitation. She wanted nothing more than to watch the light fade from the fucker's eyes.

"Get the spear thingy!" she yelled over her shoulder, pressing harder until Josef's eyes bulged.

She saw Artyom dive for it from the corner of her eye. He collapsed. Shock struck her, and she loosened her grip. The remaining Tidier had hit Artyom with the binding light strings. They whipped around him and tightened like they had on the orc.

"No!" Vana screamed. Artyom couldn't die because of her bad decision. He couldn't. Not him.

The king used her distraction and pushed her off. He

grabbed the staff and pulsed it. Vana's heartbeat sped up rapidly and shook her. Every muscle pulsed in the forceful beat. She sank down next to the suffocating Artyom, convulsing like the nachtalb had. The speed of her heart increased. Any moment now her heart would explode. She closed her eyes and hoped it'd be quick.

"What . . . ?" the king said above her. The panic in his voice reignited hope in Vana. "Let's go. Now!" he yelled.

The convulsion stopped, and her heartbeat returned to its normal state. Vana carefully opened her eyes and found Artyom gasping next to her, unbound. The king and his remaining Tidier stormed out of the infirmary. Vana looked over Artyom's shoulder and shrieked. The nachtalb she'd carried into the room had risen of his own volition and stared at her with its green light. Behind him, three other nachtalbs gathered.

Artyom pulled himself up and startled as well. "*Esh karov!*"

"What?"

"Horseshit!" he clarified, scrambling to his feet. He reached for his slingshot but didn't need it. The nachtalbs gave Vana a slow nod, then receded back into the storage room. The one she had carried into the infirmary closed the door.

Vana and Artyom stared at it for two seconds until the injured Tidier on the ground yowled.

"How could we forget you?" Artyom asked, kneeling next to the pathetic figure. He spoke a few sentences in Sap Büruÿ that Vana didn't understand before switching back to Silberfluss. "May Exitalis welcome you with arm open. May Balthos love and forgive you."

The Tidier stared at him with huge eyes but didn't move when Artyom picked up a shard. He put the Tidier to rest with one swift cut from ear to ear. There was something eerie about the calm way he handled it. He rested next to the Tidier until he was dead, then got up and turned to Vana. "All right, hothead. Damage control time. Quick."

He collected his stone shards, and Vana picked up the medical kit from the bloody mess of a doctor. She didn't know what to say or think.

"The nachtalbs . . ."

"We think and talk later about."

"Thank you."

Artyom stopped and turned to her. "You okay? You normally have no manners." Vana cracked a smile, and he returned it. "Good. Now hurry. We want be in bed floors sleeping like baby when warden returns to check."

They grabbed the rest of their tools and weapons. Vana examined the Tidiers' uniforms. They were made of good material, much better than the robes they had to clothe themselves with. She undressed them.

"What you do?" Artyom asked.

"This is great cloth, too valuable to waste." She peeked at the shards in his hand. "How did you get these?"

"Ten years of lonely boredom—you get ideas. But quick, kymbat, we need hurry."

Vana nodded and packed the rest up. "Good, so it's possible to manufacture in here." The place wasn't as lost as everyone thought it to be.

"I sharpened stone trash . . .",

She picked up a shard and cut off chunks of Tidier hair, thinking they might need more string. "No, you created our new weaponry division."

CHAPTER 30

SUBIRA

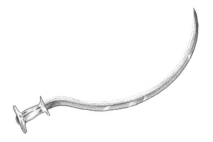

January 980 - Polemos, Virisunder

Rain swallowed the night whole. Subira wished she were in her bed, for no matter where sleep led, it could only be brighter than the darkness that presented itself to the open eye. But she needed it. The night offered this sole solace, a darkness that embraced Subira and her black stallion, Cal, in much-needed obscurity as they made their way through Polemos's forgotten streets. A nearby clock tower struck two, and she jolted upright. She had been leaning on Cal, barely holding on to both the horse and her consciousness. The rain was a comforting distraction. She tried to focus on each drop instead of the excruciating pain that had taken hold of her left side.

The night had started out like any other. Subira had been cleaning the last dish in the kitchen, quietly humming the Tribu La'am working song that filled her office nowadays.

Thanks to her new assistant's diligent work, worry no longer consumed her evenings. The military base was back in proper shape, and with Sachihiro's help, Subira had even sneaked strategic decisions past Princess Josefine. She had finally felt in control again until Gustave had reminded her that control was an illusion.

Cal stopped gently so she wouldn't fall off. Subira gave him a pat and tried to take in her surroundings. They must have reached the outer wall of the base. She pulled her cloak hood over her face. Respect was so easily lost among young soldiers who loved to picture themselves in her position before putting the work in. She had sacrificed two decades of her life to this military and wouldn't let a silly injury ruin her reputation. Plenty of snakes were waiting for the Fi'Teri immigrant to trip, among them the princess herself.

She couldn't see an entrance in the dark stone walls that protected the base and signaled Cal to go on. The reins slipped through her clammy hands, and she lost track of her surroundings. The world blurred. A second—or perhaps several minutes—later, someone shook her firmly.

"Hey, you, these are military grounds! Get your nag out of here."

Military grounds. Cal had found the gate. Finally. Subira opened her mouth to speak, but the taste of bile cut off her words. Instead, she pulled out the golden emblem of Virisunder's military. The green glow of its assula broke the darkness, and Subira could make out the guard's face. It was Soren, a thorough but cruel fellow. Alexandra had demoted him before leaving the front. Subira inhaled a sharp gush of cold air. *Please don't recognize me.*

"New recruit? Respect the curfew next time or I'll write you up. Just 'cause van Auersperg's letting anyone and *anything* join nowadays doesn't mean you can disrespect authority. You hear me?"

Oh, she had heard, and tomorrow he would surely hear from her. Assuming, of course, that she made it through this night. For now, she just nodded. It seemed good enough for Soren, and he let her through.

Few lights shone through the base, just enough to alleviate the darkness without robbing the comfort of the night. Voices wafted over from nearby barracks, muffled laughter of soldiers who would be exhausted for their early morning drills. There was something special about military grounds, a sense of community that she inhaled with each breath. *Home.* Her stiff muscles released under the sudden comfort, and she could no longer hold on. The world around her spun, and she slid off Cal. The rain had softened the ground, but the impact still tore through her. Her body took over, shaking uncontrollably while her mind desperately tried to make sense of her surroundings.

She shouldn't have waited. Was it too late? She had left the house right after Gustave had fallen asleep. It had only been a few hours. Four or five, perhaps. She would normally wait until she could visit the base doctor for a regular checkup. It was easier to explain injuries after morning drills. She couldn't visit Doctor Larrey at this hour. He was skilled, but he would write a report about the severity of her injury. Sure, her soldiers would be sympathetic, but before she knew it, they'd wonder if a woman who couldn't defend herself against her disgraced husband could defend the state. Decades of proof were easily forgotten. Gustave knew this too, and yet he had seemed nervous when she had collapsed.

Subira pushed herself up, only to land back in the puddle. *No.* She had fought in too many battles, outlived too many enemies, to let a dirty puddle pull her into oblivion. She scanned the surrounding area. It must've been Section C. The Ch'ulel cottage was in Section D, only two paths left from where she lay. She had to find the new medic, Gon Ch'ulel. Similar to their brother, Sachihiro, the orc had been fiercely loyal since Subira had approved their relationship with Zazil. More importantly, they wouldn't talk. As much as she detested the thought, if Gon tried to report the injury, she could be assured that no one would believe an orc's word over her own. The only problem was that they might tell Sachihiro about it, and she'd have preferred not to endure more questions about her husband. Worse, he might look at her differently. She'd grown accustomed to his constant praise.

She pushed a second time, but her hand lost grip in the wet mud. Her muscles begged for rest they hadn't yet earned. She thought of Xenia. Makeda's last letter had congratulated Subira on her daughter's excellence. Her little girl was becoming the glorious warrior Subira always knew she'd be. A few more years and she'd be ready for a custom weapon—the one loyal companion throughout future trials, apart from her mother, of course. Subira thought of the motus pile she had put aside, ready to be exchanged for whatever sparked her little knight's fancy. She pictured what Gustave might do with the motus instead, and defiance surged through her.

One more push and Subira was back on her feet. Her pulse shook her body in a feverish rhythm, but her hands found Cal's neck and he steadied her. Together, they slowly made their way to Section D.

To her surprise, Gon's cottage was one of the lit quarters. Zazil's voice drifted through the window. "Fuck letting go! Pier's not the enemy, Sach. I haven't heard from him in two months, and now his stupid ox of a father doesn't know where he is either?"

Subira pulled her hood lower and steadied her breathing before ringing a chain of assula-powered bells, a futile but endearing invention of her new smith. There was a rustling inside. A moment later, the cottage door flung open and Zazil stood in front of her.

"Gino, you fucker, did you get the information?" She examined the cloaked figure.

Subira tried to answer, but her muscles failed. She sank to the ground, trembling.

"Oh fuck, are you okay?" Zazil caught her before the

mud could drench her again. Subira's hood fell off, and her eyes met Zazil's.

"Captain," Zazil muttered. Realization struck her, and she yelled into the tent. "Gon! Gon, quick!"

Gentle hands lifted Subira up, soon to be replaced by stronger, gruffer ones. The inside of the tent blurred. She couldn't fight anymore. The last thing she saw were toffee-colored eyes. Then she passed out.

"Stop shushing me! Can you at least tell me how serious it is?"

"Shh."

The voices were faint, like orders from an enemy general the wind carried across the battlefield. Subira's body protested any notion of movement. She tried to open her eyes, but the weight of her lids kept them shut.

"I mean, she's gonna make it, isn't she? Of course she is. She's Captain Subira Se'azana. She's the captain. She's—"

"Will you shut up, Sachi, and let them work?"

Her tired mind shuffled the words around but couldn't make sense of them. She focused on the voice instead. *Zazil.* Subira must have left the darkness and reached the allied refuge. Her body rested on a soft surface—a base camp bed? She stretched her left leg but didn't reach the metal frame. It was strange. Her tall body rarely fit on regular camp beds. *Unless it's not designed for an elf.* As soon as her mind formed the thought, she sensed the shadow of an orc leaning over her. Their torso shielded her from the harsh torchlight, and their warm hands rested heavily on her abdomen.

"Babe . . . she is gonna make it, right?"

Was she? The urge to know pushed her eyelids open. Pink glitter hearts crushed her faith in Gon's professional abilities. They covered the medic's pajamas and closely resembled the pink of Zazil's hair, whose head rested on Gon's shoulder.

Zazil glanced between her patient and Gon with greater despair than Subira had hoped for.

"Subi, you're up. Marvelous." Zazil straightened and took her hand, which sent a shiver through her. People rarely dared to touch her. Not even Xenia approached with such ease.

"Zaz," Sachihiro said, "respect Captain Subira Se'azana."

"Shut up, Sachi, I'm respecting her as a per—"

"Stable," Gon said.

Subira expected her body to release its heaviness, but it didn't. She tried to sit up nevertheless. The estate was waiting. Gustave was waiting. If her life continued, so did her duties. A sharp pain tore through her abdomen, and she collapsed back onto the mattress with a yelp.

"Subira!" Sachihiro said. "I mean, Captain. Is she? Can I?"

His broad figure appeared behind Zazil. Her elvish body seemed comically tiny compared to the orc's, yet she commanded the room with her presence. Subira might have underestimated her.

"Hold on there, Sachi. She needs room to breathe." She placed her hand on Subira's collarbone to assure that she stayed down. "And you hold on too, Subi—I can call you Subi, right? Right. Just 'cause you're not biting the dust anymore doesn't mean you can head out to drill."

Subira wanted to argue, but her muscles agreed. She settled for a strained nod as another wave of pain shot through her.

"Yep, that's what I thought." Zazil turned to Gon. "So what's the verdict, maestro?"

Her chipper energy dwindled. Subira bit her lip. She had seen too many of her soldiers die from internal bleeding long after they were "stable."

"Tell me, Doctor Ch'ulel, have you made a diagnosis?" Subira said, firmer than she could have hoped for. Gon's grave eyes met hers. They were darker than their brother's and partially covered by their long indigo hair.

"You took a strong blow to your left abdomen, which—"

"Bandits."

"And—"

"I mean, it was bandits. I was surprised by bandits." Subira tapped her fingers on the bed and exhaled sharply. Gon gently pushed down on her stomach, and a sense of calm trickled through her.

"It doesn't matter how it happened. As I was saying, you took a blow to your left abdomen, which ruptured your spleen. It caused internal bleeding and was left untreated for . . . I'm guessing a few hours?"

She closed her eyes and nodded. How could she have been so stupid? If it had been one of her soldiers, she would have rushed them to the nearest medic immediately.

"Doctor Larrey could try to slice you open, but I believe it's too late for that."

Too late. The words hit her more than Gustave's blow. *So this is how it ends.* She would miss her little knight's graduation, miss the pride in Xenia's eyes when her dreams turned into a sacred duty, miss the chance to see what life her daughter would create for herself. All because she'd had to bring up the general position again. All because Alexandra kept pushing her to.

She tried to focus on the throbbing of her muscles. Physical pain was easier to weather than the storm that brewed inside her head. She cursed herself for losing control like this. She shouldn't have allowed Alexandra to convince her. She shouldn't have dreamed of glory on the battlefield. She had buried that dream a long time ago. Gustave had tried so hard lately to make it work. He'd been so disappointed when she'd brought up the front again. Alexandra had ruined their plans a decade ago. Why had Subira allowed her to ruin them again? Gustave had never gotten angry before Subira took the position at the base. But if his anger was justified, why could she not talk about it to anyone?

Long overdue tears rolled down her cheeks. This wasn't the dignified death worthy of a Se'azana, but she'd taken Gustave's name and it didn't require much dignity. She registered Zazil and Gon bickering without bothering to understand. She released herself into sobs and the freedom they provided. Grace, composure, none of it mattered now. Her thoughts left the tent and the body that her pathetic double life had shackled. She soared over past battlefields, remembering the rush of adrenaline, the meaning victory brought to her life. A warm hand on her forehead pulled her out of the comfort. She blinked and found Sachihiro's toffee gaze by her side. She longed to return to the field and her blessed memories but couldn't churn anger for him. He smiled warmly at her.

"One moment," he whispered, then stood up and turned to his sibling. He towered over Gon by half a head and likely doubled their overall mass. The picture exuded such authority, Subira wished he was her medic instead of Gon. "Use the Utsilo on her."

He left Gon and Zazil baffled, sank to his knees beside Subira, and started humming a sweet lullaby, likely of Tribu La'am root.

"Sachi, no. I understand the urge, but we need the Utsilo in case Pier's in trouble. Right, babe?"

Gon shifted their stance. "Her ancestors might not favor her, Sachi. Elvish ancestors aren't like orcish ones. It could do more harm than good."

"It won't."

"Babe, you're not actually considering it, are you?"

Sachihiro kept his eyes locked with Subira's browline. He tended to avoid direct eye contact. "Do it, Gon." Up close, she could see amber speckles in his large irises, as well as her own reflection. She barely recognized the woman staring back at her. When had she become so small? Se'azanas stood tall through life and war. Se'azanas didn't perish. They fell in honor. But she had succumbed to the fruitless longing for affection. Shame choked her, and she gasped for air again. This time it took several attempts for relief to set in, and another wave of pain shot through her.

Gon pulled a rust-colored bloodwood chest from underneath the bed. Letters, likely of the Tribu La'am alphabet, adorned it.

"Gon, no. What about Pier?"

"We don't know if he's in trouble," Gon whispered.

"I'm his best friend. He wouldn't just ignore me."

"It's Sachi's Utsilo."

"*What?*"

"Sachi's the chieftain, snazzle. I'm sorry. I'm doing it."

Their bickering quieted down.

"Focus on me, Captain," said Sachihiro. An impossible request, as Gon was covering her with herbs and myrrh.

"What is tha—" Before she could finish the question, a horrible feeling robbed most of her senses. It felt like someone had cut her in half, scratched her apart from the inside. The sensation quenched all comfort Sachihiro had provided. Gon must have attacked her in the moment of weakness. They'd been right—her parents, the state, they'd all been right. She shouldn't have trusted orcs, but it wasn't just them. Zazil had lured her into the ambush. She shouldn't have trusted anyone. When had all this trusting started? What had she been thinking? She lashed out, desperately trying to find her attacker.

"Guys? Guys, shit. She's splintering!" Zazil screamed.

Subira felt herself being pulled up into huge arms. She should've resisted, but the musky forest scent that crept around her distracted her from the severing of her soul.

"One minute," Gon growled.

"No, fuck no. If you're using it, use it now!" Zazil's panic was distant, buried under the slashes. Subira tried to piece the information together. *Splintering.* Gon hadn't attacked her; death had. A whirlwind of emotions and memories broke through the fog of pain. Love for Xenia. Contempt for deserters. The two emotions coexisted for a second before another slash tore into her and wiped away every sensation. She screamed.

"Do something!" Sachihiro yelled. Gon's frantic explanations and Zazil's profanities were drowned out by another cut. Subira tried to form a thought, but nothing made sense anymore. Who was she?

A black cloud rushed through the darkness. It carried with it a warm wind that encompassed her and eased the pain.

"What the . . . ?" Zazil's voice pierced through the darkness. "She stopped splintering. Fucking limbo!"

"I haven't done anything yet," Gon said.

The shapeless force around her breathed, and soon Subira breathed along. Her muscles softened with the steady rhythm, and she sank deeper into the cloud's embrace. "Please don't be upset. Your story is far from finished, my dearest." It whispered all around her.

Her eyes remained closed, yet she registered the image of a golden parchment floating in the darkness. Scratches marked the paper, but the cloud reattached all pieces with a white light. Scripture in an unknown language graced the parchment. A black ink spot in the center caught Subira's attention, and she reached for it. Her physical body didn't react, but something within her pulled the ink spot closer. It made contact and plucked her out of the cloud into yet another unknown place. She caught a glimpse of a Sap Bürüy human man in a dimly lit room. He sat on a dirty stone with crossed legs. He looked neglected with his long black hair and beard but wore a calm expression that made her heart soar. She pushed closer, and he frowned. *Did I disturb your peace?*

"Subira." The cloud's whisper picked up anew. "This man murdered his wife, like Gustave nearly did. I've found a better love for you. Do not stray away from it, my dearest." It tugged at her gently. She resisted it with any strength this strange, incorporeal body of hers carried. The man's eyes snapped open. They were the same brown as the hilt of her beloved shotel sword. He blurted a word in a language she didn't speak. The cloud stole any chance to respond. It plucked her out of the grim room and released her back into the warm, corporeal arms of Sachihiro.

She reached back toward the man, back toward the ink spot and the secrets it held, but her hand merely touched the orc's linen sleeve. Reality returned, and with it an unsettling hollowness.

"Remember when you turned the Tazadahar war around? The rebels almost lost, but you crashed the peace treaty all by yourself. Imagine the balls that took. I mean, ova-ries. I mean, ignore that part."

"Sachi, what are you doing?" Zazil asked.

"Just refreshing her memory. It'll help, trust me. So, where was I? Right, didn't those Council fools try to hide all assula magic in Tazadahar? And all the other troops had given up, but not Captain Subira Se'azana, oh no! She went over there with only three soldiers and opened the fortress, broke their defense from within. Smartest strategy I've ever read, and I read a lot." Sachihiro's gruff voice washed over the empty cracks inside of her. *Captain Subira Se'azana.* That's who she was. That's who they needed her to be. She opened her eyes and found herself cradled in his arms, as if physical containment could prevent her from splintering. The childish notion made her smile.

"Two rebel soldiers. I could only convince two soldiers to come along." The breath that carried the words also carried the pain of her spleen, but the relief in their faces to hear her speak made up for it. "Unless I don't remember correctly and you were there too."

Sachihiro reciprocated her smile and laid her back down on the bed. She noticed lines of worry on his face, but he hadn't allowed it to take hold. A true soldier, keeping a clear mind in battle.

"My study materials were incorrect then. Must be so be-cause my memory is perfect."

"Ready for the Utsilo," Gon said. Subira remembered the undefined ritual Sachihiro had insisted on and noticed the damp, itchy herbs and myrrh that covered most of her torso. "Your soul stopped splintering, but your spleen is still ruptured, so I will call upon your ancestors, but I can't promise they'll help. At least your soul is safe."

Subira expected Zazil to tell them off for their bluntness, but the smith had retreated into a distant corner of the room. Subira wished she could do the same—steal a second to think, understand what she'd seen, or more importantly who she'd seen. What had the human said?

Sachihiro nodded, and Gon pulled out an assula lighter shaped like a heart. Soon a low orcish tune filled the room, and it would've been soothing if it hadn't been accompanied by the flame. Before she could inspect it further, Gon set fire to the herbs. They ignited in a spectacular ruby tone with golden sparks that kept it in place. In another life, she might have resisted, but the cloud, the man, none of it had made sense, so she relaxed into the fire and hoped it would burn away the pain and hollowness alike.

The flames danced on her abdomen wildly as Gon's song became forceful and urgent. It peaked in a mighty throat-sung note. Three figures emerged from the flames. They weren't as shapeless as the dark cloud but moved too fast for the mortal eye to grasp their form. Gon bowed in front of them and addressed them in the Tribu La'am tongue. For a horrid moment, none of them responded. Subira caught Gon glancing at Sachihiro with concern. It reminded her of Alexandra's absurd chemistry experiments, only she had never used Subira as a test object.

Their dance slowed, and one flame figure stretched toward Subira. She couldn't make out the face, but long elvish ears formed from the flames. Another spurt of fire morphed into a familiar object, and the figure closest to her wrapped part of itself around it. It almost looked like a—

"Gon, why do they have a spear?" Sachihiro asked. "Gon? Gon!"

The figure didn't allow the medic to make sense of it. It raised the flaming spear into the air and thrusted it down into the bruise of Gustave's blow. Anguish pierced through Subira as she released a horrific yelp. The spear went into her without breaking the skin, but the fire seemed to torch her ruptured spleen.

"Gon!"

His song picked up anew, but crackling words emerged from the fire figure and drowned out the melody—Fi'Teri words. "Subira Se'azana, what has become of you?" the figure said. Tears shot into her eyes as the figure twisted the spear inside of her. "Dying by the hands of an imbecile? Disturbing the peace of your ancestors with the help of orcs? You've lost your faith."

"No," she gasped. Her whole side burned.

"And you expect us to save you?" The figure scoffed.

Sachihiro and the others shuffled, argued, and moved in a directionless attempt to stop what they did not understand. It didn't matter. Only the flames mattered—the flames and the shame they scorched her with. "Please."

"We have no choice but to help. We can't break the ethereal contract of orcs. You're lucky they wasted their spell on you."

The spear was ripped out of her without warning. No blood flowed, but she was sure her insides had been torn out along with it.

A second figure drifted toward her. "The deal. The orcs require a deal." Their voice was softer, but Subira didn't fool herself into reading any kindness into it.

"We will heal your spleen if you pledge to let no man come before your duty again. Ever. You can start by eliminating that cockroach of yours."

Gustave. She thought of what had happened hours ago. The blow. The disdain in his puffed eyes. There'd been a time when they had shimmered with the green of spring blossoms, long before rum had consumed his body and patience. She thought of the handsome troublemaker she'd found lost in the trenches during a Tazadahar sandstorm. She might have been his captain, but he had barely noticed her until that day. She had. The way he sang himself into her prettiest soldiers' beds. The way his long fingers twirled their escaped locks. The way his lips kissed the flask after a long march. She had never allowed herself to indulge in such thoughts, but the storm disrupted both their principles. They took shelter in a cave, hidden from the world for three days. The solitude made her good enough for him. The solitude allowed her to be bad. Neither she nor Gustave had had to worry about taking protective measures before, so the solitude gifted her a third miracle. Her storm baby. Her little knight. *Xenia loves her dad.*

"Cut that sentimentality from your soul. By Balthos's love, you're a Se'azana. Act like one." The flame figure jabbed the spear into her face. She held her breath, expecting another surge of pain, but it hovered in front of her like the decision she had to make.

What would a life without Gustave even look like? She tried to picture a new solitude, one that brought peace instead of gifts, and urged herself to long for it. He'd always told her what they had could never be replaced. A farewell to him was a farewell to shared beds and neck kisses. To being desired in a way that had nothing to do with her military abilities. A farewell to the pain it carried. The flinching when she heard his flask open. The studying of his face for any sign of anger. The fear that any mistake might be their last. *Her* last.

"Hold on, Captain. Gon is stopping this," Sachihiro said. Something fell into place when she heard his gruff, panicked voice.

"Don't," she muttered. Her sentimentalities for Gustave might have been toxic, but their nature wasn't. She had saved him back then not because of her affection, but because he was her soldier, and her soldiers needed her. They had always needed her. It was the one constant to rely on. Here she was, lamenting the loss of Xenia and neglecting the front. It had to stop. Her soldiers were her children now.

"I pledge to let no man come before my duty again."

The flame figures flared up. "We'll be watching." They plunged into her stomach. She expected another sharp pain, but the fire disappeared with a sensation of warm honey dripping on her aching insides. Strength returned to her body, and certainty fired through her.

She sat up without discomfort and marveled at the vanished injury. The past few minutes hadn't been as restoring for the others. She looked up to find Zazil shaking in Gon's arms. Sachihiro stared at her as if she had risen from the grave. In many ways, she had. She decided to give him something simpler to focus on.

"Sachihiro, get a parchment and quill. I need you to draft a declaration."

He didn't move. "Captain . . . what happened?"

Worry still plagued him, like it did many unoccupied minds.

"Quick, Private, we have work to do." She patted his cheek. There was so much gratitude to express, but no time. She had to get to work before the doubts caught up. "We need to inform the front that their new general is joining them."

"I don't follow."

Zazil reappeared from Gon's chest. All three of them gawked at her now. She promised herself not to disappoint them. Not now, not ever.

"Tell them *General* Subira Se'azana is taking charge of the war."

CHAPTER 31

ROBERT

January 980 - Altor Caedem, Virisunder

Robert pulled his hood tighter as thunder tore through the night sky. He loved Virisunder's stormy battles for spring, especially here in the East, where icy winds from Sap Bürüy aggravated the fight. He paused his walk around Altor Caedem's empty courtyards and watched the sky. The lightning bolts looked like illustrated paths on a black canvas. There was probably more to them, some kind of pressure exchange, or motion law, or formula with too many numbers. He'd have to ask Ally about it later. Perhaps the topic would bring her back to him and reality for a few minutes at least.

Makeda's medic had ordered bed rest after she'd fallen on the stairs, but something else had changed. He wasn't sure if Reggie's spells had stopped working or if the pregnancy put too much strain on her. Either way, she spent her days mumbling to herself, filling up parchment after parchment with illegible numbers and words until they covered her whole bedroom. It looked almost as bad as Theodosia's home.

Reggie claimed to have it under control, and Robert had to believe him. What else could he do? Ally had chosen Reggie, Elfentum's most beloved entertainer, who solved any problem with magic, who wrote stories that gifted him the heart of any lady he desired, who knew Ally, had loved her for decades, had seen her through anguish Robert couldn't imagine without falling into fits of rage. And yet, the same Reggie had allowed Josef to live instead of shooting him in the crotch and watching him bleed out slowly. The same Reggie had poked fun at the Council that had wrecked her instead of dismantling them. The same Reggie refused to talk about his strange sickness.

Robert kicked a stone into a puddle. Thunder followed, and the timing lured a smirk out of him. The thought of Reggie's mysterious ailment washed it away. Robert should've had plenty of reasons to hate him, to rejoice in his pain, but he didn't. *Reggie, you clever bastard. You got me to care about you.* The truth was that day after day, Robert sat next to their bed, wishing the demons that plagued them would manifest so he could face the pain instead. But it wasn't his place.

Once the baby was born, would it be his place? Would he be able to hold it, care for it, and sing to it like his dad used to do? But Robert couldn't sing. Reggie could. It wasn't a guard's duty to entertain a royal baby. It was the jester's. Besides, Reggie was the most imaginative, joyful, and curiosity-evoking presence he'd ever met. Ally's baby would be too smart to choose a sniper instead.

It was best for all of them that he had made his true value to Ally clear. She wanted to stay with Reggie, have a family with him, so Robert would be her guard, and that was it. It didn't matter how much he longed to curl around her delicate body at night and whisper sweet nonsense into her ear until she drifted off into a peaceful slumber, away from voices and tormentors. Or how he pictured her waking him at night with the insatiable hunger of the meadow and a throbbing beast only he could tame. How he longed to hear her moan when he shoved her downward with just enough pressure to arouse but not scare her, and feel her mouth around his—

"Cadet!"

Robert jumped. Heat shot into his face, and he cringed when he recognized the woman approaching him. Ally's grandmother. *Fantastic.*

"G-General." He saluted. His feet had taken him to the unarmed combat training ring, which the thunderstorm had turned into a mud pit. Makeda looked like she'd slept in it. Wet dirt drenched her unarmored training clothes and was crusted in her hair. She smiled in a dignified but fierce manner, as if she were riding into a tournament on a golden stallion.

"You can call me Makeda. *Robert,* isn't it? You're the guard my Ally makes doe eyes at."

"Ehm . . . I guess. What are you doing out here, if I may be so frank?"

She gestured at the mud pit. "Training."

"It's the middle of the night."

"So? Finally some peace from all the rascals running around here. You're not in bed either, and I don't remember putting your name on the guard rota."

It was true. Robert hadn't been assigned a night shift in weeks and still roamed the academy's grounds until dawn. Every time his head hit the pillow, he thought back to the staircase. What would have happened if he hadn't been there? When would Ally need him next? What if the baby came unexpectedly? It had been conceived unexpectedly, so it would make sense.

"Wanna join me for sparring?" Makeda asked.

He saw that she was serious but chuckled anyway. "You Verdains really are somethin'. Thank you, ma'am, but I gotta decline for now."

She sighed and rolled her shoulders. "I'm getting a bit

stiff anyway. It's not right for an elf to feel their age." She glanced up at the storm clouds. "I suppose our dear Caedem is telling us to stay inside. Wanna grab a beer instead?"

Robert wasn't sure if he saw despair behind her facade or if despair was the only good reason for fools to be out here in this weather. "Sure, it'd be an honor."

"Excellent, let's go to the mess hall. Peggy, my chef, should be up preparing breakfast. She always has an ale set aside for me." She led him out of the training yard and through four of the imposing stone archways until the mess hall, made of red bricks, came into sight. As chaotic as his life had become, walking through Altor Caedem awoke a childlike glee in him. He'd dreamed to roam its halls and learn how to fight like a knight with boys his age, away from the pressure his mom had put on him. At least his kid could call the academy their home.

"You're quite talented on the shooting grounds." She opened her drenched satchel and pulled a large ring with several dozen keys out. She continued to speak as she searched through them. "Were you here when Professor Urus was with us?"

"No, ma'am, don't have the kind of blood you're lookin' for."

She found the key and opened the mess hall's iron door. "Commoner?"

"Yep . . ." His stomach clenched. He didn't need to be reminded of his inadequacy.

"But you're in the royal guard . . ." She hesitated on the doorsill. "*You're* the father, not Reggie."

"I—"

Makeda shoved him against the doorframe before he could finish. She conjured a knife out of nowhere and held it against his throat.

"What are your intentions with my sugar cube?" The blade scraped his skin, but his heartbeat remained steady. He'd heard rumors not to mess with Makeda, but the ferocious fire with which she looked after Ally was better than he'd imagined. "What's funny, heh?"

She lessened the force enough for him to speak. "It's refreshin' to see someone respect her."

"Good answer. Continue." She kept the blade where it was.

"Did you make Reggie go through this too?"

"I like Reggie. That buffoon is good to her."

Robert's shoulders drooped. "I know. That's why I don't want anything from her."

Makeda scoffed and put the knife away. "You got it bad for her. Good. Well, thank you for giving me a great-grandchild to look forward to, and know that if you harm my sugar cube, I will delight in dangling your balls off our sword tower."

Robert raised an eyebrow. "Am I attached to them in this scenario?"

The mess hall chef interrupted them before he could find out. "Makeda!" An attractive woman under the elvish aging mark of 150 beamed at them. Ginger curls fell out of her bun and into her freckled face. Her eyes lit up when she saw the general.

"Good morning, Pegs."

"You're early." Peggy's smile faded when she saw Robert. "And you brought company."

"Mornin'." Robert nodded.

"Would you mind bringing us some beers, Pegs dear?" Makeda asked in a sweet voice. Peggy winked and rushed back to the kitchen. Makeda's gaze followed her until Robert spoke.

"Peggy's awfully nice," he drawled with growing discomfort.

"Oh yeah, she's, eh . . . she's a dear." Makeda gestured at the empty benches. "Take a seat. Tell me more about you and Ally."

Robert obeyed her command and sat down on a long wooden bench. Giddiness replaced the discomfort. This was the first time he'd set foot in the mess hall. He ate in the bar-racks or with Ally and Reggie (and wouldn't miss the latter), but this felt special. He gazed around the large hall, took in the tapestry of Elfentum's old battles, and tried to imagine the stories buried in this place. Thousands of young war-riors had sat here, eaten here, lived here. First loves and first heartbreaks happened within these walls. The choosing of life paths, the creation of unshakable camaraderie. What would his story have been if he'd gone here? Would he have met Ally as an equal?

"It's quite something, isn't it?" Makeda smiled at him.

He looked back at her, and the discomfort returned. She was supposed to be the mentor of Elfentum's future honor. "Don't let Ally catch you. Her grandmothers are a symbol of everlasting love to her."

Makeda stiffened. "Excuse me?"

"Would be a shame to ruin that for her. She deserves to believe in somethin'."

Makeda opened her mouth right as Peggy returned with two steins. She brushed her hand over Makeda's shoulder and giggled. "My, you are dirty. Would you like me to bring you a cloth?"

Makeda kept her eyes on Robert and didn't blink. "No thank you, Pegs. That's all for now."

Peggy pouted and left.

Makeda closed her eyes and took a deep breath. "Don't you dare tell Theo about this. She doesn't need more pain in her life."

Robert sighed. "I'm not causin' anyone pain." It was the one thing he was succeeding at. He didn't play foul with Reg-gie or Ally. He was their guard, not hurting anyone, not mak-ing anyone jealous.

Makeda opened her eyes and took a long gulp from her stein. She smacked her lips. "You have no idea what you're talking about."

Anger churned in Robert. He wasn't sure why he cared so

much about the marriage problems of Ally's grandmothers. Makeda could be dishonorable if she wanted. He knew he was honorable—he had been from the start. He'd made sure Ally was too. He might've been sick of it, but he continued to be honorable anyway.

He stretched his arms. "I guess I can ask Peggy if she knows."

Makeda slammed her stein on the table. "You disrespectful little prick."

"I'm disrespectful? Look in the mirror, General."

Makeda pulled the knife back out and stabbed it into the table. "You don't understand."

Robert leaned forward, ignoring the urge to pull his own weapon. All the frustration, anger, and confusion he'd swallowed down longed to surface. "What, you're not fucking Peggy before breakfast?" he whispered instead. To his satisfaction, the words were a harder blow than any physical violence could have been.

She let go of the knife, crossed her arms, and stared at the ceiling. Robert noticed her nose flare several times. The muscles in her face tensed until it looked like she was holding her breath. The satisfaction Robert felt was short-lived. He remembered that he was talking to a Verdain queen. "I mean, I didn't—"

"Everything was a war for Theo and me, and we *won*." Makeda sniffed once and met Robert's eyes. Her gaze hardened. "We won, but Caedem rejected us. Before you lecture me, try saying goodbye to your son the day his wife dies in childbirth because you've been exiled from the nation *you* built. Try losing your son and hearing about it in a letter. Try reading that your brilliant granddaughter is being handed off to some waste-of-skin molester." She rose from her seat, her body shaking. "Do you think I don't know what Josef did to her? Do you think I wasn't tempted to forgo the exile every fucking day of my life? Knowing that he—" She picked up the stein and threw it against the stone wall. "But I couldn't go against Caedem's will. Do you hear me, Robert? Terrible things happen to those who challenge the gods. Remember that." Robert expected her to explode into a beast of bright light like Ally had, but she collapsed back onto the bench instead. "Theo has been depressed since our son disappeared. His death was never confirmed to us, so she dies for him every day, and there's nothing I can do. Believe me, I've tried. I'm clinging to the last bit of life that's left. What is wrong with that?"

Robert froze, overwhelmed by how much he truly hadn't known. But the indisputable issue remained. "Theo loves you."

"I love her." Tears shot into Makeda's eyes, but she looked determined not to spill them. "I've loved her enough to wage war on all of Elfentum and everyone who tried to keep us apart."

Robert swallowed. "But not enough to stand by her side now?"

He had pushed it too far. Makeda glared at him like she was about to pull the knife, leap over the table, and cut his throat. She spilled a tear instead. "Robert, I don't know what else to do."

Guilt gnawed at him, but he was in the right. Theodosia had chosen Makeda, had dedicated her life to her. It made him want to scream that she was wasting such a gift. "Maybe start by givin' her the attention Peggy gets."

Makeda exhaled and nodded. "Peggy!" The chef took her time and hadn't given up her pout yet.

"Yes?"

"No breakfast for me today. Could you make a pot of hot chocolate for me to take with instead?" Her pout turned into a full-blown sulk, but Makeda ignored it. "With a bit of coconut cream; you know how the queen likes it best." The chef stomped off. "Thank you, Peggy!"

Robert clicked his tongue. "You're cold."

Makeda sniffed again, but the hardness returned to her

eyes. "I'm a general. I don't take quarters." She stood up. "Now if you'll excuse me, I'm gonna make sure she doesn't spit in my wife's chocolate."

Robert saluted and watched her leave.

"Did you make Makeda cry? Because if so, I might be genuinely terrified of you, my sexy companion." Reggie slid onto the bench and caught Robert before he fell off.

"Fucking limbo, Reggie!"

"See, I had to scare you back or I'd have fainted out of fear." Reggie winked.

"I guess so." Robert inspected him, and his heart skipped a beat. Dark circles had formed around Reggie's whole eyes, not just under them. He looked gaunter than Robert remembered and carried a travel sack over his shoulder.

"Are you okay, man?"

" 'Okay' is such a lovely, ambiguous word, isn't it? Whole tragedies could be written about 'okay.' "

Robert frowned and eyed him. He wore a muted travel coat and a black scarf. The unusual simplicity of his attire made Robert uneasy. "You're not leaving, are you?"

Reggie glanced at the kitchen, but Makeda hadn't returned yet. He turned back to Robert and eyed him with equal intensity. "What would you do if I was?" His blue irises swirled in a circle. *That's impossible.* Robert blinked at him, and the effect was gone.

"You can't leave. It would break Ally's heart. She loves you." Robert waited for anger to set in. They all threw away what he couldn't have. No anger came. Concern overshadowed it.

"You seem upset."

Robert scoffed. "No shit. I'm not exactly happy about that."

Reggie cocked his head. "Let's talk." He snapped his fingers, and the mess hall dissolved. Colors gushed around them until they settled in the beige tones of parchment. The ceiling, walls, and floor had turned into book pages with letters as large as Robert. Four gigantic books created a new room for Reggie and him to sit in.

"Don't worry. It's an illusion," Reggie whispered.

Robert ran his finger over the page underneath him, and his heartbeat quickened. He had stumbled into a story, a life grander than the narratives of reality. If getting lost in his favorite books was a drop of water for a throat pained with thirst, this was more fine wine than he could ever drink. "Where are we?"

"*Defiance of a Rose.*" Reggie smiled and looked at the letter they sat on. "I think you planted your sweet ass on Duchess Ulzhalgas's return."

Robert breathed in the comforting scent of old book pages and choked up. "It's beautiful."

"Thank you." Reggie laughed to himself.

"What's funny?"

"A lot of things, my man, a lot of things."

Robert chuckled as well. It seemed impossible not to in this pocket of wonders.

"So, Robert . . . are you unhappy with Ally loving me or with me leaving?"

Robert took a deep breath and thought about it. "Both, strangely enough."

"I don't see a problem with the first one."

"Yeah, well . . ." Robert leaned forward and punched Reggie's arm lightly. "If you see a problem with the second one, you shouldn't leave."

Reggie let himself fall onto the bed of pages and looked at the ceiling book. "I have a soft spot for *Defiance of a Rose.* Does that bother you?"

Before he could think twice about it, Robert lay down next to him. The parchment was softer than he had expected.

Defiance of a Rose *is hugging me.* He grinned. "No, of course not."

Reggie's fingers danced in the air, and the letters on the ceiling followed. "It doesn't diminish your love for it?"

A large *R* pulled an *A* closer and spun it around. Together they danced across the pages.

Reggie turned his head to look at him. Robert shook his head, then turned to face him as well.

"Then why can't Ally be with both of us?"

"She's not a book, Reggie."

"You're right. She can't belong to anyone."

Robert's eyes wandered over Reggie's face as he took in the words. They couldn't both be with Ally. It wasn't right. He noticed how surprisingly long Reggie's eyelashes were for a guy. A lot of things weren't right.

"Whatever you wanna go for, go for it," Reggie whispered.

Robert twitched, and for a horrifying second he thought he'd kiss Reggie. Then he thought better of it and sat up.

"Disappointing choice, but all right," Reggie mumbled.

"So you wouldn't mind if Ally and I were a thing?" Robert asked.

"Nope." Reggie sat up too. "I gotta confess something though."

"I'm all ears."

"I know! So many of them." He flicked his fingers, and a bunch of ears popped out of Robert's arms.

Robert laughed and shook his head. "You can't turn it off, can you?"

"Nope . . . it's all I am." He flicked another finger, and the ears fell off. He sighed. "I'm leaving because Ally's in danger and I'm making things worse. It's a thing of mine . . . spectacular shows and ruining everything."

Robert put his arm around him. "Hey, don't say that." Reggie gave him a weak smile and laid his head on his shoulder. "What danger are we talking about? I got a fully loaded pistol on me. Her name's Raptor."

"Cute."

"She ain't cute when she's shooting you in the face."

"Yeah, I can picture that a little too well."

Robert squeezed him. "Don't worry, I wouldn't shoot my pal. So what's goin' on?"

"Don't tell Ally, all right?"

That didn't seem like an honorable condition, but he couldn't say no to the jester's vulnerable, genuine face. He'd never seen him like that. "All right."

Reggie lifted his head from Robert's shoulder and took off his bag and coat. He started unbuttoning his shirt.

"Ehm . . . I-I'm not sure if—" Robert stammered.

"Relax, my man, the perfect time for a make out session already passed." He opened his shirt and turned toward Robert, whose breath caught. There were holes in Reggie's stomach, round holes that revealed darkness instead of organs.

"Wha . . . what?"

"The magic I've been doing comes at a price. All of this"—Reggie gestured around them—"ain't cheap."

Robert looked at the beautiful parchment and back at the devastating holes in Reggie. The former lost all its importance. "Then stop it. Now! You don't have to harm yourself for silly tricks."

"I thought you found it beautiful?"

"Yeah, but . . ." Robert examined his stomach closely. "Does it hurt?"

"Only when I want it to. And it's fine; this little book trick doesn't cost much. It's the bigger stuff that's getting me in trouble."

"Lifting Ally's illness . . ."

"Among other things." He buttoned his shirt back up. "I never minded, but it's catching up with me."

Robert took his hand. It was a strange gesture but came naturally. "What can we do about it?"

Reggie's eyes welled up with tears. "That's sweet, but I, ehm . . . I really should go."

"I don't know, man, this seems like a tough cookie to crack, and if anyone can figure out stuff that makes no sense, it's Ally."

Tears rolled over Reggie's rose tattoo. "A long time ago, I planned to destroy Ally. I'm afraid I'm succeeding."

Robert had sworn to harm anyone with foul intentions toward Ally, but he couldn't picture Reggie among them. He knew Bored Reginald used to publish propaganda against her, but that was long before they'd fallen in love. Or Robert presumed so, at least. He studied the blue eyes, the innocence in them, and shook his head. Reggie wouldn't harm her, and if he was in trouble, he needed Robert. He wanted to keep them both safe, Ally and Reggie. The question was how to phrase such a weird thought. "All right . . . then I'll fight you."

"What?"

"The thought of you hurting her is ridiculous, but if you try, I'll fight you. I wouldn't let it happen."

"If I leave——"

"No. Ally needs you. If what you're saying is right, she needs both of us. Oxygen or whatever she said with the molecule metaphor thing."

Reggie laughed with a sniff. "Lithium?"

"Yes, lithium. Let's be her lithium. And whatever is coming for her can deal with me first." Robert brushed the tears off Reggie's face. The fool really was sentimental. He choked up as well but ignored it.

"Staying . . . it's a very selfish thing to do."

"So what? We're only people. All we can do is be with our loved ones and try our darndest to do better."

Reggie examined him for a few seconds. "Thank you," he whispered, then kissed his cheek.

Robert drew back. "Whoa, so when I meant——"

"Too much?"

"——lithium, I didn't mean. I'm not into——"

"Got it, got it, my bad." He snapped his fingers, and the book pages morphed back into the mess hall. Robert's heart sank a little when he emerged back into reality, but then he thought of Ally. He could be with her, and it wouldn't hurt anyone. It didn't make any logical sense, but neither did parchment walls.

Reggie cleared his throat and shimmied his shoulders. The muted travel clothes changed into an elegant suit with blue and lilac stripes. "Better. Now, my fine man, how would you like to make up with Ally? She deserves to be woken up with something more pleasant than a nightmare for once. Like you admitting what a moron you've been." He winked.

Robert's thoughts wandered back to the bed, to the impossible dreams he was now allowed to act upon. Part of him wanted to run up the tower, faster than any visitor before, but concern hadn't left him. "What about you? Are you gonna sneak off while I'm up there?"

Reggie bit his lip. "You asked me not to, and I'm not good at saying no, so no—funny enough—I'm staying. Not sure if I'd made it long without her anyway."

"Look after yourself. I . . ." He wanted to say more but had no idea what.

The kitchen door was flung open, and Peggy stomped back into the mess hall. "Yeah, well have fun finding another chef, General!"

Makeda rushed after her. "You say that as if it's hard. I've got plenty of job applications on my desk."

"Reginald!" Peggy spotted him. "I have your care package prepped, like you asked."

"Oh, I don't need it anymore."

Peggy tossed her arms in the air. "Sure, why would anyone need anything from me anymore?"

"See, that's the point I was trying to make," Makeda said.

Reggie leaned toward Robert. "Why don't you go and I handle this circus? Melodrama is my jam."

Robert didn't need to be told twice and rushed out of the mess hall. The storm had worsened and delayed the morning sun's entrance. Robert sidestepped a training shield that jousted with the wind. With each clap of thunder, a fresh bolt of energy shot through him. The months of repressing any desire he'd felt surfaced and consumed him. The regular check-in with the guards at the tower's entrance took too long. He had already wasted too many moments; he couldn't spare another. He ran halfway up the staircase before exhaustion caught up. *Damn my body.* He leaned against the stone wall for a breath. A bolt lit up the sky and reignited him. He ran the rest of the way and prayed that rushing toward her wouldn't cost him his stamina later.

He slowed when he reached Ally's floor. Neither she nor the baby needed another scare. The slower pace allowed doubts to creep in. Reggie had seemed certain, but was Ally actually interested in him? She had made no advances since they'd arrived at Altor Caedem. Not since . . . *since you turned her down, moron.*

He took a deep breath and approached her door.

"Morning, Liam, mind if I head in?" He addressed her night guard and examined the beautifully carved but thin wooden door. "Actually, mind if I take over now?"

"Thank Caedem." He slapped Robert's shoulder. "Ate something wrong last night and have been holding it in for—"

"All right, don't need to hear the details."

Liam gave him a grateful nod and rushed off. Robert frowned after him. It shouldn't have been this easy to get past the queen's royal guard. But he wasn't here as the captain of her guard. He was here as Robert and sincerely hoped she'd prefer it.

He knocked gently before entering. Ally was asleep, as Reggie had predicted. Robert approached the ball of blankets and magnificence. Her elbow stuck out from under a sheet. He was tempted to kiss it but needed to be sure first that she wanted him.

"Ally?" he whispered. "Ally?"

She shifted in the sheets, her eyes still closed. "Balthos?"

Robert chuckled. "Yes, it's Balthos, king of the gods, coming for breakfast."

Ally slapped around herself and jolted upright. She struggled with the blankets, disoriented.

"Oh shit, sorry, didn't mean to—it's Robert. Just Robert."

She rubbed her eyes and blinked at him. "Robert," she mumbled in her sleepy voice. His heart beat faster. "What are you doing here?" Her hand found her belly, and she seemed more alert. "Is something wrong?"

"No, the opposite. I think. I hope, at least. Can I?" He pointed at the bed and sat down when she nodded. He looked at her round face, the fine line of her lips, and her eyes, which resembled the lilac sunrise outside fighting its way through the hazy storm clouds. "Well, shit."

"What?"

"I keep forgettin' how beautiful you are." His chest wanted to burst when her lips curled into a smile. "Makes it hard not to kiss you."

She ambushed him, swung her arms around his neck, and brought those eager lips close. He laughed gently in an attempt to appear more casual than he was. "Hold on there." His body grew impatient, hard and ready to take over, but he wouldn't settle for passion this time. "I wanna ask you first, do you, ehm, do you still want me? Not as a guard, but—"

She cut him off with a kiss, pulled away briefly to nod, and kissed him again. It was all he needed. His body took over, eager to quench the desire that had built up for months. He let go of her lips and took off the nightgown. He hadn't seen her since the change of her body.

She noticed his hesitation. "Sorry, I know I'm—"

"Holy tits." They'd been perky before with pink budding roses in their centers, but now they'd grown to a mesmerizing size. Ally's giggle turned into a moan when he pushed her backward into the sheets. He tried to follow, but her breasts weren't the only thing that had grown. *The belly.* He considered flipping her over, pulling her toward him, and taking her from behind. His brain interrupted. That might've been too forward for their first time in months.

"Different position?" she asked, short of breath.

"Let me warm you up first." He ran his hands over her legs and pressed them apart. Another moan escaped her. He stroked the inside of her thighs and pulled her closer. His pants grew too tight. He breathed slowly, knowing he'd get his relief soon enough, and took off his shirt. The look in Ally's eyes as she watched him sent another pressing wave of lust through him. He should have taken care of his business the day before. This wasn't a good time to be a quick shot. "For what it's worth, my pants have buttons this time." He hoped the joke would calm him down long enough to satisfy her.

Ally closed her legs with a grin. "Do they?"

He grinned back and slid a hand between her thighs to open them again. She grabbed his wrist, sat up, and tossed him backward against the pillows. He wrapped his arm around her waist and tried to swing her over to the pillows, but her fingernails dug into his captured wrist as he struggled. He groaned in pain and lust.

She raised her other hand and traced his nose with her finger. "I'm rather fond of breakfast in bed," she whispered. She let go of his wrist and moved down to his pants. *Fuck, it's actually happening.* He took another deep breath, eager for this dream to last as long as possible.

His eyes closed as her lips and tongue found him. He groaned again and clasped a nearby sheet. For the next few minutes, he was no longer Robert Oakley. He felt like more than that—like a god. Like Balthos, king of the gods himself.

CHAPTER 32

XENIA

January 980 - Altor Caedem, Virisunder

"So in the year 940, the armory discontinued goose grease as a cleaning substance and replaced it with nut oil mixtures. There's walnut oil. There's almond oil. There are other nut oils. There's peanut oil."

"Oh sweet Tiambyssi, swallow me whole," Nobuko whispered.

Xenia glanced at her confidant, who was playing finger tricks with her quill, and shook her head. It was inappropriate to interrupt one of their wise professors, even if it was Professor Golders.

"Hazelnut oil, pecan oil . . ."

Xenia couldn't help but groan. Why did she need to know all of this? She'd have squires to deal with menial tasks like weapon maintenance when she was a knight. Nobuko smirked at her.

Xenia leaned over. "I just made a tired noise. That's not as bad as talking during class."

"Isn't that what you're doing right now?"

Fortunately, Xenia didn't have to respond. Next to her, Chimalli let out a loud snore even Professor Golders couldn't ignore.

"Cadet Chimalli!"

The human boy startled. "Huh, what? Oh, P-Professor, yes. Sorry."

Professor Golders walked over with a ruler. Xenia stiffened. She and Chimalli had become friends over the past few months. He always followed Nobuko around, and chatting with him—or at him—was more fun than arguing with her confidant. He had been the chosen commoner for a scholarship two years ago. Altor Caedem rarely accepted Tribu La'am humans, but Chimalli was an orphan and had written a touching letter to Queen Theodosia.

Xenia had looked down upon the notion of letting commoners into the school. After all, knights were noble. She had to admit though, Chimalli was talented, especially when it came to explosives. He was sweet and fun as well, despite his commoner status, so Xenia was glad he took the same classes as Nobuko and her. He had spent the first two years at school catching up on basic education. Commoners must've been too busy picking apples to study how to write.

"Hands," said Professor Golders.

Chimalli swallowed and stretched out his shaking hand. Xenia scooted her chair closer and gave Professor Golders a large smile. "Professor, I was wondering if coconut oil would work for blade maintenance?"

He blinked at her and lowered the ruler. "No, Lady van Auersperg, of course not. Coconuts are seeds, not nuts. The oil would be a seed oil, not a nut oil. Nut oils come from nuts, like walnuts, which become walnut oil. Or almonds, which become almond oil. Or—"

A loud bang on the other side of the classroom distracted

him. A horrendous stench followed. *Stink bomb.* Xenia squinted at Nobuko, who shrugged with that annoying, innocent
face of hers. Keeping Chimalli out of trouble was a task for
two, but Xenia had handled it the proper way. No dirty tricks
were needed, just diplomacy. *Crap, I sound like Mom.* She shuddered. Maybe stink bombs were a great idea after all.

"Stay down, everyone, stay down. This smells like a
classified substance, but it might be unclassified." Professor
Golders pulled a pair of leather gloves from his desk drawer
and walked over to the stink bomb. "This is why correct clas-
sifications are the most important part of active combat and
maintenance."

The rest of the students were less tolerant of the stench.
They jumped off their chairs and struggled to hide their faces in their school uniforms. Xenia loved the stiff, half-plated
Altor Caedem uniform, but even she wished for some fluffy
fabric to cover her poor nose with.

"I'm gonna be sick," Chimalli mumbled. He did look a
little orcish around the nose.

"Let's get you out of here." Xenia grabbed his sleeve and
pulled him through the chaotic classroom. Nobuko could stay
behind and explain their absence. Or she could join them and
be a nuisance. Naturally, she chose the latter.

"Lady van Auersperg, are we leaving an active classroom
situation without permission from our commander?" Nobuko teased. Xenia ignored her and made her way to the door.
"That is not very knightly of you. I might have to write you
up to your knight captain."

Xenia took a deep breath and let go of Chimalli to push
Nobuko into the classroom corner next to the door. "There's
no *knight captain*, idiot. Knights are independent but choose to
serve their nation out of honor and dignity. Taking care of
a sick civilian?" She tugged at Chimalli, who wobbled and
tripped a little.

"Xe-Xenia, I really think I need to throw—"

"Not now, Chi, I'm giving a speech. Taking care of a sick

civilian in times of peril is very knightly, thank you very much. What would you know about knights, anyway? Vach da tìm never even had those." Xenia forgot about the chaos. Nobuko had teased her for months, but that was over now. She was a future knight, for Caedem's sake. She towered over her confidant, who was pressed against the wall. It wiped the smile off Nobuko's smug face.

"We had youxia warriors, and you can ask Golders over there, many of the old weapons came from Vach da tìm," Nobuko whispered, then broke Xenia's gaze and looked down. "You'd make a great youxia . . ."

Xenia paused and realized how close she had gotten to her confidant. Cornering someone like that was not knightly. Or youxia-ly. She would have to look up that term later. It would be embarrassing to ask Nobuko now. Xenia shouldn't have lost her temper, but somehow even the closeness embarrassed her. The torchlight caught the blue shimmer of Nobuko's hair and left a purple hue. It didn't look ugly on her.

"Ladies," Chimalli said, "I need to—"

"One moment, Chi." Nobuko smirked. "Are you gonna keep me here as your captive, or . . . ?"

"Sorry." Xenia backed off. The two looked at each other until Chimalli broke the silence by vomiting heavily between them.

"Oh gosh, Chi, why didn't you say something?" Xenia rushed to support his head. *Poor Chi.* He had a sensitive nose.

The door swung open and hit them. They stumbled, but Xenia kept Chimalli from falling.

"Ey—hello, General," Xenia blurted. *Makeda.* A thoroughly unimpressed Makeda.

"Gilbert! What is going on here? Why aren't the students in their seats?" Her voice boomed through the room. Had she practiced to attain such an awe-inspiring voice, or was it the natural gift of a brilliant general? *I should do regular vocal exercises.* They'd come in handy as a knight captain. *As a knight!*

There was no knight captain. Noboku had sneaked into her head.

Professor Golders appeared mildly embarrassed, which equaled an emotional outburst for him. "My apologies, General. The class on nut oil usage—you know, regarding the new regulations? The ones first introduced by your son—"

"Get to the point, Gilbert."

Xenia stared at her. Makeda was everything she wanted to become: strong, outspoken, authoritative, brave.

"Yes, General, of course. Well, it appears that a classified, nonharmful but nuisance-causing substance appeared in the classroom and—"

"Stink bomb," Makeda said, shooting a harsh look at Nobuko. She knew. Of course she knew. To be fair, Nobuko's nervous grin came close to a confession.

"Van Auersperg!"

Xenia jumped and dropped the faint Chimalli. She caught him before he hit the ground, but they didn't make the elegant impression she had hoped for. "Yes, General. At your service, General."

"Get Chimalli to the medic safely, then keep a close eye on Lady Phamlang during our drill this afternoon."

Nobuko dared to wink at Xenia. She did not wink back but stood taller. Xenia was worthy of Makeda's trust. "Of course, General."

Makeda nodded her approval, and Xenia's insides flooded with excitement.

"The rest of you make your way to the assembly hall. We're doing the survival drill early this year. It will take until dawn. Do not bring your belongings with you." She left, and Xenia gawked after her before she remembered her sacred knight and friend duties.

"Let's get you to the medic, Chi."

Heavy rain pattered against the windows of Altor Caedem's assembly hall as if the storm wanted to challenge Elfentum's young cadets. *Foolish storm. Nothing should mess with General Makeda.* Xenia squeezed herself into the hall, which was packed to the brim with nervous-looking students in full body armor. *By Caedem's cat!* Xenia looked down at her regular school uniform. When had they all changed?

She spotted Makeda shoving a small pouch into each cadet's hand. Xenia's stomach knotted when she noticed her grim expression. The stink bomb must have really upset her. Xenia marched toward her, but a certain black-haired elf jumped in front of her.

"Hey there, snob, ready to have some fun?" Noboku's eyes glistened with mischief, which was both exciting and worrisome.

"I didn't bring my armor." She hadn't meant to sound so whiny. She really had to work on her commanding voice.

Noboku laughed. "Don't worry, Lady Perfect, they're handing them out over there. These aren't our normal ones. They're supposed to make us miserable for the next twelve hours." The uniforms seemed to be working on everyone but her. She still beamed.

Xenia whispered in her ear, "You've got something planned."

Nobuko fluttered her eyelashes. "Me? Never! I am just an eager student. Now I suggest you get your absolutely, very much necessary pouch, van Auersperg, while I snatch you the armor you're so keen to get into."

She rushed off, and a smile crossed Xenia's face. She wanted to impress Makeda, and Nobuko was royally annoying, but somehow Xenia was looking forward to being annoyed for the next twelve hours.

Half an hour later, Xenia was equipped with her useless pouch and miserably heavy armor. The pouch held a quarter-filled water flask, a notebook, a quill, and an emergency assula to call an instructor. No food whatsoever. That hadn't seemed like a problem until Makeda had introduced the details of the catacombs survival drill. Everyone was assigned a partner, then trapped in a small cave together. According to Makeda, situations like these were a common occurrence in war, especially with the rising usage of explosives. She had implemented a yearly survival training based on it, and every student dreaded the next one—every student except for Nobuko. Xenia worried what her confidant was planning to do in that cave that had her so excited.

She didn't dread the drill either, of course. She had no problem enduring a situation like that. She had one minor disadvantage, but surely her knightly spirit would make up for that. Being scared of the dark wasn't knightly in the first place, so she had probably imagined that fact about herself. She was brave and fearless. If only Lady Icicle could accompany her on the survival drill.

"Remember to press the assula if the situation becomes too dangerous," Makeda said. "Three professors will be ready to assist you should this occur. I will not be available, as I'm taking the next twelve hours off for personal reasons. Be advised that if you do press the assula, you will repeat the exercise in a week from now. Follow me!"

Makeda led them down to the cold, clammy catacombs. She carried a torch that shone a light on the narrow pathways, but it was darker than Xenia had expected. Much darker.

"Some say these catacombs were designed like Balthos's Heretics, the prison. There are a ton of nachtalbs here," a boy next to her whispered.

"What are nachtalbs?" Xenia's voice shook. Lady Icicle would have steadied her.

She felt a warm hand wrap around her arm. "Shut it, Heath. You know that's a lie." It was Nobuko, and her hand was almost as comforting as Lady Icicle. She was annoying, of course. How dare she assume Xenia needed defending? She was a knight, not a damsel in distress. Xenia leaned into her anyway. Nobuko was her assigned confidant, which made it okay.

They turned the corner and stopped against a dank stone wall. Across from it were holes leading into even darker darkness. Xenia's stomach flipped. For the first time since she had arrived at Altor Caedem, she missed her mother. Whenever the night became too creepy, she would crawl into Xenia's bed and hold her until dawn. She had taught her that darkness was nothing to fear. It was merely a choice, and the ethereal realm was always close by, filled with people who loved their little Xenia. If she couldn't bear the darkness any longer, she could ask for Calliquium to send a message to the ethereal realm. All the people who loved her would shine down a light, illuminating the darkness. But Calliquium was a busy god, and it was best not to call upon him unless absolutely necessary. Instead, one should always try to conquer the darkness and learn from it all that one could. As weak as her mother usually appeared, in those moments she had radiated a calm strength Xenia now craved.

"Line up!" Makeda's voice echoed along the walls.

Xenia took a deep breath. *I choose darkness. I choose darkness. I choose it, and I will conquer it.* Nobuko pulled her through the line before she could convince herself.

"Hey!"

"What?"

"Stop pushing!"

Nobuko didn't slow down or apologize to the other students.

"What are you doing?" Xenia hissed at her crazy confidant. Nobuko stopped, and Xenia stumbled into her.

She pulled Xenia in close to whisper in her ear. "Do you trust me?" Their cheeks touched. The warmth of her skin gave Xenia shivers. Without sight, her other senses were more alert. She had never noticed how her confidant smelled of raspberries and warm chestnuts.

"Not at all," she replied, but even she could hear the smile in her voice.

"Too bad." Nobuko slung her arm around Xenia and pushed her onward until they reached the front of the line.

"In pairs, climb into the cave in front of you." Makeda's booming voice was right next to them now. They did as they were told. Nobuko hopped in first, with more grace than Xenia and her lanky limbs mustered. The cave was deeper than Xenia had expected and as cold and clammy as the wall had been.

"Your eyes will adjust to the absence of light," Makeda continued. "I expect you to record the experience, challenges, and accomplishments in your journal. An essay will be due tomorrow evening at six. Remember your emergency button should weakness overcome you. Good luck!"

The catacombs rumbled as heavy stones crashed outside of the caves and trapped them. Xenia had expected a small door to close, not a death trap. How would they get out now? Even if they called for an emergency, they were trapped within these dead, murderous walls. She screamed. It was so dark. Darker than any night at home had ever been. Even darker than the nights she had spent camping with her dad. She couldn't form rational thoughts. Everything screamed *dark, dark, dark* in here. She could see nothing and so much at once. There were shapes, forms, monsters perhaps? Was she standing or falling? Where was up, and where was down? She couldn't take it any longer. She had to bother Calliquium. Or better yet, Caedem. That lazy butt should've been able to blast her out of here. Some stories claimed he had paws with claws strong enough to slash any material.

She was about to call for Caedem when a soft green glow broke the darkness.

"Hey there." Nobuko's voice was much gentler than her usual teasing. She held a small training dagger that glowed green with magic. It was the dagger she'd hidden from Makeda the day Xenia had arrived. The light now illuminated her face. There she was. Another person. Something real. Something tangible in the darkness. Xenia's rational thinking hadn't returned yet, so she rushed into her arms.

"Oh, ehm . . ." Nobuko likely wanted to argue, but Xenia didn't let her. She hugged her closer, taking in all the warmth, until her breathing steadied and her calm had returned. To her surprise, Nobuko's breathing had sped up.

"Sorry, I didn't mean to make you nervous. I just needed . . . sorry." Xenia backed off.

"That's okay. You're, ehm, nice. Anyway, look, I finally contained one of the assulas we used in Explosive Studies and applied it to a weapon. I combined it with soybean oil and rubbed the blade in it. Don't tell Golders."

Xenia laughed. "I won't." She knew Nobuko was up to bad mischief, but she hadn't known that bad mischief looked so neat. More than that, her craft was brilliant and made the whole darkness survival training bearable. "Smart."

"Great, I got approval from the knight captain!" She beamed.

"That's not—"

"Let's get out of here."

Xenia must have misheard her. Out of here? Nobuko knocked against the stone wall at the back of their cave. She'd only moved two steps away, but Xenia wasn't okay with the sudden distance to the light. She sneaked as close to her confidant as she could without embarrassing herself. She could include sneaking in her essay. It was all part of the study and therefore not cowardly at all.

Nobuko knocked on several stones until she was met with a hollow sound. "Finally! Xenia, co—" Nobuko looked over her shoulder and found Xenia's face a nose length away from her. "Hey there, quite attached, aren't we?"

Xenia grinned. "Am I making you nervous?"

Nobuko scoffed and turned back to the hollow stone. She knocked harder against it until a gap appeared. She slid her hand through it and furrowed her brow. "Almost . . . almost got it. It normally comes off easier . . ."

Xenia took a step back and let her work. Something other than the darkness twisted her stomach.

"Got it!" The hollow stone slid inward, and a thin but wonderful light ray illuminated their cave.

Xenia beamed. "Marvelous! That is so much better than this horrible pitch-black scary—I mean, I didn't mind it, but I'm sure you won't be as scared now."

Nobuko raised her brow. "Sure, whatever you say, Knight Captain." Xenia opened her mouth to protest, but Nobuko cut her off. "Shush, this part is important. I am about to share the sacred secrets of our super hidden guild with you and need to make sure you're worthy."

"Of course I'm worthy!"

"We'll see. Do you swear on the honor of Elfentum to speak only to other members of the guild about the famous secret I'm about to show you?"

Xenia crossed her arms. She felt more confident now that the beam lit their cave. "How can it be famous if it's a secret?"

Nobuko punched her arm. "Don't be a stick in the mud."

"Ow! What's the stupid guild, anyway?"

Nobuko's lips curled into her annoyingly smug smile. "It's the Survivors of Survival Drills That Aren't Complete Losers Guild, of course!"

"That's not a very snappy name."

"On second thought, I might just leave you here." Nobuko raised her nose in the air and shoved her hand through the empty spot in the wall. The light disappeared.

Xenia wrapped her arms around Nobuko's waist to pull her back out. Nobuko started flailing and kicking, but as soon as the light returned, Xenia sat her down and sank to one knee in her best knight fashion. "I apologize, dearest Lady Phamlang. Please allow me entry into your guild. I promise to tell no one about it."

Nobuko blushed, and she scratched her neck. "Ehm, I mean, you can tell Chi about it. Chi knows."

Xenia nodded but kept her head down. The noble gesture made her giddy. "I promise to tell no one about the secret except for maybe Chi."

Nobuko cleared her throat and tapped the glowing dagger on Xenia's left shoulder, then on her right.

"Other way around," Xenia mumbled, but her Lady Phamlang ignored her.

"You may get up. You're now a knight of the Survivors of Survival Drills That Aren't Complete Losers Guild. Keep its secrets."

The knight ceremony planted butterflies in Xenia's stomach. She wished Lady Icicle could have been there to see it. Or maybe her mother. It was fine. They would be there when she became a knight of Virisunder.

"You're really cute, Xenia," Nobuko whispered, avoiding her eyes. "It'll get dark again for a moment, but I'm here, okay?"

"Doesn't matter to me. I'm brave." Xenia didn't recognize her own voice. Why was it so much higher than normal?

Nobuko smiled and reached through the stone gap again. The darkness didn't scare Xenia as much this time. She focused on her newly won knighthood and the warm touch of her confidant's hand.

A clicking noise echoed through the cave, and the stone wall miraculously swung outward. Behind it was a cozy, well-lit room with torches and a ton of—

"Welcome to the larder!"

The finest cheeses, meats, and vegetables filled the shelves. One nook smelled of aromatic herbs and spices. Another enticed her with the sweet scent of pastries and pies. Makeda kept each student at Altor Caedem on military rations. It was important that their bodies adjusted to the ideal daily intake needed to survive at the front. Still, Xenia missed her mother's plentiful dishes and stuffing herself as much as she wanted. A life of excess was for peasants, but surely the occasional feast wouldn't hurt a knight.

"Let me see if it's still here . . ." Nobuko searched the pastry shelf. "Makeda loves her yemar dabo. She always has some around." Xenia's ears perked up. Her mother would bake a loaf of the milky Fi'Teri honey bread whenever they traveled. She had made one for Xenia's first week, but it hadn't lasted long. The only pastry she now got to see was a piece of butter tart on Sundays.

Xenia peeked over Nobuko's shoulder, her mouth watering. "This is the best guild ever."

"What do we have here?" Nobuko pulled a parchment out of a cookie jar and wrinkled her face. She read through it, and her shoulders sank. "Personal reasons, my ass."

"General Makeda doesn't appreciate this tone."

Her confidant scoffed. "I don't care what Makeda appreciates. She's like the rest of them."

The discomfort of the darkness returned with the words. Guilt jabbed Xenia. She shouldn't have come here. She was directly disobeying the great general. All because of what? *Because of Nobuko* . . . That shouldn't have been a good enough reason. She took one last whiff of the larder and walked back into the cave, pulling at the stone wall.

"Hey, what are you doing?" Nobuko caught the door with her foot.

"Following the general's orders."

"Come back in here, please. It's no fun alone." She fluttered her stupid long eyelashes over her stupid brown eyes, as if it were endearing. Or cute. Or beautiful.

"Fine, but you need to respect the general."

Nobuko's face fell at the mention of Makeda. "You need to stop idolizing people."

Xenia stomped back into the larder and popped a piece of cheese into her mouth. "I have heroes. What's wrong with that?"

"There are no heroes."

Xenia examined her confidant. She looked like she had lost her equivalent of Lady Icicle. "My dad's a hero," Xenia said, hoping it would comfort Nobuko as well.

"I doubt that. All grown-ups turn into someone's villain. Even our precious general." She offered Xenia the letter, who took it with a frown.

She recognized Makeda's handwriting from her strategy class but had to read the lines several times to understand. When she did, heat rushed into her cheeks. She kept her eyes glued on the words as she pictured what the described inter-action might look like.

"Hello?"

"Yes, what?" Xenia looked up, and handed the letter back. "I think this is private."

Nobuko raised an eyebrow. "You think?"

"What? I-I just tried to understand what she was writing about. I didn't know women did this kind of stuff."

"My point is, our general isn't that great if she writes stuff like this."

Xenia stuffed another piece of cheese into her mouth, trying not to picture it too much. She didn't see how this made Makeda less great. If anything, it made her more interesting. Nobuko stuffed the letter back into the cookie jar with more force than necessary. "Why are you so upset about this?"

Nobuko sat down on a potato sack. She looked cornered again, tiny as she slumped down. She examined her nails and cleaned them, decidedly avoiding Xenia's gaze. "Makeda was my hero too when I first came here. I thought I could be like her . . . but with more magic. Marry a princess, become a legend. But look at the letter. She's just like all of those grown-ups. It doesn't matter if I want a princess or a prince. We all become our parents. Love's a hoax, like nachtalbs."

Xenia dropped onto the potato sack and accidentally shoved Nobuko off. She caught her and smiled. "No, it's not."

Nobuko stared at the ground. "That letter isn't addressed to Queen Theodosia."

"So? Things are complicated sometimes."

"They shouldn't be."

Xenia thought about her parents and their constant fighting. Their relationship didn't seem that complicated. It just seemed wrong. "Maybe complicated is good. It's simpler if you just become your parents." She looked around the larder with all of its sweet smells and hardy delicacies. It reminded her of her dad's favorite pub, where she'd picked him up many afternoons. He told his war stories at the pub, but that wasn't where he wrote them. No glory was found in simple comfort. No knights were forged in it. Makeda knew that. "You know it's simpler to spend the drill in the larder too."

Nobuko frowned. "It's better."

"I'm not sure. I think it's just simpler." Xenia brushed a strand of Nobuko's hair behind her ear. "I don't know what's up with your parents, but knights, or youxias, write their own stories."

Nobuko bumped Xenia. "My dear Sir van Auersperg, aren't you mimicking Makeda's and your heroic dad's stories?"

"Makeda is my mentor, that's different." She looked around the lit larder and back at the dark cave. Had her dad ever conquered the darkness like her mother encouraged her to? He spent his days in the torchlight of pubs with the finest meats and cheese, away from her mother and any challenges. Makeda had challenged him when they had arrived, and he hadn't stood up for himself. Makeda was challenging Xenia too, with darkness and confusing letters. She could sit here in the torchlight with the finest meats and cheese and ignore it all. "I guess I am mimicking my dad's story. But I don't want to be like him. I don't want to be like either of them."

Xenia stood up and looked at Makeda's challenge—the dark cave. "Let's write a better story, one where we write the rules of love and knighthood and all of that." Nobuko still looked crumbled and doubtful, but it was a knight's duty to uplift those around them. Nerves fluttered through Xenia's stomach. She ignored them, leaned down, and quickly placed a kiss on Nobuko's warm cheek.

Her confidant blushed. "Xe-Xenia," she stuttered.

"You sound like Chi." Xenia stretched her tongue out. "Now if you'll excuse me." She turned to the stone door. "I'll be in the cave, waiting for my shield maiden with the glowing dagger." With that, she chose the darkness.

"I'm not your shield maiden," Nobuko called after her.

"My magical squire."

Nobuko rushed after her. "I'm not your squire either, you snob."

She laughed and closed the door. They had twelve hours alone. Plenty of time to come to an agreement. Plenty of time to explore what else their story could be.

CHAPTER 33

VANA

February 980 - Balthos's Heretics, Silberfluss

"Are you sure it's spelled with two *u*'s?" Vana examined her scrawl in the flickering match light. *Truu.* She tried to think of another word with two *u*'s, but until a few months ago, she had never paid attention to the shape of language.

"Yes. No. I don't know. Silberfluss has lack of consonants." Artyom took the chalk from her and attempted to spell it three more times. "Husheeta! This is bullshit."

"Husheeta!" She chuckled. He refused to translate his Sap Bürüy swear words to her, but they escaped him often enough that she had caught up. They provided delightful distractions from the dread that had taken over Balthos's Heretics. The warden had threatened them with drastic changes after the king incident and had warned them they'd be implemented as soon as Princess Agathe and the Council had made a decision. Two weeks had passed since then, and the fate of Balthos's Heretics remained unclear. Not a single guard roamed the halls, the infirmary door remained locked, and they'd decreased the prisoners' regular supplies and meals. Some took it as the punishment, but Vana was sure the worst was yet to come. Or at least that was what the warden planned. Vana wouldn't allow a worse punishment. The other inmates hadn't understood what power they had, but they were a collective and they'd rise together. She and Artyom had recruited fifteen comrades so far. Once they heard Vana's speech, the support would double or triple. Artyom had helped her write it down. The spelling was atrocious, but it was the content that mattered.

She tried to write the word again. "Ah, come on, Arty, this one looks right to me."

"*Tru?* No, no, definitely not. Word looks naked, like lovely maiden." He added an *h*, then wiped it away again.

"We need to get you laid, man, if spelling reminds you of naked maidens."

He laughed, higher than usual. "Is your dirty word, not mine."

She squinted at him. "What was that?"

He avoided her eyes. "What? I do not know what you mean."

"Do you have your eyes on someone?" It shouldn't have mattered, considering their dire circumstances, but Artyom's love life was a nicer thing to focus on than their possible doom.

"Kymbat, stop."

She poked him. "Come on, who is it?" Curiosity took over. She'd never seen him speak to anyone other than her.

He stored the chalk away. "Kymbat, even if there was woman, I very much fuck up one marriage. I have no interest to fuck up second one."

"Who said anything about marriage?" She winked.

He sighed. "Fine, I will tell, but means nothing, okay? I eat too much slime and have odd reaction."

"Are you comparing your new flame to diarrhea right now?"

"Is not flame. Is not fancy. Is not nothing, okay? Is just . . . vision. Perhaps I go insane. Is deserved."

She wanted to know why he'd deserve such a thing but was too curious about the vision part to investigate. "Go on. So no one from around here?"

"You enjoy this too much, kymbat." He rubbed his face and closed his eyes. "She is elf. Fi'Teri woman. I do not know name."

Vana frowned. "So you've never actually met her?"

"No I have not . . . not that I know, but I think I remember if I had. I heard her and saw her, very real. She is strong and beautiful and hurt . . . and I think she reached to me. And I . . ." He bit his lip, then opened his eyes. "Is nothing. Is probably nothing."

A few weeks ago, Vana would have agreed that he was going insane or was having some sort of recurring dream. But that was before the nachtalbs. Before the magic she'd seen. Before corpses stood up and moved. She didn't know what to make of it, but she believed him. She took his hand and gave it a squeeze.

"Maybe—" Vana started, but a kick against their cell's entry stone interrupted. She turned around and found Clarisse holding up an oil lamp and a wishbone slingshot. Vana got to her feet faster than her mind was prepared for. She'd seen the girl around the dining hall but couldn't figure out what to say to her. Vana had heard many stories of the crime committed against her. She knew dark shit like that happened. But hearing about it and witnessing the aftermath were two different things. What could she say to Clarisse that respected the horror she'd gone through?

"Hey," she said instead.

"Hi, Vana." She gave her a brief nod. "Artyom." A smile crossed her face. "Guess what? I got Erna and the other ducklings to agree. They're waiting in the yard, willing to listen."

"Look at you." Artyom packed up the parchment he and Vana had been working on and stood up as well. "You are already big tough warrior, eh? And that is very good news. Thank you, warrior."

Vana tried to catch up. Her speech would be in the yard. They must've been waiting for her. With Erna's support, they'd have real influence among the inmates, but she needed some clarification first. "Ducklings?"

"It's what Erna calls the ones she protects. Don't worry, she has eased up on you after Artyom and you saved me."

Vana studied Clarisse. Artyom was right. She didn't look like the abused girl in the infirmary, but like a warrior in the making. Her white-blond hair was tied back in a knot, her face determined, and her grip on the slingshot firm. Whatever pain she carried, it didn't define her. She was more than that, and Vana was more than a Spiritless failure. "Happy we could be there. Next time you can save our asses. Don't worry, you'll get a chance. I get in trouble a lot."

Clarisse chuckled. "Deal."

"So you're interested in becoming a comrade of the revolution?"

Clarisse raised her eyebrows. "I'm interested in fucking shit up and am willing to listen to your plan for it. Come on, let's not make Erna wait."

She turned back to the hallway and gestured for them to follow. Vana felt jittery when she thought of the speech. She wanted to fuck shit up as well. In particular, the king and his sister, Princess Agathe. Perhaps not Queen Lunatic, after getting an idea of what the king might have done to her. She wasn't a strong warrior and revolutionary like Clarisse, but Vana couldn't blame the queen.

Clarisse's anger both invigorated and unnerved Vana. She couldn't allow it to carry her away. Not again. She couldn't create another Isa. She wanted to build a new society, not just destroy the old one. Her speech needed to make that clear. Her speech needed to make a lot of things clear.

"Read it to me again, Arty," Vana whispered as they followed Clarisse into the hallway.

"No."

"Come on, I'll only get this one chance."

Artyom put his arm on her shoulder and guided her through the darkness. "I read again, you get more nervous. You are fine. You convinced Clarisse."

Vana scoffed and leaned in closer. "You're the one who got her out of there. I went in for the medical kit. I butchered the whole thing. I even thought she was too weak to be talked to."

"We will be there in moment," Artyom called to Clarisse. She waited ahead, providing light while giving them space to talk. "Clarisse is not weak. King is weak in heart. But you know that now. Kymbat, you are eager student that is impossible to discourage. You have more belief in things and goodness than any devotee I preached to. You may screw up this. Is okay. Is lesson. But you cannot screw up that." He poked her chest. "And when this hothead catches up"—he booped her nose—"great things happen. Until then, Arty can make sure hothead does not screw up too much."

She choked up as warmth spread through her nervous stomach. "Why do you care so much?"

He shrugged. "Eh, gives me hobby." With that, he kept walking. Vana examined the darkness and took a deep breath. Uncertainty was good. She'd already created Isa and failed her comrades. Things didn't play out the same way twice. No performance of The Spirit and the Enforcer had ever sounded the same, even if they had played the same set. She'd convince these people, they'd put their trust in her, and this time they wouldn't regret it. This Vana wouldn't let them down.

She followed Artyom and Clarisse until they reached the torchlit dining hall. Its stark, bright contrast to the rest of Balthos's Heretics made her squint whenever she entered. Heated arguments echoed around the room. Several inmates messed with the supply lifts in an attempt to gain additional supplies. It looked like a fruitless endeavor.

"Let's get to the yard. People are getting too heated in here," said Clarisse. Vana took in all the stressed faces. They needed hope too. She needed to reach all of them.

"One at a time, kymbat," Artyom said, as if he'd read her mind. She spotted a Tribu La'am man in a corner eyeing the supply lifts. He seemed detached from the rest of the room, resistant to the hall's tension.

"That's Ordell Smith, isn't it?" Vana nodded at the man. "What's his deal?"

"Smuggler and forger. Stays to himself. No use recruiting," Artyom said.

Vana frowned. A smuggler could've been incredibly valuable to them. One of Ordell's black curls fell into his eye. He twitched his head to toss it back. *Don't think of Jules. Don't think of Jules.* This man was much older than Jules had been. Was this how he would have looked in his midthirties? If not for Rutilia, would he have had a wife and children? His wife and Vana's girlfriend could have sat backstage while listening to their loved ones' fantastic shows.

"Warm them up for me, will you, Arty? I'll be there in a second. I'm gonna talk to him."

Artyom sighed. "Why you always do opposite of what Artyom tell you? Okay, fine, but do not make us wait long."

She patted his arm. "Thanks, Arty." She made her way through the chaotic hall and flopped down on the bench next to him. The smuggler kept his gaze on the supply lifts but crossed his arms and legs. "Hello there. Do you speak Silberfluss?" Vana asked.

"Yup."

"Great. My name's Vana, and I—"

"Not interested." He neither looked at her nor showed any expression other than boredom. But Artyom claimed Vana didn't get discouraged, so she wouldn't. She had a point to prove.

"You sure are interested in those supply lifts." She followed his gaze and saw two bare-chested men push a third. Vana hoped it wouldn't escalate further. They would need all the comrades available when the warden returned.

"Now why would you think such a thing?"

It was obvious why she'd think such a thing, so she changed the subject. "Ordell Smith, isn't that right? That doesn't sound very Tribu La'am to me."

He turned to her but kept the bored facade. "Shoo."

"You know, my best friend was born in Tribu La'am."

"What a nonracist thing to say." He yawned. "Now shoo."

Vana laughed quietly. "You don't like me very much, do you?"

He looked back at the supply lifts. "I don't care enough to like or dislike you."

Vana bit her lip. She was running out of time, but there must've been a way to get through to him. She eyed him. He was wearing prison robes like everyone else, but they looked cleaner than Vana's. His footwear was better maintained, and he was wearing a necklace of fine leather that was certainly not part of the warden's approved items. He must have found a way to smuggle things into Balthos's Heretics. She studied the necklace closer and noticed a small wooden sword dangling from it. It was a toy, of course, but reminded her of the seax.

"Is that a Kilburn sword around your neck?"

His face dropped, and he turned back to her. "What do you mean?"

Vana shrugged. "Well, it looks like a tiny version of Richard's swords. The Kilburn Smithy of Waldfeld?"

"Kilburn *Smithy*?"

"Yup," she said to spite him. *Just a little.*

He picked up the sword, ran his fingers over it, and laughed to himself. "So Dick managed to harden the wood after all . . ."

"Dick?" Vana laughed as well. "I've only heard my mom call him that."

"Yeah, well, he's my boyfriend, so I get to as well." It seemed he was trying to recover his bored tone but couldn't hide the joy.

"Boyfriend? No way. Richard's not one of us." *One of us?* When had she become so comfortable with that part of herself? She pushed the thought aside for now.

He raised an eyebrow. "Fine, he's the last hot guy I flirted with before they arrested me. But it's easier to survive in this limbo hole if you tell yourself nice stories about the outside world. Come on, I'm sure you can imagine having a pretty lady waiting for you."

"That . . . that would be nice." The thought of Waldfeld stung. Twenty years were too long to conceptualize, so most days she didn't try. "But I've got my mom and dad waiting for me, for sure. My brothers too."

He let go of the sword and patted it against his chest. "Good for you. My tribe went a little nuts after they locked up the chieftain's wife. No one's waiting there for me."

"Locked her up?"

He scrunched his nose. "Yeah, poor thing. Esperanza wasn't the breeding machine everyone had hoped for." He stretched his hand out. "I'm Yooko. Don't wear the name out, all right?"

Vana took it and smirked. "Nice to meet you, Yooko. So, eh . . . want me to tell you more about Richard? I got some wild stories."

Yooko cracked his neck as he contemplated her offer. "Do I want you to ruin the pleasant picture my imagination has constructed?"

Vana got restless. The others were waiting for her, and it had taken too long to get Yooko on the hook. She couldn't lose him again. "Richard hasn't been with anyone since his wife died ten years ago. Probably because he fell madly in love with you." She winked at him.

"For a lesbian, you sure know how to sweet-talk a guy. All right, give me your proposal. Why are you bugging me?"

Vana exhaled. "Brilliant, thanks. I'm building a community so we'll be prepared when the warden returns. Like a tribe... not like yours though. I'll help us turn this dump into a livable place and show these noble assholes who think they can keep us miserable and quiet. It will only take a few of us to speak up and ruin the system. A man with your talents could benefit the whole, and the whole will surely benefit you."

He observed her for a few seconds before shaking his head. "Keeping low has worked well for me. It's kept me alive an awfully long time."

Vana sat up taller. Energy rushed through her. "Yeah, but what if the next long time doesn't have to be awful? What if I can get you to start thriving instead of just surviving? All I'm asking is that you give it a chance. Come to the yard with me and listen to what I have to say." He remained silent and glanced at the supply lifts. Vana didn't want to follow his gaze but caught a glimpse of a bloody mess in front of it. So it had escalated. "You know this can't be it, Yooko. There's got to be something better for us, all of us. Richard supported me, actually. He armed the mission that landed me here. He stopped accepting things. That's how his smithy became successful."

Yooko sighed. "I might be able to help you."

She jumped off the bench and rubbed her hands together. "Great, come with me."

Yooko stood up and followed her through the dining hall while mumbling, "I swear to the ancestors, if you shank me out there . . ."

They reached the yard after avoiding several heated fights in the dining hall. "Yard" was another bullshit euphemism for the scraps peasant outcasts received. It was a large round space with several benches. Four ever-burning oil lamps illuminated it, and a bright glimpse of sunlight teased them from above. The walls were high, slick, and reached so far up Vana could barely spot the end. Wet mud smacked under her feet when she entered. The whole space appeared to be an enormous dried-up well.

Artyom stood in the middle of the yard with two dozen inmates gathered around him. Vana's heart jumped. There was already more interest in their cause than she'd hoped for.

". . . and that is why Balthos loves all his sinners." Artyom spotted her. "Vana! Thank Zelission, I have not hold sermon in long time." He pushed through the gathered crowd and made room for Vana to take the center. His eyes widened when he saw Yooko.

"Howdy, everyone!" Vana said as she passed her potential allies. "How are you doing to—"

Erna blocked her way and positioned herself in front of Clarisse. Vana wasn't sure if Erna perceived her as a real threat or if it was mere habit. As hurtful as it was to be its target, Erna's protective spirit would serve the community well.

"We don't have long," Erna growled. "My Allison's wound got infected. I have to watch her fever."

"Got it." Vana nodded. "I'll be swift, but Allison might benefit from my plan as well. May I?" Erna stepped aside, and Vana moved into the free center space. She spotted a small bench that two men sat on and smirked. A bit of theatrics never hurt anyone. "Move, fine fellas, please." They stood up without complaint, and Vana pulled the bench into the center. Her stomach tingled. She'd missed the feeling of being on a stage.

"Necessary?" Artyom asked as she jumped on it.

"Necessary."

She stood tall on her makeshift stage, and her confidence returned. This was where she belonged. This was where her Spirit awaited her. With him in mind, she couldn't fail.

"Thank you all for coming to our little gathering. I promise you won't regret it. If you have one of those sad scratch calendars in your cell, mark it. Today is the beginning of a new era!"

"Good job. Keeping it small and casual, just like we talk

about," Artyom muttered from the side. She ignored him. Only a grand vision could ignite passion in those who had resigned to their fate.

"We have accepted life as a never-ending punishment for crimes defined by those who have never faced the struggles of our class, those who pushed us into the margins. I say no more! We have about two hundred mostly honest souls in here, too precious to be wasted, and among us, we have all the resources we need. At the moment, we are not using them properly. Why? Because we're lacking community, hope, and organization."

"Here, here!" one man said. He was a half orc like Erna but had a harsh Northern dialect instead of a Tribu La'am accent. Scars and brand marks covered his face and body. Vana doubted he was a petty thief and was torn regarding how to feel about him. She couldn't repeat the Isa mistake, but having scary guys on her team would increase her chances of success. She shouldn't judge him prematurely. They were comrades, not criminals.

"My ideology is simple," she continued. "I'm a political prisoner who was framed for a different crime to bury the resistance of my community. But in a greater sense, aren't we all political prisoners? It's the noble politicians who make the law, powdered cowards and cold Council trash. If we were in charge of the law, none of us would break it."

"Murder should still be illegal," Erna said, her eyes fixated on Artyom.

He smiled. "Very correct. I am scum, happy to rot." *The fuck, Arty?* Vana mouthed "not helpful" at him, but he shrugged.

"Let's not focus on the past," said Vana. "It alienates us from our potential allies. Future *murder* would, of course, be discussed in the community. We'll decide whether it was necessary for protection. Besides, Artyom committed crimes in the name of a justice he believed in." She dearly hoped that was true. "He's no more guilty than I am."

Erna scoffed. "What about Kasanovye? He killed some innocent girl."

"Ehm . . ." Vana turned to Artyom for an answer but he stared at the ground. *You're fucking kidding me.*

"I wasn't aware we're holding a discussion on everyone's crimes in this gathering," Yooko chimed in, relaxed and slightly bored sounding. "Excellent use of time for a group of convicted criminals." His dry sneering sucked the tension out of the air.

Vana gave him a grateful nod. "All right, listen. You don't have to trust one another. You have to trust in a common cause and our future. The Council was formed by former enemies because they believed in something. They believed in peaceful trade and stopping General Makeda's Crown War. They're a piece of crap now, but their union worked. The collective succeeded against dominating enemies because they believed in a united future. Give me a chance to offer you a future to believe in."

Clarisse whispered something in Erna's ear, and she nodded. "Fine, fine. My ducklings and I are listening."

Vana's shoulders relaxed. *Thanks, Clarisse.* "Wise choice! Now listen up. We're doomed because we're not standing up for ourselves. If you, dear Erna, Artyom, and I hadn't stood up for Clarisse, who knows where she'd be now! But courage and self-efficiency brought us victory. Our everyday life here works on the same principle. Escaping Balthos's Heretics is considered impossible because it is too large a task for one person. But if we build a functioning society, we can wage war on our oppressors as a force they never expected."

She searched the crowd for glimmers of rebellion and found them. "What month is it, comrades?" A good dozen smiled at being addressed that way. Vana's heartbeat quickened. She got them.

"February!" one woman yelled.

"Great. Remember this: February 980 marks the birth of revolution." Applause followed. "We'll form a community together, share all of our goods and skills among one another, smart-like instead of just giving everyone the same. For example, Allison needs medicine, isn't that right, Erna?"

Erna squinted. "Are you blackmailing us, Ackerman?"

"No, I—" She swallowed her anger. It didn't matter if Erna viewed her as a power-hungry scumbag. She had her attention. Vana could work with that. "Artyom and I still have medicine left from King Shithead's visit. You'd gain access to it."

Erna stepped forward, her arms crossed, glaring up from Vana's knees. "What do you want in exchange?" This paranoia was ridiculous. She was a community leader herself. Why didn't she understand? A piece of patent Artyom-wisdom came to mind. *Don't judge untold stories, hothead.* Erna wasn't part of the problem. Whatever had made her this paranoid was.

"Erns, I get your skepticism, really, but this is exactly my point. If we make a pact today, there'd be no need for an exchange. We'd enter all our belongings into one collective. I mean, what do we have to lose? The few old rags that we call our own? We have a much richer resource pool to gain and will each be working to increase it. I've heard two of your girls make excellent fabrics out of pretty much nothing. Eventually, I could use a fresh pair of undergarments. Haven't changed mine in months."

Yooko grimaced. "I see honesty is another resource of the collective."

The corner of Erna's mouth twitched. Was there an inkling of humor in her? Vana must've been on the right track.

"If this was an exchange, you wouldn't receive Allison's medicine until you delivered my undergarments, but we're operating on community and vision. I know that her fever is more important than my dirty ass. It would work like that with everything. Take food, for example. You and my dear half orc comrade over there must constantly be hungry, while my half elf-ness can't stomach that much mold slime. You're welcome to take some mold slime off my hands. No resources wasted. The collective strengthened. It's a win-win!"

That was the last part of her prepared speech. It had gone great, but others needed to react or she'd look like an idiot. *Three . . . two . . . one . . .*

"I want an honor codex." Erna unknowingly saved her.

"Sure! Write one up, and we'll all approve it together. The rest of you, if you're on board, make a list of all the resources you have and the skills you could bring into our community. We'll start out as a close-knit team, and soon enough others will want to join. Who's in? Show me your hands!"

"Wait," Yooko said.

"Yeah?"

"What's the use of rebellion when Tidiers can march in here and kill us all with a swing of their staff?"

Vana cracked her knuckles. She didn't want to reveal too much. She and Artyom hadn't managed to break into the infirmary yet, but with her new comrades it was only a matter of time. "Because we have some . . . unusual allies they fear. I'll share more later."

Yooko clicked his tongue. "Isn't information a resource to be shared with the community?"

Vana took a deep breath. She needed to handle her frustration with care around comrades. "Once it's fully formed, yeah. I'm sure we're all carrying a rich arsenal of knowledge that we haven't shared yet. Isn't that right, *Ordell?*"

Yooko chuckled. "Aye, aye, chief."

"Well then, let's vote. Who wants to join me in a brighter future?"

The moment of truth had arrived. Clarisse raised her hand right away. Ten others followed quickly. A few peeked around at other people's decisions before raising their own hands. The rest slowly followed. *Excellent.* Everyone except for six ladies had raised their hands. Now it was up to Erna. If she joined, her remaining ducklings would as well. Clarisse bumped her protector's shoulder.

"Fine, we will give it a try. I want Allison's medicine straight away, and if any of you abuse this collective thing to lay a hand on my ducklings, I'm out of here and all of you have made yourself an enemy. You hear me?"

Artyom cleared his throat. "If your girls get hurt, offender suffer from our hand first. Will not keep single drop of blood in body." The sincerity of his voice calmed Vana. Whatever had happened to Kasanovye couldn't have been Arty's intention.

"Thanks for the comeback, Arty. Bit morbid, but you know. Yes, Erna, we don't allow violence against our own. See it as additional protection for your flock. Am I right, comrades?"

The others murmured in agreement. Erna nodded.

"Great!" Vana jumped down from the bench and stretched out her hands. "Let's take one another's hands and raise them together." They held hands as told, and joy flooded her. She'd done it. She'd really done it. She had woken up the unheard voices of the oppressed. Those noble assholes would have their comeuppance soon enough. "For freedom, a brighter future, and the community!"

"For freedom, a brighter future, and the community!" they repeated, raising their clasped hands into the air. Together.

CHAPTER 34

SUBIRA

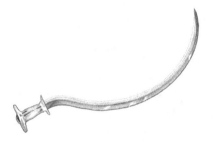

February 980 - Virisunder's Western Front Camp, Silberfluss

General Subira Se'azana of active duty squeezed her pillow closer and counted down another minute. Her eyes were fixed on the hand-size closed copper flower next to her cot. After sixty tiresome seconds, the petals opened with a chime and a tiny black figure on a horse emerged from it. The figure circled to a Fi'Teri lullaby that never failed to make her smile. *Thank you, Alexandra.* Her friend had crafted it for her when they were children so she'd never be late, but it wasn't the source of Subira's gratitude. Alexandra had given her a way out, a way back to someone she recognized in the mirror.

She jumped out of bed and grabbed the left of the two neatly folded clothes piles across from her. *Four in the morning.* Time for half an hour of independent training. After that she'd have thirty minutes to prepare for another glorious day at the front.

Joy accompanied the first plank. She had missed being alive. Today radiated even more life than the previous day. She had fortified Virisunder's weakened western front and had called the truce off a week ago. This war would rise from oblivion quicker than Agathe Heidegger could blink.

She moved on to push-ups and waited for drips of energy to pearl off as sweat. It didn't. Her excitement grew with each crunch, and new, wilder ways to release it came to her mind. Sachihiro had been catching up on the training regime rather nicely. Perhaps a private sparring match would be appropriate. The heat of her training left her abdomen and wandered lower. *Not appropriate. Absolutely not appropriate.*

She picked up the pace. Her gaze fell on the small sorted stack of letters her assistant had left with her. Sachihiro had warned her that another plea from Gustave was among them. He had intercepted previous ones, like he did with all of Gustave's correspondence, but Subira had asked him to allow one through. She had promised not to contact him—to avoid any temptation of reconciliation, no matter what doubt surged up. But she was curious what Gustave would say for himself. Would he apologize? Beg her to return? Or would he spill his anger onto the page? Part of her wanted to know, but she knew it was a dangerous game. She hadn't yet expunged every glimmer of hope for the life they could have shared. For years she had drilled herself to see the good in him, and she never forgot a drill. She suspected that Sachihiro knew that and preferred to handle Gustave-related tasks on his own. She couldn't risk an official separation, not while she relied on her reputation at the front. No priest would bless the end of her marriage, and no army would follow a sinner.

She sat up with her last crunch and felt her neck. Still no sweat. She'd have to increase the rigor of her exercises tomorrow.

Gustave's letter lay on top of the stack, unmoving and

pervading. It taunted her. She rolled her shoulders and stared at it. A spike of energy shot through her. *How dare you still taunt me?* She got up and grabbed it from the stack. It was light and couldn't have contained more than two pages. How much parchment would he need to justify what had happened to them? Maybe it contained an explanation that could make it all okay without negative implications. Maybe the years of pain had been a misunderstanding. Maybe a misunderstanding would be easier to process.

A wind gust hit the tent, and the candlelight flickered. Assula lamps were more reliable, but Alexandra had requested less magical usage at the front. Apparently, Reginald felt uncomfortable with their reliance on assulas. As if Reginald's feelings mattered when it came to military supplies, but Subira didn't want to upset her friends, not after they had urged her to return to herself.

She examined the closed letter and ran her thumb over the wax seal. As she knew Gustave, the ink had fused with alcohol. Her eyes darted to the candle. Alcohol burned well. A few nights ago, Sachihiro had told her about Tribu La'am's sacred fire festivals. Lava consumed the old to make room for the new. Perhaps the flame knew a better answer than the contradicting parts of herself.

She held the closed envelope over the candle until the fire consumed Gustave's last chance for redemption. After all the hardships, the act was strangely simple. Relief flooded her. When her assistant finished his prolonged orcish sleep, she could tell him to burn any new letters from Gustave. Sachihiro already inspected everything Gustave sent to ensure he wouldn't reveal their situation to Xenia or courtiers. He'd hardly mind the additional task.

Smoke tickled her nose and reminded her of Altor Caedem's bonfire nights after exams had finished. She'd loved to watch the flames dance and had emulated it in her secret practice. Gustave had once longed to be part of her performances. How lovely it would be to engulf him and watch as her movements turned him into ash. Gustave himself was filled with liquor. He'd make a beautiful flame.

She brushed the ash off her hands and examined the next letter on her pile. It was a spy report on Harald Heidegger's movements. The Council had visited many Silberfluss towns during the truce. Afterward, each one had improved their defenses, becoming trickier targets for the Virisunder military. This was highly inappropriate for the neutral organization, but both Agathe's and Alexandra's personal relationships to the Council leaders posed conflicts of interest that Subira had to calculate in.

She opened the report and skimmed over Heidegger's current whereabouts. *Waldfeld, Silberfluss.* The town's name sounded familiar, but she couldn't place it. She searched the map Sachihiro had pinned to her board and found the tiny dot that signified the town. A dense forest surrounded it, and there were no large cities. It would've been an easy target to occupy but wasn't on their planned route. She dropped the report back on her desk. Heidegger wasn't worth the deviation to some backward town.

She checked the pocket watch on her bedside. *Half past four.* Time for the next step of her morning. New energy rushed through her. At home, she'd barely had control over her mornings. Gustave had often returned from the pub at sunrise. Sometimes he wanted breakfast, sometimes sex, sometimes to be left alone. She'd had to figure out which one it was the moment she opened her eyes.

Not anymore. She collected the second pile of clothes, her day uniform, and headed to the bathing tent. Few soldiers tended to hygiene duties before the morning drills at five o'clock. Those quiet moments to herself fueled Subira for the rest of the day. She stepped into a curtained wash area and stripped off her training clothes. The fabric fell to her feet and revealed her naked skin. Instead of filling the washbasin, she sank down onto the stool and examined her body. No bruises. She ran her fingers over her arms, her stomach, her breasts.

Over time, Gustave's drunken remarks about her Fi'Teri skin had perforated her. It looked different in the sparse torchlight that shone through the canvas curtains. Beautiful, even. It belonged to her now. Every bit of her body did.

She listened for early risers, but the bathing tent was silent. Her hand stroked underneath her navel. There was one enemy territory she hadn't dared to reclaim. It had been conquered so long ago and had turned into a land of shame and confusion. She wasn't sure if she still recognized the territory. Her hand wandered lower, and her breathing sped up. Fear arose when she pressed down. It felt forbidden, selfish, irresponsible. She hadn't asked permission from anyone. She should've been mourning the end of her marriage. She bit her lip. *So what?* A great general made decisions, no matter how frowned upon they might be. She decided to circle her fingers, to explore, to expunge Gustave. She decided to free herself.

When she left the curtained area fifteen minutes later, she felt more relaxed than she had in years. She ensured that every braid found its place in her tight, neat bun and smiled at her reflection. Then she checked her pocket watch. *Five.* No more time for vanities.

To her surprise, three dozen soldiers were already at the training field when she arrived. This was highly unusual. She detected several heated arguments, which was even stranger. Soldiers were too tired to bicker before breakfast. The source of conflict presented itself with sparkling pink hair.

"Say that again and I swear I will shove this pommel down your throat and pull it back out of your ass!"

Subira rushed over as quickly as she could without losing authority. "Ch'ulel!"

Zazil swung around and forced her angry grimace into a smile. "General! You're . . . you're here now."

Subira sighed. She liked Zazil in social situations, but the woman was a nightmare to keep under control in professional settings. It was an easier task with Gon around. Unfortunately,

507

her spouse was still asleep, as Subira permitted them and Sachihiro two additional hours of rest, accommodating their orcish bodies. Then again, Zazil often pulled Gon into mischief with her. Not only did she keep breaking rules, but they also had a perplexing marriage that involved other soldiers—both men and women—in frequent sexual entanglements. They would've been entirely unfit for the front if they weren't both so talented.

"Explain yourself, Ch'ulel, and please do so swiftly. We have a new set of drills to get through."

Zazil grabbed the arm of a soldier. "This fu—man here, that's what's going on."

Subira hadn't memorized all the names yet, but she was sure she hadn't seen the man before. He brushed Zazil off and collected himself. Subira noticed at least ten of her soldiers lock their eyes on him. A few stepped closer. *Not a good sign.*

"You're new. What's your name and title?" Subira asked.

His lips curled into a smug smile. "Not as new as you."

An insubordinate, as she had suspected. His sympathizers watched both of them closely. She pulled her shoulders back and stood taller. "You address me as *General* and answer my questions, understood? For now, add twenty push-ups and five mountain climbers to your drill this week. I expect you not to repeat this mishap."

He looked over his shoulder and nodded at six other soldiers. They had closed in on the scene. Zazil's hand reached for her boot, likely to a prohibited weapon. The insubordinate took an inadequately long time to respond. *What a nuisance.* Subira didn't fear mutiny, but dealing with it bored her.

The insubordinate met her eyes, and his smile faded. "Mountain climbers? I signed up under Queen Alexandra, not some Fittery general. Don't you have jungles at home to climb?"

His words unleashed an array of noise: arguments, shouting, laughter. Subira's heart sank, but her head stayed level.

Nothing she hadn't dealt with dozens of times. It couldn't shake her. It mustn't.

Her first action was to reach for Zazil, and it had been the right one. She had pulled an expanding assula ax out of her boot, ready to cut the insubordinate. Loyal, but unwise. Subira kept Zazil's arm down and shook her head.

As a second action, she pulled out her assula-enforced whistle and pressed it until its shrill tone resounded over the training field. "Silence." There was no need to raise her voice. The whistle took care of it. She turned to the gathering while keeping the insubordinate in her periphery. A good number of them appeared to be on her side, but she also found uncertainty and discomfort in some faces. *Not acceptable.* Every soldier needed to trust her.

Her eyes fell on a recent recruit by the name of Goodwin, who bit his nail while glancing between her and the insubordinate. "Goodwin, bring us two combat grade rapiers from the armory." He was shocked to be addressed and rushed off. Subira turned back to the insubordinate. "If you wish to be dismissed, you are free to say so at any point, but if you call my leadership or my heritage into question, prepare to be challenged."

He scoffed. "Sure, fine, challenge me if you must, but I'm not the only one who thinks this way. You can't just waltz into our land and tell us what to do."

Subira took a deep breath and searched her troop for doubt, fear, resentment, and anger. She couldn't blame them for any of it. Alexandra's war had been chaotic and tiresome. She'd have to show them that they could rely on her.

"I know the changes over the past months have been difficult, and I hear your concerns, but we are now all foreigners on Silberfluss land, and you must ask yourself—are we conquering this land to live on, intermingle, and cultivate, or are we conquering it to nurture hate? If your answer is the latter, I suggest you return to Polemos, which provides a plentiful supply of people to hate. The one who seeks will always find it."

No one dared to comment. *Good, they're contemplating it.* "Clear a circle, please." They followed her command immediately. Another good sign.

"Soldier," she said, addressing her opponent. "What's your name? I would like to know who I have the honor of humbling."

He stretched his arms and grinned. If he thought this would give him an advantage in the fight, he was wrong. Subira warmed up the muscles required for combat every morning.

"Kalvin Mosley, ma'am."

Subira nodded but said nothing more. She didn't like the uncomfortable moments before a duel. If the parties had failed to find an amicable solution, they should get on with the forceful settlement already.

After a long minute, Goodwin returned with the rapiers. Subira handed them to Mosley for inspection, but he barely looked at them. He was cocky, unwise. If he established her as an enemy, he needed to check duel weapons before entering the fight. This inconsistency could cost him greatly with less honorable opponents.

She took one of the finely forged rapiers, entered the circle, and bowed to him. He did not return the gesture, which was unacceptable.

"Bow, asshole!" Zazil yelled.

"I'm not bowing to her."

Subira sighed loudly enough for her soldiers to hear. "Your immaturity is making this needlessly difficult. I gave you an honorable option, but I suppose if you're determined to insult the general at all costs, you leave me no choice." She pulled out a small pistol that she kept on her hip. Zazil wasn't the only one who'd come prepared. She cocked it and aimed at his head. "Last words, Mosley?"

"I, eh—" He tightened his grip around the rapier and bowed to her.

"There we go. Was that so difficult?" She pulled off the

whistle and handed it to Goodwin. "Please signal our start and blow the whistle if someone taps out. Don't grip it too tightly. Doctor Ch'ulel is busy enough without a dozen ruptured eardrums. Thank you." Goodwin remained nervous but followed her instructions. The young soldier had potential.

Mosley charged at her as soon as the whistle resounded. *Unwise.* She stepped aside and parried with an elegant upward arm twist, pointing the rapier's body down. Once he stumbled out of position, she kicked his lower back with her shin. He landed on the ground, yowling.

"Thank you for this demonstration, Mosley." She addressed her troop while he struggled back onto his feet. "This is why one shouldn't overcommit to an attack before assessing the opponent's strengths. It's a dance, and you need to understand the rhythm of your partner or you won't align with them enough to deliver a hit." She turned back to Mosley, who knocked dirt off his training uniform and glared at her. "You should also gather yourself quicker. You're giving the opponent too much room to explore their advantage."

Mosley tested the water with a thrust. His mind and body weren't in harmony, so it was easy to shake him. She smacked the rapier out of his hand with her blade. He cursed.

"Ah, as expected, your hesitant mind is sabotaging you. This is why we do strength training. It shouldn't be possible for an opponent to disarm you because of a soft grip. The sword is an extension of your arm. You need to be equally attached to it, or you will lose both."

He rushed to pick the rapier back up and seemed unsure of his next move. She decided to relieve him of the burden and launched for a redouble, starting with a light thrust, which he avoided. *Good.* She would have been disappointed if he couldn't even dodge the feint. He did not expect the second quick thrust. One precise cut adorned his cheek with educative blood drops. It wasn't Subira's favorite method of teaching, but she had studied under General Makeda long enough to know how effective it could be.

Mosley panicked and went for a rapier uppercut. She smacked it down without effort. "Parry eight. Versatile. Remember that." She didn't pause for the instruction but redoubled once more and cut his other cheek. Most of the crowd cheered. Her soldiers respected strength and honor over polemic disturbances.

The cheering aggravated Mosley, and he launched for a hard double cut. She parried the first one but appreciated the effort he'd put into its execution. The second one was poorly aimed. She grabbed the pommel of his rapier and crushed his hand. He screamed in pain. Perhaps it was time to finish this. She twisted the pommel and pulled it down until his own blade poked his throat. It wouldn't have touched him, but he screamed and stumbled into the tip. Subira smiled. A light scratch on the throat should teach him manners.

"Please . . . General . . . please."

A few soldiers laughed. Subira examined him. "Look at that; there's hope for you after all."

"You . . . you're not gonna kill me?"

She scoffed. Could she indulge in one more scare? It would fortify the lesson. She twisted her wrist and sliced down his chest. It didn't touch his skin but cut his training uniform and pulled another scream out of him. *Coward.* The troop laughed as he sank to his knees.

Subira collected the rapiers and handed them back to Goodwin. She was about to help Mosley up when something caught her eye. White ink adorned his chest. She grabbed his shock of hair and squatted in front of the whimpering mess of a man to inspect it. *Oh no, they didn't.* The tattoo was a circle of six hands clasped together. *The Council.* All members wore it to signify their lifetime commitment to Elfentum and neutrality between nations.

Rage boiled in Subira's veins. They had infiltrated her army with pathetic, incompetent spies. For how long had Heidegger sent his lackeys to sow distrust and disobedience in

Virisunder's military? Subira pitied him for thinking he could stop her with some secondhand provocations.

She clenched Mosley's shock of hair, rose, and yanked his face up so all her soldiers could get a good look at the real enemy. "Division—the tactic of cowards. They know we're too strong as a unit, and they fear us. This man is a Council intruder and a sign of reverence for our abilities. We scare Agathe enough to abuse the system that stabilizes Elfentum. I'm proud of every single one of you."

Mosley, if that was his real name, struggled under her grip, but she didn't give him room to protest. If she had wished to do so, she could have annihilated him in the first five seconds of their duel.

"Ch'ulel, pass me the weapon that I did not see you illegally store in your boot." She smirked just enough to indicate a celebratory mood for her soldiers. She wanted them to be happy about this turn of events, no matter how much anger boiled in her.

Zazil rushed over and pulled a stick from her boot. She twisted its lower end, and blades of shimmering green light expanded from the top. The assula ax was one of Zazil's most recent inventions. Subira was thrilled to soon equip her soldiers with it as hidden defense weapons in case of capture. She took it from Zazil and examined it. Two green ovals were painted on the grip.

"What's this symbol?" she asked quietly.

Zazil turned a disturbing shade of pink. "It's my, ehm, personal weapon . . . not exactly a symbol. It's Gon's ass, which—"

"Understood." Subira decided to ask Zazil fewer questions in the future. She focused back on the disgusting spy and exposed his neck with one strong yank.

"Please, please don't. It wasn't my plan. Please—"

His begging was disgraceful considering the big mouth he'd had ten minutes ago. "Ch'ulel, your handkerchief please." Zazil handed it over with a pout, but Subira ignored her reluctance. She shoved the cloth into Mosley's mouth and addressed her troop.

"I honor critique and concerns from all my soldiers, but I do not indulge in the pleas of intruders wishing to sow poison within our ranks. We cannot give them a voice. We cannot give attention to the forces that try to tear us apart. For the rest of your active duty, this troop is your family, and if you are unsure about me, know this—I do not tolerate attacks on my family."

With that, she removed Mosley's head. Her soldiers watched the lifeless body fall to her feet, then applauded. She smiled. It wasn't the lesson she had prepared for today, but it was the one her troop needed.

She tossed the head into the bloody mess in front of her. "Goodwin, call the sanitary division and let them know that there's an unexpected pile of dirt on the training grounds. Everyone else, take twenty minutes to recuperate, then return for morning drills."

They scattered, but Zazil stayed close. "By limbo, General, that was badass. I'm starting to see why Sachi is so obsessed with you."

"Ehm . . . thank you, I suppose." Subira avoided her eyes and examined the blood splatters on her training uniform instead. She'd have to visit the bathing tent again. "I wouldn't call it *obsession* though."

Zazil waved her off. "Right, we just say that to tease him. Admiration—there, that's a proper word."

Admiration. It was an odd thing to be openly appreciated. She wasn't sure how to feel about it and changed the subject. "I will need an assula brush to clean this blood off."

"Sure, I'll get you one. I have—"

A half-dressed Gon stumbled toward them, cutting her off. "Snazzle! Snazzle, a message came through the box. Oh . . . morning, General."

Subira had never seen the orc so disheveled. Their long hair was a tangled mess, and their tusks were darker than usual. *Do they polish them in the morning?* They were wearing training pants and their sleep shirt. This must've been an emergency, and from her experience, bad news brought by the camp doctor required heightened attention. "What is the matter, Doctor Ch——"

"From Pier?" Zazil interrupted. Gon shook their head. Zazil ripped the parchment from their hand and cursed imaginatively, both in Silberfluss and Tribu La'am tongue. When she looked back up, shock had consumed her face. "It's from Esperanza. How is that possible?"

"I don't know, but I haven't told Sachi yet. Pier went to Freilist and never returned."

"Fuck!" Zazil twitched and kicked the dirt.

"What is going on, soldier?" Subira looked back and forth between the two. She was both relieved and concerned that it seemed to be a personal matter.

"I'm sorry, General," Zazil said. "We have to go. Gon, Sachi, and I have to go."

Subira blinked at them, waiting for a clarification that did not come. As much as she cared for the Ch'ulels, this was unacceptable, bordering on desertion. She couldn't allow her vital assistant, best medic, and assula smith to simply leave.

"You and Sachi go to Esperanza, babe. She doesn't sound good. I'll look for Pier in Freilist."

"For the love of Balthos, what's the matter?" Subira asked.

"I'm telling her, snazzle," Gon mumbled. "General, my brother's ex-girlfriend has gone into early labor. It's not looking good."

A family matter explained the pain on both their faces, but it left too many questions unanswered. "Is it Sachihiro's?"

Zazil shook her head. "No, but——"

"Then I regret to hear that the baby and mother might be in peril, but so are my troops. The truce has been lifted. You will not be leaving, Doctor Ch'ulel."

Gon deflated, and Zazil's face turned red, similar to her previous embarrassment, although Subira suspected its cause to be volatile. "I'm going to Freilist, General. With or without your permission."

Subira ensured no one was watching, grabbed Zazil's arm, and pulled her into a nearby supply tent. Gon stumbled after them. Despite their fragile stature, they were likely to attack should anything worse happen to Zazil. Subira hoped it wouldn't come to it.

"Zazil, I'm going to be frank with you. I just decapitated a spy and will not hesitate to proceed similarly with my brilliant assula smith threatening to run to the *enemy's* capital. You wouldn't make it to Freilist before the birth anyway, so let's be reasonable, shall we?"

"Don't threaten her," Gon said.

"I'm not threatening her. I'm explaining the situation."

"We saved your stupid life," Zazil spat.

Subira hesitated. A phantom pain grazed her side where Gustave's blow had landed. She inhaled sharply. "And I will forever be in your debt, but I will not let you blackmail me with that deed in detriment to my troops."

"General, if I may." Gon stepped between them, calmer than Zazil looked or Subira felt. "This has gotten unnecessarily heated. Listen, General, Esperanza, our patient, is in Waldfeld, not Freilist—a day's ride from here, at most. We could be there by dusk. You are happy with my brother's work, right? Sachihiro still loves Esperanza. He won't forgive you if you keep him here."

Subira stiffened and reminded herself that both loyalty and Sachihiro's pleasant admiration were conditional. All affection, except for her bond to Xenia, was conditional. It would be foolish to believe different rules applied to Sachihiro. "You're still blackmailing me, Doctor. You are doing so with an added layer of deceitful amiability."

Sachihiro had a love waiting for him somewhere. She thought of Xenia's birth. It had been long and painful, but

Gustave had shown unusual tenderness during the process. He had held her hand throughout every contraction, eager to meet their daughter. No one deserved to be robbed of this moment. "Waldfeld, you say?"

"Yes, General."

It looked like she was paying Harald Heidegger a visit after all. "Fine, you may go, Doctor Ch'ulel. I was planning a covert mission to Waldfeld anyway. But I need someone for the mission who knows how to control the assula systems. Sachihiro or you, Zazil."

The smith looked pale and turned the note in her hand. Gon put their arm on her. "Pier might be tangled up in a work thing, Snazzle. It doesn't have to be bad."

"Your concern is honorable, Zazil, but you've committed to this position and this military. You're part of this family now. Please don't let it down."

Zazil sniffed. "That's . . . that's all great, but I need to find him."

Subira straightened. The risk of allowing a former Revelli with Virisunder military intel to return to Freilist was irresponsibly high. But she was right. The Ch'ulels had saved her life. Zazil hadn't told her family or anyone about Subira's marital situation. She owed her freedom to them as much as she owed it to Alexandra. "I'll tell you what, soldier. Perform well in this mission, then—and only then—you may take two weeks off to visit Freilist and find whoever Pier is."

"My brother."

"Yes, find your brother. Help me teach the Council a lesson, and you may look for your brother."

Zazil remained silent for two seconds, then nodded. "Thank you, General."

"Excellent." She ignored the sinking feeling in her stomach and turned back to Gon. "Now go get Sachihiro."

CHAPTER 35

SACHIHIRO

February 980 - Waldfeld, Silberfluss

"Brr, hush, go!" The mare did not move.

Sachihiro claimed to have studied every subject, at least to a beginner's level. The art of horseback riding must have slipped his mind. Or maybe it hadn't slipped his mind. Maybe he had never actually learned anything. He had studied people, decryption, communication, and language. How could he not have known where his Fae princess was, and worse, what condition she was in, if he was so knowledgeable? What good was his knowledge if it couldn't protect the few people who mattered? Eight months had passed since he had lost her—eight months that had passed in the blink of an eye for his human love and had consumed too large a chunk of his orcish life.

"Good lass, come on." He gave her another nudge, but the horse remained immovable. Subira had warned him to take a bull or carriage to accommodate his and Gon's body weight, but it would have taken too long. Esperanza needed him eight months ago. He couldn't waste another second.

"It's all right, Sachi. We've crossed the town limits. It can't be far now," Gon said over their shoulder. Sachihiro sat behind them, holding on to them while also controlling the horse. Or at least attempting to.

He sighed and dismounted. Esperanza would have known how to speak to the horse. She could communicate with all elements of nature's creation on a sacred level and evoke their magic within. He had envisioned her crossing over to the Fae realm for a grandiose expedition. In his imagination, the hole she had created between the realms was too small for him, so she took the journey alone. In a few years, she would have returned with all the answers she'd been looking for, and they could have resumed their peaceful life in Mink'Ayllu together. He would have been a war hero under the great General Subira Se'azana. Esperanza would have become the savior of the Fae realm. Everything would have gone back to how it used to be, only with more Fae dust in the air. But that was not how her story went, was it?

Sachihiro unstrapped Gon's crutches and helped his sibling off the horse. He examined his surroundings and recognized that Gon was right. The horse had carried them to the edge of Waldfeld. Twilight painted some beauty onto the otherwise inconspicuous town. He had pictured Pier's home posher, tidier, with a sense of self-importance, but instead found a shabby town that had sprawled out too far for its own good. His stomach added another knot to its collection. This wasn't where Esperanza should live. Waldfeld must have stolen her against her will. It would pay for it once the great General Subira Se'azana arrived.

Subira, as he was allowed to call her now, had sent them ahead while she readied the covert troop. She planned to attack the local noble manor directly, execute the duke, and claim the land in front of Heidegger. It sounded like a fantastic story for historians, but Sachihiro's excitement was lost in worry. He hoped her attack wouldn't affect the birth. He hoped Subira would be fine without him. Esperanza hadn't been.

"It'll be okay, Sachi. We'll help her."

Sachihiro managed to nod, took the reins, and walked down the main road with Gon. He had just spotted the town square in the distance when the yell of a woman startled him.

"Ey, tusks! What do ya think you're doin' here?" A redhead in a black leather coat marched toward them from a dirty-looking pub. She carried a glowing stiletto knife on her hip.

Sachihiro cleared his throat. " 'Hello' is a more appropriate greeting in most cultures, including Silberfluss, but we . . . ehm, we're looking for the Kilburns."

She pulled the stiletto knife from her hip and cleaned the gaps between her teeth with the blade tip while eyeballing them. She had no idea how to command that weapon. Subira had taught him that trained fighters trusted their weapons. They became part of their body. They didn't need to touch or flash them for reassurance.

"What's with the uniform? We ain't letting foreigner guards in here, even if they're cripples."

Gon bumped Sachihiro's shoulder. "Let's keep walking."

Sachihiro frowned at the woman. "You're very rude, but we'll ignore you and keep walking. No one has the authority to prevent someone from walking down the street without proper reason, and you don't seem to have any authority at all."

"Not what I meant, Sachi . . ."

The woman's eyes grew large. She flipped the knife and pointed it up at him. "The fuck you think you are? You're facing the leader of the Vindicators of Anarchy. My word's law around here, right after our good church."

Sachihiro looked at the knife. He could probably do the knife twist trick Subira had shown him. Or he could headbutt her, but the woman was small, so he might hurt his back. He had to clarify something else first. "That name makes no semantic sense. By implying anarchy needs vindication, you're stating it needs servants of sorts, which goes against the principles of—"

Gon pulled Sachihiro to the side right as the woman struck out with an unpleasant growl.

"Get your green ass out of here before I skin ya tuskers!"

Sachihiro tried to think of a diffusion tactic, a way of communicating that would de-escalate the situation. *Sweet vine is in labor. Sweet vine is in labor.* He couldn't think straight.

"Isa, dear! Lovely to see you." Someone else saved him and Gon. A middle-aged woman with raven hair and a simple peasant dress approached them. A sweet smile lightened her face. "Ah, you must be Mr. Kachool with the crop samples."

The woman, Isa, spat on the ground in front of Sachihiro. "They're tuskers and intruders. I'm handling it."

"My Adam told me the Vindicators are having a grand gathering today, isn't that right? He was so excited about it. I'd hate if it gets delayed because of my dear guests."

Isa crossed her arms and glanced back at the pub. She didn't seem to believe the other woman but cared about the gathering. "The tusker said he's here for the Kilburns . . ."

"Eventually," Sachihiro said, "but I'm happy to discuss the crops first." The woman gave him an approving nod. She looked like his tribal school teacher, handing him a sugar cane for giving the right answer.

"I'd love to. See, Isa dear, Richard is trying to scrounge my precious Tribu La'am secrets before I got the chance to purchase them, but we can't let this happen, can we? We need higher yielding crops, at least until Vana comes home."

Isa scoffed. "I wouldn't keep my hopes up, Mrs. Ackerman. Balthos's Heretics swallows people." She shuffled, then shrugged. "Fine, but if something goes wrong in Waldfeld today, I know who to blame." She stomped away.

Mrs. Ackerman shook her head. "Don't mind her, sweethearts, she's got too much time and not enough smarts on her hands. Gets up to flimflam now that my daughter isn't here to keep her in check. She's putting dangerous ideas into people's heads, my son included." She sighed. "What are your actual names?"

Sachihiro relaxed his shoulders for the first time since Gon had woken him up. Mrs. Ackerman spoke like maternal home. Not his home, or his mother, but her choice of words embodied the idea of home. "Sachihiro Ch'ulel, ma'am."

"Gon Ch'ulel," his sibling added.

"Lovely names. I'm Dorothy Ackerman, but please call me Dotty."

He shook her hand. "Pleasure to meet you, Dotty." Her hands had the characteristic roughness of earth workers he knew so well. Sweet vine's hands had always felt like that.

"You're shaking, sweetie."

He was sure the world was shaking, not him, but he allowed the inaccuracy. "Could you kindly show us where the Kilburns live? Or . . . perhaps you know a Miss Esperanza?"

Her face fell. "Oh, honey . . ." Sachihiro tensed back up. He detected resignation in her voice. She took his hand as if it was a natural thing to do and started leading him. "You know, your Silberfluss is quite perfect. Even more impressive than hers."

He wanted to understand her negative reaction but didn't want to scare her off with an investigation. "I'm the one who taught her, so that's more of a criticism," he said instead. They passed a loud market square. The vendors were wrapping up for the day, debating what to throw away and what to carry with them another day. "Thank you, though. You know her?"

She led them down a cleaner street filled with fancier merchant shops. Dotty had to check the house numbers to find her way. She likely couldn't afford any of the goods sold here. According to her peasant clothes, her role was to feed the merchants.

"Yes, she's a dear. A bit strange, but a dear. She came

to me for herbs and ointments. Oh, and parsnips. The little one loves parsnips. Be sure to feed them some when they're old enough." They stopped at the *Kilburn Smithy* sign. "One moment, honey." She squeezed his hand and glanced at Gon. "Just so you know . . . there have been some nasty, false rumors around Richard Kilburn and the baby. People are bored and love horror tales. You know how it is. Sadly, it hasn't been too good on poor Esperanza. Our local medic and midwife refused to assist her. Father Godfried, our priest, had a bit of a spat with Richard, so he denounced the child as a demonic offspring. Complete bogus if you ask me, but I thought you should know."

Sachihiro had a million questions. Most pressingly, when would his life stop feeling like taking an advanced master course after skipping the introduction and beginner's levels? He wondered if Dotty had an answer to that, but Esperanza couldn't wait.

"Thank you for letting me know and for taking me here."

"Sure, darling. See you around." She disappeared back into the market streets.

Sachihiro raised his hand to knock but hesitated. He wanted to prepare himself for what was to come. His mind turned blank. Was that preparation or sheer panic?

"Hey, Sachi?" Sachihiro looked at Gon's soft, familiar face. "Whatever happens in there, we still got each other."

Sachihiro pulled his sibling into a hug, let go, and knocked before he could think twice. An ashen Richard opened and said things. Sachihiro pushed past him. Everything that happened next became a blur. The moment Sachihiro stepped into the Kilburn house, he felt numb, driven only by the urge to see his sweet vine, to understand what had happened to her.

Richard seemed unhappy, but Gon handled it. Small details made Sachihiro's head spin. The creaky staircase. The flower carvings in the floorboards. The door that opened in slow motion. Then—red. Just red. The red his eyes had never seen the likes of. The red that was incomprehensible but burned itself into the walls of his skull. The entire world dipped in red, and when the spectrum of colors returned, a red layer remained over it all. It might always remain. Red, like Esperanza's blood that covered the room.

What could a linguist do in a moment that evaded words? Did the world around them cease to exist until it could be defined again? It did for Sachihiro as he stood there in Esperanza's room, staring at something he couldn't comprehend. Was time still moving? He couldn't possibly tell.

"Ivalace." A weak but wonderful voice called him by his old pet name. He stumbled forward, closer to it. His knees gave in, or perhaps gravity tugged at him. He was now face-to-face with a spectrum of brown colors. No red here. Just earthy browns. *Are you ready?* He vaguely nodded to himself.

He recognized everything at once. His beautiful Fae princess lay on the bed across from him. The blood she bathed in used to form a peaceful river inside of her. Another river sprung from her eyes. Tears. He pulled her into his arms tightly, never to let her go again. She was warm and real and the best thing he had ever felt.

"Ivalace, you came. I did it, we did it, I did it! I'm gonna find my brother and free all the Fae. All of them. Free."

"Shh, I got you."

"We made the impossletertainty!" She sobbed and laughed at the same time. He pressed his forehead against hers. "Ivalace, I can come with you now. To the tribe. We have an heir, and it will open the realm before kénos eats it, and everything will be okay."

He wiped her tears off with one stroke of his thumb. "I kept the cottage in Mink'Ayllu, sweet vine. We'll go there, okay? A lot of plants there need watering."

She laughed, which turned her face from human to pure sunlight. It was okay. Everything was okay again. "The three of us?"

"The three of us," he confirmed, although he could

hardly think of the baby. He had only found out about it this morning. It lived in the future. From now on, he wanted to live in the present, any present with her. He stroked her cheek again and noticed how cold her skin had gotten. The room was muggy, and she was sweating but shivering as well.

"Mink'Ayllu is so itty-bitty-pretty in spring." Her voice was thin. Why was her voice so thin? He dared to look at the red and saw a sharp thorn poke out of her stomach.

"What the . . . ?"

The sound of footsteps came through the door. Richard and Gon followed shortly after. His sibling didn't hesitate like Sachihiro had. They put their shoulder bag on the ground and pulled out instruments.

"Sorry, I . . ." Richard mumbled. "I tried to help her, but I'm not sure . . . she's high. It was the only thing I could do." Sachihiro glared at him. Had he dared to touch her? It must've been his child. There was no one else around. Sachihiro had trouble tracking his emotions and thoughts, so he focused on his sweet vine instead.

"We'll get you through this, sweet vine. Don't you worry."

Gon cleared their throat. "Esperanza? I will do whatever I can to save you, but I don't know if I help the . . . *child.*"

"No!" she screamed. "You have to save it, please. It can't all be for nothing. Everything I've done . . . please, you have to—" She gasped for air, then screamed with a contraction.

The red closed back in on Sachihiro. It dominated his thoughts, his vision. He reached for his problem-solving brain, the brilliant mind he allegedly possessed. He found nothing. His sweet vine was dying, and here he was, no smarter than any tribal boy. It was laughable they'd made him chieftain, gifted him the position of a leader when he couldn't even help one person. But he wouldn't have done it alone. He would have done it with the ancestors. His eyes widened.

"Gon! Ask the ancestors to save them both. The Utsilo. Use the Utsilo!"

Gon grimaced in pain and shook their head. "Sachi . . . we used it on Subira. It's gone."

No. This made no sense. He couldn't have wasted the cure for his love on his idol. It couldn't have happened.

"Oh, my changing caterpillar!" Esperanza giggled. "What a donks! Did I just hear you correctly that you met Captain Subira Se'azana?"

No. No. No. He couldn't have done this. This couldn't be his fault. He couldn't be responsible.

His eyes fell on Richard, who stood in a corner with sunken eyes. Guilty. He must've been guilty. Sachihiro let go of Esperanza, jumped to his feet, and smashed Richard against the wall.

"Sachi!" Gon yelled, but he barely heard it. This man had put his sweet vine in danger, had forced her to carry her murderer. Sachihiro had broken a snow globe for her before—he could figure out how to break a man.

"Ivalace," she pressed out between contractions. "It's not his fault."

"You don't have to defend him." He searched Richard's face for a confession or fear of punishment but found nothing in them. He couldn't break him because he was already broken.

"Ivalace, please forgive me."

He glanced over his shoulder without loosening the grip on Richard. "Sweet vine, you really don't have to—"

"I did to him what they did to me, Ivalace. I used his body . . . but, but it was for the greater good. For the Fae, and us, and our future."

He let go of Richard. The smith sank down against the wall and buried his head in his hands. Sachihiro turned back to Esperanza. "I don't understand."

"The demon said he wouldn't be conscious."

"*Conscious?*" Sachihiro urged his brain not to put the pieces together.

Esperanza's eyes bulged out, and she nodded frantically.

A false smile grazed her lips. He knew the signs. She had looked at him that way whenever he had been upset. He'd last seen it when she had ditched him to join Richard for dinner at the Zac-Cimi hotel.

"I didn't think he'd remember, Ivalace. You got to believe me."

Gon stopped whatever they were doing to help. "If this is a demonic or Fae child, I can't—"

"That's not the problem here, Gon." Sachihiro was surprised at how harsh he'd sounded. He looked at his sweet vine, his Fae princess. Esperanza, who had escaped the horrors of her tribe, left her wretched life behind to . . . *inflict it upon others.* She dropped her expression when she saw the look in his eyes. There was no longer a need for decryption, no longer a need for Sachihiro's defenses of her.

"Sachi, I love you."

"You left me." The words surprised him as well, but as soon as they left his chest, the hurt he'd never allowed himself to feel surfaced. He had married Fabia, had given up everything. His life had been over, and here she was talking about returning to the tribe together. She knew he'd longed to leave it. He had told her about the dark impulses that had occupied his youth before he'd run off to Mink'Ayllu, had told her how he didn't believe he could survive in Juyub'Chaj, but she'd left him there. She had planned the pregnancy and their reunion, so she couldn't have forgotten about him, but she hadn't contacted him either. A burning sensation plagued his stomach. He'd never felt this way toward her before, had never allowed anger to taint the perfect picture of his Fae princess. She'd lured him into a different world, one far away from his suffocating village. He'd thought they understood each other. He'd never thought she'd let him suffocate.

"I know, but—" Another contraction made her convulse in pain, but he felt too numb to care.

"You left me, and then you raped him?"

"Sachi, don't use that word. I intended—"

"Words are important, Esperanza!"

Richard stood up behind him and slid out of the room.

"Sachi . . ." Esperanza's voice shook. "You know I went through dark times too and—"

"No. No, no, no." He couldn't allow her excuses into his head. He'd end up believing them. "Zaz has too, and she would never do this. Right, Gon?"

Gon looked between the two and shook their head. "No, she wouldn't." They glanced back at the red. "You made a decision, Esperanza. We're responsible for our decisions, like the one I'm about to make. Please tell me about the Fae and the demon."

Esperanza's eyes widened farther. "Gon, you have to save this child. You *have* to."

"Tell me about the demon, and I'll decide."

CHAPTER 36

SUBIRA

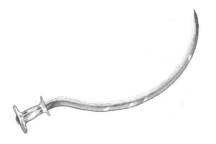

February 980 - Waldfeld, Silberfluss

Subira tightened Cal's reins around a tree at Waldfeld's forest edge and brushed through his mane. She brought her forehead to his and allowed the seconds of tenderness to harden her. Makeda had taught her that a warrior locked away their heart like the sacred treasure it was. The ones who brought their heart to the battlefield were prone to lose it.

"I will come for you soon," she whispered, then let go. When she turned to her soldiers, determination replaced all softness. She had brought six of them for the covert mission and had ordered her western battalion to follow in the morning. They could occupy Waldfeld until Princess Josefine sent a Virisunder duke to claim it. At that point, the town would no longer be Subira's concern.

Her eyes wandered over Zazil and the five other soldiers

she had chosen. Nerves stirred in her stomach. She released them with a controlled breath. It didn't matter how her last covert mission had gone. It didn't matter that her Tazadahar allies had betrayed her. These were *her* soldiers, her children.

"Let us handle this matter swiftly and with confidence. The Council has infiltrated our ranks, a breach of Elfentum trust we will not accept. Heidegger wishes to dine with the owner of this land. Let us fulfill his request and dine with him. I've heard the local cuisine is excellent." The corners of her mouth twitched upward when she saw the ease in their faces. "Rockingham and Aumale, you set off the assula explosives in the barracks. Ch'ulel designed them with sufficient reach, and the triggered explosion is delayed. It should take out everyone without putting you at risk. Understood?" They nodded. "Ch'ulel, the explosives?"

Zazil handed over a sack of vibrating glass orbs. The green lights inside looked like lightning bolts attacking the glass. "Careful with these babies. They're eager to fuck shit up."

"Language, soldier."

"Sorry, General. These babies are effective is all I'm saying. You don't wanna drop them too early."

Rockingham nodded and winked. "Got it, Ch'ulel." Zazil rolled her eyes and smirked.

More nerves sprouted in Subira's stomach. This wasn't like Tazadahar. Even if some of her soldiers had personal relationships, none of them had a vendetta against their target, Duke Belladonna. A shock of blond hair and dead eyes sneaked its way into Subira's mind. She hadn't thought of Evelyn in years. Her shoulders tensed up. She couldn't dwell on the past. This time, no innocent children would suffer.

"Here's your assula detector, General." Zazil handed her a round glowing pin. "It'll warn you before any spells are thrown your direction."

Subira and the others attached the detectors to their armor. "Thank you, Ch'ulel. Let's go." She readied her pistol in case the Belladonnas' guards made rounds outside the estate fence and stepped into the clearing. The estate was beautiful, not unlike her manor at home. Xenia had grown up in a place like this, had leaned out of large half-moon windows like this manor had, and had watched a sunset like the one embracing the world in an orange hue now. Dusk made everything possible. *Dusk will turn your mom into a war hero, honey.*

She locked the resolution inside of her heart, away from the fight and yet providing power. Her eyes wandered over the largest balcony, likely adjacent to the master bedroom. As beautiful as her Polemos manor had been, it had also been a prison. What dark secrets did the Belladonnas keep in their gallant home? They wouldn't get a chance to tell her. The war hero Xenia looked up to wouldn't let them.

She examined the wall. It wasn't high enough to cause an issue. "Ch'ulel, check for defenses."

Zazil moved her fingers through the air as if playing an invisible piano. Her chosen weaponry for the mission were eight large silver rings with glowing crystals. Subira had insisted on her carrying an additional small staff and the hidden assula ax as well but admired the ingenuity of Zazil's dangerous jewelry.

Dots of light that looked like hundreds of green fireflies rose up along the stone wall. Zazil rolled her eyes. "Simple freeze spell. The Belladonnas aren't exactly fancy, General. Nothing to worry about." She unhooked a forging instrument from her belt. It was a pistol with a glass tube as a barrel and an orb above the grip. She aimed it at the fireflies and pressed the trigger. Instead of a shot, the pistol sucked the assula energy from the wall and collected it within the orb. After she had gathered all of them, she twisted the muzzle, and the glass tube closed.

"Well done, Ch'ulel. I'm not surprised their technology is behind. The region never fully recovered from the great famine," Subira said as she approached the wall. "Safe to proceed?"

"Yes, General."

Subira gestured at her soldier, Diem, to give her a boost. He bent down to support her and lifted her up with one swift move. She stayed low to peek over the wall and noticed three guards on patrol, making rounds. Two were far enough away that they shouldn't notice the ambush. The third was too close to ignore. "Hold steady," she commanded Diem.

"Aye, General."

Subira examined the drop. She could jump and launch at the guard, hopefully surprising him before he could sound the alarm. She unstrapped the binoculars from her belt. They'd been a well-intended birthday present from Alexandra that she had failed to appreciate until now. She peered through them and noticed a glowing amulet on the guard's chest. He would sound the alarm the moment he saw her. The last seconds of his life would be too well spent.

She ducked lower and turned to Zazil. "Do you have something silent for long-range?"

"Yes, General. I can get up there and handle it, or . . . or the spell I just harvested. Yeah, that should work." Zazil stretched her arm up and handed Subira the forging instrument. "Turn the muzzle to the right to cock it. Don't break it though. It's a little delicate."

Subira raised an eyebrow. "I won't." She aimed the strange instrument at the guard's forehead. It wasn't the firearm she was used to but evoked memories of a time when she had become an arrow, a bullet, the sharp edge of a knife. A time when purpose had followed her every step and death had been a wild dance partner who did not hide in the caresses of a lover.

She took a deep breath and pictured soaring through the sky as a green light. *The assula is doing the same.* What a silly thought. Of course it wasn't. It was as lifeless as the wood splinter of an arrow. Subira's work was to breathe life into it so it could snuff out that of another. She exhaled and pulled the trigger. The guard saw what was coming. His hand reached for the alarm but froze before he succeeded. The recognition of his failure remained on his face. Subira prayed that failure would never be transfixed to hers.

"Clear," she told the others, then stored the instrument away and jumped the fence. She landed gracefully on the grass, damp from Silberfluss's ever-persistent drizzle, and turned back to assist her soldiers. They pulled Zazil over last, who shivered when she reached the wet grounds.

The smith examined the estate with an approving nod. "Adorable. Always had a thing for country nobility's quaint style."

Subira looked back at the large manor and mused how exaggerated the Revelli estate must look, but it wasn't the time for polite conversation. She handed back Zazil's forging instrument. "Rockingham, Aumale, come up with an entrance and exit strategy for the barracks. Allow us fifteen minutes to enter and locate the manor's dining room. If an alarm resounds before then, detonate the explosives right away."

They examined the quiet barracks and nodded. "Understood, General."

She laid a hand on each of their shoulders. "Virisunder believes in you. Caedem will protect you." She loved the glimmer of pride that crossed their eyes. There was nothing more satisfying than fighting for a greater good. Sometimes that greater good was a lanky girl with dreadlocks and glimmering amber eyes.

Rockingham and Aumale hurried off. Subira examined the grounds. An artistically cut hedge framed the path to the entrance. Instead of religious iconography, it was sculpted into animal shapes that could have been in a children's book. They provided decent cover from the estate's eastern side, where Subira had spotted the other two patrolling guards.

"Follow me," she said, then sneaked over to the hedge in a low, crouched position. She peered through the legs of a hedge wolf. One of the two guards was too close to the estate. She'd notice Subira and her soldiers entering through a window. Her fellow guard was closer to the hedge. Subira squinted at him and noticed the captain badge on his chest, as well as the redness of his puffy face. He must've shared Gustave's vice. It would be a pleasure to take him out.

"Ch'ulel, ready yourself to take out the woman. Silently please."

Zazil cracked her knuckles and slid her fingers under the gown of a hedge figure. Green sparks rose up the skirt, too subtle for the guards to notice.

"On my whip, Ch'ulel." Subira pulled the shotel sword off her back.

"Whip?" Zazil raised an eyebrow. "Damn, General, didn't know you were into that."

"Focus." Subira failed to suppress a grin. Her fingers tightened around the shotel grip, her old familiar friend. She hadn't used it in active combat since the Tazadahar mission but had trained with it whenever she'd felt lost in herself. The walnut-brown grip allowed a matching pair of eyes back into her thoughts. The eyes of that strange man. *Don't think about him.*

She moved to the right, closer to the guard captain, and took cover behind a hedge swan. "Ready?" she whispered.

"Ready, General," Zazil responded.

Subira copied the whistle of a nightingale. The captain frowned and stepped closer to the hedge. She whistled again and adjusted her stance. He leaned over the hedge swan's wing for a better view. Subira whipped her shotel across his neck before he spotted her. The blade sliced through his throat and the swan's. The man bled enough for both of them. The blood spurted from his neck like a miniature fountain, well suited for the quaint estate garden. Subira watched his puffy eyes close and inhaled the sweet iron scent of success.

Next to her, the woman collapsed with a gargle. Magical energy bound her hands and neck until all air was drained. Subira nodded. "Well done, Ch'ulel."

Zazil looked green around the nose, and her hands shook

as she pulled them back. Subira stepped around her other soldiers and put her arm around Zazil's shoulders. The smith had such a grand mouth, Subira hadn't considered the effect battle might have on her. She was an elf too, but the years among orcs might have softened her.

"Was that your first kill?" She leaned in close so only Zazil could hear her. The smith nodded. Subira squeezed her shoulder. "It is essential you understand its purpose then. A warrior cannot fight without knowing death."

"How surprisingly theatrical of you, Subi." Zazil's voice shook, so Subira overlooked the inappropriate address.

"Allow me to share what the great General Makeda taught me a long time ago. The death of our enemies is their failure at judgment and life. We all have the right to try, not the right to win. When you kill an enemy, you bless them by allowing them guidance of the gods. They didn't use their chance on their own, but Balthos and the pantheon will help them. Or, if you believe in Tribu La'am's ancestral after-life"—Subira thought of the fascinating trivia Sachihiro had told her—"You give your enemy a chance to join the ancestors and become so much more than they were. They can help the next generation not to repeat their own mistakes. You assist the future with your deed." Zazil avoided her eyes. Subira pushed her chin up until the smith faced her. "Zazil dear, it is the body you slay, not the spirit."

Zazil's face softened. "Thanks, Subi."

"Now let's free more of those lost souls. And don't call me Subi again." She smiled and turned back to her other soldiers. "We took out the patrol. We should have a few minutes before the bodies are discovered. We want to be inside by the time Rockingham and Aumale set off the explosives."

"Aye, General."

Together they sneaked up to the main manor. Subira signaled around the facade. They had better chances to enter near the dining hall if they came through the side. She peered around the manor's corner and saw no more guards. The dukes and duchesses of smaller towns had made themselves delightfully vulnerable in the long war. Their defense strategists had gotten used to Alexandra's military style, and the local guard relied heavily on assula rifles, some minor magical protection purchased at the Institute, and the Council's general control of the war. None of them expected General Se'azana.

Subira reached a sparsely lit window on the manor's eastern wall and peered inside. It was an office with heavy mahogany furniture, burning candles, and chaotic paper stacks. The duke could have used a Sachihiro as well. Not that Subira intended to share. The office was empty, but a guard likely stood outside the door, protecting any valuable documents.

Subira snapped to get Zazil's attention and nudged at the window. "This one."

Zazil nodded and pulled the ruby on her ring. The gemstone extended into a sharp needle. She bent her fingers and lightly brought the needle to the glass. She traced along the window's edge and left a soft green ray behind. When she brought the line to a close, the glass turned cloudy. A second later it disappeared.

"Wow," another soldier whispered. Subira's chest broadened with pride for her smith. She once again thanked Alexandra for the excellent choice.

"No sound at entry," she told them, then slipped through the window. She examined the paperwork on the desk while the others entered. Most notes were written in an elegant handwriting that differed from the duke's signature. At a closer look, they appeared to be political manifestos of sorts. The title *Princess Rutilia* appeared in all of them. Subira picked up an illustrated placard that stood out from the rest. It featured a heavily tattooed Tribu La'am boy and a boyish-looking halfer girl with a mostly shaved head. Someone had drawn a circle around the girl. The Spirit and the Enforcer was the title. Subira frowned. Waldfeld seemed to have peasant unrest within its community, likely due to the famines. Virisunder's new duke or duchess would have to focus on education and equality first, but convincing Princess Josefine to prioritize the peasantry wasn't a simple endeavor.

Subira took in the rest of the office. Its most striking detail was the life-size portrait of a young human woman with corn-yellow hair and freckles. Dead animals preserved with taxidermy surrounded her. The cold eyes of a wolfhound stared at the viewer, and the woman stroked a dead white rabbit she held in her hand. Subira stepped closer to read the nameplate set in the gold frame. *Lady Rutilia Belladonna*. She must have been the duke's daughter. She might still be a teenager, but with her political involvement it would be best to kill her as well. After the duke, of course. No parent should have to watch their child die in front of them.

"General, shall we—" Diem started, but the earth-shattering noise of three explosions closely following one another blew their cover. *Too early*. No more than ten minutes could have passed.

"Ramsay, take out whoever comes in," she barked at another soldier before rushing to the window. Ruby flames with green tips consumed the barracks and the surrounding grass. Not a single soul was nearby. Rockingham and Aumale could have escaped through the main entrance, but it wouldn't make sense. They had the order to follow them for backup. Subira's insides became heavy. The detonation hadn't gone as planned. It couldn't have. Panic fought for her attention, but she breathed it away. *A general who worries about one casualty causes more.*

There was a slash behind her, and she whipped around. Ramsay cut down the guard who had entered to check the window, but there were surely more to follow.

"Weapons ready. The noise will have startled them. Take out any guards first. Beware of Heidegger and his Tidiers. Trap civilians, don't shoot them." She pulled her assula pistol—the time for silence had passed—and rushed out of the door first. Her soldiers followed.

The office led into a wide wooden foyer with three glass wing doors to the Belladonna dining hall. It was larger than Subira had expected, with room for performers to entertain guests. Behind the glass, Subira counted at least two dozen people. The dining hall doors flung open. Two guards rushed out of the first door, rifles at the ready. One guard stormed from the second one. A Tidier opened the third. Subira aimed at the glass orb of his staff. The bullet went through it and shattered the door's glass as well. Screams came from inside. Ramsay and her other two soldiers overpowered the two guards from the first door. Zazil killed the one from the second with an air punch. A green ray shot out of her knuckle ring into the man's heart. This time, she didn't hesitate. Subira was proud of her.

"What is going on?" a man bellowed in the dining hall.

"Inside, now!" Subira yelled right as the first guests ran out of the hall. Chaos erupted as screaming ladies in fancy dresses and heels tried to escape. Their unarmed gentlemen followed. A lady with corn-yellow hair fell in front of Zazil with a sob, and the smith helped her onto her feet. Subira pressed through the crowd, searching for Heidegger.

She and her soldiers forced their way through the foyer into the dining hall. The pin on her chest vibrated. A second later, Subira found herself face-to-face with another Tidier, who swung a glowing green chain that ripped her off her feet. She rolled onto her side as soon as she landed and shot his knee. The Tidier collapsed with a yowl.

Blood rushed through Subira as the excitement of the battle took hold. The chaos. The uncertainty. The surrender to her primal nature. All of it created the drug she'd been nursed on. She was about to jump to her feet when black dots hazed her vision. Her head became heavy, and a horrid pain dripped down her temples. It felt as if her brain were melting. She blinked through the dots and found a man standing above her. The white scar on his throat was the keepsake she'd left him with on their last meeting. *Harald Heidegger.*

"Lovely surprise, Captain van Auersperg." He smiled and rotated his staff. Subira felt her brain following the movements. It seemed to circle in her skull in the same rhythm, causing a dull, nauseating pain that faded out all other sensations. The black dots grew, filling most of her sight. She sank backward.

The noise of aggressive shouting surrounded her, unlike the screams of nobility. A part of her left the hall and found itself in a different battle. The pain in her head was too heavy to make out any details, but she knew he was nearby, somewhere. The man with the shotel eyes. Perhaps he was a servant of Balthos, ready to carry her into her death when an opportunity presented itself.

"Stop it!" a girl cried somewhere close to him. "Stop it, we're not cannibals!"

"Kymbat!" This was him. She had heard his earsplitting scream before, many, many years ago. Dots of the dining hall sharpened. They grew until her vision returned. The circles of her brain slowed down. *Not today, my dear death-bringer.* She bid another farewell to the shotel-eyed man and forced herself back to reality.

Heidegger frowned as the spell's effect ebbed away. He looked at his staff, and his eyes widened. Its swirling assulas were pulled away from him. Subira's eyes followed the dancing light and found the barrel of Zazil's forging pistol. Its muzzle sucked Heidegger's magic into the pistol's glass tube.

"Not Captain van Auersperg. It's General Se'azana, dickhead," Zazil said.

Heidegger reached for the gemstone chain on his belt. Subira grabbed her pistol off the ground before he could attack Zazil and shot off his thumb. He howled as blood sputtered from his hand.

Subira noticed a leaf-green velvet mantle from the corner of her eye. According to Sachihiro, velvet mantles in the local colors were customary for Silberfluss dukes and duchesses to wear. "Ch'ulel, secure him."

Zazil nodded and grabbed Heidegger. Subira would figure out what to do with the Council head later. Killing him could spark a grander war, but she'd definitely teach him a lesson for attacking her in war territory.

She jumped up and ran after the fleeing duke. A quick glance told her that her soldiers had taken care of the remaining guards. She followed the duke into the foyer. Ramsay had blocked all exits. It was time to finish the mission.

Subira chased the duke through the crowded foyer until she had him pressed against a corner. He stared at her with huge eyes and a gaping mouth. He had the figure of a man who'd never met hardship. He'd never spent a day in the trenches. Subira thought of Alexandra's outrage at the beginning of the war, the laziness of Silberfluss's nobility in face of the famine. *This one's for you, Alexandra.*

He yanked a painting with luscious fields off the wall in a desperate attempt to protect himself. Subira hooked her shotel around it, tore it away from him, and slit his jugular with her blade. His head fell backward as crimson liquid, like the wine he'd once feasted on, gushed out of his throat. Subira watched his knees buckle before unhooking the velvet mantle from his neck and tossing it over her shoulder.

Belladonna's guests stood around her, frozen in shock and fear. She cleared her throat and spoke in her best Silberfluss tongue. "Unless provoked, no violence will be shown toward you. If it has slipped your mind, we're at war. This is now Virisunder territory. Further instruction will follow shortly." With that, she strutted back into the dining hall. She smiled when she saw the whimpering Heidegger on the ground, stuck in Zazil's assula bonds as his hand wept red for its lost thumb.

"Secured, General," Zazil said.

Subira strode toward them. Her smile widened when she met his glare. "Greetings from Alexandra. Tell the Council that Waldfeld and Nimmerwarm belong to Virisunder now." She dropped the mantle in front of him. "Welcome to *my* war."

The moment was too perfect to pass but did so ruthlessly. A crash outside the manor made both Zazil and her jump. Seconds later, a pulsating green fog wafted through cracks of the dining hall's windows.

Zazil's eyes widened. "That's not possible. That's my inve—" She looked at her hand. "Where the fuck did that ring go?"

Realization hit Subira hard. Zazil had helped a young lady with corn-yellow hair back to her feet. Subira took a controlled breath. "The duke's daughter took it. Rutilia Belladonna."

CHAPTER 37

VANA

February 980 - Balthos's Heretics, Silberfluss

The nachtalbs watched their every move, unable to distinguish between sinner and savior. *I've been there.* The closer Vana and her comrades got to the infirmary, the more nachtalbs swarmed around them. They tugged at her consciousness every step of the way. The Institute had designed them to only attack when provoked. They couldn't take over one's mind fully otherwise, but what constituted as a provocation? Questioning the system? Vana was doing more than that, so she flinched every time their thoughts intruded, anxious that they might have chosen her for the all-consuming madness. She reminded herself that nachtalb thoughts were desperate outbursts of corpses denied their last rest. Corpses that needed to be seen and heard, like any freak of the norm the upper class buried and abused. Corpses that could defend their comrades better than any living criminal in these halls.

"Son of a storm, those bastards are gonna break my skull," Sean, the scarred half orc from their community's first gathering, cussed under his breath.

"Sorry, Sean. Almost there." At least Vana hoped so. The dark twists and turns of Balthos's Heretics hid the infirmary like her grandpa hid his tobacco chews. It was a miracle she'd stumbled over it once. Searching for it again was a fool's errand. Luckily, she was a fool.

"Told you to call me Eyeball."

"Why would I call you Eyeball? You have both eyes," Vana whispered over her shoulder. She held up Artyom's and her oil lamp, guiding the way for her comrades. She'd picked seven of them to accompany her for the initial break-in. At the infirmary, she planned to share the truth about nachtalbs with her community. She wasn't quite sure what that truth was but hoped a second examination would clarify things. She and Artyom had discussed the matter in vain. Every conversation circled back to him calling nachtalbs an abomination and grumbling Sap Büruy prayers to himself. As if imaginary gods controlled living corpses.

She turned into a smaller corridor away from a pack of green rays that marked the path they'd been on and squinted into the darkness. This particular shade of dark looked familiar.

"I still have both my eyes, but my opponents don't." Eyeball grinned next to her.

"Fine. Eyeball it is."

Erna grumbled to Vana's left. She seemed smaller and less imposing without her ducklings. Allison had recovered within a day, so Erna could no longer deny the community's merit. Vana had asked her first to join this mission. The mother hen's approval had become increasingly important to her. Vana had invited Eyeball and his best friend, Skit, next. After the gathering, she'd learned that they were former pirates and would make fine protectors for the others. Yooko had weaseled his way into the inner circle too, eager to see what weaponry Vana had promised them. She hoped he'd share more of his own knowledge afterward. Then there was Daiba, daughter of a Tazadahar rebel, who was, in her own words, "a jewel thief with exquisite taste," and in the court's eyes a dangerous spy and political insurgent. Either way, she knew how to pick a lock.

Artyom's fake laughter echoed through the halls. Vana startled but forced herself to keep going. He and Clarisse had stayed behind on the main path to alert them if any guards showed up. Not that they had in the past days. Without the guards' presence in the dining hall or any outside interaction, Balthos's Heretics felt increasingly like a mass grave. Another laugh. Artyom must've been teaching Clarisse how to defend herself. *They're not attacking him. They're not attacking him.*

"Should we check on them?" Erna asked.

Vana glanced over her shoulder. "Maybe that's a good ide—"

"There we go," Yooko said, bumping her shoulder. Vana snapped back and noticed the vague outline of the infirmary door. Artyom hadn't given the danger signal, so there was no point turning back now.

"They'll be fine, Erns. Let me show you what we found first." Erna looked displeased as usual, but Vana kept on walking.

Three nachtalbs awaited them, guarding the door. The bright rays from their eye sockets hid their own appearance. She wasn't sure if she preferred to see the disfigured corpses or liked them more as a lurking threat in the dark. The first one was the correct answer, of course. Knowledge was power. It was one of Artyom's favorite lessons to repeat. Every bit of realization brought her closer to self-agency and closer to Balthos. At least that was his claim.

Vana eyed the creatures. "We should distract them in case the break-in upsets them." She glanced around, but no one volunteered. It was fascinating how a threat to the mind scared them all equally, even fierce pirates.

"Yeah, I don't want those creepsters watching over my shoulder. I mean, hello, can I have some privacy, please? Reminds me of those guys who just don't get it and—"

"All right," Vana said, interrupting Daiba. It was difficult to cut her off once she got into a story. "I'll handle it."

Daiba squeezed Vana's shoulder and pulled out the needle kit she had collected over the past few months of her stay here. "Thanks, you're quite the cool crime boss, like my pen pal Catalina Zac-Cimi," she said to Vana, then smiled at Eyeball. "She's an orc too."

"Just pick the lock," Eyeball said.

"Yeah, please Daiba, that would be great," Vana said. "I'll give you a few minutes, but the quicker the better. And I'm not a crime boss. I'm a revol—"

"Got it, my crime hoe." Daiba chuckled and knelt down in front of the lock. Vana was tempted to argue, but the nachtalb rays intensified. Two of them stepped closer. She pulled out the sharp rock knife Artyom had given her and stepped away from the group. She whistled to get their attention and hacked into the lifeless stone wall, enough of an offense to grant an attack. The three nachtalbs focused in on her, and she squinted through the sudden bright lights. Before she could prepare herself, the voices took over.

> You have no plan. No idea what to do.
> The only plan you have is leading them to their death.
> Artyom's first, and there's nothing you can do.
> Artyom will die of hands you claim do not belong to you, but they always do. They always do.
> It was your lunacy that killed Jules.
> You haven't learned. You'll never learn.

Vana's knees buckled. She knew she should ridicule them. Make fun of them. They weren't real. They were only real if she chose them to be, so why did she make that choice? Why did she give them power they didn't have? She heard scratches and the clicking of the lock behind her. *Quicker, please.* A nachtalb followed her to the ground and dizzied her with foul light. Its hand reached out to her. *Ridicule. Ridicule.* Why couldn't she do it? Anger grew in her. Rage at herself for betraying her own strength. *Come on, you useless idiot, ridicule them!*

Useless idiot.

Useless idiot.

Useless. The surrounding echoes mixed with her own thoughts until she could no longer tell them apart. Her body buzzed with the desperate need for action, for fixing things. Fixing all the mistakes she was bound to make. Fixing everything. But there were no solutions. How could she defend herself against these creatures, and why? What if they were right?

The creature touched Vana's chest and scratched a line below her rib cage. It didn't break her skin through the thin prison robe, but it sliced something else. Something deep within her.

"Almost got it, boss."

Vana gasped and looked at her chest. She was sure the nachtalb had ripped it open, but she found no wound. The room spun. The invisible tear widened.

You're lost like we are.

Lost like we are.

I'm lost like you are. A second arm reached out with alive-looking brown skin. No rot. It slapped the other arm away. *I'm lost. I'm lost. I'm lost.* She couldn't make sense of the second arm, but her sight cleared.

A man sat down next to her and sighed. "Are we going for unlovable or shame to the family this time?" He sounded utterly bored. "A combination . . . splendid."

Vana clutched her chest and felt along the rib cage, determined to find the cause of her pain. There must've been a physical manifestation of tearing apart.

"It wasn't that bad, don't worry," said the man. The voices no longer consumed her. He must have directed some of the nachtalbs' attention onto him. "You know," he continued, "you got quite the gumption, living here without pretending you're dead, at least a little bit."

Cohesive thoughts returned to Vana as she recognized the man in front of her. *Yooko*. A nachtalb clasped his shoulder. She glanced at the rest of the group, still gathered around the oil lamp by the door. She shouldn't have stepped so far away from them.

You should step farther away. Farther into the darkness.

"Take your friend Artyom for example." Yooko's voice wavered. There were cracks in his bored facade. "He's been dead inside for the decade I've known him. So have I." He flinched at a thought only he could hear. "And here you come, daring to breathe life into us all." He looked to be in pain but raised an eyebrow and sarcastically shook his head at her.

We're all dead here. You are too.

Vana blew out air. The noise distanced her from the voices, allowing her to speak. "Dead inside, heh?" Her voice shook, but it was hers. Her real words, her real thoughts. "My mom always warned me not to become one of those people."

Yooko scoffed. "You know a lot of them?"

Her chest pain traveled to her head. A throb accompanied each thought, making it impossible to think clearly. "Your boyfriend, for example," she said before she could stop herself. Yooko's face fell, losing its indifference. His little story about the outside world meant more to him than Vana had realized. "But . . . but dead people can do more than you'd think." Vana tried to save the glimmer of hope he'd brought into the darkness. Yooko rubbed his temples. The thoughts must've been circling in on him now. "Dead people can walk and react. Who knows, maybe they can find each other too."

"You're an odd duck, Vana," he mumbled.

You're lost like we are.

We're all lost.

No, we're not. I refuse to be lost. The voices quieted down as new strength filled her. She took Yooko's hand and squeezed it. "You'll see soon. None of us are really lost. They just want us to believe that."

A slight smile crossed his lips. The clicking of a lock accompanied it.

"Got it, boss!" Daiba called.

Vana jerked up, eager to free herself from the circle of dread, and tossed her stone knife in front of the nachtalbs. She inhaled and remembered—Jules, the guards, the town square. Everything. She faced the nachtalbs directly and said, "We carry no weapons. We have a right to walk these hallways." She choked up as she said Jules's last words, the ones that might have saved him if she hadn't been such a hothead.

The voices disappeared. Vana helped Yooko back to his feet. "Come on, let's get inside."

They rushed after the others into the infirmary and slammed the door closed before the nachtalbs could enter. Vana examined the place. It looked the same as it had two weeks ago, except all previously locked cabinets were open and empty.

"They've raided the place," Eyeball said. Vana pushed past him toward the storage door. She cracked it and peeked inside. The sight challenged her nerves anew, but she wouldn't freeze like last time. This was good news. *Corpses casually leaning against a wall are good news.* She'd have to repeat that a few more times to believe it. The green glow was as bright as it had been a few weeks ago, but it neither shone from the flasks that had hung next to the corpses nor from the eye sockets like it did for the regular nachtalbs. The light came from within the corpses' half-rotten chests. It shone through the skin and illuminated the wilting organs under the rib cage. Their static hearts sat right above it. Vana's hand found her own chest, the spot where she'd felt her rib cage part. It was the spot the voices had tried to tear apart. Her grandma had once told her the soul sat beneath the heart, waiting for Exitalis to collect it.

She stared at the spinning lights in the dead torsos in front of her. Exitalis had never come for them, but Vana would.

She carefully closed the door and turned to her comrades. "Don't worry, our friends are still here."

"*Friends?*" Skit asked. "I thought you found weapons."

Vana's eyes wandered over their faces. The hesitation and distrust she saw in them would have made her heart sink this morning, but the conversation with Yooko had steadied her. They had put their faith in some made-up deities. It was on Vana to restore it in themselves and their future instead. She cleared her throat. "What if I told you nachtalbs aren't inherently evil? What if I told you they saved Arty, Clarisse, and me?"

"I'd say you have a terrible memory because we just left those bastards behind and it wasn't exactly a jolly good time," Yooko said.

Vana raised her hand. "Sure, yes, *but* they were designed to be bastards. By whom? By the fucking Council and King Josef and all those noble assholes who made us into criminals. They turn us into the scum of society and then they rob us of any fucking peace death might bring. Let's take that shit back—death, life, all of it. It belongs to us." She opened the door dramatically and gestured inside. Daiba shrieked and jumped behind Skit. Yooko looked like he had swallowed an extra portion of slime. "More nachtalbs. Fantastic," he mumbled.

"No, wait, they're not like the others. These haven't been finished." Vana peeked inside and saw them clearer, illuminated with the light of the infirmary. There were eight of them. The green rays in their chests crashed against one another, which made their bodies flinch and twitch. Some leaned against the wall. Others quivered on the floor. Vana recognized the Tribu La'am human corpse that had saved them. It perked up when it saw her but seemed as much at war with itself as the others.

Vana was so focused on it, or *him* perhaps, that she

flinched when the first one of her comrades pushed past her. Erna went straight to a female elvish corpse with three tusks attached to her burnt upper mouth hole. They resembled the fangs of an oversize cat. She was of mixed Vach da tìm and Fi'Teri ethnicity. Erna crouched down to her and stretched out her hand.

"Don't touch that thing!" Daiba squeaked, but Erna ignored her and stroked the corpse's bony cheek.

"What have they done to you?" she whispered. The lights in the corpse's chest swirled quicker. More tiny bolts clashed against one another.

"Can you understand us?" Vana asked. The dead Tribu La'am man directed his empty eye sockets at her and nodded slowly. Vana's breath sped up. Questions flooded her mind, and gruesome implications of that understanding fought into the forefront. She pushed them back. She had to remain practical. "Listen, comrades, these creatures are oppressed like we are, but they're also magical. They can help us fight back against whatever is coming. All we need to do is learn their ways. Maybe they can help us defuse the hallway nachtalbs too."

"I think they're trapped souls," Erna said. A shiver ran over Vana's spine. *Don't think about the implications.* They had one lifetime, one world to change for the better, and it was all that mattered. None of them could afford to think about the possibility of an afterlife.

"How do you know that?" Daiba asked.

"The energy that keeps them running . . . it should have become ancestors by now. Our ancestors looked after our tribe in close contact. I know what their energy feels like." Yooko scoffed. "Got a problem?" Erna asked.

He clicked his tongue and looked away but muttered "fuck tribes" under his breath.

Erna rose. Her light green skin flushed brownish around her cheeks. She squared her shoulders and walked over to him. "I'm not letting some runaway insult my tribe."

Vana shuffled her feet, unsure how to proceed. "Guys, we're comrades. Let's not——"

Yooko ignored her and met Erna's harsh gaze. "Oh, and you never left yours? I didn't realize Balthos's Heretics is part of some orcish tribe. Is that why it sucks so much?"

Vana was sure Erna would punch him, but something worse happened. The elvish corpse leaped up to her feet, quicker than Vana had thought possible, and charged at Yooko. The lights crackled within her. He yelped and pressed himself against the wall. Vana lurched forward and grabbed the corpse's waist. The flesh squished under her touch. The rotting had turned the girl's body mushy. As she pressed around the waist to pull her off Yooko, the flesh gave way until Vana felt an organ. Bile crept up her throat. Vana was sure she'd vomit any moment.

Eyeball pushed the corpse back and moved in front of Yooko. The half orc didn't seem as shocked as Vana felt. Piracy must have prepared him for unexpected brawls among comrades. Vana tossed the nachtalb back into the storage room. The Tribu La'am corpse held the elvish one down for her. Vana tried to close the door, but the corpse put his foot in the way. Too much happened at once, so she allowed it to stay open a slit and turned back to de-escalate the fight. She needed to take action and forget the wetness that covered her palms.

Yooko had lost all of his detachment and yelled at Erna from behind Eyeball's shoulder. "Are you controlling that thing?"

"She's not a *thing*, asshole!" Erna snapped back.

Yooko turned to Vana. "She sicked that monster on me!"

"I didn't do anything." Erna glanced at her as well. *Fuck.* This wasn't going like she and Artyom had planned at all. She had wanted to prove to him that she could handle it on her own. Her heart sank. Apparently she couldn't.

"So what side are we on now?" Yooko spit out the question.

She needed to keep them both, but she needed to uphold their community's values as well. "Erna, back off."

The door flung open before Erna could respond, and Artyom rushed inside. "Kymbat!" He noticed the tension in the room. "Hello, everyone. Warden come from different entry. We need be in dining hall, now. So if you can rip heads off each other at more convenient time, would be great."

Erna took a step back. "Where's Clarisse?"

"I sent her down to hall."

"Alone?" Erna growled.

Artyom stretched, seemingly casual, but Vana noticed his hand brush over the slingshot. "Erna, you think that girl go somewhere she doesn't want? She is fierce like snap turtle." Erna eyed him for a second, then bumped her shoulder against his as she brushed past. Artyom gestured at the door. "Anyone else need special invitation?"

Eyeball, Skit, Yooko, and Daiba left the infirmary after Erna. Vana stared at the storage door, unsure what to do. Should she bring one? But then the warden would know they were working with them.

"We're not ready. Whatever the warden has planned, we . . ." She'd taken too long to bring them all together. They weren't a team yet. She'd thought they could understand the corpses together, strategize how to best incorporate them into their community and work against the terrible conditions of the prison. Instead, everyone had left more confused and concerned than before.

Artyom pulled a cloth from his pocket and wiped Vana's hands. "Come on, kymbat, let's go. We figure out whatever happen together."

She thought of what Yooko had told her. They depended on her, but what good had she done for them? "I failed, Arty. They're all—"

"They are people. People are stupid." He squeezed her hand and tugged her toward the door. "Give time. It'll be okay."

Vana followed his lead, and they made their way through the hallways in silence. She sensed the nachtalbs, but they allowed them to pass without intrusions. Every single prisoner had gathered in the dining hall like they had during the king's visit. Vana's stomach dropped when she saw the roughly two hundred potential comrades awaiting their fate. Thirty of them had agreed to join her community so far. Her nausea returned when she spotted the warden with his foul breath and uncaring eyes. He stood on a makeshift podium at the head of the dining hall. Instead of his normal guards, four Tidiers accompanied him. That couldn't be a good sign. The Tidiers had erected a light cage around themselves and the warden, shielding them from everyone else.

Vana scanned the crowd and found Erna among her girls. Yooko stood nearby with Eyeball, Skit, and Daiba. Vana glanced at Artyom, and while he looked concerned, his sight comforted her. His skin was no longer ashen from the ailment that had plagued him, and he'd even used those stone splinters to recover his face from underneath the shabby mess. He had cut his hair so it stopped at his shoulders and had trimmed his beard to a length fashionable outside of hermit circles. Vana's mom would have called him attractive. The thought was gross, but she was glad to watch him return to life. Yooko was right. She got this.

The warden leaned to the Tidier on his left and whispered something. The Tidier swung his magic chain, and a light bubble appeared around the warden's head. Vana perked up, hoping it would suffocate him like the victims of the king's visit, but it increased the volume of his voice, allowing each fateful word to boom around the hall.

"In the wake of recent events, Princess Agathe, with the advice of our dear Council members, has concluded that Balthos's Heretics is no longer sustainable." Noise broke out as the concern on the inmates' faces turned into frantic chatter. Noise broke out in Vana's mind as well. What did this mean? Would they move them to a different prison? She clasped

Artyom's hand. If so, she didn't want to be transferred away from him. Or perhaps the noble shits had pardoned them? They might have realized their oppression would eventually lead to rebellion and wanted to even things out before it came to bloodshed. She pictured running home over their farm's wheat fields. Her brothers would wait for her. They would no longer fight over who was the biggest troublemaker now that she'd returned. Her mom would wrap her into her arms, determined to never let go, and Vana would protest, but not really because she'd thought she would never feel the comfort of being a kid in her mom's arms again. Because she wouldn't have been a kid anymore, had they not pardoned her. She would have been thirty-six if she did her whole sentence.

"Silence!" the warden called, but the smug smile on his face revealed that he enjoyed the turmoil. "I'm certain you're wondering what this means for you. Well, you presented the princess with the choice of what to do with you. She decided to hand that choice back over to you." Vana's eyes darted across the hall. This didn't sound like a pardoning, but perhaps they would listen to ideas. She took a breath so her voice could reach over the crowd, but the warden continued before she had the chance to make a suggestion. "We are happy to offer each of you the rope. A quick, dignified execution."

"What the fuck?" Vana turned to Artyom. "No one here got a death sentence. What—"

"Alternatively, you are welcome to stay." The warden's words fell over the hall like a nettle blanket. It took a few seconds before the sting became apparent.

"What happens if we stay?" one man yelled.

"Nothing," the warden responded. "Absolutely nothing. You will not be fed, nor will you receive any further oil vials and pine splinters."

Numbness overcame Vana. She looked at Artyom for an answer while her surroundings turned into chaos. "They're burying us alive," she muttered.

Artyom seemed equally frozen, but something in her

expression snapped him back into action. He clasped her hand tighter. "No. Balthos sent you, kymbat. My second chance. I keep you alive, no matter what." He pulled her through the tumultuous crowd toward the hall's entrance right as the first people chose the rope.

Vana shook her head. "No . . . no, they can't do that."

"Is okay, kymbat. I keep you alive. I promise."

Vana glanced at the podium and saw Maya, the duckling who had insulted her, choose the rope. She'd expected the Tidiers to take those who'd chosen death out of Balthos's Heretics, but they granted no illusion of freedom. A bored-looking Tidier zigzagged his staff until a green string of light whipped out of it and wrapped around Maya's neck. The magic yanked the duckling into the air with a violent snap. By the time the string attached to the hall's ceiling, she was dead. Her head flopped to the side, and her body dangled lifelessly from above like a twisted Treaty Day ornament. A quick death perhaps, but far from dignified.

"Follow me, kymbat. Now."

More ornaments joined the gruesome display of injustice. The living became spectators to the Council's nightmare puppetry dangling above them. Vana forced her gaze off the horror and noticed Erna. She kept her other ducklings back and pushed them into a corner. If people like Maya believed this death to be the better option, what awaited those who stayed behind? The manic fear painted on Erna's face asked the same question. Whoever came for them after the shutdown, the mother hen couldn't keep them away by herself.

Vana stopped. "No, wait. We can't leave, Arty. That's what the community is all about."

Artyom shook his head and tried to pull her farther. "No, no, you cannot help. People get mad without food, without protection." She snatched her hand away from him. "Please, kymbat."

"Arty, you believe I'm your second chance? Let me be that chance for everyone." If Balthos's Heretics had no more guards, no more warden, there was nothing that could hold them back. "Maybe this is what our community needs. We start fresh. We'll figure it out." She left him there and pushed her way back toward the center. Thirteen people had gathered at the podium now, choosing execution over uncertainty.

"Vana!" Yooko called. She tried to make her way over to him right as things escalated. A huge Silberfluss man with a shaved skull and Caedem's sign tattooed on his bare chest jumped on a table and bellowed. Three men with the same tattoo tossed a bench into the crowd. It hit several people as the hall was drowned in screams and panic.

"Don't fall for the warden's word, my brothers," the man on top of the table yelled. Vana recognized him as one of the men who had beat up the guy at the supply lifts. "We, the strongest, can bond together and make this place ours!"

"Ey, that's my fucking line!" Vana yelled back over the noise before she could help herself. She didn't trust those fuckers to build a proper community.

The man's eyes locked with hers. His lips curled into a teeth-bearing grin. "You wanna challenge me, tits?"

"You fu—" Vana started, but Artyom found her and covered her mouth. She pulled his hand off. "What the fuck, man?"

Behind them, the Tidiers continued to cover the hall with ornaments of flesh. Vana needed to get through the crowd's panic and give them a reason to live, a better one than that fucker was offering.

"This is man Erna protects her ducklings from," Artyom said, and she softened. "Name is Lutz. He and friends cause many trouble. *Please* do not start fight, kymbat."

"He's right." Yooko appeared to her left. "We can't fight him directly."

"*We?*" Vana asked.

"The tribe that doesn't suck." He winked, and for a second the dining hall turned into Waldfeld's town square. The noise was applause and excitement for the change Vana was bringing them. They were together, all of them connected by the magic of music. The night might seem dark, but as long as they trusted in the next string, the next note, nothing could overcome them. Then the guards came. Then the guns came. Then Lutz spoke again.

"Seems like the little girl's got her hands full with a Sap and a Tribu fruit."

"Anyone else?" The warden's amplified voice echoed through the hall.

Lutz formed fists and slammed them against his Caedem tattoo. "You bloodsuckers aren't getting any more of our people!"

Vana was sure her head would explode any second. Memories, questions, and confusion gushed through it. How could this man say the opposite of what she stood for, followed by exactly what she stood for?

Several men pushed their way toward Lutz's table. "You have a plan?"

"Last chance!" the warden called.

"Yes I do, my brother. Yes I do." Lutz smiled at the crowd as if this were a joyous chance for them all. Acid boiled in Vana's stomach. No one should celebrate the trouble of their comrades to get in charge. More people pushed toward him, eager to hear what he had to say. Vana glanced around and spotted a nearby table. She needed to get on that. She needed to give them an alternative.

"Vana, listen." Yooko held her back and whispered, "I have a smuggle route. I can get us food."

Vana's eyes grew wide. "Enough for everyone?"

"Shh, keep your voice down. And no, fuck no. I can barely provide for myself, but . . . but I think we can take care of five, maybe six people. Artyom, you, me, Eyeball, and Skit. Maybe Daiba? I'm not sure."

Vana shook her head. "That's not enough."

"Kymbat, is good offer."

"That's not enough! We're not becoming the fucking

noble class of prison while everyone else starves or . . . or listens to that guy." She pushed them aside and forced her way to the table.

"Good luck, everyone." The warden's voice echoed through the hall. "May Exitalis pick you up with gentle and loving arms."

The podium exploded with a bang. A green cloud swallowed the hall for three seconds. When it cleared, the warden and the Tidiers had disappeared. Everyone in Balthos's Heretics was buried with no way out. Those who had escaped danced spiritless above them.

Vana jumped on a table and yelled over the panicked noise around her. "Comrades! Comrades, nothing is lost! We need to stick together and—"

"Follow my word if you wanna survive!" Lutz's voice was louder. More people listened to him. "With me, you'll never be hungry, my brothers and sisters."

"Hunger is a weapon they use on us so we tear one another apart. We are not giving them that satisfaction!" Vana raised her voice higher. Some people turned around. *They're listening.* "Remember the song we sang together, comrades? I remember because I started it." Her community shouldn't have required a leader, but they seemed to crave one. If they wanted a leader, she could become one for now. "We can figure it out together, as a whole!"

"Look at that halfer!" Lutz jeered. "Wants you to sit around and ignore the solutions right at hand. She's just like the warden, like all that damned nobility."

"What?"

"She and all of them want us to forget our strengths. Forget the rights we have! We're on Silberfluss land, aren't we? Why should we starve first when all these parasites have feasted on us?" The circle of those closest to him brought their fists to their own chests and shouted their support. Vana felt as if ice dripped down her spine. They should've been on the same team. They wanted the same thing—justice. How could he so greatly misunderstand what justice entailed? Or had she misunderstood it? She thought of Isa, and fresh anger rushed through her. Vana hadn't misunderstood anything. These fuckers twisted her words, the words of justice, to enrich themselves.

"*Comrades!* Comrades, please listen, we're all the same."

"See, she thinks you're no better than those who want you to rot here!" Lutz yelled back. *Stop twisting my fucking words!* But he continued to contort the truth into poison. "She said you're no better than the halfer tusk who keeps all our decent Silberfluss women hostage." The crowd's attention whipped to Erna. Lutz used the growing fervor and continued. "You're no better than the savage Sap who slaughtered Exitalis's Church of the Last Judge, a religious institution formed here in Silberfluss."

The crowd closed in on Artyom. Vana lost sense of the greater picture. They couldn't rip *her* people from her. Not again. "Leave him the fuck alone!"

Lutz laughed. "That's the leader who says you're no better than those animals. I say you are. I say we have a right to survive on our own land. And halfer?" He addressed her with an evil twinkle in his eye. "Your hunger is making you cranky. How about a good meal?" Vana's muscles grew stiff when she noticed the hunger that consumed the crowd. It drowned out all reason. "Do you like tobacco?" Lutz continued. "I heard Tribu La'am meat tastes like it." A few people around him laughed. "Maybe with a fruity note?"

By the time the words made sense to Vana, Yooko was already running.

"Get him!" Lutz's words ignited a feverish spark in the crowd. *Get him.* A quick solution. A simpler one.

"Stop it!" Vana cried, but they weren't listening. They grabbed Yooko before he reached the hallway. "Stop it, we're not cannibals!" She needed to jump off the table. Run after them. Do something. *Do something, you stupid fucking hothead. Do something.* The decision was taken from her when a group of Lutz's men grabbed her from behind and pulled her backward off the table.

"Kymbat!"

CHAPTER 38

RICHARD

February 980 - Waldfeld, Silberfluss

Richard stood outside Esperanza's door as one word drowned out the sobs, cries, and yelling. *Raped.* Why had the orc used that word? His heartbeat worked itself up into a senseless flutter. His stomach twisted, and sweat formed on his back. He didn't understand where this reaction came from but knew his body laughed at the concept of calmness. He thought of the other virtues Father Godfried had whipped into him: honesty, strength, the solid foundation he was supposed to provide for his family, and any womenfolk in need. Esperanza had come to him, needed him. It was his duty to protect her. It was his duty to obey the gods' word, Father Godfried's word. None of these duties could coexist with that one word. *Raped.*

Our dear friend, you're upset. We—

His Fae companion tried to continue, but Richard didn't

allow it. Not this time. He tensed his muscles and embraced each familiar ache like an old friend that led him back to *his* body. He wrapped his arms around the firm biceps that had forged a new life for Pier and him. They didn't truly belong to him. He'd lost ownership of it all long before he'd vowed himself to the demon.

Esperanza screamed too loudly to ignore, and Richard's throat tightened. She might die. They might both die, her and his child. But was it truly his?

Father Godfried would say so. A man abandoning his family was no real man. Richard's shoulders hurt from the tension he kept in them. Had he not abandoned Pier long ago in pursuit of Godfried's word? He had stayed in Pier's life with little to give. He had forced abandonment onto his son, had chased away the orcish boy who'd claimed to love him.

Dear Richard, please let us explain. Someone is stealing the essence that lines our world. The Fae realm is dissolving into kénos. We needed you to form something alive that could help us. The words meant nothing to Richard. He didn't know what kénos was, and he didn't want to know. He couldn't muster up sympathy for the alleged fate of the Fae, except for wishing that he could trade places with them. Dissolving would be easier than understanding.

A screaming sob filled the hallway, and Richard ran—away from Esperanza, away from the creature within him. He rushed down the stairs he'd once carved with visions of a brighter life and into the shop that had started it all. The drips of water echoing within his skull and the itching of thorns under his skin reminded him that there was no escape. He couldn't outrun Choravdat. He couldn't outrun the virtues that had led him here. He couldn't outrun the heat that shot into his face and the tears that fought in vain to surface.

He looked around the shop and saw the work of a lifetime. Dozens of pieces filled the shelves. They'd been crafted with the love and attention Pier had deserved but Richard hadn't known how to give. Now only the weapons remained.

His boy was gone. Pier had run to the city like Richard had run to the forest. What awaited him there?

Easy, my friend. It will be okay. Calm. Calm. Choravdat was right. There was no reason to believe the words of a tusk over everything Richard had learned to know. But the word didn't leave him. It sat in his stomach and claimed to be true. A truth too shattering to ignore.

Richard glanced at the carving of Exitalis's sign that hung above his workshop entrance and clasped his hands in prayer. "Dearest Exitalis, lady of the dead, wife of the king, mother to us, have mercy on my mortal body. Help me. I beg you to shine your light." He sank to his knees and bowed his head. His body trembled with a weakness he refused to release. "Please help me. I don't know what to trust anymore. Help me."

Crickets mocked his prayer, but no mercy found him in the last light of the dying dusk. He looked back up and screamed, "Help me!" Exitalis scorned him and his pathetic begging. "*Please.*" He struggled to keep the tears down. "I've given up everything for you, holy mother. Please show me the way."

She does not hear you, my friend. For a moment, Richard believed the soul cluster, believed that he did not matter. Then he saw him.

His vision blurred like it had when the Fae cluster had overwhelmed him, but his consciousness remained sharp this time. A worn out parchment appeared in the darkness. Before he could grasp its details, it faded into frightened eyes the color of rich cherry oak. Richard had jumped into limbo enough times to learn how to anchor his consciousness in a place that wasn't his own. He allowed his mind to catch up with his eyes, then took in as many details as he could. Black curls. Hazel skin. And a necklace. A necklace with a sword hanging from it. Richard recognized the sword. He'd given it to a guard the day he'd made the deal with Choravdat. Richard opened his mouth to say something, but the strange place's noise became audible. Maddening shouts filled his ears, reminding him of the ones that had tainted Waldfeld's air the night they'd found Brice.

Someone grabbed the man by the scruff of his neck and shoved him against a dirty stone wall. "Please, I can make you an offer," he pleaded in Silberfluss with the faintest of Tribu La'am accents. Fear distorted his handsome face. Was this how Brice had looked the night they got him? Richard hadn't been there. He'd been at church for his first lesson. Had Father Godfried known? He had never dared to ask.

Richard, come back to us. Choravdat tugged at Richard, but he yanked it off. The surroundings of the parchment vision became clearer. He was in a torchlit hall with shabby benches and too many people. A man laughed. "We're not interested in the kind of offers you're making."

"That's not what I meant. I—"

The laughing man punched him in the face. Richard flinched as if he'd been the target, and panic flooded him. He should have protected Brice. He needed to protect this man. He wasn't sure why, but he knew he needed to. *To limbo with Esperanza.* This was the person he was meant to protect. This man and his boy. Why were both out of reach?

A girl shouted something. Richard gathered energy to turn his head and take in a greater part of the world that wasn't his. The shouting girl had a bloodied face, but he recognized the shock of raven hair with its shaved sides. He recognized her halfer ears and loud voice. *Dotty's girl.* Vana Ackerman had been sent to Balthos's Heretics. That was where the man must've been.

Richard looked back at him. The recognition of his location created a thin connection. The man's eyes widened, and he muttered, "Dick."

"The fuck did you just say to me?" The aggressor had stopped laughing. He bent down to pick something up. The last thing Richard saw was a heavy stone. Then he was tossed back into his smithy.

We're here, our dear Richard. Do not worry. It will be okay.

Richard found himself lying flat on the wooden floor planks of his shop. Sweat drenched him, and a single thought dominated his mind. *They're going to kill him.* The thought pushed him to get back on his feet. Heavy breaths shook him, but he knew what he had to do. "Take me back there," he demanded from the Fae cluster.

We didn't take you there. He was simply a name written in your soul. It does not matter now, our dear friend. Return upstairs and help our child.

"Why does it not matter?" The dripping sounds inside of him turned into gushes of water. Choravdat did not want to speak. "*Why?*" Richard was done with negotiations. Done with deals.

If you saw him, he was in lethal danger. He has come to one of his story ends. Might be dead now . . . splintered, perhaps.

Richard could no longer bury the pain he felt and released it the only way he knew how to. He punched a display table and tossed its dagger onto the ground. "No! Take me there *now*. Take me to Balthos's Heretics!"

We cannot.

He'd heard enough. His failure to act had killed Brice, had killed Edel-iènne, had pushed Pier to run away without a trace. It wouldn't kill this man as well.

He searched the shop and found the zweihänder, his most precious creation. The double-handed sword was the largest piece he had ever worked on. Esperanza had helped him infuse it with her sweetest poison—batrachotoxin. She'd harvested the substance from Tribu La'am frogs. One tiny cut of the sword caused the opponent's muscle to contract irreversibly until the heart gave out. The laughing criminal from his vision had no heart, but the poison would find a way. Richard picked it up and headed to the shop door. There was no need to tell Esperanza. The orcs could handle her.

Vines shot from the ground and blocked the door. *Where are you going?*

"Get out of my way," Richard growled. *Let's stay calm and talk.* "I have stayed calm for too long." He was wasting precious time. He needed to be at the prison now. "If you're not taking me there, I will find him myself. You're a guest. You should remember that."

We're part of you. You're not alone anymore, dear Richard.

He roared and slashed down on the vines. The cluster yowled in rolling thunder, cut grass, and the suction of quicksand. The poison couldn't kill them, for they were already dead, but it hurt them. *Good,* Richard thought. The threat of loneliness had haunted him his whole life. He had taken Father Godfried's lessons to get away from it. He had married Edeliènne, had welcomed a demon into his body, and had destroyed his son's happiness, all to get away from that dreadful loneliness. Where had it gotten him? Alone, without his son, without real love of another, with no one who cared whether he breathed. *To limbo with loneliness.*

Some vines retracted back into his skin, others hung off him limply. He threw open the door to his smithy, ready to storm out, but stopped dead in his tracks. The traitor stood there, the destroyer of all. But it wasn't a traitorous celestial. It was an alleged servant of Balthos and Exitalis, the source of all goodness. Waldfeld's priest.

Father Godfried smiled at him. "Richard, we have a problem."

The priest's calm expression was a stark contrast to the surrounding mob. A dozen people had gathered behind him with torches, pitchforks, and a few proper weapons that looked like Richard had forged them himself. He recognized every one of them. They were the people of Waldfeld, the people Richard had tried all his life to impress. He spotted his brother, Reuben, and his sister, Elsie. They hadn't spoken to him since the incident but glared at him now.

"Told you the foreigners are coming for the demon child!" Isa pushed herself next to Father Godfried. Her eyes fixated on the vines hanging from Richard's torso. She'd drawn the stiletto knife he'd created two years ago. He'd given it to Vana right before her arrest. "Look at him, he's beyond grace, Father!"

Father Godfried's eyes wandered over Richard's body, and he nodded. "I thought I had saved your soul, my dear boy. It pains me to see it was lost all along."

"Get out of my way, moocher," Richard growled.

Isa raised the stiletto toward him. He had intended it to be the elegant weapon of a lady, but his intentions meant nothing. "How the fuck did you address our beloved father?"

You're not utilizing the thumb dent, Isa. He wanted to correct her but remained silent.

Father Godfried raised his hand and turned to Isa. "Don't upset yourself, dear. We must not mind the speech of the mad." He smiled wider at Richard. The wrinkles around his eyes looked like the lines of splintered wood. A veil of numbness swallowed Richard's boiling emotions at the familiar sight of the priest. He pushed back against it, clinging to the last bit of rage he'd mustered. He had broken the chains of serfdom ten years ago, but he'd never freed himself from Godfried.

"Step aside, my boy. I'll take you with me to church while they take care of the unholy offspring you sired with that Tribu sow."

His words broke through the numbness. Richard glanced at the threatening crowd. They weren't here for him. They were here for a newborn, a blessing of Exitalis, as Godfried had called Pier. Richard's grip around the zweihänder tightened. No matter whose child it was, no matter what Esperanza had done to him, this wasn't right.

Without the numbness, pictures of the Tribu La'am man came back to him, and a familiar pressure weighed on his chest. He saw the man bleeding out, forgotten on the ground of the dirty prison, but couldn't tell if it was his imagination or another vision. Hadn't the man offered him dinner all those years ago? Richard should have gone with him instead of choosing the forest. He couldn't picture what would have happened next. They wouldn't have ended up here. But Richard hadn't gone. It hadn't been decent. It hadn't been what Godfried wanted him to do.

"I'm your fucking puppet, aren't I?"

Father Godfried was so surprised he lost his infinite calm smile. "Pardon?"

"Did you know they were going to hang Brice?" Richard should have asked him twenty-seven years ago, should have defended himself when the world had turned against him. If Exitalis had shown him the Tribu La'am man, she couldn't resent Richard. If Godfried, the keeper of pious values, wanted to murder a baby, he couldn't be infallible. It was good Pier had escaped before Godfried could sink him too. Richard's eyes wandered over the crowd. They would have killed him back then. They'd kill him now. But he was no longer a helpless teenager. *Ready yourselves.*

A wind blew through his veins. The awakening of his cluster friend. *Richard, you hurt us.*

And you used me. Now ready yourselves. Richard focused on the energy in his pulsing veins and gathered as much into his consciousness as he could. Thorns itched under his skin. "Answer me, Godfried, or you'll regret it."

Isa dared to attack him with his own creation. Before the sharp tip touched his skin, thick vines shot out of his throat and wrapped around Isa's neck. He lifted her into the air and pictured thorns growing out of the vine. Blood dripped from the piercing wounds onto her hands as she struggled to free herself. He kept one eyeball on her and allowed his other one to blossom out of the socket and float toward the crowd. The younger ones screamed. The rest of the mob attacked. Richard stretched out his arm and opened his palm toward them. It widened into a flytrap. He shot hundreds of gympie-gympie hairs at the mob. Choravdat had told him that a single touch of the gympie-gympie leaf's hairs caused pain excruciating enough to madden horses. Sounds of anguish ripped the early night apart.

Our dear friend, you're going to kill the girl.

"I don't care anymore," he said through gritted teeth. Isa gargled as a thorn grew closer to her windpipe.

Father Godfried pulled out his necklace with Exitalis's sign. His hands shook, and his face had turned white. "I-I exorcize this demon out of you."

Richard directed his eye petal away from the crowd and toward Godfried. "You don't look so calm anymore, Father."

"I only wanted to help you."

The crowd's anguish echoed within Richard and fused with his rage. His chest felt like ripping apart. He roared and blasted the pain out. Flesh ripped. A spine crumbled. Godfried shrieked as her head fell in front of him. Isa was dead.

Richard trembled but refused to think about what had happened. His way of thinking had destroyed everything he loved. "Tell me, Godfried, or I swear to Exitalis your head rolls next. Did you know they were going to hang Brice?"

Godfried shook with fear, like Richard once had, but the priest's fate was in his hands now. "Richard, please, if you're in there——"

"I am. Now speak," he growled.

Godfried gulped. "Back . . . back when you were young, the world was becoming pure again. Exitalis's word was restored."

"Leave the gods out of this." Richard shot another hail of hairs at the crowd. The people who had tried to rise sank back to the ground. Richard wasn't sure if the gympie-gympie could kill them. He wasn't sure if he cared either.

Godfried nodded. "I-I will try. But see, the rotten Verdain princess and her damned general were exiled for their sins. The horrors of the Crown War had passed, faith in our good ways was restored——"

"Brice. Tell me about him."

"Right . . . I still hoped to keep Waldfeld decent. Our

community didn't include the vermin. You remember how pure and good everything was, don't you?"

Another wave of pain tore through Richard's chest. He steadied his breathing to deal with the pain. It was true. Waldfeld had been different back then. No Stag's Tail. Barely any foreigners. No music or talk of revolution. Everything in his life had been set. Richard and his siblings had been Belladonna property, raised to expand the fields of Waldfeld. His mother had thought he'd marry Dotty after he had spent countless evenings at the Ackermans'. It had been idyllic back then—an idyllic way to die without the risk of living.

Richard had almost risked living. A year before the incident, he'd seen a traveling fair in Nimmerwarm with a stall that sold beautiful woodwork. The carpenter was headed to Tribu La'am next and had offered Richard an apprenticeship. He had wanted to go, but Brice had feared the change. He'd been sure Belladonna guards would track Richard down, and he hadn't wanted them to lose their families. He had teased Richard about being greedy, always wanting more than he could have, but had kissed him nonetheless. Richard had stayed. He had lost his family anyway. Brice had lost more.

"They were in your parish. Did you know they were going after him?"

"Richard, I wanted to help."

"Tell me!" The flytrap that once was his palm snapped at Godfried, who jumped back.

"Your father paid the motus to save you, but the Ackermans didn't—"

"Pay." Richard's eye lost its blossoms and snapped back into his sockets. The vines grew limp, and Isa's beheaded body crashed to the ground. The flytrap shrunk until it was the size of his palm. "This was about motus." The words sounded as hollow as he felt. "The Ackermans didn't have the motus, so you riled up a group of men to . . . to . . ." Richard choked up again and didn't fight it. Tears rolled into his ginger beard. "Brice died because of it . . . you ruined my life for it . . ."

"My son." Godfried took Richard's flytrap hand. The other one still held the zweihänder. "I did Balthos's work." Richard sniffed as Godfried stepped closer. The priest's old smile emerged among the bloodbath that surrounded them. "I made you *decent*."

He wanted to believe him—believe that it had all mattered, that Brice had died because of a dire illness, that he had repented for the love of Balthos. But the truth revealed one crime he couldn't deny. "They would have killed Pier if I hadn't paid you."

Godfried opened his mouth and closed it again. He didn't have an answer to that, couldn't come up with a lie that would make it okay. Richard nodded. *Please return to the inside.*

Our dear Richard . . . what have we done? What have we become?

Shh . . . The vines and thorns retracted back into Richard's skin until he looked like any other Waldfeld man—broken, with his hand in Godfried's palm. He looked at the dozen people on the ground. Some were injured, some motionless. Others were getting back on their feet. Neighbors peered out of their windows. The noise had caught the attention of anyone nearby. Torchlight flickered in the distance, moving toward him. More were coming for him. He might as well give them a good reason to.

"There we go, my boy." Godfried let go and put his hand on Richard's shoulder. The touch felt like nettle balm. He could almost smell the myrrh.

Richard's other hand found the zweihänder's strength. He lifted the weapon, forged from the forest that had once been their refuge, and halved Godfried from shoulder to hip. The blade touched the priest before realization could. An undeserved smile graced his face as he welcomed death. The man who controlled the minds of Waldfeld fell into himself.

"Am I decent now, Father?" Everything was over. The good and the bad. Richard's surroundings were hazy, distant, as if Choravdat had taken over, but they hadn't. They simmered quietly within him and left him to chaos. People around him screamed and shouted. He was numb to all of them until one messenger running down the road shook him up.

"The Belladonnas are under siege! Virisunder's attacking! Virisunder tusks sighted in our streets!" The messenger slowed down when he saw Richard and the chaos in front of him. "Father Godfried murdered! Murder at the Kilburn Smithy!"

Tusks. Kilburn. His mind caught up too slowly.

Run! a thunderstorm inside him called, pushing him backward into the shop. The Fae cluster slammed the door closed in the last second before the maddened mob could get him. The situation became clear to Richard when he found himself back in the shop. He had murdered Father Godfried. He had killed their priest. The Tribu La'am man in Balthos's Heretics. He had wanted to save him, but was it too late now? The baby. The mob was coming for the baby, and Choravdat, and him, and the tusks. No, the *orcs*.

He rushed upstairs, flung the door open, and startled. Esperanza had wrapped herself around Sachihiro's arm. Gon's hands held three horns that peeked out from between her legs. A shock of bright magenta hair shone through the blood.

"You don't belong here either," Richard muttered at the horns of the child. *His* child. The decision to claim it was as instant as it was final. A fresh start. His first child had saved him. He would save the second.

"Richard!" Sachihiro called.

"We need to go." *I need you to get us out of here, my friend. Our child . . . it's dying.*

No, it's not. Get us all to safety. He felt the pull of the beyond. All directions invited him to fall.

"What?" Sachihiro asked.

"Give me your hand."

The orc looked suspicious but took the hand Richard offered. *Now.* Richard released himself into the old passage of limbo and yanked the four along. Choravdat had warned him to avoid the damned place, but their mortal world had become a harsher threat. As he fell, Richard searched for the worn out parchment he'd seen, hoping to take the man with him. He found only darkness. Perhaps the man was no longer in danger. He refused to consider the second possibility.

They landed without touching the ground, hovering in the thin, rotten air that unnerved the spirit and numbed the body. Esperanza sobbed uncontrollably as the child tore its way out of her. "What is happening, Ivalace?"

Sachihiro lifted her into his arms. "Shh . . . I'm still here." He swayed her gently. Gon mumbled Tribu La'am prayers. Richard took his eyes off them and examined their surroundings instead. The place they had landed in was unlike the limbo he knew. The foul scent and milky darkness remained the same, but it wasn't empty. Rows of huts, if one could call them that, lined the spot Richard hovered on. They had been constructed from misshaped wooden planks, shipwrecks, cracked stones, and wild scrubs. Someone must have taken the discarded chaos of limbo and shaped it into a town.

Richard didn't get a chance to process the strange place before something more pressing caught his attention. A familiar blond woman ran toward them. A large chunk of her face was missing.

"Darling!" She reached him and swung her arms around his neck.

He patted her back in complete shock. "Edeliènne."

CHAPTER 39

ALLY

February 980 - Altor Caedem, Virisunder

A lly stirred as the pain of another lifetime woke her from a nightmare. Like last time, she had sunken into her pillow with the rousing butterflies of a new love until an intruder stirred her back up. But this child wasn't an intruder. It wasn't Josef's mark. It was a fresh start, rousing like the butterflies.

She gasped for air until the first contraction passed, then sat up. The bed was wide and emptier than she liked. Reggie had enlarged it with a surprisingly long-lasting illusion, but the pillow to her left hadn't been used yet. Robert must've been on evening patrol. Another contraction ran through her, and she cringed. *Breathe.* Ally had spoken to her grandma Theo about the best breathing methods once, but both of them had given birth such a long time ago, they barely remembered.

Mentioning her dad caused too much pain for her grandma, so Ally hadn't brought it up again. Now she wished she had.

Reggie was fast asleep to her right. She tried to wake him with a kiss but knew it was a hopeless endeavor. Her Reggie needed his beauty sleep to dream up fantastical show ideas. At least that was what she told herself. Without the charming story, her mind convinced her he was dead. She held her finger under his nose to check for breath, like she had done many times before, but another contraction reminded her of tonight's urgent priority.

"The little warrior is coming," she whispered, placed another kiss on his cheek, and scooted off the bed. Reggie had recovered enough to gift her a week free from voices, and Robert had promised to go no farther than the tower's lookout platform for his patrol, aware that the baby might arrive any day. He couldn't sleep alongside them for more than two hours. Insomnia that he poorly played off as excitement had plagued him for weeks. It would be beneficial this evening. As long as she managed to climb up the flight of stairs, he'd be with her and alert enough to help.

She was reaching for her night-robe when a wave of vertigo pushed her against the wall. *Breathe in. Breathe out.* That couldn't be the whole breathing exercise, but it was all she remembered. *Breathe in. Breathe out.* She recovered enough to put on her night-robe.

It was a short-lived victory, as her water broke seconds later and drenched her clothes. She sighed. The baby definitely possessed a talent for melodrama. Or perhaps Ally had absorbed Reggie's and Robert's discussions about dramatic storytelling and her body functioned accordingly now. Either way, she needed new clothes. If only Reggie were awake and could fix the mess with a snap of his fingers. She held her stomach as another contraction passed through and made her way to the closet. She reached for a fresh robe, but more water ran down her leg. Nothing would stay dry for long. *Fuck this*. This was Robert's first child. He wouldn't be occupied with Ally's looks.

The bedroom door creaked when she opened it. She glanced back, hoping the sound might stir Reggie, but he remained motionless as a corpse. *Don't think like that*. She closed the door, giving up on the hope that Reggie would be with her during the birth. The baby should have picked daytime for its arrival.

Ally struggled up the stairs. The pain intensified, and she felt the baby sink lower. Her warrior not only had poor timing but was also in an inconvenient hurry. She wasn't sure if she could make it to the top like this.

"Robert," she panted, not as calm as she had wanted to sound. She didn't want to freak him out. Reggie had been terrified during her first birth, and she couldn't picture Robert handling it any better. Then again, he was a sniper and a quick thinker in battle. He had trained to be calm in tense situations. Why had she not thought of that first? Perhaps she didn't know him as well as she thought. Perhaps they were rushing into this strange new relationship. Ally stopped halfway up and blinked. *Look at that, now I'm freaking myself out*. She shook her head. There was no time for this nonsense. He didn't hear her, so she pushed her way to the tower platform and collapsed against the archway. "Robert."

He had been leaning over the tower railing, watching the last glimmer of sunlight disappear into the night. Ally preferred to sleep in the evenings and wake at midnight when her mind was the sharpest. Robert startled when she called out for him and spun around. "Ally, what—"

His eyes widened when he saw what a drenched, panting mess she was. "By Caedem, it started."

Ally nodded faintly as he rushed over to her. He made a few bumbling arm gestures somewhere between hugging her and lifting her up. She chortled, but the smile turned into a grimace as the next pain wave hit.

He nodded frantically. "Oh limbo shit . . . okay, okay, it's coming." Ally's initial concerns about Robert's reaction might have been correct. She knew him after all. "Okay, it's coming. A baby."

"I hope so," Ally said with another smile.

"All right, ehm, just . . . just stay here. I'll get Makeda and Theodosia."

He tried to rush past her down the stairs, but she caught him by the scruff of his shirt. "We're giving birth on the platform?"

Robert stared at her unintelligently before shaking his head. "Right . . . sorry. Sorry, I should probably take you with me."

"Brilliant idea." A stronger pain hit, and vertigo followed. Ally sank to the ground, and the platform turned pearl white.

"What's happening?" Robert asked. She was trying to tell him it was a heavy bout of vertigo when the ground shook. *Oh no.* If it wasn't the vertigo, it must've been—

A figure materialized in the middle of the platform before she could finish the thought. Ally and Robert both turned their heads, and her love collapsed at the sight.

"Robert!" Ally screamed.

"Don't worry about him. He is not part of this." The figure flicked his finger, and the surrounding light evaporated. Ally could see him clearly now. Her eyes could, at least. Her mind couldn't fathom what she saw and attempted to turn it into a processable picture. He was a man, of sorts. Beautiful beyond anything she had ever seen. More beautiful than existence should allow. He was blue. Her mind stumbled over that last part. *Blue.* She squinted at the figure and noticed that he didn't have blue skin but was made of a shining crystal. The color reminded her of Reggie's eyes. She shivered at the thought. It couldn't be him. He was fast asleep in their bed. She paused. *Too fast asleep.*

"My sugar . . ." He stepped closer. Ally's brain failed to comprehend the details of his glistening form. His blue crystal body appeared to be solid but traveled through space like liquid. She didn't trust her perception of his face. He looked like a mortal man to her because it was an image her brain could process. Did his appearance disrupt the limitations of her own senses? Was it possible to see something one was unable to see? The more she thought about it, the more she saw Reggie in him.

"Sugar is what you like to be called, isn't it?" Ally sank lower. Another shiver shook her. She kicked Robert on the way down and panicked. *Robert.* What was happening? Was he alive? A long time ago, she had asked Reggie to call her sugar. It gave her a sense of family. Safety.

"Reggie?" she asked with a trembling voice.

"Balthos." There was an edge to his voice, an anger that made Ally's skin crawl. "It's time to come home, Alames."

Another contraction hit her, and she groaned in pain. Her warrior protested as much as her mind did. She reached for Robert and shook him, but he didn't move. "Robert? Robert!"

Balthos sighed. "If you're trying to make me jealous with a mortal, it's not working." The god snapped his fingers, and Robert's body floated into the air. Ally tried to protest, but before she could utter a sound, Balthos flicked his wrist and tossed Robert over the tower railing.

"*No!*" Her scream could not save him from falling to his death. Pain flooded her mind and all reason. Robert had been unconscious. He hadn't even seen it coming. He hadn't faced death like the brave soldier he'd been. He'd just . . . *fallen.* She screamed. It was the only thing that felt right.

"Shh, my sugar. Don't upset yourself over one mortal soul." Balthos was a few steps away from her. The closer he got, the less Ally understood what he looked like. He stretched his hand down to her. "So many more fell when they turned you into the Traitor, but I knew my Alames wouldn't remain a splintered monster forever. I had faith, if you will. Come now, home is waiting."

She shied away from his hand until the ground gave way

to stairs. She tumbled backward against a wall of white light. Balthos beckoned the light closer until she could no longer get away. More pain rattled her. She wasn't sure if it came from her bleeding heart or if the warrior was eager to claim life. A widening between her legs confirmed the latter, and she panicked. She couldn't have the baby. Not here. Not like this. They would take it away from her again.

"I'm not Alames," she sobbed. The voice of Balthos had made this claim two months ago, but no matter how hard she'd tried, she couldn't process it. It couldn't be true.

"You don't remember," he said. She flinched as he reached for her forehead. "Don't be scared. Our war is over, sugar." *Reggie.* He couldn't be. It couldn't be him. He wouldn't harm Robert. He wouldn't hurt her like this. *But he did hurt me.* Memories of their first meeting came to her. She had visited him in her palace dungeon. He had dangled there, helpless, or so it had seemed. She had planned to hang him for slandering her as Princess Lunatic and the many other titles he had invented in his plays and songs. He had riled up the commoners of Virisunder against her, had hurt her in any way possible that hadn't involved violence.

She had gone to the dungeon to understand. She'd had nothing more to live for, and still he'd wrecked her. Why bother destroying a teenage princess when her mind did so on its own? The first time Reggie saw her, shock had painted his face. For years he had claimed that she stole his heart the moment she took off her hood and allowed the light of her lantern to illuminate her face. It was almost as if he had recognized her that day.

"I remember," Ally muttered, overwhelmed with questions too large for one mind to hold.

"I'm glad, sugar." He dared to smile at her.

"Your magic . . . your illusions . . ."

He laughed. "Illusions don't exist, sugar." He took her hand. "Can we please go home now? We will talk more. I'm not sure what mortal ailment plagues you, but we will cure you of it."

She felt the contraction when he said the words "mortal ailment." Her hand darted to her stomach. The little warrior wasn't an ailment. Where was home? "My baby."

Balthos grimaced. "Demigods . . . they're not a good idea. Caedem, that imbecile, tried it once. It is too messy of an endeavor."

Pain shook her harder. She felt a tear between her legs and noticed blood drip into her wet robe. "I'm. Not. Going. Anywhere without it," she panted. "You said you wanted it too!" she screamed when enough breath had traveled into her struggling lungs. Robert. The baby. He had ripped it all away from her.

Balthos jerked backward. "Fine, we'll keep it." He paused and frowned. "Although . . . there's nothing to keep, sugar. I don't hear a heartbeat."

No heartbeat. No heartbeat. Ally expected to faint. Or maybe she longed to. Nothing made sense anymore. Nothing made sense. When she thought it couldn't be worse, the dam that had held the voices broke.

It's dead. Ripped from you before you could ruin it.
Murderer. Murderer.
She didn't kill it. She's just too rotten
to keep anything alive.
She wanted it dead. She murdered it
before it could defend itself.
Like you murdered Robert.
Like you murdered Robert.
We told you not to trust Reginald.
We said you wouldn't exist with him.

"Alames, you're coming with me. Don't make me use force. I know the centuries in limbo must have been hard. We'll fix it. We'll start a new world. One to your liking." He touched her chest as the voices devoured her. She could no longer fight him, no longer argue. His hand stroked lower until it reached the bottom of her rib cage. His touch caused an eruption of euphoric ecstasy so all-consuming it must've been death. It snuffed out the pain and cleansed her mind and heart of anything that wasn't him. Ally longed to surrender to it forever, let it swallow her. She no longer cared.

I'm sorry, this is gonna suck real bad.

The loving voice of a woman pierced through the perfection of Ally's state. She hated it immediately.

"Wait . . ." Balthos's voice followed next, and he withdrew. The ecstasy drained out of her like a vortex. "You're not . . ."

Ally wanted to tell him she could be anything he needed her to be, but the female voice spoke again.

Take a deep breath for me.

Ally refused and held her breath, hoping to contain the last drips of euphoria. She blinked through the white light. The tower platform became visible again. As soon as she recognized it, darkness swallowed all sight.

She fell.

She fell in all four directions.

CHAPTER 40

SACHIHIRO

Outside of Mortal Time — Limbo

When they were children, Gon used to ask Sachihiro for detailed accounts of his dreams. Every morning, his sibling sat by his bedside with a quill and parchment, eager to decipher what messages the ancestors might have sent their big brother. To keep up, Sachihiro started waking up an hour earlier than Gon and collected beautiful words from any book he could find to weave a dream narrative. His actual dreams overwhelmed him. Taking in more than three images at once was too much because he couldn't form words fast enough to process them.

The place Sachihiro found himself in now was a construct of a hundred dreams. Every sensation, every flash of color, every illogical image overwhelmed him further. He tried to take a deep breath, but not even his lungs followed their common function. Air reached him without traveling through him, or at least he couldn't feel it. The warm essence of former love ran down his arms. Esperanza bled out. She panted. He comforted her, not knowing if his voice belonged to him or the dream. Next to her was Gon. They had taken one crutch with them into the dream. They held a knife, an image Sachihiro wasn't sure what to make of. Behind them was the smith and a woman, or parts of a woman. Most parts. All parts but her left eye, eyebrow, cheekbone, and ear. Richard had called her Edeliènne.

Sachihiro's head throbbed when he tried to process the dream landscape beyond the familiar figures and the incomplete woman. A town, his eyes argued, but he disagreed. A town was defined as a settled area, and this place was the most unsettling phenomenon he'd ever seen. Its huts defied all knowledge of construction. His gaze caught on two walls of smudged archway windows that could belong to a forgotten palace. They were attached to five wooden carriage doors that made up the hut's other two walls. Six old-fashioned Virisunder hoopskirts filled with banana leaves created a roof. *That's not how you build houses.* The alleged town looked like the fever dream of a mad jester. Or perhaps it was Sachihiro's fever dream. Perhaps he shared Esperanza's physical pain while he processed what she had done.

"It's suffocating," Gon said.

"No! No, please!" Esperanza screamed.

Richard let go of Edeliènne and turned to them. "Save my child, Doctor."

This wasn't a dream, no matter how nightmarish it seemed. The realization overwhelmed Sachihiro. He recognized every detail: Esperanza's desperate look as he held her in his arms. The sweat that pearled off Gon's forehead. The sudden signs of life in the smith's face. The gathering of incompletes behind Edeliènne. And finally, the bright magenta curls in Gon's hand and the shining knife in their other. The blade reflected Sachihiro's face. The lost tribal boy he'd once been stared at him, but he was the assistant of the great *General* Subira Se'azana now, and that man didn't freeze up.

"Gon, deliver the child," Sachihiro ordered. His head throbbed harder when he noticed sharp spikes peeking through Richard's tattered clothes. *Demon. Fae. Faemani.* Whatever was fighting for life from Esperanza's womb could be declared a blessing or curse after it had taken its first breath. "Mother thought you were cursed too, Gon, but Dad insisted on saving you. We need to give this baby the same chance."

Richard opened his mouth as if to support the point, but Edeliènne interrupted. "Your child? Are you not dead?"

Sachihiro focused on Gon instead. His sibling hesitated, then nodded. "Okay, but only because we're family, Esperanza."

She shook harder when they called her family, buried her distorted face in Sachihiro's chest, and hid under the curtain of her limp curls. The curtains of his fertility dance had shielded Sachihiro from the prying eyes of his tribe, but they had offered no absolution from the shame and displacement he'd felt. Her note and the faint memory of a life they'd once lived had brought solace.

"Let me take you to my hut." Edeliènne tugged on Sachihiro's sleeve. "We can lay her on my bed."

Gon shook their head. "No time. Esperanza? You know you won't make it if—"

Esperanza emerged from Sachihiro's chest. "Go ahead. They lied to us, but it's worth it. It'll all be worth it."

"Stand back," Gon said to Edeliènne and Richard. They looked like their father back when he'd introduced surgical procedures to Juyub'Chaj. Gon had been too young to remember, but Sachihiro did. Nothing could go wrong as long as his father's calm certainty had filled the air. "Distract her, Sachi."

Sachihiro covered Esperanza's face with his hand and pressed her gently back into his chest when the blade hit flesh. He hoped his moss-green palm would remind her of forest protection instead of tribal curtains. The screams that followed echoed painfully in his chest. She'd have to endure one last torturous act. No matter what she had done, she didn't deserve this. Sachihiro pulled her closer until he smelled her familiar scent through the foul, sick stench of blood. Flowers should've accompanied it. Flowers had always accompanied her scent.

"Sweet vine?" His quiet voice barely made it through her sobs, but he didn't want Richard to overhear him. "I am very angry with you right now."

"I know," she pressed out.

"But our lives are cursed with mortality, aren't they? So we're walking around with decaying brains. Mine feels like that constantly." She rubbed her cheek against his palm. More liquid dripped down her side, but Sachihiro banished the sound from his mind. All sounds. He only granted her scent to matter, for it kept him talking. "I'm sorry your brain failed you."

She chortled between sobs. "Is that an 'I love you'?"

"That's an 'I will forgive you.'"

She kissed his palm and grew heavy. "I look forward to it on my daffodil walk . . ."

Before he understood the weight in his arm, four things happened. A gong created a sense of union among the random shambles of this strange dream place. A dark cloud formed above the town, pulsing with the energy that had caught Sachihiro when he had tumbled into his volcanic death. A baby opened her swollen eyes and cried for the loss of her mother. An invisible woman spoke with a voice that sharpened the haze and eased the knots in Sachihiro's body.

"My beloved spirit buddies, please seek shelter, not just in one another's arms, but in the nooks and crannies we call home. We are awaiting a celestial refugee, and I am afraid the presence of untainted light might attract some of our least favorite friends. Knights of the Rose, ready yourselves for intruders."

A gigantic orc yelled at the cloud, "Alames! Alames, we can't protect a celestial! We can barely keep the Ouisà Kacocs away as it is. Alames, where have you gone?"

White light crackled in the dark cloud. "Trust me."

The cloud disappeared, and the crying baby reclaimed her moment.

"Say hello to your little girl, Esperanza." Gon smiled, focusing on the miracle in their arms as if the surrounding nightmare didn't matter. Sachihiro blinked at his sibling and the infant. Esperanza's last efforts had smeared its face with blood and things he refused to put words to.

"She's asleep," he muttered. The words would make it true. They had to. Well-picked words wouldn't lie to him.

"Our goddess told us to hide. We should follow," Edeliènne said with a voice as hollow as Sachihiro felt. Gon's face dropped when they saw the sleeping Esperanza. His sibling hadn't expected her to fall asleep that quickly, but his sweet vine had always been full of surprises. They cut the lifeline between mother and child. The baby protested harder.

Richard gave his zweihänder sword to the disturbed Edeliènne and stretched his hands out, strangely detached from the somber moment. There was joy in his eyes. Excitement. What displaced emotions. He looked like Pier before holding a public speech. It shouldn't have brought him joy, but it did. "Can I hold her?"

Gon nodded. "Of course. I can't clean her though." They handed the child over to Richard. Sachihiro noticed the shocked expression on Edeliènne's face as she examined the infant but couldn't bring himself to process its appearance yet. Esperanza was asleep in his arms. That was all he wanted to know for now.

"Let . . . let us go," Edeliènne said, then led them into the chaos that pretended to be a town. At least three dozen people ran across the main road of smoky air. If the landscape possessed a firm ground, Sachihiro couldn't define it. Each step felt like a brief fall that ended without his foot finding resistance. The people who scurried into their strange huts were even more diverse than Mink'Ayllu's population, but the missing pieces of their bodies made them look alike. Some were dressed as knights of an old order, wearing plate armor that had gone out of use centuries ago. A rose graced their tarnished breastplates. Sachihiro had read that black roses were the Traitor's sign, but these flowers were alive, blue and blossoming.

"This place is peculiar, isn't it, sweet vine?" Sachihiro nudged Esperanza. Her head flopped to the side. *That means yes.* It was a gesture. Nonverbal communication. Not a loss of body control.

"Dear, I don't think she made—" Edeliènne started.

"Leave him for now, please," Gon said. She nodded and continued walking until they reached a hut with a large cohesive structure. It was a small merchant ship turned upside down with a door carved into the front. As strange as it was, it followed a logic the neighboring homes didn't. Sachihiro had to crouch to get through the door but could stand in the ship with a slight hunch. The inside was laid out with ripped blanket strips sewn together into an eerie quilt. It felt like walking on hammocks, but the existence of a floor and the wooden ship walls grounded him in a reality he understood.

Edel: ènne led them to three haystacks with another quilt strapped over her. "You can lay her down on my cot." Sachihiro nodded but made no moves to let go of Esperanza. The bed didn't look comfortable. She needed comfort. They all needed comfort.

"Little one's beautiful," Richard whispered next to him. "Do you have something to clean her up?"

Edel iènne rushed off into the ship-hut's second room. Richard swayed the infant in his arm, and it stopped crying. Sachihiro swayed Esperanza as well. Nothing happened.

"Sachi?" Gon put a hand on his shoulder. They leaned against the ship wall, physically exhausted but as calm as they'd seemed in the open. "I don't condone it, but I learned a Faemani resting prayer in my Soul Passage class. Why don't we lay her on the bed and guide her to peace?" Their hand wandered to the arm Sachihiro held her with and pushed it down with gentle force. He followed the push and laid Esperanza on the uncomfortable cot. Gon propped themself on the haystack, carefully sank to their knees, and circled a hand over Esperanza's face, performing tribal forest signs and speaking beautiful Faemani words. They pronounced them wrong, but Sachihiro didn't protest. The prayer guided him to peace as well. With each word of the Fae language, the body in front of him became less asleep and more . . . *paramicha*. A story once told, as the Fae said.

A tear rolled over Sachihiro's cheek. He brushed it off and mumbled, "Paramicha Esperanza." She had left him again. He hoped she'd find peace this time.

The scream of a man sounded from the road. Sachihiro peered through the bullseye above the cot and saw an elvish man with brown hair, a pistol, and a rifle on his back drop out of the dark cloud and tumble onto the street. He jumped up in a frenzy, yelling, "Ally! Ally!"

"Nothing to worry about. Souls are often confused when they first arrive," Edeliènne said behind him. Sachihiro startled, as he hadn't noticed her return. She handed Richard a linen shawl, and the smith wrapped the infant in it. Sachihiro's eyes widened when he took in Esperanza's daughter for the first time. She was neither human nor orcish and yet looked like the perfect child of sweet vine and him. The little girl had skin the color of pale spring clovers, and dark ivory tusks grew not from her jaw but her head. They were horns, he recognized. Three of them. Two curved toward each other while the third was longer and grew straight in their middle. Bright magenta curls surrounded them. A tail that looked like a thorny vine sprouted from her lower back.

"She's a miracle," Sachihiro muttered.

Gon struggled their way back to standing. "No, Sachi,

she's . . . she might be dangerous." They held Sachihiro back and addressed Edelienne. "What do you mean souls arriving?"

She forced her eyes off the child and looked at them instead. "Right, yes. Our dear goddess Alames assembles as many splintered souls as she can find."

"Demons," Gon muttered.

Edelienne paled. "No . . . the demons of limbo are lost. No one can save them from the Ouisà Kacocs. Our goddess finds the splinters of one single soul and ties them back together. Demons form on their own, shape themselves from conflicting splinters of many souls that were never meant to fuse. I got lucky. Alames has lost her grip on limbo in the past forty years. I'm one of the last souls she assembled." She peeked out of the bullseye herself. "I can't believe she spoke to us. It has been an eternity since I've heard her voice."

Richard cradled the baby closer. "Alames no longer exists. This is the Traitor's realm."

Edelienne walked over to him and kissed his cheek. "There are things only the dead understand, Rich." She looked at Sachihiro and Gon. "So how did you get here if you're not dead?"

That was a great question, almost as good as asking how they could leave this place. General Subira Se'azana awaited them. So did Zazil. Sachihiro's eyes wandered over his wilting sweet vine. Whatever happened, he needed to bring his sibling back to their wife and make sure Esperanza's miracle made it out of here.

The smith's face twitched. The hairs on his forearm rose and vibrated. He closed his eyes, breathing heavily. "No, you're not touching her."

Edelienne frowned. "I'm sorry, Rich?"

"She's under *my* protection. You're not using her as an experiment," he growled. Edelienne exchanged looks with Gon and Sachihiro. If Richard didn't want Edelienne to hold the girl, he wasn't using his words wisely. The smith's face twitched again, and green bruises bulged around his neck.

He gasped and pressed the girl into Sachihiro's unprepared hands. "Keep her safe," he groaned before sinking to the ground, holding his neck with both hands.

"Rich!" Edeliènne crouched next to him.

The baby flung her arms wildly and cried until Sachihiro rubbed his thumb over her forehead in slow circles like his father used to do for Gon. The girl's cry stifled with a hiccup. She batted her magenta eyelashes at Sachihiro, and his heart melted.

"I know, this is quite the tumultuous arrival. But Sachi's here," he whispered. She hiccupped again. A tiny butterfly left her lips and flew into the other room. Sachihiro's mouth fell open. He and Esperanza had searched for a portal to the Fae realm, something that could open the gate to another world. She and Gon were right. This girl was Fae wrapped in a humanesque body. Esperanza hadn't been able to find the bridge, so she'd created one instead.

"Make her open it." Richard's guttural roar sounded unlike the smith's normal voice. He trembled on all fours like a hurt animal. The next words he spoke were in Faemani. "Open it so we can go home."

Edeliènne shrieked and let go of him. Sachihiro didn't think Richard spoke the language, but it didn't increase his trust. He pulled the girl against his chest and shielded her from the smith's beastly glare with his large palm. Esperanza had studied the Fae realm her whole life. As magical as this little girl was, Sachihiro couldn't picture her opening a portal large enough for a human within the hour of her birth. The butterfly alone was a magnificent accomplishment.

Gon made a throaty noise that turned into a melody. High priestesses sung it to ward off evil spirits. Richard didn't react to it, but it must have worked, for seconds later a white light shone through the bullseye and overwhelmed Sachihiro. When he closed his eyes, the light tickled his eyelids and filled his chest with a pulsing longing, an urge as beastly as Richard's stare had been. Images of battlefields and bloodshed crossed his mind. Of triumph, admiration, and the pleasurable release of rage. Darkness snapped him back to sanity.

"Caedem," Edelìenne groaned. Sachihiro squinted into the dark hut with a racing heart. He'd never felt such rage, never found such pleasure in it. Caedem was the Elfentum god of warfare and strength. What was this place?

Richard propped himself off the ground and gestured a religious sign. The bruises on his neck had disappeared.

"The Elfentum god?" Gon asked. Even they couldn't maintain calmness any longer.

Edelìenne nodded, looking as if she might faint. Gon supported her with one arm while keeping their other arm on the crutch. Sachihiro tried to catch up. The little girl looked as flabbergasted as he felt.

"I-I don't know as much as the knights," Edelìenne said, "but Alames taught us that the gods messed with mortal minds, made us crave destruction and submittal to their will. Our ancestors—our true ancestors—were free before the Celestial War."

"The Traitor said that?" Richard asked between heavy breaths.

"No, there is no traitor. Everything we learned in church is wrong, Rich. I know it's a lot, but . . ." She checked the bullseye again, shaking. "The treaty saved us from the gods. They do not care about our lives, Rich. They do not care about life at all. If the treaty is broken . . . if the gods are coming for us again . . . we're all lost. Alive or splintered, it won't matter."

"But there are ancestors here to protect you?" Gon asked.

"A few." Edelìenne bit her lip and stretched her neck to get a better view of the road. Her eyes widened when she spotted something. Sachihiro pushed his head next to hers to see as well. A woman had appeared in the road. She had long white hair and pale skin but looked like a regular elf. She held her large belly and panted the way Esperanza had.

"There's another woman in labor. Gon, we need to get out there," Sachihiro said. He was halfway to the door when he remembered the girl under his care. Had the intruders arrived yet? He couldn't risk putting her in danger.

Richard pushed past him. "I'll bring her inside. The doctor can take care of her."

Sachihiro opened the door for him. Richard hurried toward the woman. The dark cloud was forming around her now. It shaped itself into a hand that brushed the tears off the woman's cheek. Richard had almost reached her when they arrived. The monsters. The most horrid defiance of reality yet.

Nine figures emerged from red steam and charged at the woman and any dead person near her. Three of them had gaping flesh wounds with flickering red glimmers as eyes and skin filled with pus. Purple veins ran down their limbs and necks, and sharp fangs pierced out of their skin, surrounding their mouths. Two others looked like giant flesh-colored worms that twisted around themselves as they glided forward. Hairy tongues stuck out of clefts in their middle. Yellow eyes sat on top of the tongue. Another two possessed no face at all. Instead, their tawny skin was covered in toxic-looking rods and ashen arms. They all doubled Sachihiro in height.

The sight of the remaining two caused bile to shoot up his throat. The largest of them all charged into the middle with a demonic creature on a leash. The pet most closely resembled a bird, but Sachihiro's brain was desperate for any association. Its body looked like a crystallized tar pit. Bloodshot eyeballs covered it with feathers for eyelashes that blinked with each leap it took.

Its owner, the nauseating figure, was triple the size of Sachihiro and consisted of a twirling fire core with two muscle clusters throbbing inside of it. The core was attached to a dozen corpses, some fully sewn onto it, some cut in half to improve the core's mobility. The bodies were orcs, elves, and humans. One of them shifted between different animal shapes, likely a Fae. The demon walked on two human necks that crunched with each step. One charred arm stuck out above the core. Its insides were filled with more muscle clumps and ripped pieces of skin.

The woman screamed, and the cloud that had surrounded her shot toward the demons. The armored knights followed and attacked the monsters with a battle roar that feigned a bravery they couldn't possibly possess. Sachihiro was glad he'd neither pissed himself nor vomited. The cloud built a wall between the town and monsters, but white sparks flew from it as the demons fought harder. The remaining civilians ran away from the crumbling defense, except for one man who ran toward them. Sachihiro recognized him as the man who had fallen from the sky.

The woman sobbed when she spotted him. *"Robert!"*

Before Richard could reach her, vines grew out of his side and shot toward Sachihiro, who jumped backward, trying to protect the baby in his arms. The vines avoided him and gripped the hut's doorframe instead.

"No, wait!" Richard yelled, but the vines didn't listen. They yanked him back into the hut, away from the woman and any help he could have provided. The largest, most monstrous demon broke through the wall with its pet. It stopped its charge at the woman and turned to the hut instead. Fifteen pairs of corpse eyes focused on the doorway.

"Richard Kilburn, thief of my Fae." Its voice sounded like the cracking of glass splinters, the mockery of people, and the gushing of blood that had left Esperanza's body.

The vines slammed the door shut before the monster could utter another word. Edeliènne and Gon had made their way to the entrance and gaped at Richard. Sachihiro frowned, putting his thoughts together. "You stole a Fae demon from a . . . a . . ."

"Ouisà Kacoc," Richard finished for him. The smith's face had lost its color. His freckles stood out harshly against the gray skin. He closed his eyes. "We have to end this, my friend." A terrible growl resounded from the outside. The ship planks around them shook and creaked. "Edeliènne, where's my sword?"

"No, darling, you can't go out there. That thing has a soulcreeper. The knights will handle it."

Richard pushed past her and found the zweihänder on a nearby stone table. The walls trembled harder. Sachihiro wondered if he should take off his armor and use it to shield the child. Richard leaned over her and placed a kiss on the infant's forehead. "You deserve peace," he whispered, smiling at her for a second before turning back to Edeliènne.

"Rich, you can't—"

"Edeliènne, darling." He clasped her shoulder. "Forgive me for my inaction. I should have fed you. I should have helped you with your addiction."

"Richard, I wasn't a—"

"It doesn't matter now." He squeezed her forearm and turned to the door.

Fear overcame Sachihiro at the thought of getting near the monster that lurked outside, but General Subira Se'azana wouldn't let a fellow soldier face doom alone. "Is there anything we can do?"

"Keep my little girl safe," Richard said, then adjusted the grip on his zweihänder and rushed out the door.

"Stay away from the soulcre—" Edeliènne called, but the door closed in front of her.

The trembling stopped, and silence replaced the growling. The only noise still audible was the muffled sound of battle.

"What now?" Sachihiro asked.

"Now we wait," Gon said, then put a hand on Sachihiro's shoulder. "Wait and pray for the ancestors' victory. Pray for Alames's victory."

CHAPTER 41

ROBERT

Outside of Mortal Time – Limbo

He had drowned again. Drowned in all four directions. Sunk into a darkness none of his books had prepared him for. But like last time, the brilliant light of his love flooded him until he drowned in her instead.

"*Robert!*" she sobbed. He had searched for her as the town became as mad as it looked. There she was, at the spot he'd sunken into, shining her light and needing him. He ran toward her like the gruesome enemies on the other side of the road. Robert didn't dare to look at them for long. He wanted to keep a clear mind. Unless he needed a shooting target, their appearance didn't matter. Only Ally's did. She sat on the nonexistent ground in her drenched robe, clasping her belly with his child that was so eager to see the world.

A snap of green broke his focus, and he saw thick vines pulling a human man, who looked more alive than the rest of the lot, backward into an upside-down boat. Robert's hand found the pistol in his holster, ready to shoot the vines, but they didn't attack Ally. He kept running. Ally gaped at a tall enemy, no farther away than twenty steps, who roared at the vines. There was another enemy on its leash, half-animal, half-monster. Robert made the mistake to look and stumbled when its countless feathered eyes blinked at him.

He sped up and crouched beside Ally before the thing could reach her. "I got you." He lifted her and his unborn child into the air, cradling them.

She swung her arms around his neck and sobbed harder. "You're alive."

He kissed her neck and pressed her close. "Let's keep it that way."

He spun, eager to find a safe hiding place for his love and queen, as a gruesome voice twisted his insides. It sounded like the ripping of pages, the dull thump of hitting stone, and the last gasp for breath his mother took.

"Richard Kilburn, thief of my Fae." Robert looked up at the monster that had spoken. The world spun at its sight. If the man on top of Altor Caedem's tower had been beautiful beyond comprehension, this creature was the opposite. An accumulation of carcasses throbbed around a fiery muscle cluster core.

"Ouisà Kacocs," Ally whispered. "Evil demons."

Her voice snapped Robert back into the moment. He glanced down before he could process the other monsters. One at a time was enough to deal with. "Got it. Let's get the fuck away from them." He turned and ran.

"It's coming!" Ally screamed in his arms. "I can't hold it in any longer."

"Shit, shit, shit." Robert scoured the area for a hiding spot. About a dozen armored soldiers brushed past him with drawn swords and archaic spears.

"In there, lad!" one soldier yelled, pointing at a stone building made of large limestone and what looked like the contents of a riverbed. Robert noticed a piece of leather strapped above the door with a potion painted on it. *Infirmary.* He rushed toward it.

They had almost reached it when the tormenting voice of the Ouisà Kacoc spoke again. "Kilburn is mine. The rest of you, destroy the god seed and the man carrying her."

Robert was forced to look now. Seven demons stared back at him, their appearances more horrifying than any monster he'd ever read about. A wormlike miscreation screeched and charged at them. A soldier jumped in its way, but the worm rolled over him without slowing down. Two other Ouisà Kacocs with pus-filled skin and wounds for eyes howled and closed the distance. They were quicker than the worm. Robert pulled his pistol and fired a shot at the eye closest to him. Its outcry became angrier, and it reached for them. Robert jumped back, but the tip of its claw caught in Ally's hair.

Robert aimed at the hand. Before he could fire, the dark cloud that had saved him wrapped around the demon's torso and tossed it backward.

Please run, the cloud said in the voice of a woman that warmed his heart. She sounded familiar. Robert ran to the infirmary. He was five steps away when the hairy tongue of the worm curled around his neck and tossed him to the ground. Ally slipped out of his arms and fell with a grunt that turned into a panted scream. Robert rolled around in time to see the worm strike out at Ally. His hands shook around the pistol. There was no time for breathing. No time for technique. Robert Oakley never missed a shot, and he'd better not start now. He aimed at the mouth cleft and pulled the trigger before he could make the conscious decision to. Worm flesh sprayed backward. A terrible shriek followed. It convulsed and shrunk into itself.

Robert turned to his love, whose hands pulled at something between her legs. He could smell her sweet blood. Too much of it. "Are you—"

"Robert!" she screamed, but it was too late. The worm

had regained strength and leaped onto him. It buried him in pulsing flesh that sent shocks through his skin. Everything around him became the worm. No glimpse of limbo made it through the demon's all-encompassing body. Robert couldn't breathe under its weight. Sores formed on his limbs and neck, anything his uniform didn't cover. Above his face, the demonic worm's tongue left its cleft and pushed down on Robert's throat. He couldn't move his arms, couldn't feel his pistol nearby. The sores deepened until he smelled the first drops of his own blood. Worry required breath he no longer had. He pushed against the force one last time, but it was in vain. He hadn't saved himself in the river, hadn't saved himself on the tower, and couldn't save himself now. The sores spread to his chest and tore into his hurting heart. His muscles grew limp, and he did what no Oakley should do—give up.

We're not giving up, my man. Real bad timing. The woman's voice rang through his heart and patched up the sores. The pressure on his throat eased enough for him to breathe. Ally remained hidden behind the wall of worm flesh, but the dark cloud ripped the cleft's hairy tongue into shreds, which rained down on Robert. *I. Hate. This. So much,* the voice cursed while doing so.

The worm's skin became translucent and revealed tattered parchment pieces bound with thick burgundy sap.

Here I am, hanging out with my limbo buddies, and you spooky weirdo-nians have to ruin it for us. Two cloud hands formed and ripped the parchment pieces apart. The worm shrieked and began to split. It struck out once more with such force Robert was sure it would crush him. The cloud squeezed in front of Robert's face and kept the monster's body two fingers away from his nose.

Let's leave Mister Baby Daddy alone, all right? The woman's voice rang in his mind. He couldn't tell if she was speaking to the Ouisà Kacoc or performing for him to keep him sane.

Performing. She performed. *My man.* She had called him that. She wasn't the first person to call him that.

The worm split in half, screeching in pain.

I know, I know. Splintering sucks, my dear. Flesh flapped down on both sides of Robert, keeping him trapped in the monster. The sky should have cleared, but the cloud hovered above him. He saw the vague outline of someone he knew in it.

"Reggie," he whispered.

The cloud figure brought the shape of a flowing hand to her face.

Shh. She dove onto Robert. The flesh and monsters around him disappeared. He became part of the cloud, hovering in something greater than his mind could grasp. An ecstatic peace replaced all aches. Awe surged through him. A single truth followed and stole the power of any pain the future might hold. He was loved.

They call me Alames around here, or did your ears fall off again, my man?

"The Lost Goddess," he muttered. Alames laughed. Tears covered Robert's face when the blessed sound reached him.

Got some nerve calling me lost. I'm saving your booty right now, and not for the first time tonight.

"I . . . Ala—but . . . Reggie, Bored Reginald . . . Alames." His head pounded as he tried to understand, but the pain couldn't break his happiness.

Robert dearest, are we done stammering? Her cloud created the shape of a woman in front of him, so beautiful he could barely breathe. Her shadow glided close to him, and she stroked his cheek. The touch of her smoke made him tremble with a confusing longing. He tried to read an expression in her smoke face. Was it sadness? How could she possibly be sad if her touch ignited happiness strong enough to illuminate limbo's darkness?

Ally can't know about this. No one can, you understand? There's a lot at stake. This stays between me and my favorite mortal.

Robert remembered the urge he'd felt weeks ago. The desire to kiss Reggie had made no sense. He raised his shaking hand to touch the shadow as her words trickled in. *Favorite mortal.* "Ally—"

—is not exactly mortal. You won that cup, butterscotch. She moved closer to his face. An icy wind followed her. *Tell me I can trust you. We're lithium. Three components of one element, like Ally said. Promise?*

Hundreds of thoughts swarmed Robert's mind. Ally. Reggie. The baby. Mortals. Gods. The man on the tower platform. *Balthos.* He still couldn't make sense of the glorious beast Ally had turned into in the depths of the Hard Rime River, and he couldn't understand the jester's celestial transformation. All he knew was the desire pounding in his chest. *Protect them both.* He reached his hand for the back of Alames's cloud neck and pulled her close. Her face lost its clarity as her cloud skin leaned into him. "I promise."

His heart fluttered as she dissolved under his touch. First his queen, now his goddess. Robert was in over his head.

The figure disappeared as the cloud around him spoke. *Thank you. Now, I need you to do exactly what I tell you. Shit's about to get messy.*

"Got it," he whispered.

Magnificent. Let's meet your child. Without warning, the cloud collapsed, and Robert fell back onto limbo's idea of solid ground. The dead worm lay split beside him. Ally cowered several steps away, curled around something she held in her arms. Battle noises filled the air as the knights fought off the remaining Ouisà Kacocs. The demons had advanced farther into town. They were getting too close to Ally.

Robert rushed to her side. A blood puddle floated in front of her, dripping in the strange air. He wrapped his arms around her cold shaking body. "I got you."

She lifted her head. The look on her face sent a shiver down his spine. Her pale skin had turned as white as a corpse, and all life had left her eyes. "She's dead."

"What?" Robert followed her gaze and saw what she was holding. His infant girl, blue instead of rosy, slept limply in her arms. He'd seen the discoloration before on a baby that had suffocated in his village. Tears shot into his eyes as he tried to catch up. The girl had fine strands of shimmering white hair, delicate lips like Ally's, and an Oakley nose that looked particularly large on a baby's face. He ran a finger over her tiny fist, clenched in anger over the life that was stolen from her.

Numbness replaced the happiness Robert had felt. He shook his head. "No . . . no, you said . . . you said I'd get to meet her."

"I said what?" Ally asked faintly.

Take the little girl into your arms and give Ally a kiss. This won't be easy . . .

The last thing Robert wanted was to rob Ally of this faint comfort. He couldn't take the girl away from her already. *I promised.* He bit his lip. "Can I hold her please?"

Ally clutched the girl tighter and shook her head. Blood-curdling screams came from the battlefield. The terrifying feather monster dashed at a man.

Don't look.

"What is that thing?" Robert asked. Ally curled up and frowned. He needed to comfort her, be there for her, but they were still on a battlefield. He needed to know what they were dealing with.

A soulcreeper. It traps its victims in their darkest moment until they offer up their soul. The quicker we act, the fewer of our friends have to endure this fate. Take the girl.

Ally flinched when Robert kissed the top of her head. He swallowed hard. "I'm so sorry. I have to take her away for now."

She stared at him as if he were a demon himself. "You're not taking my baby girl away. No one is taking her ever again." She shied away from him, leaving a blood trail between them.

"Love, please, I've never taken anything away from you. Just let me hold her." For a second, her face softened, and Robert thought she'd hand her over. Then the transformation began.

Ally snarled while her mouth grew into a snout. Her sharp elvish teeth extended into bladed tusks. White light radiated from her expanding body, but Robert was close enough this time to see the beast she was turning into. Her hands transformed into furry paws that struggled to hold the infant's corpse, and her legs swelled with muscles until they broke the night-robe. The skin on her face stretched apart and revealed the hollow skull of a gigantic angry boar. *Her* skull. It was attached to a wolflike body with white fur and strong, defined muscles. She grew larger with every second, transforming from the curled-up woman to the towering beast.

Fear struck Robert, but he pushed it away. This was still his Ally, the eccentric scientist, the brilliant mind, the passionate lover. This was the beast that had kept him from drowning. "Ally, my love? Are you . . . can you hear me?"

She growled, but Robert wasn't sure if it was a good or a bad sign. The answer came with a raised paw and a slice that cut the front of his uniform. It drew a thin line of blood. *No chance for reason.* He plunged forward and ripped the infant from her paw. She roared louder and tried to crush him in her palm. Alames's cloud pushed her backward before she succeeded. The goddess's smoke crackled with white light as Ally slashed her tusks through it.

Robert backed off and wrapped his dead daughter in the torn fabric of his uniform. Ally snatched a stream of Alames's smoke in her paw and yanked it out of the cloud. A white lightning bolt tore through limbo's sky.

"Alames!" Robert screamed. A huge, ancient orc in knight's armor ran toward them and raised his sword at Ally's arm. "No!" Robert pulled Raptor and shot the hilt out of the orc's hand. He yowled and dropped it.

"This is our goddess, you heretic!" The orc grunted and picked up his weapon with the other arm. Robert glanced between him and Ally. He couldn't let anything happen to Reggie. He couldn't let anything happen to Ally. *Fuck!* Reggie was a goddess. She could handle it.

Robert kissed his daughter on her cold, lifeless cheek and placed her onto the floating ground, away from the active combat. She looked as peaceful as Reggie did when he was asleep. No, when *she* was asleep. Perhaps it was a good sign. The orc raised the sword with his healthy hand. Robert jumped onto his back before he could strike and grabbed his neck.

"She's not a monster," he called, but the orc ignored him and swung the sword over his right shoulder, cutting into Robert's side. The slash ran from his shoulder muscles to his hip, deep enough to bleed without tearing him apart. The orc sliced into Ally's beastly leg next. Robert clung on tighter, pulled him into a headlock, and yanked him backward off-balance. Ally snapped her snout into Alames, who gushed out of her way in the last second. The goddess must have noticed Robert's weak attempt at holding back the knight and split her shapeless self in half. One part swirled around Ally as she bit wildly into the air while the other circled the sword blade.

"Sir Muwaan, stop." Alames's voice filled the air. The sound soothed the burning pain on Robert's back. "She's not Caedem. Let her be." She lowered the orc's blade.

He stopped struggling under Robert's grip. "My goddess, she——"

"Bring this man and the infant to the crypt's entrance. *Trust me*, please." She released the blade and floated back to Ally. Robert recognized the manic despair in Ally's beastly eyes. He'd seen it the day in her tent. He wished he could toss a blanket over her again and take her to a world without invisible enemies and monsters.

Sir Muwaan grabbed Robert's leg and pulled him off his back. "The goddess has spoken. Pick up the corpse and follow me."

Robert scrambled to his feet, ignoring his back pain and the tightness in his chest. *Corpse.* How quickly had his baby girl turned into a mere corpse? As he bent down, a thin stream of smoke crept up his chest and into his nose. The world around him spun, and he fell backward. Sir Muwaan caught him. "Careful."

Warmth spread within Robert, and the certainty returned. *I am loved.* A part of Alames must have entered him. He felt as light and sheltered as he had in the mornings when Ally had traced her favorite formulas onto his forehead with her finger. She had started doing so two weeks ago. Alames's warmth inside of him convinced Robert that he'd return to such peace. After the darkness, the beasts, and the stillbirth, Ally might still run her fingers over him and remind him of daylight's glory.

You know who else was a stillborn, my man? Her voice was only for him to hear now. *Bored Reginald. And he developed quite a personality, don't you think?*

"What?" Robert stumbled.

"The infant," Sir Muwaan said, then handed him his daughter wrapped in the tattered uniform. Behind them, Ally whimpered. The last glimpse of her snout disappeared in a cloudy haze.

I'm keeping her safe with me until she's regained control and this mess has cleared.

Sir Muwaan examined Robert's back. "The cut is not deep. Your mortal skin will heal." He gestured for Robert to follow him as he walked away from where Alames had taken Ally. Robert hesitated. How could he trust the words of an invisible goddess? It all sounded too absurd, yet he knew it to be true. He shouldn't leave Ally on a hunch, but he had promised to follow Alames.

"Are you coming, mortal?"

"I—" Warmth poured through him and quenched the doubts.

Don't worry, I'm still inside of you. Although you'd probably prefer the other way around, eh? The Lost Goddess had made a sex joke in his mind. What had become of this night? It all sounded like a Bored Reginald show, which was reason enough to trust it. Robert held his daughter's body tighter and followed Mu-waan. "Let's do this."

You will find everything we need at the crypt.

Robert glanced over his shoulder toward where Ally had been. Even the cloud had disappeared. *You better not harm her, or I'm splitting this lithium atom thing,* he thought.

I'm pretty sure lithium is an element, but don't worry. I'm more Lady Erasyl than Duke Alikhan. The *Defiance of a Rose* reference soothed Robert further. Ally would be fine. She'd taken a bite out of a goddess. Nothing could mess with her.

He followed Sir Muwaan away from the infirmary and back to the main road. Alames had lessened the burn of his cut, but Robert felt its impact as he tried to keep up with the orc's large strides.

"My brothers and sisters are falling. Let us hurry," Sir Muwaan said. Robert checked the battlefield. He spotted few-er knights than before. What happened when a corpse died?

The terrible howl of a man came from underneath the feathered monster. "The soulcreeper got someone," Robert said.

"The fate of our stories takes cruel turns. Their sacrifice will protect the rest of us from the Ouisà Kacoc's greed." The man's anguish did not seem to bother Sir Muwaan. "Besides, it is Kilburn the soulcreeper was after. The man has sinned against my kin."

An uncomfortable weight dropped in Robert's stomach. This wasn't right. No soul should be exposed to such mon-sters. He thought of the worm's flesh that had suffocated him. The fate of his story had told him to die there, but he hadn't. Not every story was meant to be read. Some needed to be lived and changed. "Alames?" he whispered to himself.

Listen, my man, I—

"I take the deal!" the Kilburn man screamed behind them. Robert didn't wait for Alames's answer; he pushed his infant into the orc's arms.

"Keep her safe," he called as he sprinted toward the soul-creeper. He pulled Raptor on the run, his finger firmly on the trigger. He could handle a feathered beast. He was the best shot in Elfentum.

Robert, you bloody fool, said the jester.

CHAPTER 42

RICHARD

Outside of Mortal Time - Limbo

Richard had been numb to the world for over two decades, displaced among all its beauty. A weight fell off his shoulders as he stepped into the chaos outside of Edeliènne's hut. For the first time, what he saw matched the turmoil buried inside of him. The sight of demons could not shake him. The people of Waldfeld counted him among them, and they were right. He'd lost his humanity long ago. Godfried had taken it with every coin of motus meant to save his soul. The Traitor had claimed his soul despite it, but it wouldn't collect a chained man. Richard Kilburn was not the serf of Waldfeld, the serf of the church, the serf of the Traitor, or the serf of limbo, and by the spirit of the forest, he would make that clear.

Our friend, go back inside. The child. We force the child to make a portal. Bring us home. Flee from evil!

"You can't flee from evil," Richard whispered to the drips of a panicked creek running inside of him. "You became it long ago."

Choravdat pulled on Richard's consciousness and pushed through the limits of his body to regain the control they'd lost. To bring him back. To make him hide again. To use his daughter as a cowardly escape from the monster they'd been running from. Neither Richard nor the Ouisà Kacoc would give Choravdat that chance.

Richard took in the battlefield ahead. Six vile demons fought their way through the knights' defense. Three had broken through the line and chased the pregnant woman and the man who had come for her. More would soon follow, as the knights struggled to hold their ground. One faceless Ouisà Kacoc covered in toxic rods pressed a knight against its lethal body and splintered the poor soul into smoldering pieces.

The foul smell and heat of a godless fire crept closer to Richard.

We need to hide. Now.

"No!" Richard yelled, then raised his zweihänder and spun around to face Choravdat's master, the Ouisà Kacoc that had called his name. Its fiery core lit up and roared. Richard joined its outcry and slashed his sword through a mauled elvish leg attached to the demon's core. It fell off. He twisted the hilt, ready to slice off another limb. The Ouisà Kacoc's charred arm above the throbbing fire reached for Richard, but he dodged its grip and cut upward into its bone. Its roar grew louder, angrier, and its core heated. A boiling gush of wind pushed Richard backward. Limbo's hovering grounds eased the impact of his landing.

"You dare to steal my possession. You dare to challenge me." The Ouisà Kacoc sounded like the scratches of skin on a rope, the opening of nettle balm boxes, and the joyous squeaks Edeliènne had let out twice, then never again.

You promised to protect us from it.

"You want to be free?" Richard growled at his former

companion. He didn't care if the Ouisà Kacoc heard him. It could know what was coming for it if it wanted to. "Let me free you." He struggled his way to his feet, back into his fighting stance.

A tar-black creature dashed at him from his left. Richard lifted the zweihänder, but the beast with a hundred feathered eyes jolted around him before he could cut into it. Its feathers brushed Richard's arm, and a sharp pain pulsed through his pelvis. He gasped for air as a memory rattled through him, a memory he'd forgotten long ago.

"Dare to attack me again, and Vasirétis, my pet, will have some fun with you. Now return my Fae." The soulcreeper pet returned to the Ouisà Kacoc's side.

Vines tugged on Richard, desperate to pull him back into the hut. He pushed against them with all the force he could muster. Choravdat would not lead this monster to his new-born daughter. He wouldn't allow it.

You're giving us up. The words sank him like a waterfall.

"I'm not," he said through gritted teeth. It wasn't an option. But what if the Ouisà Kacoc found out about the little Fae miracle inside the hut? He charged again, aiming at the core itself. The charred arm punched him before he could reach it and tossed him to the ground. He lost grip of the zweihänder, which slid away from him. *By the love of Exitalis, help me fight it,* he commanded Choravdat, but they ignored him.

The Ouisà Kacoc grabbed Richard's leg before he got to the sword and drew him closer. Its touch scorched Richard's thigh. The smell of his burnt flesh covered the demon's foul scent. He gritted his teeth harder and focused on thorns, vines, anything to defend himself, but the Fae coward trembled in his chest. The demon's grip torched through Richard's pants, and his skin peeled. He could no longer suppress a scream. An orcish foot attached to the Ouisà Kacoc stomped down on his back. Richard felt a vertebra crack. *Help me!*

Promise to run, dear Richard, and we will. His back cracked louder, and tears shot into his eyes. *I* . . . He thought of the little girl's magenta curls, the peace he'd seen in her face. His spine groaned under the pressure. This monster wouldn't let him go even if he exposed Choravdat, and his former companion wouldn't keep his daughter safe. She was a tool for them. The only way for her to be safe, and him to be free, was to slay the monster. *I can't, but trust me, my friend, please.*

Vines wrapped around his torso and squeezed hard, forcing another scream out of him. The burning pain on his leg intensified, then stopped. He lost all sensation in it. *This is your last chance, or we will consider our deal broken.* Choravdat's voice spilled through him.

"Your last chance, mortal. Give me the Fae." Feathers brushed over his cheek and caused a nausea wave. Four of the soulcreeper's eyes blinked at him. They turned into Godfried's eyes, then his father's. Panic surged through Richard when his father looked away. He couldn't look away. He couldn't be fine with this. A father was supposed to protect their child. This wasn't protection. Neither was threatening a naive orcish boy. Pier's heart had broken in front of him, and he had looked away. As if looking away was a virtue and not a sin.

Richard twitched, and his confusion cleared. Those had been the soulcreeper's eyes, not his father's. Anger boiled in his chest as hot as the fire that burned his leg. How dare this creature use his son against him? How dare Choravdat use his daughter? He rolled to the side, shaking the demon's orcish foot off, and ripped himself free of the vines. He stretched for the zweihänder, but the Ouisà Kacoc was quicker. It let go of his leg and grabbed his throat instead. The boiling touch cut off his airways. He gasped. *Exitalis, have mercy.*

A white lightning bolt struck the sky and illuminated the darkness for two seconds. The Ouisà Kacoc's grip loosened, and the monster slumped into itself. Richard used the moment to free himself and grab the zweihänder. He struggled back to his feet. His right leg didn't follow his commands, but his arms were strong and his mind set. He would half the monster like he had halved Father Godfried. The sharp edge of his blade could cut through any muscle cluster. He readied himself to slice the Ouisà Kacoc's core in half right as its power returned. The blade had almost touched the core when something snatched the zweihänder from Richard's hands.

His head spun to the new enemy, but his mind couldn't process what he saw. The enemy next to him looked like an unseen color, the inside of the womb, the uncertain certainty of death. *My Fae cluster.* They had stolen his zweihänder. The vines he'd once controlled wrapped around his shoulders and pushed him into the Ouisà Kacoc's arms. Fire torched his body. Drips of water echoed in his mind one last time. *It pains us that you have broken our deal, but we created the child portal to our home, and we will use it. Distract it for us. We wish your splinters good luck.* Then they were gone.

The Ouisà Kacoc roared when Richard was thrown at him and tossed him back to the ground. "Give me the Fae, *now!*" Choravdat's plan had worked. The Ouisà Kacoc had missed their escape.

"They're no longer inside of me," Richard panted. Another gush of air hit him and scorched every freckle that had graced his cheeks.

"*Liar!*" The heat disappeared. "Get him!"

Richard forced his eyes open. His burnt skin stung with every facial expression. There was no time to recover. Above him, the soulcreeper reared up and leaped onto him.

He expected more stings, more burns, more pain. Instead, he landed softly in an ancient stone hall. In front of him was a black door with Exitalis's sign hanging above it. Torches illuminated the letters written underneath it: *We serve as we wilt to bloom again in your embrace.* An icy shiver ran over his back without soothing the burns. He knew this place. He knew it better than he had ever wanted to. The soulcreeper had brought him to the catacomb of Waldfeld's church of Exitalis. Behind the black door was Father Godfried's ceremonial hall, where Richard's parents had inaugurated him into the church, where he had married Edelienne, and where—

Eyes with feathered lashes opened and stared at him from everywhere—the walls, the ceiling, the floor. Only the black door and the sign remained untouched.

"Do you like games, Richard?"

His hand reached for the zweihänder but gripped air instead. The Fae cluster had left him helpless. He opened his empty fist and frowned at the rough skin of his palm. The sun had burned it, not the Ouisà Kacoc. He froze when he saw his bloodied knuckles. He had hurt them a long time ago when punching a brick wall in his hopeless search for redemption. The wounds were fresh. This wasn't the hand of the weaponsmith Richard Kilburn. This hand belonged to a scared seventeen-year-old serf boy.

"I like games. Let's play as long as you can resist me."

Richard's breath sped up. He'd left that boy behind two decades ago. He'd buried him, suffocated him until his foolish misery could no longer hurt Richard.

"Tell me when you'd like to stop, and we'll strike a deal."

"No more deals." He wanted to sound strong, but his voice was high and cracked. The harder he tried to breathe, the less air traveled into his lungs. This wasn't real. It couldn't be. This stupid boy, Dick, didn't exist anymore. Richard had willed him not to.

"You know who doesn't like games?"

All eyes shut and left him in the comforting dark that didn't last long enough. The torches flickered brighter and illuminated the rest of the hallway. It looked as real as it always had.

"Say your prayer."

Richard startled at the voice of his father, but his body didn't move. It was bound to the memory's progression. He tried to shake his head, protest, run, but he stayed as still as he had back then. A foreign excitement rose in him. It was the first time his father had spoken to him in three days. No one else had. He had spent the last three days without food or comfort, had slept next to the pigs and felt sick from the constant stench. No, he hadn't. Richard was forty-three years old. A grown man, not a boy. The hollow pains in his stomach disagreed.

"Exitalis, wife of the king, mother to us, thank you for the breaths you have not yet taken." His mouth moved and words came out, but none of it was under Richard's control. "Thank you for the life you have granted. Take the passing of today's time as a sacrifice and have mercy on my mortal body. My bones are yours."

Richard's father continued the prayer. *Mercy.* The word lost its meaning when it left his father's lips. Richard's heartbeat quickened, but he couldn't tell if it belonged to him or the boy who wasn't supposed to exist. He focused his energy like he did to control the vines. Nothing happened. The memory had put him in unbreakable chains. Could he destroy the boy who contained them? Pierce his soul before it could wander? Before the black door opened. Before fate was set. But if the boy hadn't walked through that door, Pier wouldn't exist.

There was another way out. The soulcreeper. He summoned his thoughts as if to speak to Choravdat and directed a question at the monster. *How much will you show me?*

"As long as you want to play. Let's get to the good part first, shall we?"

Father Godfried opened the black door. Richard tried to picture the lifeless halves that had fallen to his feet, but the priest's everlasting smile overshadowed the image.

He flicked his hands in Exitalis's blessing. "James, good to see you."

Richard's father nodded without a smile. Emotions had always been below him.

"Have you avoided contact as I suggested?" Godfried asked.

His father nodded. "Yes. My wife is struggling with it, but she's doing her best. Elsie, Camon, Justus, and Reuben are avoiding him as we discussed."

The picture of Reuben and Elsie collapsing under the hail of gympie-gympie hair made its way back to Richard's mind. They'd fallen in front of the Kilburn Smithy. Had he killed them? Had they been right to avoid him? *No, don't think like that.* The soulcreeper was playing with him. He couldn't risk playing along. *Clear your mind. Calm. Calm.* But calmness had left him the moment he saw that Tribu La'am man at Balthos's Heretics.

"Excellent." Godfried's smile widened. "Your family will be restored in no time."

Richard's body tensed up. His siblings had never spoken to him again, even after the silence order was done. His mother had. Too little, too late.

"Let's speed this up a little, shall we?"

The hallway blurred. The body of Dick went through a hundred little movements that Richard couldn't track. Further formalities were exchanged. They entered the ceremonial room. His father took a seat in the room's darkest corner, far enough off that he could look away when it suited him. Godfried prepared the table and the nettle balm. Richard felt something rip in his chest, like a wound that had failed to become a scar. *How much longer?*

*"Until your soul belongs to my creator.
Make the deal, and I release you."*

He didn't belong to anyone. No one. Never again. He could make it through this one memory. As much as he'd tried to snuff out the boy who had lived through it, he had evidently survived. He could again. Richard could survive it again.

*"I think you misunderstood the rules of
our game."*

Godfried pulled out a wooden box and blessed it with both Exitalis's and Balthos's signs. He opened it and revealed the silver shaft kept inside, then dipped it in stinging nettle balm.

*"I can replay this lovely moment infinite-
ly. You can live in it forever."*

Richard screamed, vomited, fainted, anything to release the fear. His seventeen-year-old body did none of it. "Dad?" he heard himself saying instead. "Dad, please look at me. What's happening?"

His father looked up, his face wooden and empty. Richard had never looked at Pier like that, had he? "Father Godfried will make you decent, boy."

Godfried nodded. "Bend over, son."

I take the deal. Please, I take it. The Ouisà Kacoc can have my soul. Nothing could be worse than this. He'd brave future torment if it allowed him to release the past. Eyes appeared everywhere around him and fluttered their feathers in different rhythms.

*"Repeat after us: As long as gods exist,
my soul belongs to—"*

Something ripped through Richard before the soulcreeper could finish. It tore into the aching wound beneath his ribs and burned as harshly as the Ouisà Kacoc's touch.

"No, no, no. Creator, what is happening?"

The body of the boy Richard used to be faded away with the memory. His real chest replaced it as the chaos of limbo welcomed him back to reality. Blood seeped through his chest. His heart raced with the traitorous bullet that had ripped it apart, desperate to win. For a peaceful moment, the Ouisà Kacoc, the soulcreeper, and Richard stared down the end of a barrel together. Behind it was an ashen Virisunder man who looked as if he had just met death. But he hadn't met it. He'd brought it.

"I . . . I missed," the man stammered.

Thank you. But Richard's lips no longer spoke the language of the living. He collapsed into the only freedom life had offered him. The last voice he heard washed away his anguish.

Hey there. Alames loves you. She always has.

CHAPTER 43

VANA

February 980 - Balthos's Heretics, Silberfluss

She knew it before her head hit the dining hall's stone floor. This was it. This was the moment they'd been singing about. She and Jules had thought they could recognize oppressors by their garments and fancy talk. It was the hate in their speech they should have looked out for.

The fall's impact struck through her body, but Jules's last song rang in her ears and soothed all physical pain. *Kick us, oh one more time, and we'll bite back. Back. Back. My spirit spreads.* His spirit was with her, if only in memory, and these fuckers with their corrupted view of justice had kicked her one time too many.

Four men had pulled her down from the table. One of them pressed his human hand on her mouth and nose, cutting off her breath. Vana licked her half elf teeth and bit down as hard as she could. Their sharp tips broke his skin, and he let go with a yowl. Before the others could react, Vana jolted her boot into the air and kicked one attacker in the balls. Another yowl. Another lesson taught to those fuckers.

One of the two remaining reacted quicker than she'd have liked. He threw himself on top of her, pressing her down with his body weight, and landed a hard punch on her face. Blood spurted out of her nose, and tears shot into her eyes. Hundreds of sewing needles seemed to prick her face when she took the first breath. Her eyes swelled up, making it difficult to see her opponent.

"Kymbat!" Artyom pushed his way through the crowd toward her. The man on top of her struck out again, but Artyom reached him before his fist wrecked Vana further. She expected him to throw the man off of her, but Artyom had a more brutal idea. The asshole collapsed onto her chest, bleeding freely from his open throat and a gaping cut from his lip to his eye. Vomit rose in Vana's throat as the warm liquid drenched her.

She wiped the blood off her own face and squinted at Artyom, who was struggling with the last of her attackers. More of Lutz's men surrounded them, but he hadn't noticed yet. He clenched a sharp stone shiv as long as his arm and stabbed the man's face and throat. Vana froze when she saw the wild rage on his face. For the first time since her arrival, she could picture her caring, paternal friend slaughtering two dozen people. Her first kill pushed its way back into her mind. Her helplessness. The fear on the guard's face. The guts that had spilled on her feet. The way her seax had taken over. She had frozen back then, like she froze now. Maureen and the others had paid the price. They'd died because of her hesitation and the weakness she'd shown toward Isa. These men were no different than Isa, and if Vana didn't harm them, her people would pay the price again.

Three others joined the fight against the raging Artyom. Vana pushed the dead man off and rolled to the side. Her broken nose protested, but she pulled herself off the ground despite of it. A short Silberfluss man with a shining blade sneaked up behind her beloved friend.

"Arty, caref—"

The man buried the blade in Artyom's side. Vana finally understood how the seax had felt. She jumped over the dead body, grabbed the short man's hair, and hurled him to the ground. *Forgive me, Mom.* Without allowing another thought, she raised her foot and stomped the back of his neck. The crack brought satisfaction, then shame. What was she doing? Why was she celebrating violence against potential comrades? No, these weren't potential comrades. She could no longer put her faith in every stranger. These were enemies, and they would die as such.

"Arty!" She swung around to help her real comrade, but he'd already thrown himself back into combat. The blade sticking out of his side did not faze him. He fought off two men at once, no sign of exhaustion in his once tired eyes. Vana was about to join him when Yooko's scream reached her. *Shit.*

Artyom's eyes met her own. They'd have to get to him now, or it would be too late. Vana kicked an approaching woman with a Caedem tattoo in the stomach and freed some space. She squeezed her way deeper into the riot. Artyom grabbed her arm and pushed a sharp stone into her hand.

"Was not prepared for big shit-show, but here. Can stab eyes if another swine come close." The blade was so sharp it scratched her palm. She adjusted her grip and nodded at him. The farther they pushed, the fewer of Lutz's men surrounded them. They were concentrated around the table Vana had left behind, Yooko, and Lutz's table. Vana and Artyom now found themselves in the heart of the hall, among panicked prisoners that needed guidance and were presented only with violence.

"Hey!" Vana yelled at a Silberfluss man and woman nearby. "You know this isn't right. Join us!" They hesitated, but she saw a spark of justice in their eyes. If they didn't join

her, they'd at least think twice before joining Lutz. She continued to yell at whoever they passed.

The crowd ahead of them cleared and formed a half circle against the wall. Vana struggled to push her way through
it as the men became larger and less willing to make way.

"The fuck did you just say to me?" someone said.

"Step aside, kymbat," Artyom whispered, then pressed
past her. He raised his long shiv and jabbed it into the shoulder that blocked their way. The man arched his back, howling. Artyom sliced the blade down to his hip, leaving a long
gashing wound. He pulled out the shiv, and Vana kicked the
man down, creating a clearing to the circle.

A massive man had backed Yooko against the wall. He
carried a heavy stone in his hand, ready to bash their comrade's head in.

"No!" Vana called, jumping over the injured man she'd
kicked down.

"Finish him!" Lutz yelled behind them, still safely on his
table surrounded by his own people.

Artyom was right behind her, but neither of them reached
the man before the stone came down. Vana closed her eyes
instinctively. She couldn't watch him die like that. He looked
too much like Jules.

Uproar came from the surrounding crowd. The sound
of a heavy body dropping to the floor tore through Vana's
heart. She couldn't save him. She couldn't save any of them.
All she'd given them were broken promises.

"You're not hurting our tribe," someone growled. It was
the familiar voice of a disgruntled woman. Vana dared to
open her eyes and found Yooko's attacker lying stretched out
on his back, staring blankly at the ceiling. Erna stood in front
of Yooko with her ducklings nearby. Eyeball and Skit had
pushed their way over to them like Vana and Artyom had.
Erna stretched out her fist, and Vana realized she had crushed
the man's windpipe with one well-placed punch. "You will
leave my people alone, or you'll regret it."

Silence stole the crowd's panicked noise. Everyone stared at Erna. Hope washed over Vana. She hadn't let them down. She'd taught them they were a union, together, even if Vana herself acted too slow or too stupid.

"Make room!" Lutz bellowed. Vana bit her lip when the crowd obeyed. Did they not realize they didn't have to obey him just because he was the loudest or the simplest to follow? She stumbled over to Erna's side and wiped off the fresh blood that had poured out of her nose. Artyom followed her.

She glanced at Yooko over her shoulder. He looked like a bronze statue, unmoving and captured in an expression of utter shock. "You okay?"

"I saw someone," he muttered, definitely in shock. Vana wanted to give him a hug or a pat on the shoulder, but Lutz reached them before she could act on her impulse. He broadened his shoulders and faced her small group of misfits. She examined her wounded comrades, a minority among the prisoners, and the hope longed to drain out of her, but she didn't let it. They needed her to believe in them.

"I hope you all saw that," Lutz boomed over the crowd. "This halfer tusk killed one of our men, unprovoked. He simply executed the wish of the majority."

Vana pushed herself in front of Erna. "They know you're full of shit."

"Do they?" Cold provocation flickered in his eyes. "We can find out what happens when I tell them to tear you all apart."

Vana's eyes flitted over the dozens of riled up people. Her mom had warned her to never underestimate a scared mob. If they charged as one, they couldn't lose, no matter what cause they were fighting for. It was the core of Vana's belief. If she let them attack her people as a union, her point would be proven, and Balthos's Heretics would be lost. She couldn't do that. She'd have to use a dishonest noble method instead.

"Looks like he needs you to fight for him," Vana said as

loud as she could. "Scared to face me yourself?" She wiped the blood off her nose and squared her shoulders.

He scoffed. "You wanna duel me, halfer?"

"If you dare." She cracked her knuckles, hoping that preparing her body would somehow prepare her mind. How could she defeat that monster of a man? She waited for a revelation to arrive, but nothing came. This was a job for an unrealistic hothead.

"All right, if you want to slow things down." Lutz looked around the people and raised his voice. "I'll show you what happens to those who prevent the common good of Silber-fluss's righteous people." He slammed his fists against his chest and roared. Everyone around Lutz backed off to make room, but neither Artyom nor Erna left Vana's side.

"Kymbat, what—"

"I know what I'm doing," Vana said with no idea of what she was doing. "Step away." She glanced across the hall and caught sight of the archway that led to the yard. A plan formed in her mind. She leaned closer to Artyom and Erna so only they could hear. "Make your way to the yard with the others. It'll be easier to barricade if . . ." *If I lose? When I lose? If I lose.* She could do it. She could defeat a gang leader with her little experience. It was the heart and fighting spirit that counted. And if she couldn't, she could at least distract him long enough.

"I am not leave you."

"Arty, you said you believed in me, in us, and in this community, right? So save them. For our new society, please."

He sucked in air and teared up. His brown eyes looked like driftwood. "I make sure they sneak to yard, but I stay near. Good luck, kymbat." He twitched as if to embrace her but thought better of it and handed her his shiv instead. Vana took it gratefully and returned the smaller one to him, then watched her comrades leave her side. The circle around her widened. She scoured her memory for the fighting lessons her dad had taught her. *Find your center. Find your stance. Never lose it.*

She bent her knees slightly and kept her feet hip's width apart. *Five minutes.* She'd only have to last five minutes for her comrades to reach the yard and block it. How many of the two dozen she'd spoken to last week would follow her core group? How many of them would survive? She couldn't allow herself to worry about them.

Lutz laughed as she readied her shiv and protected her chest with her other fist. He paced in front of her, not bothering with fighting stances or protecting his bare skin. A few people cheered him on, but most of them watched tensely, as if the fight decided what kind of people they could be—the cannibals or the hopeful.

Vana hummed the last notes of Jules's song and charged. She caught Lutz off guard, jumping as she reached him and cutting him across the cheek. Artyom's shiv left a long red gash like the seax had, but she was in control this time.

The jump threw her off-balance, and she cursed herself. *Find your center. Find your stance.* She recovered from the landing with a turn and a cut, ready to slice this fucker's throat, before he even knew what was going on. She spun too quickly for a proper aim. The blade hit his chest instead of his throat. It tore the skin, and she yanked it through his pecs. For a moment, there was victory. Then she saw the slash through his Caedem tattoo. Thick drips of blood blossomed from it like roses. They ran down his skin over the tattoo. Blood and ink. Blood and ink. Jules flashed before her eyes, and she stumbled.

Lutz roared with anger over the wounds she'd caused. Vana forced herself back into the present moment, but it was too late. He snatched her wrist, grabbed her head, and rammed his knee into her face. She fell backward while he kept his firm grip on her wrist. Her wrecked nose cracked further, and her head felt like a carriage wheel going full speed. Lights flared up everywhere. They looked like the noble fireworks she'd once seen at a Grievance March festival. If she died here, the lights of a beating would be the only fireworks she or any of the victims of Balthos's Heretics would receive.

Silberfluss cared more about some made-up dead goddess than its own people.

A horrible sting shot through her arm. A crack followed. It took Vana several seconds to understand what had happened. The haze of light and pain made it tough to form clear thoughts. Lutz had stomped on her left arm and snapped her elbow. He let go of her, and she hit the stone floor hard. The pounding pain and haze dared to sink her, but she struggled for her consciousness. If she stayed down too long, Artyom might do something stupid. Perhaps it took a hothead to recognize another. She thought of the days they had spent in their cell, talking about big ideas and playing with his makeshift backgammon set. Or rather losing, in Vana's case. That life was still possible. It must've been. There was always a possible life to fight for.

Lutz was gloating over his alleged victory, riling up the crowd further. Vana used his arrogance to grab the shiv she had dropped and pushed herself off the ground. He turned around too slowly. She raised her healthy right arm and stabbed the shiv into his knee joint as hard as she could. He screamed as the kneecap popped off, then sank to the ground. She tried to pull the shiv back out, but it stuck in the joint muscles. *Fuck.*

He used the second of her yanking at the shiv to grab her hair. Vana's spinning head protested at the sudden movement, and bile rose up her throat. Lutz gave her no chance to recover and shoved her face into his chest, rubbing her across the gashes. "Taste the blood of Caedem, halfer!"

He pulled her off so she faced him. Vana swallowed down vomit and squinted at him through the curtain of blood soaking her vision. Her disorientation slowed her reaction. She felt like she had fallen into a surreal world that ran at half the speed of everyone else's. Had five minutes passed yet? *Find your center.* Where was it? Did this throbbing body even belong to her?

The control over it didn't. Lutz headbutted her full force,

and she collapsed back onto the floor. The impact was so strong, she was sure it thrust her soul out of her body. The fireworks blended into one white lightning bolt that shot through her. Through it, she noticed the silhouette of Lutz, ripping the shiv out of his leg and approaching her. *He's gonna finish me.*

Vana realized she'd never grappled with the possibility of death before. Sure, she'd spoken of it, embraced the glorious concept of martyrdom. But she'd never considered what it entailed. She'd never believed in the gods or the saving of souls. Would she become a nachtalb? Could she even? What else was there? Cold panic rushed through her. She felt as unprepared as she'd been in the barracks during her first kill, pressured for an answer to a question she'd forgotten to ask.

Death came with a whistle. Screams. Green light shining onto her broken body.

"Touch 'em at your own risk, losers!" What a strange thing for death to say. Vana searched her torso for the shiv. Her neck. Her head. She couldn't feel any new wounds. Had she become numb, or had Lutz not stabbed her yet? "They'll pluck your eyeballs out, just ask Eyeball! It's true, I'll tell ya!"

Eyeball. Why would death mention him? Why was Vana talking about death as if it were a god she submitted too? She forced her eyes open and found the hall in renewed chaos. People trampled over one another, desperate to get as far away from the green lights as they could. Vana turned her head toward the lights, struggling to stay conscious. Her face throbbed harder. For a brief second, she wondered what she looked like before pushing away such vanity. She was alive. Somehow.

The lights revealed the reason. Prisoners were running from ten nachtalbs with illuminated chests, not eye sockets. They advanced quickly, wrapping their arms around several of Lutz's people. Instead of sinking them into nightmares and panic, their light attacked their victims' bodies. One person close to Vana convulsed as if lightning had struck them, then collapsed into the nachtalb's arm. It dropped them and moved toward Vana. She tried to get up, but her left arm reminded her of its fate. The nachtalb leaned down to her. Her heart sped up when she recognized him. *Jules.* No, not Jules, but another lost Tribu La'am soul. It was the nachtalb she'd pulled off the hook.

"Everyone, stay calm!" Lutz yelled. The panicked crowd no longer listened to him. Survival instinct had taken over. Most had never seen a nachtalb in torchlight, let alone been physically harmed by one. "It's the halfer! She's working with the warden, sending monsters after us."

Vana wanted to spit at him, to spew bitter questions about why she and her people had been left to fight him if she were a traitor, but her mouth was filled with liquids she did not care to examine. Her facial muscles refused any movement that stung her battered face further.

The nachtalb slipped his icy hands under her body and lifted her into his arms. The movement made her hazy, but she found a strange comfort in the dead man's arms. He'd seen the worst of it, had paid the worst price, and still acted of his own volition. *Second chances.*

She spent her last energy battling her swollen eyelids and processing what she saw. Lutz raised the shiv and charged, baring his teeth. Anger contorted his face, likely over the loss of authority instead of the deaths of his people. She should have feared him with her snapped arm dangling uselessly by her side and her body too heavy to dodge, but she didn't. Time moved too quickly for fear to catch up.

Instead, her numb brain barely watched the shiv rush toward her. It stopped a finger's length away from her face as someone jumped Lutz from behind. A blond girl with a wishbone slingshot clung to his back, throwing him off-balance. He roared and tried to grab her, but she evaded his hands with her swift movements. She stabbed a sharp stone shard deep into his ear. He sank to his knees, his hand failing to stop the fresh wound's bleeding. The girl slid off his back, yanked

Artyom's shiv from his hand, and threw her weight against his shoulder, tossing him to the ground.

"Everyone's in the yard. Bring her over," the girl said. *Clarisse.*

The nachtalb followed her command and carried her through the chaos.

"Oh, thank Zelission, Balthos, Lost Goddess, pantheon. Thank fucking all." Artyom's familiar voice wafted through the crowd. Vana forced her eyes open one last time and found Clarisse walking by her side.

She leaned in with a smirk. "You were right. Didn't have to wait long to save your ass." It lured a chuckle out of Vana, too much movement for her battered muscles. She faded out of consciousness with a fuck ton of pain and a smile.

Vana awakened with the uneasy certainty of being watched. The act of opening her eyes took enormous willpower, and she regretted it immediately. Not one person watched her. Everyone did, dead and alive. She shuddered and blinked at the green glimmer surrounding her. It focused on her body like a limelight.

"Kymbat!" Artyom sank to his knees in front of her and covered the lights. He was shirtless, and his side was bandaged. He was hairier than Vana had thought. "Is okay. Slow breaths. Will fix all fucked-up face in time. For now just very careful, okay?"

"Fucked-up face?" Vana mumbled and discovered how raw her throat felt. She'd have to choose her words wisely.

"It ain't pretty, but it gives you character. I dined with a guy once who had a scar as large as his—"

"Thank you, Daiba," Artyom interrupted her. "You alive. All that matters. I thought I lose . . ."

She decided the pain in his eyes was worth spilling more words over. "Ey, you can't get rid of me that easily, Arty."

"Kasanovye would be just little older than you now," he muttered, barely audible, then spoke loud enough for the group to hear. "Okay, you seem not too confused. Let us explain what happened."

Vana rolled onto her back to take in more of the room. The first thing she noticed was the floor's warmth and surprising comfort. Had they somehow brought her to the infirmary? She squinted harder into the green light and recognized Erna's outline above her. The warmth beneath her was Erna's lap.

"I still got a bit of that medicine you gave me for Allison," she said when she noticed Vana's eyes on her. "We'll patch you up." The rawness in Vana's throat pounded harder as she choked up.

"Thanks, momma-duck."

Erna scoffed, but the inkling of a smile flitted across her lips.

"So we make to yard, like you tell us to," Artyom continued. Vana looked around, trying to understand. They were indeed in the yard. Her core crew—Artyom, Erna, her ducklings, Yooko, Daiba, Eyeball, and Skit—was there, along with three dozen others huddled together next to seven infirmary nachtalbs. The Tribu La'am nachtalb stood nearby, watching Vana closely. He'd saved her. She wasn't sure how much he understood and felt, but he'd saved her nevertheless. Vana had never thought she could feel such gratitude toward a corpse.

"Daiba kept close to hallway and—"

"Yeah, no offense, but I wasn't jumping into that flesh bazaar." So it was Daiba's voice she'd heard, not death's.

"Yes, so she saw special friends lost in hallways and brought them in to clear path to yard. You safe. More people can join thanks to unholy abominations I now call friends because they save kymbat and I am weak." She could hear a smile in his voice too. She could breathe for the first time since the warden had arrived, and even though it stung, she savored it. She had left the infirmary door unlocked because she hadn't been able to shake the thought that the nachtalbs would be on their side. They wanted salvation, wanted to be part of something like everyone.

Her gaze fell on the blocked archway, and her chest grew prouder. They'd worked together to barricade themselves with tables, stones, and whatever else they could find. Even if Lutz's men wanted to face the nachtalbs again, they couldn't do so easily.

Her enthusiasm dwindled when she realized how crowded the yard had become. They had no food, no sleep accommodations, no water. All they had was the damp ground of a former well and a hint of daylight teasing them from above. The latter wasn't even present at the moment, as it appeared to be nighttime.

"Arty, how—"

"It worked," Yooko said behind her. She tried to turn her head, but her neck protested with a crack. She couldn't see past Erna, whose lips had become suspiciously thin.

Artyom didn't look pleased either. "Good, good . . . enough for all?"

"Yep, enough for all. Should be supplied for a year if he's not a prick about it." Yooko sounded much happier with himself than anybody else seemed to be. "Which I suppose is always an option. But he's such a rarity, Zan should get a good price from him."

Vana frowned and discovered that her forehead stung as much as her throat. "Who's Zan? Who's him?"

"Yooko made deal. Is . . . best option we have," said Artyom. That didn't sound good.

Yooko walked around Erna until Vana could see him. "Zan's my little brother. He's been my smuggling partner since I got here. We have a bit of an *arrangement* with a Silberfluss duke. The yard's walls are less impervious than you'd think."

He must've been certain if he talked so freely in front of their new comrades, but Vana grew more and more uneasy as to what he had traded.

"Can you get us out of here?" she asked.

He clicked his tongue. "Unfortunately, no living thing can pass the threshold. The Council made sure of that. But we have seven of them left, so it should give us a good eight years before we run out of supplies."

Vana couldn't imagine what eight years trapped in the dark yard with a large group of people would look like, but it wasn't the most pressing matter. "Seven of them?"

"The nachtalbs, of course. They'll be going for enough motus to feed us all." His eyes sparkled with excitement and pride.

Vana was sure she'd throw up. "You sold them as . . . as . . ."

"I traded one, Vana. The living matter more than the dead, don't they?"

"Easy, kymbat. Is only choice we have."

This was wrong. This was all wrong. She searched her tired mind for another solution, anything that wouldn't make them as bad as the warden, as bad as Lutz had described her to be. Her throbbing head went blank.

"Look, I know this deal is uncomfortable, but—" Yooko gasped and clenched the bottom of his rib cage. He sank down in front of them, coughing.

"Yooko!" Eyeball rushed to his side. The coughing subsided when Eyeball helped him sit up. The pride and excitement had disappeared. Ashen terror painted Yooko's face.

"What happened?" Eyeball asked.

Yooko looked down at his chest as if he expected to find a hole there. "I . . . I lost something."

Vana glanced at the nachtalbs behind him. "I think we all have."

CHAPTER 44

SACHIHIRO

Outside of Mortal Time - Limbo

Edeliènne's haystack bed was too small for the three of them, but Sachihiro squeezed his way next to Esperanza's body anyway. He half sat, half hovered on the haystack like he had in Subira's office, cradling the precious miracle in his arms. Richard had left the hut seconds ago, but it felt like an eternity had passed. The baby stopped crying and listened as attentively as the rest of them to the doom outside of the hut.

Sachihiro studied Esperanza's resting face. Despite everything, she looked peaceful, like Richard had when he bid farewell to his daughter. *Peaceful.*

"Gon?" His sibling was leaning against the ship wall, humming an orcish lullaby to drown out the noise from outside the hut.

"Hmm?"

"What do you think of the name Frieda? It's an old Silberfluss name for peace." The baby hiccupped, and a caterpillar crawled out of her mouth. She laughed, flung her arms, and squashed it. When she removed her hand, a butterfly emerged. "I think she likes the name."

Edeliènne returned to the room with three steaming tea mugs. "That'll be Rich's decision when he returns." Her remaining eye narrowed at Esperanza, but she recovered her apathetic expression quickly.

"When he returns?" Sachihiro asked, too aware of the horrible screams coming from outside their hiding place.

"Things will work out as they should," Gon said before Edeliènne could answer.

She nodded. "Yes . . . of course. Anyway, have some tea. It calms the nerves."

Sachihiro took the hot mug gratefully. He welcomed any sensation that established normality away from the chaos. He inhaled the sharp steam and frowned. It smelled like his and Esperanza's less sensible college nights.

"Opium?" Gon asked.

"Laudanum tincture, just a few drops. Works the same way. It's hard to get anything good here, but I'm close with a knight, so . . ." She forced a wink, then took a big gulp. Sachihiro and Gon exchanged glances. What would General Subira Se'azana say to intoxication in the middle of a mission? Sachihiro hoped he'd get the chance to find out. To get her opinion on little Frieda's gift. To see his idol again one more time. He hadn't made her proud yet.

"So, if you two know Rich, do you know my boy too?" Edeliènne asked and took another gulp. "How's Pier? He was always so good to his momma."

Sachihiro considered taking a sip himself to avoid the question. Luckily, Gon answered before he could tell Edeliènne the full truth. "Pier's in Freilist. My wife is his best friend, and, ehm . . . we'll visit him soon, I'm sure."

Edeliènne finished her mug and chortled. "Your wife?"

Had there been alcohol in the tea as well? Sachihiro trusted their hiding place less and less, so he pulled Frieda tighter. She nuzzled happily against his chest.

Edeliènne eyed Gon, lingering on their braid with weaved in pearls. "Poor woman must have missed some signs . . ." She tilted the mug one more time, discovered it was empty, and set it aside. "Well, anyway—"

"Liar! Get him!" The roar of the horrid creature tore through the hut and diminished all pretense of normality.

"Rich!" Edeliènne screamed, staggering to the door. It blasted open, and a gush of wind blew her backward. A creature stormed into the room, so absurd Sachihiro wished he could read a dozen theses on it first before having to face it. He jumped from the bed and begged his mind to perceive it in any form possible. In the hall, Edeliènne shrieked and pushed the door closed.

"Give us the portal child," the creature said in the sound of a rainstorm echoing in Sachihiro's head. It carried Richard's zweihänder sword.

"What did it say?" Gon asked, and Sachihiro realized it had spoken Faemani. That helped. It was a Fae. A Fae demon. Sachihiro's mind put the pieces together enough to recognize a cluster of vines, thorns, and magenta light. The scent of moss and flowers tickled his nose. For a strange second, he wondered if it had come for Esperanza's soul so she could rest on a bed of clovers until her tortured soul grew into plants, void of all sins. Then he realized what it had actually come for.

"No." Sachihiro ripped the quilt from Edeliènne's bed. He wrapped his little Frieda into it, desperate enough to hope the fabric could protect her. A net of vines sprouted around Sachihiro until he saw nothing but green. A hand, or a barren autumn branch—Sachihiro could not be sure—jolted forward and snatched Frieda from his arms. Her cry broke his heart. He launched after her, but more vines wrapped around his neck and tightened. Thorns grew from the vines, first scratching his skin, then piercing holes.

"Home, bring us home. Child of mortal and Fae, open it. She said it would open it. She said that. Why is it not obeying? Open it!" The words rained around Sachihiro. With every sentence, the creature's impatience grew frantic, and its grip tightened around his neck. Frieda cried and swung her tiny mint-green arms around. Gon and this creature were wrong. Frieda was a baby, not a portal, not an abomination, not some otherworldly power. Just a little girl in need of care.

Sachihiro tensed his muscles against the vines, struggling to free himself, but their grip didn't loosen. The creature dangled Frieda by one leg and shook her. Flashes of purple light formed around her middle horn. "If you don't open the Fae realm alive, your soul will." The demon raised its sword. If the thorns didn't kill Sachihiro, her confused cries surely would.

A golden hue swallowed the darkness. Edeliènne screamed, and the vines grew limp. Frieda fell from the creature's grip. Sachihiro dove forward and caught her in the last moment. He pulled her back into his trembling embrace. "I got you. Sachi's got you."

He looked up and almost screamed himself. The golden shadow of his father stood above him. The contours of three other familiar-looking orcs surrounded him. Together they summoned golden waves into the room that made the creature crumble into itself and caused Edeliènne to collapse. Sachihiro glanced at Gon and startled. His sibling's eyes were rolled backward. Their hair had broken out of its braid and hovered in limbo's strange air. They mumbled incantations and pressed against their rib cage, where the golden hue radiated from.

Ancestors. Gon was summoning ancestors. Sachihiro looked back at the figure closest to him. "Dad . . ."

His translucent hand of pure gold touched the top of Sachihiro's head. Memories dripped down his spine. Their first game of pitz. Their nights on Juyub'Chaj's volcano finding patterns in the stars. The books he brought back whenever he went on expeditions. Sachihiro shuddered when the hand was lifted. "You will be a good father, my son."

Tears shot into Sachihiro's eyes as he tried to process what was happening.

"I take the deal!" Richard's scream wafted through the cracks of the front door. None of them could pay attention to it.

The light of his father embraced Sachihiro. "The three of you need to get back to your world. There is so much more life waiting for you. Do not despair over the loss of your love. Another name is written on your parchment, but she does not carry it yet."

Another name. "Do you mean—" The sound of a gunshot stopped him from finding out.

The ancestors' light flickered. "Come, son, pick Gon up and follow us. Someone has stolen kénos from the realms. It is blasphemous, but there's a rift in limbo that you can escape through and—"

The sound of breaking glass, ripping pages, and Esperanza's screams cut him off. It was not an echo of her suffering, but the terror-inducing voice of the Ouisà Kacoc Richard had faced. "You stole my mortal plaything. You will take its place." A bolt of white light flared up. "Your splintered goddess can't save you. Pet, find the Fae and bring them back to me while I take care of this."

Gon trembled, their hand less steady on the crutch. Sachihiro got to his feet. "What now?" he asked his father, but the ancestors' shapes weren't as defined anymore. They bled into the golden hue around the room. "No, no, Dad, stay with us."

Gon's hair dropped, and foam formed around their tusks. *Shit.* Their body collapsed into Sachihiro's arms, who struggled to support them and hold Frieda. From one second to the next, the golden hue disappeared. The room became darker than it had been before the ancestors arrived. Sachihiro looked at the bullseye and almost dropped Frieda.

The yellow stare of feathered eyes twisted his heart and lured another memory of his father to the forefront. The last time he'd seen him. Sachihiro had never felt comfortable with hugs, so his father had put a hand on his head and told him how proud he was. Gon's voice echoed over the image. *Dad lost the K'aah Ki'ik. He lost the fight. Lost the K'aah Ki'ik. Lost the fight. Lost. Lost. Lost.*

Sachihiro snapped out of it at the same time Edelièenne regained consciousness and rose from the ground.

"What—" he started, but Frieda's cry stopped him. Vines circled her body. *No.* He failed to clasp her tighter, and she slipped out of his hands toward the Fae creature. It had risen alongside Edelièenne the moment the ancestors had disappeared.

Frieda floated in the air toward it. Gon shifted. Green flashes of light burst through the creature's vine flesh. Sachihiro caught Frieda for the second time, then turned to Gon, who breathed heavily, holding their crutch like a weapon. The pretty crystals Zazil had attached to them glimmered with the distinct green of assula magic. She had claimed the crystals' purpose was to improve stability, but Gon seemed to know better.

"Run, Sachi! You heard Dad. Get her away from this thing!"

"Gon, I—" A vine whip lashed toward him, and he thought better than to argue. Gon shot another light ray at it, which dissolved the whip in the air. Sachihiro held the crying Frieda closer to his chest and dashed past the creature out of the hut. Branches reached for him but were met with green bolts before they could hurt him.

He stumbled back onto the absurd town road. A bloody battle had taken over the town's entrance to his left. The main road led to a faraway town square to his right. The Ouisà Kacoc that had called for Richard dashed down the road, leaving a lifeless body behind. Sachihiro shielded Frieda's eyes. She'd already watched her mother die and needed no more tragedies burned into her memory.

The soulcreeper circled Edeliènne's hut, so Sachihiro chose the main road, unsure where else to go. He ran away from the hut and creatures as fast as he could. "I know this is uncomfortable," he told Frieda. She must have understood, for she stopped crying and buried her head in his chest.

He passed a stone building with an infirmary sign and stopped. Could he hide in there? Before he made a decision, limbo's sky erupted in white bolts once more.

"Ally, no, stay with me!" The beautiful voice of a woman resounded through the sky. Sachihiro looked up to see where it had come from. Instead of a woman, a beast burst out of limbo's clouds. It was no less majestic than the voice had sounded but far more terrifying. Its vivid wolf-body ended at the neck where it turned into an eerie hollow skull of a gigantic boar. The beast jumped over Sachihiro's head with a realm-shattering roar and galloped down the road.

"Give. Me. My. Child." Its beastly voice came not from its mouth, but from the surrounding air, crackling with white light at each word. It left Sachihiro's sight as suddenly as it had appeared, running in the Ouisà Kacoc's direction. Sachihiro stood there, stunned, until the fatal touch of vines crept up his neck. He swung around, but it was too late. The creature had stolen Frieda and took her through an alley next to the infirmary.

"Give me my child!" he screamed with the urge to burst into a beast himself. But he wasn't a beast. He was just Sachihiro. And all he could do was run. So he did.

The town ended behind the infirmary. Limbo's grounds became even less tangible. Sachihiro hadn't thought that was possible. All directions were obscure here. He couldn't tell for sure if he was running on the ground or in the sky. The air changed from inscrutable to a distinct rotten smell. Sachihiro's stomach turned when he discovered its source. Corpses floated around them, some intact, some in strange pieces. Was this what happened to the incompletes that couldn't escape the demons? His heart sank when he thought of Gon. What if the soulcreeper got them?

Don't think about it. Just keep running. So he did. The horizon ahead circled and became smaller until he ran in a constantly decreasing tunnel. The creature produced magenta rays from the tips of their vines. They tore a hole into the end of the tunnel through which sanity shone. *A kénos rift.* Sachihiro saw glimpses of a forest, a real forest with the mossy ground of tangible earth. He wanted nothing more than to take Frieda there and escape this place. *Wait, but Gon.*

He stumbled, unsure whether to follow the creature and save Frieda or return to his sibling. He'd promised Richard to keep her safe. She needed him, but so did Gon. The brush of feathers decided for him. He glanced over his shoulder and found dozens of horrifying yellow eyes staring at him. *The soulcreeper.* It rushed after the creature like Sachihiro did. The terror of its single touch sped him up until he caught a branch of the Fae demon that had stolen Frieda.

The glimpse of reality enlarged. Frieda screamed. The creature jumped. Sachihiro clung to the branch, the only chance of saving his little miracle. Something clung to him with equal urgency. Together they tumbled into a world worth grasping. Sachihiro fell in all four directions, focusing on Frieda's call.

He hit the ground hard. Images of his dying dad haunted him. He gasped for air until the monster let go of him and charged its actual victim. Sachihiro jumped off the ground and ran after the Fae demon and the soulcreeper through a thick forest. It was dark, but the air was pure and alive.

The forest cleared after a minute of chase. The scream of a woman caught the Fae demon by surprise, and it faltered.

Both the soulcreeper and Sachihiro lunged, eager to use the demon's startle. The soulcreeper buried the mess of vines and branches under its tar-colored body. Frieda disappeared with it.

"No!" Sachihiro howled, punching into a yellow eye, but it ignored him. A rainstorm rattled the forest without a single drop falling. Was the creature screaming? Sachihiro's body threatened to freeze, but he commanded it not to. Frieda was somewhere in there. Somewhere in the terror. If the soulcreeper showed them memories of despair, what could a newborn see? Would she simply relive every waking moment? Her life had been nothing but terror. "Move!" he yelled again, as if it helped.

The woman who had screamed stepped into his periphery. She had recovered from her initial shock.

"Help me!" Sachihiro called, then immediately regretted it. The young human watched with glee as the soulcreeper devoured the creature. A glowing green assula ring graced her finger.

"Rutilia Belladonna, you fucking bitch!" Someone came running toward them from the forest clearing. *Zaz?*

Rutilia smiled. "I see my prayers have been answered."

CHAPTER 45

ZAZIL

February 980 - Waldfeld, Silberfluss

"Rutilia Belladonna, you fucking bitch!" she screamed after the young noble who had dared to steal from her. *The cloud ring of all things!* It was Zazil's newest and most precarious invention. So precarious she didn't dare leave it behind at the camp. The cloud it produced was not meant for combat use but as a fuel to assist with the queen's ideas. Zazil had managed to make items hover with the assula-molded substance, not exactly safe enough for Alexandra's flying constructions, but a start. This stupid noble girl had released it all on the manor, and Zazil had no idea what it could lead to. She'd told Subira to get the others out of there as fast as possible.

Zazil chased Rutilia into the forest she'd ran off to, as if the dark woods could shield the silly girl. She spun her moonstone ring to illuminate the night. Rays revealed her and, unfortunately, much more. Zazil stumbled forward when the light reflected off a hundred yellow feathered eyes. She slapped her hand over her mouth to stifle a scream. *Demons. Fucking demons.* Zazil had hated Demonology at college and had skipped it whenever she could, but this was an Ouisà Kacoc if she'd ever seen one. Worse, this was a soulcreeper, an Ouisà Kacoc designed by one of its own.

It had already found its victim. Another demon, from what it looked like, but an Asynár. This type formed from incoherent soul splinters, causing confused, animalistic thought processes without creating a distinct body to house themselves in. Not as dangerous as Ouisà Kacocs, but nothing to be toyed with.

The orcish man next to the demons seemed determined to brawl with them anyway. He punched the soulcreeper's eyes. *Idiot. Wait . . .* That idiot looked familiar. Why was that idiot staring at her like that? Why did he look so much like her dear spouse, but taller, broader, and distinctly more awkward?

"Sachi?" she called before she could stop herself. Rutilia swung around and pressed the stolen ring once more. Not much substance was left, but it caught the soulcreeper's attention.

"Creator, I caught the Fae. Creator?" The demon's haunting voice echoed through the forest. "Where is my creator?"

"Vasirétis," Rutilia said, answering its cry. "Come to me."

Zazil didn't wait for an explanation and fired an assula beam from her hematite crystal ring at the noble brat. The soulcreeper leaped in front of the beam and swallowed the green light in its tar body. The hematite on Zazil's finger cracked in half.

"Frieda!" Sachihiro screamed, hidden behind the soulcreeper and Rutilia. Zazil had no idea who he was talking to. It was Sachihiro, wasn't it? Her stomach dropped when she thought of the assula-molded substance in her lost ring. She must have miscalculated its creation and accidentally produced a hallucinogen. *Yes, that's it.* That was why Rutilia thought she knew an Ouisà Kacoc by name and Zazil saw her brother-in-law being a moron. She'd had weirder trips with hallucinogens in the past. None of this was real. The thought steadied her. The Belladonna girl was no match for her alone.

Zazil pulled the small assula staff from her hip and charged at the ridiculous feather-eyed vision. Soulcreepers had looked way better in her textbook. She swung the staff, producing a green light whip that struck the demon's bottom side and whirled around its body. The monster was surprisingly heavy for not existing, but she shoved it aside with condensed focus. That should've been enough force to evaporate her silly vision.

Rutilia stood behind it, next to the imaginary Sachihiro holding a mint-green baby with horns wrapped in a dusty quilt and the bound Asynár. Zazil blinked at the strange picture, then shook her head and yanked the light whip back, ready to put Rutilia in assula chains and drag her ass to Subira.

She raised it above her head to gain momentum as the soulcreeper jumped back in front of Rutilia.

"You shall not harm her. She knows my name." Its voice crackled among the trees. It would have been terrifying if it was real.

Zazil forced herself to laugh. "Sure, Rutilia, you're friends with all the soulcreepers." Rutilia must have messed with the ring cloud's hallucinations. Somehow.

The soulcreeper's hundreds of eyes squinted both at Zazil and Rutilia. "Where is my creator?" The demon slid around Rutilia, eyeing her from all sides. "You're not like them. Not all strong. Not all malevolent."

"Feed me Choravdat, and I will be."

Zazil gulped. This was getting too absurd for her taste. Sure, she'd seen weird shit in opium hazes before, but the combination of drugs and her mind had never created cohesive narratives, let alone conversations between real and fake creatures.

"Zaz, the demons are real! We escaped limbo!" Sachihiro

yelled from the other side. *Nope. Nope. Nope.* Limbo was an inescapable place. Why would Sachihiro even come from there? He and Gon were helping Esperanza with her birth. If Sachihiro was here, where was Gon?

The sky erupted before she could find an answer. A flash of white light broke the night's darkness. The soulcreeper screeched. Zazil looked up, and for a heart-stopping moment she thought the stars were falling from the night sky. Tiny spots of light floated down from the world's painted constellations. Their glow kissed the dark grounds and melted into the earth. The sky wasn't falling apart, but it snowed. It snowed stars. A breeze of celestial singing followed. It evoked a peace in Zazil's chest she'd never felt before. When the starry snow touched her shoulders, all anguish disappeared from her life. It kissed away hate, rage, injustice, and self-loathing until she felt like a perfect creation meant to roam the world in search of love and light. War and bloodshed were constructs of the past, constructs that should never have existed, for she was meant to adore the patterns dots drew on ladybugs and dance to the sound of fiddles. Tears streamed down her face. She was whole again. They were all whole again.

As soon as it had started, it stopped. The snow ceased to fall, and the night's grip lured them back to their twisted reality. She lost the images of ladybugs and the frivolity of dancing. She lost all peace.

"The rift," the soulcreeper's damned voice hissed through her pain. "It closed. My creator . . . I lost my creator . . ." *We lost so much more than that, you foul limbo-hound.* Zazil cursed herself for the thought. She'd admitted it was real. The Ouisà Kacoc, the Asynár, the strange baby, Sachihiro . . . they were all real. Which meant Gon was . . . where was Gon?

"You know your creator and I talked. I haven't brought them Kilburn yet, but I am here now," Rutilia purred. "Let me be your mistress." Her confident tone sent a shiver down Zazil's spine.

The soulcreeper spun circles around Rutilia, creating a

whirlwind of red smoke that rose from her feet. "Here's the Fae, mistress," it hissed back.

Sachihiro dashed out from behind her, toward Zazil. "Go, go, go, Zaz. *Run!*" But she was frozen in horror as the Asynár's watery voice screeched through the air. It struggled to grow roots strong enough to hold on to the forest. The red smoke devoured every vine that sprouted from its magenta core and forced it closer to Rutilia. The noble lady stretched out her hand, ready to receive the soulcreeper's gift. Red smoke tore her mouth open.

"Zaz!" Sachihiro screamed. The baby in his arms joined him. She stumbled backward, still unable to take her eyes off the horror playing out in front of her.

The sound of invisible waterfalls surrounded them. Heavy rain showers. The tears of a creature knowing its doom. The red smoke strangled the Fae Asynár in the air, tossed it over to Rutilia, and crushed it until its essence fit into her gaping mouth. She swallowed it whole. This was no symbiosis. It was ownership. Magenta light pierced out of her eyes. She quivered until thorns burst from her skin. The sight was enough to shake Zazil back into the moment. She spun around, grabbed Sachihiro's hand, and ran.

"Kill her, and get me that magical child." Rutilia's voice resounded with an unnatural edge, like wind rattling autumn leaves.

"Fuck!" Zazil screamed, aiming her staff over her shoulder. *Destroy. Disarm. Do something, anything!* She commanded its stored assula magic, unable to form a clear strategy. Sparks shot out it, but nothing slowed the soulcreeper down. It leaped onto Zazil's back and tossed her onto a shining marble floor. The fall knocked out one of her rounded teeth. Her sharp elvish chompers hadn't grown in yet. *What is going on?* Familiar hands gripped her from behind.

"Mom!" she heard herself scream.

"They don't care. Let's go back to our room." Panic flooded her mind when she heard Marcel's voice. The soulcreeper was fishing for memories she'd drowned in liquor, sex, and opium.

"*Mom!*" Her old self cried wet, useless tears.

"Zilly . . ." Marcel breathed into her droopy ear. They hadn't grown their sharp points yet. She must've been under nine in this particular buried torture. He pulled her backward. Zazil was sure her mind would break. Her soul couldn't endure reliving it one more time.

A blessed voice saved her. "Run, soldier!" said the great General Subira Se'azana.

The soulcreeper screeched and staggered off Zazil. The reality of the forest field returned. The Belladonna manor reappeared. Her shaking body longed to kiss the muddy earth beneath her, the present that saved her from the past.

Sachihiro pulled her off the ground. She stumbled to her feet and found Subira in a vicious dance with the soulcreeper. An elegant pirouette, as quick as the wind, followed each deadly shotel slash. Feathers flew around her as she tore into the howling beast. No fear graced her face, just a calm determination and focus as sharp as the blade she wielded. If captured in paint, the moment could've graced the ceiling of a cathedral. Nothing Zazil had seen in religious artwork had looked as holy as the general did in that moment.

"Evacuate our troop and as many civilians as possible through the back," she commanded while leading the soulcreeper away from the manor's gate, back to the forest.

As much as Zazil hated to argue, she had to. "No, General, the manor isn't safe. The green cloud that filled the dining hall is—"

The ground slipped away from underneath her feet before she could finish her sentence. What had been grass made way for dirt and stone. She spun around and found Rutilia, or what was left of the human woman, standing at the edge of the forest, summoning another horror that should not belong in the sober mind. Rutilia's limbs stretched far away from her torso and turned into thorny vines that gathered the surrounding earth, yanking it off the ground like a blanket and piling it up next to her. Her eyeballs left their sockets in flower petals, watching from above as the soulcreeper and Subira fought. The nature she summoned turned hostile, heaping around her like a tidal wave waiting to consume the manor.

"The forest by the side fence. Where your horses are," Sachihiro called. "We can seek shelter there."

"Our soldiers!" Subira bellowed. Zazil looked back at the gate and saw Diem from her covert troop running toward it. The rumblings of the earth must have been noticeable in the dining hall, and the soulcreeper's screeching had surely alerted everyone in the vicinity.

"Sachi is right, General. We must—" Zazil started, but terror cut off her words once more. All starlight disappeared as Rutilia's forest wave arched over them. "Run!" she screamed, then grabbed Sachihiro tighter and pulled him toward the side of the manor, where the demonic noble lady didn't control nature. Vines struck down next to them like lightning. Sharp leaves fell from the darkness above. Zazil dared to peek at it and nearly tripped. A ceiling of pointed thorns, branches, and toxic-looking moss threatened to crush them. She looked at Rutilia, whose floating petal eyes focused on the manor. Was she trying to wrap it in demonic Fae magic, or did she want to destroy it all? It was her home. It had to be the former. It had to be.

Flashes of memory fought for Zazil's attention again, but she pushed them away. Feathers brushed her left side. She didn't slow down to check but hoped to the ancestors it meant Subira was nearby, preferably winning. They ran past the front fence until they'd almost reached their horses. It felt like an eternity ago that Zazil had secured her mare on a tree and readied herself for a simple covert mission.

Subira groaned. Zazil aimed her staff to the side without slowing down. *Injure. Injure the soulcreeper.* Her heart leaped when she heard the monster screech. She wasn't completely useless.

"General!" Diem yelled from behind them. Zazil glanced over her shoulder and saw him at the gate with a pistol at the ready. The green cloud from her ring wafted behind him. Her eyes widened. She hadn't tested how the substance reacted to sparks.

"Don't shoot!" she called. He aimed at Rutilia's terrifying form. She advanced toward the manor, taking her heaping Fae wave with her. Each step she took decreased their escape route. Trees near the fence's corner were ripped from their roots and became part of the nature that threatened to flood them.

"Quicker!" Sachihiro yelled as it circled in on the manor. It had almost reached the corner. A little farther and it would hit their horses.

"I got her, General!" Diem called, then fired.

"No!" Zazil screamed, but it drowned in the noise that followed. His gunshot ignited the cloud behind him. The fire traveled up to the manor in less than a second, answering Zazil's question. The fuel she'd been working on was indeed flammable. Very flammable. The quaint Belladonna manor exploded with a blast so earth-shattering she was sure the people of Freilist heard it. Its shock wave sent Zazil and Sachihiro flying backward. The soulcreeper yowled and dashed to its new mistress. The explosion's impact ripped holes in the ceiling of vines and branches. Thorns broke off and shot down all around them.

Zazil's mind seemed to burst as well. Her body rolled out of the way, dodging the deathly tip of a thorn that headed for her torso, but her brain could no longer process it. First the stars had fallen from the sky, now nature did.

Something pulled on her. Muscular arms. Smaller than Sachihiro's, but just as strong.

"On your feet, Ch'ulel," Subira snapped. The strange normality of a military instruction roused her off the ground.

Follow, Zazil commanded, as if she herself was an assula weapon. Then again, wasn't she? She had been no different from a raw, pulsing assula, lethal to touch, easy to manipulate. But she'd taken that essence of her lost self. She'd taken that energy and shaped it until it could be of use to the world. Tears ran down her face. She never wanted to be raw again. Where was Pier? Where was Gon? Where were those who had forged her into something beautiful?

Subira whistled through her fingers. The sound of hooves followed. Zazil stumbled toward it, numb to the surrounding chaos. She looked at the burning manor. A man, engulfed in flames, spread his wings above the roof and flew into a star. *Wait, what?* There was indeed a man. A winged man. She blinked, and he was gone.

"Sachihiro, take her mare and free the other horses," Subira barked. "Zazil is riding with me."

"Her head—"

"I know, we'll bandage it at the earliest opportunity."

Her head? Zazil touched her hair. It was sticky and damp. She looked at her palm. *Wet.* Red liquid drenched it.

"She's in shock," Sachihiro said as he mounted a horse. Where had that horse come from?

Subira yanked Zazil to her side right before another thorn struck the ground. A second later and it would have hit Zazil. She squinted at it, trying to understand. One thought formed in her mind. *Ouch. Ouch. Ouch!* Every sensation turned into pain. Her head was on fire. It must've been. Her knees gave way, and she fell to the ground. No, into arms. Firm arms.

"Let's get you onto Cal," Subira said, then tossed her horse's saddle onto the ground. Zazil stumbled over to her general's black stallion, but her legs were too heavy to lift. "Hold on." Subira picked her up and gently laid Zazil over her shoulder. New stars clouded Zazil's vision, but she doubted anyone else saw them. Subira held her tightly, then mounted the horse and slid Zazil onto it in front of her. "Keep your arms around my neck if you can. Let's get out of here."

This wasn't right. She was injured. Someone was always there when she was injured. "Gon . . ."

"Sachihiro, where's Gon?" Subira asked and spurred on the horse. They galloped quicker than Zazil had expected. Her stomach protested with aggressive nausea. The scream-ing baby in Sachihiro's arms made her head throb harder. The wind soothed the explosion's heat, but no answer soothed her mind. After several moments of silence, Subira cleared her throat. "We'll get you to a doctor as soon as possible, sol-dier. Nothing to worry about."

But Sachihiro hadn't answered the question. Why didn't she ask again? The question. Zazil needed to know. Nothing else mattered. "Where's Gon?" she muttered.

"Don't worry about that now," Subira whispered, then placed a kiss on her forehead. Her advice would have been impossible to follow if Zazil hadn't passed out at that very moment.

CHAPTER 46

ROBERT

Outside of Mortal Time - Limbo

He'd last missed a shot on his eleventh birthday. Target practice first, then cake. That was how a good soldier, a good Oakley, was raised. So there he'd been—hungry, impatient, and half a finger too high for the bottle he was supposed to hit. Back then it had cost him the adventure collection his father had obtained as a present. Robert could still see the bonfire devour the book after his mom had tossed it in there. *If you miss a shot, you lose something dear to you, Bertie.*

The Kilburn man was dead before his head touched the ground. Robert wondered if the dear thing he'd lost was his sanity. The man passed with a hint of peace on his tortured face. Perhaps sanity was a price worth paying. His tormentors didn't give Robert a chance to contemplate the matter.

"You stole my mortal plaything," the monster said, but from where Robert could not say. "You will take its place."

The pulsing muscle core jolted forward. Robert tried to fire Raptor, but his pistol clicked its beak helplessly. The assula had run out of charge. It'd be useless for at least fifteen minutes. Rotten arms grabbed him with sharp nails that tore into his flesh. Love left him. *No, not love. Alames.* The thin part of her cloud that had traveled inside of Robert burst out of his chest and against the monster's core. The arms that captured him loosened enough for Robert to free himself. He swung the rifle from his back. The core and Alames's cloud flared up red and white as they fought. Robert squinted into the bright light, unable to tell the struggling entities apart, but he had to. The crackling sounded dangerous. No one was allowed to hurt her on his watch.

He aimed his rifle at the creature's main bony arm above the core right as the light cleared. The arm pressed Alames's cloud against its fiery body, causing the crackling. Robert's heart dropped. Gods were immortal, weren't they? *The Lost Goddess.* If they were immortal, why did the world assume Alames was dead? Why would Balthos assume it?

"Your splintered goddess can't save you," the monster taunted, then snapped at the soulcreeper. "Vasirétis, find the Fae and bring them back to me while I take care of this."

The one second of distraction was all Robert needed. Or it should have been. He had aimed the rifle at the arm, certain he could shoot off its wrist without hitting Alames. Certain, if only he could hold his hand steady. *Come on.* He couldn't doubt himself now or ever. He wasn't allowed to falter. But what if he missed again? What if his bullet tore through the cloud like it had through the man? What if—

Alames's incorporeal form flickered brighter. *Pain,* he realized, then pulled the trigger. As long as he was standing, nothing would harm his loves. The shot tore through the monster's wrist as planned, and Alames escaped. Robert's heart jumped. He did it. He still had it in him. Alames's crackling steam rushed at him, whirled around his feet, and pushed him backward. The monster roared as it struggled to reattach its hand. Robert prayed to Balthos that it couldn't. *No, not to Balthos. To—*

Why don't we figure that out later and move our own freaking feet? Her voice had returned to his head. He looked down at his feet and realized Alames ran him away from the scene by her volition. Robert stumbled, then started to sprint himself.

There we go, my man. Her voice kept its playful tone, but she sounded terribly out of breath.

"Are you mortal?" he pressed out as he ran back to the spot where Sir Muwaan and his stillborn had been.

Sticking with the easy questions, are we? Soft wind brushed through his hair. *In some ways, we all are. In other ways, no one is.*

Robert glanced over his shoulder at the monster as it welded its wrist back onto the arm. "And without the riddle?"

Showing me the tough guns, eh?

A quick shock stung through Robert's head. Crackling accompanied it. She must've been injured. He focused back on the road, running as fast as he could. *The crypt.* He'd promised to get to the crypt. Maybe she could rest there. His heart jumped when she continued to speak.

Sorry about that. So, mortality. Well, the essence that makes up our soul lives forever. Only kénos can destroy it. The question is whether our consciousness remains attached to it. I'm celestial, my dear, so unless someone molds my soul splinters into a new person, or let's say—random example—a floating fucking sky city, I got dibs on them.

Robert spotted Sir Muwaan ahead, close to the infirmary where they'd first fought. "So you called dibs on your splinters and are living through them?" *Please be immortal. Please be immortal.* He didn't know how to protect her if she wasn't. How could he guard incorporeal splinters?

Living through them is one fine illusion, isn't it? I have, or am, about 50 percent of my splinters. Oh my, Ally would hate this vague calculation, but around 30 percent of them are keeping her busy right now, so she won't know. My limbo splinters are a little less conscious than the ones living it up as a sexy jester.

A terrifying roar resounded from behind. Robert dared

to look once more without slowing down. The creature had attached its wrist and charged after them.

But tonight you got the full show, my man. Only kept a sliver in that lovely mortal body to make sure his dead heart keeps beating.

"There you are!" Sir Muwaan yelled as Robert reached him. "What—"

Robert ripped his lifeless daughter from his hands and kept running. "Go, go, the thing, it's after us!"

Sir Muwaan readied his sword once more. "You have upset an Ouisà Kacoc?"

Robert didn't have time to fight, but he had no idea where the crypt was. "Alames?"

Little. Busy. Right. Now. Ally, calm down! Her voice echoed from far away, as if she called from the bottom of a well.

"Follow me!" Sir Muwaan led him to the most bedraggled hut he'd seen so far. Its walls were a rusted chain fence with empty parchment pages to fill the gaps. Burgundy velvet curtains that reminded of the theater made up the roof and the entrance.

"What is this place?" Robert asked when Sir Muwaan pushed the curtain aside.

"This is where she used to live. Before the treaty was broken. Before she left to rinse the world from celestial influence and failed."

"She didn't fail," Robert said as he entered. He barely understood what the knight was talking about, but he sounded no different than Ally's disrespectful lieutenants at the front. Robert's breath caught when he saw the inside of Alames's hut. Letters of a language he'd never seen were scribbled on all four walls. The yellowed parchment papers that formed them also served as a thick carpet. Robert stepped on stacks of them with each step he took. Alames's handwriting was both tiny and impossibly intricate, as if the grandest cabaret show had been condensed into a finger puppet theater. Broken quills littered the floor, and ink drops stained it. The only piece of furniture was a black granite armchair with stories chiseled into it. Robert noticed writing at its top, enclosed in a heart: *To my Poet, this gift is but a fraction of your beauty. Your Smith.*

The hut's ceiling was the only place not covered in parchment. The velvet curtain dipped low inside, and hundreds of tiny granite ornaments hung off it. Robert tried to take them all in, but they told too many stories to be grasped in seconds. He saw ladybugs, orcish boys, fiddle players, and twirling girls. It looked like a land of pure peace, so very different from the nightmare of limbo.

A roar came from outside the hut, making it impossible to admire its beauty like it deserved. The ceiling shook. *Shit, the monster.*

"Stay here," Sir Muwaan said with his sword raised, then he pushed the curtain aside. He hadn't needed to bother. The monster's charred bone grabbed the curtain door and ripped it out. The fences trembled, and figurines crashed down from the velvet. Robert wanted to catch them, but he was holding an even more important treasure. At least that was what he had promised to believe—that the girl wasn't lost, his daughter wasn't dead.

Sir Muwaan sliced into a limb and caused the monster to shake. It struck out again, toppling one of the fence walls. "No!" Robert screamed as he ran out of it. This place was holy. It couldn't become another part of limbo. He shifted the infant in his arm and struggled to aim his rifle.

"My treasured goddess!" Sir Muwaan bellowed without a hint of admiration. "Give up the celestial refugee. The Ouisà Kacocs are after her, not us!" He buried the blade in the monster's side. More pieces of its absurd body fell to the ground, but the monster, or Ouisà Kacoc as Sir Muwaan had called it, barely noticed.

"She's not what we thought, Sir Muwaan." Robert startled when he heard Alames's voice outside his body. He should have been relieved that she was okay but felt strangely empty without her inside.

"You can't know that, my go—" Sir Muwaan started,

but the Ouisà Kacoc caught him and swung him into the air. Robert fired his rifle into its core. It howled so loud he worried his eardrums might burst, then it let go of Sir Muwaan, who tumbled to the ground. Robert searched the air for Alames's cloud. Was she nowhere? Was she everywhere?

"You will regret this!" the Ouisà Kacoc roared, convulsing over its center.

Sir Muwaan struggled back to his feet and yelled at the air, "Give her up, I beg you! You've abandoned us for four decades, for what?"

"She's not a monster like the others, I promise." Alames's frantic voice echoed from all around them. Robert readied his rifle for the next shot when a massive beast with white fur, the skull of a boar, and muscles stronger than an ox jumped at the Ouisà Kacoc.

"Great timing, Ally! *Really?*" Alames's cloud wafted around them. White light pulsed inside of the goddess, matching her strained voice. The people of limbo didn't know about Ally. Why not? Questions flooded Robert's mind, but he couldn't dwell on them. He jumped backward in the last second to avoid Ally's huge legs and pulled the infant closer to his chest.

Ally bit into the Ouisà Kacoc that flailed around itself. Its heat smoldered Ally's fur, but she did not seem to care.

"The crypt, Sir Muwaan. Now!"

The knight rushed back into the ruined hut. Robert was about to follow him when the Ouisà Kacoc lifted Ally up and smashed her into the hut's remains. It pounced on Ally, pressing her down farther. She snapped wildly.

Sir Muwaan escaped their impact in the last moment and rushed off. "My knights need me."

"Muwaan!" Alames's cloud called after him, but he ran back to the main road. The Ouisà Kacoc and Ally were caught in a vicious battle. Ripped parchment danced around them. Robert stumbled backward, out of the battle's line. The promise of the infant's lost life was the only thing that kept him sharp. The last of the hut collapsed into itself. Robert choked up at the thought of all the lost stories, the last remnants of his goddess's lost time.

Ally yowled. Robert pushed his useless sentimentalities aside and readied his rifle again. It was impossible to aim for the monster without hitting his love. They were engulfed in a battle worse than he could fathom.

Alamès's cloud wrapped around the Ouisà Kacoc's body from behind to pull them apart. It hooked itself firmer into Ally. She growled and ripped an elvish torso out of its mass.

My man? My man, you there? The voice as sweet as honey dripped through his insides once more. He nodded. *In the nicest way possible . . . may I possess you?*

"What?"

The cloud yanked harder on the Ouisà Kacoc, and Ally ripped another piece out of it. Its core flared up. Its defenses became uncoordinated, desperate. The cloud's force pulled them backward, away from the hut's ruins.

Ally's got this, all right? Can I take over this fine body now, please? She struggled to keep the hopeful cheer in her beautiful voice. Her cloud left the two beasts and encircled him once more. *I won't if you don't want me to, but by this rotten limbo mess, it would make shit easier.*

"O-okay," Robert said, right as Ally slashed her claws into the monster's core.

The honey he'd felt inside spread until all his muscles were like warm clay, ready to be molded. He kept his senses, but they drifted away from his direct experience. He merely observed the touch of parchment under his feet. His daughter's soft skin as he stroked her cheek. The wet, ghastly sounds of flesh ripping. The sight of the granite armchair buried in ruins. The force he used to uncover it, and its smooth surface under his fingers when he pushed it aside.

You're doing great.

Robert fell into the back of his mind like he'd fallen into Reggie's—no, *Alamès's*—bed of pages several weeks ago and watched her magic unfold. Underneath the armchair was a circular trapdoor. Robert's body knelt down and opened it. Tears ran down his cheeks. *No, don't cry.*

I'm sorry, my man. This is just . . . this mess is all my fault. Robert longed to comfort her through the distance of his own body, but it was as fruitless as comforting an actress onstage. *But I'll be damned if we can't steal something beautiful from it and revive our little girl here.* Smacking sounds came from behind. Robert knew without checking that Ally had finished her monstrous prey. *Well, I'm damned either way, but the world would be a little less so.* With that, Alames dove through the trapdoor. Robert felt his daughter clenched tighter against his chest as he observed the strangeness of the fall. The trapdoor led down a long, dark hole, and yet he seemed to be floating upward.

They landed softly on another stack of parchment in another miracle. It took several seconds for Robert's distant consciousness to grasp the place's majesty. When he did, Alames was already walking him down a narrow brick path. It led through the nave of a cathedral with pointed arch ceilings as high as Virisunder's palace. Flying buttresses supported it that connected to wide limestone pillars with sculptures carved into them. They portrayed elves, humans, and orcs of all nations, as well as animalistic nature creatures that must've been Fae. Their depictions faded into one another, dancing and frolicking together in a peace that had never existed. At least not to Robert's knowledge. The cathedral's gray limestone arches turned into black granite walls at Robert's height with thousands of tiny holes from which white light shone. It was like walking through the night sky with star constellations no other man had seen before.

A river of paper flowed on both sides of the path. Its stream followed the cathedral arches down into the starlit arcade. Robert couldn't spot the end of it and wondered if there even was one. This place was so surreal, so beautiful, he could have fallen into the depth of existence, the essence of life itself.

"Not quite that dramatic, but I like the way you're

thinking. Welcome to my crypt," Alames said with Robert's voice.

Robert's consciousness focused on the parchments that danced in his periphery. *What are these?* A shiver ran over his skin, and he sniffed, but they were her movements, not his. *Don't be sad, I'm here.*

"I never thought I'd show this place to someone," she said, then hummed a divine melody with Robert's voice that echoed around the cathedral. The stars in the granite walls hummed along, easing the loneliness it held. "These parchments . . . they're my story and that of every soul I lost."

Robert was walking through a bookshop, but instead of stories, the ink's curves told of life. Then again, where was the difference? His drifting consciousness swam in circles around a reality he couldn't grasp. A decade ago, Polemos's simple bookshops had overwhelmed him. If that Robert had only known what rivers ran in Alames's crypt.

"It's a special kind of anguish, wandering through the world, reading stories that might never find their ending." Warmth spread through Robert's body. A hug, perhaps? The granite stars twinkled along. "Your parchment's got quite the story on it. Liked it the first time I read it back at the Polemos recruitment office."

Understanding trickled slowly into Robert, but when it did, the warmth disappeared. *You know how I will die?*

"No, I know how you *should* die. But more importantly, how you should live. I read the names of your protagonists, the people playing the memorable roles of your life. I saw your little girl long before Ally wrote me she was pregnant. I hadn't realized Ally was bonded to a name until we ran into you. She's hard to read . . . terrible handwriting, but what do you expect from a physicist?"

His daughter, resting from a life she never lived, weighed heavily in his arms. *But the little girl . . . she didn't make it out alive.* More tears pearled down his cheeks. Robert couldn't tell who they belonged to.

"Yeah, that's my fault, but I . . . I will make up for it. I erased your and Ally's memories a few weeks back."

What?

"Harmless, I promise, and necessary for reasons best discussed over a cup of tea. You know, the kind with a lot of rum? Anyway, it took enough celestial power to attract my damned ex."

If his mind had swum moments ago, it was now drowning. *Your ex . . . Balthos, king of the pantheon.*

"Oh, please don't blow even more steam up his ass. Yes, *him.* He's suspected that our beloved Ally might be me for quite some time now. He knows my splinters would reassemble one day to something that contains my consciousness. I tricked him once, claimed my knights had distorted me into a monster like the ones he's created."

The Traitor.

"Bingo! But no offense, mortals alone can't form a new immortal god. He thinks they're still holding my splinters hostage, but he's been searching for glimpses of my light. Unfortunately, I glimpsed a bit too much."

Memories of Sunday school flooded Robert's mind. The Traitor. Balthos. Alames, his lost love. She was gone, and any reincarnation of her had fought Balthos in the Celestial War. *But you're his enemy?*

Robert's body wavered as he continued down the path. "Hmm . . . you see, I'm not the greatest at breakups. Shocking, I know. Our darling *king* sees himself as a widower. Except for the splinter he kept, that is."

He has a piece of you? Another shiver ran down his spine. He took that as a yes. *Fuck him, we need to get that back.*

A chuckle. "Have we forgotten our tower tumble already, my fine man?" The amusement left Robert's body as quickly as it had arrived. "He can never know the names of mortals dear to me. If he knew what Ally meant to me, if he knew I loved her, she wouldn't exist anymore. You're a good shot, Robert, but not *that* good."

He sank deeper, away from any purpose he'd once possessed. His mother had wanted him to be a sniper, but he was no impeccable shot. He'd longed to be a guard, but his daughter was dead, the women in his life powerful beyond his understanding, and Ally had saved him more times than he'd protected her. What good was he?

"Anyway, after I used my power to erase your memory—I know you have questions, mainly why I'm such a goddess damn idiot, but we'll talk about that later—he came for Ally with no regard for her disposition or the baby."

My daughter died that day on the stairs. Robert thought he'd caught Ally before anything bad could happen, but he'd been too late.

"Balthos has a talent for shocking you to death." Robert's heart grew heavier. Once again, he couldn't tell if it was his own or hers that submerged in pain. Perhaps it was both of theirs. "We're here. Ready?"

There was nothing to be ready for. The path continued as it had behind them, and the starlit arcade remained endless. Alames raised Robert's hand and spoke in a strange language that made his skin tingle. "For the love of the Poet and the Smith," she finished in Virisunder.

The air in front of them turned solid, and light shaped itself into two figures too divine for Robert to process. They parted the air like a curtain, creating the entrance to a modest cobblestone cellar. It could have belonged to a Virisunder monastery were it not for the diamond coffin in its center. They stepped inside, and the invisible curtain closed. The coffin itself was the only source of light, but its sparkle reflected off the stones.

"Have you ever read about the Poet and the Smith, Robert?"

Can't say I have.

"I thought not. It wasn't them anyway, but I do believe I depicted them well. A bit of a memorial to my creators." She spoke as if the information wasn't overwhelming to his mortal mind. His pounding head confirmed that it was.

She stepped around the coffin, grazing his hand over the smooth diamond texture. Underneath its glimmer lay a woman so beautiful Robert lost the last bit of consciousness he'd been given.

The next thing he heard was a snapping through the darkness, then her voice. "Come on, you charming bastard. That's very flattering, but we've got a job to do, and Ally's waiting."

Ally. Robert forced his consciousness back into the moment and faced the goddess laid out before him. The coffin had been opened while he was gone, and he saw her even better now. He longed to faint again, not deal with the overwhelming awe her image brought, but he pushed through the sensations. *Ally.* Ally needed him. He'd managed to look at Ally for a decade now. How bad could this be?

Bad. His vision swam right away, and his head seemed to burst. A soothing touch ran down his spine. Her delicious whisper followed. "It's just me. Just Reggie. Just boring old Bored Reginald."

Deep breaths traveled through Robert's body, and he saw her. She was made of blue crystal. "Kyanite."

Underneath its surface, she was an unnaturally blue river running like the parchments had. She looked like an elvish woman, but perhaps it was what Robert wanted to see, what he could understand. When he focused on her ears to check his theory, his vision blurred once more. There was a scene in *Defiance of a Rose* when the Rainbow Giant was submerged in the ocean of dreams. Its water fulfilled his every longing at once. It almost killed him when he returned to the surface and breathed in banality. Robert wondered if submerging in Alames would feel the same.

He blushed. "I can hear your thoughts. You know that, right?" More heat shot into his cheeks. Robert was sure it came from him this time.

Ehm . . . so . . . that's your dead body?

"Can you make this any more awkward, my man?"

He examined her face, uncertain what he saw. *You know, I read a children's tale once where a prince kissed a dead princess back to life.*

"Creepy." A chuckle ran through him. "I see you *can* make this more awkward. Let me make it worse. I need you to reach into me, and it's not gonna be as fun as either of us hope for." The body of his daughter shifted so that Robert could move his right arm freely. It stretched out until it hovered a finger's length over the goddess's chest.

"I'll send you into dreamland for this, if you don't mind."

I'm already there. The energy coming off her corpse vibrated through him, even from a distance. His fingertip touched the kyanite, and he dove back into a darkness as consuming and protected as a womb. When his vision sharpened again, he held a lilac Quill in his hand. He must have pulled it out of her chest. Its feathers were delicate and soft, but it exuded an energy that trembled through his body. Sentences in the strange language Alames had spoken hissed through him.

"You're okay?"

Robert tried to nod, forgetting that he'd given up his body. Alames understood anyway. "Magnificent. Let's make a baby!" What should have been funny struck fear in him, for her voice was thin and shaken. He found himself kissing his daughter's forehead, then carefully placing her on the diamond coffin lid.

How do we—

"Remember the spooky shit Josef threw at us during the Ceremony?" Alames asked as she led them to one of the curved cobblestone walls. Rage shot through Robert's body at the mention of that cockroach. He imagined it was a shared sensation before remembering that Alames had let Josef live. She'd been with Ally for decades and the monster still dared to breathe.

A sigh. "I don't murder people, Robert. I reap them. And

yes, a goddess reaping mortal souls again might draw Balthos's attention. My hands were bound. That being said, Josef has greatly wrecked my belief that all mortals are worthy of worship. The Poet would have never written a sick creature like him." Alames pressed his hand against the wall. The cobblestone's rough corners caused friction against Robert's skin. The harshest cracks reflected the diamond's light. "What else is there to do but meet this evil with love? And that I have provided Ally plenty of, albeit never enough."

She inhaled heavily through his lungs. *What are you scared of?*

"Kénos. The only substance that can erase you and me alike. The only substance that makes us equal." Another sigh. "And also the only substance life can be formed of. I don't have the Chisel to create what Balthos has made." Robert's voice cracked as she spoke the king's name. "But I believe with a little luck, this should do."

Before Robert could ask what she meant, an energy rushed through him that threatened to tear him apart. White light shot out of his fingertips and stretched the cobblestone wall until reality ripped. Kénos. The forsaken substance lurked behind it, hovering around the reality he perceived like the twist of imagination turning dreams into nightmares. A white glimmer traveled up his hand as he reached toward it. She hesitated.

Can you touch it?

"I think so. I've done it before with the inherent magic of my soul, but . . . but if I can't, we're both fucked."

Nonexistence. What a strange threat. *Do it. I trust you.* With that, she reached into the kénos. His heart stopped when his fingers clasped the elusive substance, but it didn't devour him. She'd succeeded.

Together they pulled out a sliver that pulsed in his hand, eager to feast on his flesh. Only her white light kept it from doing so. She raised his other hand that held the Quill and brought it to the kénos. *Will it not destroy it?* The Quill looked even more fragile than his skin against the haunting substance.

"It didn't when I wrote the stars, but I suppose that was a long time ago."

Robert had a thousand new questions. It didn't matter. *What are we writing?*

She filled him with a deep breath, and a smile crept onto his face. "Your little girl's soul. She didn't get a parchment like mortals do, but this should work. Stories have come from stranger places." She brought the Quill's tip to the kénos and painted symbols foreign to Robert into the darkness. "Do me a favor, some inspiration, think of all the joys of life you want your daughter to have."

She started to write in the foreign language. Robert's consciousness sank into visions of a life grander than he, Ally, or anyone had lived. Exciting adventures, enough love to fill four hearts, the most beautiful women. *Wait . . . oh well.* Alames chuckled despite the sweat that had formed on Robert's forehead from concentration. "If you say so, baby daddy."

More visions crossed his mind until one sharpened, fueled with desperate anger. *Balthos. My little girl is going to destroy Balthos.*

"What the—" Alames tried to protest, but it was too late. White sparks flew off the kénos cloud and crackled in the air. "Okay, enough. Good soul. Good life. No apocalyptic war needed. All good," she mumbled frantically through Robert's voice. It formed a stark contrast to the calm he felt. His daughter could do it. He was sure of it.

Alames spun his body around and returned to the girl's corpse on the diamond coffin lid. *What now?* His heart fluttered painfully, consumed with Alames's anxiety.

"We put the soul in her body. It should breathe life into her. That's vaguely how it worked for little Reggie me, at least." Robert's hand shook harder the closer she brought the kénos soul to the infant's lower ribs. "I will let go of the kénos now."

Do it. Robert wanted to give her a squeeze, some sort of encouragement, and hoped the thought alone would comfort her. Together they placed the impervious substance into the girl's body. His hand traveled through her skin and flesh without harm. Alames released the kénos soul and pulled Robert's hand back as quickly as she could.

"There we go. Give it a second, and our little Robert-and-Ally will scream at this mess of a world."

It could have been a reassurance or a prayer. Either way, it didn't work. Right after she uttered the words, the kénos soul announced its birth in a volatile outburst. It was Alames who screamed, not the child. The infant's rib cage fell into itself. Grisly tentacles devoured it, climbing out of her chest in search of more matter to consume.

"No, no, live in the body!" Robert's voice distorted until it was Alames's pitch that screeched. Her cloud left him in her panicked attempt to stop what was happening. He collapsed to the ground, unprepared for the sudden task of managing his own limbs. His senses returned when he hit the cold stone. "Don't erase her! She's you!" Alames screamed above him.

Robert's mind raced but caught up quickly. His daughter had a soul forged with love. She had a body made of the same kind of love. But how could soul and body come to harmony? He thought of *Defiance of a Rose.* It was the wrong time to think of fiction. Except . . . hadn't he seen their own lives written on parchments, existing in words as all stories did? In the last book from his beloved series, the Rainforcer's child was turned into a desert. She ripped a chunk of herself out of her chest to save her child and bring life back to the desert. Ally's and his daughter couldn't survive on her own because the two of them were three. They were lithium, and a component was missing.

Robert jumped off the ground and pulled Raptor from his hip. *Please be recharged. Please be recharged.* The assula pistol glowed, ready to fire, and his heart beat faster. It had to be Raptor. No other barrel should ever be aimed at her. He ran around the coffin, away from the devouring soul of his daughter, and aimed at the goddess's dead kyanite chest.

"My man, what are we—"

"Trust me," he said, then fired. Holy crystal shards blasted in all directions. They cut Robert's cheeks, his hands, his neck, but he didn't care. He picked up a shard from her chest and shuddered when his skin touched the kyanite. His consciousness threatened to slip away from him again, but he refused to let it. *Focus on the destruction.* This wasn't a goddess. This wasn't a woman. The real one was floating through the air in a panicked frenzy. The real one lightened up their bloody world with Bored Reginald's grand shows. The real one was the only one that mattered.

He clasped the shard tighter, ignoring the blood that formed around its edges, and sprinted back to the other side of the coffin.

"What? Why? What? Why?" Alames's cloud blew through the cellar aimlessly.

"I got you," Robert said. "Both of you." He picked up his daughter against all better judgment. Her kénos soul had eaten her stomach and crawled up her throat. The black tentacles lashed out at Robert, confused about an existence that didn't make sense to her. They brushed over his skin, causing an anguish unlike anything he'd ever experienced. Peaceful memories of Coalchest and his father threatened to dissolve as his daughter's kénos burned patches of his skin, but he yanked away quick enough to avoid permanent loss.

"I love you," he said, then stabbed the kyanite shard into her heart. Everything erupted into white light. The impact tossed Robert backward, and he fell into a land of peace—a world that swallowed him with its beauty, a world that lived the greatest story ever told—and he fancied himself part of it. All desires melted away until his pure blissful soul shone through. It had but one desire: to lie on a meadow among it all and watch as the story retold itself.

Perfection slipped through his grasp as reality settled

back in. The white light condensed itself into stars that fell from the cellar's ceiling like snow. His snow empress had given birth to a miracle. He lay there in the falling stars until Alames's sobs reached him.

"It worked. But she's . . . she's . . ."

Robert got back to his feet like a sleepwalker and approached his daughter. The kyanite had fused with her. Her once elvish body had turned as translucent as Alames's dead shape. The kénos soul filled her insides, swirling with undeniable life. Through it, her shining blue kyanite heart beat. Despite her strange translucent form, she looked like the girl Ally had birthed. Like their girl.

"She's . . ." Alames stammered again.

"A goddess."

The girl agreed with him, for when she opened her mouth, she did not greet her world with a scream. She dipped it into divine song.

EPILOGUE

February 980 - Altor Caedem, Virisunder

I gasp for the breath that never belonged to me, the air only mortals are worthy of. My stolen body protests the illusion more than it ever has. *I know, my friend. I know.* It has been a long night. The first glimpses of dawn shine through our bedroom window, releasing me from my prison once more.

They have returned from my prison as well. Just this second. It took more than I could give to carry them back to me. I gave it anyway. My hand wanders under the warm cotton blanket. Oh, what delightful comforts mortals seek. I rather seek them myself nowadays.

I reach for my trusted belly, the flesh that invited me to lavish feasts and showed me what havoc butterflies could wreak. My hand finds nothing. Emptiness. Except it isn't empty. It leads back to my prison. Back to limbo. I don't push down on the holes. I'm breathing. Another day is gifted to me, and I do not risk losing it.

I prop myself up, ready for them. She should not know. Nothing can help me if she knows. I don't know what I'll do if the celestial seed in her sprouts. Not now that she finally tastes the true joys of mortal life. I would pray for all to be well, but I rarely listen to myself.

The hand I steady myself with aches. I grin at the loving pain of a body that's in touch with me, but the joy leaves my face when I notice its source. Two holes pierce my hand and lead to limbo once more. They remind me of boar tusks. Oh, Ally, could you not have taken a bite of me another time? I suppose timing has never been our strength.

"Reggie! Reggie, it's a miracle!" Footsteps rumble down the stairs. My heart jumps. *Reggie.* I've never been happier to hear this name that isn't mine. She doesn't remember. Thank me! *Thank yourself, dummy.*

I hide my hand in my pocket before they enter, get out of bed, and yawn as eccentrically as I can. No illusions. The breath traveling through my dead lungs is the biggest illusion I can pull off today.

I see her face first. It lights up the room like it always does, like it did that night in the dungeon when she took off her hood and showed me what a fool I had been. I came here to rid the world of a monster, of a crime against the treaty that saved us all. Instead, I found a blessing.

"Are you okay, my love?" Ally rushes toward me, her daughter in her arms. "You look like you're the one who just gave birth."

"Funny." My eyes flicker to Robert, who steps into the bedroom after her. He knows. There's no doubt about it. I smile when I notice that my treacherous heart doesn't mind. It is almost mortal in its folly.

"Look at her," Ally demands. I obey with pleasure and examine the sleeping celestial in her arms. I was meant to leave no trace on the mortal world. Neither was Ally. Now here's this girl, the daughter of a mortal, a demigoddess, and a goddess.

"She's perfect," I say. It scares me how much I mean it. Her existence ridicules my illusions. I arrived here holding on to my two favorite treasures from the World Before. Humor and stories—the only pieces of perfection Balthos had overlooked when he wrecked the world in his image. But he had overlooked love too, and so did I. Figures both of us wanted to forget about that particular piece of perfection that had turned our world into a nightmare.

Robert steps forward, saving me yet again from my fretful thoughts. "We're thinking of calling her Rose."

Ally nods and strokes the cheek of her daughter, a logical impossibility. *Rose*. Do they know the Poet wrote me on rose petals?

"I'm not sure what happened," Ally says, "but she certainly defied death."

A chuckle escapes me. They named her after *Defiance of a Rose*. Of course. The intense look in Robert's eyes tells a different story. I shudder and play it off. "Great name. She can get a matching tattoo with me when she's old enough. If you can tattoo blue crystal, that is."

"Kyanite," Robert says with a voice that fills the holes in my body. I wish it really could. "She's made of kyanite. It's a long story."

"I'm sure," I mutter. Ally smiles widely at me. I'm glad we reunited her with her miracle like she deserves.

I sigh at her sight. There are many foolish things I could have done in this beautiful mortal world. Falling in love with Caedem's daughter was the worst of them.

I lean down and kiss my Ally. I don't regret it.

To be continued

LEARN MORE ABOUT THE AUTHOR AT

WWW.LEAFALLS.COM

patreon.com/leafalls

Instagram: @leafallswrites

@forgottensplinters

Twitter: @leafallswrites

YouTube: Story Manifestors

TikTok: @leafallswrites

SUPPORT & CONNECT

Please consider leaving a review on Goodreads/Storygraph and wherever you purchased your copy. Reviews are the best way to support independent authors. Even one line can make a great impact. Thank you so much for your support!

If you enjoyed GODDESS OF LIMBO and don't want to wait for the sequel, join our Patreon family and get exclusive short stories, background snippets, and updates about the Forgotten Splinters universe.

Stay in touch by signing up for the newsletter and be the first to hear about any writing & publishing developments!

GLOSSARY

Virisunder

God: Caedem, god of war and strength
Species: Elves
Characters born in Virisunder:
Alexandra "Ally" Verdain, Princess of Virisunder
Josef Verdain, born Heidegger, Prince of Virisunder, now in charge of
        the Council's Institute for Assula Magic
Lady Josefine Verdain, Alexandra's and Josef's daughter
Harald Heidegger, Head of the Council
Agathe Heidegger, elvish Princess of Silberfluss
Bored "Reggie" Reginald, palace jester
Robert Oakley
Dillon Calgery, Alexandra's personal guard
Gustave van Auersperg
Xenia van Auersperg, Subira's and Gustave's daughter, mixed ethnic-
        ity (Fi'teri)
Theodosia Verdain, former Princess of Virisunder, Alexandra's
        grandmother
Talbot Cox, Prince of Tazadahar
Fergus Ackerman, Vana's father

Silberfluss

God: Exitalis, the lady of the dead & King Balthos' wife
Species: Humans
Characters born in Silberfluss:
Richard Kilburn, a serf of the Belladonnas
Pier Kilburn, a serf of the Belladonnas, Richard's son
Edeliènne Kilburn, a serf of the Belladonnas, Richard's wife
Vana Ackerman, half elf, guitarist of 'The Spirit and the Enforcer'
Zazil Revelli, daughter of Silberfluss's elvish assula smith family, assu-
        la smithing & people studies major at Tribu La'am
Dotty Ackerman, Vana's mother
Clarisse Lautrec
Rutilia Belladonna, daughter of Waldfeld's duke

Fi'Teri

God: Calliquium, keeper of language, thoughts & knowledge
Species: Elves
Characters born in Fi'Teri:
Subira Se'azana, captain of Virisunder's military, residing in Virisunder's capital Polemos
Makeda Verdain, born Amanirenas, former general of Virisunder's military, wife of former Princess Theodosia, principal of the military school Altor Caedem

Tazadahar

God: Squamatia, the serpent
Species: Humans
Characters born in Tazadahar:
Badih Jalil, a rebel fighter
Huda Heydari, a rebel fighter
Daiba Roshan, daughter of a rebel, convicted criminal, Catalina's pen pal

Sap Büruy

God: Zelission, the shape-shifting trickster & protector
Species: Humans
Characters born in Sap Büruy:
Artyom Yuldashev, pantheon priest, convicted criminal, residing in Silberfluss

Vach da tìm

God: Tiambyssi, the time-waver
Species: Elves
Characters born in Vach da tìm:
Nobuko Phamlang, a student at Altor Caedem

Tribu La'am

Belief system: Ancestral worship, independent from Elfentum's pantheon
Species: Orcs & Humans

Characters born in Tribu La'am:

Martín Zac-Cimi, orcish heir of the Zac-Cimi crime family in Mink'Ayllu

Sachihiro Ch'ulel, son of the High Priestess of the orcish Juyub'Chaj tribe, language & decryption major at Tribu La'am University

Gon Ch'ulel, nonbinary child of the High Priestess of the orcish Juyub'Chaj tribe, ancestral magic and medicine major at Tribu La'am University

Catalina Zac-Cimi, Martín's sister, part of the Zac-Cimi crime family in Mink'Ayllu

Yooko Tlatoa, a human from Tribu La'am, resides in Silberfluss under the name "Ordell Smith"

Esperanza, a botany major at Tribu La'am University, of nomadic Faemani origin

Erna Kaax, half-orc/half-human, residing in Silberfluss, a convicted criminal

Jules Maguey, Tribu La'am human, residing in Silberfluss, singer of 'The Spirit and the Enforcer'

The Original Gods

The Poet & The Smith, creators of the world

Alames, former celestial reaper, "The Lost Goddess"

Balthos, former celestial reaper, creator of the new pantheon, "King of the gods"

Terminology

Assula: magical energy; originally discovered in Tazadahar; now controlled by the Council of Elfentum

Assula smiths: a smith capable of forging magical energy into tools and weaponry

Asynár: a demon formed from incoherent soul splinters with an animalistic thought process; residents of limbo

the Celestial War: The war that erupted after Balthos created the new pantheon; Balthos and the new gods fought on one side, while the Traitor and mortals, trying to restore the old peace, fought on the other; ended in the Treaty

the Ceremony: A Virisunder exception to Balthos' marital and family law, created by Princess Theodosia Verdain and her wife General Makeda Amanirenas; a way for noblewomen otherwise unable to conceive a child to have an heir; involves a

Tribu La'am fertility potion and the blindfolding of both the noblewoman and the donor

Conchs: Elfentum's weight measurement unit; 1 conch = 5 pounds

the Council: a former merchant union that capitalized on assula magic and expanded its influence into becoming a governing body of Elfentum; run by the elvish Heidegger family

the Crown War: An all-of-Elfentum encompassing war, started by Princess Theodosia of Virisunder and the Fi'Teri general Makeda Amanirenas; initially started to legitimize their marriage, then expanded into the failed attempt to unify Elfentum under the Virisunder crown

Faemani: human nomads, living in Tribu La'am, who have both human and Fae ancestry; a people keen on establishing a spiritual connection to the Fae realm

the Fertility dance: A Tribu La'am tribal ritual for the wedding night of the new chieftain and high priestess; tribal members gather around the curtained-off bed, chant, and let notes with wishes rain down on the newlyweds; a fertility potion guarantees conception

Impetu Caedem: Virisunder's elite military troop trained in quick charges and executions

the Institute for Assula Magic: The Council's assula research and production facility; run by Prince Josef Verdain of Virisunder

K'aah Ki'ik: the ritual of bitter blood; a battle to the death in Tribu La'am tribes to determine the ancestors' true will and rectify dishonor

Kénos: a substance that dissolves everything yet existence is made out of; the Poet & the Smith created the world from it

Kymbat: "Precious child" in Sap Bürüy

Limbo: The realm of chaos and demons, where everything that does not belong to the story integrity of reality goes; the Traitor's realm; the place where splintered souls go

Magic-bearer: someone trained in wielding assula magic

Ouisà Kacoc: a demon formed from the malevolent splinters of many souls; evil in nature

the Pantheon: The six gods Balthos created from the splinters of the Poet & the Smith, and one of Alames' snatched splinter

Soulcreeper: a demon created by an Ouisà Kacoc; the creature is often used as a means of psychological torture and is capable of trapping victims in traumatic memories

Splintering: The fracturing of a soul whose life story was not supposed to end that way

Tidiers: The Council's guards; pledged to neutrality

Trigger Warnings

Dear readers, this story addresses a lot of heavy subjects. Please be aware that there will be graphic descriptions of violence, death, gore, and body horror. Mental illness, psychological struggles, and the effects of trauma are also explored in detail.

Sexual assault, suicide, and child marriage are referenced. Reclaiming one's autonomy and agency after trauma is a main theme of the book, hence it will come up frequently. However, none of the assaults are graphically described and the focus stays with the survivors. Please reach out to me via my website or social media if you'd like more details on the specific triggers before reading.

Triggers by chapter:

- Ableism: 13, 15, 23
- Birth complications/Reference to miscarriage/Stillbirth: 1, 34, 35, 39, 40, 41, 46
- Body horror: 11, 17, 27, 29, 37, 38, 40, 41, 43, 45
- Cheating: 31, 32
- Child marriage/Pedophilia: 3, 4, 18, 28
- Domestic Abuse: 8, 20, 26, 30, 34
- Drugs: 5, 9, 13
- Eating disorder: 11, 25, 27
- Homophobia: 10, 11, 16, 18, 37, 42
- Mental Illness/Depression: 4, 15, 18, 19, 21, 23, 24, 31, 39
- Psychological horror: 11, 22, 37, 42
- PTSD: 11, 13, 16, 22, 25, 27, 31, 38, 42, 43, 44, 45
- Racism/Xenophobia: 9, 11, 26, 27, 34, 35, 37, 38

- Religious trauma: 7, 16, 38, 42
- Sexual assault/harrassment: 14, 16, 17, 27, 28, 29, 33, 35, 38, 42
- Sexual situations: 7, 9, 10, 12, 19 (uncomfortable), 31, 34
- Suicide: 5, 6
- Transphobia: 11, 13, 23
- Violence/Death: 1, 3, 10, 12, 14, 21, 29, 30, 33, 34, 36, 37, 38, 39, 40, 41, 42, 43, 44, 45, 46

ACKNOWLEDGMENTS

This moment has bedazzled me for years. Writing the acknowledgments meant the book is finished. Here I'm sitting, writing the acknowledgments, and you, my dear reader, have finished the book. Unless you're like me and read the acknowledgments first, in which case: Welcome!

Thank you to my dear friends Void and Nick, who unknowingly started this journey with me when they agreed to play DnD. (Yes, my lovely wife was there too, but she's getting a whole paragraph later, so shush.) Thank you both for your creativity, for your love, and the improv joys we've shared. Thank you, Void, for disintegrating the world when the chance presented itself.

Thank you for the warm welcome I received at Air France, and to the wonderful people I shared the office with. This story was born in the break times, the early mornings, the late nights, and you made the return to the normal world pleasant.

Thank you to my early readers. Thank you to my wonderful friend Emma, who read the story's first glimpses with enthusiasm when I barely knew how to write. Thank you for the invaluable input my beta readers gave me. Thank you especially to Robert, who pointed out all the times I assumed I'd written something but forgot to put it on the page. You were my first completely unbiased reader and released me from my fear of having written incomprehensive gibberish for two years. Thank you for gleefully yelling at me after the plot twist. That moment will motivate me for the years to come.

Thank you to the Yale Writers Workshop and everyone I've met there. It was a dream come true and you helped shape that Subira chapter into perhaps the best part of this book. We gave the general what she deserved.

On that note, thank you to my incredible teachers at AAU. Thank you especially to Melissa, Andrew, and Dyan, who provided the shovel that I unburied my voice with.

Thank you to my family, who supported me and made this moment possible. Danke an meine geliebten Eltern. Danke, dass ihr immer an mich geglaubt habt. Thank you to my mom for making it possible to find Elfentum on a map. Thank you Brian for helping me haunt you, readers, with creepy worship symbols.

Thank you to the Enchanted Ink team, who turned my manuscript baby into the book you're now holding. Thank you to my editor Natalia for her keen eye, kindness, and for taking on this mammoth with excitement. Thank you to my amazing cover artist Franzi (Coverdungeonrabbit) She took my mess of ideas and turned it into a masterpiece. I'm still crying over it.

Thank you to my kitty boys for the endless purrs, snuggles, and reminders to take breaks. Thank you for keeping me company in all the health struggles I've faced while writing this story.

Thank you to my love for your never-ending compassion, patience, humor, and creativity, and your unshakable faith in me. Every time I fell apart, you picked up the splinters and put me back together. You reminded me what it's like to play, to imagine, to create. You refused to let me live as a shadow of myself and shone a light on me until I could produce it myself again. This book wouldn't have existed without you. From your creation of Josefine, Rose, and god wars, to our long London walks discovering Ally, all she was and would be, to searching for Bored Reginald towers. Thank you for the hours and hours of improv scenes, in which we found the characters' voices. Without you, they wouldn't have been able to tell me who they wanted to be. Your enthusiasm and your magic mean the world to me. Our souls will be like this forever.

Thank you to my readers. Please know that to express my full gratitude and glee, I'd have to write a longer book than this one, and who's got the muscles to carry that around? I love you. Thank you.

And lastly, thank you to my characters for finding me when I needed you. I feel blessed to walk this journey with you.

LEA FALLS is a writer, actor, and passionate lover of

stories. Equally drawn to page and stage, she's written plays, screenplays, poetry, short stories, and two novels, and has acted in numerous short films, plays, and improv shows. She earned her BFA in Acting at the Academy of Art University in San Francisco and attended the Yale Writers Workshop. After a brief call and response with Londontown, she now lives in NYC with her wife, two cats, and a slither of skyline that never fails to inspire her. There, she spends her days murmuring lines over a keyboard or a script. She's recently learned the meaning of "free time" and has since acquired a taste for annihilating virtual aliens with her wife, steering her coffee robot through D&D battles, and getting hopelessly lost in cities.